# THE
# BOUNTY LANDS

*by William Donohue Ellis*

*Cleveland ★ New York*

THE WORLD PUBLISHING COMPANY

JH WB RG JM

*Library of Congress Catalog Card Number:* 52–5196

**FIRST EDITION**

HC 952

TO MY PARENTS

who know about frontiers, their hazards

and their violence, this side of

the bounty lands.

# CONTENTS

GEORGE WASHINGTON, *President, The United States\* America*

To all whom these presents shall come,

Greeting:

Know ye that in consideration of military services performed by:

JONATHAN WOODBRIDGE, Private

as a member of the Continental Establishment in the Great Rebellion, there is granted to said veteran in lieu of monies:

100 acres

in the United States public domain known as The Northwest Territory, to be surveyed from the tract known as The Military Bounty Lands. Said tract and all appurtenances thereto shall be to said

JONATHAN WOODBRIDGE

and/or his Heirs & Assigns, to have and to hold, *forever.*

G. WASHINGTON


*Indorsement:* To Thomas Woodbridge, son & heir. J. Woodbridge. (Tom, do not yield up this share in the Bounty Lands until ye hold in hand the deed.)


. . . but immediately the warrants soured in their powder-stained fingers.

For between the warrant and the deed stood:

A thousand road miles of Senecas, Mingoes, Delawares, Miamis, Wyandots.

The statesmen of six coastal states who swore by their satin breeches that the Northwest Territory belonged, not to America, but to the original colonies under charter from Charles II, who had carelessly written . . . "from coast to coast."

The most adamant school of idealistic statesmen who ever tried to plat a country by blueprint, decimal point, and maxim.

The hungriest horde of land jobbers who ever fattened on a soldier's bounty . . . and the unwitting Congress who helped them haul away the public domain at ten cents the acre.

But from the dwindling muster list and/or their Heirs & Assigns there rose now and then a truculent Thomas Woodbridge who held to his bounty warrant with a vast red wrath in a fist that was big enough to make the warrant good. And because of him:

Our streets generally run east-west or north-south instead of kitty-cornered.

Our state, if it's west of Pennsylvania, is nearly square, as is our county, our township, our house lot.

Our western boundary is the Pacific instead of the Mississippi.

Our nationality . . . American.

# BOOK I

# Chapter 1: *THE WARRANT*

ALTHOUGH he grudged the time for the gesture, Tom Woodbridge washed his large square hands. He washed, not because he was going to Mr. Shuldane's house, nor because Miss Shuldane might be there, but because he was about to open "the document box."

His father had always washed his hands first. And since this was the kind of worthless concession a son makes before a major disobedience, Tom Woodbridge washed carefully.

The town of Concord in the Massachusetts Commonwealth was already being called "the seat of independence"; and old-timers still gathered on the Mill Dam every nineteenth day of April to talk about "that day at the bridge" twenty-four years ago.

They argued.

Some said the old Reverend William Emerson was the first one to show up at the bridge with his gun. Others said young Buttrick and Sam Hosmer. But Hosmer always claimed it was Jonathan Woodbridge who had cut across country to the Buttrick farm to head off the British detail that left the square. Jonathan Woodbridge himself never said.

Concord families, especially those which had lost someone, already referred to the anniversary of that fight as "the independence day." But for the redheaded Thomas Woodbridge, son of Jonathan, there was in the town neither independence nor concord.

The lack of peace within the man—no one thought of Tom Woodbridge as a lad—was the worst kind of trouble which could come to his kind, for it was a vague, diffuse opponent on which he could get no grip with his big red hands.

His trouble came mixed with unassailable friendship and favors. It stemmed from some scrivening upon a parchment between his late father and Mr. Shuldane, who was a friend. The share-farming document with Mr. Shuldane was a lenient arrangement, but it amounted still to indenture. And Woodbridge was no closer to owning the fifty acres than his father had been. They belonged to Mr. Shuldane.

Independence? Mr. Shuldane had called for the two Bedford shoats

3

to be delivered to his kitchen for the big meeting. Woodbridge knew the two Bedfords were worth their weight in gold as breeders, and it was a form of murder to eat them. But the delegates to Congress, en route to Philadelphia to write the new Western Territory land policy, were stopping off to get Mr. Shuldane's views on the subject. They would lap up his "views" along with his Bedford hams and the vision of his daughter Veronica presiding at table.

From his doorway Woodbridge scowled in reproach as the two little Bedfords frolicked in the mud as if they were ordinary young pigs, unaware that they romped at the end of twenty years' breeding and a bribe-bought trip across the Atlantic. The stubble on Woodbridge's flat cheeks glinted red in the sunlight, but a small white crescent grew on either side of his mouth. And at that moment was born the incredible possibility that there might be, on the Shuldane table that night, ordinary hog. And the Western land policy just might mean more to Thomas Woodbridge than to all the lawmakers in New York, Philadelphia, Boston, and Mr. Shuldane's house.

Woodbridge dried his hands, unlocked the walnut box, and took out the four papers with a kind of guilty reverence. To compensate for what he was about to do, he handled the papers as delicately as his hard fingers would allow.

The indenture paper he knew by heart. He folded it into his chest pocket. The pedigree letter for the two Bedfords went into his pocket as well. The large paper which was fraying at the folds he spread out carefully. In the lower right-hand corner it said:

> Platte of the Village of Mesopotamia in the
> U.S. Military Reserve.
> The Ohio Country, Northwest Territory
> Lat. _____ Long. _____
> Prop. Elnathan Shuldane
> Title Patent issued by U.S. Land Office

With a pencil Woodbridge drew a careful X through the lots which had been sold in the past month according to the duplicate plat nailed up in the post office. That still left most of them vacant, including the big in-lot in the center of town and the accompanying out-lot along the river, both of which were circled on Woodbridge's plat and on his heart.

The last paper was the one for which his father had built the box. It was to be the last treasure to be forsaken. It was the first thing to be saved in case of fire: the Bounty Land warrant. On the back it was endorsed to "Thomas Woodbridge, son & heir," together with the note in his father's writing: "Tom, do not yield up this share in the Bounty Lands until ye hold in hand the deed."

Woodbridge felt guilty as he put the document in his pocket, as though his father were watching him. The late Jonathan Woodbridge had died easy in the knowledge that he had left his son a free and clear estate of one hundred acres of the new Republic.

General Washington had told the veterans that as soon as the Indians were cleared from the Northwest Territory the western lands would rise in value to $20 and $30 and $50 an acre and that each man's discharge pay, his bounty warrant, would amount to a fortune. Jonathan Woodbridge had solemnly ordered Tom to hold onto his warrant at all costs until the general's prophecy came true. But in the impatient opinion of Thomas Woodbridge, who now rode into Concord Center with a pocketful of paper, General Washington and Private Jonathan Woodbridge had been wrong.

As he rode through the town, though, it seemed to Thomas Woodbridge that every man who saw him knew what he was about to do.

Nor did he feel any more at ease when for the first time in his life he knocked on the *front* door of the Shuldane house. To wait outside the Shuldane doors was an experience calculated to humble the most brazen. The double doors were so extremely shut that they appeared never to have opened, and they were so massive and obviously such a trouble to open that the caller needed, of course, a good reason to knock. Woodbridge was prepared to stop the house woman from exclaiming over his front-door appearance, so he was at a loss when Miss Shuldane opened the double panels in person, turning the doorway into a picture frame.

"Morning, Miss Veronica. I'd like to see your father."

"Tom, if it's about the pigs, he wants them around at the kitchen."

"It's not about the pigs, Miss Veronica."

"He's awfully busy, Tom, getting ready for the land-law delegates. Could you wait until—"

"Would you tell your father I come on land business too?"

She was surprised for a moment into silence, and Tom could see her thinking what to do. The house woman would not have gone to so

much trouble. She would not have taken Tom's request seriously for
one instant.

He wished now in a way that it had been the house woman; he
could have coped with her answer. But Miss Veronica made it difficult
because of her courtesy and her honesty.

"Tom, you'll get a much better hearing from Father if you catch him
some other day." Her brown eyes made her statement a promise. "I'll
see he comes out to the farm one day this week."

"Got to see him now, Miss Veronica."

"Come in then, Tom. I'll tell him."

Standing inside the door, he watched her flow up the stairs in a
rustle of crinoline. At the bend of the first landing it was her turn to
study him, and during the examination he gravely picked at nothing
inside his hatband.

He knew shortly by her coming all the way back down and over to
him that the answer had been "not today." Otherwise she would have
beckoned from the landing. His hat was already on his head when she
said, "You're to come up, Tom."

Her statement seemed to surprise her as much as him.

Shuldane's surprise was near the surface when Tom entered his huge
study; but Elnathan Shuldane was not a maker of enemies, and his
presence of mind was as quick as his daughter's, who explained, "Tom
says it's very important, Father."

"Come in, Tom!" called Shuldane. "Sorry I haven't been out to the
farm lately. But I've known it's in good hands."

The man spoke as handsomely as he dressed and looked. Woodbridge stood awkwardly with his feet wide apart, aware of his mud-
crusted boots against the wine carpet, and of the fact that he was at a
disadvantage to do his business here. He could hear his father's words:
"Shuldane has done a lot of good, boy. He breeds success. Men who
work with him do well. But never try to fool him, because he can let
you down as gentle as melting ice eases a boulder to the bottom of the
pond in spring. Give him your best, short only of the Bounty Land
warrant, which you owe to no man."

Woodbridge acknowledged an introduction to a fluff-shirted, young
Boston lawyer with self-assurance written in his easy posture and his
handsome face.

Shuldane asked, "Bring the pigs, Tom?"

"I didn't come about the pigs, Mr. Shuldane. But since you mention it, I brought this."

Woodbridge laid the Bedford pedigree letter in front of Shuldane, who pushed it back with a ruler, unread.

"I know, Tom. You had big hopes for these. But there are bigger things afoot, my boy. Sometimes a Bedford in the belly of a delegate is worth more than a breeder in the pen, eh, Blair? We'll get others, Tom."

"I could furnish you two very tender Woburn Blacks, Mr. Shuldane, but these are the only two pure-bred Bedfords in the Commonwealth, sir, as you can see by this paper."

But Shuldane had made all the effort the matter was worth.

"Bring the Bedfords around to the kitchen, Tom. Now what was the important business?"

"Mr. Shuldane, I'd like to buy a lot in your Mesopotamia."

The law fellow suddenly straightened up. Veronica dropped a copy of the Boston *Columbian Centinel* and came to sit on her father's left. Shuldane leaned forward across his desk. The three of them faced Woodbridge like some shocked tribunal of inquiry, its leniency violated.

Woodbridge could see from their surprise that of the few men who had come to trade Bounty Land military warrants to Shuldane for land in Mesopotamia, none had been bound apprentices like himself. Shuldane explained at length why it was a poor move for Woodbridge, adding, "Who shall I get to run the farm?"

"I'll not be hard to replace, since you mostly want to grow asparagus and hogs for the pantry. Your house man could do as much in Miss Veronica's flower bed."

"But I thought we were building together, Tom. You and I." Shuldane looked injured. "You'll own half the farm in another year."

"I was supposed to own half by last December, sir, according to the agreement."

"But the revenue hadn't come in, Tom."

"It would have, sir, if you'd not used our best stock for your table."

Woodbridge could feel the change in Shuldane, and he remembered his father's talk: "Give a lot, lad, before you make Mr. Shuldane feel his mistakes. He's a good friend but a bad enemy. Got ways of spreadin' himself; and he's got a spider web spread across the Republic from Philadelphia to Boston. He knows how to get along. In rough-neck Pittsburgh he goes by 'Nate *Shul*dane.' In fancy Philadelphia he does his business as 'Colonel Elnathan Shul*dane*, the Second.' And if he sets against you, boy, he could take everything but your Bounty Land."

Shuldane leaned back in his chair and made a church with his finger-tips in front of his face. "Tom, how old are you?"

"Nineteen, sir."

Shuldane blew down the church. "And what do you propose to do about the indenture clause which goes until age twenty-one? Can you buy your time from me?"

"No, sir. But if you'll remember, that was to be voided if I didn't own half, time I was nineteen."

Shuldane turned a searching eye at the young lawyer. But the law man only smiled an uncomforting smile, and Shuldane reached with some resignation for the plat of Mesopotamia, 23,040 acres of wilder-ness which Shuldane had never seen, west of the Scioto.

"Very well, Tom. At least you chose to settle in the best part of the Bounty Lands. Here's the plat. Pick your lot."

"Already picked it, sir."

"Good. How do you intend to pay? Cash?"

"With a Bounty Land military warrant. My father's."

"Let's see. That would be a private's warrant. Right?"

Woodbridge winced, but laid it on the desk.

"Yes."

Shuldane examined it thoroughly, as if the wounds and early death of Jonathan Woodbridge weren't sufficient to make it a bona fide Revo-lutionary Bounty Land warrant.

"Then that'll give you thirty acres," he said.

"But the warrant's for one hundred acres!" said the red-haired lad.

"Of course, Woodbridge. And if you want to wait until the govern-ment gets around to surveying, they'll give you one hundred acres for it. But that may never be. The only reason there's any Mesopotamia to go to is because a few men like me got tired of waiting for the gov-ernment. We sent out surveyors, ran the lines for the village, bought the block from the government so that men like you could buy small pieces and move onto it right now. That cost me money. I'm offering thirty cents on the dollar for Bounty Land warrants. Go down to the blacksmith or the store or the bank; they'll give you twenty."

Woodbridge picked up the warrant, folded it carefully, and put it in his chest pocket. Shuldane continued, "Now do you want the land or don't you?"

"Yes."

"Then let's have the warrant."

Woodbridge reached for his pocket. Then he dropped his hand.

"Well, Woodbridge?"

But the boy asked, "Do you have an agent on the site, Mr. Shuldane?"

"Yes. Sam Hosmer can make a transaction for me out there if you like, but time you get there the value of your warrant may have dropped."

"I'll have to take that chance, I guess. I've picked my lot, but I'd like to see the ground first."

"The land's all equal, and if you've got your lot picked you're better off to let me cash your warrant now. I'll make out your title right now. That's how it's done."

"My father told me to be standing on the land when I made the deal. I should hold out the warrant with one hand and take hold the title with the other. Then 'twas all right to let go the warrant. Not before."

"Um-hum. Well, your father was a good man," granted Shuldane. But the compliment left something wanting. Shuldane rose, though, to what was expected of the biggest land jobber in eastern Massachusetts. He put out his hand. "Good luck to you, Woodbridge. I'll come out to the farm before you leave. Don't forget to bring the Bedfords around to the kitchen."

When the door had closed after the red-haired farmer, Veronica picked up the plat of Mesopotamia. "Father, I still say someone in the family should go out there and see the settlement. Me, at least. How do we know what kind of land you're selling?"

Shuldane leaned back and smiled. "We'll go, my dear, when they get troop protection out there. As for the land . . ." He picked up a handful of dirt from the box which had been shipped back to him, then let it fall from his hand, which he wiped carefully with a handkerchief. "The land is good, or we'd have heard from Sam Hosmer and Amos Exeter and Jim Hawkins."

Veronica persisted. "Still, I'd like to visit the place. I'd like to see if they're keeping up our cousin's grave. Seems when our own flesh and blood has gone down to the Wyandots there, we might at least go out once."

Shuldane had already overtaxed his restraint.

"It's too early for you out there yet. Now Blair and I have work, if you'll excuse us. And see the cook woman follows instructions on those shoats. The fire should be bright coals. No flame."

When the door closed after Veronica, Jonathan Blair resumed his reclining position, and with the presumptive confidence of the eternal aide, the eternal deputy, he added one more dose of gall to Shuldane's worst day in a week.

"You made a mistake, sir."

By any measure Shuldane was a young man. Forty-six was young to have the ear of the Congressional delegates who were about to throw around millions of acres of water-cheap western land as lightly as they had given out the Bounty Land warrants to the Revolutionaries. Forty-six was young to have bought up bounty warrants for 23,040 acres, and to have lobbied a bill through the Congress permitting him to survey it, occupy it, and resell it in parcels to settlers. Forty-six was young for that, but as Shuldane turned now to face his assistant's last impertinence Blair could imagine for a lucid instant how he would look at sixty. The free and easy exhilaration of a hundred close deals was being replaced in Shuldane by a cautious calculation. The handsome face was puffed a little, and the voice cracked like the tip of a stage driver's whip.

"What's a mistake, Blair?"

"You make a mistake when you send a man loose in the West with bounty warrants on his person. That man, at least. He's free to stop short of your Mesopotamia. Take up land anywhere within the Government Bounty Tract—and a full hundred acres for his warrant instead of thirty. Why should he go on to your Mesopotamia? Farther to travel. Closer to the Indians. Would you?"

"He's got to settle on land that's already surveyed."

"It'll all be surveyed eventually, and more accurately than yours. Government's starting already on the near side of the Territory, west of the Pennsylvania border."

"Your information's out of date, Blair. Delawares and Mingoes drove them off that survey a month ago. Besides, the government won't accept bounty warrants for less than a four-thousand-acre block. So the Woodbridges must go on to Mesopotamia."

"That won't last. The West is clamoring for sales as small as a half-section—180 acres. Harrison made a powerful talk at the last session. Made them listen, too. Why not? Smaller sales mean more sales. More immigration west, more buffer against the Wyandots. More money in the federal treasury. Or less debt. Same thing."

"It won't go through, Blair."

"Why?"

"Because of you and me."

"Me?"

"You and I are going to convince the Honorable Joseph Varnum, before he leaves our little party tonight, that the only way they can sell off large amounts of the West is to sell big tracts—whole townships —to land jobbers like me. And I've a good case in sample in Mesopotamia. He'll see."

"You still made a mistake to let Woodbridge go with his warrant. Why won't he join with thirty-nine other men who hold hundred-acre warrants, and take up four thousand acres? When others see that, why should they go out to your Mesopotamia and your other projects?"

Shuldane quietly congratulated himself on finding Blair. Blair saw that he registered, and moved in like a skillful prosecutor.

"A man named Hogland has organized the squatters out there. Urges them not to sell their warrants for cash. Tells them to squat on the land until such time as the government honors their warrants at face value. He even set himself up as governor of the squatters."

"I know about him. But St. Clair's troops ran him out."

"Some say not. Some say he just changed his name. Hangs around Pittsburgh. Meets the settlers moving west. Tells them to hold on to their warrants. Tells them the day will come when a hundred acres are worth $5,000."

"It will!" snapped Shuldane. "But the ones like Woodbridge aren't looking to that!"

"Sounded to me like he was."

"He's just a surly lad. His father worked for me. Asked me to keep the boy on. I know him."

"Uh-huh. Then I presume you knew he was planning to leave your employ?"

Shuldane got the point. Blair bore in.

"Did you know, too, that he had it all figured out . . . down to the part about your forfeiting the indenture if he didn't own half by December?"

"No-o."

"Did you know he'd even selected his lot from the village plat? And did you know he had saved his father's land warrant all this time?"

"Never thought about it."

"Well you'd better, Nate. I never saw the lad before, but already I know that if there's many more like him the West'll belong to his kind, and to hell with the Elnathan Shuldanes."

"Quiet, Blair!" It was not the least of Shuldane's strength that, though he hated a well-grounded critic, he instantly used the criticism. "Go find Woodbridge," he ordered. "Tell him that he cashes in his warrant here, or he gets no land in the village."

"I wouldn't put it just that way to Woodbridge."

"You're right again, damn you! Tell him, if he turns in his warrant before he leaves, he can be sure of forty acres. Make it fifty. But hurry! He lives toward Sudbury."

When Jonathan Blair rode up to the Woodbridge place, he found no one at home. This was because Tom Woodbridge was at that moment at the Shuldane house again, at the back door this time.

The cook woman examined the hairless bodies of the small pigs with disdain.

"How come you dressed 'em for me this time?" she asked. "I kind of wanted to see these special critters with the hair on. Supposed to be all white, aren't they?"

"Yeah."

"They told me these were to be so special. Special instructions how to stuff them and turn them just so. Look like plain pigs to me."

The cook closed the door, and Woodbridge rode back to his place. There was a note stuck in his door to see Shuldane immediately. But Woodbridge drilled a hole in the bottom of the two-wheeled wagon, under the seat. He bolted the document box to the floor of the wagon. Except for the warrant in his chest pocket, he returned the papers to the box and locked it.

As darkness set in over the Concord River, Tom Woodbridge was loading his wagon.

Up at the Center, at the fork of Sudbury Road and the Mill Dam, there was a light in every window of the Shuldane house. There were carriages around the circle driveway, and in the dining room a distinguished company was hearing about Tom Woodbridge, how he had been at such pains to import two pure-bred Bedford hams.

"The King ordered no exportation of Bedford foundation stock," explained Shuldane. "But my lad arranged by letter to smuggle this pair out on His Majesty's ship *Sussex* as part of the ship's larder. Then Woodbridge had me pay a fortune to the ship's cook and two seamen to see that the animals were withheld from the captain's mess en route. The seaman who delivered them carried a letter from the farmer proving they're by the boar Duke, out of Regina, primmest dam in England. Shall I cut you some more, Senator Varnum?"

Joseph Varnum declined, and Shuldane wished the meat could have better supported his story.

But Joseph Varnum had not come to talk hog husbandry. He cited young William Henry Harrison's plea for smaller land sales in the West as a stimulant for immigration and settlement.

Shuldane had his argument well organized.

"He makes a convincing point, sir. On the surface it would seem the fastest way to fill up the West. But notice it would burden the federal land office with maintaining a staff to handle hundreds of small sales, and these scattered over four hundred miles of woods from Fort Pitt to Cincinnati and Fort Harmar. Impossible administrative problem! Eat up all the revenue from the land sales."

Shuldane's sharp eye or ear, or perhaps it was his uncanny, absorbent soul, noticed that he was not drawing the usual reaction from his listeners. But he continued. "Whereas if settlements like Mesopotamia form the pattern for development, the government makes a single, clean-cut transaction."

Joseph Varnum smiled. "Some of them have been singular enough but not too clean-cut, Mr. Shuldane. Judge Symmes has defaulted on his second payment for the million acres between the Miami rivers. He's going to have to give back some of that land from which he's already sold sections to settlers. Also, his surveyors miscalculated many thousands of acres in his favor."

Shuldane chuckled, deprecating such carelessness.

"Well, the judge bit off more than he could sell."

"But at any rate, Colonel Shuldane," continued Varnum, "the first consideration is not convenience for the government. And if men will more readily settle smaller land purchases, it's our duty to be at a little trouble to sell it that way."

Shuldane frowned. Veronica offered Mr. Varnum another glass of wine.

Thinking that the word "duty" had recently clouded much good clear thinking, Elnathan Shuldane said, "But the large allotment-type purchases make for more solid settlement." He had caught onto something with a dutiful ring, and he pressed it. "A scattering of twenty settlers over a hundred miles is easily wiped out. Take the massacre along the Scioto River. Whereas our concentrated settlement at Mesopotamia has withstood three major Wyandot raids, one by the Delawares, and one by roving Mingoes. In fact, because of the concentration, it's now quite safe out there."

"How safe, Shuldane?" asked Varnum. "You going to move out there?"

"Later. I have reserved a town lot and a farm lot there."

"How much later?" persisted Varnum.

It looked as though Elnathan Shuldane were staring at the chandelier, reflecting when he should move, but it was more likely he was staring pointblank at a daring and dramatic argument for large land sales.

"As a matter of fact," he replied, "my daughter Veronica is planning a trip out there shortly."

The men looked at Veronica at the end of the table. Veronica stopped her glass halfway to her lips. She was surprised; but the Shuldanes were quick, and she smiled and touched her glass to Blair's.

"To my trip, gentlemen, if you will," she said.

"My God, Shuldane!" said Varnum. "You're not letting that lovely little thing go out there!"

"I wouldn't, Mr. Varnum, if I didn't know that the township method of settling land is invincible and that she will be quite safe."

He turned casually to Blair. "Mr. Blair, did you manage to contact Woodbridge?"

"No, sir. I suspect he's left."

"Then as a matter of fact, gentlemen," said Shuldane, "Mr. Blair is leaving on an errand to the West for me tomorrow morning. He will be all the protection Veronica will need."

Veronica smiled. A few looked at Blair, searching in vain for his protective powers. A few looked at Blair with envy. Mr. Varnum said, "By God, Shuldane, if that girl makes it out and back safely, you'll have a case for the efficiency of block land sales."

He raised his glass to Veronica, as did the others. "To your safety, my dear . . . and to the settlement of the Bounty Lands."

Shuldane was the last to leave the dining room as the others followed Veronica to the library. He looked with some disappointment at the two platters bearing the barbecued pigs. With his fingers he tasted another small sliver, thinking that the Bedford pig was no more tender nor succulent than ordinary hog.

And in this conclusion he was justified, for at that moment Thomas Woodbridge was heading out the old Mohawk Trail with one horse in harness, another in tow. In the boot behind Woodbridge's wagon seat was a crate. The red-haired youth turned occasionally to lift the lid and inspect the two small white shoats that slept fitfully there.

Woodbridge turned off the Mohawk Trail to the west onto the Boston Post Road. And as he did so, he realized that it was a devil of a long way beyond Worcester, Massachusetts, to the Ohio Country and Mesopotamia, or Hosmer Village, as it was known to ordinary folks who remembered when Sam Hosmer took a small group west over the same road.

With a nervous gesture which even in the last hour had become habitual, Woodbridge touched his chest pocket to hear the reassuring crackle of one hundred, or at least thirty, acres of Bounty Land—if a piece of paper meant anything.

# *Chapter 2:* THE SHULDANE PURCHASE

WOODBRIDGE'S arguments with the world in general exactly paralleled his trouble with the fuming Forbes Road tollkeeper. For the redhead sat relaxed on his wagon seat, looking down at the sputtering man as disdainfully as his own nigh horse studied the tollkeeper's yapping hound.

Slowly approaching Pittsburgh, Woodbridge had been driving his team over the dusty Forbes Pike, absorbed in watching the white clouds move west with him. When Woodbridge jogged with the road, the clouds jogged with him. This secret harmony between Tom Woodbridge and the universe had never been explained, even to Jonathan Woodbridge, for it was too presumptuous to be believed.

Part and parcel of this presumption was the fact that the road ahead of Tom Woodbridge sprang to life as he approached it; and as it fell away behind him, it ceased to exist. The limit of his vision constituted for him the earth's outer boundary. So ingrained was this vanity that it seemed to surprise him when the road behind his wagon failed to dissolve but ran after him and caught up, as it was to do very shortly in the person of the sweating tollkeeper.

Woodbridge's rig plodded through the afternoon into the sinking sun. He judged he was nearing Pittsburgh by the fact that cabins now appeared every two or three miles or so. Two stages and three riders overtook and passed him, powdering the left flank of his nigh horse and causing the shoats to sneeze in the dust.

The road led up a long slope. Against the low sun the rocky ridge line looked like the Reverend Emerson's description of the ultimate edge of the earth at the rim of hell. The horses' heads bobbed alternately as they strained over the crest, and Woodbridge found himself staring down into a canyon so deep and wide that a vaporous chunk of Hades seemed to show through. In the shadowed bottom a few straggles of cabin smoke rose from Fort Pitt to mingle in the wispy fog forming over the Allegheny and the Monongahela rivers.

It grew darker as Woodbridge descended, and when the opposite escarpment cut off the sun he pushed his arms into the sleeves of Jonathan Woodbridge's old Continental greatcoat. The abrupt descent into a cold layer of air woke the shoats, who stirred themselves to huddle against the end of their crate. The wagon doubletrees crowded forward against the haunches of the horses, causing them to brace in a stiff-legged descent.

Tom Woodbridge looked ahead at Fort Pitt, where the lights were coming on; but he thought back to Concord, reflecting that if Shuldane had not offered independence he had at least offered security and protection, which seemed suddenly important. No one had done much for Tom Woodbridge, but what had been done had been done by Elnathan

Shuldane. He remembered that to get a new plow blade, to have a horse shod, to buy a bag of salt, it had always been enough just to say, "It's for the Shuldane farm." He wondered what he was doing in a lonesome pair of ruts halfway down the sides of this strange canyon.

Below him Woodbridge saw two lanterns sputter to life astride the road in time to call to his attention the toll station there. A pair of shallow ruts slanted off to his right through the woods. It was a steep descent, but several travelers obviously had found the risk worth twenty-five cents. Woodbridge nosed his team into the shallow ruts, and when his wagon was well off the main road, and under cover, he set the hand brake, which hardly broke the wagon's momentum. He jumped down off the seat, ran ahead of the team, grabbed the inside harness, and pushed back.

"Easy, Prince! Steady. Whoa, Jock!"

The ruts leveled off on a shelf which Woodbridge could see led back to the main road, neatly bypassing the toll station. But a voice came from almost directly overhead.

" 'Whoa, Jock,' is right!"

Woodbridge looked up through the dusk to find himself directly below the toll cabin.

"A single hoss can get away with it, mister! But you shoulda known better with that rig. March 'em right back up here!"

Woodbridge led his team along the shelf and out onto the main road. The tollkeeper was waiting for him there. Woodbridge reached into his pocket and presented a quarter which the keeper ignored.

"Naw, sir. When ya get caught, the sporting thing is to do better by the keeper than that."

Woodbridge held out two quarters.

"Ordinarily that'd do it, stranger. But in your case there's a party comin' along behind that's interested in catchin' up with you. I 'magine it'll be worth more'n that to him to find you waitin' for him when he gets here."

Woodbridge put his fifty cents back in his pocket. The tollkeeper, watching him, urged, "So if I was a runaway prentice, or was in any kind of trouble, I'd outbid anybody that might be followin'."

"I'm a freeman. Thomas Woodbridge. Nobody's looking for me."

"That's what they all say, and I don't blame 'em. But y' see, Forbes Road is the main haul for the big woods in the Ohio Country; and in order for that to look good to a man, things've got to be pretty bad behind him. So you just wait here with me, and we'll see what comes along."

Woodbridge climbed up onto the wagon seat.

" 'Fraid not," he said. "I'll be goin' along. Far as I know, you've got no authority to hold me."

The tollkeeper raised his rifle to the head of Woodbridge's dappled stallion, Prince.

"You'd be right, there, Woodbridge, except for one thing. When ya tried to skip payin' toll, ya 'powered me to hold ya for the sheriff. Now if you'll just get down off that wagon and lead your team back a little east of the toll cabin."

Woodbridge led his team back to the east of the toll cabin, yielding up his rifle to the keeper. He put feed bags on the horses and waited. The valley below faded into a hundred pinpoints of light in the bottom of a velvet bucket.

While the horses munched in their feed bags, Tom gazed between them, watching where the tollkeeper placed his rifle and gauging the distance from the tollhouse to the outer rim of the lantern light.

Little more than an hour passed before a single flickering lamp jiggled downhill from the east. It decorated a light, underslung chaise-type surrey with a trunk in the back boot. The rig passed Woodbridge and came to rest under the toll-cabin lantern, bouncing lightly on its springs. It tipped as a man of medium height got out on the right to talk to the keeper.

From his distance Woodbridge could tell there were questions and answers, and as they walked toward him he could hear the keeper.

"Yes, sir, I held him right here. He's the one, all right. Red curly hair and carries himself like he was General Washington."

A slightly familiar voice chuckled, "That's the one."

Close to Woodbridge a short, solid silhouette materialized, and from above a chest full of white ruffles came the pleasant drawl of Jonathan Blair.

"Hello, Woodbridge. I'm glad I found you."

The tollkeeper's disappointment was obvious as Blair extended his open hand. Woodbridge left it begging.

"You the one that was looking for me, Blair?"

"I inquired about you, Tom. But I didn't authorize these turnpike men to hold you up. However, since it's to both our advantages, we won't report them."

The tollman's mask of authority dissolved in the presence of Blair's much better one.

"Our advantages?" asked Woodbridge.

"Shuldane figured I might overtake you, and he sent along a new offer for your Bounty Land warrant."

They moved over by the light of the toll cabin. Blair's pleasant manner and the fact that he was someone from home melted Woodbridge, who asked: "How far you going? And why?"

"Business for Mr. Shuldane," Blair answered. "We're headed for the Mesopotamia tract."

Woodbridge caught the plural. He stepped over to look into the intimate, leathered interior of the low-slung chaise surrey.

Her eyelashes were powdered with road dust a little, and her face under the framing bonnet had taken color from the wind, but her throat was very white against the black velvet collar. A man would be willing to trade places with the horse that pulled the surrey, to see she didn't get jostled too much. But she shattered the sentiment.

"Hello, Tom." She said it as though he had just delivered some roasting ears to her house in Concord. And he said, "Hello, Miss Veronica," as though he had just dumped them on the kitchen table. He looked his surprise at Blair, who explained: "It was her idea. She wanted to come. We're taking it in easy stages, stopping at friends of the Shuldanes along the way."

Woodbridge looked into the surrey again, as if to find a third person. Blair stiffened a little.

"Miss Veronica's Uncle Webster started the trip with us," he explained quickly. "But he was taken unwell at Hartford. Miss Veronica decided to continue anyway."

"What about the offer, Mr. Blair?"

"Fifty dollars for your warrant, right here and now."

"Can you tell me right here and now what kind of a piece of land I can get in Mesopotamia for $50 . . . and make me out title to it, here and now?"

"No. Sam Hosmer will make out the title when you give him the money. But anybody knows that cash makes a man more liquid than a warrant."

"I'd like to look around the land office in Pittsburgh tomorrow to see what I can do. The government meant a man to get a hundred acres for a hundred-acre warrant."

"You'll be lucky to get twenty."

"I'll look anyway. Waitin' ain't hurt so far."

Blair shrugged. He looked down into the dark valley and said: "Well, we'd better get down to the Eagle Inn. You'd better come with us."

Woodbridge could see nothing of Fort Pitt in the dark, but after the lonesome haul across Pennsylvania it was good to be going up the steps of the inn with people he knew, however slightly. From the doorway came light and noise. The proprietor surged forward to greet them. His voice was warming, like the smell of cooked meat that came from inside.

"Welcome, Miss Shuldane. We got your father's postal. How do you do, Mr. Blair. We'll see to your horse. Come in."

Woodbridge put one foot over the threshold. But there was an arm across the door, and the proprietor's voice.

"Good evening, my friend. The wagoners' taproom is the next door down."

Woodbridge looked up in surprise, caught awkwardly with one foot over the threshold. His lower jaw slid forward. As he turned to leave, he heard Blair say, "He's with us." Beyond Blair's shoulder he glimpsed Veronica's surprised face becoming aware of the situation.

Recrossing the puncheon porch toward the road, Woodbridge heard the proprietor's stammering apologies and suddenly felt him groping for his left forearm.

"Please, I'm covered with shame. I saw you drive up in a separate wagon. Naturally, I thought you'd prefer the quicker service in the wagoners' taproom. Do come in."

But Woodbridge snapped his left arm free with a jolt that trembled the jowls of the proprietor.

There was a guffaw from a leather-clad figure at the hitching rail, and a stream of tobacco juice arched across the porch, landing on the receding boot of the proprietor.

A toothless hole in the face of the leather-clad opened in a grin. "Guess you can go in now, mister, if you still want."

"No thanks," answered Woodbridge. "Is there another place?"

"Right across there on the corner of Front Street, mister. Not such good eats, but better company by a damn' sight."

"You eat yet?" asked Woodbridge, who wanted to find someone to ask about land.

"Yeah, but I'll come along for a jolt of Monongahela. Name's Navarre. Slover Navarre."

"Woodbridge."

In the tavern on Front Street, Woodbridge looked down at his plate and ate.

Navarre said, "Well, what d'ya want to know?"

Woodbridge looked surprised.

"Well, you're jumpin' off from here, aren't ya?"

"Yeah. How'd you know?"

"So's everybody else that goes through. That's what these natives live off. Everybody's either on their way out, loaded up with hope, or on their way back, loaded down with grief. I only come in to bring in pelts, and git out. But I know enough ta tell ya what ya want t' know."

"Where's the land office?"

"There's two. Best one's upstairs over this eatery. But neither one's any good."

"Why?"

"They're sellin' land they never seen. Givin' out titles that ain't surveyed right. What you want with them?"

"Swap a land warrant for a land title."

"Don't. They won't give you what it's worth."

"Figure I'll try, anyhow. Where's the store?"

"What kind?"

"Hardware and like that."

"Go to Higgins. Don't buy everything he tries to sell ya. But take an ax. A good one. And some rope and canvas. Got a good rifle?"

"A Jaeger. One-ounce ball. Smooth bore."

"Fair. You got plenty of shot?"

"Six pounds, I guess."

"H-mm. How far you goin'?" asked the trapper.

"All the way, I guess. Up toward the Erie Lake. Just south of the Greenville Treaty Line. Mesopotamia, they call the place."

Navarre looked surprised. "What for?"

"Raise hogs."

"There's better places."

"I got my lot all picked," said Woodbridge as he forked in the slumgullion before him.

"Better take twenty pounds of shot lead, then."

"I thought it was all quiet this side of the Greenville Indian Treaty Line. We stay south of it. The Wyandots stay North."

"Huh!" The trapper signaled for another Monongahela. "Look at it this way, lad. Taken you're a Wyandot, a fractious critter like in Chief Rontondee's clan. You're accustomed to huntin' all over the Ohio Country for your meat. Now comes along a treaty—which you can't read. Neither can your Chief. But your Chief tells you: 'Commencin' now, if you're chasin' game to the south, and the game crosses this here imaginary Greenville Treaty Line to the south—this line that you can't see—well, you stop dead in your tracks. Don't cross it.' Now bear in mind, you tried huntin' up north and you found they didn't leave you no room hardly. You run right smack into Lake Erie. And the deer's got awful scarce up there. So's everything else. So you got to hunt south if you're gonna eat. And you come to this line. Are you gonna know where that line is, lad? And if you did know, are you gonna stop? And supposin' you was to make a fair guess at where the line was, and you meet a white man, like me, say, crossin' over in what you know's your side? And he don't give a hang about the line? Are you gonna shoot him just when he steps over the line? Or are you gonna go down a little south of the line and get him before he even gets close?"

Woodbridge took the question seriously. "I s'pose I'd maybe venture a little south, at least to see how many whites was there."

"Damn' right ya would! And when ya got down there, you'd find white men staking off the ground right up to the line, and some of 'em across the line, and no intentions of stopping anywheres short of Lake Erie. And what would you do, lad?"

Woodbridge stared out through the door to his horses. "Y-e-a-h," he said.

The man who seemed to be in charge of the eatery sloshed some yellow liquid from a crock into Navarre's mug. "There y' are, Hog."

Navarre's face jerked up to freeze the proprietor as he stood. The mug ran over. The proprietor swabbed the table with a rag and left hurriedly.

Navarre studied Woodbridge's face.

Woodbridge looked back at his plate. "Yeah," he said. "I'll get twenty pounds of shot."

The trapper showed Woodbridge where he could get a bunk for the night. But looking at the loungers that hung around the front of the place, the red-haired lad drove his wagon into a small stand of trees a little way off from the houses. He fed the shoats, crawled into the back of his wagon, and spent the night under Jonathan Woodbridge's great-coat.

Pittsburgh in the daylight was 110 cabins and a thousand people jammed in the flat triangle in the bottom of the valley between the Allegheny and the Monongahela rivers. Woodbridge judged that the people who looked like contented spectators at a hanging were the natives; the rest—that is to say, most of them—were either coming or going. For Pittsburgh was the conditioning ground between civiliza-tion and wilderness. If you were "going out," Pittsburgh was the last look at women with brushed hair and lace cuffs. If you were "coming in," it was the first.

As he walked up Front Street to find Higgins's Store, Woodbridge saw smooth-shaven men walk briskly down toward the river landing. And he saw heavily bearded men walk sluggishly up from the river landing, gawking around as if squinting in the bright light of the clear-ing called Pittsburgh.

The Higgins of Higgins's Store showed Woodbridge an oil lantern. "Very good, they tell us on the frontier, if you take your own oil." Woodbridge shook his head.

Higgins pointed to a barrel of iron bolts. Woodbridge bought a few and twenty pounds of ready-made shot and twenty pounds of bar-shot lead. He also bought a canvas tarpaulin, one hundred feet of rope, and an ax, and then walked down to the tavern where he'd eaten supper the night before.

An outdoor stairway went up to the second floor. The sign at the bottom said:

Miller and Zane
Western Land Agents
Bounty Land Warrants Honored
Western Land Business Handled for Eastern Owners

Three loungers reluctantly moved away from the stairway, and Woodbridge went up.

Miller was polite. He pointed to the plats nailed up on the walls. There were men grouped around them, studying. "We can give you good tracts in several locations. The time is right to buy in the Ohio

Company Purchase at Marietta. They have a good store there now. Safe, too. There's a detachment of troops due to be quartered there soon."

Woodbridge said, "I'm interested in the Mesopotamia Tract."

Miller seemed not to hear. "We get very favorable reports back now, too, from those settling in the Miami Purchase, Judge Symmes's tract. Very little Indian trouble."

"I want to be in or near the Mesopotamia Tract," said Woodbridge.

"Lad, you make a mistake," answered Miller. "Too far north. Just under the Greenville Treaty Line."

"Got my lot all picked. Can you sell it to me?"

Miller lifted his gaze over Woodbridge's shoulder, and his voice held more respect: "Back again, Mr. Blair? Can I help you?"

Woodbridge turned around. Blair said: "No, we're looking for this young man. Go ahead, Tom."

Veronica nodded to Tom, and the men in the room turned to look at her. Woodbridge's voice sharpened to pin Miller down to business. "What about Mesopotamia?"

"I'm sorry, sir. Mesopotamia is the one development I can't offer you. Nate Shuldane won't let us land agents handle any part of it any more. Wants to control the settlement of it himself, I guess. He took it out of our hands."

Woodbridge stiffened. "How long ago?"

"Why, since you ask, just this morning. Mr. Blair, here, brought—"

Woodbridge's neck turned red. "What'll you give me for a hundred-acre Bounty Land warrant?" he asked. "Cash."

"Twenty dollars."

"That's only twenty cents an acre."

"Your warrant's only a piece of paper until the government surveys."

"I was offered thirty back east."

"You should have taken it, mister."

Woodbridge turned to leave. Veronica forbore any comment. But the wisp of a smile reproached him as she and Blair preceded Woodbridge down the outdoor stairway. The loungers at the base of the stairs were rewarded for a month's loafing when Veronica passed through them, and they took their reward from head to foot.

When they got to where Woodbridge's horses were tied, Blair said, "Woodbridge, have you made arrangements for boat passage down-river?"

"No."

"Well, if you want to go with us, I spoke for passage for you and your team and wagon on our boat."

"Appreciate it. But I plan to look around Pittsburgh a few days to see what's the best trade I can make for my warrant."

"I think I can arrange that for you too, Woodbridge." There was a wonderful comfort in Blair's words, somehow. "Shuldane authorized me to use my judgment if you rejected his first offer. I guess he knew you'd drive a hard bargain. I'm certain I can make you an arrangement you'll find very acceptable when we get on the boat."

It seemed as though Blair could have told him some details about the arrangement. But looking into Blair's open face, Woodbridge had the feeling that this time it would be right, and Veronica's smile reinforced the promise.

Woodbridge noticed the small blue veins that showed through the crystalline skin under Veronica's eyes. She was a self-possessed china doll with a pulse. He said suddenly, "I'm ready, except there's one thing I'd like to buy at Higgins's Store first."

"All right," Blair said. "Suppose you take Miss Shuldane with you while I see to getting her trunk and the surrey down to the boat. Meet me at the river. Ask for the boat owned by Platt Thayer."

At the store Mr. Higgins said, "Ha, back for the lantern, young man?"

"No," answered Woodbridge. "How much is a pane of window glass?"

"Man, don't spend your money like that. Take the lantern or more nails or shot or an extra knife."

"How much for the glass?"

Higgins sighed and looked at Veronica as though measuring her for a window.

"How big?" he asked.

"Big enough for light. Small enough not to break."

"A dollar," said Higgins. As he was wrapping it, they heard a clattering of horses in front of the store as two soldiers rode down toward the waterfront to the hazard of the pedestrians. Miss Shuldane looked surprised.

Higgins explained. "Looking for that one that calls himself Governor of the Northwest. He comes in here every so often to recruit westbound squatters. Helps them find the good places."

"You ever seen the man?" asked Woodbridge.

"Nope. And don't know anybody who has. But the squatters call him Governor of the Northwest Territory."

Veronica said: "Is it some sort of joke? Everyone knows, of course, that General St. Clair is governor of the Territory."

"The government doesn't take it like a joke. You saw the soldiers."

Platt Thayer's keelboat was of the large type. And as the boat began to be caught by the current, he shouted at the passengers from his position at the stern steering sweep.

"Now try to understand this. A keelboat is nothing but a big keel with a little hull built around it. That means ya don't go runnin' all of ya to one side of the boat all at once. One of the crew'll come around and show ya how to lash down your wagons. Keep your animals still. And stay out of the way of the pole men on the catwalks. If ya hear the yell, 'Indian!' get under the housing. If we upset, swim for the south bank, not the north. Better chance to keep your hair. There's two ladies aboard. They'll be in that forward compartment. See that none of ya go stumblin' in there by accident or otherwise."

The first four days were quiet as the sixteen passengers studied the boat and the shore and each other.

On the fifth day Woodbridge was on his knees feeding the shoats when one of them scrambled out of his hands in fright. Woodbridge recaptured the young pig and looked behind him. He followed a pair of leather leggings up to a leather hunting jacket and a leather face. Woodbridge had not seen the man get on the boat, nor had he seen him in the five days afloat. But such were the ways of Slover Navarre.

Without preliminaries Navarre said: "Soon's you can afford it, Woodbridge, get rid of that Jaeger musket. Get some kind of a gun with riflin' in the bore."

"This gun was good enough for my old man in the Rebellion."

"Sure. But out here you'll get only one shot at a deer to feed yourself. And one shot at a Indian to save your hair. As for reloadin', you'll never get the chance. To shoot like that, you need riflin' in your gun."

On the sixth day Woodbridge was leaning on the housing near the stern, looking toward the bow where Veronica and Blair were talking. Navarre appeared soundlessly beside Woodbridge.

"Day'll come," he announced, "when that'll all be worth $10 an acre, maybe $20."

"What will?" asked Woodbridge.

Navarre looped an arch of tobacco juice shoreward into the wind so that its trail eloquently described several thousand acres of the north shoreline.

"All that," he said.

"What you gettin' at?" asked Woodbridge.

"Did you cashier your warrant?"

"Nope."

"Good."

"Don't know as I was so smart. Got myself in a position now where I pretty near got to accept what they offer."

"Don't ever believe it, boy. Hang on to that warrant till you can cash it in on its face value to the government. Nobody can offer you the kind of money that land'll be worth in a few years when the survey's through."

"But meanwhile I got to have land to live on."

"Ain't that enough for you?"

"What?"

Navarre spewed out an all-encompassing rainbow of tobacco juice.

"All that out there," he said.

"But that don't belong to me."

" 'Course not. But you can live on it till the government gets its survey made. I can name you a hundred families out there now, and I can find three hundred more livin' just like they owned it. Squatters."

"Nobody chases 'em off?"

"Yeah, every so often. But they move right back on soon as St. Clair's troops leave."

"That wouldn't do for me. I'm plannin' on hogs."

"No. I guess it wouldn't suit you."

"But it means I can hold out for a good price for my warrant. I could squat if I had to."

"That's right, boy. And if you do it, and if you should get in trouble by it, ask around for Slover Navarre."

"What can you do? You're a trapper."

But Navarre had already turned and was walking aft.

On the seventh day Slover Navarre was put ashore at a place called Belpre. From the river four cabins were visible; but there were more people than that on the beach, and they greeted the skinny leather-clad trapper with motions that Woodbridge took for affection.

On the eighth day Woodbridge and Blair stood amidships watching the Indian shore. The fog almost obscured the north bank, but that only increased the impression that millions of acres were going by.

"How come Shuldane named the place Mesopotamia?" asked Woodbridge.

"I take credit for that," said Blair.

"Credit?"

"Yes. I persuaded Shuldane to name it Mesopotamia."

"You've been out here, then?"

"No."

Before he continued, Blair's face relaxed with the look of a man about to tell a story for his own benefit. "You see, Mesopotamia, they think, was the beginning of civilization. The one over between the Tigris and the Euphrates, I mean. They think they were the ones who made the first handwriting. And the first set of laws—the Code of Hammurabi."

"I don't figure there'll be much writin' or lawmakin' in this place."

"No, but up where we're going they're sort of starting all over again. They'll make everything new, to suit themselves. They'll band together to propagate themselves. The old Mesopotamia was the first real democracy. Even the gods had to submit their propositions to a kind of Continental Congress, a group of interdependent men. They invented justice in commerce."

"How about land?" asked Woodbridge. "Justice there, too, in this old Mesopotamia?"

The film of glory, like the third eyelid of an eagle, vanished from Blair's face, and he reverted abruptly to Shuldane's shrewd, sharp-eyed assistant.

"It's only a name," he snapped.

The fog turned into a light drizzle. As they stood watching a million acres of wilderness go by, land seemed plentiful. The time was right for Blair to speak of Shuldane's proposal, if he was going to; but he did not. Woodbridge said, "Mr. Blair, you spoke of a new offer from Shuldane."

Blair looked ashore and then astern. But it was Woodbridge's habit in conversation to focus both of his eyes on one of his companion's, and to wait for his answers in such an attitude of attention that he physically blocked all avenues of conversational escape.

"Yes, Tom. Shuldane will go as high as $70 cash for your warrant, providing you turn over the warrant when the final offer is made—which is now."

"What difference if we make the deal now or when we get to Mesopotamia, where I can see the land I'm to get?"

"Tom, Shuldane doesn't want that warrant to get to Mesopotamia. All the present settlers turned in their warrants for cash at a considerable discount because of the risk Shuldane took in putting up the purchase money. It happens now that Shuldane can make a better offer for warrants; but no sense in waving that in the faces of the men who already settled there at ten and twenty cents on the dollar for their warrants."

"Don't quite add up, Mr. Blair. Nobody needs to know."

"Maybe not. But mix that in with the fact that you might take your warrant and join with others who hold warrants and settle somewhere else at full warrant value after the government surveys. That could start a lot of people doing it. Be hard after that for Shuldane to sell off the rest of Mesopotamia if that got started."

Blair seemed not unkind. Woodbridge even had the feeling that this was a roundabout suggestion from Blair. But he couldn't quite figure it.

"I kind of had that loose in my mind," said Woodbridge. "When the land's surveyed, the government'll cash warrants for full acreage value."

"That'll take a while," said Blair. "Meanwhile, you've got to have a place to live."

"It's not so crowded a man couldn't kind of borrow a piece of land for a while."

"Woodbridge, you're a fool. Everybody else was glad to settle for twenty and thirty cents on a warrant acre."

"Could be their warrants didn't cost them as much as my old man's cost him. It'd kind of be like sellin' my old man for seventy cents."

"Eighty dollars for your warrant, Woodbridge."

"There's some say a hundred acres out here will be worth $1,000. If that's so, the lot I got picked out will be worth ten times that, the way it's situated. At that rate I can settle for less land than a hundred acres, but not for less money."

The drizzle increased to a rain which was wetting Blair's fine dark-blue twill coat. He brushed some drops from his sleeve along with his patience.

"Woodbridge, it's up to you. One hundred dollars for your warrant now. Or keep your warrant, and I don't know what it'll be worth in Mesopotamia. I'm carrying a letter from Shuldane to Hosmer. I don't know what's in it. But I advise you to take the hundred."

"My old man must have had a good reason to tell me to see the land and the title before I gave over his warrant. He held the warrant ever since the Rebellion, waiting for 'em to survey and tell him he could go stake his claim. I'll hold it till I see the land. Funny, Shuldane objects to that."

"Perhaps, but Shuldane has the respect of the people in Mesopotamia. He furnishes them a contact in Philadelphia. He has lent them money when they needed it. He is working to get troops up there to patrol. No matter why he does it, it means respect for Shuldane. He means to keep it that way. I wouldn't foul his intention. What's your answer, Woodbridge?"

"I'll give over the warrant when I see the land."

Blair turned away and went down two steps to go inside the housing. The rain pelted down now, plastering Woodbridge's blue shirt against his chest muscles in the shape of a molded armor breastplate. He walked aft to his wagon. With his knife he ripped a three-foot strip from the length of the canvas. Placing the small strip over the shoats' crate, he said, "I guess if our warrant's worth $100 out here on the water, it'll be worth a good-sized chunk of land in Mesopotamia."

Muffled corroboration came from under the canvas. Woodbridge took the remainder of the canvas, pulled it over the backs and heads of Jock and Prince, and told them, "It begins to look like Jonathan knew what he was talking about when he said land is worth more than the money they can offer us."

He took the warrant from his pocket, dried it off on the underside of the canvas, and locked it in the document box. He crawled under the wagon and pulled his father's coat over him.

By noon of the ninth day, Woodbridge's loaded wagon sat next to Blair's surrey on the Fort Washington dock. Blair said: "Here's the plan, Woodbridge. We go up the Miami about a mile, where we get on another boat that takes us up north. Shuldane arranged for a squad of troops to accompany us and escort us over to Mesopotamia."

"Thanks," said Woodbridge. "But I've got no more boat money. I'm going up the land trail. Faster, anyway, I hear."

Veronica got out of the surrey. Blair said, "What's the hurry, Wood-bridge?"

"Just want to get things settled."

"You know the route?" asked Blair.

"I'll find it."

"I'll draw you a map."

Blair went to the other side of the surrey to draw his map. Veronica said, "Tom, Sam Hosmer wrote that there are places on the trail north that a wagon can't manage."

"I'm pretty handy with a horse and wagon, Miss Veronica. But would you have room in your plunder for my pane of glass?"

She took it from him and placed it inside the surrey.

The trail was packed down hard in the center, where it had once been a footpath. Woodbridge walked on the hard center, ahead of the horse and wagon, looking to the front. He carried his gun with both hands, across his front, wondering how a man could keep this up. That was when he heard the wagon-wheel squeak change tone behind him, as if under some new weight. He whirled around to find himself looking down the end of a long-barreled Kentucky-type rifle. The rifle-man was sitting on Woodbridge's wagon seat. But instead of a threat, the man's beard parted in a wide grin. Slover Navarre released a stream of tobacco juice, and said: "You're doin' pretty well, lad, except for one thing. You'd do better to watch more to the rear. Not much trouble ever comes from dead ahead."

Woodbridge grinned. The leather-clad trapper continued.

"Another thing, if you ever get startled like that again, and if you're going to keep that old Jaeger, don't whirl around so sudden that you jerk all of your primin' powder out."

Woodbridge shoved his frizzen forward and looked into a nearly empty flash pan.

Navarre explained that he was on his way north, waiting here to meet another trapper. They began to prepare supper in a lean-to Navarre had thrown up. Woodbridge let the shoats out of their crate to feed them.

Navarre looked on with curiosity. "Never see any little white critters like that out here," he said. "Only them skinny, homely lookin' brown woods pigs. Land sharks, they call 'em. Never saw any chubby little critters like yours out here."

"Nope. You won't for a while, either," said Woodbridge.

"Don't look like they'd thrive in the woods like these wild fightin' rascals they got out here."

"They can't. These y' got to take care of like babies. They're kind of helpless, but they'll grow fat and heavy."

"You sound like they're somethin' awful special."

"They are. Bedfords. Pure-bred. From England."

"How'd a fellow like you get 'em?"

Woodbridge's flickering cheek muscles cut off further questions. He looked around at Navarre's lean-to. "I was going to ask you," he said, "how come for a trapper I don't see any traps?"

Navarre grinned and sluiced a bullet of tobacco against a tree trunk. "All right," he said. "My mistake. We'll quit the questions."

When they finished eating together, Navarre said: "If I'm not out of bounds again, what you doin' so far east and south? Change your plans?"

"No. Why?"

"Thought you were goin' up north to the Mesopotamia settlement up under the Greenville Line."

"I am. Following this map right here."

Navarre studied the map that Woodbridge pulled out.

"Where'd you get this?" he asked.

"Fellow named Blair made it for me."

"Friend of yours?"

"An acquaintance, I guess you'd say. Why?"

"Well, you'll get there this way. Maybe. But it'll take you two weeks. Any reason he might want it to take ya that long?"

Woodbridge studied the man who called himself a trapper. He looked over at the document box in the wagon.

"Draw me the short way," he said.

With a burned ember Navarre charcoaled a trail on the paper. It went up roughly parallel to the Miami River, but straighter than the river. Navarre drew in several small squares which he explained were cabins. He wrote the names of the occupants beside the cabins, and verbally named the cliffs and streams and clearings.

"How do you happen to know all these settlers?" asked Woodbridge.

Navarre grinned. "Where'd you get your fancy pigs?" he asked.

On the following morning Woodbridge pointed his wagon back west

toward the Miami River, where he would pick up a new route for
Mesopotamia, or Hosmer Village, as it was called out here, where a
man's name was more reassuring than a Biblical symbol.

# Chapter 3: MESOPOTAMIA

ON THE land sellers' maps in the East, in the
conversation in Concord, and in the Shuldane advertisements in the
Boston newspaper Mesopotamia was a glorious citadel.

Vaguely, the existence of Mesopotamia gave a little shade of independence to the tone of voice of the apprentices and bound men along
the seaboard. It gave a slight inflection of arrogance to every debtor
and tradesman and small merchant, for Mesopotamia was a vague
sanctuary somewhere in the West. In the fancy of the easterner,
Mesopotamia was a place to go if anything went wrong.

But in the fact, Mesopotamia was eleven log cabins and a certain
stubbornness.

Arrival there was a severe disappointment. When a newcomer suc-
ceeded in finding his way safely to that particular six square miles out
of the whole vast forest of the Northwest Territory, he felt full of his
triumph, as though he were the first to discover the place, and he expected a heroic welcome. The present settlers, on the other hand, knew
very well that the wonder was not that the newcomer had found them
but that anyone had survived for him to find. Hence the initial greeting between Sam Hosmer and Tom Woodbridge, though civil enough,
was like a handshake between a right and a left hand.

Tom Woodbridge pulled up to a stop in front of Hosmer's Store. He
crawled down from his wagon.

"By God, I actually found it!" he said.

And Sam Hosmer looked around at the four visible cabins and at the burying yard in the center, and said, "Yeah, we're still here, some of us."

The very first settler in Hosmer Village had been there only twenty-six months, but already the lines of protocol were sharply drawn. The newcomer quickly learned that the Hosmers and the Stikes and the Fitchburgs were there first and that the Masons came four months later. Each family thereafter preserved its time of arrival with the jealousy of a first lieutenant of militia guarding his date of rank.

It was unnecessary, though, for they wore the information on their faces and their clothes.

Within an hour the presence of the new wagon in the center of the village brought most of the settlers to the store. Woodbridge hardly recognized Hope Emerson. She must have been one of the early ones, for her cloth clothes were gone and she was in deerskin like Sam Hosmer and Mike Stikes. Her face was just as firm and mannish as he remembered her in Concord, but her long straight jaw line was more severe. The blonde hair was now cut short. It was combed straight back by the fingers of her hard brown hands, which were becoming square, like a man's. Woodbridge had heard that a year ago she had pulled out the arrow that had widowed her, buried Harvey, and finished the harvesting before she unhitched the ox that same day. Her one feminine gesture, perhaps, was that her hand went unconsciously to her breast in relief when she saw that it was Woodbridge.

"Oh, I was afraid it was my young brother John come out here," she said.

She extended her brown hand to Tom.

Mike Stikes's gaunt face was as cavernous as Woodbridge remembered it. The vertical gray hair was toward white now, and his leather blacksmith's apron had shaped itself to his lanky legs like part of his skin. He clamped Woodbridge's hand in a bony vise.

Morgan Brady was a medium old-timer, having gone to leather breeches, but still preserving his wool shirt as long as it would last.

Jim Hawkins still wore his eastern clothes, though they would not last much longer obviously. His hair was long, and it was apparent that Hawkins had had a serious thought or two in the last half-year. Woodbridge noticed, too, that he was now called Jim, instead of Jimmy, by the men in the village.

The quick, concerned glances of the people warned Woodbridge that there was good reason not to take offense at Loretta Shane's spontaneous disappointment upon seeing him. Woodbridge had never seen the woman.

"I'd thought may be it was Shane back safe," she said.

The people here with southern accents were strangers to Woodbridge.

But this was no one-way inspection. The cold face of Mesopotamia drew mixed judgment upon Thomas Woodbridge, as though they had not known him before, or would not credit his past record.

The thick forearms that hung loosely at his sides were all to the good. The knotty bicep that strained the fibers of his rolled sleeve when he patted his chest pocket was good, though the gesture itself was puzzling. The maturity in the face was good. The broad-based stance and the jutting chin—well, some thought it firmness and some "cussedness."

Woodbridge noticed that though old man Hosmer didn't raise his voice, the store quieted for his remark.

"Folks, Tom's gonna take a lot and settle. For the benefit of some of you new ones from Virginia, Tom's from Concord. Son of Jonathan Woodbridge. You bring your title with you, Tom?"

"Shuldane said you could make the transaction, Hosmer."

A few of the elders snapped their heads resentfully toward the newcomer. If Shuldane and Hosmer didn't command a "mister" from this redhead, whom might he respect? But Sam Hosmer, the father, founder, and patron saint of Mesopotamia, asked calmly, "What you going to pay with, Tom?"

"My father's Bounty Land warrant."

"Good enough. Which lot you want?"

"I picked my land from the plat. But I'd like to look at the ground a mite 'fore I surrender the warrant."

"Good sense, boy. Some of us that picked from the plat found ourselves on the side of the cliff or in a swamp."

"That's what I mean."

"Take yourself a look around tomorrow," said Hosmer. "Then Thursday everybody can come into the store and you can pick your lot and get title."

Woodbridge looked surprised. Hosmer explained: "Don't mind everybody gawkin' at your transaction. Only reason we do it that way: say you picked d'rectly back of the Widow Emerson, for instance. Well, everybody knows she's got her eye on that little level spot, soon as she can afford it, to plant flax on. And we all want her to do it so we can have some clothes around here. If you were to pick that spot she would speak up."

"It agrees with me," said Woodbridge. And the people went back to their work in Mesopotamia, which Woodbridge noticed was here more often called Hosmer Village.

Woodbridge stayed the night with Jim Hawkins.

Slightly after noon on Thursday, the settlers began to drift in to the store again. Sam Hosmer was pegging the Mesopotamia plat up on the wall of the store where the inside of the logs had been hewn flat. Amos Exeter hoisted himself onto the store counter beside the pile of blankets, Mike Stikes leaned against the wall near Hosmer, and some stood around and talked in the middle of the floor. The women were looking at Judith Dolk's baby, though Hope Emerson stood apart from the group.

The murmuring voices quieted down when Sam Hosmer said: "Well, somebody's gonna get a new neighbor today. Let's find out where Tom picked."

The crowd closed in, leaving a small circle of open floor around Sam Hosmer, who stood beside the plat on the wall. Under iron-gray hair his brown face was short and broad, like that of some aged and genial snapping turtle. The network of crinkles was shaped to a grin today because Woodbridge was further evidence of the permanency of Mesopotamia.

From the back of the room Morgan Brady yelled, "Sam, it's gettin' so crowded here that some of us'll have to be pushin' on to the north."

Stikes said, "It's not so crowded yet that Jim Hawkins didn't have to stand Indian watch on his weddin' night."

Hawkins blushed. There were grins until Hope Emerson wiped them off. "Anybody pushes more'n five miles north of my place," she said, "and he'll wish he had a crowd with him. I was missing another sheep this morning. And there were footprints."

"I know it, Hope," said Sam Hosmer. "That's just one more reason it's good we've got one more man now. Tom, step up here and mark an X in the lot ya picked out."

Woodbridge took the charcoal from Sam Hosmer. Directly opposite the site of Hosmer's store, and at the end of the long oval common, the plat showed a large pie-shaped lot. The common was not yet on the ground at Mesopotamia, but it was on the plat. It would include the area where the graveyard was now. The lot south of the common would be the logical center of the village, Woodbridge thought.

"Ever since my old man turned a copy of the plat over to me," said Woodbridge, "I've had my eye on this lot right here."

He reached up and drew a heavy **X** through the pie-shaped lot on the common and through the adjoining acreage. He handed the charcoal back to Hosmer. But Hosmer did not reach to retrieve it. He was staring at the **X**.

The room hushed to the point where the new baby's cry was a shriek.

"What's the matter?" asked Woodbridge.

"Ye got to pick over again, Tom," said Hosmer.

"What's the matter with that one?"

"That one's reserved for Mr. Shuldane."

Woodbridge looked around at the faces for a better explanation. But Judith Dolk looked down at her baby. Mike Stikes looked out the door. Jim Hawkins bent over to remove a burr from his trousers.

"I suppose you picked a second choice, didn't you, Tom?"

"No, I didn't. And I'd think a man on the site would have first call over a man that's a thousand road miles from here."

But Hosmer was no longer listening, nor was anyone else. Out in front of the store two mounted soldiers had ridden up and were tying their horses to the posts. The villagers could have been no more surprised if a city-rigged coach and four had appeared, but at that they were little more surprised than one of the soldiers whose voice floated into the store.

"By God, Thompkins, you win! I would of sworn there wan't two live white men north of Boxford's Cabin."

The one with the chevrons answered, "See you pay up, then."

"I'll pay," answered the short one. "But will you take the same odds they ain't here this time next year when we come up squatter huntin'?"

The villagers stared at each other in hopeful amazement. Some even thought the soldiers might be part of the troops Shuldane had promised to secure for protection. But the people were in for a greater surprise, for the two soldiers were followed immediately by a surrey that was like no vehicle ever seen in Hosmer Village. Two more soldiers brought up the rear, and Mesopotamia was on its feet walking out onto the porch of the store.

Blair and Veronica Shuldane got out of the surrey. Blair shook hands with Sam Hosmer. Woodbridge and his land, or lack of it, were forgotten as the people crowded around Blair on the porch, leaving Woodbridge standing beside the plat inside the store.

Woodbridge looked at the plat. Jonathan Woodbridge had not known the half of it. "Shuldane has got a net spread from Philadelphia to Boston," the old man had said. But the fact was, the net of Elnathan Shuldane reached a thousand miles out into the big woods, even up under the Greenville Treaty Line. But it wasn't the kind of a net you could get your hands on and tear up. It was a net of legalities. It was a net of strange loyalties that owned the souls of men like Sam Hosmer.

Alone in the store Woodbridge studied the plat. There was a lot that fronted along the river just west of Buttrick's cabin. The other side of it faced the common, and there appeared to be some high ground on the west end of it that would keep pigs safe from the cold night fogs of the river. It was located near the center and it would appreciate in value.

Having made his decision, Woodbridge walked out onto the porch. Watching from the far rail of the porch, the red-haired Woodbridge was surprised that such a dapper popinjay as Blair should be the center of such deferential attention out here where fluff-fronted shirts would seem to solve no problem. But they pressed close around Blair, men and women both.

"Is it true, Blair, that the survey's gonna start soon?"

"Did Shuldane get any of the delegates at Congress to holler about St. Clair not sendin' any troops up here?"

"Do they know back East that Chief Rontondee ain't even givin' lip service to the Greenville Treaty? Do they know that Tecumseh's stirrin' up tribes from Lake Erie to Orleans and that the British are helpin' 'im?"

Woodbridge could not hear the answers from Blair's urbane voice in the center of the crowd, but he could see the law man nodding affirmatively most of the time, comfortingly; and his answers seemed very satisfying to the eager questioners.

"Is it true," asked Hosmer, "that Harrison has got the Congress ready to approve small government land sales as low as a hundred acres on twenty years' credit?"

Blair's answer did not seem to come so readily. As the men leaned forward to catch the answer, Woodbridge wondered why Sam Hosmer, who had led a party out here before there was even a guide map, should listen to Blair as though he stood at the feet of the prophet.

Woodbridge noticed that one other beside himself stood apart from the crowd. He noticed, too, that a miniature inquisition was taking place. Miss Veronica had obviously put great thought into her costume. There was not a stitch of silk or linen showing. The hat was a plain gray felt bowler. The coat was beautifully cut, but it was stark gray from her throat to six inches from the porch floor. Nor did any bright-colored skirt project below the coat, only small black boots. Woodbridge noticed that even the little black strip of velvet, which had made her throat so white that night on Forbes Road, had been stripped off the collar. She had been to great pains. How could she know that even this would not be enough?

The inquistion was not noticed by the rest of the men, it was that bitterly quiet. Except for Hope Emerson, the women all greeted Veronica, took her hand, or brushed an arm around her back briefly, inquiring after her father's health. But it was pointedly brief, and cruel on both sides.

As the women looked at Veronica's translucent complexion and brushed hair, their hands went automatically to their own heads. But Judith Dolk caught herself in the unfamiliar motion and stopped her hand mid-air, studying its square-cut nails and bramble scratches. By her expression she was looking into some brutal mirror that reflected the past beside the present. The mirror was Veronica.

The women then moved quickly to the crowd around Sam Hosmer and Blair, leaving Veronica to contemplate the backs of their righteously fading dresses and a few deerskin skirts.

Woodbridge watched Veronica furtively unfasten a gold wristlet and slip it into her pocket. She saw him.

"You're here so soon?" she said.

But Faith Hawkins at that moment detached herself from the crowd to speak to Veronica.

Faith Hawkins, who still owned Mesopotamia's only unfaded dress, reached up to pull from Veronica's gray collar a long black thread.

"That collar looks almost as if it were made especially to have a little velvet band around it, Veronica," she said. "A pity they didn't put one on. You must come over to our cabin and I'll sew one on for you."

The suggestion that there was an inch of velvet in Mesopotamia obviously surprised Veronica.

"Oh, yes, you'd be surprised," said Faith, "at a lot of things out here. Why, just the other day Sam Hosmer was saying that a lot of fifth-rate

eastern lawyers have come west to Cincinnati expecting to be Territorial judges right away." She let her eyes play over toward Blair. "And
then they're surprised to find that out here they're still fifth-rate
lawyers."

Veronica stiffened. But the Shuldanes were quick. She smiled and
said: "Faith, I'd like it if you'd fix this collar. I'll bring it over."

When the devastation was over, Woodbridge thought Veronica
looked like a poor little china doll lost from its shelf, and he wanted
to reach out and put it carefully back where it belonged. He went over
to her, in fact, for that purpose. But, close up, the small intricate face
with the delicate nostrils and high cheekbones defied assistance, and
Woodbridge's remark came out unintentionally harsh.

"Looks like even your fifth best coat was a little too good, Miss
Veronica."

She looked over at Blair, who was still answering questions.

"Just because a man happens to make a reputation for himself while
he's still young . . ." she began.

"I was talking about coats, not lawyers," said Woodbridge. "But
since lawyers are on your mind, if there were a few less lawyers it might
be easier for a man to get a piece of land."

"You had a better chance than most for your land," she said. "And
a better offer for your warrant. But you don't trust your best friends."

"Not when they're so interested in cutting a soldier's warrant down
to thirty acres in a dicker that forgets how he earned it."

"Well, it was your father who earned it. And it seems to me he never
went around asking for the world to be handed to him."

"No, he didn't," answered Woodbridge, "and mighty little of it he
got. What with worryin' that everybody else got theirs. Includin' your
old man."

"I can see you plan to correct that mistake."

Woodbridge nodded. "And then some," he said.

His emphatic answer carried to Stikes, who looked over at Woodbridge.

He yelled to Hosmer: "Sam, we're forgettin' what we come for today.
Woodbridge is entitled to pick his lot so he can get a roof over his head
before snowfall!"

As they moved into the store, Blair saw Woodbridge for the first
time. Woodbridge grinned at the surprise on Blair's face, and through

the crowd he saw Blair reach under his coat and pull out an envelope which he handed to Hosmer.

When they were reassembled inside the store, Hosmer asked, "You got a second choice yet, Tom?"

"Yeah."

Woodbridge walked forward and took the charcoal off the bench.

While he was doing so, Sam Hosmer absently opened the envelope he'd received from Blair. As he read, though, his attention to the letter increased to the point that the network of facial wrinkles slowly realigned themselves into Hosmer's perpetual concern for Mesopotamia.

Woodbridge walked up to the plat and drew an X through the riverbank lot next to Asa Buttrick's cabin.

"Since I can't have the big one on the common, I'll take this one," he said.

Stikes said: "What about it, Sam? He's picked a good one. Any reason he can't have title right now?"

Hosmer turned slowly from the letter toward Woodbridge and the plat. "Yes, it seems there is," he said. "I just got a letter here from Shuldane. It says: 'Effective upon delivery of this letter, no more of my lands in the Mesopotamia settlement will be sold directly for military bounty warrants. You will accept, on my behalf, only currency, or notes on banks known to me.'"

The people sat in a sort of stunned silence, staring at Woodbridge.

Hosmer said, "I guess that means you, Tom."

Mike Stikes protested, "What does he give as a reason, Sam?"

"None."

"Then it seems to me, Sam, that since Woodbridge didn't get his first choice because he picked the Shuldane reserve lot, like most of us did, he should be allowed to pay by warrant. Unless Mr. Shuldane gives a good reason why he shouldn't."

Sam Hosmer spoke slowly. "Half the men in this room owe Mr. Shuldane for part credit on their land, and the other half owe him for their lives when he arranged to get that shipment of corn up to us during the famine winter."

Brady interrupted. "It's not as though it wasn't added to our mortgages, Sam."

Hosmer's short corded neck snapped his head around, "Ye didn't ask for a free ride when ye come here, did ye, Brady?" His voice softened. "So if Mr. Shuldane wants to adopt a certain policy about the land he owns, he's not obliged to explain to us why. I'm sorry, Tom."

Blair said: "Tom, I'll be going back East in a few days. You go back down with me far as Cincinnati. I'll take you to a couple of land offices there where we can get you some land for your warrant."

Woodbridge ignored the lawyer. He pointed to the extreme western edge of the plat of Mesopotamia. "Who owns this strip?" he asked.

"I own it," said Hosmer.

"How much of it would you sell me for my hundred-acre warrant?"

"None of it."

Red seeped up the back of Woodbridge's neck. "Why not?"

"Because I figure you intend to live on it. And it's not safe that far out from the village. Sittin' off by yourself, you'd draw Wyandots. We'd only have to come out and bury ye. And likely some of us would get scalped doin' that."

The color worked up to Woodbridge's ears. "I'm not asking you to worry about me! I'm asking you to sell me a piece of your land!"

Veronica saw Mike Stikes straighten up and close his bony hands. She guessed that an affront to Hosmer was an affront to Stikes. She knew that suddenly Tom Woodbridge stood alone in the room. But Hosmer remained calm.

"Tom, I served the same as your father, and I knew his feeling about the warrant he left you. I'll not let his son spend it on a piece of ground that'll likely be his own grave."

"Is it that, Hosmer?" flared Woodbridge. "Or do you fear our Mr. Blair here will report back to Shuldane that you sold me a piece of land when he's afraid to?"

Until that moment Tom Woodbridge had had a friend in Sam Hosmer. But now Hosmer lost his calm. "Ye've an awful presumption in thinkin' Mr. Shuldane would have any reason to fear an ungrateful brat like yourself . . . unless it would be because he doubted he'd get paid. And I'm wonderin', if I was to sell ye twenty acres, would I go beggin' for the warrant like Shuldane is for his thanks for harborin' ye these last years?"

The blood rushed to Woodbridge's head, and in that red instant he threw away a lifetime of Jonathan Woodbridge's advice.

He pulled the warrant from his pocket and clapped it against the puncheon bench, leaving his hand on top. The report was a slap in the face.

"Make out the title!"

Even the soldiers, watching out of curiosity, knew by the mutterings in the room that the redheaded one had made some kind of mistake.

Sam Hosmer reached quickly into a cubbyhole at the end of the puncheon counter for a piece of paper. He scrawled on it hastily with a quill, and shoved the twenty-acre title paper at Tom Woodbridge, who slowly took his hand off his warrant.

As Woodbridge released his warrant, sickening realization flushed the strength from his body, and he paid to Elnathan Shuldane the respect of hatred.

Jonathan Blair, watching intently, was not so fortunate. For as he watched the redheaded farmer lose his battle, he found no clear-cut, satisfying object for his own refined hatred. He could not hate himself, for this was the mission he was sent to accomplish. He could not hate Elnathan Shuldane, because Shuldane had obviously been correct. The hot-tempered, short-thinking, poverty-driven Woodbridges would never inherit the West from the keen entrepreneurs of the East. He could not hate Veronica Shuldane for the sympathy which stood naked on her face toward the redhead, because he loved her. He could not hate Woodbridge, because one does not hate an enraged bear who runs upon the knife of the bear baiter.

Woodbridge looked at the land title angrily, folded it into his chest pocket, and strode across the store to the door. It was not as Jonathan Woodbridge would have liked it, he knew. But then the old man had neglected to explain that a warrant to the glorious Bounty Tracts did not become a ticket to the promised land until you reinforced it considerable.

Though it was apparently more for the worse than for the better, there was a new landowner among the Mesopotamians who stood in front of the store watching Woodbridge ride off toward the West and his own personal twenty acres of misery.

# Chapter 4: UNDER THE GREENVILLE LINE

MESOPOTAMIA DID NOT exact homage; but it did expect from newcomers a certain docility, a certain willingness to accept advice. This usually presented a problem, because the type of man who would hold a bounty warrant and who would come to the Ohio Country had already established a firm habit of ignoring advice. Woodbridge was no exception.

Mesopotamia's advice, however, did embody a certain tyranny in that behind its spare tones often lurked the harsh alternative: survival or extinction.

For example, it was Sam Hosmer's custom to assemble all the men in the village, excepting those on Indian watch, to raise a cabin for the newcomer. By working together, they could erect the cabin in a single day. The newcomer did not get discouraged to the point of going back East, and he was then free to help the village in the harvesting or planting or in keeping the Indian watch. Hosmer never volunteered this service until after the newcomer had struggled to make a beginning. This insured appreciation.

Now that Woodbridge had made a beginning on his twenty acres, Sam Hosmer called the men together at the store. Some women came along. The group had decided to go out to Woodbridge's place on the following day when Amos Exeter spoke up.

"Sam, I went out to have a look. He's started a cabin, all right; but he's not building a plain one-room cabin like the rest of us. He's got staked out on the ground one of those big double cabins. Two sep'rate cabins side by side, about ten feet apart, with a roof between them, makin' a kind of covered-over passageway between the two. I don't see myself buildin' a big affair like that for him when my own ain't floored in yet."

The store murmured agreement.

Hosmer turned to Amos Exeter. "Did you explain to him, Amos, that the rest of us just built single cabins?"

44

"I did better'n that. I told him if he'd put up a simple one-room cabin like the rest of us, we'd probably come put it up for him."

"What did he say?"

"Said he didn't remember askin' any help."

Veronica noticed that everyone in the room took it as a personal affront, and she wondered if Exeter was helping the story along. She also noticed that Sam Hosmer shrugged his shoulders in a way which left Tom Woodbridge strictly on his own.

"All right," said Hosmer. "We've got more important work anyhow. Stikes has finally got the plans sketched out for our blockhouse. Since Mr. Woodbridge doesn't need our help, we'll start building that tomorrow, first thing. Brady, you take Hawkins and Miller and Mason and go after the foundation logs. Stikes and Slasher will fit the corners as usual, after they're notched by Isaac Shane."

Hosmer stopped abruptly. The room was silent except for the sound of two women who moved over beside Loretta Shane quickly.

"I'm sorry, Loretta," said Hosmer softly. "There's nobody can cut the notches to fit like Isaac Shane, and I naturally . . . I forgot. We'll find him, Loretta."

The two women took Loretta Shane out of the store.

Veronica heard Hosmer say: "We'll need every man at least two days a week. Can't be anybody turn up sick or missing. Even so, we'll be lucky to finish before we need it."

"Yeah," said Exeter, "and I doubt we can figure any help from Woodbridge, since he's buildin' a castle."

Woodbridge lifted the top log off again. It would not fit into the saddle notch of the one below it. The cabin, or one wing of the double cabin, was up six logs high. Holding the ax just below its blade, he widened the saddle in the fifth log. Sweat from his forehead dropped onto the ax blade. He wiped it off with the palm of his hand, but that, too, was wet, and the rust seemed to form on the ax blade faster than the cabin went up.

Woodbridge fitted the sixth log into the notch of the fifth. It seemed to settle in fairly well. He jumped down on the outside of the cabin and walked off fifty feet to look at his work.

It was the first he'd noticed how the near corner was growing slantwise out toward him like the prow of a boat.

Woodbridge charged back inside the cabin and began throwing off the logs he'd just laid. He threw them off to the outside in all directions, reducing the cabin back down to the base logs. It was a matter of a few minutes. He was on the ground squaring up the base logs again when he saw a pair of sorrel kneecaps shimmer up and down. Following up to the saddle, he stared into the handsome, quiet face of Jonathan Blair.

"Hello, Tom."

Woodbridge did not answer, but rose to stand broad-based with his arms ajar.

Riding up beside Blair came Miss Veronica on the chestnut mare.

"Well, we found you," said Blair.

"You had the advantage of having no map," said Woodbridge.

Blair made no apology or explanation to the taunt.

"Well, what's on your mind, Blair?"

"Matter of fact, nothing, Tom. I came along to help Miss Shuldane find the place. She had some errand with you."

Woodbridge looked to the girl. He seemed to catch her unready.

"I—I came to see if you were ready for the glass pane I carried for you," she said.

Woodbridge pointed to the helter-skelter pile of timbers.

"You can see I'm a long way from ready."

"That was a little on my mind, too," said Veronica, coming to the real point. "I remembered about the hog shed you built for father. And I knew building things was not your—ah—best strength." She smiled, inviting Woodbridge to smile at himself. But he let her struggle on alone.

"I thought you ought to know, Tom, that they're going to work on the blockhouse tomorrow morning. Everyone's going to turn out. I know they'd take it well if you were to come help. It would be a good-appearing thing to do."

"What good to me is a blockhouse six miles to the east?" asked Woodbridge.

"That would make the gesture appear the more generous," she answered.

"It seems that you've studied hard from your father's book, Miss Veronica, on what appears well."

Blair cut in. "What Miss Shuldane means, Woodbridge, if you'd help with the blockhouse they'd probably build your cabin for you."

Woodbridge noticed resentfully that they already talked like man and wife, finishing each other's thoughts.

Blair continued, "Any settlement like this must band together for its biggest works. That's how the ancient Mesopotamians were able to build their great fortresses."

"I don't know anything about them," said Woodbridge. "But I wouldn't be surprised you can overdo that bandin'-together business."

Veronica said, "They'd especially help, Tom, if you'd build just a single cabin. Why do you want a big double cabin so much finer than the rest?"

Coming from her, the question angered Woodbridge. There was a good-enough answer; but if he were to put it into words, it would sound preposterous. It left him without a civil reply. "I might ask the same about your house in Concord," he said.

"Will you be there tomorrow?" she asked.

"No."

Blair and Miss Shuldane rode back toward Mesopotamia. Tom Woodbridge resumed his building, beginning from the foundation again.

In the village, on what was to be the common, the blockhouse was rising perceptibly every day. Each man was to work every alternate day. But some of them, like Mike Stikes and Stanley-the-Slasher, worked every day.

It became Brady's genial custom, near the middle of a morning, to shout over at Amos Exeter, "Well, Amos, how's the Woodbridge castle progressin'?" It was when the walls of the blockhouse were head high that Brady asked the question, and the sound of chopping ceased. The men leaned on their axes, whimsically expectant.

"Well, Monday mornin' I seen it," said Amos, "and it looked like some new kind of an arrangement made especially so's Woodbridge'd have plenty of fresh air between the timbers."

The chuckles encouraged Amos Exeter to clutch for a fragment of fame.

"Then next I seen it on Tuesday," continued Amos, "and it was *all* air, and no timbers a-tall."

Exeter flushed a little under the laughter, and his tongue loosened.

"Y'know, it kind of sets on a side hill. Well, it seems Woodbridge didn't believe in peggin' the front foundation log in, and the first thing

His Royal Highness knows his foundation log is rollin' down the hill
with half his front wall rollin' after."

Veronica Shuldane looked down into the massive stew which she
and Faith Hawkins were cooking for the blockhouse workers.

Amos Exeter reached for his draw knife and concluded, "Awful nice
touch with an ax that boy has—like a buffalo in a henhouse."

The axes began cracking into the fresh, tight timber.


Three days later Exeter reported with less good humor that the
Woodbridge cabin was up about eight logs high and looked pretty fair.

That was the day Veronica and Blair took the pane of glass out to
the Woodbridge place.

"Thanks," said Woodbridge.

"The blockhouse is almost finished, Tom," said Veronica. "They
could use a little help with putting in the floor tomorrow."

"I guess if they've come so far, they wouldn't appreciate any last-
minute help from me," said Woodbridge.

Veronica said, "I heard Mike Stikes and Sam Hosmer saying that the
one thing they lack is some iron bolts for the door-locking bar. Didn't
you buy some at Fort Pitt?"

Woodbridge did not respond, but he seemed in a good humor, she
thought.

On the following day, which was Sunday, the men were chinking the
cracks in the blockhouse and splitting puncheons for the floor. From
the porch of Hosmer's Store Veronica saw Tom Woodbridge walking
over to the blockhouse on the common. She was pleased that he had
apparently taken her advice, and she felt relieved.

Woodbridge wondered at the unfamiliar look to the town, until he
realized that the timber cut for the blockhouse had opened up a
hole in the forested roof of the Ohio Country. It had changed Mesopotamia.

Others saw Woodbridge coming, too. The men working on the floor
inside seemed suddenly to find reasons to work on the outside. Conversation ceased as though each man were rehearsing his own little speech
of reproach. But Woodbridge gave them no chance to voice them. He
addressed Mike Stikes. "Would you tell me how those flat roof boards
were made? And how were they locked onto the roof?"

"Rive the slabs out of the midle section of small timbers," said Stikes
with pointed economy. "Use your ax. Then stick the thick end of the

riving under the ridge pole, bow it out over the rafter timber, and lock the thin end of it under the eave timber. Then cut off the uneven ends."

Woodbridge turned around to leave, but Brady wanted to see some fun. He yelled over: "Hey, Tom! We're havin' a little dedication ceremony t'night. Kind of a housewarmin' for the blockhouse. You comin' in?"

Every head turned to hear the answer.

Woodbridge studied the crowd briefly.

"Yeah," he said. "I'll come."

When Woodbridge had left, Morgan Brady sank his ax into a stump, and his laugh boomed out over the common. "By God!" he roared. "Whatever else, you can't say he ain't got guts!"

For answer the axes of Mesopotamia bit angrily into the puncheons.

With his cabin so nearly finished now, Woodbridge drove himself impatiently to get the roof on. Cutting the roof slabs was agonizing work, for sometimes in splitting off a slab the grain of the wood ran away with the cut, giving him a slab too short or too misshapen.

Dusk brought a light rain, but Woodbridge continued to split off roof slabs. He was at that point of fatigue where it was an effort to lean over to pick up the ax.

Woodbridge walked down into the gorge to the northwest of his cabin where he had his horses spanceled and his wagon hidden. He fed the shoats, picked up his rifle, and started back toward the cabin. Instead of climbing out of the gorge over the steep bank, Woodbridge followed up the bottom because it was easier walking. As he climbed south, the gorge grew shallower until he had to stoop to pass under a shaggy bark hickory which had fallen across the top of the cut.

His foot caught in a bramble that sent him headlong on the ground. Woodbridge rolled over on his back. It felt good to be off his feet. Until that moment he had not acknowledged the fatigue. It was raining quite hard now, but he lay there to rest for just a moment. The raindrops drummed against the shaggy bark hickory that bridged the draw over his head.

The drumming in his dream changed from the clopping of the hoofs of Prince and Jock across the Forbes Road to the tramp of the keelboatmen's feet on the catwalks of Platt Thayer's boat. Suddenly the beat slowed down to the measured thwack of his own ax into the beech-tree trunks. Each stroke of the ax seemed to jar Woodbridge's body, even in the dream. It sent a tremor into the ground under his

feet and it jostled the leaves and the branches up above so that chips
of bark fell into his hair and onto his sweaty face. He could feel them
falling annoyingly into his face even now.

Woodbridge clapped his hand to his face and sat up, leaning on one
arm. He was surprised to find that he was not chopping wood, but
lying in the dark in the gorge, wet through. The rain was pelting down
now. He was not chopping trees, yet when he took his hand away from
his face it held a piece of bark from a shaggy bark hickory. He was
wide awake, but the beat was still there, very faintly.

Holding the chip of bark, Woodbridge looked overhead. Four feet
above his face, silhouetted against the slightly lighter sky, was the fallen
hickory which bridged the shallow end of the gorge. As he stared at it,
a shadow crossed above the hickory in that same thumping cadence.

Woodbridge was about to rise when a tiny twig followed the chip of
bark and fell on his forehead. But Woodbridge made no move to brush
it off. For on top of the fallen hickory there was the silhouette of a
figure. The silhouette moved silently from west to east and was gone.
The beats were footsteps; not sounds, but vibrations coming lightly
through the ground. The figure was gone, but in a few seconds it was
followed by another.

As Woodbridge's eyes adjusted to the dark, he could see that it was
a column. Each figure carried a rifle, some slung across the back, muzzle
down. Most of them carried at the alert, in both hands across the front.
But there were pieces of leather or cloth wrapped around the firing
locks of the rifles.

The twig which lay on Woodbridge's forehead itched, but he made
no move to brush it off, remaining frozen. Some of the chests of the
figures were naked and shone just a little with the rain water on them.
The heads of some of them shone, too, where they were shaved.

Rain water flowed around the twig on Woodbridge's forehead and
drained down beside his nose into his mouth, which was open to quiet
his breathing. He longed to take a deep breath, instead of short ones,
to relieve his awkward, frozen position. But he did not. For Thomas
Woodbridge was looking for the first time in his life at what was called
an unfriendly Indian. Not one, but a column of them.

Occasionally two would cross on the log simultaneously, and there
would be short, throaty exchanges. As Woodbridge watched, he had the
feeling that he was looking at some highly developed animals, not because of their appearance, but because of the way they accepted the

rain and the darkness. The illusion was furthered because Woodbridge could not understand the noises which he took to be a language, and he knew they would not understand his.

Some unruly nerve set Woodbridge's left arm to quivering in protest against its intolerable half-bent position as it supported him, but he sat still. The twig on his forehead itched unbearably. He wrinkled his brow to move it, but it slid into his eye. His right hand darted automatically to his face. The sudden motion caused his rifle to roll off his leg, making a sound which halted the Indian on the log above.

Except for the quivering of his left arm, Woodbridge froze his body. He held his right hand motionless over his right eye, allowing only enough breath to pass back and forth over his teeth to sustain himself. The silhouette of the Indian stared down into the draw from the log, not moving, except to bring a rifle to bear toward Woodbridge.

Keeping the rifle pointed into the draw, the Indian edged slowly to the east end of the log, where he waited until the next Indian in the column arrived. There was a short exchange of throaty sounds, and the second Indian shoved the first along the trail with an impatient grunt. When they were gone, Woodbridge brought his arm down and shifted his weight off his quivering left arm. Two more silhouettes passed over the log, and then no more.

Woodbridge had not thought to count them, but he had an impression of about fifteen. That is, fifteen since he'd been awake.

He rose slowly so that his knee joints would not crack. Taking his rifle, he moved to the head of the draw, but he did not inhale deeply until he had continued a good two hundred steps away from the hickory log. He let his left arm hang loosely, shaking his fingers to bring the blood back.

Hosmer had said that the warning alarm was three shots. Woodbridge moved into a dense thicket in case the shots should bring the Indians back. He pointed his rifle west and drew back on the trigger. There was only the hopeless click of the wet flint against the frizzen.

Woodbridge put his thumb in the flash pan. The powder was a wet paste.

Every part of the rifle was wet, as was every part of Woodbridge's clothing. He broke another powder charge. But the vacuous click changed the Jaeger from a gun to a worthless piece of wood and iron.

With haste now, Woodbridge tore back the mat of wet leaves, feeling for drier ones underneath. Kneeling, he crushed a handful of them into a feathery tinder. Shielding them from the rain with his body, he cocked his rifle again and fired a spark into the tinder. But the leaves were damp and coarse, and would not take the spark.

Woodbridge visualized fifteen Indians filtering into Hosmer Village, spreading out silently among the dark cabins as they were said to do. Mesopotamia made a big thing of its so-called "Indian watch"; but it was raining tonight, and so dark that the Indians had not seen Woodbridge four feet away. Nor could Woodbridge have seen the Indians if he had not been below them so that he could raise their silhouettes against the sky.

He shivered in his wet clothes, and pulled the trigger again. A good spark jumped to the tinder leaves. Woodbridge bent over it. The spark ate a circle of red into one of the leaves, and Woodbridge blew gently. The circle of red brightened, and a lick of flame developed which spread through the tinder. He had fire.

Clawing under the wet leaves for toothpick-sized sticks which were dry, he placed them gently in the small flame, turning each one until it kindled. Suddenly a bright flame caused Woodbridge to recoil from the fire.

As he did so, the rain pelted the fire out.

In the sudden darkness Woodbridge could not see, but in his mind he visualized the fifteen leaning silhouettes closing on Mesopotamia, or Hosmer Village as it had been called by those who slept in the burying yard across from the store.

Inside the blockhouse at Mesopotamia, the inspection and the fort-warming ceremony were so nearly over that Judith Dolk had already left to take the baby home to bed. The new blockhouse, with its formidable exterior of frowning gun-port slits, gave the village such a new-found security that Jim Dolk had let his wife walk home alone.

Flannerty stood his Indian watch conscientiously in the cupola of the blockhouse, but since he could see nothing in the rainy blackness the watch was more for the purpose of demonstrating the new Indian watcher's perch high over the heads of the celebrating villagers below than for security.

The Flannerty youngsters climbed up the ladders onto the riflemen's balcony which ran around the four sides of the blockhouse, projecting out over the first story. There were holes in the floor of the balcony at intervals, so that a rifle poked down through the overhang forbade the enemy the ground next to the foundation of the blockhouse. A small bastion at each corner permitted riflemen to enfilade the walls in case of a scaling attempt, and in the center of the blockhouse there was a tripod of logs from which hung a deerskin siege bag for water. To-night, though, it sagged deflated, except for a couple of remaining quarts of house-warming whisky in the bottom.

In one corner Mike Stikes was proudly explaining to a group of women how to find the section of the split-log floor which opened into a hole for storing meat and powder. The women listened with unhear-ing courtesy while they reflected that if half the loving care had gone into their cabins there might be fewer dirt floors in Hosmer Village.

Morgan Brady saw Stikes talking to the women, and bawled, "If there's gonna be any speechmakin', Mike, make it to the whole of us!" And Stikes was propelled to the center of the blockhouse in the middle of a crowd.

The gaunt, humorless Stikes, who had staunchly and bitterly argued Stanley-the-Slasher into searching three days for a forked log angled precisely to support the cupola roof, now lost his voice when faced with a friendly speech. Prodded by their demands, however, Stikes took a deep breath and began.

"Well, about all I have to say," he struggled, "we still have no proper lock on the door. I don't think it'll hold against a ram. Soon as I can get some iron bolts with threads, we can fix that. Meanwhile, the last man in should always set the jamb pole in its floor socket."

For Stikes's sake they tried to look concerned about the lock. Then they asked Blair to make a speech. He said precisely the right thing.

"When I spread the word about this blockhouse back in Boston, it will increase the migrations out here. I'll see to it there's a piece in the Boston *Columbian Centinel* about it. An outsider like myself can't help being impressed by the fact that this blockhouse represents the work of every man in the village."

Veronica, noticing glances exchanged among the crowd, wondered if Blair had deliberately pointed up the one glaring absence.

Sam Hosmer began without a preface.

"When three rifle shots are fired," he ordered, "every man drops what he's doing and reports his family directly to the blockhouse. Only those in charge of rations bring any animals. There's no room here for your livestock. Exeter is responsible for keepin' the water bag filled. Stikes brings the bar lead. Now go on home; and just because we got a blockhouse, that don't make the woods any safer."

Stikes climbed up into the cupola to relieve Flannerty on Indian watch, and Hosmer stayed to talk to Stikes.

Out in the woods, six miles west of the blockhouse, Tom Woodbridge's eyes slowly became accustomed again to the blackness. The fire was so completely extinguished that it was hard to imagine there had been one; and he wondered how long it took an Indian to walk six miles. He tried to enumerate every possession he owned to find one that would burn. None of his clothes were dry. The only dry items he could think of were the papers in the document box and the hair on the horses' tails. But even if they would kindle, he still needed dry wood to make a fire big enough to be seen six miles.

A bolt of lightning cut the black. In that instant Woodbridge saw his cabin, rising twelve logs high on one side and ten on another. The logs gleamed wetly. But there was a floor in the cabin. The underside of the floor could be dry. On the downhill side the floor was about two feet above the ground.

Woodbridge took his rifle out into the clearing and crawled up under the cabin. Under the floor he assembled some dry tinder and chips. But before he pulled the trigger to make the spark, he paused. From underneath he observed how closely the puncheons fit together. How thick they were, and how many strokes of the ax had gone out of him to split the logs in half to make the flat floor! He felt the giant eighteen-inch foundation logs, and remembered how he had sharpened his ax four times on that one tree alone, reducing the size of the blade visibly. He felt the pile of chips under him, and each chip seemed to be a hunk of his life span.

It could be, too, he thought, that the Indians were not going to Hosmer Village, or if they were the townsmen might already be well alerted because of the ceremony at the blockhouse. Lying on his side under his cabin, Tom Woodbridge considered these things.

In the Indian-watch cupola atop the blockhouse in Mesopotamia, Stikes said: "It's a good structure, Sam. Why are you so worried?"

"Because people like Dolk are already actin' like a blockhouse means we won't get any more raids."

"And you're of the mind it'll work just the opposite?"

"For a while, yes. If Rontondee is the one, he'll figure he's got to test the blockhouse so's he'll know how many red devils he'd need to break it. And if it's Tecumseh hears about it, he'll figure to teach us a lesson right away; and he'll pick some special night to impress everybody—like Christmas night, or some special time."

"Figurin' like that, Sam, it was a mistake to build it. We just made it tougher on ourselves."

"Don't ye always if ye defend yeself?"

"Yeah."

Mike Stikes stared out thoughtfully through the cupola's western firing port.

"I can see ye don't agree," said Hosmer, "but something's got to be—"

"Sam! Look!" Stikes pointed to a glow that reddened the western sky.

Hosmer reached for his rifle. "I knew they'd do it!" said Hosmer. "They got Woodbridge! And there goes his fancy cabin up in smoke."

Hosmer fired, loaded, and then fired twice more into the rainy night.


A single night's fighting had changed the blockhouse from an arrangement of logs to a storied place. The smell of fresh-cut green timber had changed to that of acrid burnt gunpowder.

It was still dark inside, but through the frequent cracks between the logs Veronica could see that it was lightening outside. The people lay prostrate in complete sleep all over the blockhouse floor, except for one vigilant shadow pacing slowly around the rifle balcony. It called periodically to another voice up in the watcher's cupola, and a sleepy voice came back in monosyllables.

A crack of light showed Blair sleeping beside her. His face was handsome despite the beard and the powder-blackened white shirt. She took his coat off her shoulders and laid it over him. Then she rose, walked over to the wide ladder, and climbed to the rifle balcony.

Henry Flannerty lay sleeping face down on his rifle beside one of the holes in the balcony floor. Flannerty's rifle extended over the hole. But up through the port came an awful quarreling of dogs, and she kneeled to look down through the hole at the ground.

Three hounds covered some important object over which they squabbled in anger. The large black dog finally sent the other two scurrying off to a new attraction, leaving Veronica Shuldane staring at the naked back of an Indian, lying face down. There was a small round hole in his back, and Veronica thought for an instant that she knew now the appearance of war. She was surprised that she could look so calmly.

At that moment, though, the big hound seized the corpse by a stiff arm and turned it over on its back. Veronica barely regained her balance. Both hands went to her mouth, and she kneeled with her face to the wall. A tremor of sickness shuddered her taut head and neck, and she knelt there a moment trying not to take in air that had touched the mass below. She had not the strength to move. For the first time she knew what was inside the human body.

The measured step that paced the balcony approached. A hard hand took her elbow and raised her up. She was forced to breathe finally by nature.

"I'll get you down off here," said Hosmer.

Her hands were weak on the wide ladder, but Hosmer's arm was around her waist, and they went down side by side.

Reaching the floor, she looked at Hosmer's face, and it seemed to Veronica that she could visualize him as he would look, killed. She looked around at the people sleeping on the floor, and she saw them suddenly not as people, but as meat. She broke into uncontrolled sobs.

"Will he look like that?" she asked.

Sam Hosmer was not an unkind man. But he was tired and he was sixty, and he was nervous at being absent from the rifle balcony.

"Who?" he asked curtly. "Oh, Woodbridge? He'll look worse. There's the matter of the token they always take, you know."

"When do we go out there?" she asked.

"We don't, for a while yet."

Veronica sobbed into her hands, and Hosmer said: "I know. I know. But don't forget, we told him. And there's no sense gettin' killed to bury a man."

Veronica walked back to her corner. But by now people were stirring in the grayness, and as she passed Amos Exeter and Asa Buttrick she could hardly believe her ears. "They'll take his horses, of course," said Exeter, "but they'll leave the wagon. They never take a wagon."

She knelt beside Jonathan Blair and shook him.

"Come, Jonathan!" she said, repeating it until he got to his feet and moved groggily toward the blockhouse door, uncomprehending.

She struggled with the jamb pole. But Hosmer's voice cut through the gray. "No one goes out yet! Not till it's light enough to look around good."

Jonathan Blair sank to the floor beside Veronica and went to sleep, for he had had a night's work last night—the first in his life, in fact.

From her corner Veronica sat and watched as the patrol went out to look around. She watched, then, as Hosmer sent out a burying detail. Two armed men went out for water.

The activity increased throughout the next hour and finally woke Jonathan Blair, who reached out for Veronica. But she was not there.

They looked all over the blockhouse. Then they looked in Faith Hawkins's cabin. Miss Shuldane was not there, but her small chestnut mare was gone from Hawkins's shed.

Blair and Hosmer and Stikes and Hawkins saddled up. But even as they headed out the trail to the west, Veronica came splashing across the ford in the river. She drew up in front of them on the village side of the stream.

"He's alive," she said. "Badly burned, but alive."

Hosmer was surprised.

"The Indians didn't find him," Veronica continued. "He was lying in the gorge back of his place when they went by."

"It's a wonder they didn't root around the place and find him after they fired his cabin," said Hosmer.

"They didn't fire his cabin. They went right by."

"Then what was the fire that warned us?"

"It was his cabin, all right. Burned to the ground. But Tom fired it himself."

The four men stared for an explanation. Veronica looked at Sam Hosmer.

"You told him that any man that didn't give the warning was a murderer, Mr. Hosmer. The cabin was the only thing that would make a signal."

Comprehension came over Hosmer's face, but then it was quickly replaced by a question mark. "Why not his rifle?" he asked.

"Wet," said Veronica.

It was early that afternoon that Woodbridge was pushing a pole through the ashes, fishing for a pane of glass. The activity stirred up the throbbing in his left forearm, which was wrapped in a piece of

white cloth of finer weave than Woodbridge had ever seen. One edge
was frazzled where it had been hastily ripped. The other edge, though
mostly well tucked under, revealed here and there a small corner of
delicate lace which looked odd against the dirty red freckled arm.
Woodbridge lifted the arm and the cloth to his nose, and found there
a faint perfume and a vague excitement.

He stood foolishly looking at the bandage and smelling it, and suddenly he colored and drew the bandage across his chin, as though wiping
off the soot. For out of the tunnel through the forest, Sam Hosmer
rode into the Woodbridge clearing from the east.

Behind Hosmer rode Mike Stikes and Jim Hawkins. Behind them
came Morgan Brady's wagon carrying Hank Flannerty, Exeter, and
Buttrick. Another wagon followed Brady's. It was driven by Elizabeth
Hosmer, and carried some women. Two men with alert rifles walked
on either side of the second wagon. Hope Emerson, cradling a rifle,
walked behind the wagon. Other men followed.

Hosmer stopped in front of the smoldering pile of black logs, and
the others pulled up beside him. Tom Woodbridge faced Hosmer, but
neither had any word for the other. Men with axes began to jump out
of the wagons, staring at the smoldering ashes and at Woodbridge as
if they looked at some ghost.

Hosmer made no explanation. But he remained mounted and
shouted to the others who assembled around him.

"Hawkins," he yelled, "you and Slasher set out to find ten good
eighteen-inch foundation trunks."

"Right, Sam."

"Dolk, you take your crew and start cuttin' timber for the side logs.
Eight to ten inches or better."

"How many, Sam?"

"Just keep cuttin' till we stop ye."

Woodbridge stood dumb while Hosmer scanned his people.

"Brady," said Hosmer. "You and Exeter get me eight big flat foundation rocks for the corners. Oughta be eighteen to twenty inches acrost."

Brady moved quickly toward his wagon. But Exeter was not so quick.
"How come eight?" he asked. "One for each corner is four."

Hosmer said, "This here's to be a double cabin with a kind of an outdoor hallway joinin' the two, as I understand the idea of it."

"A single cabin's good enough for the rest of us," said Exeter.

Hosmer's square wrinkled face looked like that of an angry snapping turtle. "Apparently ye've not heard how this here fire started," he said. "I've not time for explainin' now, Amos. I only say to ye that if ye were to build a hull five-room house out of solid rock for Thomas Woodbridge this day, ye'd still be his debtor. Now git movin'!"

Woodbridge was surprised to see that Hosmer had put Blair to work with the gang dragging down the cut logs to the site. He was more surprised to see a dead seriousness on Blair's face.

In this Woodbridge perhaps underestimated Blair. For, though Blair paid strict attention to the way Flannerty fitted the notches together, he paid more attention to the greater skill with which Sam Hosmer raised Flannerty to a man of importance.

Lowering his voice a shade, Hosmer said: "Flannerty, you're the one worked closest to Isaac Shane. You think you caught his way of fittin' those corners so's they'll tighten as the timber dries out?"

As Flannerty bent closer to his work, the lawyer allowed himself a small smile of appreciation for Hosmer's ingenious leadership, though it's doubtful that he noticed how he bent his own back lower as the Old Man watched the lawyer raise the next timber.

As the walls grew above the heads of the fitters, skids were used to roll the logs into position. The dazed constraint had worn off Woodbridge, and he was now everywhere among the men, handling the heavy logs. He was amazed that thirteen men could do so much more than thirteen times what one man could do. Every time he looked at the cabin, it had grown.

As he worked on the inside of one wall, he heard Hosmer on the other side talking to Exeter. "Amos, go help Flannerty cut some wedge-shape' slats for chinking the cracks."

"Clay was good enough for the rest of us, Sam."

"That's no reason we shouldn't improve. I saw a slat-chinked hut down at Boxford's Cabin."

As the ridgepole went up, Hosmer spoke his first words to Woodbridge.

"I understand you got some iron bolts with threads, Woodbridge."

Woodbridge said, "I don't know what to say to ya, Mr. Hosmer, about building the house."

"I asked ye about the bolts. I been keepin' them in mind for pinnin' the ridgepole extra solid to the rafter beams. Ready for 'em now."

"I got other ideas for the bolts."

Hosmer shrugged, affronted. "Well, they're your bolts."

Woodbridge reached over to the back of his wagon. He picked up a heavy package and unwrapped the bolts. They were rusting a little, but the threads were sharp and even. He handed them to Hosmer.

"I heard there was some need of bolts for the gate to the blockhouse," said Woodbridge. "They don't make much beside what you done for me today. But they're bolts."

Hosmer accepted the bolts in a hand that was like an old apple-tree branch.

"Thank ye," he said. "As for who owes who, ye need worry none. The cabin shows up like a lot, but the men know it's a cheap-enough ransom for their scalps."

# Chapter 5: THE REVEREND

IT was in a way surprising that Sam Hosmer and Elnathan Shuldane held each other's loyal esteem, for two men seldom so misunderstood each other.

Sam Hosmer, agent for Shuldane, ran Mesopotamia almost as though Shuldane were watching with deep interest. Yet the projects which earned Hosmer's gravest concern always puzzled Shuldane, such as Hosmer's laborious effort to get the Steubenville circuit rider to extend his circuit north for an occasional church service at Mesopotamia. However, if in Hosmer's judgment a preacher was needed to keep the people happy . . . well, who could argue with Hosmer's leadership?

In like manner, Hosmer so little understood Elnathan Shuldane that when the fat letter arrived by Asa Buttrick on Friday morning, Hosmer took it as further evidence of Shuldane's openness and trustfulness that he enclosed in the same envelope a letter to Blair. The letter to Blair was merely marked "Personal . . . to J. Blair."

Hosmer was a man to honor such small trusts, so he dutifully set aside Blair's letter without unfolding it. There one also for Veronica.

---

Hosmer's own letter from Shuldane was rather light. It expressed hopes for good spring planting and good seed. It told Hosmer that Lots 21 and 23 had been sold, but not to expect the new owners for some time. It said that he would like Veronica and Blair to return to Massachusetts as soon as the road out was passable; and it complied with Hosmer's request:

"Sam, through Bishop Fearing in Boston I have arranged for the circuit rider to continue services once every two months in Mesopotamia. I have made a bequest to the diocese here which will cover these visits for one year."

Blair squirmed as he read his own letter, for he knew that Shuldane had enclosed the letter with Hosmer's expressly so that Hosmer would read it. He assumed that Hosmer had read his letter, and he admired Shuldane for the technique, filing it away as a lesson to be remembered.

But it bothered him immensely because Hosmer now would know about Veronica and himself, having read, of course, these paragraphs:

"I should like you and Veronica to leave immediately for Massachusetts to be married. I have made arrangements with St. Clair, through Joseph Varnum, for a squad of troops to escort you down to Cincinnati. They should arrive almost as soon as this letter.

"I desire this for reason. Varnum is not backing the land legislation properly, and I have determined to run for delegate to Congress to see to these matters. I shall need your full assistance in gaining a seat, and later at Philadelphia. The wedding itself will call important attention to my candidacy, if held in Boston. And I have taken a house in town which will serve you as a home and us as a campaign headquarters. It will be necessary for Veronica to receive properly certain county leaders and their wives. Therefore lose no time. It is also my wish that Veronica shall speak at various gatherings, describing the safe living conditions in the West. I know that many are holding back from buying our lands out of fear for their women. Veronica will be living proof that there is no danger there. The land sales are not going fast enough for the fulfillment of my plans."

When Blair saw Veronica that noon outside the Hawkins cabin, he searched her face to see if her letter had been the same. She saw the eagerness in his face, and neither quenched it nor reflected it, ignoring the important subject.

"I know," she said. "We're to go back."

"Buttrick said the soldiers stayed down at Boxford's Cabin last night. They should be up here tonight."

"Yes."

"Then we'll leave tomorrow, if that gives you enough time, Veronica. We can stay tomorrow night at Boxford's Cabin. Then with a full day's ride after that, we'll make the inn on the north part of Dayton's Purchase."

She suggested that after the noon meal they go separately around the village to say goodbye to people, and then meet toward evening at Hosmer's to finish Shuldane's business with Sam and to say goodbye.

After he had eaten at Hosmer's, Blair dismounted in front of the Hawkins cabin and walked out to Hawkins's shed to saddle up Veronica's chestnut mare. But when he got there, Hawkins was already completing the task. It gave Blair a twinge of jealousy to realize how completely Veronica had taken over Mesopotamia, especially the men. Jim Hawkins, who would wave to his wife as she carried two wooden buckets of water from the creek, found it quite fitting to come in from the field to saddle up Veronica's mare.

In further everlasting credit to Veronica, Blair noticed that she accepted these tributes without injuring the women of Mesopotamia. Blair tried Shuldane's studied habit of analysis to examine the power of Shuldane's own daughter. He noticed that once in the saddle, chatting with Faith Hawkins, Veronica fingered the velvet on her collar as though she were always half aware of it and of the fact that Faith had sewed it on. And while she talked to Faith, her left hand lowered knowingly on the opposite flank of the mare to accept the rein which Hawkins placed carefully in her palm.

They started north across the common, but they had not gone four rods when Faith called and came running after. Would Veronica arrange her packing so as to be free tomorrow morning? The women, and the men, too, had planned a little something for her.

"A farewell party?" asked Veronica.

"Some'at a sight more special than that," answered Faith. She looked at Blair as though they shared a secret.

Veronica turned to Blair. "But you wanted to leave in the morning, Jonathan."

"We could stay over another day."

Veronica rode northeast to see Hope Emerson, then Mrs. Fitchburg and Mrs. Mason. She stopped briefly to see Mrs. Exeter, spent quite a long time with Hank Flannerty's wife and little Camelia Flannerty, and then went to Polly Stikes's.

Blair made a similar circuit, going out into the fields to talk to the men. They all asked him to get Shuldane to arrange some kind of troop protection, if only a patrol, and most of them gave him letters and messages to take back East.

Late in the afternoon, though a light rain was falling, Blair rode south across the river and then turned due west toward the Woodbridge place. He had left Woodbridge for last. And as he rode, he tried to analyze why, with time so short, he should trouble to ride six miles out and six miles back to see a redhead who would be even less pleased to see him. He told himself that it was his duty as Shuldane's emissary, for of all the threats to Shuldane's empire, he thought that Tom Woodbridge was the greatest.

Blair imagined himself explaining this to Shuldane. And he imagined Shuldane's piercing, "Why?" It would not be a contemptuous "Why," for one of Shuldane's strengths was the ability to recognize a power which did not look like one, and to be able to recognize weakness which looked like power. Shuldane never wasted his strength against a gutless title. At the same time he would spend a precious half-hour cultivating a certain minor government clerk whom others mistakenly ignored.

But concerning Woodbridge, Shuldane's query would be searching, and Blair's answer was laughable. "Because, Nate, he has a great scorn in his eye?" Ridiculous. "Because he has nothing to lose and the whole West to gain?" Doesn't make good sense. "Because he does not have sense enough to be afraid of you, Nate, and your kind?" Shuldane would write that off as an emotional answer. "Because he acts. And others might follow him?" Not much proof of that.

But put them all together. "Because he has a great scorn in his eye . . . has nothing to lose . . . is not afraid of you . . . and he takes action . . . swift, unconsidered, but drastic. That's why, Nate."

Blair caught himself talking out loud. But that was his answer. Shuldane just might understand that. And Blair told himself that was why he was looking in on Woodbridge.

The rain began to fall with force. It was turning the trail into a small stream underfoot. The drops were cold and steamed off the flanks of the sorrel.

Blair was surprised when he looked up to see another rider in front of him about forty rods. He urged his sorrel into a gallop. When he had closed the distance by a quarter, the silhouette seemed familiar, but he couldn't place it. He called. The rider's face turned briefly and then seemed to bend to the mount and ride faster. It was understandable enough. On the West Trail one didn't care much to meet another rider, what with some of the Wyandots wearing white men's clothes now.

Blair could make this trip tomorrow morning while Veronica was attending Faith Hawkins's affair. He turned back and pulled his collar up against the rain, which was beginning to soak down his neck.

He stopped at the Hawkins cabin to ask Veronica if her trunk was packed and ready. But Faith Hawkins said, "She's gone, Jonathan."

"Where'd she say she was going?"

"She didn't say till I asked," explained Hope in exasperating detail. "But she went out to Woodbridge's place."

"What for?"

"She had a pane of glass with her. Reckon she was to deliver it to him. I thought you'd be going out with her."

Blair looked out at the rainy sky and he thought about the rider he'd seen on the West Trail and how he . . . it . . . had picked up speed.

"I naturally expected you'd be going, too," repeated Hope.

"Yes, of course. That was the plan. I'll catch up with her right away." But he did not go. She would be back any moment now, he thought.

It was a different Woodbridge that Veronica found. He was on his way from the cabin toward the hog shed when she led her wet horse up the slope, and he seemed distraught and impatient at being detained to greet her.

She did not know exactly what his reaction would be to the startling news that she was suddenly leaving and was to marry Blair, but she expected him to say something. However, Woodbridge acted as though he had not heard her.

"Go in out of the wet and set," he said as he left the cabin. "I'll be right back."

But he did not come right back.

As she sat in the cabin, she felt ridiculous. She realized now that she had come somewhat breathlessly to tell him the news and to leave immediately. Now here she sat, having told the news, and it made not enough difference to deter this redhead from a trip to the hog shed. Initially, it had seemed a nice, casual little thing to do. She had merely come out to say goodbye, with the hope of leaving Woodbridge with a better feeling toward her father, toward Blair . . . and perhaps toward herself. But her plan had somehow gone awry.

She rose and was about to put on her wet coat to leave when Woodbridge came running back into the cabin holding something cupped in his two large hands as though it were precious. He did not speak, but sank quickly to his knees in front of the fire. He gently laid the small pinkish-white object on the warm stone and bent over it.

It was Veronica's first look at a new piglet. But this one lay as still as the man who bent over it, holding his breath.

She started toward the door, and was about to speak, but she froze at Woodbridge's command, "Quiet!"

The redhead leaned over and placed his ear against the animal's tiny wrinkled flank, listening. He picked it up and held it up to the doorway as though he would look through its nearly translucent body. But it was not breathing.

With his back partly to Veronica, Woodbridge brought the animal close to his mouth. His chest swelled his shirt as he inhaled. His mouth was against the animal's snout, and Veronica's hand went to her lips. Woodbridge blew gently several times. The flanks of the tiny animal expanded ever so faintly. Then they shrank and expanded again. The faint motion could only be detected by the alternate wrinkling and smoothing out of the satin hide.

Woodbridge lowered his great cupped hands to the stone. He opened them delicately, and out of them wriggled a small white body which stood a moment on spindly legs and then toppled, got up, flopped again. But it breathed.

A rare and beatific smile lighted Tom's worn face.

"Happens that way to one sow in a hundred," he said. "Young are born without breath."

With less delicacy now, he scooped up the animal in one hand and carried it out of the cabin, returning directly, empty-handed.

Being full of the events of the last hour, and the birth of the first

Bedford piglets in the West, he stood waiting for her to say something about them. There was silence on both sides until Woodbridge remembered with a rush why she was here.

"I'd got out of the habit of thinkin' of you goin' back," he said. "Either you or Blair."

"I'll remember you back home to—" Veronica realized that her usual remark was inappropriate. "We had almost gotten out of the habit of it ourselves," she amended.

Both turned to the doorway as a rumble of thunder unleashed a torrent that plastered the grass against the slope in front of the cabin and hammered tiny rivulets into the soil.

"I better put your mount inside my shed," said Woodbridge.

She started to speak, but he said: "There'll be room. I'll crowd my critters over." He left before she could object.

When he returned, he ran a big hand over his red hair and whipped the water into the fireplace, where it sizzled.

"Never seen it come down like this," he said. "You can't go for a while."

She said nothing, and her silence heightened the importance as well as the awkwardness of the moment. Veronica did not realize that Woodbridge's remark was no mere banality. He *had* never seen rain like this. It drilled through the grass on the roof to drum against the slabs, driving occasional drops through the joints. It startled the horses. It slathered against the door and ran off in sheets. Drops pelted down the chimney to sputter in the fire. The rain seemed to dump out of the sky, causing Woodbridge to close the cabin door. He wondered if the foundation stones would ooze out from under the cabin.

But Veronica, in her preoccupation, did not notice until Woodbridge said, "You'll have to stay for supper." He spitted a small woods shoat which he had cleaned.

She unwrapped a shiny object from a piece of wet paper and handed it to him.

"What the devil?"

"It's the broken window glass," she said. "From the fire. Mr. Stikes fused it somehow in the forge."

It was smaller than before. The edges were uneven. Black soot was glazed right into the glass now which contained bubbles and swirls of distortion. But he handled it carefully and with pleasure. He held it up to the light and looked through it. You couldn't see anything very

clearly, but what you could see was rather pleasantly distorted, Woodbridge thought, giving the view a kind of grandeur, like the paintings
in the Shuldane house. Then, remembering the day he had bought the
glass in Pittsburgh, he asked, "You think you'll come here again, Miss
Veronica?"

"I'd like to. But I'll stay, of course, where Father is. Being all he has
left."

"You saying he'd be lonesome?"

"Yes."

"Always seemed to me you was more like an ornament to him and
his house and his business—like them regimental eagles he's got over
the doorway."

"Would that make it a smaller kind of loneliness than some other
kind?"

He felt the sudden little wall of silence she built, and said: "But
that's none of my business. Guess I was just lookin' for a way you
might be back."

"It might be he'll come out here," she said. "He's reserved a lot for
us."

Woodbridge did not point out that he had bitter reason to know it.
But his silence gave no encouragement to the arrival of Elnathan
Shuldane in Mesopotamia, with his daughter or without.

"He wants very much to come," she continued. "He lives for
Mesopotamia."

"Does he? I had the idea it was the other way 'round."

"You haven't seen what he's done for the village."

"S'pose not. But I've seen what the village has done for him. Take
this twenty acres. When I get it improved, it'll be worth maybe $100
an acre. So will all the ground that surrounds it. Your old man will get
the benefit of that."

She gave him no answer.

"Take you," he continued. "He sent you out here, 'stead of comin'
himself. That'll help sell the land out here—a woman comin' out and
gettin' back alive."

"He's exactly the same as you in that," she said.

"Be hard for me to see that."

"He'll mortgage his life to succor Mesopotamia. Then he'll sell it
off to the highest bidder. That's the same as you're doing."

"Huh?"

"You take a young pig and pamper it. Then you turn around and kill it and sell it."

"So?"

"So, it's as cruel—more so than the land business."

"That's different. It's a kind of a treaty. The farmer guarantees an easy life, plenty of food, a good shed. The animal pays back."

From a small square of thick tinfoil which had been a tea package, Woodbridge was cutting ten small strips with his knife. The strips were an inch wide and three inches long. He rolled them into small tubes and then bent each tube into a U shape.

"What are they?" she asked.

"Best thing I've got to make clips for the ears of this litter."

She took one idly and bent it around her finger, noticing how it held the shape it was given.

"Why clips for the ears?" she asked.

"When my herd builds up, I've got to be able to tell which hogs are the best breeders. I'll mark this first litter with a clip in the left ear. Of course, I'll never sell the two special ones that I—" Woodbridge caught himself, but she finished his sentence with a faintly impish smile.

"—that the delegates were supposed to have eaten in Concord?" she asked.

They ate a slow supper, and afterward sat on the floor in front of the fire. A drop pelted through the roof onto Veronica's face. Woodbridge saw it, and it caused him to take the canvas from under his bunk. He opened the door to go out. Veronica said, "It's not enough of a leak to bother with, Tom."

"I know it," said Woodbridge, opening the door. "But same thing could happen in the hog shed where the new litter is."

She looked at the door he had slammed behind him, wondering about a man who would go out in a rain like this to cover a litter of swine; but almost in the same thought she realized that she had to go out in it herself. She could not well stay here any longer. It was dark outside. She rose just as Woodbridge slammed back into the cabin.

"Tom, I've got to get back to . . ."

But he moved swiftly to the fire and poured water from a cask into the pot on the fire. He was severe.

"Never should have left them alone," he said, reaching for the lid.

He didn't notice that she was putting on her coat. "Next one's coming right now. Hand me that poker."

"Tom, I must go."

"I should have known. I should have known. I said hand me that poker!"

His voice impelled her to obey him.

"Now fetch a stick of fire to that lantern. Hurry."

While he roughly bunched together some bundles of straw which he tied into a matting, she stood helplessly fussing with the sooty awkward contraption which he had called a lantern. She didn't even know how to light it.

"The others'll be born in a sack, too," he grumbled. "If I can just get breath in 'em, and get 'em through the night. I should have known. Give me the lantern."

But he saw now that the lantern was not even lit.

"What have you been doin', woman?"

He snatched the lantern, lifted the glass, grabbed a coal from the fire, and touched off the grease wick. The coal burned his hands, and he dropped it. He was out the door with the lantern, the hot water, and the straw mat.

The room seemed strangely empty without his tumultuous presence. She picked the coal off the floor where he had dropped it, and she in turn dropped it, wondering how he had held it in his fingers long enough to light the lantern. She nudged it back onto the hearth with the poker.

The cabin, which had been relatively neat when she arrived, was now in disorder. She reflected that Thomas Woodbridge would probably leave a similar disturbance behind him all his life. And she felt more and more ridiculous sitting there as the minutes passed. She would wait for him to return, then she would tell him that she must go, and she would go. But as the time passed, she realized that she had no idea how long it took to give birth to a litter of pigs. She had better leave.

She was opening the door to test the rain when Tom burst back in, his soaked shirt plastered to his chest. He brushed roughly past her. His leather shirt caught on a projection in the doorway. She reached to unhook it, but he pulled impatiently through, ripping the shirt the length of his back.

"Two more. Same way. Quick. Come."

He laid one piglet on the hearth. Water from his hair fell on it, and he cursed, brushing the piglet dry. He took the second one in his own hands and began to treat it as he had the very first, blowing into its snout. Then he looked up in anger to see her standing helpless and aghast.

"Pick it up! Take it! Do like I do!"

"But, Tom, I can't put it—"

"Pick it up!"

She bent over the tiny form with the closed eyes. She was afraid to touch it. She was afraid not to.

"Pick it up!" he bellowed as he worked on his own animal.

Gingerly she reached for it.

"They're not coming regular," he said between breaths. "I got to get back. May be more already."

He worked over his animal.

"Rain washed out the footing under the shed. It's sliding. Got to get back and fix it."

He released the tiny piglet on the hearth, where it tottered and fell, but breathed.

"Got to go back. Get yours breathing."

He was gone, leaving a pool of water where he had knelt, and a pool of fear in her heart. The animal in her hands was very still and growing cold. She blew into its face ineffectively. But she could not touch it with her mouth. She looked at the other one lying on the hearth, breathing. She heard pounding noises coming from outside, and she could imagine the great redhead out there shouldering the shed back onto its base and driving stakes to hold it against the torrent that was turning the slope into a landslide. The pounding made her heart beat faster; but when the pounding stopped it beat faster still, for she knew he would be back.

The door flung open, and he stood in the noisy torrent with the lantern raised, staring in angrily at her as she held the piglet ineffectually. But he stood only an instant before he was charging into the cabin. The action panicked her into pressing her face against the piglet, and she blew.

He stood over her threateningly, yet not daring to move lest she was about to succeed.

His voice was hoarse. "Quick! It's only a few minutes they can last!"

She was amazed at herself. It was not as bad as she thought, and she relaxed as she concentrated on breathing into the white little being. In her fingers she felt a tiny swelling, and then a contraction, and she concentrated with an intensity which surprised her.

She placed the piglet on the floor, where it moved; and she stared at it. The redhead dropped to his knees over it. Drops fell from his face, but he caught them and moved away slightly.

She sat down and began rocking back and forth with her hands clasped tight in her lap. Woodbridge looked at her, and his great angry mouth spread into a smile. Her arms felt a million tingling pricks, and she also felt suddenly tired all over.

They stood staring at the animal for a moment, and then Tom was on his feet.

"Got to go back. If only I had a clock, I could tell."

"Tom, I must leave," Veronica said.

"Keep them warm," he ordered, and was gone again.

She rose quickly and followed him to the door, but there was no calling over the torrent. She started out into the rain. The driving water soaked her in an instant, but she felt that she must tell him. Then she remembered his last order, and returned to the cabin. Quickly she put the two piglets in the old greatcoat which she found on the bunk. She arranged and rearranged the coat several times, not knowing how it should be. Finally she left the little snouts exposed to get air, covering the rest of them. One sleeve covered them both.

It was a long time before he returned, but she dared not leave them alone.

When he did come back, he was breathing hard, but he was quieter.

"Be a while yet before the next one," he announced. "Cleopatra's easier, but still scared, what with the shed moving on its pins and the rain pounding and all. I got two lanterns burning for heat."

He looked at her. Her dress was molded to her from the rain, and her hair was soaked. She shivered, and he brushed off a section of log and shoved it close to the fire.

"I'm sorry," he said. "Sit here by the fire, Miss Veronica. I forgot. I got everything in those Bedfords. Everything."

"Tom, I've got to go. I can't stay here any longer."

"Go? You can't. Didn't you see that rain?"

"I can't help that. I can't be here."

"You can't do else, Miss Veronica. Your mare couldn't navigate. If she could, you couldn't go alone. Them red devils use the night."

"Not a night like this."

"Especially a night like this. Remember the night of the fire?"

She was silent under the weight of the truth.

"Rain is cover for them."

"Then you must take me in to the village, Tom."

Woodbridge looked shocked.

"With five or six yet to come?"

She could see what she asked. But he tempered her disappointment.

"It shouldn't be long now, Miss Veronica. When we're done, maybe the rain'll be done too. I'll take you in then, rain or not."

"Then I've got to go by myself," she said.

"I didn't ask you to come here, but I'll not have your killin' on my hands. And don't try to get your mare, Miss Veronica. I'll cover her and put her where you won't find her."

She was angry, but the answers to all her charges were written on his face. He had everything at stake tonight. A pair of Bedford shoats might be only a meal to Nathan Shuldane, but to this great angry redhead they were life. He hadn't asked her to come out here.

"Where's your fancy law man?" he said bitterly, ending all talk.

He went back out to the shed, and they worked together into the night.

The fourth time he returned to the cabin, he found her asleep on the floor before the fire, exhausted. He put a new log on the fire, and as the dry bark flared up he saw how its light was reflected against the whiteness under Veronica's chin. Her throat was so white and exposed, and her clothes were so shaped to herself, that he felt a man oughtn't look. He sat down again to wait awhile on Cleopatra, feeling that the faint perfume in the cabin would make tomorrow night and every night after that tasteless.

It was almost dawn when the farrowing was over. The nine piglets were snuggled safely on the straw mat, covered with more straw. Cleopatra slept. The rain had stopped, and a great calm was in the night.

He saddled Veronica's mare and Prince, and stepped to the cabin door.

"We'll go now, Miss Veronica," he called.

But there was no answer. The rifle was gone from the wall.

He tied the mare's rein to Prince's saddle, and rode as quickly as the darkness would permit toward the lighter sky in the east.

Blair's awakening could have been from several causes. It could have been from the rain on the roof of Hosmer's Store, which stopped so suddenly, or it could have been the vision of Faith Hawkins. For as Blair sat up, he dwelt on Faith Hawkins's vague invitation to Veronica to be free for a little get-together tomorrow morning—rather *this* morning. "Something a sight more important than a going-away party," she had said. He remembered then how Faith Hawkins had looked at him, as if he were supposed to be party to some cozy secret.

It dawned on him that Faith Hawkins had had time to hear from Hosmer about the marriage planned between himself and Veronica. The little affair Faith Hawkins planned was undoubtedly in the nature of a betrothal party.

There was more to Blair than a handsome face and a keen legal perception and a ruffled shirt front. He knew as surely as he sat up in his bunk that Veronica would marry him. In the first place her silence through the years of presumptuous references by Shuldane became tacit consent. In the second place Elnathan Shuldane wanted the marriage. But Blair also knew that anything stronger than friendship would have to come later. He knew that under such a mute arrangement Veronica would not take it kindly if she thought he had announced to Mesopotamia that they were to be married. It would be highhanded.

He could visualize the scene in Faith Hawkins's cabin. He could see the hurt surprise that would come to Veronica's face when the matrons of Mesopotamia welcomed her into their own dubiously happy state of matrimony. And he could feel how her lovely person would cool toward him. He knew she wasn't ready yet. It was even possible she wouldn't tolerate it. The party, or whatever it was, must be called off.

By the time Polly Stikes's rooster crowed, Blair was at the Hawkins place, sparring around the edges of a difficult subject with Faith, who was now up. But his veiled inquiries brought no results in the face of Faith's labors at the fireplace, where she was making surprisingly large amounts of corn dodgers and barley coffee. Blair plunged in direct.

"What I mean, Faith, is this. Is it by any chance a kind of betrothal party you've planned for Veronica this morning?"

"How did you find out?" she asked. "It was to be a surprise."

"I didn't find out, Faith. I guessed."

"Quiet, Jonathan." Faith pointed up to the cabin loft. "She'll hear you. She'd be up now except you must have kept her out at Wood-bridge's awful late last night. I didn't even hear her come in."

Jonathan had forgotten that Faith thought he had gone to escort Veronica home last night.

"I suppose Hosmer told you about Veronica and me, Faith?"

"Nope."

"Veronica told you herself?" Blair's voice was hopeful.

"No." Faith resented this question. "But if a letter is lyin' around in my own house . . ."

Blair's disappointment was deep after the fleeting hope. "Don't you see, Faith? Veronica didn't tell you anything about it because she's not sure she wants me. It's kind of being pushed onto her. Now she'll think I told the whole town, and she'd have a right to quit me. She's not ready to marry me yet."

Faith grinned at Blair's modesty. She put her hand on his arm, but he was impatient.

"Faith! You don't understand. This could spoil everything! I know what I'm saying!"

"Quiet. She'll hear you, Jonathan." Faith grinned. "Or maybe that's your intention."

"Faith, you've got to listen. I tell you, it'll spoil it all if you don't cancel this thing."

But Faith Hawkins, still playing the role of Mesopotamia's bride after twelve full months, had hold of something new to take the grim routine off the frontier. She intended to make the most of it.

"Please, Faith!" Blair pleaded.

"Seems to me the way to do," said Faith slowly, "would be for me to go up and ask her privately, Jonathan."

Faith was on the ladder immediately, climbing up to the loft.

"No! Let her sleep, Faith," Blair begged.

"Plenty of time for that after." Faith winked down at him.

Blair stepped forward quickly and grasped a fold of the hem of her skirt. Faith looked down at his hand with an impish grin.

"Let me go tell her," said Blair.

"It's not your place yet," grinned Faith. But the idea rather appealed to her, and she climbed down.

Blair climbed up the ladder. At the top his eyes adjusted to the dark, and he saw an empty loft. Faith could not see the tenseness on his face. He stayed there a moment as the truth flooded over him. At the top of the ladder he leaned into the loft, as though talking to someone, and mumbled a little. Actually, he was thinking about what he must do. He must go out to the Woodbridge place and get Veronica back here as quickly as possible, and by some roundabout way. Slowly he climbed down the ladder to where Faith waited for him.

"She says she'd like you to call it off, Faith," he said.

"Aw, Jonathan Blair! She's just shy! It's natural. I'll go up and tell her."

Jim Hawkins came in from feeding the stock, alarmed.

"Veronica's mare broke loose! It's gone!"

Faith looked at Blair and then at the loft. She started quickly up the ladder. Blair grabbed for her, but she was already halfway up. Blair watched helplessly.

Faith reached the top of the ladder and looked into the loft, then down at Blair in wonderment. Her surprise gave way to breathtaking understanding. She climbed slowly back down the ladder.

"I can see why you'd not want a party," she said.

"Now, Faith, wait a minute."

"She's stayed the night out there in Woodbridge's cabin."

"We had to stay out there because of the rain," explained Blair. "I was there too. The three of us were together."

"Looks to me like you're here and they're out there," said Faith stubbornly.

"I just came in, just now, to talk to you about canceling the party. We three were together."

Faith Hawkins looked pointedly at his clean clothes, which showed no signs of rain or being slept in.

"I changed my clothes before I came to your cabin," protested Blair. But the more he explained, the more he needed to explain. "I see now I should have wakened her and brought her in with me, but I didn't think how it would look. I was that worried about the party."

Faith's smile was a taunt. Such righteous innocence was uninteresting.

"Looks like you lost out all around, Jonathan."

"But Faith, you've got to call off the affair."

Faith walked to the door, looked up toward the blockhouse, and returned.

"Little late for that. They're coming already."

Blair looked up at the blockhouse to see people entering, some carrying pots from which steam issued.

"Guess you can explain to them," said Faith, "same as you did to me."

Blair could have beaten the woman, for she now set to work assembling her part of the breakfast with an alacrity very like anticipation. It was apparent that the affair would be more of a success than she'd hoped.

When Tom overtook her, Veronica rode the mare and he rode Prince. He was depressed to notice that Veronica set a fast pace. In fact, she covered the distance toward town so quickly that he experienced the same sinking feeling he'd had after he had brashly handed over his warrant to Hosmer for a miserable twenty acres. He felt now that he had missed another chance. Something important was rapidly going out of his life.

They had only about a mile to go when Woodbridge heard a laughing voice issue from the woods.

"That's a hell of a way to wear a gun!" it said.

When Tom pulled up, Veronica reined the mare down too. Woodbridge unslung his gun clumsily, getting the reins mixed up in the sling.

A grinning, bearded figure rose up out of the brush.

"By the time you got through jugglin' that firin' stick, you would have been a dead hog farmer," laughed the stranger. "And it wonders me ya didn't shoot yourself."

"Navarre!"

"You'd oughta carry your gun handier. Lot of times them red devils are just sneakin' back to the Greenville Line this time in the mornin'."

"What are you doin' here, Navarre?"

Navarre's glance asked the same, with impudence, as it took in the two of them.

Veronica looked away. Woodbridge reddened.

"Miss Shuldane's just goin' back East. Not that it's your business."

"Me and a couple a others tracked four soldiers up in here," said Navarre. "They went into Mesopotamia. We aim to see what they're up to. Squatter hunters, we figure."

"There were some soldiers coming up to take Mr. Blair and me down to Cincinnati," Veronica said. "Those are probably the ones."

"Thank you, ma'm. That relieves me some. Though I'll keep watch of 'em all the same."

As they rode the last mile into town, Veronica kept silence. She had had the first faint evidence of what she might face.

They were finishing up the breakfast at the blockhouse. Blair had explained to the whole town that Veronica had not formally consented to marry him and that it would embarrass his cause with her if this were called a betrothal breakfast.

Morgan Brady hollered for the coffee, and said: "Well, it don't have to be a marryin' party! Get her up here! We'll call it her goin'-away party!"

Blair explained that Veronica could not come out, implying illness. It was no time to tell the truth, in Blair's judgment. Few times were.

The women turned to Faith Hawkins, who corroborated his explanation. But she did it with such cryptic and interesting inflections that the subject of Veronica's illness would not die.

Little Camelia Flannerty, on her part, could not bear the thought of all this joy and the angelic Miss Veronica alone, sick in bed, so she quietly went out of the blockhouse and found her way into Faith Hawkins's cabin and up the ladder. She returned back in tears to announce: "Miss Veronica is nowhere. She's gone. Bed ain't even been slept in, it looks like."

The youngster pulled a hank of her yellow hair into her mouth to hold back the grief, but the tears made paths down her cheeks.

Faith Hawkins tried to quiet the child with some limp possibility about Miss Veronica perhaps being out in the shed to get some water or something. Among other skills she had the ability to refrain from gossiping while in the same breath inciting others to do it.

Judith Dolk logically pointed out: "Faith, your water bucket's not in the shed. It's at the well."

Mrs. Exeter inquired, "Faith, did you talk to her this morning?"

Faith was forced to admit that she had not. Through it all none observed that Camelia Flannerty had slipped out again to continue the search.

Woodbridge and Veronica rode silently into the village. Veronica was surprised and pleased that there seemed to be nobody about. She rode toward the Hawkins cabin.

"I hope everything will be all right," she said.

"It will if I get right back there, and if Cleopatra can feed them all right," answered Woodbridge.

"I didn't mean that," she said.

Woodbridge looked puzzled.

They were nearing the Hawkins cabin and were about even with the blockhouse when Camelia Flannerty spied her angel.

"Come here, Miss Veronica, quick!"

"What is it, Camelia?" asked Veronica softly.

"Oh, I was so scairt, Miss Veronica! Come!"

"Scared, Camelia? What could frighten you so?"

"I thought—I thought—never mind. Come. You've got to come right now!"

Veronica had never seen the child so excited and frenzied, but Tom urged her to wait.

"It'll only take a minute," said Veronica. "And the child is obviously troubled."

They followed Camelia toward the blockhouse.

Inside the blockhouse people heard the little girl's excited, eager voice.

"In here, Miss Veronica! You was almost too late!"

The youngster yanked open the door with Woodbridge's help, and Veronica stepped over the sill log to face the angry, the curious, and the expectant.

Camelia pulled at Tom Woodbridge. But he said: "I've ate already, Camelia. And I've got a brand-new litter of Bedfords to tend to."

The little by-play took place in view of the entire party, and Tom withdrew, leaving eyes free to converge on Veronica, who was being led gently by Blair to a place at the table.

She observed his clean clothes and then looked down at her own.

The presence of Veronica Shuldane in Mesopotamia had done many things for the women of the settlement. They knew it. They had even told her so. One was an improvement in their appearance. But now, ironically, Veronica's unkempt appearance struck every woman in the room. She was still the most beautiful and her dress the finest, but no one had ever before seen her hair so tangled and her dress so wrinkled.

She smiled timorously around the room in greeting, but the smile was stricken from her face by the stark curiosity of the stares as she sat down at the table.

Every motion of Blair's body offered her forgiveness, forgiveness he thought was needed. It hurt her. She granted him no attention by either word or gesture. She confined herself to the barest motions necessary to eat. She was not hungry, but she could not bear to speak any unnecessary words of explanation to the unnatural, unspeaking group around her. She had not been sure, at first, what they were thinking. But as she ate, the extreme attention of Blair, and the complete absence of conversation about the rain and how she was stranded at Woodbridge's, left her no doubt.

Blair didn't see Veronica again until noon. When he did, he told her that the soldiers had arrived, and asked her how soon she could be ready.

"I'm not leaving here until I get this straightened out, Jonathan."

"Veronica, I—"

"Hear me out first, Jonathan." She explained gently everything that had happened. "I'm not going to leave until everybody understands. Until they know the truth."

"Veronica, you don't have to bother. We can leave this afternoon."

"Can't, Jonathan."

There was nothing he wouldn't have done to right the wrong. And she knew it. She knew that he was writhing with regret, but she could give him no comfort. She had too much trouble herself. She was sick about the suspicion which she now met everywhere.

"Tomorrow, then?"

"No."

"Why not?"

"I'll go to the church service. They'll see that I'm not hiding, and it will give me a chance to tell them. I'll tell them about Tom's pigs and the rain."

"Veronica, don't go to the church service. Don't go."

"Why?"

"I haven't given you much reason for confidence. But believe me this once. Do not go to that church service. I've heard about this preacher."

"I'm going, Jonathan."

What Woodbridge actually came in for on Sunday morning was not the circuit rider's church service, but to see if Sam Hosmer had some hog or cattle tonic. However, as Woodbridge was leaving the store Brady followed after and said raucously: "You're lookin' a little peaked this mornin', Woodbridge! But I envy ya!"

Woodbridge stopped and turned to Brady, who stood there leering. "Must be that curly red hair that gets 'em!"

"What are you rantin' about?" asked the redhead.

Brady's grin faded under Woodbridge's questioning stare, and he moved away.

Woodbridge stood for a moment, thinking. He turned back toward the store to find Amos Exeter staring at him from just inside the doorway.

Woodbridge walked back into the store. Conversation died out until Exeter broke the silence. "Somethin' you forgot, Woodbridge?"

"No." He looked around at the cold face of Mesopotamia. "No. But I suddenly got the idea there was somethin' goin' on pertainin' to me."

Seth Gershom, the lanky, cadaverous circuit rider, took a step forward. "Perhaps you'd clear up any doubts that might assail you if you stay to the meetin' that begins in an hour in the blockhouse."

"I got a feverish sow and nine piglets that need tendin'," said Woodbridge evenly.

"And you've got a hellish streak in your soul that needs it worse." The black-clad giant's voice seemed to come from a dungeon.

"Seems to me you know a lot about the color of my soul," Woodbridge answered, "for only seein' me twice in your life, Rev'rend. I think maybe I better come to your service. But I recommend your lesson be founded on better than the talk y' might happen to pick up in Hosmer's Store this morning."

When the people began to assemble inside the blockhouse, Woodbridge climbed to the guard post in the northwest bastion.

The circuit rider's service brought to Mesopotamia the thrill of the theater, the shrine, the courtroom, the confessional, the gallows. The Reverend Seth Gershom knew well the mixture of emotional thrills that was expected of him. And he was prepared to fulfill that expectation. With the material available, his performance would be consummate. He even set his own stage well.

As Veronica came into the blockhouse through the west door, escorted by Faith and Jim Hawkins and Blair, Gershom raised his head from his Bible to look. He removed his glasses with his left hand, the

better to study Veronica, and with a long bony finger flipped his Bible
closed as though the time had come to begin. Gershom then lifted his
eyes to the northwest bastion, where Woodbridge returned him a dis-
trusting scowl. With his head thus raised, the preacher closed his great
eyelids and converged the fingers of his right hand on the bridge of
his hawklike nose. It was easy to see that the tolerance he was about to
ask from Above was out of all reason.

The congregation watching the good man fidgeted in anticipation
and looked at the group on the front bench.

Veronica shivered despite her resolve. She began to understand why
Jonathan had told her not to come.

Gershom saved the best until last. There was a blessing for the new
blockhouse. There was a prayer for the return of Isaac Shane. There
were prayers of thankfulness for certain dubious blessings; and when
the miscellaneous clerical chores had all been covered with a sprin-
kling of personal first-name references, almost every member of the
village was left flushed with pleasant embarrassment. Stikes was com-
mended for his blockhouse design; Hope Emerson, for her courage.
Judith Dolk was blessed for her baby. Asa Buttrick was lightly rebuked
for the high price of his cloth imports, but in a way that left him the
character of a likable, mischievous boy. One way or another, the circuit rider gave most of the men and every one of the women a wonderful feeling of inclusion in the sight of the Maker. The people were
now solidly behind the minister, whatever he might do.

Then came the long pause. Blair prayed that the service was over.
From the northwest bastion Woodbridge eyed the minister suspiciously.

Finally the great head rose to reveal such an expression of injured
long-suffering that it startled the women and children and fascinated
the men. The grim mouth opened and the storm broke.

"Stolen waters are sweet, and bread eaten in secret is pleasant!"

Gershom pointed up his vague reference by glancing down at
Veronica on the first bench and then up at Woodbridge in the northwest bastion. The congregation followed his scowl.

Then Gershom's unmerciful tirade reverberated at length around
the walls of the blockhouse with such authority that it held motionless
on the rifle parapet even the small restless boys, who ceased swinging
their legs out over the people below.

Veronica sat looking at the floor. She had had no idea such degrada-
tion could be cast upon her, and she broke under it. Blair found a host

of things to do for her. He placed her Bible on the floor. He handed her a new handkerchief when she wept.

One thing the Reverend Gershom did not perceive: the real basis of Hosmer Village's anger at Woodbridge was not the suspicion of sin, but the fact that he had turned a kind of angel into clay. For there was not a husband in the blockhouse who had not secretly pictured Veronica tenderly binding wounds which he had received defending her from some vague danger. Woodbridge had seemingly created a kind of mass jealousy. If it had been Blair, it would not have been so bad, for Blair was not of them.

The women's malice against Veronica was allied. They had used her as a kind of confessor, telling her their troubles. She had been to them a tower of sympathy, above woman. They had been duped.

Veronica sensed their resentful stares on her back.

Gershom had built up the imagined sin now to such heights that the rest of the congregation felt extremely virtuous by comparison. Obviously, it would take a mighty advocate to intervene with the Maker on behalf of Veronica and Woodbridge. Gershom paused to gird himself for the fight, and the people bent forward to see how such a momentous thing could be attempted. But in the pause a voice from the northwest bastion, almost as vibrant as Gershom's, shocked the congregation.

"You'll excuse the interruption, Gershom. I call for a replacement on Indian watch here! I'll be leavin' for my farm."

Every neck in the blockhouse turned. A pool of startled faces lifted up to Woodbridge.

Gershom's face was granite. "If you've the cowardice to leave this woman alone here to face the town, then you'd best go, for I can do nothing for you."

"I've better reason," said Woodbridge, walking east along the riflemen's catwalk to the ladder, "to be at my place, where I've an ailing sow, than to be here listening to the ravings of a suspicious man!"

"I should have expected you'd show more concern for an animal than for a human life you've wrecked," said Gershom. He had to look up sharply now at Woodbridge, who stood above him at the top of the ladder, at the east end of the blockhouse. "Go, then. And leave the woman to face it alone."

Woodbridge's jaw slid forward and his cheeks turned white.

"I'd no intention of leaving her alone," he said, "if you're meaning my wife—Mrs. Thomas Woodbridge."

The only sound in the blockhouse was that of Woodbridge's feet scraping down the ladder. Veronica's tear-stained face had a stunned look. Blair stared at her with unbelief, as did everyone else.

Woodbridge reached the bottom of the ladder and turned to face Veronica across the first bench of people.

"Come, Veronica!"

It was a command, and it brought Veronica involuntarily to her feet. Once up, though, she wondered why, and stood there sobbing. Her lips were parted. And as her left hand lifted to her mouth in a motion of indecision and anguish, the sun sparkled on the tinfoil on her finger.

Woodbridge raised his voice. "If the ring on your finger means anything, Wife, come with me now!"

In her confusion Veronica looked about her, at the cold face of Mesopotamia and at the shocked countenance of Seth Gershom; and in that sea of hostility she saw a redheaded pillar of angry strength that looked like shelter.

Like a woman walking in her sleep, she moved across the front of the congregation, hesitantly at first, toward Thomas Woodbridge. By the time she reached the middle of the blockhouse, she was walking upright, and through a haze of tears she saw an outstretched arm covered with red-gold hairs that glinted in the sun from the rifle port. She walked quickly now to grasp it with an impulse that was at least gratitude.

She held Woodbridge's forearm with both hands. It was warm and substantial and strong, and it guided her slowly through a double row of swimming faces toward the door.

Jonathan Blair watched them walk toward the door, and it was as though something were being stolen from him, like life. His brain would not work fast enough as he rose to his feet dazed, in utter disbelief. But as the pair reached the doorway, he cupped his hands to his mouth and shouted, "Wait!"

Woodbridge stopped and turned an angry, inquiring face toward Blair, who called out, "I should like to know the name of the witness to this alleged marriage—if there be such!"

Woodbridge stood still, speechless. The faces of the congregation began now to turn in anticipation from Blair to Woodbridge.

The silence was broken by a shuffling in mid-congregation as a dirty bearded figure stood up to face Blair. He was dressed from head to foot in leather, and he slouched against his standing rifle, which he gripped by the muzzle. A black hole opened in the middle of his beard, and with the overt challenge of a man who tells a bold lie, he said, "I was the witness to the marriage. Slover Navarre."

Veronica stared in surprise through moist eyes, but she could not bring the man into focus, nor did she have time, for the steady arm of Thomas Woodbridge was guiding her out into the strengthening sunlight.

Seth Gershom and Jonathan Blair were left alone in the blockhouse as the astonished villagers crowded out to watch a dappled horse carry a man and a woman west across the river which divided the settled part of the village from the unsettled—the east part from the west part —and the crowd from Thomas Woodbridge.

# Chapter 6: *I CHARGE THEE*

WOODBRIDGE impatiently wiped the rain water off the ax blade with a hard palm. Then he rubbed a piece of hog fat over the iron. The relentless summer rain would rust the head off an ax while a man stood looking at it. It was the cause of every trouble on the Woodbridge place. It had rotted half the seeds in the ground, so that his corn was even spottier than it should be for a first year's crop in green ground.

The ever-drenching rain had apparently even drowned the soul of Veronica since she had come to the cabin with Woodbridge. She had no kind word to say. He caught her staring at him as he ate, as though he were some gross hog. She spoke when spoken to. She was unrecognizable as the loving spirit who had softened the cold face of Mesopo-

tamia. She would not go in to the store. She would not step off the
Woodbridge place.

The rain was the very cause of Woodbridge's work today. The woods
hogs which Woodbridge had acquired ran wild and took care of themselves capably. They were tall, long-legged, skinny animals carrying
very little pork, but able to run from a wolf or counter the claws of a
painter with their long sharp tusks.

The Bedfords, though, were delicate, and three of the young ones
had died. Woodbridge blamed the dampness. He was building a platform inside the sow's shed to keep the young ones off the wet ground.
He split off a slab and looked at the clean heart grain of the wood. As
he looked, a brown stain appeared on it. Not until Woodbridge had
looked overhead and on both sides did he see the leatherclad figure
behind him, so quiet was the arrival of Navarre.

"You're askin' for trouble this far away from your gun, Tom. Won't
help ya any over by the cabin, there."

Woodbridge grinned and relaxed.

"I try to keep it halfway between Veronica and me," he said. "So's
either of us can reach it in a hurry."

"Then you better get two of them, livin' way out here."

"I aim to. Stikes sent for barrel iron. But meanwhile we've got only
the one."

"Then you better keep Veronica with you, or you stay with
Veronica," advised Navarre.

Woodbridge looked at his boot. "That's easier said than done,
lately," he said without explaining. "But I never got a chance to thank
ya, Slover, for what ya said at the church service in the blockhouse that
day."

"You're gonna get a chance right now." The trapper studied Woodbridge's face for any sudden disinterest. "I was up here for a purpose
that day, you remember, trailin' them federals."

"I remember."

"Government's cleanin' out squatters, Tom. Serious now, they
moved in on six settlements south of here with twenty men. Point
is: I want you to harbor five women and three kids for a few days.
Families of men squattin' down near Boxford's Cabin. We're gonna
make a stand there. Want the women and kids safe out of the
way."

Woodbridge's face hardened a little, and he shook his head.

"Slover, I'm 'debted to ya. But I want no hand in squatter doin's. Squatters took their way of gettin' land, gamblin' for the cheap price. I paid for mine. Seems t' me like they got to stand by their own gamble."

"Fair enough, Tom, if ya don't agree with squattin', and if ya figure you'd be doin' it for the squatters only. But I wasn't puttin' it to ya exactly that way."

"How, then?"

"I was askin' ya to do it fer me, personal."

"What are the squatters to you?"

"That's got no more to do with it than how come you got such fancy imported pigs."

Woodbridge squirmed. "How do you know the government men'll pick on the squatters near Boxford's Cabin?"

"They came up the Miami and burned out the men squattin' on Jonathan Dayton's part of the Miami Purchase. We figured next would be north of that at Packer's place. 'Twas. And time they arrived we was layin' for 'em. Drove 'em off. We give it to 'em again at Jamison's. Now ya draw a likely line of march north from Jamison's, y' know the government men are headin' for Boxford's. We'll be waitin' for 'em again. But we want the Boxford women out of it. Just be two or three nights' shelter we'll need for them."

"Why not take 'em into Mesopotamia?" asked Woodbridge. "Safer. Why bring them out to my place?"

"Reasons enough. Mesopotamia's mostly like you. Feel pretty righteous, payin' for their land and gettin' cheated at it. Don't like squatters. You got a big double cabin. You could put the women in one half."

Woodbridge looked down at his boot.

"Slover, no reason you would've known. But we use both halves of the cabin, nights. That's the way it is."

Navarre looked in wonder at each half of the double cabin. Then with vast understanding he blasted another round of tobacco juice against Woodbridge's fresh-cut slab as a black mark against all womanhood.

"You're married, ain't ya?"

"Nope."

"If a man declares in public he's married to a woman, and if she takes his food and his roof, then she's married."

"Not with her kind of woman," said Woodbridge. "Got to be a preacher and all that. Way it is now, it works on her mind. If I brush against her by happenchance, she gets goose bumps all over, like it was unholy."

Navarre opened his mouth to speak, but Woodbridge cut him off.

"Oh, she tries to be good to me. But fact is, I just happened to be on her side when there was nobody else. I should of known better'n try to brand a pure-bred like her. But I got so mad in the blockhouse there that I figured I could treat her better'n any of them was doin'. Now I can't undo the damage."

"You sayin' she wouldn't have you even if you was preacher-married?"

"Why should she?"

"Then why does she stay?"

"Don't know for sure that she would if she had a choice, though I guess she gives me a little somethin' for what I done at the blockhouse that day. She was that hurt at the time."

"What does she want, then?" asked Navarre.

"To go back to Concord is my guess. Though 'twould hurt her pride some."

"Then why don't ya let her go, Woodbridge?"

Navarre waited for an answer that didn't come.

"It's only right," he persisted. "Ya got no right to prison her here."

Woodbridge's teeth ground together, shaping a diagonal line under each cheekbone; and under the bleached eyebrows Navarre found himself staring at the humblest yet most presumptuous visage in his experience.

"My rights and my wants," said Woodbridge, "are two different things."

Inside the east end of the cabin Veronica and Navarre and Woodbridge ate a midday meal in silence until Woodbridge spoke.

"Veronica, I didn't say we would, nor we wouldn't. But Navarre here asks us to harbor eight squatters for three days."

Veronica spoke to Woodbridge, but she looked at Navarre, not knowing exactly what to make of him.

"I thought you didn't believe in squatting," she said.

"I don't," answered Woodbridge. "But Navarre says these are women squatters and three kids."

Veronica's brown eyes queried Navarre, who told her about the expected government action against the three huts near Boxford's Cabin, adding: "They'd be no trouble to ya, ma'm. They could sleep in your west cabin, leaving this part to you and Tom."

A kind of panic tightened her face, and she inadvertently glanced at the single bunk in the corner.

Woodbridge noticed. "I'd bunk in the shed," he said.

Her relief was obvious. "Then we should take the women in," she said. "Between the two cabins we'll have room enough."

Out in the shed Navarre used Woodbridge's ax. He very quickly set two short uprights and connected them with a long stringer that would form the edge of a bunk for Woodbridge. Navarre cut an unusual notch into the top of the uprights with a minimum of ax strokes. It was an inverted V with a small gap at the apex. Then on each end of the stringer he cut a tongue of the same shape which he slid into the inverted V. It made a kind of dovetail joint. Woodbridge watched carefully at first, but then his interest drifted to the big question.

"Seems t'me this'll make it tougher on her," he said. "She'll be worryin' what tales those women'll be carryin' around."

"You missed somethin' important, Woodbridge," answered Navarre. "That woman in there is past worryin' about what *people* think about her. She's worried about what *she* thinks of herself. You notice what page she had that prayer book open to?"

"No."

"The marriage ceremony, like she was memorizin' it."

Navarre asked Woodbridge if he could leave his rifle there and take Tom's large-bore gun instead, explaining that he expected close-range work, where he wanted short power and heavy ball. Woodbridge agreed.

The bunk was completed in the shed, and then Navarre's quick ax helped Woodbridge complete the wooden platform in the special hog shed. When it was finished, the trapper's quick knife slid in and out of a long thin chip, cleaning out the soft grains, making a wooden comb. He handed it to Woodbridge. "Take this into her for the meal I et, and then bring your fancy pig critters up to their new house."

Woodbridge found the sow, Cleopatra, and led her back toward the special shed, her litter following single file. When he returned, Navarre's rifle stood in place of Tom's gun. Navarre had left.

In the back of Hosmer's Store, Blair shaved, uncovering a smooth, handsome face; but to Jonathan Blair the reflection from the scratched fragment of polished steel was that of a pusillanimous coward.

Blair had so thoroughly learned the methods of Elnathan Shuldane that he knew the mechanics of them better than Shuldane himself. By planning every possible move of his opponents at law, by devising a counteraction for each of these potentials, by seeking always the real motives of his opponents, Jonathan Blair had become the most promising young attorney in the Massachusetts Commonwealth.

Yet, once away from the influence of Shuldane, he had lost the simplest of contests. He had been bested by a simple man of impulse. Jonathan Blair had sat ineffectively in the blockhouse while an unthoughtful redhead, in a burst of emotion, took away the dearest woman ever set on earth, and without benefit of love.

As he shaved, Blair steeled himself to use the best and the coldest logic he could muster, but the flow of thought was drowned out by the booming laugh of Morgan Brady, which came in to him from the front of the store.

"All right, Exeter," Brady said, "maybe they were and maybe they weren't. But one thing's certain. They're good and married *now!* And there's nothin' anybody's gonna do about it if I know Woodbridge."

"Yeah, but if it was a preacher marriage or a justice-of-the-peace marriage, where was the justice or the preacher? And when did it happen?"

"I don't know. But there was a witness."

"Yeah," admitted Exeter, "but who was he? And where did he go? I never seen him before."

"Doesn't matter anyhow. By now it's a common-law marriage, if it's nothin' else."

"Not so sure about that," said Exeter with implications.

"Huh?"

"I was out to see Woodbridge, and nobody was home."

"So you snooped around a little, as usual."

"I couldn't help seein' the little single bunk in the cabin. And out in the shed there was another bunk with Woodbridge's old coat on it. Don't look like they're keepin' comp'ny like man and wife."

Blair halted his blade in mid-air and listened with sudden hope.

Brady said: "I guess if it wasn't legal, Blair wouldn't be packin' up to go back East. He ain't stupid, that one. He'd do somethin' about it."

Blair heard Sam Hosmer's voice join the conversation.

"What's going to bring trouble to Woodbridge is those squatter women he's keepin' out there. There was a shootin' argument down at Boxford's Cabin yesterday between squatters and government troops. There's some got shot. That'll bring trouble."

Blair could not see the faces, but Hosmer's information brought a stunned silence to the store.

As Blair approached the Woodbridge cabin, he inspected his dress, not in vanity, but because he hoped deliberately to remind Veronica of a way of life she was forsaking. Over his arm he carried her fine gray wool coat. It would furnish something to say to postpone the inevitable awkwardness of their meeting.

As he rode toward the cabin, Blair was glad to observe that the squatter women would help his cause, for to the west of the shack he saw one of them rolling something into a skin. In all his life, even along the docks at Boston, Blair had never seen such an animal-like human being.

The woman looked up at him, startled, and her eyes followed him, as at some curiosity. Blair guessed that Veronica's imagination had already projected herself into such a primitive state. And he guessed also that it had frightened her.

The door to the east half of the cabin was open, but Blair knocked. "I brought your coat out to you," he said.

Veronica motioned him in. She sat on an upturned section of an eighteen-inch timber, and Blair was struck by the change in her. He attributed part of her paleness to fatigue, but the lifelessness and the unsmiling face he blamed on Woodbridge. She stroked her gray coat that he'd brought, feeling the softness of it, and Blair took the opening.

"Veronica, you're not reared to this kind of a life."

She nodded her head in lethargic agreement, but said nothing. In fact, she gave him no verbal answers to his personal remarks. Blair felt as though he were talking to a sick woman. The sight of her languid, lifeless figure brought him to his knees on the floor beside her. And it was not Blair, the man of reason. It was a simple, ingenuous Blair, talking fast, pleading almost for his own life.

"Veronica, we both know this is not a marriage, in spirit or in fact.

Even if it were, it wouldn't matter to me. I'd give my right arm if I'd been the one that did what Woodbridge did."

He would have given more, because her silent, accusing eyes reminded him that he had not been the one.

"In five days I can get the soldiers back up here. We could leave Sunday morning. I'd leave without the troops, except I'd never forgive myself if anything . . ."

He reached out and grasped her hand, but she detached herself gently.

"I'll send word down tonight by Brady," he said. "The troops will be here Saturday night. We'll leave Sunday morning. You won't have to say anything to anyone. I'll handle that. You just be ready."

She said, "No." But it was such a despondent No that it made Blair strong. It cried out to go with him. In that moment, too, Jonathan Blair took a lesson from Thomas Woodbridge.

"You don't have to say anything, Veronica. I know. I won't make you say Yes or No. Just leave it to me. It'll all be my fault. You can always remember that. What happens now will be my fault."

He stood up, not caring that the squatter woman on the threshold had probably heard.

The women were ready to leave, and as they came in to say goodbye their gratitude to Veronica came from the heart. But the ragged one looked at her long and intently and said: "Don't forget about sucking the ginseng root. It'll spice up your blood."

Outside the cabin Slover Navarre indicated Blair's horse with a long looping stream of tobacco.

"Whose?" he asked.

"Blair's."

"He the lawyer that come down with her?"

"Yeah."

"The same one that asked for the witness in the blockhouse?"

"Yeah."

"What's he doin' in there?"

"Talkin' to her, I guess."

"What about?"

Woodbridge shrugged his shoulders. "I been out here with you."

Navarre looked at the ground and shifted the bulge in his cheek thoughtfully. "Tom, the squatters owe you a lot for keepin' the women. And they keep count of favors. When you need somethin', ask."

Navarre left, leading the three horses he had brought to spell off the five women and three children during the long walk ahead. He left his rifle with Tom, for he had lost Woodbridge's gun in the scrap.

Woodbridge put one foot over his own threshold, but Blair and Veronica were staring at each other in such silent privacy that Tom felt like an intruder in his own house. He needn't have, though, for he was unnoticed. Their backs were to him as they faced the fireplace.

"Sunday morning," said Blair. She gave him no answer, and Blair repeated it, "Sunday, Veronica. Keep count of the days."

Woodbridge did not know what was meant, but it had the ring of a contract, a private one, and a possessive anger surged up to redden his neck. He turned away quickly and strode outside to the front of the cabin where he could see Navarre and the women disappearing into the tunnel of forest to the east.

"Navarre!"

Navarre turned around and walked back to meet Woodbridge. When they met halfway, Woodbridge asked, "Where can I get a preacher?"

"A preacher?"

"That's right."

"You think she'll marry you?"

"Going to find out."

"You won't like the one I'd get. But the squatters have been supportin' a preacher down Steubenville in pretty style. Long way for him to come, though. Could you meet him part way?"

"Where?"

"The river ford twenty miles down the South Trail, below Boxford's."

"How soon?"

"Take me two days to get down there. Two days back. One day for leeway. Make it Monday, about midday."

"Too late," said Woodbridge. "Got to be Sunday."

Navarre looked up sharply at Woodbridge's presumption. But he said, "All right. Sunday."

The week passed largely in silence on the Woodbridge place. The rain let up on Wednesday for part of the day, and Woodbridge made use of the break to cut timbers to make a walk through the ankle-deep mud, so that Veronica could go to the shed without getting her feet wet. Veronica watched his shirt darken with perspiration from the labor. She saw the loose fibers of his shirt strain across his breadth, revealing the deep groove that ran down the center of his powerful back. And at such moments she felt a deep tenderness toward him as he drove his strong body to spare her feet.

But at night, when they were close together at supper in the cabin, the great squareness and thickness of his hands on the table made him a stranger to her. While carrying the water to the table, her bare arm brushed the coarse, granulated hide of his elbow, and she looked at him from behind, as though he were another species. He retired early to his half of the cabin.

Sunday morning, though, she wakened with a start to find him kneeling beside her bed. It was barely light outside.

The aroma of cooked bacon was in the cabin, and in Woodbridge's great palms was her prayer book, open.

"Veronica, Navarre's got a preacher coming to meet us, to do it like you want."

She sat up startled, clutching her gray coat around her.

"It leaves you with the same man, Veronica, but at least it makes it a preacher marriage, like you been readin' here. Don't that help?"

He held the book out in supplication.

"As for the man you're gettin', Veronica, you don't know it now, but it's strength to build whatever you need." He held out his open hands, palms up, fingers spread, then turned them over and doubled them into fists until the knuckles whitened.

"It's ruggedness to protect you from anything that could ever happen."

He flexed his shoulders forward like a brainless savage putting himself up for sale.

"And before I'm through, I'll put you back up where you belong, askin' nothin' back, except you be here. I'll live in the other half of the cabin."

Her eyes filled, and she buried her head in the coat she used for a cover.

"I'll get the horses ready," he said, and left her.

They rode through Mesopotamia before anyone was about. Woodbridge glanced anxiously up at the cupola on the blockhouse, but no call came.

As they turned south at the common, Veronica turned her head toward Hosmer's Store, where Blair slept. But she neither slowed her horse nor turned off the path.

Woodbridge saw how her knuckles whitened on the bridle, but he merely crimped his lips and dropped a half-length behind her. Not until they were a half-mile south of the river did he lengthen out the gait. By midmorning they were well south of Boxford's Cabin, and the rain started again.

Although he could not see the sun, Woodbridge felt it must be about noon when they approached the river. He could hear the river before he could see it. As they rode out from under the heavy cover at the ford to glimpse the fast-moving swirls in the center of the current, he spurred ahead of Veronica, anxiously, to the edge of the water.

It was not a normal riverbank.

The stream had overflowed beyond the rushes that once marked the edge, and there was no ford visible. The trail led abruptly into the murky water, and the usual well-trodden bank that marked the approach to a ford had disappeared. The tops of the reeds were under water, with the exception of an occasional tall one which slanted sharply downstream under the brisk current.

Woodbridge urged Jock forward, and the stallion sank a half-dozen reluctant steps into the water, mushing mid-shank deep in the mud. Tom jogged in the saddle, but Jock stood still. The rein flicking across his withers only caused his wet hide to ripple.

They turned back to the shore. Without explaining his suspicions to Veronica, Woodbridge cut a stout sapling pole and jabbed the bottom of the stream. The pole met with such little resistance that Woodbridge saved his balance only by stepping forward into the water, which quickly rose over his short boot.

"There's someone on the opposite shore," she said lifelessly.

Through cupped hands Navarre's voice came very faintly across the wind: "You can't cross, Tom! I been up and down the shore. There's no footing to be had!"

Woodbridge looked upstream and down. His eye measured the height of the tallest tree against the breadth of the stream. Again Navarre shouted across the stream. "No use, Tom. I can't even have the preacher swim across to ya. He can't swim."

Veronica had retreated from the water's edge to a tree, where she stood with Jonathan Woodbridge's greatcoat over her head. The coat had turned dark blue with the wetness, and Veronica's face seemed small and white under it.

Woodbridge approached her with weighted steps. As if it were pertinent, he said, "You know that I'll never let anything happen to you, don't you?"

She nodded, shivering in the cold rain, and said: "Tom, it's not meant to be. We'd better go back."

Her remark was hard to ignore, because he had the same feeling. But he continued, "And you know, don't ya, that if it comes to anything real important I'll not slight it for you?"

"I guess so, Tom."

"It's important you do. Because the ceremony is going to be slighted a bit. But there's gonna *be* one."

Woodbridge led her down to the water's edge. He cupped his hands and yelled across the stream to Navarre, "Where's your preacher?"

"Back here resting!"

"Get him up to the edge of your 'bankment!"

On the opposite shore Navarre brought his hand down from his ear and stood confused. Woodbridge shouted back, "It don't say anything in the book about—about the distance apart."

Navarre stood a moment, uncomprehending. Then suddenly he slapped his side in vigorous appreciation and disappeared behind the south embankment.

Veronica looked at Woodbridge in hypnotized unbelief. He tried to reassure her with his arm and his voice: "It'll be the same words. The distance doesn't matter."

"But a wedding at the top of the lungs!"

In Mesopotamia, Blair cursed Polly Stikes's rooster for picking that moment to crow. But he pointed the sorrel toward the west road and lengthened the leather for the borrowed horse he was leading. He noticed that the surrey stood loaded behind Hawkins's cabin. It would be ready. He cursed again when the voice of Amos Exeter shattered the morning stillness.

"Where you goin', Blair?"

Blair looked up to the top of the blockhouse, but he spurred the sorrel and splashed across the river, heading out the West Road. He had an extra horse in case there should be a hitch in getting Veronica's mare out of the Woodbridge shed. In fact, he had planned for the worst, and he felt the club of iron under his coat. Blair was not above learning from a man of action. He'd use no Shuldane strategy here. No matter what Woodbridge said, Blair would not waste time with answers. He would keep moving no matter what happened.

Blair was surprised to find both horses gone from the Woodbridge shed. But that was good; perhaps there would be no trouble.

He nudged the cabin door open six inches and stood back. There was no response, and he shoved it all the way open.

The emptiness inside was as nothing to the emptiness in Blair's chest.

He moved around the room aimlessly, picking up objects and putting them down.

There was an empty paper box lying open on the table, and on the cover were the words:

PRAYER BOOK
Confirmation Gift of Bishop Fearing, Boston

The book itself was gone.

As Jonathan Blair rode back into Mesopotamia, Amos Exeter was coming off watch at the blockhouse.

"I could have told ya, Jonathan."

"Which way, Amos?"

"South."

He had more to explain, but he talked to the air, for Jonathan Blair had thrust the lead rein of the extra horse into Exeter's hand and was splashing across the ford to the south on the other mount.

At the river south of Mesopotamia, Veronica Shuldane shivered in the rain and in the sight of the harsh redheaded stranger who had taken over her will and her life. They saw the mounted minister loom up over the opposite bank, rising a notch for every step of his horse. At this distance he was mostly a silhouette, and so tall and gaunt as to be a kind of specter.

A little cry escaped Veronica as she clutched herself to Woodbridge's chest. Even Tom stared with mouth ajar, for he was looking at the hawklike silhouette of the Reverend Seth Gershom.

Gershom himself was calm enough. He studied the couple on the north shore for only a moment. Then slowly and deliberately he turned his horse around and receded from view below the embankment.

Woodbridge thought he caught fragments of excited voices carried over on the wind, and then the silhouette reluctantly reappeared. Beside it this time was the figure of Slover Navarre, whose mount stood broad flank toward Veronica and Tom. Slover stood on the ground behind his horse, his legs showing under the horse's girth, his head extending a little above the saddle.

Woodbridge saw Navarre's mouth working. Then the minister raised his hand over his head and his deep voice carried across the water, "Are you ready to proceed?"

Veronica's clenched hands pulled Tom's wet shirt so tight against his chest that his collarbones were outlined under it. She looked into his face. "No, Tom! It won't be right! He hates us!"

He faced away from her toward the opposite shore. "Go ahead!" he yelled.

Veronica thrust him away, but his arm went around her and bound her to him. From across the stream the minister's voice came intermittently as the wind favored it or blew it away.

"We are gathered together here in the sight of God and . . . face of this witness . . . join together this man and this woman in holy . . . which . . . honorable estate . . ."

As the wind lessened, the voice sank to a lugubrious reverberation which caused Veronica to listen with wide eyes and strict attention.

"I require and charge ye both as ye shall answer at the dreadful Day of Judgment, that if either of you know any impediment why ye may not be lawfully joined in matrimony, ye do now confess it!"

The quivering fearfulness of Veronica's body as she heard the words conveyed itself to Woodbridge, and he found himself listening carefully to Gershom, who shrieked, "Have ye some'at to confess?"

Veronica started to speak, but Woodbridge wrenched the prayer book from her hand and opened it to the ceremony which she had marked. Though the rain spattered the thin paper into pulpy crinkles, Tom could read through the part Gershom had just intoned, to make sure what was "required and charged."

Gershom impatiently repeated, "Have ye aught to confess?"

Woodbridge hurled his voice, "We have not!"

There seemed to be words between Navarre and Gershom, but the minister resumed.

"Woodbridge, wilt thou have this woman to thy wedded wife?"

The wind rose again, blowing apart the sentence, ". . . to live together after . . . Wilt thou love her, comfort her, honor . . . keep . . . in sickness . . . forsaking all others . . . so long as ye both shall live?"

Woodbridge lifted his voice over the wind to Gershom, but it entered Veronica's breast in a resonance from his ribs.

"I will!"

"Veronica Shuldane!" continued the strident minister, "Wilt thou have this man to thy wedded husband?"

The wind erased most of it. But they could see when Gershom lifted his head from his book to wait for her answer.

She pushed away from Woodbridge, who held her with a rigid arm, yet gave her room to move within the arm, as strong fingers englobe a crippled bird to mend a wing.

"No, Tom! This is wrong!"

"Then tell *him* so!"

She turned to the opposite shore and called her answer.

"No!"

Woodbridge dropped his arm to free her, and she looked into his naked, wounded face.

Gershom put his hand to his ear, and partly turned his head.

As she faced Gershom to repeat her answer, she suddenly saw the silhouette of his half-turned hawklike profile as it looked that day in the blockhouse. She saw Woodbridge standing straight in the blockhouse, holding out his muscled arm to her before the hostile gaze of Mesopotamia.

She cupped her hands to her mouth and inhaled. "I will," she called. "I will."

And she bent her head against Woodbridge's chest. He could not see her face, but he gripped her tight, even on those terms.

Gershom turned his horse and started to ride away. But Slover Navarre's reprimand came across the water in the storm's lull.

"Give 'em the last part too, Rev'rend."

As Tom and Veronica stood in each other's arms, Gershom rode back reluctantly and intoned, "Almighty God, bestow upon these Thy servants, if it be Thy will, the gift of children to the honor and glory of Thy name."

The minister turned away, but again he was stopped by Navarre.

"There's more yet, Rev'rend."

Gershom flung it over with finality: "Those whom God hath joined . . . let no man put asunder. Amen."

Veronica secretly blessed Slover Navarre for that last. It seemed
directly to answer a question in her, and she swayed hard against
Woodbridge. He stared down incredulously for a long moment to see
if he misread the glowing upturned face in his arms. Then he bent a
wet curly head down to claim her.

They turned back to the waiting horses with quickened steps. Nor
was the exhilaration lessened for Woodbridge by what he saw over his
shoulder as he cast a final look back across the river.

Navarre's horse hawed around to follow the retreating minister,
leaving Slover Navarre standing suddenly unshielded, and Woodbridge saw what had not been apparent during the ceremony. Slover
Navarre's rifle was leveled hip high at the very spot where the minister
had been.

# Chapter 7: THE OPEN LETTER

As Tom Woodbridge listened to the reading of
the letter in Hosmer's Store, along with the rest of the villagers, the
red color of guilt seeped up his neck from under his collar. For as
Hosmer read the letter from Shuldane, it became apparent to Thomas
Woodbridge that he had misjudged Mr. Shuldane.

Sam Hosmer evidently thought so, too, for he looked up repeatedly
from the paper, deepening the color of Woodbridge.

The redhead was just now beginning to see how Shuldane won the
respect of men like Sam Hosmer and Mike Stikes and his father,
Jonathan Woodbridge. He always delivered what he promised.

Woodbridge thought back over it. Shuldane had told him that he
would do better to buy his land in Concord. It had worked out that
way. Shuldane had told Hosmer that a preacher had been arranged for.
And though Shuldane sat over a thousand road miles away, a preacher
had arrived in Mesopotamia, as promised. Shuldane had promised to
arrange for troop protection, and though no troops had arrived two

soldiers had come through to say that later in the summer a squad
would be assigned to patrol Mesopotamia.

Hosmer had said that Shuldane had the interests of Mesopotamia
closest to his heart. And here was a letter in which Shuldane talked
more of the settlement than of the daughter he had lost. Hosmer read
it with an accusing accent.

"Naturally, as an overly fond father, I was shocked to learn of
Veronica's marriage when I had other plans for her. Also, I had hoped
for her assistance in Boston and Philadelphia, where I am shepherding
some legislation favourable to our Mesopotamia settlement. However,
I shall carry on as best I can, with the help of Mr. Blair. Our every
effort is in behalfe of Mesopotamia."

Woodbridge looked neither left nor right. But he sensed the townsmen glancing at him occasionally as the picture of Mr. Shuldane came
through to them, sweetened the more by Hosmer's reading voice, a
tired, harassed gentleman, working against odds, beset now by the
additional burden of loneliness. Not a few of the women were thinking
about "that nice Mr. Blair," too.

The letter took the whole village into Shuldane's confidence and his
plans:

"I want to inform you all of a development of concern to you. Mr.
Blair discovered on his recent visit to you that our original survey was
in error by a thousand acres. As you all know, the survey was made
under the most difficult circumstances, and such errors are not uncommon. I have considered this carefully, and have arrived at a decision. Mr. Blair astutely pointed out to me that if I volunteered to
return this extra parcel to the federal government, it would make a
good impression and perhaps gain us the consideration we desire in
matters of troop protection and other favours which we shall need
from time to time.

"It has worked out precisely so, and I am told that the Congress and
the Land Office were well impressed by our honesty. We shall not lose
by it."

Shrewd winks traded among the men, admiring this stroke on the
part of the proprietor of Mesopotamia.

"I shall informe you later which portion of the village we shall return to the government. Mr. Blair is working on it now. It will affect some of you, but I shall compensate whoever is inconvenienced. Good planting to all of you and God bless you.

Elnathan Shuldane"

As Veronica and Woodbridge rode out the west trail, which was already being called the West Road, Woodbridge said: "I'm afraid I misread your father, Veronica. I see it's like the others think. He's got the town at heart."

Veronica's honesty forbade complete agreement; her loyalty precluded disagreement. She said nothing.

"The lawyer, too, I was hard on," said Woodbridge. "I had in mind he'd not forgive. And I had the idea he'd outmatch me for you some trick way, with law and the like. But I guess he bears no grudge."

Woodbridge leaned over in the dusk to see why he got no answer from her. Though she faced straight ahead, she looked down toward the swingletree hitch, causing Woodbridge to reconsider what he had said.

A couple of miles later, as though answering a question, she said, "Strange there was no letter enclosed for me."

Woodbridge felt that he should grasp some special meaning from her remark, but before he could think it out, she murmured, "And yet, of course, it is not strange at all."

He waited for further explanation, but none was forthcoming by the time they had reached the cabin. He unhitched Prince and bedded him down. He said good night to Veronica and walked out to his own bunk in the west half of the cabin.

Each day with Veronica since the wedding had impressed Woodbridge with the honesty of the woman he had captured. Her reverence for a bargain or a promise demanded a similar scrupulous response; and since Woodbridge had promised at the time of their marriage to demand nothing more than her presence, he kept his word.

Now, more than ever, though, he had reason to worry about their distance from the blockhouse, for he had also promised her safety.

On the way to his bunk in the other half of the cabin, he looked at the blackness under the trees around the clearing, wishing fervently that the troops promised by Shuldane would hurry. He considered fitting his half of the cabin with bunks to make it convenient for the patrol to stop off there.

Inside the dark cabin he took off his shirt and his boots, and in the blackness felt for the rolled coat of Jonathan Woodbridge which served as the pillow on his own bunk. What he felt caused him to spring back and grab his rifle, for where the coat should have been his hand sank down to touch the bare puncheon slabs of the bunk.

Clutching the rifle at the ready, Woodbridge slipped his feet into his boots and retreated into a corner, leaving only his front exposed. But he could hear no sound in the dark cabin beyond his own breathing. He approached the bunk again and felt for the wool blanket which he used. It, too, was gone.

Woodbridge went quietly out the door and looked around. He could hear nothing but Prince disturbing Jock in the shed. Rifle still in hand, he walked into Veronica's east cabin, "Somebody's been here, Veronica. I can't find—"

He stopped. Rolled up on the bunk beside Veronica's pillow was the faded blue greatcoat of Jonathan Woodbridge.

Her smile was timorous and fleeting, and it asked him to call no undue attention. But she reached up to clasp her cool hands around his neck.

"From now on, Tom, we shall need to combine our strength."

He looked down at the rifle in his hands, which was between them, harsh against her. She opened her arms for him to move it aside.

He held her lightly lest he drive away the moment. But as the warm softness of her met him, his fingers felt the tremor in her waist and back, and he enfolded her closer. Her breath came against his neck in a whisper.

"For better or worse, Tom. But . . ."

"Anything. Always." His voice rumbled through her.

Whatever she had found to fear was a mystery to Thomas Woodbridge; but it could be an army now, and still be nothing, he thought. For on this night her lips languished pliant under his, receiving his total, uncautioned strength.

The very fact that Sam Hosmer came out to the Woodbridge cabin was significant enough, for he had not been out since the raising. It was Hosmer's custom to transact all his business calmly and easily in the store as the townsmen came and went.

Hosmer did not even look around the clearing or the cabin. He took from his pocket a folded paper which he handed to Woodbridge without explanation.

"Y' might's well read it now, Tom, while I'm here."

Veronica asked Mr. Hosmer to sit down. Though he declined, he took off his hat and looked around the cabin. For Woodbridge, Veronica's simple invitation changed his cabin from a pile of timbers to a station in life. The pride of ownership swelled through him as he casually unfolded Hosmer's paper with the scant attention of a man who cannot be hurt by anything from outside his boundary lines.

Hosmer stood as if braced.

Woodbridge only had to hold the paper to the light from the fireplace for an instant to recognize that Sam Hosmer had handed him back his own Bounty Land warrant.

"How come, Sam? This a gift?"

"'Fraid not, Tom. I'm askin' you to give me back the deed I gave you to this place."

Woodbridge stood still, uncomprehending. Veronica walked to his side, unsurprised.

"I got the letter here from Mr. Shuldane," said Hosmer. "He's givin' this strip back to the government. Survey was bad."

Woodbridge's menacing silence hurried Hosmer into getting the letter out of his pocket. He walked over to the fire to read it, stooping to catch the light.

"The explanation comes from your own wife's father," said Hosmer. "He writes: 'Mr. Blair informes me that of all the tracts in Mesopotamia, the easiest way to return a thousand acres to the government is to measure it from the western edge of the village. This will inconvenience the fewest people. Also, it will rid us of the strip in which you and Mike Stikes hold the soil suspect because of the cleared place where you found no trees. This arrangement is especially pleasing to the government because it throws the west edge of our township in line with the north-south survey range lines which they are planning to run across the whole of the Revolutionary Bounty Land Tract. In fact, Mr. Blair cleverly worked it out that way in cooperation with Mr. Hutchins, the national geographer. In exchange for this cooperation, I should have no trouble getting troops to patrol Mesopotamia shortly, Mr. Hutchins having done several real-estate favors for the governor of the Northwest Territory, General Arthur St. Clair. Sam, I am re-

turning your money plus a consideration for your trouble. Will you
be so kind as to forward my deed? I will stand the loss for the thousand
acres, since I know you men made the survey under bitter conditions.
Elnathan Shuldane.'"

Woodbridge snatched the letter from Hosmer and threw it in the
fireplace.

"That's all right for you, Hosmer! But what about me? What about
the cabin and the sheds and the trees I cleared? You sold me this! I got
your deed to prove it!"

"Tom, I'll turn over to you your share of the refund money Mr.
Shuldane sent me."

"A-ah!" Woodbridge cut him off. "When a man holds a deed, he
owns the land. That's law, any place!"

"True," said Hosmer. "And I don't like the way it turned out, Tom."

"Then why did you give Shuldane back his deed?"

"Tom, I've buried six men, three women, and four children, without
scalps. I want those troops out here."

Woodbridge's red face was fierce in the firelight. His forehead was
wrinkled, and his lips were drawn back in uncomprehending rage.

"'Mr. Blair informs me.' Mr. Blair this! Mr. Blair that! Mr. Blair
and Mr. Shuldane have been very busy. Now I see a lot of things!"

"Tom, I know it's not fair to you," said Hosmer stubbornly, "but no
matter who gets hurt we got to have those troops. And you need 'em
worse'n any of us."

Woodbridge crumpled the Bounty Land paper in his fist. "Hosmer,
the law's on my side in this, and I'm holdin' you to your deed."

Hosmer put on his hat.

"If that's the way you're going to take it, I'll have to take my
chances."

But even as Hosmer said it, it became sickeningly clear to Woodbridge that the older man actually took no chance at all. How do you
hold a man to a piece of paper out here in the woods, up under the
Greenville Line?

# Chapter 8: THE SQUATTER

WOODBRIDGE had planned to finish replanting the field that afternoon, but for a thing like this even the corn could wait.

He had straightened up to rest his back from replanting the rain-rotted hills. That was when the sparkle of light caught his eye from a good fifty rods south. He could not believe it at first, but as he squinted downhill the tiny forms moved up the slope like a column of shoats behind a homecoming sow. As sure as the sun glinted off the gun barrels, it was a squad of troops approaching the lonesome Woodbridge development.

Woodbridge threw down his leather seed bag and ran to the cabin. But Veronica had already seen. Together they watched the little squad approach, and it was a wonderful sight. For three years Fort Washington had promised protection to the fringe settlements. Each month there had been excuses. But it was here now.

They watched the figures grow into blue uniforms. Even when they tramped along the lower edge of the reseeded cornfield, Woodbridge said: "They got no way of knowing there'd be new planting this late. Y' know, at times like this you can see the Republic is finally aware of the West."

Veronica said, "Doesn't look like many men to send to guard against the Wyandots."

"There's twelve of them," said Woodbridge. "And the way they slant their hats, they must be the same ones that was with Wayne at Fallen Timbers. With them, twelve is plenty."

Woodbridge was not a demonstrative man, but today he could not wait for the troops to reach his cabin. He went down to welcome them.

"Ensign Armstrong out of Fort Washington," the young man said.

"Glad to see you, Mr. Armstrong. Mighty glad. Come up to the cabin."

"I'm afraid you won't be so glad. Are you Thomas Woodbridge?"

"Yes."

"My errand is to clear the territory of squatters. And because of the

land-title and boundary mix-up—well, that means you, Mr. Woodbridge."

Veronica closed the door so that Woodbridge could not see half the
squad of regulars chasing one of his small razor-backed woods hogs
while the other half erected a spit over a fire.

From a small cask which she lifted from under the floor, Veronica
poured a noggin of whisky in front of the ensign who sat opposite her
husband. But the damage done across the table by Woodbridge's vio-
lent language could not be repaired by a cup of whisky, though she
knew that the officer was trying to mirror his new-issue uniform in her
facial expression. She also knew that the ensign held the advantage
only by virtue of his squad of regulars outside, who seemed to be enjoying their bloodless campaign against their countrymen.

Woodbridge snapped the silence.

"I tell you, Armstrong, I'm no squatter. I've got a deed!"

"Then it's between you and whoever gave you the deed. This land
belongs to the government."

"I'm willing to pay for it again, then. I didn't come out here to
squat."

The ensign's patience was maddening.

"I know all that, Woodbridge. But in the eyes of the Congress you're
a squatter. This land wasn't ready for settlement yet. It's got to be
surveyed first. Then it can be sold. Not before."

"Blast it! Let them survey it! How will I interfere if I stay?"

The ensign's patience increased unbearably.

"They want the whole Northwest Territory surveyed into regular
squares to prevent what's happened in Pennsylvania and the East. A
man buys eighty acres of valley, driving his stakes so they include only
where the dirt is black. That means his property may come out in the
shape of a snake. His neighbor in the next valley does the same thing.
That leaves a misshapen strip of ridge ground in between them that
nobody will buy from the government."

"Good God! The Territory's big enough so it won't hurt the government to lose the revenue from a few scraggly parcels!"

"It's more than that. It makes such a helter-skelter pattern that back
East, if one marker stone gets moved, the property lines can never be
reestablished. That's how *you* got in trouble. Bad survey."

The ensign preened his knowledge of affairs.

"Winthrop Sargent already showed the Congress where the cost of land-claim litigation in the New Jersey courts right now is over double the original cost of all the lands in the state. Sargent showed that if the government doesn't evict the squatters and survey the land into regular squares before it sells, the whole country'll be in court for the next hundred years."

The ensign's smile brought no reflection from Woodbridge, and he dropped his civility. "I told you my orders, Woodbridge: to evict all squatters and burn the cabins."

Veronica emphasized the young man's title. "Ensign Armstrong, our land was part of Hosmer Village. That should put us within the square."

"I'm sorry, ma'm, but you're outside the lines now. This land will fall in another range of townships."

Veronica saw her husband's neck turn the color of a gobbler's wattles, and she left the room. Woodbridge slammed the puncheon table.

"All the more reason to leave us be! We're all that stands between the village and the Wyandots. Is this the thanks a man gets for breakin' his back out here?"

The ensign stood up, and behind his young beard was the coldness of all officialdom since Caesar.

"Woodbridge, I've been patient. You're a squatter. I've got to burn the place. You going to be in it or out of it?"

Woodbridge walked to the window and brushed aside the skin that hung over it. He looked at the squad of soldiers lounging near his shed, as though estimating their strength against his own. The soldiers had spitted one of his small hogs and were roasting it.

"Armstrong, one cabin won't matter. Far as anybody would know, I moved in here after you inspected."

"Hardly. I'm detailed to patrol this area until the survey's over. If I let you stay, Major Sargent would find out; and he wouldn't sit still till you were burned out."

"What Sargent is that?"

"Major Winthrop Sargent. He's in charge of the survey party for the fifth range. That'll come somewhere through here."

"Where's this Sargent startin' his survey from?"

"Killbuck Creek. Northeast of here."

"When the survey's done, can the land be sold?"

"Yeah, but if you're thinkin' about buyin' your own place back you'd have to be the first one in line. Anybody could buy it, y' know."

Woodbridge was silent.

"I'll give your wife safe escort to Fort Washington," said the officer, not ungently.

"No thanks, Armstrong. I'll see to my own wife."

The ensign put his three-cornered hat squarely on his head.

"Then I'll leave a four-man guard with instructions to burn the place. They'll give you till noon tomorrow."

Veronica heard the rattle of gear as the platoon got up and straggled off to the north, two men carrying the half-roasted hog on the spit.

In the cabin she saw Woodbridge slumped over the table, his head suspended between his big-knuckled fists, each of which grabbed a handful of his short red hair. Though the room grew dark and the rain drove in the window flap, he did not move.

Veronica made two dozen strokes through her hair with the wooden comb and covered it only partly with a knitted shawl. She went out into the darkness toward the four huddled silhouettes streak-lighted by the embers from the roasting pit. The four rose, and a voice cut the black.

"Stay where you are!"

"It's only Veronica Woodbridge. I thought you'd want to keep dry. Use the shed and the other half of the cabin."

Inside the shed she handed over a kettle of soup. To the one who seemed to be the sergeant, she said: "You may as well sleep dry. It took a lot to build this place."

The authoritative one took off his hat and accepted the soup.

"But we're still bound to execute the ensign's orders, ma'm, when you've left the place."

She stood a minute looking at his shaggy face.

"I know," she said. "But maybe just the shed would make enough flame to suit a young ensign that wears his hat square on his head?"

The sergeant fingered his beard, but made no commitment.

"Would you answer me a true answer to a question, ma'm?" asked the sergeant, deferring her question.

"Certainly."

The sergeant kneeled down beside Woodbridge's old bunk in the shed. He wrapped a big hand over the corner joint and strained back and forth against it. The veins in his hand thickened and diminished, but the bunk was unyielding.

"Who joined these timbers here?" he asked.

"My husband, I presume."

"Nobody come and done it for him?"

"Not that I know of."

"He always go by the name of Woodbridge?"

"Yes, of course. Why?"

"Somehow, lookin' at ya, I believe ya. You're different from most squatters."

"We're *not* squatters! Our land was bought and paid for. Bad survey."

The sergeant had seen it happen before. He didn't challenge it.

"Why did you mention the bunk?" Veronica asked.

"There's a squatter reptile, ma'm, that we're huntin'. Killed one of our men down at Boxford's Cabin."

"What's his name?"

"Calls himself Governor of the Squatters, ma'm."

Veronica's cheek dimpled in a near grin.

"Yes, it would be a joke, ma'm," continued the sergeant, "except for one thing."

"What's that?"

"The squatters also call him Governor of the Squatters."

"Are there enough of them to matter?"

"They outnumber the deed-holders about twice. We figure there's two thousand of them hid in the Territory. And this governor rascal helps 'em all. Helps 'em find the good places. Helps 'em defend theirselves. Even helps the new ones build their huts. And he's one of the few knows how to mortise a corner joint like this one. Dovetailed like that, so's it gets stronger as the wood dries out. I was just wonderin' if you knew him."

"If you're going to be in this vicinity long," said Veronica, returning to her original purpose, "I should think you'd leave the cabin standing. It could bunk your whole squad, come cold weather."

The sergeant fingered his beard thoughtfully, but he gave no answer.

When she reentered the cabin, the change in Tom Woodbridge startled Veronica. When she had left to take out the soup, Tom was

absolutely motionless, with his red head in his hands, defeated. Now
he was on his feet, and there was a ruthless vigor in his motions which
repelled her strangely. He said nothing to her, but continued moving
rapidly around the room. As she watched, she saw him unlock the
document box.

"What are you doing, Tom?"

His lips were clamped tight over his teeth. He took one paper out
of the box and put it in his chest pocket, then moved swiftly to the
fireplace and lifted off an iron pot. From the pot he poured a silver
liquid into a small iron bullet mold.

"Tom, what are you doing?"

He poured cold water over the iron box, causing steam.

"I'm gonna hold this land, Veronica."

While the lead cooled, he broke segments of bar lead into the pot,
which he put back on the fire.

"How?" she asked.

"Don't know, for sure. But if the surveyors are gonna have the say
on the land, then I'm gonna be with the God-damned surveyors!"

He snatched a piece of canvas off the wall and laid in it a hunk of
smoked ham and some extra gun flints.

"But where are you going right now?" she asked.

"Got to see Navarre and his squatters."

"Tom, don't get mixed up with the squatters."

He rose from his work, and his face was red.

"Why not? I'm a damned squatter myself!"

"We're not."

"I sure as hell am. And squatters help squatters, don't they? All
right. I need 'em." He moved quickly to the fireplace and poured
another mold of bullets.

"And after that?" she asked.

"Then I'm goin' to find this survey outfit."

"You'll be gone?"

"That's right."

"How long?"

"Long as it takes," he answered with a finality that took Veronica's
breath and pierced her with its callousness.

"And me?"

He rolled the canvas into a tight cylinder and wrapped it with a
whang strip.

"Hosmer'll see you're sheltered. After what he and Shuldane done, it's the least he can help."

"You'll actually leave me?" Her eyes were wet with injury and disbelief. He looked up.

"What else?" he asked. "You can't come where I'm goin'. I got to save the land. I'll be back."

She looked at him from vast disillusionment. This was the man who had bent by the side of her bed and offered his person almost as her slave. This was the man for whom she'd come six miles beyond oblivion. This was the man who had sworn to her protection and devotion, humbly, in the absence of any other qualifications. She cried out to him from withering distress.

"You said 'always, forever'! You and I!"

He brushed it aside cruelly. "Can't you understand? I've got to save our land. That's you, too. Your land as well as mine. Can't you understand?"

"I understand that the land and I are the same to you. Only the land is more. The hogs, too. Your land and your hogs and your woman! Is that the way it is?"

She was suddenly face down on the bed, shaking.

It was the first time that Thomas Woodbridge had ever seen a grown woman cry, really cry. He dropped his packing. Never had he witnessed such racking desolation. He was on his knees beside the bed.

"Veronica, it's only that it's the land. Yours and mine. What is a man without it? What can I give you without I have land? Everything comes from it. Everything I want for you."

She gave no answer. He touched her elbow. Instantly she pulled it away.

Thomas Woodbridge had never felt such helpless defeat. Words would explain nothing. Words were not trusted. He had to hold her so that she could *feel* what he meant about the land. He had to crush it into her with his arms. He took her two arms to turn her over, but she stiffened at his touch.

Woodbridge pulled her to her feet and held her by the shoulders.

"Listen to me, Veronica! Listen!"

But she stood rigid under his hands.

Her tears demanded an explanation, but her mind refused to hear it. The intolerable frustration of trying to make her understand forced the gentleness out of Woodbridge and thwarted, heedless anger flooded in.

"It's the same!" he said. "It's not deserting you. It's the same. Saving the land is saving *you!*"

He gripped her so hard that he hurt her. He wanted so desperately to take back the hurt, that he gripped her still harder, compounding the torment until there was no breaching the anger which widened between them.

"Can't you understand!" he yelled. "It's the same! The land and you are the same!"

At last she spoke. And the sound of her voice lacerated him. She was utterly spent, empty, beyond caring.

"I understand," she said softly. "Your wife and your land, it's all the same. And your hogs."

His face was stricken. Those were his words but not his meaning.

"And the things we said before, Tom, the first night we . . ." Veronica abandoned the effort, and shrugged. He dropped his hands from her limp shoulders. "The fact that I need you," she resumed, "the fact that I'll be among the people who accused me . . ." She looked over his shoulder at the wall.

If she would rail at him, if she had enough consciousness to see what he meant, it would help; but her utter desolation and resignation defeated him.

"Veronica, I'll prove it to you. I'll prove it's for you. Let me go and I'll prove to you."

"How can I stop you?"

"If you could only—" But he stopped, for she was right. He was leaving her in a town which had hurt her. He was leaving her when he should be with her. He had promised her anything in the world. And now she was only asking him not to leave. That was all she asked. But . . .

They went about their preparations in hopeless silence. Veronica packed her trunk. Woodbridge was in and out of the cabin, stowing items in the wagon.

"Have Hawkins come out for the rest of the corn," he said flatly.

She did not answer.

"And come out and look at the place every once in a while."

There was no reply, and he asked her again if she would.

"If I stay in Mesopotamia," she said.

Woodbridge dropped his pack and grabbed her shoulders roughly. His blue eyes were fierce.

"What did you say?"

She looked up at him with a steady, uncaring gaze.

"You must realize how it will be for me," she explained. "And I'll not know when you'll be back, or *if* you'll be back. I'll be like Loretta Shane."

"You stay in Mesopotamia!" he said hoarsely. "Be here when I get back! You belong to me! You will be here! Do you understand?"

Her eyes widened under his violence. It was an order, a threat—and a plea. But she did not answer.

They separated at Hussong's cabin, halfway to Mesopotamia. Woodbridge crossed the river to the north on foot, and Veronica drove the heavily loaded wagon down the ruts along the south side of the river to the lower ford. Then she crossed north to Hosmer's Store.

Hosmer said: "We couldn't help it, Veronica. And we wanted to help out. That's why we arranged it so Tom could borrow that little piece of ground in close here. Why did he turn it down?"

Veronica studied Hosmer a moment. "Tom Woodbridge will never again farm another man's land," she said.

"Stubbornness is a fine luxury if you can afford it."

"I thought so too," answered Veronica. "But when you know him, Mr. Hosmer, you know he can't afford to farm any other man's land."

"Huh?"

"You see, if he ever left that land, or lost it, had to go to another place, he'd leave behind part of himself."

Hosmer's face crinkled in tolerance.

"No, I don't mean it as ornamental talk," said Veronica. "I mean, when I cut the hair from the back of his neck he threw it in the field. Added it to the soil. Same as he plowed his old shirt under when it wore out."

"But he's already lost his twenty acres," said Hosmer.

"You can't make him believe it. He has a plan."

"How far north has he gone?"

"Up where the survey starts."

"But that's way up at the Greenville Line."

"I know."

"For how long?"

"Long as he has to, he said."

"When we heard he was goin', we talked to Asa Buttrick. So's you'd have some cash to fend with, Buttrick will pay in silver for the wagon and your plow and horse. That'll easy pay fare and food to Fort Pitt. You can take your hogs there and sell. That'll get you back to Massachusetts Commonwealth."

Hosmer had always thought that Veronica was too fragile for the frontier, and he'd never understood why Shuldane had let her come. He was relieved she was going back to the Commonwealth.

But Veronica said, "The wagon and things aren't for sale, Mr. Hosmer."

"We're not urging you to sell, Veronica. 'Twas just to be a convenience for you and Tom."

"I'm to get along by trading our hogs for keep, except for Boss and Cleopatra."

Hosmer said: "Well, whenever you're ready Buttrick'll have the cash for you. Meanwhile Faith Hawkins said to come up and stay with her. She's expecting you."

Veronica's face fell. Of all the cabins in Mesopotamia, she least wanted to enter the Hawkins cabin. Vaguely, and with no evidence at all, she felt that Faith Hawkins had not helped her in her trouble.

When Veronica walked into Hawkins's cabin, Faith was grinding corn into meal. Veronica picked up the nearest ear and began to shell off the kernels. But Faith took the ear out of her hands.

"Veronica Woodbridge, after everything you've been through, and nobody makin' it any easier for you, you're going to be a guest in this cabin. Don't lift one finger. Just sit there and tell me what your plans are."

"For now, I'm here with you, Faith."

"And welcome."

"I might be here quite a while."

"Well, you just rest up. Don't turn a hand. Sam Hosmer and Asa Buttrick are arranging everything to take care of you."

Veronica was surprised by the warmth of Faith's reception. She had expected some difficulty; for a woman with no man to support her, a woman that had to eat and be looked out for, was a liability in Hosmer Village. That is, a married woman was, that no man could hope to turn to his chores by marrying. Veronica had learned that already.

She relaxed while Faith Hawkins rattled on. It was good to have friends who would take you in, no matter what. Suddenly she caught a phrase in Faith's gushing stream of warm talk that pulled her away from her reverie.

"There's not a man in Mesopotamia, Veronica, but wouldn't like to tell him straight off, after what he did."

"What? Tell who?"

"Woodbridge, of course." Faith looked up from her corn grinding in surprise. But she was more surprised by the sudden sternness she met in Veronica's wide-set eyes.

"Why?" asked Veronica.

"For runnin' off, leavin' you, of course."

There was a silence.

"And you not used to this," said Faith. "And plenty of other men, like Jonathan, that would give their right arm to see you comfortable . . . and church wed—I mean, in a big church."

Veronica's face colored.

"Tom Woodbridge has seen to my comfort," she said. "And there's not been any question of running off."

She withheld any further explanation, for there was none. But it was plain to Faith that the Hawkinses were seeing to Veronica's comfort. Not Tom. And as for the running off, Faith demolished Veronica's statement gently.

"I'm sorry, Veronica. I must have heard it wrong. Where's Tom?"

"Up at the Greenville Line."

"The Greenville Line stretches from the Cuyahoga River west to Heaven knows where?"

"He didn't know exactly. He's never been there."

"Oh."

"I'll likely hear as soon as he finds it."

"When'll he be back?"

"He couldn't say for sure."

"Oh."

Faith Hawkins worked in a punishing silence for several minutes. But when she looked up, she was smiling pleasantly.

"Veronica, when you see your father would you ask him if it would be all right if we sent our next land payment in the spring?"

"What?"

"I said, when you see your father—"

"Faith, I'm not going to see my father. I'm staying right here until Tom sends word."

Faith stopped pummeling the deerskin in which she was pounding corn into meal.

"But it's all planned," she said. "Sam Hosmer and Asa Buttrick made arrangements with the keelboat. With no cabin, how will you—"

"Faith, I'm staying. Tom left me fixed to pay my way. The hogs, you know."

Faith Hawkins sagged noticeably on her puncheon stool. The invitation to stay was not rescinded, but Faith picked up a handful of ears and passed them to Veronica with a scraper for removing the kernels.

# Chapter 9: THE BOUNDARY LINE

MAJOR Winthrop Sargent sat under a square of canvas in the surveyor's base camp at the mouth of Killbuck Creek, eating. Woodbridge walked out of the rain, and under the canvas, with his hat on. The two men did not shake hands.

"Hello, Sargent."

"Major Sargent," corrected the surveyor.

"The war's over," said Woodbridge.

Sargent finished a mouthful and wiped his mouth on a braided coat cuff. He looked at Woodbridge as though appraising a new mount.

"They tell me you want to sign on with me as chain bearer. But the fifth range crew has no vacancies."

"You have now," said Woodbridge. "Three of your men just transferred to the second range crew."

A shadow of injury crossed the major's face, but he said, "With that recommendation before you, why do you select my crew?"

"Couple a reasons. For one, I know you from Boston when you had Battery B, First Massachusetts. In garrison duty, that was."

Sargent made no concession to the reference to his noncombat command. He continued eating.

"Surprises me the more," he said. "I'm not the type that usually inspires the so-called loyalty of the troops."

"You don't. But you're just cussed enough to get this job done right."

"What difference to you if it gets done right?" Sargent seemed eager for the answer.

"Private reasons," said Woodbridge. "Do I get the job?"

Sargent leaned back with a cold smile. "Did you know I drew the fifth range? The outside one? Nearest the Wyandots?"

"Yes."

"Pay'll be in Spanish gold coins. A half-joe a month, plus any loot from the squatters' cabins. I furnish the chain, but you furnish any powder and shot that's needed, which could be considerable."

"If it was for the pay, I wouldn't be here," said Woodbridge.

"What proof have I that you can handle the surveyor's chain?"

"There's not so much to it I can't pick it up."

"If I find a mistake of a half-rod, you'll run the line over again."

"I'll measure the lines right if you can read the compass right."

"If your endurance matches your insolence," he said, "I'll try you."

The surveyors in the camp were as miscellaneous as their reasons for being there. Woodbridge had not seen so many human beings in one place since he left Pittsburgh. Here and there was a bona fide surveyor studying the guidebook with professional interest in the great project that would measure off a whole nation in squares for the first time in the history of the world. There were representatives of the eastern land companies, sent here to find the choice tracts, to make careful note which lands had water, which had salt, and which had walnut timber. There were also a few veterans who had been discharged from Wayne's army with land certificates instead of cash. The rest were frontier misfits; and among them was Ira Crumley, who reminded Woodbridge of the raccoons which ate what the hogs left.

Woodbridge took the guidebook Sargent had tossed at him and read how the new land was to be covered with squares. For the first time he wondered if he could handle the job. He understood the part that said the purpose was to form square farms, square townships, square counties, and square states, packages of real estate which could be sold handily in standard shapes. It would simplify bookkeeping, map making, road building, and empire building. But the process itself made complex reading to Woodbridge:

"The geographer's line, or base line, shall extend due west from the southwest corner of Pennsylvania, and all other base lines, which shall ever be plotted within the territorial limits of the Republic, shall be based from this line. The principal meridian shall be . . ."

One hundred and ninety men began the trek west along the geographer's line. At the end of the first six miles the first range crew of thirty-eight men stopped off to drop their range line to the south. Six miles farther west the second range line crew of thirty-eight dropped off, as did the other crews at the third and fourth range lines. When they reached the fifth range line, Winthrop Sargent halted his crew on a high point where they could see out over the swaying ocean of treetops. He was sternly reviewing the rules when a plump man named Faulkner, whom Woodbridge had spotted for a land speculator's representative, interrupted Sargent.

"Major, according to the agreement we're supposed to have troop protection. Where are they?"

"They'll be here later," said Sargent dryly, "as soon as General St. Clair can spare them from making parades at Fort Washington."

"Well, Major, I'll not work the outside range without troops." He looked to the rest for support. Mr. Sargent handled this stray boar as though he had expected the difficulty.

"Murphy," he ordered, "take this man's place. We move out immediately."

The portly one threw down his chain and walked back east along the base line.

Woodbridge was in charge of a crew of four which moved south, down under the roof of trees, and the lines began to be drawn on the land.

One hundred and twenty chains south from the geographer's line, Woodbridge cut off a shaggy-bark hickory and blazed the west side of it:

R5
T1
1/4S

He watched Sargent write in the field book: "Range 5, Township 1, 1/4 Section, shaggy-bark hickory stump."

Sargent snapped the book shut almost in Woodbridge's face.

"All right, Woodbridge, keep right on moving to the south."

Woodbridge worked his way south, 66 links to the chain, 80 chains to the mile, 6 miles to the bottom of the first township, fifteen days to measure off the township and divide it into sections and quarter-sections.

When Woodbridge had measured off his bottom line six miles to the east, he put his last spike in the middle of a small creek at the base of a knoll in a clearing. Ira Crumley cut a maple post for a marker and turned to Woodbridge. "Which side of the creek shall I sink it? Can't set it in the middle."

Woodbridge said they'd wait until Sargent arrived before they set it.

Crumley's beard parted in the shape of an unfriendly grin. "Happen you mean we missed connections with the fourth range crew, Mr. Woodbridge?"

"They must have forgot they agreed to leave two men at this corner to see if we connected with them. But their stake must be nearby. Look for it."

Ira Crumley threw down his post in disgust.

Woodbridge said they'd go up on the high ground to get a view of where the fourth range crew's stake was.

The sun was at the treetops when Winthrop Sargent arrived with his runner and his orderly. "Aides," he called them.

"I see you missed it, Woodbridge."

"Don't think so, Sargent. I should be right."

"Obviously you're not, though. There's no post here from the fourth range crew."

"Could be the fourth range crew missed the mark."

"You're off course, Woodbridge. And I know where you slipped. I noticed your tracks. You skirted the swamp back there to keep your feet dry. You'll run the line over again tomorrow and go right through the swamp like you're paid to."

Woodbridge said: "If you'd have done a good job of snooping, you'd have seen I made a perpendicular offset of eighteen paces and came back on course. I got two men with no bottoms on their shoes."

Sargent caught the wink that passed between his runner and his orderly, and he added it to the score against Woodbridge. "You'll run the line over again tomorrow," he repeated.

Sargent's orderly had started a fire to cook the major's ration. The orderly was not a regular orderly. He was hired as a chain bearer. But then in many ways the major was not a regular major. His promotion had not been earned in the line, but had been given him so he'd be a suitable aide-de-camp for General Edward House. In some mysterious way the regulars and the veterans all seemed to know how the major's rank had been acquired, even young Captain Harrison. Thus Sargent had an "aide" to prepare his supper.

Suddenly Captain Michael, the Indian, came charging up the slope. He kicked the major's fire apart with his moccasins, stamped out the tinder, and glared at the group. Sargent was about to grab the Indian when Woodbridge jabbed the chain pike into the ground in front of him.

"If Captain Michael says no fire," he said, "I'd consider did I want my rations worse than my scalp. Captain Michael thinks we're being watched by Wyandots."

Captain Michael waddled back down to the creek. As darkness set in, Woodbridge watched the Indian walking in ever-widening circles around the place in the creek where the sixth mile had ended, looking for the fourth range crew's stake.

The night passed slowly because of the rain, and Woodbridge spent the hours on a border line of sleep and consciousness. He reviewed his measurements of the past day. The offset around the swamp, he knew, was accurate. When the blackness diluted to gray morning, Woodbridge was wakened by Sargent's voice.

"If you had more respect for mathematics and less for your men's feet, you wouldn't have missed it, Woodbridge."

There was a snapping of branches down by the creek. Woodbridge rolled over on his stomach and brought Navarre's rifle to bear on the creek while he looked for a red man's skin. He saw a figure emerge from the creek bushes dragging something extremely heavy behind him in the grass.

Woodbridge heard Sargent's hammer click back from the safety, and he said: "Don't fire, Sargent. It's Captain Michael."

As the Indian struggled to the top of the hill, they went to meet him. When they came up to him, he dropped the maple post, with its double burden, into the mud. The carving on the post said, "Range 4, Township 1." Woodbridge could not read the rest, for the markings were hideously obscured by the rain-soaked and bloated bodies of Naylor and Faulkner of the fourth range crew, bound to opposite sides of the post by a surveyor's chain.

Woodbridge was surprised to see how the face skin shrank from a scalpless human skull. He turned his eyes away in time to see Winthrop Sargent swallowing hard. The major's face was suddenly stippled by small bumps which rose at the base of each whisker as he stared at the two surveyors bound with their faces toward the pole.

"Face to face," said Sargent. "They made them watch each other get it."

Sargent and Woodbridge grated on each other's souls. Together, however, they ground relentlessly against the crew, pushing the line to the south, but for different reasons.

When they reached the last corner of the second township, Woodbridge faced the same problem again. He had failed to strike the stake that should have been placed there by the fourth range crew.

Sargent came up with his two "aides."

"Well, you missed it for certain this time, Woodbridge."

"Maybe."

Woodbridge turned to Captain Michael and pointed to a small draw that led away from the creek. Captain Michael vanished up the draw.

While Woodbridge studied the terrain through a glass, he said, "You talked to any of the Indian guides, Sargent?"

"They've all deserted from the other teams. They can't afford to be caught with us if Wyandots strike. Your guide is the only Indian left, and he doesn't talk, does he?"

"No," said Woodbridge, "but he made some pictures in the sand for me. The Wyandots believe the land belongs to all men. No fences. No squares on the ground. He gave me the idea Rontondee and Tecumseh have heard about us with the chains. What are you going to do about it, Sargent?"

"We'll continue, of course. Did you have any question?"

"Just sampling your intentions, Major," said Woodbridge. His use of the title could have meant anything.

The men in Woodbridge's team were boiling some water that was to become soup, but they stood up and watched suspiciously when Captain Michael came trotting out of the draw and up to Woodbridge. The Indian held out a curling piece of birch bark. Sargent reached for it, but the Indian handed it to Woodbridge. Sargent leaned over, and both white men read the charcoal message:

> To Fifth Range Crew
> Informs you 2nd, 3rd, and 4th range crews have
> left the field. Returned to camp. Wyandots.
> We lost 7. This our last stake. R4, T2, SW.

Ira Crumley and Ault came over to stand in front of Woodbridge as he finished reading. Crumley spoke.

"Anything you'd ought to tell us about, Woodbridge?"

"Yeah," said Woodbridge. He stuffed the bark into his pocket slowly. "Captain Michael found the fourth range crew's stake. Everything's fine. Eat, and we'll move out to measure the third township."

Crumley's face challenged Woodbridge for a moment. Woodbridge busied his thumb, wiping rust off the frizzen piece of his rifle, but his upward glance met Crumley's long enough to turn the two men back to their soup.

When the sun was dead overhead, they moved out, measuring to the south.

In a small clearing near the first section stake for Township 3, Ault, one of Woodbridge's team, stopped at a place where the line on the land went right through an empty one-room cabin which stood there. Woodbridge was inspecting it with special interest because he noticed that some of the joints were unique, dovetailed. He also noticed that Ault took out a charcoal pencil and a piece of paper. He made some notations. Woodbridge came up to him.

"As far as I know, Ault, you're not hired for any clerical work. You're hired to lug that chain."

"Your knowledge doesn't go very far, Mr. Woodbridge. I'm also hired by a land jobber to note down any places like this where the land has already been cleared. They'll buy this and resell it as 'improved' property. And now if you'll help me start a fire, I'll just touch off this cabin."

"That won't be necessary," said Woodbridge. "You just handle the chain."

"Sargent said we were to burn *all* squatter huts."

"I know the orders," said Woodbridge, "but you can stick to hauling that chain."

However, Major Sargent arrived on the scene and ordered Ault to proceed with the burning. Ault knelt over his tiny flame, shielding it with his hands to keep the wind off it. Suddenly Ault jumped up as the fire seemed to explode in his face. The report followed immediately, and Woodbridge saw some leaves fluttering on the bushes across the clearing as the result of a muzzle blast. The bullet had spattered the fire.

Ault's heavy face was white. Woodbridge led the break for the lee side of the cabin, and the others followed.

"Indians!" said Ault.

Sargent was surprisingly calm. "I don't think Indians shoot that straight," he said. Woodbridge, hugging the protective wall, found his eye about six inches from one of the corner joints of the cabin. It was a dovetailed joint, and Woodbridge swallowed hard, knowing now that the Indians would be the lesser of his worries. He wished suddenly that in this he were still on the side of Slover Navarre. For by the accuracy of the shot and by the dovetailed joints of the cabin, he recognized a fearsome trademark—fearsome to a man who had broken faith with the squatters, or who appeared to do so.

They finished running the fourth horizontal line of the third township and made camp at dusk. Woodbridge did not pair up with any of the white men in the crew. He sat instead with Captain Michael. Woodbridge did not speak because he was preoccupied. Captain Michael did not speak, presumably because he had never been known to use the English language.

There was a rustle in the bushes twenty yards to their front. Captain Michael had just gone out of sight to investigate when Woodbridge suddenly felt his right arm pinioned to the middle of his back and twisted upward sharply. He could not twist out of the grip, for another equally strong force pulled his jaw back in the opposite direction. A dirty hand was over his mouth and his head was hard against a hard-breathing chest.

"Very little trouble ever comes from d'rectly ahead, Woodbridge."

It was the voice of Slover Navarre. He thrust Woodbridge deep into the brush before releasing him. Woodbridge shook his arm to relieve the pain. It was a different Navarre, a grim specter, calm and deadly.

Navarre's beard barely parted to let out a streak of tobacco juice and profanity.

"Why didn't ya tell me ya were throwin' in with these survey rats, Woodbridge?"

"You wouldn't have understood my plan," answered the panting redhead.

"That's sure I don't," spat Navarre. "They're burnin' our cabins, shootin' our people. Now they're gonna sell off our land. This is what we get for takin' ya in when ya said you was declared a squatter!"

"I told you I have a plan. That's why I asked you to get the bounty warrants from the squatters."

Navarre looked at Woodbridge with the scorn he usually saved for federal soldiers.

"On nothin' but good faith and them two hogs for security, I got ya the two-hundred-acre warrant and the three-hundred-acre warrant ya asked for. Said ya needed to borrow them just to make good your own hundred-acre warrant. I didn't ask any questions. I trusted ya. I just got ya the warrants. Now I find ya makin' your bed with these stinking government men."

Navarre spat on Woodbridge's boots, and his blazing black eyes invited Woodbridge to do something about it.

"Well, now you'll give 'em back to me!" Navarre held out his hand.

"I haven't got them with me," Tom said. He flinched as Navarre roughly ripped at his pockets. When Navarre failed to find them, he rapped his knuckles on Woodbridge's chest, bringing the blood to his face.

"Where are they, Woodbridge?"

"You'll get them back, or the land for them, when I've finished what I'm about," said Woodbridge. "And I'll be doin' a sight more for your blessed squatters than you ever did with your killin' and sneakin'. You can't win that way. It's got to be on paper. You can't keep fightin' off the army. And you can't make a squatter out of me. If you were as much as you pretend, you'd stand up in daylight for what's your right, instead of sneakin' around in the woods."

"Give me back the warrants."

"I haven't got 'em with me. I gave you the two Bedfords for security. They're worth more'n these warrants by twice."

Navarre was defeated. He heard Captain Michael returning. His lips curled, and his words were measured. "Tom, you made a bad mistake, because you just put you and me on opposite ends of a gun barrel, and I ain't never been winged yet. I'll hunt your surveyin' party through the woods till you'll wish you'd stayed East. I'll be at every cabin you come to. And I'll be there in the end to collect them warrants."

With his rifle pointed at Woodbridge, Slover Navarre backed into the woods and was gone.

As the teams within the fourth range crew crossed each other's paths periodically, all the men noticed that the teams were smaller now, and Woodbridge watched them huddle in clannish little groups that broke up sullenly whenever Major Sargent passed close by. Woodbridge felt that he was being watched from the woods every minute, and the sensation kept him constantly on the alert and on edge.

The woods were silent under a hot September as the crews threaded back and forth across the fifth range, dividing it into square townships and the townships into sections. Crumley shambled up alongside Woodbridge.

"Is Sargent going to pay part wages at the end of the fourth township, Woodbridge? Like it was agreed?"

"I don't know anything about that part of it. Why?"

"You don't notice the woods game much, do ya, Woodbridge?"

"Nope. Hogs are my critters."

"You don't know, I take it, that these woods should be full of game now. Well, they ain't. They can smell humans a mile off. And there's more humans in this woods than just us."

Woodbridge scratched on a maple shaving, indicating five chains.

"You don't know, I suppose," said Crumley, "that all the men have noticed we ain't tied into a stake from the fourth range crew since we finished the second township. They're wondering why."

"Crumley, I'm just hired to haul this chain, like you," said Woodbridge.

"You don't act like it. Looks to us like you got ideas Sargent's gonna take care of you with the Congress. Maybe a nice tract as a bonus."

"You're wrong," said Woodbridge, pulling the chain tight.

"Then you'll oblige the lads by making a tracing off Sargent's map tonight, so we can find our way out of here after the payin's done."

Winthrop Sargent approached with his ever-present aides, and Crumley dropped back to blaze a half-section marker.

At the west end of the bottom line of the fifth township, Sargent ordered a hold-up until all the teams assembled for instructions on completing the survey. Of the original thirty-two men there were only sixteen left. In the dusk the men from the various teams mingled by a fire, exchanged information, and glanced up to where Sargent sat alone, marking the field book. Some looked at Woodbridge, who also sat alone, honing his long knife.

Woodbridge suddenly saw Sargent moving toward him through the men. He saw the men's eyes follow Sargent's progress, and he knew that he had been forced into an unhealthy alliance.

Sargent said, "Woodbridge, I appreciate your sticking by me."

"No call for that. I'm here for my own reasons."

"What are they?"

"What difference?"

Sargent sat down. "Woodbridge, I don't know why, but I have a certain confidence in you. Kindly bring your Indian and stand guard while I count out each man's money. I don't like the mood of this crew tonight."

"I wouldn't hand out any money here if I were you."

Sargent ignored the remark.

"We've lost sixteen men through desertions and Indian killings," he said. "That leaves me a better margin on the survey. I intend to pay you at the rate of five joe the month, since your loyalty has been valuable in continuing the survey."

"If you pay the men tonight, Sargent, you'll have no crew tomorrow."

"Why do you warn me about this now?"

"What difference?"

"Well, I've had two messages from Thomas Hutchins ordering me to stop the survey because of the Indian pressure."

"And you want to know how much you can count on me if you decide to go ahead."

"Yes."

"Sargent, my reasons have to stay my own. If you're looking for encouragement to finish the survey, you'll have to use the same that's kept you going so far."

"You presume to know what that is, I suppose, Woodbridge."

"You're figuring that Hutchins doesn't stand very strong in Washington. If you were to finish the survey against his orders and give the government some land to sell to put some cash in their hands, it might look like you ought to be the head geographer instead of Hutchins."

"Woodbridge, when you're paid off you can turn your chain over to Crumley and leave the survey!"

Woodbridge interrupted his honing to wave the blade toward the crowd of fifteen men who were slowly approaching in a sullen body.

"I don't know if you can afford to say that to me, Sargent, unless you've got a pretty good story for these lads."

The men crowded around, and their spokesman shuffled forward. It was Crumley. He began with the menacing deliberation that comes easy to a man with fourteen backers. "Major Sargent," he said slowly, "we've come for the money as promised."

Woodbridge felt that even now Navarre was watching from the darkness.

When the inevitable argument began to get out of hand and dangerous, Crumley said the men would not lift another chain without pay and troop protection. Woodbridge studied the faces as the men glared at Sargent. He had to admit to a certain admiration for Sargent's consistency. The man maintained his haughty tone as though the title "Major" were bulletproof. Twice Woodbridge expected the men to rush Sargent's person, but something in the major's cold eye held off even these fifteen.

Crumley finally demanded to see the money. Sargent hesitated, and Crumley stepped closer, pressed by the crowd behind him.

Woodbridge stood up and yelled, "Wait!"

He knew he had gained only a moment's worth of silence. But if the men were paid, they'd leave the survey immediately. He talked rapidly.

"Major Sargent just told me there's less than half of us here now than started. If we finish the whole survey, he'll divide up the money that would have gone to the ones that aren't here. Twice the money for each man at the end of the survey."

Sargent stood up in protest, "Woodbridge!"

But Woodbridge continued: "And he goes tomorrow to get troop protection from Fort Washington. That right, Sargent?"

Sargent opened his mouth to object, but Woodbridge, with superb timing, walked directly into the crowd, which split apart to let him through.

"Now let's get a guard out around this camp," he yelled, "before we get ambushed like an ox in a hog slough!"

And the command was no more for the benefit of the surveyors than for the unseen ears in the woods.

In Mesopotamia, or Hosmer's Village, as it was called, Veronica Woodbridge walked up the path to Asa Buttrick's cabin. It would have been easy to talk to him two months ago. But she had let his offer of cash for her loaded wagon lie for four months. Now it was an empty wagon she had to offer. And the hogs she had were all expended.

As the months had rolled by, with no word from or about Thomas Woodbridge, his name was less frequently heard in Mesopotamia. When it did come up, it would be followed by shoulder-shrugging remarks.

"Huh. We've seen the last of Tom, mark me."

"We'd a heard by now, if we was gonna."

The more trusting Morgan Brady decided, "Wyandots got him."

Once a rumor came from Cincinnati that a redhead named Wood-bridge was back in Pittsburgh and heading East.

But the more these hints reached Veronica, the more frequently she used the phrase, "When Tom comes back . . . " and the more she used it, the more vigorously she said it.

Some thought Veronica used the words because they made her feel better. They were wrong. They made her feel worse. For Veronica Woodbridge did not believe them.

And therein lay a difficulty. For it was hardly possible any more to attempt a kindness toward Veronica, without speaking, demonstrating, or implying the failure of Thomas Woodbridge. And to do this was to close a door, a civil, but firm little door which Veronica Woodbridge presented to all those who made the error.

Particularly was this subtle insinuation against Woodbridge apparent in the advances of women. Men more often offered their assistance or casual companionship without talk, without subtle references to Tom. But this also became difficult, because the wives of Mesopotamia were not anxious to have their husbands repair Veronica's wagon, or recommend a tonic for Prince when the horse was sick. Nor were they able to extract any satisfactory news about Veronica from their husbands when the men returned from such small favors.

For there was about Veronica a quality of honesty and womanliness, almost saintliness, which a man liked to lock up in a secret place in his mind and keep guard over. Even Morgan Brady. It was not a thing to discuss, for it was a sheepish rendezvous of thinking that reddened a man's face when he caught himself at it; but it explained why a sergeant had left half of a double cabin standing out on the West Road despite orders to burn it.

Veronica found Asa Buttrick outside his cabin. She wanted to be able to pay Faith Hawkins for her keep. Jim Hawkins had repeatedly assured her that she was welcome forever, and not to worry about such matters; but Faith's hospitality did not wear so well.

Veronica explained to Asa Buttrick about the wagon she had. She also said that she could spare one of the horses. Buttrick was a trader, dealing largely on the Cincinnati dock in produce he brought down from the woods. Therefore, better than anyone else in Mesopotamia, he recognized a bargaining position when he found himself in one.

"My dear, I might be able to get you a few shillings for your wagon and your horse, but not enough to pay your passage to Boston."

"I didn't mention anything about Boston, Mr. Buttrick."

"However, there is a keelboat bound for Fort Pitt on which I have the principal cargo. I could get you passage on that vessel. And I'd be along to see to your comfort."

Veronica Woodbridge declined, and returned to the cabin where her comings and goings were no longer marked and where Faith Hawkins more frequently asked her, "Do you think Tom will be back soon?"

The oft-reiterated question, in addition to her desolation, partially explained the quick thrill of warmth she felt when suddenly she saw the familiar, well-set, and well-booted figure of Jonathan Blair walking across the common from Hosmer's Store toward the Hawkins cabin.

Faith Hawkins stood at the store with her arms crossed, examining the back of Jonathan Blair from the boot heels up the thick but well-muscled legs which trimly filled tight breeches, on up to the good shoulders and the curly brown hair. She approved immensely, but she resented his having gone directly to Veronica without even noticing or speaking to her, the lady of the cabin.

Blair and Veronica stood facing each other in silence. Then he took her hand again, in an impulsive second greeting, but when he reached for the other she withdrew it gently.

His freshness was good to see. His well-being was good to see, too, and his rich voice good to hear.

"Veronica, I make no apology for what I did to him. It was my scheme. True, we had to give back the acreage. But I selected the area. I don't know what it's cost you. But I left here seething. I deserve nothing, yet I ask everything."

"I thought at first you came as a friend, which is your only place. And not entitled to that, after what you've done."

He looked at her in renewed wonder. "So right," he whispered, and turned to go.

"Jonathan!"

It was hardly audible. But it was beseeching, and in it was such stark loneliness that he turned instantly and reached for her hands. But she withdrew them and bit her lip.

"Just stand there," she whispered.

That was when he noticed.

"Veronica. A child?"

Her eyes filled, and despite every intention he moved to her and took her against his chest, where she dropped her head and released herself in tears.

"And he's gone. Gone so long."

He held her closely, comfortingly, until at last she lifted her head and pressed him gently away.

"Veronica, anything! Just a friend; but let me *be* one. Let me make up for it the rest of my life. Let me take you home from here, for the birth . . . in your own home."

She shook her head. But Veronica Woodbridge, who had given comfort to so many, had in turn received comfort. The first in a long, long time.

Sargent did not recover from his rage after Woodbridge had promised away his profits, but he seemed glad enough to make the trip to Fort Washington for troops.

The first morning after his departure was critical. Woodbridge found that in Sargent's absence a certain uncontrollable independence broke out in camp, and he realized for the first time the power Sargent had held by his austere demeanor and the simple title "Major." But by assembling all the crews into a single crew, for protection, he persuaded them to continue, always pushing the reluctant surveyors to the south.

Woodbridge made it a policy never to be alone. But in the middle of the fifth township the men slowed down again. Woodbridge was walking back to check a section corner post when Slover Navarre walked quietly up behind him.

"Woodbridge, you've worked yourself down into my territory now. And the farther south you go, the more squatters I can call on . . . and the less men you'll have. You gonna give me them warrants now? Or wait till we lay a couple a dead men at your feet?"

Woodbridge looked quickly to the south.

"No use," said Navarre. "Your men are sittin' t'other side a that knoll. They're tired, they're disgusted, and they're scared. Won't hardly be no trouble at all to finish 'em off, if you're gonna be stubborn."

"I tell you, Navarre, my plan'll work," said Woodbridge, "if you'll just let me be."

"Maybe. But after watchin' you work, the boys think you're actin' an awful lot like a government man, the way you're drivin' this survey. And we don't see how you got our interests figured in. So you better tell me where you got them warrants hid."

Woodbridge thought a moment.

"Navarre, you got no faith in me. But I've got nothin' to hide. Put a couple of your men on my crew. They can watch me every second. That way you got me covered day and night. And I can use the men."

"Don't see anything wrong with that from my point of view. Won't be too good from yours, though."

"Why?"

"Because I'll send the two that own them warrants you borrowed. They'll be especially conscientious. And they got no love for you, Woodbridge."

Their names were Mitchell and Adams, and they looked as if they were partly animal. They were dressed much like Navarre, except that their hair was longer. They kept Woodbridge between them day and night.

They worked three days under the new arrangement, but on the morning of the fourth day Woodbridge woke to find Adams standing over him. His shoulders were wet from walking through the dew-covered brush. Adams spoke well enough, but briefly, as though disuse had atrophied his tongue.

"I saw him just now," he said.

"Who?" asked Woodbridge.

"The—that is, Navarre."

"So?"

"Message from your woman."

Woodbridge was on his feet.

"She wants you to come to her," said Adams. "Says it's important."

Woodbridge studied Adams carefully for a long, suspicious moment.

The squatter said, "Navarre don't lie."

Woodbridge reached down for his rifle and called for Ira Crumley and Ault. He asked Crumley if he understood how to carry on the survey, and told Ault to continue marking the field book. He said he would be back in a few days, and then stepped between Adams and Mitchell. But as he did so, he found the way blocked by the crossed barrels of their rifles. The redhead looked up at Adams.

"You can go as soon as you give us the warrants back," said the squatter. "Not before."

Woodbridge looked at Mitchell, who nodded in confirmation. Crumley and Ault looked puzzled.

"What does she want, Adams?"

"Don't know. But it's important."

"Let me talk to Navarre."

Adams shook his head.

"He must have told ya what it was about," said Woodbridge.

"No."

"He must have said what she looked like, or where she said it, or how she got in touch with him."

"No."

"For God's sake, Adams, it's my wife!"

"You can go to her."

Woodbridge moved to go.

"Just give us the warrants," said Adams.

Woodbridge stood looking from one to the other. His spirit yearned out to Veronica, wondering what was wrong, remembering the ugly parting. But the survey was near the end. The men watched the redhead intently.

"Give us the warrants and you can go."

Tom's lips clamped over his teeth. Slowly he placed his rifle on the ground, lock uppermost, and sat down. It was clear that Thomas Woodbridge had made his decision. It was also clear that it had been a costly one.

"I take it you're stayin'," said Adams.

Without lifting his head, Woodbridge answered in a low, deliberate monotone. "I'm stayin'," he said. "God help me if I'm wrong. God help me."

There was a silence as they looked at his bent head. And into their silence he spoke, just above a whisper.

"And if I'm wrong, God help you, too."

Woodbridge drove the survey relentlessly south, like a man possessed. He hardly allowed time to eat. He kept them going into the dusk until they could no longer see to blaze the markers. He got them up in the morning when it still looked like night.

When they closed off the sixth township, Sargent returned. He had taken time out in Fort Washington to procure a new pair of boots and a new mount. He had also brought back assurance from Territorial Governor St. Clair that a platoon of troops would join them later under an Ensign Armstrong who was presently on patrol duty to the south. Sargent was pleased that Woodbridge had picked up two new men, though he was startled at their surly response to orders, and puzzled that they would not leave Woodbridge.

Woodbridge could not keep his opinion crystallized about Sargent. That the man ran on cruel personal ambition he was sure. Yet to select this thorny path to fame took a strange sort of courage that might easily be confused with patriotism. He had begun to feel kindly toward Sargent until they closed the seventh township and started north to cut it into sections.

Sargent said: "Woodbridge, they told me at St. Clair's headquarters that up ahead about three miles we should come upon a farm with standing crops. The squatter has been driven out, but the ensign failed to burn all of the cabin. We'll spend tonight in the cabin, and when we leave in the morning see that it's burned."

"No we don't, Sargent."

Sargent stopped in his tracks.

"Woodbridge? Insubordination?"

"Put it this way," answered Woodbridge. "If you think you can run this crew without me, burn the cabin."

When they reached the cabin, Crumley went wild with delight. He swung his chain pike crashing through the corn stocks. "Look Woodbridge! Corn! Fresh corn!"

Woodbridge grabbed his arm.

"Take what you want to eat," he said. "No need to ruin the rest of it."

Ault, standing nearby, said: "What's the difference, Woodbridge? You heard the major. It goes up in smoke tomorrow."

Woodbridge saw Ault looking at the stand of corn, making notations in the little private ledger he carried. Tom half moved to grab the book, then thought better of it and walked into the cabin to join Sargent, who had already made himself at home. Adams and Mitchell followed.

It was the first good ration they had had all summer. The men ate outside, and Woodbridge and Sargent ate inside the cabin. Even Sargent warmed up a little after he had finished eight ears of corn.

"A long time since we've had a roof overhead, Woodbridge."

"Yeah."

"And something besides unsalted meat to eat."

Woodbridge examined a new ear of corn critically, sticking his thumbnail into one of the kernels. Sargent leaned back expansively and said, "Now if we only had a little ration of brandy or—"

Woodbridge said, "There's some whisky in that—that is, they probably kept it in that floor drop if they had any."

Sargent found the floor drop and lifted the lid, but he was looking at Woodbridge. He reached in and brought out a small wooden cask, then sat down, studying Woodbridge intently.

"Well, it was the logical place," explained Tom.

He opened Sargent's field book quickly and said, "Sargent, you sure this northwest corner post is set right?"

"I declare, Woodbridge, it's awfully late in the survey for you to be getting concerned about precision."

"And this east-west line," asked Woodbridge, "the spring falls inside it, you're sure?"

"What spring are you talking about? Do you expect a surveyor to remember every spring on a strange tract?"

Woodbridge stared at the book for a moment, and then changed the subject in some confusion.

The messenger who came that night gave the men the strange sensation of being near civilization. The message was for Sargent. It was from General Richard Butler, Superintendent of Indian Affairs. Sargent wore a smile of satisfaction as he folded the letter.

"The Wyandot pressure is so great that we are ordered to complete this township and then stop the survey," he said. "But I am to report back to Washington to plan the rest of the survey for the whole territory and to supervise the land office in the sale of what we've surveyed here in Range 5."

Sargent slept with a smile on his face that night. Woodbridge went outside for a while to look around.

Sargent was up early in the morning, full of authority as he ate the roasted corn his aide brought in for breakfast.

"Woodbridge, tell the men to assemble, and start them back to the surveyor's camp at Killbuck Creek. We'll pay them there. They can finish marking these last two sections on the way. I have some business at Hosmer Village nearby, and I'll join you on the trace above."

"I guess you'll have to do that yourself, Sargent. I'm not going back."

Sargent put down his ear of corn. "You'll not what?"

"But there's one thing I want you to do for me when you get back to Washington. This range will go up for sale now, won't it?"

"That was the object," said Sargent. "But the land office isn't set up yet for this tract."

"But you could take an order back. And the pay, and give me a receipt? Make you look pretty good in Washington, Sargent. Sellin' and surveyin' both."

Sargent appreciated the fact.

"I want you to enter an order for me at the land office and see it made out proper and legal."

Adams and Mitchell stepped close to the table in surprise.

"You know, of course, that the new minimum government sale is one whole section," said Sargent. "That's 640 acres."

Woodbridge spoke slowly. "Order for me, Thomas Woodbridge— mark this down so there's no mistake—order for me in the northwest quadrant, Section 15, Township 7, Range 5—640 acres."

Woodbridge laid three dilapidated land warrants on the table. Adams impulsively reached for his, but Woodbridge stopped him with an imperious gesture which Adams obeyed in confusion.

Sargent looked at the warrants in surprise, then opened his field book as if in a trance.

"I'll mark your purchase right next to the survey designation in the book," he said. "Northwest quadrant, Township 7, Sec—why, that's this piece we just surveyed—with this very cabin!"

"That's right."

Sargent looked up at Woodbridge and then at Adams and Mitchell. There was the ghost of an uncertain smile coming over Adams's face.

Sargent asked: "Where shall I send the papers? The deed?"

"Make it three deeds, in the same names and in the same amounts as on those warrants. And give me three receipts. The extra forty acres you can take out of the pay you owe me. And send the deeds to my home."

Adams was looking at Woodbridge as if seeing him for the first time, and the grin that wrinkled his face was pathetic under the water that welled up in his eyes and rolled down into his whiskers.

Sargent said testily: "Of course I'll send it to your home. But where's *that?*"

Thomas Woodbridge rose, hung his rifle over the hooks on the stone fireplace, and his hat over the muzzle.

"Right here," he said. "Right here, Sargent. And as you go through Hosmer Village, leave word at the store that Mrs. Woodbridge is to come home now."

Winthrop Sargent stared at the back of the red-necked hog farmer with an expression of surprise that changed slowly to something akin to admiration. But that too changed, and suddenly Sargent jumped to his feet and brushed the warrants onto the floor angrily.

"I won't do it! You've been a miserable squatter all the time! And on my payroll!" He threw his pen down on the table.

Mitchell moved quickly to the door and kicked it shut. Adams raised his rifle off the floor, and Mitchell followed with his.

Though water was running off Adams's cheeks and into his beard, his quivering monotone was the fiercest kind of command.

"Make out the receipts, Mr. Sargent, like he said."

Sargent sat down slowly. Mitchell picked up the pen and handed it to him gently, handle first.

Sargent looked at the redhead. "You tricked me, Woodbridge. But you taught me, too. It's all right."

It was perhaps the first time that the major's bare soul had shown through. He repeated, "It's all right, Woodbridge."

And reached for the pen.

In the cornfield that afternoon, Thomas Woodbridge found a leather seed bag, much molded from exposure. He carried it to the cabin and was rubbing the dirt off it with a pair of calloused hands when a young ensign, with his hat square on his head and leading a small platoon, stopped at the Woodbridge cabin to inquire for a surveying party that he was to guard. Woodbridge directed him where they had gone.

The young officer suddenly drew himself up as he recognized the hog farmer in the doorway. But before he could speak, Woodbridge showed him a receipt over the signature of Major Winthrop Sargent. It said: "Northwest Quarter, Section 15, Township 7, Range 5: 100 acres by warrant, 40 acres by cash . . . Thomas Woodbridge."

# BOOK II

# *Chapter 10: THE STRANGER*
## *(1801–1802)*

WOODBRIDGE scooped up the shavings in his big hands and threw them out the door. He backed off and took a look at the new shelves that filled the corner from the floor to the loft. Veronica would be surprised. She would come back to a frontier that was one year less primitive.

The shelves weren't all that would surprise her. She would come back to a husband whose devotion would overwhelm her, a man who pledged a lifetime to compensating for his one great default.

For Thomas Woodbridge believed that he would never forget the day, almost a year ago, when he had come down off the survey. He had sent word into Hosmer Village to let Veronica know that he was back, that the place was secured. Waiting for her to come to him, he had walked tirelessly over the place. He had been surprised to find things in such good condition. He had even thought what he would say when he first saw her.

He would pull the land receipt from his pocket and hand it to her. "Now wasn't it worth it?" he would say. "And no one can take it away from you!"

He had been up on top of the hill when the hoofbeats reached him, and he had raced down to the cabin.

But it was Jim Hawkins.

"Tom! You made it back!"

Woodbridge had grinned. "Yeah."

"We'd given you up, some of us. No news."

"Yeah?" Woodbridge's grin had stretched.

"Tom, did you—ah—" Hawkins wasn't sure of the best way to ask. "Did you do what you set out to do?"

Woodbridge hadn't answered. Just pulled the paper from his pocket and held it in front of Hawkins.

"Woodbridge! A hundred forty acres! Right here? Including your own buildings and everything?"

"Right."

"How did you work it? Nobody in town knows what you were up to exactly. Except we knew you was fightin' eviction some ways."

"Later, Jim. Where is she?"

Woodbridge's grin had wilted as instantly as the surprise that flooded Hawkins's face.

"You mean you didn't hear anything about Veronica yet, Tom?"

"What? Hear what, for God's sake!"

"Veronica went back East."

Woodbridge remembered how the place had changed before his very eyes in that moment. The cabin was suddenly a forsaken pile of logs.

"How'd she go?"

"With Blair."

"Blair!"

"It's best for you it was Blair, Tom."

"Best!"

"There's nobody in the world that would look out for her so careful. And she was in need of lookin' out for."

"How?"

"I figured you knew. That's why she sent for you. There's to be a child. You didn't come. She left. It could be you paid dear for your 140 acres, Tom."


That had been the homecoming. More details came out as the first month passed, none of them calculated to comfort Woodbridge.

One thing and another had kept her from returning. First, the babe was too tender for the trip; then the winter; then the muddy roads in the spring.

But now it was 1801, and it was autumn and he'd have a chance to make good.

Woodbridge looked at the cabin interior. Slasher had made the shelves, and Woodbridge had pegged them in. Mike Stikes had fashioned the iron firedogs. Woodbridge had burned out the inside of the three-foot log and then shaved out the black part and put rockers under it. He rocked it with his foot. The babe would have outgrown the cradle by now.

Woodbridge took the little soap that was left and went down to the creek. It was cold, but it had to be done. He peeled off his doeskin hunting jacket and soaped his chest. Most likely Veronica would come back accustomed to the lavender scent that clung to the Boston men who crowded her father's house on political business. She'd have to get unused to that again, but no use in it being a shock to her.

Back beside the cabin Woodbridge honed his knife to a razor edge and shaved off the beard that glinted red in the September sunlight.

As he drove into Hosmer Village, Tom felt strangely self-conscious, more so than when he had driven to the river to marry Veronica more than a year ago. He tried to think what he should say to her the first instant. He had a picture of how she would look, the whole woman, but he could not sharply remember her individual features. For it was a quality of Veronica's that in her presence she made one more aware of himself than of her. It was as if he were going to meet a stranger. It was hard to believe that he had sat beside her, eaten with her, touched her, and he wondered if at this very moment she was trying to remember what Thomas Woodbridge was like.

His apprehension increased as he drove past the Shuldane Reserve. The sight of it did not anger him so much any more, but it reminded him vaguely that Veronica was coming back to a slightly different Woodbridge. For in the last year the redhead had come to put his faith in one man only. He knew now that you did not depend on the powerful Elnathan Shuldanes for help. Neither did you depend upon the men of principle who oppose the Shuldanes, like Slover Navarre, for they would have you share their risks and pull you down to a squatter. Nor did you depend upon the fatherly help of the Sam Hosmers, for they would have you settle for twenty acres.

If you were Thomas Woodbridge, you looked only to Thomas Woodbridge.

Perhaps Veronica would be different, too. On the long ride east with Blair, certainly she would have compared the two men, to Woodbridge's disadvantage.

In front of Hosmer's Store a little crowd waited for Morgan Brady, the teamster. He always came back from meeting the downriver keel about noon of the tenth day after he left the village. Today he was late, and all the people who were expecting cargo or a letter from the East were waiting for Brady. It could be that he drove slower today so that Veronica and the babe would have a smoother ride.

Mrs. Hosmer looked at Tom Woodbridge's smooth-shaven face and his linsey shirt, but spared him any comment. Jim Hawkins, though, looked and whistled. Woodbridge turned red, but he grinned and took his place with the little crowd looking down the road to the south. It was a bigger place he took now than a year ago, being the holder of 140 acres, instead of twenty. Also, he was the first really freeholder in the village, being the only one who had his land direct from the government, with no economic encumbrance to Elnathan Shuldane.

They could hear Brady bellowing before they could see him; and then the double team came splashing around the bend, and the schooner leaned over until the springs screeched against the axles. It righted itself and came charging on. Woodbridge did not mind Brady's putting on a show to make the people think he came that pace all the way from the landing, but with a babe and Veronica along he might ease off.

When the schooner springs came to rest and the dust settled in front of Hosmer's Store, the crowd looked as one man at the empty seat beside Brady.

Brady jumped down with his usual gusto and began to untie the tail gate, shouting his usual chant about whose cargo he had inside. But he stopped abruptly as he felt the big hand on his forearm. Dropping the ropes, he faced Tom Woodbridge.

"She wasn't on the boat. That's all I know, Tom."

Woodbridge had intended to turn under some new sod that fall, when he plowed his corn stubble to plant winter wheat. However, now there was no Veronica to look out the window and be surprised. Woodbridge sank the iron plow point into the ground at the place which marked the edge of the old field, a little inside, in fact. Though the plow moved through the earth faster than it ever had, it sank deeper, too, and caught on new roots which had not been disturbed before.

New boulders were working to the surface, too. It was one of these that started the trouble. What first took Woodbridge's eyes off the furrow was the thwack of an ax in hardwood across the still valley. He looked down across the trace and saw a tiny figure there whose ax flashed in the sun. When the distant tree began to hover and topple, Woodbridge remembered his plow. He instinctively lifted it high and pulled back against the horses, but he was too late. There was a screech of iron on granite. The axman below looked up, and the two stood facing each other across a fifth of a mile of silence and malice.

At Hosmer Village Mike Stikes put down his sledge and reached for the two pieces of iron. He rubbed off the dirt and fitted them together tenderly. With a punch he marked four tiny circles astride the break where he would drill.

"Only be temporary," he said.

Woodbridge nodded.

"How'd you do it?" accused the blacksmith.

"A man caught my eye. I hit a rock."

Stikes looked up sharply.

"What man?" he asked.

"Don't know. Couldn't find him when I went to look."

"That's probably him."

"Who?"

"The Stranger," said Stikes. "He came in here to have his rifle rebored. Said he's a trapper. Said he'd pay in a month. Said he's staying around here. But he don't look permanent to me."

When his ground was finally ready, Woodbridge went to see Sam Hosmer about seed. Hosmer pulled skins off the tops of five barrels of seed, and explained.

"This is that stuff Exeter grew this year. It was this high last of May. This barrel here Asa Buttrick brought up from downriver. Claims it does good in wet weather, but I'm not sayin' so."

"What's in that short barrel there?" asked Woodbridge.

"That's the best."

"That's what I want."

"Not for sale," said Hosmer. "I'm saving that for the village sale about Christmas time."

"What's the village sale for?"

"We're going to raise some hard money to buy a cannon from Pittsburgh for the blockhouse. For an Indian alarm. Everybody brings something to sell. We need $94."

Woodbridge took an eighth-barrel of Hawkins's seed, an eighth-barrel of Exeter's and a quarter-barrel of the seed that Buttrick had brought up the river.

"Price and terms, Sam?"

"Same as last year, Tom—that is, unless you got reason to want to square up before winter."

Woodbridge looked surprised. "Any time suits me," he said. "How come you put it that way?"

"Veronica's not back. Could be you'd have plans of going back East yourself."

Woodbridge's pale blue eyes fixed on Sam Hosmer, who protested:
"Now don't get excited, Tom. You asked the terms. I answered ya,
that's all."

The other men in the store stopped talking and turned to watch, but
the conversation was interrupted as the door swung open. The Stranger
looked neither to the right nor left. He walked straight to the counter
and paused as though he expected a greeting. There being none forthcoming, he laid an empty powder horn on the counter.

"Salt," he said.

The Stranger stood a head and a half above Sam Hosmer. He wore
moccasins instead of boots, and he was clad in leather from top to
bottom. He showed no general curiosity about his surroundings, as
though he were at home anywhere. He was alert enough, though, to
notice that Sam Hosmer was filling his horn with the coarser crystals.
With an offhand wave at the other salt, the Stranger corrected him.

Hosmer laid the filled horn on the counter, keeping his eyes on the
Stranger, who, in a preoccupied fashion, picked up a package of tea
and a package of gunpowder and placed them with the salt. Then,
after deliberating, he reached for a luxury, one of the gray wool
blankets, placing it with the salt and the tea.

"How much?" he asked.

"In what currency, Stranger?" asked Hosmer.

"The name's Maloney. You can compute it in Continental money."

"Then it'll be $4.37½, Stranger."

The Stranger made no effort to reach for the merchandise. He said,
"I'll pay by the first frost."

Hosmer reached over and took away the blanket, leaving the tea and
the salt and the powder.

The Stranger protested, "I aim to be here steady."

"That's what the last trapper told us."

"The blanket was for my boy."

"If you're still here in December, come after the blanket. Meanwhile, I'll write you up for $1.12."

But as Hosmer began to mark on the paper, the Stranger picked up
the tea and replaced it on the tea stack. He looked at the gunpowder
for a long time, then pushed it away from him reluctantly. He emptied
the horn of salt onto the counter and started for the door, hesitating
only to examine Woodbridge for a moment.

When he had gone, Woodbridge said, "Kind of hard on him, weren't you, Sam?"

"You won't think so," said Hosmer, "time you see three, four transients go through town, leavin' us all the poorer, contributin' nothin', takin' everything."

"He said he was going to stay around."

"All trappers are transients, specially his kind. Notice them skinny legs, but shoulders wide enough to measure doors with. That's from paddlin' canoes. That's from travelin', not from stayin'."

"But he made a point of saying he was staying."

"Fair enough," said Hosmer. "When he's invested something in the town, the town'll give credit. Until then—" Hosmer shrugged. "Trouble with you, Woodbridge, you weren't here the hungry winter when the food we gave the trappers might have saved some of us that's now in the buryin' yard."

Mike Stikes supported Hosmer. "The Stranger's already into me for reboring his rifle."

Hawkins said, "You don't see him building a house, like a man that was going to stay."

"He's got a lean-to," said Woodbridge. "Furthermore, it's on my land. Not hurtin' anybody else."

Tom's land was not a beloved subject among the elders. It was a subject to be admired, yes. It was a subject of importance. And Tom's land made it necessary to look at him in a different light. But Tom's 140 acres was also a reprimand to those who urged him to settle for twenty. It was the source of prodding doubts to those who *had* settled for twenty. It caused young men in the village to speak more boldly to their elders.

Hosmer said: "All right, Woodbridge. Let him leech on to you if you like, I'm not sponsorin' him."

"I'm not either," said Woodbridge. "God knows, nobody did me. I'm only saying if he can make his own way, it's no concern of mine, one way or another."

"It will be, Woodbridge."

Sam Hosmer tilted the barrel to the counter and scraped the salt back into it.

In the two weeks that followed, Woodbridge didn't see the Stranger. When Brady was due back from meeting the next keelboat at

Cincinnati, Woodbridge did not wait publicly at Hosmer's Store. He saddled up and rode south of the village to intercept the wagoner on a bend.

Brady saw Woodbridge waiting at the bend, stopped the schooner, and climbed down.

"She wasn't on it, Tom. But this came for you."

Woodbridge opened the letter and read. Brady asked, "The next boat, maybe, Tom?"

"Doesn't say." He jammed the letter in his pocket and mounted Prince.

Brady said, "Uh—up at the store, folks'll ask me."

"Just say her father thought she should wait a while yet."

When Woodbridge returned to his cabin, Boss and Cleopatra, the Bedfords, set up an expectant dinnertime clamor among the hogs. It was time to feed. But there was a pointlessness to it all today, and Woodbridge ignored them. Inside the cabin he read part of the letter again:

. . . and I would like to come to you now, especially since I know at first hand the bitter pain of waiting for someone who does not come in response to a call. But I am afraid that to leave Father now, when he is beset on all sides by reverses, would be to repay him badly for a lifetime of devotion and protection. I owe him at least my presence.

Do not believe this decision is easy, for I know well enough that my place is also with you. Yet I cannot blame myself too much, remembering that I would still be out there in Mesopotamia had you found it important to come to me when I learned about the baby and sent for you on the survey.

Woodbridge tossed through the night, alternately on a bed of guilt and anger, and rose in the morning to an overriding loneliness.

It surprised Woodbridge that he didn't see the Stranger close up again; in fact, he seldom saw him even at a distance. However, he frequently encountered the Stranger's woman, or the Stranger-woman, as she came to be called, walking with the Stranger-boy, in the pair of ruts called the West Road.

At the store, Hosmer was trying to plan for the village sale that would finance the alarm cannon. Buttrick had contracted for it and had signed the paper. Now he was urging Hosmer to be sure the town would meet the commitment. Hosmer was figuring.

"Let's see, the winter-wheat seed I'm contributin' should bring ten, twelve, fifteen dollars. Hawkins, you're offering seed too. Say, seven, eight dollars' worth. Dolk has promised a cow. Say, twelve, thirteen dollars."

Hosmer began to add.

Hope Emerson pledged two dozen charcoal pencils and ten yards of linsey.

Mike Stikes promised two kegs of nails.

Woodbridge said, "You can figure me for ten hogs, butchered and smoked, towards the cannon."

Hosmer laid down his pencil in surprise. Stikes looked at Woodbridge, as did Hawkins and Dolk.

Their surprise galled him.

"Well, what did you expect? Twenty?" he exploded.

Stikes answered. " 'Tain't that, Tom. It's just that we weren't figurin' you in at all."

"Why not?"

"We guessed you'd be headin' back East by then," said Stikes.

"What led you to that?"

"Well, Veronica was first waiting for the thaw, then for the roads to harden up. Now for some other reason. Appears a better guess would be her gov'nor's keepin' her there. He never wanted her to come out here in the first place. Not likely you'll stay on alone."

Exeter said: "There's been, all told, four couples where one-half went back for some reason and the other half followed for keeps. No crime in that. But the rest of us like to know who we can count on for sure."

"Don't worry yourselves about Veronica," said Woodbridge. "She said she'll be back. That means she'll be back. And you can lay your land and your cabin and your stock on it."

To lend authority to his boast, Woodbridge added: "That reminds me, Sam. I want four yards of that white cloth. Put it to my account and give it to Hope Emerson when she's in. Tell her to make me up a set of curtains. Want to fancy the place up a bit before Veronica gets back."

It seemed, these days, that whenever Woodbridge went to the store there was trouble. The argument in November started when Stikes and Exeter had compared with Hosmer on what was owed them by the Stranger. Woodbridge had snickered at the talk, and Sam Hosmer had accused him of siding with the Stranger. The hog farmer's face showed two spots of white beside the mouth.

"I'm not sticking up for him," he said. "I'm just saying that if you're going to kick him out of town, get it over with! Stop sniggerin' and chiselin' at him behind his back."

Hosmer pounced. "All right, Woodbridge, if you're so forthright, we elect you a committee of one to do it."

"Why me? I'm not the one that cares."

"Don't be crawfishin'," said Hosmer. "You spoke fine. Now let's see you do it. He lives on your land, anyhow."

The white spots beside the hog farmer's mouth grew larger.

"All right! I will! It'll be a damned sight easier on his woman and his boy than what you're doin' to 'em!"

As Woodbridge worked at cutting rails for a third hog pen, he saw the Stranger come down the West Road with a heavy beard and a light pack of skins. The Stranger may have seen Woodbridge; but neither waved, and the trapper cut south into the woods on what was now a faint path into his lean-to.

At dusk Woodbridge went down the path. The Stranger-boy was the only one there. With the edge of an ax the boy was scraping a round dowel he had obviously cut to fit into a hole in a three-inch section of maple trunk. The boy's eyes met Woodbridge's calmly.

"They're away right now," said the boy. "Be back soon."

"What you making, lad?"

Before the boy could answer, a deep growl from the rear caused Woodbridge to turn toward a wolf-like animal which charged to the end of a vibrating leather strap. The boy ran suddenly toward the beast and adjusted a splint that ran from its paw to its shoulder. He calmed the wolf, which lay down, glaring at Woodbridge.

As though nothing had happened, the Stranger-boy returned.

"It's a spinning wheel I'm making," he said.

"Tell your father I'd like to see him tomorrow. I'm the one up on the hill with the hogs."

"I know," said the boy. "I'll tell him."

It was midmorning when Woodbridge saw the Stranger coming up the path. He busied himself measuring out the hog feed and rehearsing his ultimatum. He mumbled it out loud. "Stranger, I've been appointed by some of the citizens—I've been asked by the people in the town to tell you that—"

The Stranger arrived silently and quickly, before Woodbridge had emptied the feed bucket. Tom faced him. "Stranger, my name's Woodbridge, and—"

"I know," said the Stranger abruptly. "I come to ask if I could borrow your woman's wheel for a spell. We judged you wouldn't be needing it while she's off."

"Hanging in the cabin," said Woodbridge, surprised at himself.

The Stranger took the spinning wheel and walked back down the path with long easy strides. Woodbridge watched his receding back. Then he picked up the bucket of wet meal and dumped it savagely into the trough, splashing it on the heads of several hogs, who flicked their ears absently and continued eating.

Woodbridge went back down the path to the lean-to that night. The Stranger and the boy and the wolf were gone. The woman was alone. Woodbridge was surprised to find that his carefully nourished indignation had left him and that he was in complete confusion. The woman was handsome. He wondered how she managed to make the front of a dirt-floor lean-to seem as private as the great double door to Mr. Shuldane's house in Boston. She was not timid or deferential, but matter-of-fact, like the boy.

"We thank you for the loan of the wheel, Mr. Woodbridge. It's possible we could return the favor if you need any woman's work done, like sewing. I guess you're alone lately."

Woodbridge found himself wishing he could put a floor in the lean-to for her. He said, "I've no needs at the present, except to talk to your husband on town matters."

Her voice was pleasant.

"I'll tell him," she said. "He'll likely stop by tomorrow."

But he did not.

It was at the late harvesting at Hawkins's place that the subject came up. Woodbridge carried a sheaf of cornstocks to the wagon. A group was listening to Sam Hosmer.

"If the Stranger or even his boy would turn out to help on days like this, it would be different. But they don't."

Woodbridge cut in.

"How can he? He's a trapper! He's got to be away!"

"You break the news to him yet?" asked Hosmer.

"I went over to his place."

"How'd he take it?"

"He wasn't there. Just the woman."

With a teamster's delicacy Morgan Brady chimed in, " 'Bout now that musta looked all right to you, huh, Tom!"

"You tell her?" asked Hosmer.

"I don't deal with women. I'll talk to him face to face."

"You sure that's all that's keepin' you?"

Woodbridge threw his armload of cornhusks into the wagon where Hawkins was packing. Hawkins buckled in surprise under the force of it.

Mesopotamia's patience was fast running out, for there was little good will toward men—transient men—in Hosmer Village. Woodbridge hailed Stanley-the-Slasher on the West Road. The Slasher was one of those rarely gifted woodsmen who had the knack of making a small cut on one side of each tree in a stand. Then by selecting the proper key tree and the proper wind, he could knock the whole forest down in one great slashing torrent, using the same principle that a small boy uses in knocking down a string of dominoes. He was known to have knocked down an acre and a half in one slash. The Slasher's services came high because they saved a man two months' labor. But Slasher spoke first.

"Tom, I notice the Stranger's got no sod banked up around his lean-to."

"So?"

"I notice, too, he's brought none of his skins into town to pay up with."

"You notice a lot, Slasher."

"Enough to know he's fixin' to fly the coop. Or maybe you got to him with the message."

"Haven't had a chance. He's always away to his traps."

"Huh, funny ya wouldn't see him once in a while. What ya want of me, Tom?"

"I want to put in more winter wheat before Veronica gets back. So I want you to slash that patch of oak east of my house."

"Wheat don't thrive in green land."

"I've heard that. But I'm going to try. Like to get the timber off in a hurry."

"Sure," said the Slasher. "When I wasn't busy, you tried to cut down the whole forest all by yourself. Now I'm busy, you're in a hurry. Well, hurry costs, Tom."

"I can pay. One-half of the winter wheat next spring."

"Tom, from you it's got to be cash."

The hog farmer's neck and ears reddened.

"Why single me out?"

"Nobody's very sure that winter wheat of yours'll ever get planted, Tom. And if it does, will it get harvested? A single person seems to winter-kill out here."

"I'll pay cash," said Woodbridge. "I want to start tomorrow."

Woodbridge finished a meal as tasteless as all his food had been. In Veronica's absence he ate at irregular intervals, and then only to quiet his stomach. The great shoulders were more bony than usual, and the huge hollows beneath his collarbones seemed deep enough to hold a pint of water each. In fact, as he worked, stripped to the waist in the unseasonably warm rain, the water spilled out of the hollows and seeped down through the frizzly red hair on his chest.

As he hoed, he watched to the south, as he had watched steadily now for two weeks. Today, though, his watchfulness was rewarded, for the Stranger came down the West Road and turned south into the path that led to his lean-to.

Woodbridge went to his cabin, put on his hunting shirt, and started down the path toward the lean-to, nursing his vague resentment of the Stranger. It was difficult to avoid the fact that he now had more in common with the Stranger than with any other man in town. It occurred to him as he walked that if he had a favor to ask now, he might better ask it of the Stranger than of anyone else. It occurred to him also that the Stranger had a slight advantage, for the trapper at least knew wherefore he worked. He worked to feed his woman and his boy. But it was suddenly doubtful to Thomas Woodbridge why Thomas Woodbridge should continue to raise hogs for a woman and an heir who were living well in the Bay Colony. It was true, however, that the Stranger must go. He contributed nothing. It was truer still that he himself had said he would send the Stranger out of town. And Mesopotamia's memory was long, accurate, and vindictive.

The wolf dog did not growl, but ran toward him barking. The Stranger-woman called, "Down, Wolf!" The raindrops suspended like jewels in her fair hair made Woodbridge suddenly conscious of his sweat-stained and unkempt leather hunting shirt. He asked for the Stranger.

"Gone to the store to see Mr. Hosmer," she said. "For some tonic. It's the boy. Chills."

Woodbridge bent over to follow her into the lean-to. As he stood close to her, his hands suddenly felt extra large, and he noticed a heady smell of pine soap which had grown strange to him in the past year. He wondered how the Stranger had got such a woman.

Someone had gone to great pains bleaching her doeskin blouse and slitting the tasseled fringes which yolked the back and the breast. She wore her leather soft side out. It enfolded the fullness of her gently so that the extremely fine-slit fringes rippled faintly with her motion. This vibrancy emanated powerfully to Woodbridge, although he avoided looking at her.

But the Stranger-woman's attention was all for the boy, who was lying on a sort of pallet, a skin stretched tight over two maple stringers. The serious young face was damp and pale. The boy said, "Hello."

To the woman, Woodbridge said, "Not likely your man'll find much in the way of medicine at Hosmer's Store."

"You mean he won't find it, or won't get it?" she asked.

Woodbridge walked out of the lean-to and rode up the path to his own cabin. He returned with a small wooden cask of whisky which he placed at the entrance of the lean-to.

"Heats up the body," he said.

The woman said, "Thank you," and the Stranger-boy asked: "You going away some place, Mr. Woodbridge? You got your fancy cloth shirt on this time. Just before, you had the buck shirt on."

The hog farmer's neck turned red, and he looked down at his shirt.

The Stranger-woman looked too. The slightest crinkle of a smile broke the smooth line of her cheek. But she said graciously, "We haven't given you a chance to tell us what you came to see us about."

"When your husband gets back, tell him I need to see him."

But the Stranger never came to the Woodbridge cabin. He passed by occasionally, within waving distance, but without waving. Woodbridge felt like a man who was being laughed at.

In a harvest way it had been a fair year for Mesopotamia. The Wyandots knew this, and because the early snow limited their game supply they came to the settlers for handouts. The requests became more demanding as the Wyandots joined Tecumseh's faint but sprawling empire, and the alarm cannon for the blockhouse in Mesopotamia became more important. It was decided to hold the village sale on the evening of December 15.

On the morning of the day of the sale, the men were moving the puncheon benches out of the blockhouse to make room for the produce.

Hosmer said: "Woodbridge, there's a chore we'd a sight rather have you handle than this. The Stranger's already into me for $20 worth."

"How he ever managed that I'll never know, Sam, careful as you are about such things."

But there were no answering grins in the crowd. A handful of men drifted over.

"What you're leading up to, I guess," said Woodbridge, "is it's my fault now if you all got stuck."

"It wouldn't be," said Hosmer, "except you agreed to send him out of town. Since then the Stranger's made everybody in town poorer by something. And we're layin' that on your doorstep."

"I tell you he's away most of the time," said Woodbridge.

Stikes said, "Best thing is for a bunch of us to go up and tell 'em today, since Woodbridge can't stomach it."

"The devil I can't!" Woodbridge exploded. "I'll have them out of town before the week's over. Now let's go back to work."

"That's not soon enough, Woodbridge," said Sam Hosmer. "They got to go today."

Woodbridge hesitated, looking into each face.

"All right. I'll tell 'em tonight on my way to the village sale. They'll leave tomorrow. That suit you charitable people?"

"We'll let y' know when they've left," said Stikes.

On his way to the blockhouse that night, Woodbridge stopped his wagon at the path that led down into the Stranger's cabin. The snow crunched under his feet, sending ahead a warning that should have alerted the wolf dog. But there was no barking.

When he stepped into the Stranger's little clearing, he found it lifeless. The fire had even gone out at the opening of the lean-to. On closer examination he noticed by the blackness and lack of fluff in the ashes that the fire had been put out with water.

Standing by the Stranger's fire pit, Woodbridge gazed out into the gloom of the forest. He was relieved. It looked as though the hard, horny soul of Mesopotamia had driven the Stranger and his woman out. The so-called freedom and equality of the West, it seemed, was a figment of Boston advertisements for western land. As he gazed into the blackness, he wondered about the Stranger-woman, and if she might be thinking of him. He thought of her calm beauty, of the unsatisfactory bed her husband must make for her in the forest, and of how she endured her life, loyally, even proudly.

Unfairly, his thoughts led him to Veronica. He compared the handsome, stoic Stranger-woman following her trapper into the woods to his own wife warmly enclosed behind the massive protection of the great doors of the Shuldane House in Concord.

Woodbridge drove his wagon over the West Road and into the village, where the sale had already begun. He was occupied for a while in setting up his hogs in the front corner of the blockhouse. He brought a section of an oak log on which he could saw off portions of the meat for people who wouldn't want a whole side. When he was finally ready to do business, he straightened up and faced the crowd that was scattered through the blockhouse, buying the products of its fellow-citizens. That was when he saw Mike Stikes staring at him in quiet impeachment. The voices in the room quieted noticeably, and as he looked around he saw many people watching him, as if to observe his reaction to something.

Then he saw the Stranger-woman.

Standing at the far end of the room, where the circuit rider always stood, were two lonely figures, a woman and a boy. The blockhouse was crowded, but they stood apart like a contaminated island in a sea of hostility. Woodbridge flinched as he met their calm glances.

Jim Hawkins was insistent at Woodbridge's ear.

"Tom, didn't you see who came?"

"Yes! Yes! I saw! She has a right, doesn't she?"

The crowd went back to buying the produce of Mesopotamia. Mrs. Hosmer's stand was busy. In Mesopotamia it was good sense to buy a little of Mrs. Hosmer's maple sugar, though almost everyone made his own.

Mike Stikes's stand was busy. Everybody could use a few iron nails. Woodbridge's pork was selling and he was busy, but not too busy to notice that the Stranger-woman and the boy still stood alone. The boy had a raccoon knee-length jacket over his arm. He stood behind a spinning wheel which he had made and brought to the sale.

As Woodbridge watched, the boy pushed a bench behind his mother and the Stranger-woman sat down. As a queen might, Woodbridge thought. In her lap she held a pair of red ruffled curtains which she had brought for the sale.

Though no one appeared to see the articles the Stranger family had brought, their attitude was a walking lie, because the fur jacket was a prime piece. A spinning wheel ranked with a rifle and a plow, and the red curtains were the most vivid item at the sale. They stood out like a kind of flag, Woodbridge thought.

Woodbridge noticed that Polly Stikes's chickens were selling well, and as he watched he heard her comment to Faith Hawkins, "She might have known she wasn't to come, since no one told her about the sale."

"Maybe someone did tell her about it," answered Faith, looking at Woodbridge. He turned away in some confusion, and Faith encouraged Polly to continue. "Those curtains are about the kind of useless contribution you'd expect from a transient."

It occurred to Woodbridge then that Hope Emerson had never made his white cloth curtains. It also occurred to him that Hosmer had probably not given her the material, in view of Woodbridge's waning credit.

Exeter came over to Woodbridge's stand.

"You won't have to wait until *after* the sale to tell 'em, Woodbridge. Guess you saw who showed up yonder."

"I got eyes, Exeter! I'll tell them tonight, like I said. No need to stand around and stare at 'em!"

The produce which had lined the walls of the blockhouse had dwindled by eight o'clock, as the villagers carried their purchases out to their wagons, but the people remained. Some stayed because the sale had become a kind of social event. The rest stayed because the sale had become a sort of public hanging.

When the front door opened at about half after nine o'clock, a cold wind swept into the blockhouse. But what suddenly froze the conversation in the big room was the tall Stranger, who stood on the threshold, leaving his hat on and his rifle slung. While he brushed the snow from his leather hunting shirt, his eyes traveled around the room. As he strode into the blockhouse the crowd gave way in his path, forming a corridor leading directly to the seated Stranger-woman and the boy.

As the Stranger moved toward his woman, Hosmer came up beside Woodbridge.

"It's a hard thing, Tom, but it only gets worse by postponin' it. If ye've got to be too much of a neighbor to 'em, I'll tell 'em. Though I don't fancy the job now that ye let it get so far."

Woodbridge shook him off. "I'll see to it! Leave off!"

The Stranger walked directly to his woman and the boy. He looked slowly around the room at the cold faces of Mesopotamia. Then he bent over and picked up the red ruffled curtains from the woman's lap. When the woman rose, the Stranger handed the spinning wheel to the boy. He took the Stranger-woman by the arm and started his family back through the crowd to the door.

The people unconsciously closed in behind them. All eyes turned to Tom Woodbridge. The fiddler ground to a stop as if entranced.

As the stranger approached the door, Woodbridge stepped over to intercept him, and Mesopotamia seemed to hold its breath in the quiet blockhouse.

Woodbridge said, "Say, Stranger!"

The Stranger altered his course enough to avoid the hog farmer. But Woodbridge stepped effortlessly in front of him again. "I was talking to you, Stranger."

The man stopped. A rafter creaked and the crowd closed in.

"My name's Maloney, if you mean me."

"I was just coming over to have a word with you."

The hog farmer looked down at the raccoon fur jacket over the boy's arm. "I was going to say I'd admire to buy that 'coon jacket you brought to the sale."

Mesopotamia seemed to choke, and Hosmer stared at Woodbridge. The Stranger's answer was calm, and his voice was as deep as Woodbridge's.

"Seems to me you had plenty of time to buy it if you fancied it much."

"Didn't know if the price was suitable," said Woodbridge. "And I don't like to dicker with women and boys. But if $12 would take it, I'd admire to have it."

The Stranger addressed Woodbridge. "Mister, I judge you're the one does the talking for this crowd, and I'd—"

"No," Woodbridge interrupted. "But maybe it's time I did. I'd like to own those red ruffled curtains there, too. Like to spangle up my cabin a little before my wife gets back."

Woodbridge said the last part good and loud, and he looked around the room before he continued. "And that wheel the boy's got there, there isn't a woman here wouldn't admire to own it. 'Twouldn't be fair to sell it to one and deprive all the rest. Sam Hosmer, that would make a nice item for you to have in the store to rent out the use of."

Hosmer was speechless with surprise.

Woodbridge raised his voice to the crowd. "What about that, you folks? Shouldn't Mr. Hosmer have a wheel in his store for the public use?"

Except for those standing close around Sam Hosmer, the sullen face of Mesopotamia suddenly cracked into a grin. They registered a timorous chuckle of approval.

"What would you say would be a fair price for that wheel, boy, to Mr. Hosmer?"

The boy did not answer.

Woodbridge addressed Hosmer. "How much we lackin' for the cannon, Sam?"

"About $9. But what in—"

Woodbridge snapped a question to the boy. "Would you guess $9 a good price, boy?"

The Stranger-boy's face was serious. "I'd say so," he said. Woodbridge took the wheel and held it out to Sam Hosmer, who ignored it.

"There y'go, Sam. The boy gives you a good price on it. What do you say?"

It seemed like a joke, but most people knew it was not.

They looked at Sam Hosmer. Hosmer looked around the room and at the serious face of the boy. He reached in his pocket and pulled out six paper dollars and six silver halves.

"I guess it's a good price at that," he said.

Mesopotamia seemed to exhale, and Tom Woodbridge addressed the Stranger. "Your boy's that handy with his woodworking that if he has any extra time this winter I'd pay to have him build me a bar-and-slot hog fence—that is, if he's going to be around this winter."

The Stranger unslung his rifle. "He'll be around."

Woodbridge hollered to Morgan Brady, the fiddler, "Hey, Brady, get back on your stand and play us a tune! This here affair has just begun!"

"What tune you want, Tom?"

"If you remember how it goes, play us that tune about good will toward men."

Briefly there was in Mesopotamia good will—even toward transient men.

# Chapter 11: THE RED CURTAINS (1802)

At the store Hosmer had the sale money spread on the counter in two piles. One pile contained English money, Spanish money, and twenty-two Continental dollars. Those were easy to calculate. Converted to dollars they totaled fifty-eight. The dubious pile, though, was the one that contained a note on a Virginia bank, a note on a Kentucky bank, some Pennsylvania bank currency, and a personal note on Judge Symmes.

"No telling what they're worth," frowned Buttrick, as though contemplating a skunk under a cabin; "but to be safe, compute the face value in dollars, then deduct 30 per cent and add the balance to the fifty-eight good dollars."

Sam Hosmer's charcoal pencil figured a moment. "If we do it that way, Buttrick, we've got only $83. Eleven dollars short of $94."

Mike Stikes turned to Buttrick. "Asa, for $94 you said we get a portable carriage with that cannon?"

"That's right."

"If they'd give us just the cannon for $83, I could probably rig a mounting for it on the blockhouse wall. Wouldn't be portable, but 'twould hold."

Hosmer asked Buttrick if he could arrange it.

"If it was anybody else but me went up to Pittsburgh to talk to them," said Buttrick, "they maybe would. But me, they'd figure it was a dickering maneuver, being a trader."

Woodbridge spoke perhaps too quickly then. "I'll take the money up and buy the cannon."

He was suddenly the center of attention. "Who'd tend your hogs while you were gone, Tom?" asked Hosmer.

"I could teach the Stranger-boy to see to the Bedfords. The wild hogs I could drive over to Adams's or Mitchell's place."

Mesopotamia was still not used to the idea of Woodbridge's association with Adams and Mitchell and the unspoken strength which they gave to him—strength which did not come from within Mesopotamia, but from outside. Mention of the names Adams and Mitchell always made folks take a second, longer look at Tom Woodbridge. For it reminded them of the staggering thing that he had done. He had said that he would establish a farm six miles outside the safety line, and he had done it. He had survived. In the face of a Territory-wide convention that a government bounty warrant was worth only 20 per cent of face value, Woodbridge had acted as though he should be an exception and should get a full hundred acres. And he had got it. True, the time factor was in his favor because Congress reduced the minimum purchase from 4,000 acres to 640. But he handled himself well. And not only that: he had got it by himself, unassisted. And he had dragged up with him the squatters Adams and Mitchell.

So when you looked at Woodbridge now, you looked, not at a red-headed boy, but at a hard-faced force who spoke for at least three men, perhaps four, if the Stranger owned such a quality as loyalty.

These thoughts were not expressed in the village, but they were undercurrents—a quick glance from Mike Stikes to Sam Hosmer, the impulse which caused Asa Buttrick to bristle up when Woodbridge said: "I been wantin' to see for myself how that market works at Fort Pitt. Might take a few shoats along with me."

Buttrick's heavy jowls quivered. "You sayin' you aren't satisfied with the prices I've been gettin' you, Woodbridge?"

"I didn't say that, Asa. But I *am* wonderin' why you're bringin' me back slaughter-hog prices for Bedfords when no man in his right mind would use any one of them for anything but breedin' stock."

"Tom, I'm tellin' you they don't know what to make of those white hogs. They admit they grow heavier than any brown woods hog; but what they don't understand, they don't trust."

"They will in time."

Hosmer voiced the real question in the minds of the men. "Woodbridge, if you were to go to Fort Pitt, would you be comin' back?"

The room went silent. Woodbridge looked around at the cold face of Mesopotamia, and his ears reddened.

"If that's what's goin' through your minds, what if I didn't? I can still buy the cannon and get a receipt and ship it back to Fort Washington on a keel. Brady can wagon it up from there."

"I wasn't worried about the cannon gettin' back," said Hosmer. "I was wonderin' about you."

Woodbridge stood up. "You don't own a man, you know."

Hosmer shook his head slowly. "That's true. Y'might pay fer him two-three times over. But you don't own a man. And as a matter of fact, Tom, you'd be a pretty good one to dicker with these iron people. Suits me if it suits the rest."

Asa Buttrick looked at Woodbridge as though he pitied the iron merchants, and Hosmer pushed the money forward.

Tom walked to the counter and picked up the money. "I'll leave with Brady when he goes south next."

Hank Flannerty stopped Woodbridge as he rode by one day. He held out a smeared piece of paper, folded, with the edges sealed in wax.

"Tom, when you go to Fort Pitt, would you deliver this letter for me?"

"Sure."

"Obliged."

"Can I find the party all right in Fort Pitt? Place has grown, they say."

"You didn't look at the address. It's to Shuldane in Concord."

"Concord. Why give it to me?"

"Because you're goin' to Concord."

Woodbridge handed the letter back. "I didn't say anything about Concord. Only Fort Pitt."

"No, but everybody knows it."

"How come?"

"Everybody says that's the only way you'll get Veronica back from Shuldane."

"Why shouldn't Shuldane let his daughter come to her husband?"

"Any way you look at it, Shuldane's got nothin' but grief to thank you for. You run off with his two prize pigs."

"He didn't give a damn about them," said Woodbridge.

"P'raps. But he does now. Blair said the old man's done some studyin' up on that question after you run off. Even tried to get some more like 'em out of England. Got a man tryin' to get some out of England right now. They won't ship."

"He's got no less hogs now on my account than he would have had anyhow," said Woodbridge.

Flannerty grinned through a ragged beard, for everyone knew the story now about the special dinner for the Honorable Joseph Varnum.

"I know that, Tom," said Flannerty. "But that's only the half. The next thing, you run off with his daughter that he's savin' for that fancy lawyer. And then ya come out and show a bunch of men how they can get together with other warrant holders to get their full value out of the warrants. That don't help him any when he's tryin' to buy up warrants at thirty cents an acre. That's what that letter's about. I want my warrant back from Shuldane."

Woodbridge was astonished by Flannerty's naïveté, and still more by his nerve.

"Don't you know you're wastin' your paper, Flannerty?"

"Better not be wasted, Tom."

Woodbridge glimpsed a fleeting, ugly resolution in the other's large flat face.

"You seen Hosmer about this, Hank?"

"Yeah. He said I shouldn't write. But I'm givin' Shuldane this one chance."

"He'll laugh at you, Hank."

"Not more'n once't."

When the Boston fellow arrived at the store in Hosmer Village, he was well dressed and he spoke with the Britishness of the seaboard, but politely.

The settlers gave him the rapt attention of men anywhere who seek news of their origins. They asked him about things in Boston and along the seaboard.

He spoke genially and of large affairs. Statehood. There were increasing rumblings and rumors, he said, that the eastern half of the Northwest Territory, that is, the Ohio Country, would be split off from the Territory and given statehood. There was a big fight about it.

The Territorial governor, General Arthur St. Clair, did not want statehood for the Ohio Country. It would put him out of his governorship. For the new state would elect its own governor. He was claiming there were not enough people in the Country for statehood. The hotheads at Chillicothe, on the other hand, had gone over St. Clair's head, presenting a petition to the Congress requesting state status, claiming by some mythical count and by some special arrangement of boundaries an excess of 16,000 free white male settlers. There was an argument, too, about where to break off the proposed new state. It would be the seventeenth in the Union.

The Easterner had other news. There was an inn established just west of Zanesville, on Zane's Trace. There was a ferry across the Scioto River at Franklinton. The federal land office was closing in on Judge John Cleves Symmes for nonpayment on the million-acre Symmes Purchase between the Miami rivers. On the other hand, settlers who had received bad titles from Symmes were trying to sue him. But Symmes was the Territorial judge. Meanwhile, the bad titles made the settlers legally squatters, and many of them were being run off.

Some fool named William Hogland was still trying to organize the squatters behind him and become Governor of the West. But there was at least enough behind it to cause Governor Arthur St. Clair to put on a special drive against squatters; partly because he was against the stealing or preemption of land, but mostly because if some wild man in the woods set himself up as governor it would be reason enough for his statehood opponents to claim he had no proper control over the West, which would be the truth.

There was the breath of change in the Easterner's talk. He called Fort Pitt "Pittsburgh" without explaining. He called Fort Washington "Cincinnati."

The Easterner had come to see Woodbridge, but he had found the Woodbridge cabin empty.

In answer to his question, Sam Hosmer explained that Woodbridge might be at the Adams or Mitchell cabins.

"Is he well?" asked the Boston fellow, whose name was Lot Webster.

"Little light of flesh, but otherwise seems fit," said Hosmer. "Why?"

"My name is Webster," the man explained. "Cousin to his wife, Veronica. I was to deliver a message and get an answer."

There were seven people in the store besides Sam Hosmer. At these words they dropped all pretense of store business to gather around Webster. The Stranger-woman remained apart, examining a roll of cloth.

There were some introductions, and then Webster explained. "You see, it's a rather delicate matter, but my cousin wonders if he's been receiving her letters."

"He has," said Hosmer. "Is she coming back here?"

"That's the problem of it," said Webster. "It's rather important she stay East a while yet to help her father in his campaign to go to the Congress, but she wants to know what Woodbridge thinks. There's no one to be hostess at her father's house and to manage."

"There's no one to be hostess at Woodbridge's house, either," said Hosmer.

Young Webster studied Hosmer and had the sense not to smile. "I believe there's a particular friend of Woodbridge's here, Jim Hawkins. Perhaps he could best advise me what to tell my cousin. She has a rather grave choice to make."

"Then Veronica's the only one can judge," said Hosmer, "whether it's more important for her to stay East."

The matter might have rested there, but a clear feminine voice from the cloth counter spoke.

"If I were you, sir, and I had my cousin's best interests at heart, I'd carry back the message that she should remain in the East."

They all turned to stare at the Stranger-woman, like a startled jury. But she stood still with great presence and a certain audacious regality.

Webster was obviously impressed by the straightforwardness and conviction of her remark.

"And who should I say advised this?" he asked.

"That's the important part," answered the Stranger-woman. "Be sure to say that her new next-neighbor told you this; and be sure to say a woman."

The unsmiling face of Mesopotamia darkened in Hosmer's Store. But the Boston fellow grinned, and rode south that afternoon to take an eastbound boat from Cincinnati. No one thought to ask what the man's principal business was in the West.

Brady didn't haul south all week. Woodbridge finally asked him how the road was to the river.

Brady didn't know, and Hosmer explained: "Tom, you'd better not leave yet. Brady won't be going for a while. The Stranger came up that way. Said the cabin at Boxford's was burnt. Captain Michael was through and said there's Indians on the move. Four of those Mission Indians were down demanding provisions again. We need the alarm cannon, but we need an extra rifle around worse."

For the next two weeks Brady stayed off the road to the river, and the Stranger stayed out of the woods. Three men stood watch every night at the blockhouse; and the families that lived on the west outskirts, Mitchell, Adams, and the Stranger, for the most part kept someone on guard all night. But at the end of the third week Brady considered it safe to make the trip down to the river. Woodbridge borrowed a pack from the Stranger and put his cloth shirt and trousers in it.

Hosmer and Stikes were on guard duty at the blockhouse. The Stranger was supposed to be the third man, but he was late. Dolk and Exeter and some others were there, talking. Woodbridge walked in about nine o'clock. He addressed Mike Stikes.

"Mike, I'm going for the cannon tomorrow and I'm leaving you my horse Jock. That square me for mending the plow point and all the sharpening?"

Stikes sat up straight. "Why settle up now? You claim you're comin' back."

"Sure. But might as well be now as any time. Something could happen to me."

Stikes studied the hog farmer, disappointed. "All right," he said. "The horse suits me." His resignation implied that a horse that was sure to stay was better than a man that didn't know his own mind.

Woodbridge turned to Exeter. "Amos, I'll leave you two sows. That take care of what I owe you?"

"It'll suit."

Woodbridge offered Sam Hosmer five hogs and his plow to settle his store bill.

Hosmer sat hunched like a molting owl.

"A man givin' up his plow," he said, "doesn't sound like he's plannin' to be around after the thaw."

"Thought I might get an all-iron one, Sam."

"Tell you what, Woodbridge, instead of leavin' me the hogs, bring me a small iron stove from Fort Pitt." He looked at the hog farmer pointedly. "When you come back," he added.

"Maybe you'd better take the hogs, Sam."

"I'll risk it."

"I'd rather you'd take the hogs."

There was no answer, and Woodbridge explained.

"Stove might be unhandy to carry."

At that moment the Stranger came out of the darkness into the circle of firelight inside the blockhouse. He had his woman and his boy with him, explaining, "Don't like to leave them so far out tonight, even though Woodbridge's cabin is fairly close by."

Hosmer said: "Good idea. We can make them comfortable. Besides, Woodbridge isn't in his cabin. He's here."

The Stranger looked around the circle of light and then out into the fringe of darkness until he found the hog farmer. "Pardon me, Woodbridge. I don't generally give unasked advice, but maybe you don't know it's a bad idea to go off and leave a light when the red devils are out."

"I didn't leave any light," said Woodbridge. "Haven't been there since noon."

"Y'did though," persisted the gaunt Stranger. "We just came by your light. My boy said we ought to warn you to come into the blockhouse tonight. I said you knew enough. But the fact is, the light coming through those red curtains 'ud draw the red devils as sure—"

"I never put any curtains up, Stranger. You must be—Are you certain you saw a light in my place?"

Suddenly Woodbridge picked up his rifle and bolted out the blockhouse door.

The Stranger was surprised, and he looked his question at his wife.

"To his cabin, of course," the Stranger-woman answered. "It's a long time since there's a light in the Woodbridge cabin."

Sam Hosmer leaned forward to take a coal for his pipe, and though he still had the problem of getting the cannon out of Pittsburgh, he thought it was more important not to be short one rifle in Mesopotamia, or Hosmer's Camp, as it was known to the hungry Wyandots who ventured closer to it lately.

# *Chapter 12: THE REPRESENTA-TIVE (1803)*

WOODBRIDGE ignored the army officer who sat in his house.

The babe was almost three. It pleased him that she had her mother's chestnut-brown hair and the delicate groove from the nose down to the center of the lips and his own pale-blue eyes. His huge red hands turned the child to the light, and he bent to scrutinize her critically. The way he studied the child, as if she were a calf or a colt, bothered Veronica. But it shouldn't have. For he was marveling that in her the blood lines were running true. But as the officer resumed his talk, Woodbridge's face clouded. He put the child quickly down on the floor.

"You know well enough I'm no squatter, Armstrong! Why keep comin' back to me for information about 'em? I got nothin' to do with 'em."

"I know you're no squatter, Woodbridge," said the lieutenant, "but you *were* one. Hogland might come to see you. Just tell me where to look for him."

"I don't know him. Don't know where he is. And prob'ly wouldn't tell ya if I did!"

"Seems funny you don't know him, when it's known that Mitchell and Adams knew him. And you brought them here."

"Seems funny to me, Armstrong, how come it's more important for you to find this Hogland than to keep the Indians off us?"

"Because in Washington they're saying Governor St. Clair can't control the Territory. They're joking that this squatter Hogland is more gov'nor than he is, and my orders come from St. Clair. The Jeffersonians down in Chillicothe are using it as a lever to get statehood for the Ohio Country. The Federalists want the squatters out so the statehood people can't count up enough male settlers to apply for state status."

"Seems to me you're workin' against us, Armstrong. Seems to me we'd be better off under a state government that knows what's worryin' us. Why should we be under a representative from Washington like St. Clair, that sits down there in Chillicothe and Cincinnati and sends good troops out whackin' the bushes after a few harmless squatters while we're up here worryin' about them red devils?"

When the lieutenant pulled out with his squad next morning, Veronica worried over his coolness to Woodbridge.

And the autumn turned to winter.

Though Woodbridge was not an observant man, he was observant enough to notice that Cleopatra was off her feed and sticking close to the shed. He was observant enough to know that it was time to get her clean straw so that she might arrange it and rearrange it until it satisfied her as a birthing place for the precious sons of Boss that she carried. He was observant enough to notice that she was a bit mean and that it was probably because he had neglected to greet her.

"Always," he said to the Stranger-boy, who worked on the Woodbridge place now, "when you come to your hogs in the morning, have a friendly word for them, by name. Reassures them. Specially around farrowing time."

"But these white ones are an awful troubulation to you, Mr. Woodbridge. Wouldn't it be better to have all brown ones?"

"Ah-h. There you came to the thing, boy. Sure, the white ones are a terrible trouble. But they'll pay ya double in pork."

"But they don't seem to care about that down at the village."

"No. But they will."

"Horses and sows I think I'd rather raise," said the boy.

"What you don't see, boy, whenever meat's needed in a hurry, lots of it, it's the hog that breeds the biggest litter. It's the pig that'll feed your armies, and it's the pig'll lift the blasted mortgages off men's backs, boy."

Woodbridge was observant enough to notice that Cleopatra's time would be in about eight days. But when he went into the cabin to tell Veronica so, he was not observant enough to notice that she drew in a little in his presence. He was not observant enough to notice the haggardness, the trademark of sustained worry and fear.

But in the winter of 1803 several things troubled Veronica. And today, as she looked at her child, doubts crowded in upon her, adding up to discontent, and distaste for this open space in the woods.

She had studied every square foot of the cabin to determine what she would do with the child in the event of an Indian attack. She had concluded in favor of the trap door under the floor.

The babe, almost three, sat facing the fire, struggling with both hands to move the foot treadle of the spinning wheel. As Veronica looked at her, she seemed to see, not her own baby, but another little woodsie like the Flannerty urchins or the Adams and Mitchell children.

"Elizabeth, don't touch that dirty boot," cautioned Veronica.

"Zabeth. Zabeth touch it?" echoed the child, shortening her very name to a barbarous woods-born exclamation. Vaguely, Veronica charged it against the forest and the West and Thomas Woodbridge.

She also harked back to the blessing that Gershom, under protest, had flung across the river at them like a curse: "Bestow upon these Thy servants, if it be Thy will, the gift of children."

She loved the dark-haired babe, but its vigor and roughness were a constant source of self-blame. There was another source, too.

When she was East with Shuldane, guilt had followed her from rising in the morning to bed at night. For she could clearly see Woodbridge struggling alone in Mesopotamia. Alone in the field in the day, alone in the cabin at night. She even visualized physical injuries happening to him, and the inadequate care he would take of them. Strong surges of concern for Woodbridge impelled her West.

But now that she was with Woodbridge, she visualized just as clearly her father, alone but for unconcerned servants, in the big house in Concord, beset frequently by keen, powerful opponents who matched his own skill in affairs.

If she could be with them both! Yet that might happen. And it would be worse. For if Shuldane should come to the West soon, she knew why he would come.

Statehood was being discussed for the eastern part of the Northwest Territory, the Ohio Country. And statehood would put her father diametrically opposed on every count to her husband.

She had heard her father talking to a dinner table full of Federalists just before she had left him to return to Woodbridge. She remembered the determined lines in his face. "Gentlemen," he said, "if you permit statehood for the Ohio Country, you immediately lose control of your holdings in the West. The States or the people living on the site will make all the laws pertaining to your ground. They can, if they wish, tax it right out from under you. To retain any value, we will have to go ourselves, or send our own people out into those capitals at the moment of statehood. I'm in better circumstances than the rest of you. I could probably get Blair into the new state legislature. Or go myself.

THE REPRESENTATIVE (1803)                                    171

But the fact remains, gentlemen, give the Ohio Country statehood and you lose it."

Veronica remembered how joviality had left old Uncle Webster's face, how he had surveyed his own son, Lot Webster, at the table, and said: "All right, Nate. Granted. But give us a plan!"

"There are a few things to do," Shuldane had said. "First, they must prove the existence of a sufficient number of male citizens to qualify for statehood. They're trying hard. Counting squatters and any male who looks twenty-one, including runaway slaves and apprentices. St. Clair has little control over the Territory, but he's as anxious as anyone to prevent statehood. He wants to remain Territorial governor. We've got to see he gets the troops, and then uses them, to drive off the squatters. If they can't find 'em, they can't count 'em."

"St. Clair's been trying," said Uncle Webster.

"Not enough," answered Shuldane. "Blair tells me this William Hogland already calls himself Governor of the Squatters. We've got to get him out of there."

"Surely St. Clair knows about that."

"Of course. But his patrolling is incompetent."

That was when Lot had spoken up. "When you sent me out to check on the statehood sentiment, I met an Ensign Armstrong at Fort Washington. Seems to be doing most of the squatter patrolling. Seems like an ambitious lad, and capable. But he's been an ensign a devil of a long time. I had the impression that if there were more incentive, there'd be more patrolling."

Uncle Webster had lowered a forkful of duck. Veronica's father had stopped his brandy halfway to his mouth. They had all abandoned the dinner and left the table immediately for the library, for they all saw the clear path indicated by Lot Webster's remark. Veronica stayed through the animated conversation to the point where they were all slapping young Lot on the back and wishing him well. Then she had heard her father's authoritative instruction to her flushed young cousin: "You may assure the young officer of unlimited support and a good future. I suggest you leave tomorrow."

When she had heard that, she slipped upstairs and quietly packed the baby firmly into a hooded basket. Next day she had intercepted Lot Webster at Framingham, and they had come West together. The memory of leaving the house without saying goodbye to her father stabbed her.

That had been over two years ago. But it seemed like yesterday, because at that moment Ensign John Armstrong was riding onto the Woodbridge place. Except that it wasn't Ensign Armstrong now. It was Captain Armstrong.

Behind Armstrong were five riders. Four of them were soldiers, and they had boxed in among them a man who sat his horse awkwardly. As Veronica looked out the window, she saw that it was because the fifth rider's arms were tied tight against his sides at the elbow. She saw Armstrong motion to her husband to come over, and she saw Tom start slowly toward Armstrong, studying the situation as he went. Veronica joined her husband.

Armstrong was haggard and short-tempered. He pointed to the abject bearded captive in buckskins on the horse.

"Woodbridge, is that William Hogland?"

"I told you I don't know Hogland."

"Is it a man named Navarre then?" demanded Armstrong.

Woodbridge had never heard the two names connected before, and it made him suddenly thoughtful. But the figure before him was not Slover Navarre.

"No," said Woodbridge. "It's not."

The newly made captain smiled cryptically.

"All right, Woodbridge, I just wanted to be sure you were positive."

Armstrong turned to one of the soldiers. "Corporal, tell them to bring up the other one."

The corporal yelled, and Woodbridge and Veronica saw another party of five soldiers ride out of the woods, also with a captive rider in the middle. Woodbridge's face whitened. The captive was Slover Navarre.

"Now then," said Armstrong. "Is this Navarre?"

Navarre gave no sign of recognition. He looked down at the back of the horse. He was tied in the same manner.

"Well?" asked Armstrong. "Is he?"

"I don't know," said Woodbridge. But his voice was thin.

Armstrong exploded. "What do you mean you don't know? If you know Navarre well enough to know this first man isn't he, then you know well enough whether the second one is or not!"

"I never said I knew Navarre," balked Woodbridge.

Armstrong was about to dismount in anger when Veronica said:

"Just a minute, Captain. What Tom meant was that he was sure this first man was not Slover Navarre, because we know who he is."

The captain's face fell in astonishment. Woodbridge studied his wife, puzzled. Veronica continued.

"He's your own sergeant. Perhaps you forget, Captain, you left him to burn our cabin when you drove us off here before the survey."

The captain sucked air through jaws rigid with pained disgust. But Veronica's grin was not malicious. Somehow it merely exchanged mischief with the officer, giving him credit for his attempt. He looked quickly at Navarre, who had the sense to study the ground intently.

"Which is the shortest way to Mitchell's cabin?" Armstrong demanded.

When they had left, the hog farmer turned to the Stranger-boy. "Boy, take Jock and ride through the gorge to Mitchell's place. Tell him the trick!"

After the boy had left, Tom studied his wife with astonished admiration. That night Woodbridge acted once more as he had before the preacher-marriage, as though he had in his house some gifted and delicate princess, an attitude which had been trampled for some time under the frontier mud and under the vague estrangement of the unanswered questions between them.

Five new families had come to Mesopotamia in the past year, giving rise once more to the recurrent optimism among the settlers that the long-heralded immigration and land boom were beginning.

A sixth newcomer to Hosmer Village was new only to Woodbridge and to those who had come after him. Although it was a revelation to see the new color in Loretta Shane's face, Woodbridge was not favorably impressed with the return of the missing man he'd heard about so long—Isaac Shane.

The village had no other topic of conversation for the first week after his return.

It seemed that Adams and Mitchell had followed Armstrong's squad, at a distance, up into the survey toward the Greenville Line to see what they could do about freeing Slover Navarre. They reported that they lost track of Navarre, but seemed to think he would be all right somehow.

The singular event of their trip, however, was the discovery of

Isaac Shane above the Greenville Line. The story was not clear in every detail, nor did Woodbridge much examine it. He had heard how Loretta and Isaac Shane had led a strange existence, apart from the rest of the village. They had been squatting on a nearby tract before Hosmer and Stikes arrived in the Territory. When Hosmer and Stikes settled Mesopotamia, the Shanes moved over and bought land so that Loretta would be near someone when Shane went off trapping. Hosmer had always said that in traveling alone like that, a day would come when Shane might not return. And from one trip, four years ago, he had not returned.

Though Woodbridge found him strange, he was somehow drawn to the man. But Shane never had anything to say to Woodbridge.

Shane had a new pair of cloth trousers and a new buckskin shirt. They said he was near naked when they found him. He had not as yet a hat of any kind, and his hair was scraggly on top. He joked that he was lucky to have a scalp, let alone hair.

He was extremely thin, and his face had a weird cast because the forehead was dark and weathered and wrinkled, while the cheeks were pale, white, and smooth, like those of a man who has shaved off a heavy beard. He kept his rifle closer to him than was now customary in the village proper. Stikes charged it to Shane's experience with the Indians.

As winter melted, Woodbridge watched the last strongholds of snow disappear from the shaded corners. Daily now he pulled back a few hundred years of matted leaves from the floor of the woods to find white threads of vegetation sprouting underneath.

When the white threads turned pale green, Woodbridge went to Hosmer's Store for seed. While he was there, the ponderous Asa Buttrick came in, fresh from Cincinnati, and Mesopotamia crowded around to hear the news.

It was no wonder that John Armstrong was in a sweat to catch up with William Hogland. An outlandish thing had happened. There had been an election down along the river. The Ohio Country was a state, all right. And she had elected a governor and a legislature.

"But the amazing thing," said Buttrick, "was the voting. They say strangers kept stragglin' into town all during the election. They weren't landowners, but they came in and voted. Turned out they were squatters. Came in from all over. Some of them couldn't write, but they had scraps of paper with them to copy from. Caused a lot of commotion. Some towns counted those votes, some threw 'em out."

"How many threw 'em out?" asked Woodbridge.

"Don't know," said Buttrick. "Point is, when it was all over, it turned out these men had all written in a name for the legislature, a William Hogland. Spelled it all kinds of ways: Will Hogland, Billy Hog, William Hog, but darned if they didn't elect him."

"The squatters elected a man to the legislature!" Hosmer was amazed and hurt. Hosmer Village had not even figured in the election.

"That's right," said Buttrick. "Through him they're gonna work for legislation to let them keep the land they're squattin' on, and buy it by easy payments, long-term credit, small parcels, or by bounty warrant."

Brady let out a horse laugh. "More power to 'em!"

"But now there's a real battle on," continued Buttrick. "The Federalists say if this Hogland has the gall to try to take his seat April 1st in the legislature, they'll arrest him for murders committed against the army by squatters, and for a whole list of offenses. The Jeffersonians say if Hogland takes his seat in the legislature, he's immune from arrest while he's legislating."

Veronica, however, took the news more seriously than Tom had expected, and it puzzled him.

By the notches on the wall at Hosmer's Store, it was March 13 when the trouble happened at the store. While Woodbridge waited to talk to Hosmer, he studied the profile of Isaac Shane, who was sifting Hosmer's gunpowder through his fingers.

Here was a farmer who came to the store in person to select his gunpowder, but sent his wife to the store to select his seed. Here was a man whose nose and forehead and ears were weathered, brown and wrinkled with rough living. But his cheeks and neck were white and smooth and soft-looking. Shane was a man who looked careless of his person, yet he wore clean new buckskins and he shaved his face more often than the others. Woodbridge was lost in this puzzle when a lately familiar voice grated across his reflections. Captain John Armstrong spoke louder than necessary.

"Woodbridge, I've been waiting for you to come in town."

The hog farmer flooded with resentment.

"We've pretty well located Hogland up on the survey. I understand you're one around here most familiar with it."

Woodbridge turned slowly to face Armstrong, but he stood silent. The officer had never experienced such cold resentment as came from the redhead's pale, ice-blue eyes, and it put him at a loss for words.

Brady hollered across the store, "Looks to me like this here Hogland outranks ya now, Captain, bein' a member of the legislature." He laughed. "Besides that, it looks like he's got a bigger army'n you got anyhow. Least they git around more."

Armstrong had the sense to avoid an argument with Mesopotamia's popular clown, but his resentment surged out against Woodbridge.

"You'll get ready to leave with me this afternoon, Woodbridge, for the survey."

"Get Captain Michael, the Indian. He knows the survey."

Armstrong brushed this aside.

"I want you to lead us up there, Woodbridge, to the place he's most likely to be. He'll see you eventually and come up to talk to you. I'll be behind with a squad, and we'll seize him then as an enemy of the United States and the State of Ohio."

The men in the store now formed a ring of intent faces.

"You're a fool, Armstrong," said Woodbridge. "You think he'll be alone? There'll be at least a dozen squatters with him, any one of 'em willing to die for Hogland, I hear. The way word travels through the squatters, they'll know as soon as you step onto the survey—and they'll know why. What's more, they'll see I'm leadin' ya up there. They'll shoot me down as soon as look at me if I'm with you."

"Then I see you are quite familiar with squatter habits, Mr. Woodbridge. We'll move out tomorrow. You'll lead."

"Armstrong, you're forgettin', I'm not one of your boys. I'm Woodbridge, private citizen, freeholder. I don't lead anybody any place unless I feel like it."

"I didn't want to use this, Woodbridge, but I see I'll have to. There was a matter of a murder—a shot soldier—at Boxford's Cabin."

"What's that got to do with me?"

"The word is that the squatter women stayed at your cabin during the fight. That makes you an accomplice, way the army will see it."

Woodbridge silently cursed the squatters and Navarre for involving him in the Boxford's Cabin affair. Aloud, he cursed the captain.

"And there's another matter," continued Armstrong, "of two surveyors killed by squatters. You were on the survey. I hear you were even in charge of it part time. Then when the survey's over you and two other squatters end up owning land. It'll make interesting listening down at the Chillicothe sitting of the circuit court—if it gets back there. No reason it should, though, if you lead me to Hogland."

Woodbridge spoke through stiff jaws. "You got a way of workin' things around, Captain, that makes a man no better'n a muskrat in a trap!"

"The governor has a habit of giving me assignments that call for that. We'll leave this afternoon, Mr. Freeholder Woodbridge."

Hosmer broke in. "Just a minute, Captain. We're for helpin' you catch this Hogland, within reason. But you don't go marchin' Woodbridge or anyone else out of here against his will, leavin' his wife and babe alone in the cabin. Especially not Woodbridge, since he lives out on the edge. Go get Captain Michael."

"Woodbridge isn't compelled to go with me, Hosmer. But it seemed to me he just made a kind of a bargain with me."

"I doubt if Woodbridge has got anything to hide. You care, Tom, what he says about these squatter women?"

Woodbridge warmed to Hosmer. He wished he could reassure the brown, wrinkled face. Hosmer waited for an answer. But it came from Armstrong, who turned to his sergeant.

"Bring in our evidence, Sergeant."

"Yes, sir."

The sergeant was gone only a moment, but during his absence Hosmer studied Woodbridge.

"Ye're not mixed in that Boxford Cabin killin', Tom. Tell him so!"

But Tom turned to see what the sergeant was bringing. It brought a red frustration to his face and an expression of stupefaction to Mesopotamia.

Hosmer's disappointment cut Tom, for the sergeant had placed on the counter a rusting Jaeger musket.

"I believe you're all familiar," said Armstrong quietly, "with Mr. Woodbridge's Jaeger smooth bore."

No one spoke. The officer resumed. "I'll leave a guard at your cabin, Woodbridge. We'll move north this afternoon."

That's when Woodbridge saw Isaac Shane elbow forward, prying his way between the muscular hulk of Brady and the tall, gaunt frame of Mike Stikes. His thin small body lounged against his rifle, and he addressed himself to the officer.

"Strikes me you're baitin' the wrong trap, Captain." The impertinence was so flat, nasal, and assured, that the captain was at a loss.

By virtue of sheer gall the skinny one had command of the store. "Strikes me, Captain, if your Squatter Gov'nor, so called, is still up in the survey hidin' out, it means he's afraid to come down out of there, and you got no worries anyhow."

The captain managed a face of pained tolerance.

"But if he ain't afraid to come down," continued Shane, "and if he does expect to sit on this here legislature by April 1st, he'll be easin' down toward Chillicothe about now. And it 'pears to me you might look just a mite derelict sittin' way up here in the woods if he's down there at Chillicothe."

The captain's mask slipped long enough for Woodbridge to notice his hungry attention. But he recovered.

"I thank you, sir, but I have men stationed at gateway points on all the major trails south. If he's headed south, they'll intercept him."

"Where are your men stationed?" asked Shane.

"Why I've got two waiting at the ford at —" The captain's eyes narrowed. He stopped unrolling the map, and rerolled it briskly. "I'd prefer not to say," he said.

"Doesn't matter," shrugged Shane. "If this Hogland is all they claim, he ain't gonna be caught at any what you call 'gateway points.'"

The captain's answer was closer attention.

"But there's one way you could intercept him, no matter which direction he slips into Chillicothe from."

"Pray, what is your infallible plan?"

"I don't know if you're maybe too late already," said Shane. "If I was him I'd already be south inside Chillicothe, layin' low. Be the safest place for him, what with all you soldiers out stompin' up the woods t'the north."

"So? The plan?"

"You'll have to hurry some to do it."

The army was exasperated, but also worried, and impatient for Shane's revelation. But the thin one handled the officer like a strayed pig. He dribbled the corn out one kernel at a time, making the captain water at the mouth for the whole handful.

"Hurry where?" demanded the captain.

"Fact, you could hardly make it even if your men were all mounted."

"Where?" stamped Armstrong.

"Why, I'd hurry them soldier boys right down to Chillicothe, and I'd spread 'em in a ring around the outside of Chillicothe. I'd straddle 'em across every road and trail and path into the town. I'd stop every wagon comin' in and search it. I'd lay 'em around that town so thick that a stragglin' muskrat couldn't swim between 'em. And that's how I'd catch me the King of the Squatters."

Woodbridge scowled at Shane. He had never met William Hogland, but he shuddered for him because Isaac Shane's plan was so formidable.

The captain squirmed at the good sense of it. "I must confess you've a point."

"A point!" bellowed Brady. "He's got a dang sight more'n that! In fact, now that he puts it that way, what in thunder are you doin' up here, Captain?"

Woodbridge lashed out: "Whyn't you men let the captain catch his own squatters? What did this Hogland ever do to you, Shane?"

"You helpin' the squatters, Woodbridge?" asked Armstrong.

"No! Blast them! But I been one, and it pleasures me none to see one trapped like a rat!"

Shane brushed off Woodbridge with a curiously gentle smile, and proceeded to pour more coals over the burning officer. "But I doubt if you got time to get there ahead of him, Captain."

"I'll take the South Road this afternoon."

"You'll never do it, Captain, unless you're familiar with the old Shawnee cutoff past Bluff Rock. You know it?"

"No."

From Shane's description every man in the room could picture a certain William Hogland somewhere out there in the big woods filtering swiftly toward Chillicothe.

"It's the shortest way down," said Shane. "Awful tricky to find, though. Fades out in a couple a places."

The captain's disappointment was unconcealed. He asked each of the three soldiers with him if he knew the trail. "Never heard of it." Shane let the captain pace up and down the store a few times. Then, "Tell you what, though," he said. "I got reason to go to Chillicothe."

Loretta Shane looked up, surprised.

"And I'm a little squeamish about takin' the Shawnee Trail alone," continued Isaac. "In exchange for your protection south, I'll lead you the short way down. Then when we get there, y'see, you can keep your troops outside the town so they don't rile up any suspicions. I could go in and ask around town for you, while you're watchin' the approaches."

"Good. We'll protect you, all right. Can you leave this afternoon?"

"Tomorrow morning, early," Shane said.

Three of the soldiers were to remain in Mesopotamia. It was the troop protection Shuldane had arranged for. He always made good on a promise. Three soldiers were far short of adequate, but more were to come later. Meanwhile, that afternoon, Mesopotamia pitched in to erect living quarters for the three soldiers inside the blockhouse.

Woodbridge dumped an armload of small timber at the feet of Hank Flannerty, who was making a corner joint for one of the bunks. He paused to watch, not so much out of interest, but because of the captain's intense interest.

"That's a mighty neat joint you make there, mister," said Armstrong.

"Thanks," said Flannerty without pausing.

Armstrong seemed to be digging at something. "I saw a few like that up on the survey recently, in squatter cabins."

Flannerty looked up from his work.

Woodbridge became alert to the crackle in his voice.

"Where'd you learn it?" asked Armstrong.

Flannerty didn't answer. But Sam Hosmer proudly and innocently gave credit where credit was due.

"Flannerty learned that trick from Isaac Shane," he said. "Shane's a master at it."

Woodbridge saw Shane edging out of the blockhouse. But Armstrong called to him, "Oh, Mr. Shane, a word with you please."

Shane approached slowly. The sergeant stood in the doorway. Sam Hosmer continued, like a proud father exhibiting his sons: "Yeah, Isaac made all our joints when we first settled here. Fortunately, he taught Hank here the trick. Still, we were lackin' somethin' awful for joints when Isaac was away."

Armstrong became flatteringly interested. "Oh, was Mr. Shane *away?*"

Woodbridge saw Shane standing off a double pace, listening carefully. Vaguely he heard Hosmer continuing, delighted with the captain's sudden attention: "Yeah, we almost lost Isaac. He was gone four years."

Armstrong turned to Shane behind him. "Where were you, Mr. Shane?"

Shane's talk was not so glib now, and Woodbridge watched him with a strange sense of recognition.

"Where were you?" asked Armstrong again.

"Oh, up above the Greenville Line."

"Trapping?"

"Nope. Indians. Captive."

"Wyandots?"

Woodbridge had the odd feeling that Armstrong was a sentry challenging for the right password.

"Which branch of the Wyandots?" persisted Armstrong.

"Turtle clan," answered Shane.

"Rain Cloud still chief there?"

"Uh . . . yeah."

Armstrong grinned. "My error," he said. "Rain Cloud is from the Panther clan, isn't he?"

Shane's face darkened and he looked down at the ground, unleashing a bullet of tobacco juice. Woodbridge felt that there was more to the cryptic exchange than Indian talk.

"Anyway," said Armstrong with a new lightness, "we'll leave in the morning. Right, Mr. Shane?"

Armstrong turned away, motioned his sergeant out of the doorway, and together they walked out of the blockhouse. Woodbridge saw him call over three of his soldiers, who dispersed, each going directly to talk to another soldier briefly.

Shane started to leave the blockhouse, going a few steps out of his way to pass Woodbridge. In a very low voice he muttered, "Not much trouble ever comes from dead ahead, Tom."

Woodbridge's jaw dropped.

Shane walked out of the blockhouse and toward the East Trail with a mincing gait that Woodbridge now recognized. Tom saw a couple of soldiers cease cleaning their rifles to stroll off casually behind Shane. Woodbridge and the Stranger-boy followed them. They overtook and passed the soldiers, reaching the Shane cabin shortly after Shane had entered. Woodbridge went to the door and knocked. Loretta opened the door and Woodbridge stepped in.

The man's back was toward him, but he turned around quickly.

They stared at each other. The settler in the cabin arched a brown stream out the window. Woodbridge could get out only one word.

"You!"

"That's right, son," laughed Slover Navarre. "And slow you were to see it."

"How should I, when you once fooled even your own people under the name of Navarre at the blockhouse?"

"They had less chance than you. I left here over four years ago. They never knew me in a beard, and so dirty and scarred up and skinny."

"Well, who are you? Shane or Navarre or maybe Hogland?"

"Maybe each is part ways right."

"Well, mostly you're a fool! Armstrong knows now that you're his man! He's got two soldiers coverin' this place right now."

"Yeah. But I reckon you'll admit I had a slick plan for gettin' the captain to escort me to Chillicothe before he caught me lyin'. Right?"

Woodbridge thought back over the talk in the store, and every word that had been spoken suddenly took on opposite meaning. It had been a clever scheme.

"But you're in hellish trouble now," said Woodbridge.

"Set yourself, Woodbridge, and figure a minute. This here Armstrong is pretty cute in the head."

"That's why you're done for."

"No. That's good. Y'never know what a blockhead'll do, but a smart man you can figure."

Loretta Shane's quiet resignation was suddenly impressive. What a secret she had kept!

"Figure this way, Woodbridge. If he was smart enough to catch me lyin', he's smart enough to know everything about me now."

"Of course he does. That'll why he'll kill you."

"But notice he was also smart enough not to say anything about it. He didn't arrest me. He didn't holler. He didn't call me a liar. He didn't let on. That means he's gonna pretend he don't know. He's gonna let me think I'm leadin' him down to Chillicothe tomorra."

"Then he's gonna git rid of you in the woods!"

Loretta Shane winced. "Isaac!"

"Don't think so, Tom. I think the captain's got bigger plans than that—like deliverin' me to his colonel."

Indignantly and self-righteously Woodbridge sighed. "Well, we'll get you out of here tonight, somehow."

Navarre's eyes snapped. "No ya won't. Just don't worry about me!"

"You just said Armstrong's gonna take you down that trail and turn you in."

"I said he's gonna try. But the way he's gonna do it gives me time to think. That's all I ever needed, Woodbridge."

Woodbridge got up. "Then you're on your own!"

"Always have been. That's a long time before you came along, Woodbridge."

Navarre smiled. Woodbridge left abruptly, smarting.

Back at the Woodbridge place, the hog farmer sent the Stranger-boy north to get Adams and Mitchell. But Adams was not in his cabin. Mitchell was not on his place either. Woodbridge fumed. "If his own blasted shiftless squatter friends can't be rallied, Navarre's done for."

Woodbridge tossed on the bunk through the night, and in the morning early he and the Stranger-boy rode into Mesopotamia. Several men and women were up to see the squad off for the south. The soldiers were grouped by the porch of Hosmer's Store. But they glanced frequently across to where Navarre stood talking to Woodbridge and Loretta Shane and the silent Stranger-boy.

Armstrong called over: "Lead off, Mr. Shane! We're ready!"

Navarre blasted a bullet of tobacco into the dust, and he shook his wife gently by the shoulder. He grinned at Tom, saying, "The captain don't know, Tom, that trouble don't come from the front." He winked and shambled down the South Road toward the river.

Woodbridge watched the soldiers close in behind Navarre, and he decided that he was watching the squatter's champion walk to the gallows. It filled him with a helpless, fuming wrath.

Loretta wiped her eyes and hurried away, leaving Woodbridge standing beside the silent Stranger-boy.

"Damned if there's any sense to his kind," he grumbled. "Makes his wife suffer, makes his friends worry. Gives all of himself to a damned cause that ain't worth the grunt out of a foundered river hog."

Woodbridge stood still as he watched the last of the soldiers disappear around the bend, completely surrounding Navarre.

He looked over to a stump where sat Adams. "There's the kind of shiftless lard hog he's dyin' for. Navarre is dyin' and Adams sits on a stump."

But a great and wondrous understanding suddenly came over Wood-bridge. For as he watched, he saw Adams rise up slowly, sling his rifle casually over his shoulder, and amble off down the trail in the direction of the troops.

As Adams became a small figure disappearing around the bend, Woodbridge saw Mitchell rise up from another stump and stroll leisurely off behind Adams. As Mitchell disappeared around the bend, Woodbridge saw another figure rise up from the burying yard to saunter off aimlessly in the same direction, cradling his rifle carelessly in front of him. When the third figure turned the bend, Woodbridge was startled at a rustle in the brush behind him. Turning, he saw another ragged woodsman rise up from the cut-over oak bushes. He meandered slowly toward the river, keeping his interval behind the man ahead.

Even the Stranger-boy grasped the significance. "And I suppose they'll be squatters droppin' in behind like that all the way down the trail past Boxford's Cabin," he said.

"And beyond that, even," finished Woodbridge. "Till there's an army marchin' behind those unwittin' soldiers that's big enough to storm into Chillicothe in broad daylight. They'll be enough to set Mr. Navarre or Shane or Hogland in the front row of that there legislature."

The redhead and the Stranger-boy stood watching in speechless wonder and admiration until Woodbridge turned to his horse.

"Navarre's had time to do his thinkin'," he said.

# Chapter 13: RONTONDEE (1804)

THE Reverend Seth Gershom was cold; but he could no more allow himself to shiver in the presence of Captain Michael than he could drink his warm whisky from the common gourd shared by Michael and the other mission Indians.

Gershom therefore moved toward the hut's fireplace slowly, as though from habit rather than from cold. He bent his great hawklike face to the floor, and it was apparent to the Indians that he was communicating the great problem to the Great Spirit.

Actually, the Reverend's thoughts had wandered far from the serious Indian dilemma; he was communicating with Seth Gershom on the subject of Seth Gershom.

Why was he sent way up here, north of Mesopotamia, in the forsaken, disputed wilderness tight up under the Greenville Line?

Gershom lifted the gourd and transferred the amber liquid to a silver lacework of a goblet that was lined with glass. The glass gave the impression that the Reverend's brandy was suspended mystically in mid-air in this leaky silver vessel. This worthless piece of glass and silver separated him from the Indians in the bark hut.

But tonight, unfortunately, it did not separate Seth Gershom from himself, nor from the necessity of sending an answer immediately out to Chief Rontondee's audacious demands.

The Reverend Seth Gershom was a worldly man. And on this count he was self-conscious, comparing himself to his colleagues, whose dedication he never had understood. There were some visions he had not seen, some divinity which had been withheld from him. He had watched his brother seminarians pray years ago in school, and he had seen by the rapture in their faces that they received answers. But when he bowed his own head, he saw only the hobnails in the boots of the kneeling seminarian in front of him. And since divinity would not show in his face, he had made the black vestments and the silver goblet and the language of theology set him off. He had so mastered his accouterments that even the bishop seemed to consider him one of them, though Gershom had not been absolutely certain even of that.

Gershom's fault, however, was a matter of degree. Had he been a little more earthly, he might have known or guessed at the reason for his being relieved of a growing, promising parish in Steubenville to be shipped up under the Greenville Line to this forsaken, freezing Indian mission.

He would have made a study of the politic names, and he would have known that you don't tie a Shuldane to a big woods-talking hog farmer. Or, failing that, he might at least have associated the large bequest to the Massachusetts Episcopal Diocese—the Shuldane Seminarial Scholarship Fund—with the name of the proprietor of Mesopotamia. He might then have understood why four years ago the bishop had ordered him to extend his circuit up north from Steubenville to include the Shuldane tract.

Which connection would naturally have led him to notice the name Veronica Shuldane, when he married her without published banns to a big redheaded nobody. Which in turn would have shed light on the bishop's severe and summary action in banishing him from the Steubenville circuit to this cold, miserable Wyandot mission.

The cherubic young minister who had come to Steubenville to relieve him had brought a message from the bishop. "The mission requires our best and most experienced man. It is our noblest and most productive work." There had also been a sealed note from the bishop ordering that the publishing of the banns of marriage three times before the ceremony henceforth be strictly observed.

The Reverend Gershom reflected angrily that the bishop had never perhaps looked into the black muzzle of a long rifle held by an agnostic squatter.

But the mission Indians now stirred impatiently as they watched the great hawk pace up and down the hut. Gershom wondered what to tell them.

The twenty-six domesticated Indians at the mission needed all the corn they had stored to get through the starvation-fraught winter. It was little enough. But the roving, hunting, untamed Wyandots up north of the Greenville Line had none. Chief Rontondee's rebellious clan had not planted. A few hungry Shawnees, too, joined Rontondee. They knew that the mission Indians had planted last year. Worse, they knew exactly which of the rickety bark huts contained the harvest. And at this very moment nine of them waited outside, demanding a gift, a handout.

Captain Michael spoke impatiently in Wyandot to his son, Silver Pigeon. Silver Pigeon then rose and addressed Gershom.

"Father Gershom, Captain Michael says if the Great Spirit makes no suggestion or advice, we should refuse corn to Rontondee. Tell them to go to the Mesopotamia town for corn."

Gershom was always taken aback by the excellent English spoken by the handsome Indian boy. But he said: "No, Silver Pigeon. That will not do."

Gershom pointed a bony finger to Thomas Running Fox, who rose, almost too quickly, Gershom thought, and with a kind of sardonic deference. In giving the mission Indians Christian names, Gershom could not help naming Running Fox for Doubting Thomas.

"Thomas, give the Wyandots four skinfuls of corn and tell them that is the end of it."

"Rontondee know better, Father."

"Tell them it's the end of it," insisted Gershom. "And as soon as they have gone, we will build a new granary deep in the woods."

Running Fox opened the door to execute the order. Gershom frowned as the open door admitted a swirl of snow and a freezing wind which coagulated the mucus in the preacher's great nostrils. He was about to yell at Running Fox, when he saw that worse than dalliance kept the door open. Running Fox crouched, transfixed by something outside.

A shot split the air, and a yell. Running Fox snatched his rifle and bolted. Captain Michael was out the door, with Silver Pigeon after him.

Gershom reached the door in time to see the long-haired Wyandots running toward the woods, carrying deerskins of grain. One mission Indian lay on the ground on his back, another kneeled in firing position.

Running Fox stopped, brought his rifle to his shoulder. Gershom yelled, "Halt!"

Running Fox lowered his rifle an inch and turned his head reluctantly back to Gershom. But Gershom could not stare him down, and the Fox raised the rifle to his cheek.

"Stop!" Gershom's imperious voice paralyzed the Fox long enough for the Wyandots to make it safely out of the clearing.

"Forgive their trespasses," commanded Gershom. "It is the way of the Great Spirit."

"How many times does the Great Spirit let them trespass?" accused Running Fox in a level, loaded voice. "Who will feed the Christian mission Indians when the corn is gone to the Wyandots? The white men, perhaps?"

The Reverend Seth Gershom was at the moment only faintly concerned with the Great Spirit's recommendation. But he was deeply and fearfully concerned with avoiding a scalping war between his twenty-six helpless Indians and Rontondee's Wyandot clan and the fiercer Shawnees.

He lowered himself onto the bench, muttering; and the bishop's ears should have burned, back in Boston, Massachusetts.

It was two weeks later, in mid-January, that Captain Michael shuffled into Hosmer's Store and placed himself and his son in front of the door, their feet wide apart. Captain Michael stamped the snow from his feet overzealously, but even this did not interrupt the argument in process. Buttrick had just returned from Cincinnati with an empty wagon. He was on the defensive.

"We might just as well face it," he said. "Grain's not to be had."

Hosmer refused to face it. "Asa, you can't tell me there's not corn in Cincinnati, stored for the troops at Fort Washington, or lyin' in stills."

"Listen, Sam. I saw that Captain Armstrong out on the dock offerin' the labor of thirty soldiers for seven days for eighty bushels of wheat to feed his garrison. He didn't get it. I saw John Piatt post a notice offering $2.75, metal money, cash, for ordinary Kentucky squaw corn. He got none."

Woodbridge swore. "Those blasted Kentucky bandits!"

Captain Michael stamped his feet again, though the snow had melted. The short Indian was built much like Hosmer, including the square, wrinkled face. He shoved Silver Pigeon. The Indian lad started forward toward Asa Buttrick, but the old chief stopped him with a grunt and pointed to Hosmer. Woodbridge noticed that the young Indian was about the age of the Stranger-boy.

"Come to speak about corn," said Silver Pigeon to Hosmer. "Wyandots hungry. Take corn from mission. Father Gershom say whites give corn to mission Indians. Mission Indians give corn to Wyandots!"

Hosmer heard the boy's speech to the end, and sighed. He turned a withered face on Hawkins. "How much can you give, Jim?"

Hawkins faced the old man without answering.

The faces in the room were thinner now. Even Asa Buttrick had slimmed some, and the once meaty jowls were deflated and sagging. Stikes was gaunter than ever, and Morgan Brady's laugh was seldom heard.

Hosmer held Hawkins's stare until the latter stammered, "Sam, you know I already lost the cow for lack of feed."

"How much can *you* give, Dolk?" asked Hosmer.

The stolid Dutchman wanted to name an amount. But his wife, Judith, stared him silent.

Exeter spoke up. "There's not a man here can afford to give away two ears of corn. Let the missionaries feed the mission."

Stikes shifted his weight.

"Exeter's right, Sam. We can't spare the corn for the mission."

Woodbridge exploded, "You're all crazy! Ya can't afford *not* to send somethin' up there! Listen what he's tellin' ya! The mission Indians'll pass some of it along to the Wyandots to keep Rontondee quiet. Otherwise he'll be down here on our necks."

"And they'll take it home inside our scalps," added Brady.

"Where's the difference?" asked Stikes. "If we don't give it over, they attack. If we do give it over, we starve."

"We don't starve right away," said Woodbridge.

But there was more logic on Hosmer's side.

"Tom, it won't work. Be like tryin' to fill up the gorge north of your place with corn. It'll be blackmail. They'll take more and more and more, and when it's all gone . . ." He made a gesture across the top of his head that blanched Judith Dolk's face.

"I know that," Woodbridge persisted. "But before that maybe Navarre will have got the state or the federal to send up troops."

"I was coming to that," said Buttrick. "Navarre's not in good favor. They don't like his manners or his clothes or his talk. He gets up in the legislature and asks for troops for up here. They argue him down, sayin' these aren't towns up here under the Greenville Line. Just scattered settlements. Militia's all staying home anyway, trying to feed their own families. Navarre demanded troops and rights for the squatters until the Federalists dug up his record as William Hogland, and it looks like they found a way to arrest him."

Silver Pigeon said, "Captain Michael wants your answer about corn."

Sam Hosmer shook his head slowly, and the two Indians left.

Woodbridge stopped over at Mike Stikes's shop.

"Make me a small squirrel rifle for the Stranger-boy. Like Veronica's."

"But the boy's still too young to handle one of my rifles, Tom."

"Looks like he'll have to grow up to it," said Woodbridge. "And right sudden."

The Reverend Seth Gershom heard the report from Silver Pigeon, corroborated by the nodding head of Captain Michael. Gershom's face blackened as his black brows beetled down over his deep eye caverns, leaving only a fierce half-moon of white showing under the eye pupils. He made no comment.

Silver Pigeon continued, "But Captain Michael says he knows where to get corn, Father Gershom."

"Where?"

"From Mr. Woodbridge, the fire-topped one."

"No!" Gershom slapped the puncheon bench, reddening his palm and startling Silver Pigeon.

"We'll take no corn from Woodbridge!" Gershom modified his tone. "One man cannot give enough corn to do any good for twenty-six Indians. Was there no other message?"

"Just one," said Pigeon. "As we left, the Hosmer squaw asked if Father Gershom comes Sunday to preach."

"The answer is No!"

Running Fox's dark, taunting face showed teeth in a way that discomfited Gershom. "The Great Spirit does not forgive the white ones' trespasses, yoi?"

Gershom stood up. "You're right, Running Fox. I'm wrong. I will preach them a sermon Sunday." Gershom looked into the fire. "I will preach them a sermon they will not forget."

Gershom inserted a thumbnail into the big book and ripped it open to the place where it said: "Judge not, that ye be not judged! For by what judgment ye judge, ye shall be judged. And with what measure ye mete, it shall be measured to you again."

Wetting his fingertips, he roughly flapped more pages over. With a bold stroke of the charcoal that tore the page, he marked beside the passage, "For your brothers have asked of you bread . . . and you have given them a stone!" Then he slammed the book shut.

Woodbridge cut the woods hogs off from any corn at all. He led them up into the thickest part of the woods, where the snow could be kicked back to uncover frozen layers of rotting leaves, acorns, frosted moss. The woods hogs were on their own. Woodbridge had no idea how many would survive. Each day there was a new carcass or two being devoured by the rest of the hogs.

But the Bedfords had to have corn. Left alone in the woods for a day, a Bedford would not feed itself one morsel. It was the price of domesticating an animal. But he cut the corn ration in half. The Bedford herd was up to eighty-two hogs now, though. And each day's ration made a gaping hole in the bins behind the shed.

When Captain Michael arrived, Woodbridge let him have four skinfuls of corn. That emptied the first bin. When Captain Michael returned the third time, the second bin was emptied. Woodbridge had already decided that when Captain Michael came back the fourth time, he would refuse him any more grain. So, just after the first of February, when he saw Captain Michael and Silver Pigeon approaching, Woodbridge framed his refusal. But he never got a chance to say it.

Silver Pigeon was out of breath.

"Captain Michael says you go! Leave cabin!"

That was the beginning. Everyone knew it.

Woodbridge moved Veronica and the babe into the town and into the blockhouse at once. The Mitchell and Adams women and children went with Veronica and the Stranger-woman.

After unloading the women and their gear and the children at the blockhouse, Tom turned to leave. It took Veronica by surprise.

"Tom!"

"What?"

"You're not going back?"

"You didn't think I could leave the hogs for them!"

"Tom, don't go back there!"

"Veronica! The hogs!"

"The hogs! Last time it was the land. You said never again."

He walked out of the blockhouse.

"Tom!"

Woodbridge returned to the cabin to figure out what to do with the Bedford hogs. Mitchell had returned to his cabin, so Tom knew he was not alone. However, he knew that Adams had not come back.

The in-town women moved into the blockhouse with their children while their husbands pried loose the stores and valuables from the cabins and carried them into the blockhouse, crowding it to capacity. Yet casual observers such as Morgan Brady noticed how small was the stack of rations being piled in the center of the floor.

More careful observers, such as Faith Hawkins, could not escape the feeling that the small amount of corn brought in by Amos Exeter was not his entire larder. Her feeling was bolstered by memory of four bags she herself had hidden in the woods.

Hope Emerson moved her sheep into a cave behind her cabin. Throughout the village men sought sheltered places in the woods for cattle and horses which they turned loose.

The first morning after depositing Veronica in the blockhouse, Woodbridge was surprised to find Stranger-boy in the shed. Together they worried about where to hide the Bedfords so that the animals could survive. The cabin already had a deserted feel, and it seemed to watch reproachfully as Woodbridge and the Stranger-boy loaded corn into the wagon.

Woodbridge grumbled, "If they'd only made the blockhouse big enough, while they were at it, to hold the stock."

"Bein' an emergency, wouldn't they let us bring the Bedfords inside?"

"Nope. No stock inside, except butchered for rations."

There was hard breathing behind, and a growl from Wolf. Woodbridge whirled around and reached for his rifle. But it was Captain Michael.

It was the first English Woodbridge had ever heard from the old Indian. But he wouldn't even have had to speak. The frenzied gestures and sweaty face were enough.

"Go!"

"Where are they?" asked Woodbridge.

"Go!"

Silver Pigeon caught up with his father. "Adams' cabin!" he said. "Ashes!"

Woodbridge looked to the northwest, as if it were possible to see anything except the trees at the top of the ridge.

The chief motioned to Woodbridge to hurry. The hog farmer turned to the Stranger-boy, "Take Prince and the wagon! Ride in! Tell everybody! Put the corn in the blockhouse."

As he said it, he picked up Cleopatra by main strength and threw her into the wagon. He also grabbed a young boar and threw him in, too.

The Stranger-boy was on the wagon seat. "What about you, Mr. Woodbridge?"

"I'm bringin' the Bedfords. I'll find a place for them somewheres along the way."

Stranger-boy clucked to Prince, but to the chief's disgust Woodbridge stopped him and ran into the cabin. He came out with the document box and threw it under the wagon seat. Almost in the same motion he slapped Prince on the rump. The wagon rattled away.

Woodbridge put Boss in the lead, headed down the West Road, and drove the other Bedfords out behind Boss. Captain Michael gestured wildly and let out a stream of Wyandot. Silver Pigeon said: "He means, forget the animals, Mr. Woodbridge! Go!"

"I got to try, Silver Pigeon! Got to!" And he rapped the hogs unmercifully into a run, walking fast beside them. He looked back to see that the tail of the column was clearing the pen. Captain Michael poised his rifle, butt down, over the column of hogs, and there was a question on his face. Woodbridge nodded consent, and Captain Michael lowered his rifle into the column, turning back the last fifteen hogs or so, for himself and the mission Indians. Woodbridge figured the chief wouldn't have been so bold if he expected the hogs to survive the raid. It caused him to hurry.

Once under the heavy cover of the forest on the West Road, Woodbridge kept the hogs moving as fast as Boss would move. Desperately he searched the woods along the road for some gorge or crevice or especially dense patch where he could hide the animals. He found a couple of thickly brushed stream lines leading down to the river. But each time he hoped for a better place up ahead.

The hogs tired of running and slowed to a walk. The pace was insufferably slow. Some lay down in the snow along the way and would go no farther. When one animal lay down, others always followed the example. By noon Woodbridge had been on the road two hours, and the ones which were lying down now could not be made to rise. Nor did the redhead stop to try. For Thomas Woodbridge had heard the warning cannon fired from the blockhouse, and suddenly he knew fear, the kind that had stopped his breathing under the hickory log in the gorge on the night that he had burned his cabin. He felt that the hog hoofs crunching in the snow must be audible to the Indians.

Woodbridge walked backward much of the time now, watching to the rear. At the head of the column Boss waddled along, grunting whenever Woodbridge hurled a stick of wood at his rump. It was like a dream Woodbridge had often had, wherein he tried to hurry away from something but his feet would not move.

There was a ground tremor of pounding horse hoofs from behind, and Woodbridge abandoned the hogs to jump into the woods. He stopped running when he saw it was Mitchell, wild-eyed, driving his horse and wagon as fast as the snow would permit. The hogs blocked Mitchell, and Woodbridge came out of the trees.

Mitchell yelled, "You seen Adams?"

"No! Not for three days."

"His place—"

"Yeah, I know. Was he in it?"

"I don't know. But get in and come on!"

Woodbridge looked at his hogs still moving forward on the road and shook his head.

Mitchell's voice went to pieces like shattered pottery. "I said get in! Fool!"

Woodbridge went close to the wagon, but he did not get in. He bent down and scooped up two young pigs and threw them into the wagon atop a hodgepodge of goods.

"Get in, you fool! To hell with that!"

Woodbridge threw in two more young pigs. Then he pulled out one gilt and replaced it with a sow in-pig.

Mitchell yelled: "The hell with that, I say, Woodbridge! Are you comin'?"

Woodbridge reached for another pig, but Mitchell whipped his horse wildly down the ruts to the east.

When Mitchell was out of sight, Woodbridge felt very much alone and exposed. The herd was down to about forty now, Woodbridge guessed. He drove them unmercifully.

When the sun was well over to the west, Woodbridge saw Prince jogging toward him, the wagon on behind. The figure bouncing on the seat as the wheels bumped over snow-covered tree roots must be the Stranger-boy. But as the wagon rushed closer, Tom saw the fur jacket he had purchased from the Stranger. The hood was pulled up over the head of the driver. Woodbridge stared as Veronica pulled up without a word, turned the wagon around, and jumped to the ground. She caught hold of a medium boar, but couldn't lift him, and reached for a shoat instead.

"Good girl, Veronica!" he said.

And they both fell to grabbing hogs and throwing them into the wagon. Tom worked with a fierce callousness, but the woman could only put in the smallest ones, and often they wriggled away.

"Hurry, Tom!" she panted. "It's to be a bad raid!"

"The other ones get in all right with Stranger-boy and Mitchell?"

"Yes. But not inside the blockhouse."

"Wouldn't they even let Cleopatra inside? Hosmer knows how important she is!"

"Not one."

The hogs darted out of Woodbridge's way to avoid the manhandling. He tugged on Boss, but Boss was too heavy and he grabbed others.

"Where are they then?"

"Stranger-boy's keeping them herded right on the common!"

When the wagon was as full as Prince could haul with any speed, Woodbridge closed the tail gate and yelled: "Go now, Veronica! And don't chance another trip."

"You're coming, too!"

"Veronica, I got to get Boss in."

"Tom, it's enough we've saved! Come now!"

"No."

The wagon rattled east.

As Woodbridge and the remaining eighteen hogs closed the distance to the blockhouse, the plodding column passed the Hussong clearing. It was deserted.

The hogs had slowed down now to an exhausted dalliance. They would not respond to Woodbridge's switch. Once down on their bellies, they could not be prodded. That would have been all right except that this time it was Boss who was flat on his belly. Woodbridge shoved a three-inch branch under him and lifted. The stick pressed into Boss's soft belly, but Boss did not move. Woodbridge sawed the stick back and forth to irritate the heavy hog. Boss raised up a little, but when Woodbridge moved the stick he flopped back down again, his big jowls deep in the snow.

Woodbridge was cutting a heavier pole when Veronica returned a second time. Prince was lathered up and excited.

"I told you not to—" But Woodbridge stopped talking.

He drove the wagon into a slight depression in the ground. Leaping from the wagon, he laid the tailboard from higher ground to the bed of the wagon. With vicious haste now, he prodded Boss across the tailboard gangplank into the wagon. He put the tailboard back on the wagon and slammed home the bolts. He looked back to the west nervously.

"Go now, Veronica!"

"Both of us this time!" panted Veronica.

"No. One more trip'll do it."

"No! Now!"

Woodbridge looked at his wife's strangely knowing and adamant face, and jumped to the wagon seat. He slapped Prince.

"They still won't let 'em inside?"

"Not one. They say white hogs are no better'n woods hogs."

Woodbridge slapped the knotted end of the rein unmercifully across Prince. "I got no place else to put 'em," he muttered. It made the woman uneasy.

When they reached the blockhouse, Woodbridge commanded, "Get inside!"

Veronica went inside.

Outside, Tom saw that Stranger-boy was still holding the Bedfords in a neat pack. He completely unharnessed Prince, patted the animal's sweating neck gently, and then, without warning, struck the stallion across the haunches with the flat of his rifle stock.

"Good luck, Prince!"

From the rifle parapet Veronica called for Tom to come inside, as did Hosmer and Stikes. But Woodbridge dumped the Bedfords roughly out of the wagon, rounded up the others, and drove them to the block-house door.

The door did not open. Stikes called from the rifle parapet, "Nobody else brought theirs in, Tom! You don't either!"

"Mike, listen to me!"

But the redhead was drowned out by the yells from the parapet. The Stranger-woman called to her boy to come inside. Woodbridge particularly heard Exeter's voice: "We got women and kids in here crowded bad enough without you bring your swine in on us!"

"I tell ya I can't get more if these are gone! It's only the Bedfords. Not the others."

But his voice was lost in the confusion, for Hank Flannerty had just yelled from the lookout cupola that smoke rose over Hussong's place. Hussong's face appeared above the parapet, gazing west.

Woodbridge spoke quietly to the boy, who then walked up to the gate carrying the document box from the wagon.

"Let the boy in!" yelled Woodbridge.

The gate opened. The boy took one step forward. Woodbridge let out a piercing yell and drove the hogs for the opening. The gate swung quickly toward closing. But it stopped with a thump that shivered it on its hinges, leaving a two-foot gap. The men strained to shut it, but the Stranger-boy's document box was lodged firmly in the opening at the bottom. The hogs jarred the boy's sturdy body as they scraped against his legs, funneling into the blockhouse. A few turned to one side or the other, but most of them went through the gate.

Only a few of the hogs were abandoned outside when the first bullet splattered above the blockhouse gate, dropping bark chips down Woodbridge's neck as he dived for the door opening.

The first hour was such confusion that only fleeting impressions remained. Woodbridge remembered a moment of panic inside the blockhouse when he looked for Veronica and couldn't see her. When he did find her, she was bending over Flannerty, who had been knocked out of the lookout cupola in the first few minutes. He remembered he had studied her for a moment from a distance of about forty feet. The picture of her came to him in interrupted flashes, only a few seconds each, for people swarmed back and forth, cutting off the view. But he saw Veronica's mouth clamped tight against a monstrous nausea as Flannerty writhed, spreading the blood over Veronica's skirt. He saw her put a knee over his flailing arm and work over him. And he marveled at his wife.

He remembered seeing Fitchburg bending his height as he ran along the rifle parapet. He remembered seeing Hope Emerson climb to the parapet with her rifle. He remembered seeing Morgan Brady pull back from the parapet, seriously studying a hole in his fur hat. He remembered seeing Zabeth sitting on the floor. He remembered Stranger-boy struggling alongside him as they arranged piles of goods to form a fence, hemming the hogs into one corner. He especially remembered Jim Hawkins's fleeting, accusatory glance from the parapet. That reminded him of where he was supposed to be. He grabbed his rifle and climbed to the northwest bastion.

Hawkins and one of the three soldiers were already at their assigned firing ports. Hawkins was firing west. The soldier fired to the north. Woodbridge poked his rifle through the middle port that faced northwest. But he did not lay his cheek to the stock, and he kept his head well out of the opening. For it seemed to him that the hole was as big as a window and that every Wyandot in the northwest was watching the hole, waiting for his head to appear in it. He looked at Hawkins's back, wondering how the mild Hawkins first brought himself to put his eye to the firing port.

Hawkins pulled his smoking barrel out of the hole to run a ramrod through it. His powder-stained face turned toward Woodbridge reproved the redhead's cold gun, and in that instant Woodbridge suddenly understood that the difference between a veteran and a recruit is a matter of minutes. He lowered his head against the stock of his rifle, and looked for something to fire at.

A little flurry of snow flew up fifty yards to his front, and a patch of white smoke grew there. He thought he heard a report from that direction, but in the din he couldn't tell. By then there was another flurry of snow to the right of the first, and another patch of smoke. Woodbridge shifted his rifle, but there was nothing to fire at. Some dried brown scrub oak leaves fluttered violently to the north, and a patch of black smoke grew over the bushes. Woodbridge squeezed his trigger, but when the smoke cleared he felt he'd sent good lead for nothing. He felt useless, inept, a waste.

As he reloaded, a scream from his left jerked Woodbridge's head around in time to see Jess Hussong reel back against the railing, his mouth open, his hand to his left eye. Bright red ran down his left forearm toward the elbow.

Woodbridge shoved his rifle through the port. Now, for the first time, he sensed clearly the murderous synchronism between the tiny muzzle blasts in the snow and the simultaneous flat slap of lead against the blockhouse walls. He fired at the snow flurries and at the smoke. He fired at the odd bulges on the sides of trees and at foreign brown patches in the snow. He fired quickly and with hatred.

There were more Indians here than merely Rontondee's clan of Wyandots. There were a few of the long queues of black hair from the Shawnees. There were some that Stikes said were Delawares.

Hosmer walked along the catwalk.

"Every other man go down and eat!" he said. "Make it fast and get back up so's the others can eat!"

Woodbridge was the alternate man. He climbed down the ladder. At the bottom rung Veronica stood waiting for him with a trencher of hominy and a noggin of sassafras tea. He shook his head, dismissing the food, not unkindly, but completely. He put his hand on her shoulder.

"You and the babe all right?"

"Yes, Tom. I watched you up there," she said.

Because she seemed proud of what he had done, what he had to do now was hard.

"Veronica, if I do something you think is wrong, I don't ask you to like it, but only to—"

However, others were coming down the ladder, and he was suddenly separated from her in the crowded blockhouse. Veronica did glimpse his red hair moving toward the east wall as he shouldered his way toward the hogs.

Tom found that in the rush and confusion his bulk corn had been piled with that of others. Though he couldn't tell which belonged to him, he began throwing ears of corn behind the barricade of personal property which fenced the hogs off from the women and children in the blockhouse. Since it was precious, Woodbridge threw the corn carefully, distributing the ears evenly among the hungry hogs. Occasionally he stepped among them to move the shoats and young pigs to one end where they'd have a chance at feeding. Old hogs nipped the young ones, snapping the cobs away from them.

Hope Emerson's large iron kettle was on the pile of property. Woodbridge grabbed it and walked to the tripod from which hung a deerskin full of water. Crouched on the floor, Woodbridge was untying the leg which served as a spigot to the bag when he noticed the crowd crystallizing around him.

Exeter said, "What you aim to do with that water, Woodbridge?"

"The hogs."

"That's what I thought. I'm in charge of keepin' that bag full. And I say no water for swine while there's people needs it for drinkin' and swabbin' the wounds of them that's up where they belong, at the rifle ports."

"The hogs ran half the way in here. They're without feed and water since morning."

Exeter's answer was not to the point, but it was telling. "Jess Hussong's without an eye. His wife may be without a husband. Your hogs can go without feed and water."

Without taking water, Woodbridge tied up the water bag and walked back to his hogs. The crowd did not break up, but drifted over behind him. The corn he had fed to the hogs had only made them hungrier. Woodbridge was throwing in more ears when an angry hand stayed his arm. It was Fitchburg.

"You devil! You can't go feedin' that corn to hogs while there's humans here!"

Woodbridge shook off Fitchburg's grip.

"I sent in a load with the boy. I can feed my own corn."

"I don't know anything about you sendin' in any corn. But even if you did, critters don't eat durin' siege!"

The crowd pressed closer.

"If you could see to the end of your nose," yelled Woodbridge, "you'd know these hogs should eat even before the people! Your cattle and your horses and your ox are in the woods. What are ya gonna eat if we get out of this?"

Fitchburg tried to break in, but the hog farmer was raging now.

"And if you're not lyin', there's not a man of ya's gonna come through with anything left over for seed. Most of ya claim ya can't feed your kids through March! Those hogs are the only brutes that'll breed fast enough and grow big enough ta feed ya. You're either blind or lyin'! Else you'd be beggin' me to take care of these critters!"

It was logic and the truth; but it was sacrilege in the face of Jess Hussong's shot-out eye. It was as though the redhead had stuck his thumb in the searing wound on Hank Flannerty's chest, and the crowd would not stand for it.

Fitchburg yanked Woodbridge off the pile of gear where he stood scooping bulk corn into the hog enclosure.

Several angry hands grabbed Tom, but the redhead's hard body was charged with a fury beyond the strength of muscles. Even as they tugged at him, he grabbed a deerskin of someone else's corn and flung it at the wall over the hogs so that it burst and showered corn down into their enclosure. As the hogs swarmed over the corn, the crowd dragged Woodbridge down off the pile. That was when Hosmer wedged through the mob angrily. He grabbed Fitchburg and Exeter and shoved them toward the ladder.

"You fools! You want to live or die!"

The men took new powder and ball and climbed aloft to the parapet. They were firing rapidly in the dark at a clamoring horde of savages who seemed to have smelled the food inside.

Woodbridge was about to climb to the rifle ramp. At the foot of the ladder Veronica met him with an apron full of lead bullets and a horn full of powder. Her face was a noncommittal mask, but she was there. Woodbridge knew by her silence that she was humiliated; but he also knew by her presence, waiting for him, that she was worth every woman in Mesopotamia. He also knew, in the same moment, that if she were only his friend as well as his wife, he could outface the world. As Thomas Woodbridge climbed the ladder, he was a lonely man.

Woodbridge stepped into the northwest bastion to his firing post, but his place was taken. Hawkins loaded his rifle without looking up to explain why Hope Emerson fired from the redhead's port. Woodbridge walked along the parapet and found an empty port between Stikes and Exeter. But as he poked his rifle through, Stikes said: "Mitchell's there. Just went for a ramrod."

He walked along toward the southwest bastion. But it was a relief when Hosmer came by, grabbed him briskly by the arm, and said, "Woodbridge, I need you over by—"

There was a yell from Brady. "The devils are burnin' my place!"

Indian firing seemed to slacken as Brady's cabin illuminated the area north of the blockhouse. As the men stared through the ports to the north, Buttrick yelled from his post on the east wall, "Fire in the store!"

Hosmer went below. Rifle fire from the Wyandots had almost ceased, but a light also broke out beyond the store, about where Hope Emerson's place was. The sky was turning red. There was one red reflection in the sky way out to the west.

The panic that broke inside the blockhouse welled from the sickening realization in every man that Rontondee had changed to demolition tactics. There was no defense from inside the blockhouse, and each man knew that the next patch of light might be his own cabin.

The rush was started by Brady, who left his post. He spurned the ladder and jumped down from the parapet. He ran for the west door, yelling. Hosmer grabbed him by the arm, but Brady shook the older man off and drove for the door. Hawkins jumped down to follow, and the surge for the door was begun.

Brady had pried loose the log that jammed the door closed. He was partly out when Stikes grabbed him and jerked him back. The press of men fortunately jammed the door shut. Together Stikes and Hosmer stood before the door and yelled, but Mesopotamia was not listening.

Woodbridge had dropped from the parapet to the top of the pile of goods beside the hogs. He grabbed an ear of corn and fired it over the heads of the crowd against the door so that it peppered hard kernels among them, startling the panic to an instant of quiet.

"Wait! Wait!" he yelled.

"Wait, hell!" Exeter challenged. "They're burnin' the cabins!"

"And you won't stop them by goin' out there!"

As Woodbridge and the mob exchanged insults, Hosmer worked himself into a better position to hold the door.

"Stop your miserable babblin'," yelled Woodbridge, "and help me shunt these hogs out there! Those Indians are hungry!"

Stikes and Brady got the idea immediately, and others followed. They jumped over the barricade and opened a path for the hogs to the gate.

"Wait a minute! Save the sows! Send the boars!" But Woodbridge's command was drowned in the frenzy. The men drove the hogs out indiscriminately.

Woodbridge spotted the Stranger-boy.

"They're out of their heads, boy! Try to hold back the sows!"

With both hands, Brady was heaving corn out in front of the hogs, forming a trail which the hogs followed toward the Indians. Woodbridge saw Cleopatra being herded toward the door by the butt of Exeter's rifle. Tom leaped over several hogs and rammed his elbow into Exeter's chest, knocking him to the floor. Cleopatra was out the door. Woodbridge followed, ripping loose from Stikes's grip. Sliding on his belly in the snow, he caught Cleopatra's hind leg with both hands. The frightened animal shook her hind leg powerfully, and dragged him for several rods through the snow as the other hogs trampled over him. She dragged him over the sharp stumps of small cutover brush. His foot caught a small stump and held.

He got to his feet and dragged Cleopatra back toward the gate. It was the first time Thomas Woodbridge had ever heard the special hurtling *whang* of death-close flying lead. Struggling back against the current of frightened onrushing hogs, Woodbridge dragged Cleopatra inside the blockhouse. Stikes slammed the gate.

The men had scrambled back up to the rifle ramp, but Hosmer yelled: "Don't fire! Let the Indians come after the hogs!"

Veronica was beside the panting redhead, opening up his shredded leather shirt. Woodbridge was looking frantically around the inside of the blockhouse, searching. Veronica said, "The boy's got him safe over there."

In the southeast corner Stranger-boy was building a barricade around Boss.

The night was filled with the intermingled screams of hogs and

Wyandots. Despite Rontondee's screaming, the red men abandoned the cabin-burning to converge on the hogs. From the rifle ramp, by the light of the three burning cabins, Mesopotamia watched the carnage as the Wyandots fell upon the white animals, leaving the snow dark with the blood of the Bedfords.

And if there was also spilled onto that snow some of the lifeblood of Thomas Woodbridge, it was best known to Veronica and the Stranger-boy, who watched silently as the hog farmer's big hands unconsciously wrung the empty deerskin corn sack that he held. His sweating face glistened red as he stared out through one of the lower rifle ports. The shrieks and squeals of the Bedfords sliced him like bayonets.

Small fires could be seen throughout the area, glowing behind a cover of trees or a rise of ground. But they were not cabins burning. The Wyandots were roasting hogs.

There was some desultory firing throughout the night, but for the most part the hungry Indians had given themselves up to feasting. And Rontondee could not rally them.

Although Hosmer ordered the men at every alternate rifle port to sleep, they could not sleep. Most of the men stood alert throughout the night.

The cabin fires had died to a dull glow when Stikes announced the faint knocking at the southeast corner. Stikes and Hosmer and Dolk stood debating whether to open the door. As they argued, the knocking moved under the floor. And as they followed the sound, it led them to the trap door which Stikes had built into the floor for storing rations. Stikes and Exeter trained rifles on the trap while Hosmer pulled it back. Up out of the dark hole came Elisha Adams.

They grabbed him quickly by the arms and pulled him out.

"I got word to Navarre," he said. "He's comin'."

"With troops?" asked Hosmer.

"No. Troops are promised, but not coming fast enough."

"What good's Navarre without troops?"

"He's got better'n that. Got squatters."

Men had come down from the rifle ramp to listen. Hosmer's growl ordered most of them back to keep guard. Adams continued.

"Navarre's workin' north from Boxford's Cabin. Probably about here now. They knew down there already that you were drove in. So Navarre says don't fire in the morning till it's light enough to see what you're shootin' at. And don't fire into the cabins. He plans to occupy 'em under darkness. Then if the devils attack the blockhouse, he'll close in. Or if they go for the cabins, they'll get theirselves a hot welcome."

The plan was spread from man to man along the rifle ramp. Lucy Adams and Loretta Shane hugged each other as the men asked Adams whispered questions about Navarre.

"Navarre says it isn't workin' out in the legislature," Adams explained. "He can't talk good enough to make 'em take notice."

"Did he ask for troops?" said Hosmer.

"Yeah. They put him off with promises. Besides, they're gonna put Navarre in jail. Can't do it while he's legislatin', but if they catch him away from the legislature they can arrest him."

"For what? Those murders Armstrong talked about?"

"Nope. They can't prove anything about that."

"Then what can they jail him for?"

"Treason, they're gonna call it."

Loretta shook in sobbing anguish, and Lucy Adams held her tighter. Stikes's face froze with his lips drawn back in disbelief.

"Treason?"

"Treason."

Adams lowered himself back into the hole, but Lucy Adams tugged at his shirt. "Why must you go back to him?"

"He's expecting me, Lucy."

"But the men here all know the plan. There's no need you should risk the trip out. Why must you go? Why?"

Adams's simple answer revealed to Mesopotamia, as nothing yet had, the power that lay in the hands of Slover Navarre.

"Because Navarre's expectin' me, Lucy." And he slipped down into the hole.

On the following morning the people of Mesopotamia had further evidence of Navarre's strength. So did Rontondee.

For Slover Navarre sprung his trap.


The Wyandots were less wary on full stomachs, and as Rontondee began his very first assault on the blockhouse the Indians moved in boldly. Since little fire was returned from the blockhouse, they began to spurn cover, running and firing in the open.

The reports from Navarre's rifles behind the Indians did not at first register with them, for the advancing braves assumed that they came from other Indian rifles. But from the northwest bastion Woodbridge saw the realization come to Rontondee as his Indians slammed to the ground, face down. As Rontondee whirled to face the mystery to his rear, a slug from the blockhouse split the stock of his rifle. He spun back to the blockhouse and a shot from the rear grooved the muscle of his forearm and bloodied the snow at his feet.

Rontondee ran screaming to the north.

Those Indians who could find a way out of the trap fled into the woods.

Captain Michael seemed to feel that in view of Indian concessions the white man should at least learn the savage tongue. And as Woodbridge and Veronica arrived at the cabin, he let out a stream of Wyandot and gestured to the cabin with his open hand, as though making a grand presentation of some kind.

Silver Pigeon translated. "Captain Michael said this is his gift to you. He stayed here and told the Wyandots to spare it, saying the red-top had given much corn to Indians. The Wyandots took the corn and left the redtop's house stand."

Captain Michael took Woodbridge by the arm and led him forcibly out to the shed, to which he pointed, again waiting with an expectant grin.

Silver Pigeon explained. "Redtop's horse came back. Captain Michael tied him."

But as Silver Pigeon spoke, the beatific grin faded instantly from the old Indian's face to be replaced with reproach and disappointment as he studied the puny remains of the great hog herd which Stranger-boy drove out to the pen. His guttural Indian language spewed out in an angry stream.

"Captain Michael asks," said Silver Pigeon, "where is the great tribe of heavenly white hogs?"

Woodbridge drew his finger across his neck and said, "Rontondee!"

Captain Michael shook his head slowly.

Jess Hussong's funeral was held on Sunday, and Woodbridge and Veronica went in. The crowd gathered around the burying ground, waiting for the Reverend Seth Gershom. It was a day and a half down from the mission, and they were not certain that the minister would come. Knowing this, the village was angrily predisposed against him;

but before the sun was dead overhead Seth Gershom rode slowly out of the woods.

Woodbridge noticed that Gershom's clothes hung looser on his bony frame. The eye caverns were deeper now, and the cheekbones appeared almost to stab through the white skin stretched over them.

A few minutes after the preacher arrived, Silver Pigeon rode out of the woods, and two rods behind Silver Pigeon came Captain Michael. Stretched between them were the Bedfords that Michael had appropriated on the day of the raid. As everyone watched, Captain Michael drove them up to Woodbridge.

"Only one we ate," said Silver Pigeon. "Captain Michael gives them back. Says Fire Top needs the heavenly white pigs."

Woodbridge laid a hand on Michael's shoulder.

"Thanks, Cap'n Michael. But take them back. I can't feed them. That would give me a total of twenty-two."

A stream of insistent Wyandot came from Michael.

"Red Top will find a way to feed," translated Silver Pigeon.

Woodbridge grinned feebly at their confidence in him.


Woodbridge noticed that Gershom's sermon was delivered in a quieter voice than usual. But in the middle of the service he looked up from the mound of hard, chipped dirt surrounded by snow and glanced toward the river. Then he looked quickly down at Loretta and Isaac Shane. Drawing himself up, his voice boomed out with all its old strength, but with a mysterious emphasis. The words did not seem to follow the previous sentence.

"And if there be one here who at this very moment carries upon his soul a burden of blood and a fear of pursuit, let him rise up now and hide himself in the forest of oblivion." Gershom dropped his voice, but he pointed a long, scraggly arm directly at Isaac Shane and enunciated with deep overtones of doom, "For the soldiery of Heaven and Earth pursues ye."

Loretta Shane's hand went to her breast, but Navarre's face split in a sacrilegious grin.

Gershom took a step closer to Navarre, and the intensity in his eyes wiped the grin off Navarre's face. Slover glanced nervously in the direction of the river, then rose and left the group, walking quickly behind the blockhouse.

The crowd turned to see what Navarre had seen. Splashing across the river on horseback came a platoon of regulars. Well in advance of the head of the column rode John Armstrong.

Mesopotamia stirred and broke into a murmuring grumble.

"Four days too late, they come."

"Lookit their pretty blue uniforms. A pity Jess Hussong couldn't see 'em."

"They prob'ly been moseyin' up from Fort Washington. Coulda made it if they'd pushed."

The soldiers saw the black mound of earth in the snow. They advanced sheepishly, and Woodbridge noticed that Gershom's voice suddenly boomed out in benediction for their benefit:

"And may the humble cross on the grave of Jess Hussong stand in eternal rebuke to those who dally in the fleshpots of ease dressed in the garish trappings of officialdom while men perish on the fringe of civilization in plain leather skins and with empty bellies!"

Tom knelt by the hearth working with the fire when the knock came at the Woodbridge cabin door.

It was Sam Hosmer, Mike Stikes, Exeter, Fitchburg, and Hawkins. Woodbridge lowered his gun, but it remained for Veronica to ask them in.

Hosmer stepped over the sill and removed his hat.

"Hello, Veronica."

There was some shuffling for position as they arranged themselves awkwardly in the small room. They faced Woodbridge, who said with little warmth, "Yes?"

Old man Hosmer spoke.

"Tom, it's talked around that ye took a half-skin of corn from Hawkins and a half from Fitchburg."

"I bought it, if that's what you mean by 'took.' And aim to pay somehow. It's too late to give it back, if it's your thought. It's gone. Didn't last a full day."

"Point is," said Hosmer, "ye got no corn."

"That's right."

"Well, point is, Tom, it 'pears perhaps lot of us could be indebted t' those hogs of yours, the ones that was kilt, for our cabins standin' today."

Woodbridge's face relaxed its guard. Hosmer continued.

"Well, we got no corn to turn over to ye, in bulk. That is, no man likes to take a dip out of his larder and give it away. He'd maybe give away more'n he can spare. But we figured what with table scraps and a little corn now and then, well, prob'ly each family could keep one hog alive till thaw, when maybe they can survive on grazin' and such. Or at least maybe we could each keep one of your hogs alive till you could figure out somethin' and take 'em back from us."

Water came into Veronica's eyes as she saw Tom's face soften with understanding.

There was no food in the house to spare, but Veronica poured a noggin of whisky for each man. Her activity covered the silence of Woodbridge, who seemed unable to answer.

" 'Course, if you'd be worried," continued Hosmer, "about how we'd treat the hogs . . ."

Woodbridge's nostrils dilated as he struggled for speech. His face colored.

"Tell you what I'll do." Tom paused for control of his voice. His rock-like chin crinkled and melted. He pulled an old rag from his pocket and blew his nose violently.

"If you'll do that, I'll board out with ya all sows that've been served. Any man brings a sow through to farrowing for me . . . he can keep all the boars in the litter for himself for ham meat."

# *Chapter 14: THE ELECTION (1805)*

As the spring of 1805 seeped in, all bounte-ousness faded from the United States Bounty Lands.

On very slim rations the men rebuilt cabins for Brady, for the Hussong widow, for Hope Emerson. At Hosmer's insistence his own cabin-store was the last to be rebuilt. The rebuilding was not so rapidly completed as the original raisings had been.

No new settlers had arrived, for news of the Indian raid had reached the East, and settlers stayed away from the hostile Greenville Line.

True to Hosmer's prediction of long ago, the Stranger had left. So little of the place had clung to him, that his leaving, with all his gear, had been the work of an hour. There were no goodbyes—none, at least, that anyone could hear. For none saw the probing intensity of the gaze from Tom to the Stranger-woman, in which he wondered "Why? And what will happen to you out there in the big woods?"

Not even Tom could read the stoic answer on her handsome face. All he knew was the question she asked aloud.

"Can the boy stay with you?"

Stranger-boy stayed. He did twice as much work as a twelve-year-old boy should, but because of it he ate more of the Woodbridge store of roots and salt and pork and coffee than a twelve-year-old should.

Veronica was pale and wan, and Zabeth was thin.

Boss and Cleopatra had lost weight. The hogs which the settlers had boarded for Woodbridge through the winter showed their ribs. Even the woods hogs had not done well.

Woodbridge's temper was as short as the fleeting March warmth that came only at high noon, and then only in the lee of the cabin.

In the matter of Woodbridge you had to take sides. You were either for him or against him. You might change sides often, but you changed all the way—either for him or against him.

In March, 1805, the five men in Hosmer's Store were against him.

Woodbridge entered the conversation late, but soon enough to despise what he heard.

Sam Hosmer was saying, "So ye see, the time has come when we need a board of trustees to run the town. We need an overseer of the poor, one constable, one property appraiser, one justice of the peace, two fence viewers, and one treasurer. Spread the word there'll be a meetin' here tonight, and we'll figure out how to run this election."

Stikes nodded his head thoughtfully. Brady said, "Sure."

Hosmer turned to Woodbridge. "Can you get the word to Mitchell and Adams, Tom?"

The redhead exploded.

"A-ah! Y'make me sick! Half of ya fought the King, or your fathers did, to git free of gover'ment. Now you're startin' it all over again out here. Fence viewers! Tax appraisers! Overseers of the poor! Petty royalty!"

Stikes's voice was calm.

"'Tain't that a-tall, Tom. Fact is, havin' no town government has been an almighty burden on a few of us."

"And havin' one'll be a sight more burden!" said the redhead. "We'll have rules and regulations and pronouncements and bylaws; and all I want is to raise my hogs and be left alone! I come out here to be rid of that nonsense."

"You been pretty much left alone, Tom," said Stikes. "Sam Hosmer's been carryin' most of the load of gettin' things done around here."

Stanley-the-Slasher concurred. "And Sam can do it with one hand tied. But—beggin' your pardon, Sam—Sam won't be here forever."

"Hogwash!" said Woodbridge. "Just what you been doin', Sam, that's so blasted hard to handle? I see ya runnin' down to county on some nonsense once in a while, but—"

"Watch your tongue!" Stikes stepped forward.

"Let him talk, Mike." Sam Hosmer was unruffled. "What's your idea about it, Tom?"

"My idea is it's time somebody talked up to you, Sam. Everybody around here jumps when you hoot. Well, there's a few around town that—"

"That would like to see Tom Woodbridge running things?"

"That's right."

"And I've been glad to see it, Tom, hopin' you'd take hold of some of the chores around town. But I've not see ye doin' it. So we'll just go ahead with our meeting tonight to plan the election."

"A-ah!" The redhead moved for the door. But as he reached for the handle he froze, because pegged to the wall was a piece of newspaper torn from an old copy of the Boston *Columbian Centinel*.

"Elnathan Shuldane, in his new prospectus advertising lots for sale in his tract in the Bounty Lands, states that there will be an election of town officials there this spring. The presence of town officials on the tract called Mesopotamia will control the infiltration of squatters on the lands and will secure better recognition for the settlers at county seat and at Chillicothe, the new state's capital. But principally, Shuldane declares that the town government will assure prospective buyers of a high state of civilization and justice, contrary to reports about lands situated so close to the Greenville Indian Boundary."

Woodbridge yanked the clipping into a wad which he tossed on the floor. "How much did this have to do with us needin' a gover'ment all of a sudden?"

Woodbridge went to Hawkins's cabin and spoke without preliminaries.

"Jim, I'm building a hog shed tonight. Need your help."

"Make it tomorrow night, Tom. There's a meeting tonight at Hosmer's."

"Got to build it tonight, Jim. For good reasons."

"But—"

"The hogs served you well enough through the winter. You got a litter of eight. Least you can do is help me build a hog shed—tonight."

Christian Kilgore had built a cabin just west of Hussong Creek. Woodbridge stopped there, and Kilgore agreed to come to the shed raising. Mitchell and Adams came also, though they called it strange that a hog shed should be needed in such a hurry with Tom's herd so depleted.

During the building of the hog shed, Hawkins noticed that Woodbridge didn't have the same interest that he had had when the last one was raised. And when it was finished there wasn't the same satisfying feeling, nor the comradeship. The men left soon after the job was done.

As Woodbridge and the Stranger-boy rode past Hosmer's Store next day, the men on the porch failed to answer his wave. Woodbridge and Stranger-boy rode up toward Amos Exeter's cabin.

Woodbridge asked Exeter, "How was the meeting last night, about the election?"

"Why, there was no meeting, just as you planned it, Woodbridge, when you pulled those men out to work on your hog shed."

"No reason not to have the meeting, just because some of us didn't come."

"You knew well enough you killed the meeting. And you made a mistake, Tom."

In the next few days the hog farmer saw an unaccustomed flow of traffic crossing the West Road to his place. Hope Emerson rode up to the first hog pen, where Woodbridge was feeding the shoats which Mesopotamia had returned to him from the sows he had boarded out. Her voice had the alto of a young man's.

"Tom, I stopped to tell you the Flannerty children in town are in trouble. Kids haven't eaten in couple days. Hank's down in county jail. The woman's kind of dauncy."

"Why tell me?"

"Can't let 'em hunger t' death."

"'Course not. Go do somethin' about it."

"I have, for about a month. But it's to the point where I can hardly get by myself."

"Seems odd you should come way out here to tell me when there's so many others in there."

"I told Sam Hosmer first. He sent me out here. Said you'd know what to do."

Woodbridge put down his bucket.

"Hosmer said that?"

"Said you'd understand."


Woodbridge left for Hosmer's Store on Thursday to catch Buttrick before the trader left for Cincinnati. Buttrick could stop at the county seat and see about getting Flannerty out of the jail. However, when Woodbridge reached the freshet that poured into the river by Hussong's cabin, the east bank had washed away, dropping the east end of the bridge into the creek. Woodbridge unhitched the wagon, and Prince stepped gingerly over the fallen bridge, causing it to sag more.

At the store Woodbridge had missed Buttrick, but Stikes and Exeter and Jim Hawkins and a few others were there.

"Need a few hands to help fix up the bridge over Hussong Creek," Woodbridge announced.

The redhead was surprised at the stony silence. It was as if they had never heard of Hussong Creek.

"East bank, washed out," he explained. "Timbers dropped down into the water. Only two hours for four, five men."

On such occasions Hosmer usually grabbed his hat, named off the best-suited men within his sight, and the job was begun; but on this day he turned around, walked slowly into the back of the store and into his cabin.

"Well, who's comin'?" chafed Woodbridge.

No one answered. Woodbridge looked at Amos Exeter.

"Come on, Amos."

"Sorry, Tom. Don't have time."

"Neither's anybody else, I see. But most everybody uses the bridge a time or two a week."

"Can't deny that, Tom. I'll be glad when you git it fixed."

Woodbridge stiffened. "All right! Brace your feet like cranky hogs if you want. But if it comes down to it, you *got* to help. The state says every man gives two days a year to the road, and a team of horses if necessary!"

Hawkins looked down at his boots. Dolk stood stolid and mute. Exeter said, "Maybe that's the law, Woodbridge, but where's the constable to make us do it? You don't favor electin' one."

"You always did it for Hosmer without a constable."

"Sure. Old Man Hosmer carried my store bill for ten months. But I ain't beholdin' to you, Woodbridge."

As the hog farmer slammed the door shut, he heard the voices come to life behind him, including Brady's big laugh.

It was dark before Woodbridge had half the bridge repaired. He was down in the creek shoving one of the stringers into place with his back when Mordecai Mason rode up. Woodbridge hollered for him to grab hold of the end of the stringer and lift. " 'Bout time somebody showed up to help."

"I'll lift the stringer, Tom, but I can't stay to help. Just stopped to tell you I come by the blockhouse, and there's nobody on Indian watch there."

"It's not *my* night. Why tell me?"

"I told Hosmer. He said tell you."

Woodbridge lowered the timber and straightened up.

"What in tarnation for?"

"I don't know. But if anything happens, don't forget I told ya."

He saw Hosmer's method. But two could play at that. The blockhouse watch served the in-town people more than those to the west anyhow. They'd best stir themselves to worry about the watch. But the receding hoofbeats of Mason's horse had left a gnawing echo that whispered, "If anything happens, remember I told ya."

Woodbridge yanked the store door open, but Hosmer left his back to him and let him stand there while he sat reading an old copy of the Scioto *Gazette*.

"There's nobody on Indian watch," said Woodbridge abruptly.

"Says in the *Gazette* here, Tom, that there's land down at the mouth of the Scioto bringin' $20 an acre. Can you figure that?"

"Sam, I said there's no watch!"

Hosmer turned a page. Woodbridge burned.

"I see you don't intend doin' anything," fumed Woodbridge. "Tell me who's supposed to be on. I'll get him."

Hosmer continued reading, absently handing over the guard list. Woodbridge studied it, but it was all crossed over and altered and hen scratched, with arrows reversing the order of names.

"I can't tell anything from this, Sam. Least you can do is tell me who's due. That's simple enough."

Hosmer put down the paper.

"Glad it's simple for ye, Tom. Never was fer me. Stikes was on last night, but Polly got sick. So I had Exeter relieve Stikes 'bout midnight, little after. Now tonight's Exeter's regular night, but he's not back from Boxford's Cabin yet. So you tell me. Who should be on?"

"Simple. I'll get Stikes to take over for Exeter tonight till midnight. Then Exeter'll be back to relieve him."

"Uh-huh. 'Course time Exeter gets back, will he be fresh enough to keep good sharp watch the rest of the night?"

Woodbridge scratched his head. He thought he detected the faint shape of a grin among the myriad wrinkles astride Hosmer's mouth, but he couldn't be sure. He stomped out of the store.

By the time Woodbridge was ready to start home over the West Road, he had heard five bona fide excuses why five men couldn't stand guard that night. He had finally got Hawkins to do it. But it was as though he had asked a personal favor, and even in the dark he slumped into the slinking posture of the unwilling debtor. He got home at midnight.

When the maple leaves were the size of squirrel ears, Woodbridge wanted to get his seed in. But Hope Emerson came to the cabin to say that the Flannerty children were hungry. Woodbridge dropped his planting for the two-day trip to county.

He was relieved to find that the sheriff was a man more like Mike Stikes. He had expected a fancy man like Blair, who would comfluster him with law talk. The sheriff's name was Job Hill, and his tone was reasonable.

"Mr. Woodbridge, we don't want to keep this Flannerty here any more'n you want us to. We didn't even want much to arrest him. Fact, we didn't even have a jail to put him in. Had to build it, special. But for what he did, the commissioners said he'd have to be locked up."

"When can he get out?" asked Woodbridge.

Hill was disappointed at the redhead's lack of curiosity about Flannerty's offense, but he was impressed by Tom's singleness of purpose.

"Flannerty can go any time now, Woodbridge."

"Good, I'll take him with me now."

"Not so fast. The county wants some money to pay for what he ate and part of the cost of buildin' the jail. But Flannerty doesn't have any money. So that leaves the county only one way to get its money back. We got to send him down to Fort Washington to the army. They'll pay his fine, they're that hungry for troops."

Woodbridge's jaw clamped, bringing out a diagonal line in each cheek.

"How much does the county want to let Flannerty go?"

"Fifteen dollars."

"Fifteen! What did Flannerty do that's so bad?"

"Ask him. He tells the truth. Be better if he didn't."

Flannerty had not suffered much. He was clean, and apparently had been fed regularly. But Woodbridge thought Flannerty's bewildered face was like that of the Stranger-boy's dog, Wolf, when he was not permitted to follow the men into the cabin at night after working with them in the field all day. Flannerty pounded his knuckles against the log wall.

"Tom, I came out here with two one-hundred-acre bounty warrants. Mine and my brother's. Gave one to Shuldane for my twenty acres in Mesopotamia. I was clutchin' the other for my oldest boy. But when they made the law sayin' a man had to have four thousand acres' worth of warrants before he could occupy, why then I gave up. The hungry month came, and I sold the warrant to an agent down here. A pig named Ault."

"For how much?"

"Eight dollars. For eight cents an acre I sold my brother's warrant."

Woodbridge swore, as much at Flannerty as at the agent.

"Then," continued Flannerty, "Buttrick told how they changed that law so's y'only needed a thousand acres of certificates. Then they cut it down again so's y'needed only 640 acres in one purchase. Then I heard how you and those two squatters worked it, puttin' your warrants together and gettin' your full warrants' worth of land. And I thought about how I gave mine away for eight cents an acre, and I come stormin' down here to find the agent. I found him in the tavern and I—"

Flannerty's voice cracked. But Woodbridge looked at the skinned knuckles on Flannerty's left hand and motioned the Irishman silent. "Yeah, I see."

Woodbridge's stony countenance was at once contempt and sympathy for Flannerty and hatred for the warrant agent. But Woodbridge reserved a special kind of bitterness for the end man in the transaction.

"Who bought the warrant from the agent?" asked Woodbridge.

Flannerty choked, silent with rage.

"Who bought the warrant from the agent?" asked Woodbridge.

"Shuldane." Flannerty hammered the wall. Woodbridge stared out the door.

Woodbridge had ridden down to county contemptuous of Flannerty, wanting to get him home just to take care of his own kids. He now rode back to Mesopotamia wanting to get Flannerty free for another reason. He felt a kinship with the unfortunate Irishman.

The trip had also been good for him. He had had a somewhat intimidating idea about county seat. But "county" was nothing but a group of men like Stikes and Exeter and Mitchell.

But the most important information was that Shuldane was buying more warrants. Why? Woodbridge didn't talk about it at the store. He wanted to think about it, first. But they all listened eagerly as Tom explained about Flannerty. When he told about Hank's warrant going for eight cents an acre, Stikes swung Hosmer's bung mallet against a projecting rafter dowel, driving it flush. But the men's interest seemed to cool off when Woodbridge got to his point.

"So we got to raise $15, somehow, to get Hank out."

There were no volunteers.

"You're handlin' it, Tom," said Mason.

"Now if we had a duly elected town treasurer," Exeter said, "it'd be a simple matter. But we don't."

Woodbridge got fifty cents from Mitchell and fifty cents from Adams. Veronica got fifty cents from Faith Hawkins, and when she casually remarked that it was the same contribution the Adamses had made, Faith added twenty-five cents more. It was her estimate of the social differential.

Asa Buttrick gave Woodbridge nothing, but when Veronica approached him he contributed a quarter-eagle. Veronica had not seen a $2½ gold piece since she left Massachusetts. Stikes, approached privately, put in a dollar. But in all, Woodbridge had only $8.50. It had come reluctantly, and mostly, Woodbridge feared, from those who had their mind on a return favor from him.

In the following week Woodbridge tried to get his seed in, but while trying to get his own corn sown he was also supporting the Flannerty kids and trying to raise $7 more to get Flannerty out of jail.

Hosmer's tacit plan was well understood by now, and Woodbridge hated to go in to town. There was always some exception to the guard roster. Someone always had a good reason not to stand his regular night. Woodbridge stood two nights in one week himself.

The question of repairing the door of the blockhouse came up. There was some talk that Exeter had no business plowing up the ground where the common was going to be located. Woodbridge let that go; but whenever he came to town there was some other problem shifted to his shoulders.

Over the weeks Veronica watched those shoulders sag. She saw his defensive withdrawal when Brutus Christofferson walked into the cabin one evening to introduce himself.

"Brutus Christofferson's the name. Got a bounty warrant for a hundred acres. Didn't feel like sellin' to one of them land sharks. But I can't locate on only a hundred. Hosmer, in town, said you'd found a way of workin' it somehow."

When he'd left, Veronica said, "You should rest more, Tom."

"Veronica, I've got to have some help. I went down to county and offered them the $10 for Flannerty, puttin' in two of ours. They wouldn't take it. They're sendin' Flannerty to the army next Wednesday. And somebody's got to check the fences and keep the guard roster, and who's gonna look after Flannerty's kids?"

"Tom, let's post a notice of a public meeting in the blockhouse. Tell the people about the Flannerty children and about the system that's needed."

Woodbridge looked at his wife as he had on the day she recognized Armstrong's sergeant. He got her one of Hope Emerson's charcoal pencils and gave her the old guard list, turned over on the blank side.

"Write it out, Wife."

She wrote the notice and he was out the door with it.

"Wait," she said. "Tomorrow morning's time enough."

But he had gone.

On the night of March 28th, Tom Woodbridge and his wife sat in the blockhouse waiting for Mesopotamia to come to the meeting. Stranger-boy pulled the rope on the new bell which hung in the cupola. But the Woodbridges waited alone.

"They might just be late," Veronica said.

"A-ah! The bell's been ringin' a quarter-hour!"

Mitchell and Adams came, and Brute Christofferson came with them. But Woodbridge had told them by word of mouth about the meeting.

Christofferson went back outside the blockhouse and inspected the fragment of the notice which remained. He said: "Y'know, Mr. Woodbridge, that sign don't look to me like it blowed off. The way it's ripped so's none of the writin' is left a-tall, it mighta been tore off deliberate. Is that possible in a place like this?"

Brute's voice echoed in the blockhouse so that Woodbridge felt the hostile emptiness of the place. He remembered that it was possible for Mesopotamia to go to the village fair a few years ago without speaking to the Stranger-woman. He remembered that it was possible for Mesopotamia to refuse to sell him the Shuldane reserve lot because it was one of the rules they went by. He remembered how they had refused to admit his hogs to the blockhouse.

"Yeah," he answered. "It's possible."

There were some footsteps outside the door, and Jim Hawkins walked in. Veronica walked forward to meet him. "Jim, you came!"

"Yeah, Veronica. But I think there'll just be us that's here now."

"They're over at Hosmer's Store, I suppose!" challenged Woodbridge.

"The main ones."

Woodbridge clamped his jaws.

"We could go over there, Tom," Veronica suggested.

"We'll stay right here."

But the Flannerty girl came in and asked, "Where are all the people, Mr. Woodbridge?"

"They didn't come, Camelia. What are you doing here?"

"Miss Veronica said tonight you were going to find out about the money so they won't send Pap to the army."

Veronica said, "I guess we better go over to the store, Tom."
But Thomas Woodbridge sat down. And the sitting was a decision.

Though he was a stranger to Washington, the city quickly opened to Jonathan Blair its most luxurious and formidable doors, as he had expected it would. The magic key, used by Blair with exquisite carelessness, was the phrase "on an errand for Colonel Shuldane." Blair experimented with the phrase as he had with his first boyhood spyglass, which had once amazed him for an entire afternoon by bringing each more distant object under his observation. As he used the phrase in Washington, Blair was even more impressed with Elnathan Shuldane than when he sat beside the man in Concord.

He observed that the name was more magical when dropped gracefully before the older, white-haired delegates, the powerful "Signers." From younger men, especially those from the Territories, the name drew sharp attention; but Blair was quick to notice that it also induced in them a stiffening of the back.

Perhaps the most exclusive club in the nation in 1805 was the Cincinnati, formed by the veteran field-grade officers of the Rebellion, close around George Washington. Blair was surprised to be invited by Colonel Brigham to enter the sacred Cincinnati Hall, which had a special entrance of its own in the side of the Harper House. The dark interior, further darkened by walnut tables and chairs, was principally illuminated by a fire from the huge hearth, reflected richly from the burnished copper wall emblems of the Virginia Line, the Putnam Artillery, the Connecticut Establishment, the Massachusetts Light Infantry. The engraved and embossed and inlaid furnishings only heightened the splendor of the colonels and general officers who moved around oblivious to the grand environment, violating its hushed elegance with loud, callous voices.

A tall stately general entered who carried himself almost in imitation of Washington. He stopped for a word with Brigham, who said: "General Wilkinson, this is Jonathan Blair, down on an important chore for Colonel Shuldane. And for that matter, for all of us."

"How do you do, sir," said Wilkinson. "Would you two gentlemen go to mess with me?"

Brigham accepted speedily, and Blair pulled out a chair for the general. But Wilkinson did not sit. Instead he led them to a small door marked "General Officers' Mess." The first room, which had once seemed grand, now became a common taproom beside this tiny cubicle of tapestry.

Seated, Brigham explained to Wilkinson: "Blair is to barrister a case before the Territorial—that is, the new State of Ohio—Supreme Court against that William Hogland who gave General St. Clair so much trouble. Colonel Shuldane is lending Blair, you might say, for this case. And Blair wants to study the General Land Office records to make a case against squatting on Bounty Lands reserved for Revolutionary veterans. Can you secure him access to those records, General Wilkinson?"

The general indicated that it would be a trifle, but expressed surprise that such thoroughness was required in the case of an out-and-out squatter.

"Besides," said Wilkinson, "I thought the charge was treason."

"Well, it is, sir," said Blair. "But as I get into it, I find it's neither clear-cut nor particularly well founded. And Colonel Shuldane wants the thing done right."

Wilkinson postponed a large bite of duck. "And don't you consider his assumption of the title 'Governor' to be clearly treasonous? And didn't I understand this Hogland threatened to deliver up the Territory to the Spaniards?"

"Many understood that, sir," said Blair. "But better witnesses claim he only said that if the Republic did not soon provide for the protection of the people, and if land were not made available in small quantities to the bounty warrant holders . . . why, then he would set up his own country. That he acted treasonably in uniting the squatter veterans for their own protection is another thing to prove—unless I can show that the lands occupied by his squatters were in such amounts and locations as to constitute an invasion of the public domain or a preemption or a hostile infiltration. To search for such facts I'd like to study the land titles in the Doomsday Books at the land office."

Wilkinson craunched his celery, ending the cordiality.

In the land office a veteran with a wooden leg sat at a high desk pasting canceled Bounty Land warrants in six enormous blank books. The man was working on Volume VI. Blair could therefore make free use of the other five volumes.

Blair approached the volumes without sentiment. They recorded a nation's payment to the soldiers who had won for the Republic a vast public domain to the west and independence from the King. But the wooden-legged clerk was a sample of the Revolutionary. And they were hard to worship.

Blair did not know exactly what he expected to find. But he began by flipping back the edges of the warrants, those the clerk had not pasted down flat, to see who had cashed them in. The name of the veteran on the front of the warrant meant nothing, but the name on the back showed who had bought the warrant from the soldier. They were big names.

Blair recorded them, and toward the end of the second day he had tabulated some figures which surprised him. For page after page of warrants bore the same names on the backs. The notes on his pad read as follows:

| | | | | | | | |
|---|---|---|---|---|---|---|---|
| E. Backus | cashed in | 151 | warrants for | 22,561 | acres of land. | | |
| J. Higbee | " | " | 137 | " | " | 24,000 | " " " |
| J. Stanberry | " | " | 309 | " | " | 40,000 | " " " |
| J. Symmes | " | " | 306 | " | " | 36,000 | " " " |
| E. Shuldane | " | " | 157 | " | " | 23,000 | " " " |

But the next entry brought Blair up short: J. Dayton cashed in 721 warrants for 90,900 acres of land.

Blair quickly flipped back the pages of the Doomsday Book and looked at the endorsement side of several of the warrants. Most of the warrants Dayton had bought for $10. Ten cents an acre.

"Fool!" said Blair.

The clerk looked up, "Me, sir?"

"Oh, pardon me. No. The veteran. The veteran has given away his Bounty Land for ten cents an acre! Not one in five hundred of these warrants was actually cashed in and settled by the veteran!"

"You just findin' that out, sir?"

"He gave his land away for ten, twenty, thirty cents an acre!" accused Blair.

The clerk looked at his wooden leg, and his tone was defiant.

"What else could he do? When he got out of the army he had no money. The govermint wouldn't let him settle on his Bounty claim until she cleared title from Virginia and Connecticut and them states that claimed they owned the public domain by charter from King Charles II."

"All right," said Blair with disgust. "But that was straightened out. All he had to do was wait five years. Hold on to his warrant."

"Huh!" The clerk took off his iron-rimmed glasses and looked up and down at Blair's clothes, at the uniform of the bright young man of Boston.

"Yeah. It was straightened out. But then the govermint says: 'No. Y'can't go out there yet. Not till we git it all surveyed into nice pretty squares.'"

"All right. There was a reason for that. Why didn't the veterans hold on while the surveying was being done?"

"Huh! They tried. But they been surveyin' it now for ten years. Indians bust up the survey once a month."

"But there's a lot of it surveyed now. A hundred-acre warrant is better today than $10—" Blair interrupted himself. "Oh-h! I see what you mean. Then they came along with the speculator laws saying a man had to have four thousand acres' worth of warrants before he could settle. They cut it down gradually. But he's still got to have 640 acres' worth."

The clerk looked smug, as though he had made the argument himself.

"Still," said Blair, "a man's better off holding on to his warrant. Lord knows they were hard enough come by."

"Ha! Easy enough for a sprig like you to say he should have held on. But you're forgettin' the veteran wasn't gettin' any younger. He's been waitin' that long he's disgusted. He needs money, too. And $10 cash is better than hangin' the warrant on the wall. Likely he's got souvenirs enough."

The clerk thumped his wooden leg.

Blair picked up his pencil and did some more figuring. When he had finished adding up his figures, he found that of the 2,560,000 acres of the Bounty Land initially reserved for the veteran, 70 per cent of it was now owned in huge chunks by 115 men.

By the fourth day of his study, Jonathan Blair had discovered that Volume IV was the most interesting, and his notebook included many startling observations. Lunch was repeated with Colonel Brigham and with General Wilkinson, who was in a patronizing good humor.

"Well, Blair," he said, "I see that notebook goes everywhere with you. Just what does a lawyer write in his notebook in a treason case?"

Blair flipped his notebook open. "It's been most revealing, General.

I find that for certain of the veterans, the Bounty Lands have been truly a bounty."

"For certain ones? For all of them, I should think."

"Well, I notice in the book, sir, that you hold 6,000 acres. General von Steuben had 15,000 acres near Steubenville in the Bounty Lands. Patrick Henry held 2,000 acres. Part of that acreage was granted to them. But part of it they bought in bargain warrants."

"Yes?" The general frosted over like the Atlantic Coast in January. He had a sudden distaste for the conversation.

"However, in adding up a bit, I find that of the 9,900 Bounty Land warrants so far issued to veterans, 7,500 of them have come into the hands of only 115 men, mostly *non*-veterans."

The general patted his lips with his napkin, and over the linen his gaze attacked the relaxed face of Jonathan Blair. Suddenly Blair's completely civilian status irritated the general.

"Just how, Mr. Blair, do such notes contribute to the prosecution of William Hogland?"

"I have been asking myself the same question, sir." Blair's grin bounced off the general's granite eyes, and the lawyer dived for his coffee in retreat.

"Then one more question, Blair, in which I trust you will be ahead of me. May I?"

"Certainly."

"Enlighten me, Mr. Blair, how would a professional lawyer, let's say one as thorough as yourself, proceed? Suppose, for example, that the notes he takes in his little black notebook should seem not to favor his client. What then does our hypothetical lawyer do?"

"Why, I suppose in court he does his best with a weak case."

"But suppose our hypothetical lawyer knows that his 'best' with a weak case will be far superior to opposing counsel's 'best' with a strong case? Then what does he do?"

Colonel Brigham did not know why, but he knew that the air was beginning to crackle and snap between General Wilkinson and Blair, and he busied himself with trying to drink more soup from an empty bowl.

"My question, Mr. Blair?" prodded the general.

The lawyer took a mouthful of bread to excuse himself from answering. For Jonathan Blair had only this morning asked himself this same question.

"General," sparred the lawyer, "the case has become almost too hypo-thetical for me to follow well."

In the blockhouse in Mesopotamia, Thomas Woodbridge and his wife and Jim Hawkins sat where Seth Gershom always stood to preach and where Sam Hosmer always stood to make announcements. Facing them sat Adams and Mitchell and Brute Christofferson in silence. Between the two groups stood Camelia Flannerty listening to the bell which the Stranger-boy was ringing. She also looked toward the door, and she asked, "Why didn't the people come to your meetin', Mr. Woodbridge?"

Woodbridge didn't answer.

"Does that mean they want Pap to go to the army? Mama said she didn't think the people'd let him go to the army because she said he's so good at joining timbers."

Veronica's eyes dampened, and Brute Christofferson reached a great paw out to pull Camelia to him.

"But maybe Mama could be wrong again."

The adults in the blockhouse studied Woodbridge. The hog farmer sat staring at the floor between widespread knees which supported his elbows. He pounded one fist brutally into his opposite palm.

Brute Christofferson's deep voice combined outrage and sympathy. "Don't seem to me, Camelia, anybody could want anybody's man to go to the army whether he could join timbers or not."

But the reassurance alerted Camelia, and she pushed away from Christofferson. "You think they do, though! That's why you're so nice to me."

The girl's defiance crumbled into unrestrained tears, and Veronica left her husband's side to walk over to her. "It's not *your* papa they're mad at, Camelia."

Jim Hawkins also walked over to the girl.

No one saw the redhead get up and walk out of the blockhouse.

It was hard for Woodbridge to grip the door handle to Hosmer's Store tonight, especially since it was filled with a kind of taunting laughter and gaiety which he knew would die as soon as he shoved open the door. It did.

Amid the silence the hog farmer walked slowly to the center of the store. He stood with his feet wide apart.

"Well, you didn't come," he challenged.

It would have helped if someone had thrown his defiance back at him. But the complacent silence goaded him and charged an angry strength through his body.

"All right! Since you didn't think enough of my meetin' to come, I'll bring the meetin' to you, and I'll have my say anyhow!"

By now feet were scraping on the porch outside, and Woodbridge yelled, "Bring that kid in here!"

Veronica edged into the room leading Camelia. Mitchell and Adams and Hawkins and Christofferson followed.

"I'm gonna show ya what you're doin'! I'm gonna tell ya that if ya don't get organized and get somebody to round up some money to pay our share down to county jail, you're gonna send Camelia's ole man to the army! And every time y'see Camelia, you can thank yourself for makin' her an orphan!

"And while I'm at it, I'm gonna tell ya somethin' else! Since y'don't think enough of me to come to my meetin', you can get yourself another fool to black your boots. There's too many here willin' to stand around in the store and let just a few go out and sweat about the bridges and the guard watch! You better get somebody in charge of keepin' track of the lot boundaries in this town. And somebody to say whose critters kin eat off the public common and whose can't. And since you're so blasted lazy you better get somebody with the power to drive ya out to fix the roads. And you better do it quick or this place is gonna be a patch of misery with no standin' down to county nor anywheres else, including out on my place! You can suit yourselves, because for me I don't give a God damn! I can take care of me and mine, but there's some here that can't!"

Amos Exeter jumped down off the counter to answer, but Sam Hosmer, with his eyes on Woodbridge, extended a restraining hand toward the acid-tongued Exeter. The old man did not seem displeased with Woodbridge, but his voice held a challenge.

"So that's what ye think now, huh, Tom?"

"That's what I *know*, Hosmer!"

"Ye wouldn't be sayin', I don't suppose, that what we need is a town government?"

The redhead pulled his feet closer together and looked at the floor.

"I don't care what you call it, Hosmer."

It was a defeat, obvious and final, and the victors crowded in.

Exeter jumped down off the counter again and said: "If you'd a thought of that before, Woodbridge, you'd a maybe had Camelia's ole man back a month ago."

Stikes's long fingers closed like a claw over Exeter's shoulder. His voice was deep and quiet. "Hosmer's talkin' good enough, Amos. Shut up."

Elisha Adams looked like a man betrayed. He stepped toward Woodbridge with a hurt face.

"How come ya changed? All them things you said got done before with no town government!"

The redhead kept his eyes on the floor and traced a crack in the puncheons with his boot.

"Yeah, that's right, 'Lisha. But that was when there was a dang sight better man than me runnin' it. And Hosmer won't be around forever. Y'better git this here election under way."

Sam Hosmer had the paper. Stanley-the-Slasher made a vote box out of planed ash. Mike Stikes forged an iron clasp that would accommodate the lock off the blockhouse gate. Faith Emerson brought over four charcoal pencils. The vote box was placed in the blockhouse.

On the morning of April 1, 1805, Thomas Woodbridge saddled Prince.

"Don't much lavish to go up to town and face 'em, Veronica. But I guess they'd snicker all the louder if I didn't show myself at the voting."

"They won't laugh, Tom. You'll find your name up for trustee, along with Sam Hosmer and Stikes and Buttrick."

"My name! Who put it?"

"After you left the store with Brute Christofferson to take Camelia home, Sam Hosmer told them all that after what you went through the past few months there's not a man in the state—himself excepted only —that knows more about running a town than you."

"Hosmer said that!"

On that first Monday in April, Thomas Woodbridge rode into town to cast his ballot for three trustees, two fence viewers, two overseers of the poor, one constable, and one treasurer.

On Tuesday morning that particular patch of the Bounty Lands looked no different than before, but Asa Buttrick rode down the South Road toward county seat with $15 in his pocket for the county sheriff. For Asa Buttrick was treasurer, and government had come to Hosmer Village, or Mesopotamia, as it pompously signed itself this day.

# Chapter 15: BY DUE PROCESS
## (1806)

THE reunion between Woodbridge and the law man was the less fortunate because Woodbridge was in a hurry.

Even as the wagon raced downhill toward the ford, Woodbridge called for more speed, and the wrath inside him overflowed against the person of Asa Buttrick.

They splashed across the ford faster than Prince liked to go, and the wagon rumbled up the bank toward Hosmer's Store.

Now the unwritten but unbending protocol of Mesopotamia tacitly left open the center hitching post at Hosmer's Store for Tom Woodbridge. But today, as he dropped from the seat of his wagon, he saw that the center post was already wrapped with a well-soaped bridle rein, and his eye followed it off to a fresh-curried white mare with a copper-garnished saddle.

The voices hushed as Woodbridge barged into the store. He instantly spotted the newcomer, who stuck out like a boar in a sheepfold because of his short black forktail coat and English boots. Blair was back.

Jonathan Blair stepped forward with his hand stretched out to Tom, but Woodbridge brushed past and went straight to the counter to confront Sam Hosmer.

"Sam! You heard what Buttrick's pulling on me?"

Sam Hosmer turned away, ostensibly to examine the muzzle of his rifle in a better light. Even Hosmer found it hard to think straight in the direct glare of the hog farmer's pale-blue eyes. Woodbridge continued.

"Buttrick is trying to take the Stranger-boy off my place!"

Hosmer wrapped a new cleaning swab onto the end of his ramrod, thus furnishing the pause for the grainy voice from across the crowded store.

"Don't tell your troubles to Hosmer, Woodbridge."

It was Asa Buttrick.

"Here I am, right here."

Woodbridge turned around as Buttrick moved through the parting
crowd with the majesty befitting the trader who brought in most of the
hard money that circulated in Mesopotamia. He took the produce of
Hosmer village down the river or over the trace to the East, and
brought back money. He offered no explanation about his markets or
methods, but Mesopotamia expected none in the face of results.

"I'm not taking the Stranger-boy permanently, Woodbridge. Only
offering him a chance to work off the debt his old man owes me. He
can do it in one year."

Woodbridge was not one to examine the reason for Buttrick's assured smile. Nor did he consider the fact that Mesopotamia's money
man had never been known to err. He said: "Buttrick, that boy is indentured to my place. And any business concerning him you'll address
to me. Not to the boy."

Buttrick, strangely enough, was a rigidly honest trader. His honesty
was cold and extremely simple. It stemmed less from his soul than from
his economics. He was ostentatiously honest because in forty-seven
years he had learned that any variation from that course merely rendered a short, quick profit at the expense of the long, continuous commissions. It left him in a towering, unreproachable position, as he
intended. Hence he hooked his thumb over his belt, taking his time,
as a man who holds a good bargaining position.

"Woodbridge, when the Stranger and his woman left town they
owed me £15 English. Stake for a season's trapping and for one new
rifle barrel."

"Then your deal's with the Stranger. Not the boy. The boy was indentured to me at the woman's request when they left town. Hosmer
was there."

Hosmer agreed.

A respectful silence usually followed any remark by Hosmer. But the
lawyer in the British boots brought an outsider's ignorance.

"Gentlemen," and Blair said it as though he believed it, "may I
make a suggestion?"

"Little early for that, isn't it, Blair?" asked Woodbridge. "Especially
since the trouble concerns Buttrick and me, and you don't know any
of the details."

To Mesopotamia's surprise, Blair continued.

"Didn't you elect a justice of the peace in the last election? That's
what he's for. You should put the mechanism in motion."

Woodbridge cut him off. "The justice of peace was elected only for how it would look down at county. Sam Hosmer here settles all our troubles. Always has. Always will, far as I know."

Blair persisted, causing expectant glances to trade among the crowd.

"The advantage of a court is that it forces one side or the other to crystallize the point of difference so that that point alone may be argued, cutting away all unrelated matters, at once establishing the question and narrowing down the laws which apply to it. You have the means of law by due process here. Why not use it?"

"A-ah!" Woodbridge's derision was devastating. "Your blasted court law is nothin' but a spider web. It catches the little ones. The big ones break right through. We don't need that. It's a simple matter. The Stranger-boy belongs to me!"

"If it's that simple," said Buttrick, "let's take Blair's suggestion. Try the justice court. See if it works. We elected Jim Dolk justice of the peace."

"A-ah! Did we also elect some divine brains into his head? How's Jim Dolk to know what's right and what's wrong?"

Buttrick had a good answer, and he knew it.

"Woodbridge, just a minute ago we were about to let Sam Hosmer settle this thing. What's the difference?"

"The difference is Sam Hosmer's most always right, and everybody knows it. Far as I'm concerned, that makes him the law till I know more about how Jim Dolk decides things."

Blair interrupted. "Under the law, the justice of the peace can appoint a six-man jury to help him decide if he wishes."

"And if Dolk should decide the Stranger-boy should work for Buttrick instead of me, you think I'd let him go?"

"The justice can order your elected constable to execute his decision," answered Blair.

"Hah! How would Amos Exeter get the boy off my place if I said No?"

Buttrick stepped in. "Well, Woodbridge, I'm willing to try this due process of law here in our justice court. And what's more I'm going to engage Blair here to start it off."

Woodbridge's reply precluded any retreat by either party. "Count me out! This is the first I knew the lawyers hawked their services by starting the trouble. I would have thanked you, Blair, to let me handle my affair with my neighbor in peace, especially since you're not established here."

Blair stood steady in the blast of the redhead's bristling hostility. "I hadn't had time to tell you, Woodbridge," Blair answered. "I'm staying here to run for the legislature."

Woodbridge stared at Blair in surprise, then abruptly started for the door.

Asa Buttrick addressed the newcomer in a voice that carried to the door, "Well, how do we get this due process of law started, Mr. Blair?"

Woodbridge walked to the door of his cabin and threw it open.

"Come in out of the wet, Amos!"

But Amos Exeter stood outside.

"I better not this time," he said. "You're to read this paper and mark your name here."

Woodbridge reached for the paper, which he read aloud.

"'To Thomas Woodbridge, greetings: I, James Dolk, do command you—'"

A red color spread up the back of his neck toward his ears. He looked at Exeter. "*Command* me?"

"Finish it first, Tom."

"'—do command you to appear before me on the first day of frost at Hosmer's Store to show cause why the boy called the Stranger-boy should not be transferred to the household of Asa Buttrick, plaintiff, in satisfaction of a debt of £15 owed the plaintiff by the parent of the boy called'—Why, that blasted—why I won't show up for this thing. You know that!"

"I know it," said Exeter, offering one of Hope Emerson's charcoal pencils, "but sign it here to prove I delivered it."

Woodbridge slammed the door and resumed sharpening his scythe. Until today Jim Dolk and Amos Exeter and Asa Buttrick had been merely neighbors to Woodbridge, individual men with whom he dealt simply and directly. But now, suddenly, Jim Dolk became justice of the peace. Amos Exeter stood behind a piece of paper that said "Constable," and Asa Buttrick stood behind the ruffled shirt of an outsider, a law man, and was called, not Asa Buttrick, but "Plaintiff." And together they set in motion a strange, elusive force upon which Tom Woodbridge could get no grip with his big red hands.

Between the man Woodbridge and the indentured boy who was still called the Stranger-boy there was never talk of anything but the chores at hand.

Side by side, a scythe handle apart, they mowed down the sweet-grass patch in silence, both blades swinging in unison. At the far end of the field they pivoted without a word and mowed their way back down. The man noticed the boy only when he had to slow his pace a little to let the boy catch up. But the boy, from his position just a half-step behind, was exactly familiar with the way the man's biceps bunched and flattened rhythmically under the freckled red skin. He observed how the great bony shoulders pivoted as the man's blade reached well back to his right and followed through on his left, leaving a neat mat of sweet grass flat on the ground.

Woodbridge measured the remainder of the field against the height of the sun and increased his pace, forgetting that the Stranger-boy was still a boy. The boy observed the back of the man's neck, exactly how the thick columnar chords ran down from each ear and disappeared in the great hollows behind his collarbones. He noted how the trunk twisted, and adjusted his own stroke in imitation of Tom's as they approached the far end of the field.

"Where do you stand on the thing, boy?"

The Stranger-boy said, "If my kin owed Mr. Buttrick, I ought to work off the debt, I guess."

"Then you want to go, don't you?"

"I didn't say that," the boy answered. "I said, 'I ought, I guess.' "

They mowed to the end of the field, pivoted, and started back toward the setting sun.

"You're thinking, I suppose, that Buttrick will make a trader of you and you'll get to see Cincinnati and Pittsburgh and Steubenville."

"He said I'd go with him to the markets, keep the accounts straight. Whose stock was sold to whom for how much. Like that."

"A damned teachified, triflin' bookkeeper he'll make of you," said Woodbridge. "I suppose he talked up an easy life and fancy. No wonder you want to go."

"I didn't say that. I only said I ought."

"Same thing. Give way with your blade to the right a little."

The boy chose the nighttime to go see Asa Buttrick. And he chose the back door for two reasons. First, the approach to Buttrick's back door was concealed from the square by the heavy trees along the river-bank, and the Stranger-boy did not want anyone else to know of his visit. Second, the Stranger-boy had a back-door stature in Mesopotamia.

His parents had come into Mesopotamia as transient trappers, making no contribution to the community. They had been known as the Stranger and the Stranger-woman; and they had left toward the north-west as suddenly as they had come, by the back door. Hosmer had always said it would happen.

Tonight the Stranger-boy wanted to talk to Mr. Buttrick. It could have been that the boy needed some honest advice. It could have been that he wanted to ask about the trading profession as a way to spend a lifetime. It could have been that the Stranger-boy was truly a stranger, and did not wish to be.

The Buttrick cabin was long, consisting of three rooms and a shed for the trade goods. Though the door was open, the Stranger-boy raised his fist to knock. But he held it in mid-air, for he heard his name mentioned from inside by the granulated voice of Asa Buttrick. The boy backed to one side a little.

Buttrick was answered by the well-spoken newcomer, the law man.

"You see, Buttrick, I've obtained a copy of your Ohio statutes from Chillicothe. There aren't many yet, but they're very specific in the matter of indentured servants."

"They give those laws out to anybody that wants?" asked Buttrick.

"No, but there's a printer in Chillicothe. He prints the laws as they're passed by the assembly for anybody who will buy or rent this book from him. Other books, too. Now see, here it says, 'The master shall be required to furnish the indentured apprentice with a Bible and two suits of clothes.'"

From outside the cabin the Stranger-boy could not see Buttrick, but he heard him say, "Veronica Woodbridge has a Bible, but I doubt the boy has two suits."

The law voice continued.

"But here's the important thing. It says, 'The master shall be required to teach the indentured servant, if male, to read and to cipher to the rule of three.'"

Buttrick said, "Then we've got Woodbridge right here. The boy can't read."

The law man asked, "How do you know?"

"I expressly asked him," said Buttrick, "because he'd be much more of a help to me in the markets if he could."

The Stranger-boy heard the stools scrape back. He flattened himself against the cabin as the two men came to the door.

Buttrick said good night and added: "Blair, this is all based on the assumption that you can get him to come to the trial. I doubt if you can."

The law man stood within ten feet of the Stranger-boy, but he faced the cabin light. "I can," he said with a quiet assurance. "If worst comes to worst, the constable can deputize up to six men to bring him by force from anywhere in the county."

"It won't be easy, though, Blair, to find six who will go after Tom Woodbridge."

"It's illegal to refuse a deputation."

The Stranger-boy waited until the footsteps had crunched out of earshot. He was just turning out of the shadows of Buttrick's path onto the edge of the West Road when the clomp of a westbound horse and wagon behind him came to his ears. The boy crowded close to the trees on the edge of the road and walked faster, but the road would soon converge him with the driver of the wagon at the river ford. The driver seemed to increase his speed to match. The wagon came abreast of the boy, and a voice cut the blackness: "Hello, Buttrick. Stop a while."

The Stranger-boy remained silent and walked faster. There was a slap of reins in the dark, and the wagon rumbled up beside the boy again.

"I say, Buttrick, stop a while. I want to talk to you. Well, blast you! It's me! Woodbridge!"

The boy gave up and stood still. The wagon came up close beside him and stopped.

Woodbridge said, "You?"

They stared at each other a moment, and then the man said, "Get on if you want."

When the boy was seated, Woodbridge gee'd the surprised Prince with an unwarranted slap and the wagon jerked forward at an unnecessary speed.

They rode across the ford in silence, and then another half-mile over the road without speaking. Finally, with his eyes still to the road, Woodbridge said, "Well, you've picked your friends, then."

He allowed time for an answer. When none came, he punished his horse over the remaining six miles.


Wednesday was make-ready for the "raising" on Thursday. That is, Stikes, Exeter and Hosmer, Brady, Hawkins, Slasher and Flannerty

were coming to raise a hog shed for Woodbridge. They arrived early
Thursday morning. Woodbridge was whetting an ax by the fire. He
told Veronica to have the boy lead the men up to the site.

"He must be up there already," said Veronica. "He did the morning
chores early."

Zabeth, always quick to take Stranger-boy's side, added, "And I
found these potatoes here that he unsprouted for the men's dinner."

Woodbridge ceased sharpening the ax and led the men up to the site.

Hosmer directed the laying of four boulders for the corner supports.
Stikes began whittling pegs to the size of his auger, and Brady and
Stanley-the-Slasher sharpened their blades in a leisurely manner.

When Hosmer had selected his base logs, he set Hawkins and Flannerty to work cutting them into the lengths he wanted. He shouted
across the clearing: "Woodbridge, where's your ox? You can start pulling the base logs over."

Woodbridge answered, "The boy's likely on the way up with him
now." But he went to look.

In the barn the chores were done, but the ox was still in the stall.
Nor was the boy in the house.

Woodbridge yoked the ox himself. He attached the draw poles and
signaled to the ox to move. The massive beast stood rooted, and when
he swung his huge head resentfully to see what heavy hand was this,
Woodbridge cursed the absent Stranger-boy. Not knowing what private
signals the ox answered to now, Woodbridge hauled the logs with great
difficulty and the aid of the whip. But under Hosmer's easy, autocratic
direction the hog shed went up that day.

At one o'clock Stikes called for an iron wedge chisel. Woodbridge
went to the shed to look for it. He looked in the chest under the
wagon seat and he looked in the boy's bunk in the shed. It was neither
place. "I've let the kid take over so I don't know my own shed."

A shadow across his arm stopped Woodbridge from mumbling to
himself. He turned and confronted the clean-shaven face of Jonathan
Blair. "Yes?" he said, with the defiance of a man who stands well within
his own property line.

Blair wore what he probably imagined to be work clothes. That is,
the sleeves were rolled up above the elbow, but they were white sleeves,
as were the arms they exposed. The legs were short and well muscled,
but they were also encased in well-cut breeches that tucked into boots
that were old but unscratched. He had in his hand a new timber adz

from Hosmer's Store. As he stood in the barn door, he looked to Wood-bridge like a fancy house cat gingerly exploring the entrance to the hog house.

"Hello, Woodbridge. I came to offer a hand."

"What kind of roundabout is this, Blair? We stand on opposite sides of things."

"I'm trying a case for a man who makes a claim against you. But I have no feeling against you."

"You saying you don't care how it comes out?" asked Woodbridge.

"No. I shall do everything I can to win the case for my client, just as I expect you do everything in your power to sell your hogs without in-tending harm to your competitor who thereby loses."

"A right comfortable fancy, Mr. Blair. But not my way of doin'. If a man's against me, he's against me. And no half way about it. I can't savvy how your kind hires out so quick to one man as to the next."

"When a man is in trouble, he needs the use of a knowledge of law as badly as he needs ham when he is hungry."

"Maybe, Blair. But you're selling yours to Buttrick, so you've picked your side."

"At the moment it seems Buttrick could offer the Stranger-boy more, and in addition has the law behind his claim. But the boy's attitude should count. What is it?"

"I thought you'd know more about that than I," said Woodbridge.

"Where's the boy?" asked Blair.

"I think you know that, too. He's gone."

Tom Woodbridge returned to his rising hog shed, and Jonathan Blair started back toward the West Road to Mesopotamia.

In front of the Woodbridge place Blair had one foot in the stirrup, but he stood there untwisting some leather. There was nothing seriously wrong with the bridle, but he could feel Veronica's presence. He told himself he would be aware of her in a thousand-acre forest.

How do you break a silence of five years? How do you say the first audible word to someone you've carried with you absurdly for five years?

How do you act as if you've forgotten an appropriate number of details, suitable for a five-year absence, when you vividly remember the hollow at the base of her throat, the faint throb there. . . . When you remember exactly how her back tapers to just where the hips curve outward? When you know the vibrancy of her waist under your hand?

When you've trespassed in dreams a thousand times into the secret parts of the house, how do you now talk like a stranger at the outside door?

"Jonathan, I saw you. But I thought you'd stop at the house before you left."

"Veronica!"

His picture had been exactly right. There were five years of washing and wear on the linen clothes, but the figure was eternal. Her eyes brushed away time, acknowledging that it was right to carry a vision for five years.

"I was going to, of course, Veronica. But, well, Tom didn't seem to need an extra hand. I thought I'd best leave."

"Tom is a single-minded man, Jonathan."

"I know," he said.

"To a fault at times," she said.

But he knew it was not a regret. It was only a courtesy apology.

He looked up at the solid cabin and at the land and at the woman. He looked at the wagon, and at all the physical equipment on the place. A single-minded man had won this. This was what a single-minded, simple-thinking man had achieved for himself—a man who couldn't hold his own among the cunning maneuvers on Beacon Hill, a man who couldn't even manipulate among the schemists at county seat. Or could he?

"With Tom it's either for or against." He grinned. "And I happen to represent 'against.' "

She gave no answer.

"I'd have been better off if I'd been that way myself the night we came here to say goodbye six years ago," he said.

She colored at the base of her throat and changed the subject.

"You've come for the legislature for Father?"

"Which means I'll be on the other side in most everything, Veronica. I hope it won't mean that . . . "

He didn't finish.

"Then there's the Navarre trial. I'm to prosecute."

"You'll not be able to, Jonathan."

"Why?"

"When you've been here a while, you'll not believe in your case."

"But if I do, how will you—"

He searched her face.

"If you do, I'll know you just don't understand," she said. "But you won't."

On the second night after the hog shed had been raised, Woodbridge went to Boxford's Cabin with Brady to pick up five woods hogs that were roaming down there. The settler who reported them said they were extra large. He had heard that Woodbridge was peculiarly interested in such hogs. There was a small trade involved.

It was late on this night that the Stranger-boy returned to Mesopotamia, and the wolf dog set up a furious barking.

The boy whispered, "Wolf!" The barking ceased, and Wolf was all over him in frenzied recognition. His playful bites hurt, though, and tore the cloth bag the boy carried, for Wolf had not gentled like a dog. He retained the roughness that had been on him when he limped out of the forest six years ago.

Since it was after midnight and the cabin was dark, the boy did not go in. He went straight for his bunk in the shed, but Wolf hung back. He lowered his head and set up a deep vibrating in his throat.

The Stranger-boy opened the shed door, and Wolf continued to growl. The boy walked through the darkness to his bunk, set his sack on the floor, took off his doeskin hunting shirt and his boots and felt with his hand for his bunk.

His hand rubbed over something warm which moved. Wolf stiffened and growled. The boy pulled the cover back, and suddenly there was a scramble. A figure sat up in the bunk, grabbed the Stranger-boy by the neck, and choked him.

"Who are you?"

The boy could not answer. He groped for the figure in the bunk, but the choking arms held him off too far.

The voice yelled, "Get him, Wolf!"

Instead Wolf leaped onto the bunk, and suddenly the figure let go and called: "Get him off! Get that devil off me!"

Stranger-boy grabbed Wolf by the collar, pressed his thumb and forefinger roughly against the hinge of the animal's jaw, and pulled him to the floor.

When the door was opened to let in the moonlight, the man in the bunk said: "They thought you'd gone for good. I'm to take your place."

The Stranger-boy curled up on the floor, truly a stranger in his own shed.

As the days shortened on the Woodbridge farm, so did the tempers, and the Stranger-boy felt like a trespasser.

On the first day after his return he knew he would be allowed to stay because Miss Veronica wouldn't have the heart to send him away and scold him, both.

"Tom was surprised you picked Thursday to go to Chillicothe," she protested. "The work was heavy here, raising the new hog shed."

"There was something I had to get up there," he said.

"You should have picked a rainy spell."

"I will next time, Miss Veronica."

"Next time! Will you go again, then?"

"I must," he said.

The new man, who was now installed in the boy's bunk, entered the cabin at that moment, carrying wood for the fire. The boy watched him tramp his boots across Miss Veronica's circle rug, which the boy always skirted, and he left the cabin and the conversation. Little Zabeth followed him out, and Wolf followed Zabeth.

It was not clear in his mind what the arrangement about him was to be from now on. He knew that when Woodbridge returned there would probably be words between him and Miss Veronica. But he found things to do.

The Stranger-boy first learned that Woodbridge would make a trip to Cincinnati when the new man, Simmons, received his instructions from the hog farmer, who took no pains to do it privately, but spoke openly in front of the boy.

"I'll be gone about two weeks," he said. "I'll take every woods hog over a hundredweight that can make the trip on foot, and any Bedford culls. When I leave, be sure to feed these special ones like I've done, and mark it in the book."

The boy said, "I can mark the book."

Simmons glanced resentfully at him and then back to Woodbridge. His tone was confidential.

"You want me to be in charge here then, I take it."

The Stranger-boy picked up a bucket and found work to do. Wolf was a watery blur of black beside him.

When he went on errands to the village in the following weeks, the boy felt the eyes of Mesopotamia on him. When he entered Hosmer's Store, he caught sentences that ended in the middle.

One night, as he was about to enter the Woodbridge cabin with an armload of firewood, he heard bursts of conversation punctuated by the long pauses which lately meant the Woodbridges were discussing him. He had his foot on the doorsill when he heard Miss Veronica.

"Asa Buttrick has always brought you a good price from Cincinnati for the hogs, and always in hard money or good notes. He's too smart to do else."

"I know that. But he'll not market my hogs while he covets any part of my household. A man can't deal *for* you at the same time he's dealing *against* you."

"But Buttrick knows the market, and he has connections with the flatboat men and with New Orleans. You don't know anything about that."

"I'll learn."

"You should be here watching your new ones."

"Simmons can handle them."

"I'd rather see the boy handle them," said Veronica.

"Hah. The boy! He was late again to the field this morning."

"I had some house chores for him."

"You mean he overslept because he was up late again last night with those books. I saw the light. And why? Because he's learning to cipher so he'll be a help to Buttrick, as he thinks, in the trading business. And him asking for a new suit! I'll be better off if he goes to Buttrick."

"Will you go to Cincinnati before or after the trial at the justice court?" asked Veronica.

"Neither," said Woodbridge. "I'll go *during* the trial, and to make sure they don't take the boy I'll take him with me."

The Stranger-boy's load of wood was getting heavy as he listened outside. He turned away from the cabin.

It was about an hour after dark when Zabeth entered the shed. With no talk, but with considerable understanding, she handed Stranger-boy a half-loaf of bread and half of a roasted pigeon.

The first day of frost was November the 12th.

Mesopotamia was self-conscious on the day set for the first trial at the justice court. As they gathered about the front of Hosmer's Store, the people glanced anxiously to the west from time to time. They had come for an event, but knowing Tom Woodbridge they knew they might be cheated out of it.

Veronica knew that if Woodbridge failed to appear at the trial, he would make the town ridiculous. And Hosmer Village would never forgive him. But she was helpless, for Woodbridge was at that moment lining up the hogs for the trip to Cincinnati.

Even as she called to him, he channeled a number of the spiny-backed, mud-crusted hogs between himself and her so that her voice was lost in the drumming of their hard hoofs and the dust they raised. She crossed over to him ahead of the next bunch.

"Tom, Faith Hawkins said they've already deputized six men to bring you in if necessary."

Woodbridge whacked an independent hog with his pole and got him back in line.

"Hah. They'll need at least that," he answered.

"They'll be mounted," she continued, "and you can only go as fast as the hogs."

"Are you thinkin' they'd stop me by force?" He signaled to the boy to move on down the road at the head of the hogs.

Woodbridge brought up the rear of the column of hogs, leading the big stallion, Prince, behind him. The Stranger-boy led the column on foot. As they dipped down the valley road toward the west bank of the river, Stranger-boy could see a group of men on the near shore at the ford.

When the column reached the river, Amos Exeter held up his hand and Stranger-boy halted the column. Wolf ran across the backs of the moving hogs to police both sides of the column, which was losing shape as the lead hogs stopped.

From the tail of the column came the raucous, outraged voice of Thomas Woodbridge.

"Get those hogs on across the ford!"

But it was impossible for Stranger-boy to advance in the face of the line of men, and the column closed up on itself. The men fidgeted as the column closed tighter and tighter. They were armed.

Woodbridge dismounted and strode through the hogs to where Exeter stood.

"God damn you, Exeter. What did you tell the boy?"

"Tom, I got to take you to the trial."

"You shouldn't have troubled, Amos," said Woodbridge. "You know I won't be at that trial. I'm marching these hogs right past the store and out the East Road a ways, then straight down the Shawnee Trace to Cincinnati."

Woodbridge turned to the boy.

"Take Prince across, boy, and hold up about fifteen rods from the bank and wait till the hogs get bunched up! Then go ahead!"

Exeter said, "No, Tom. I'm to take you to the justice court. We'll decide right here whether you'll go easy or otherwise."

Woodbridge studied the men. Jim Hawkins was one of them, and he singled him out.

"I didn't think you'd be a party to this, Jim."

"He deputized me, Tom. They showed us where it's illegal to refuse a deputation."

"Hah! Then they must pay you each seventy-five cents a day to come get me. And Exeter gets twenty-five cents for delivering the mandamus. Dolk gets twenty-five cents for writing it out. And the jury gets seventy-five cents apiece for sitting. Looks to me like justice is up for sale."

Hawkins looked tormented. The constable's deputy certificate was heavy in his pocket.

Exeter said: "Tom, I don't want to lay a hand on ya, but if ya don't agree to come along I'll have to have the boys grab holt of ya. See. Read it here."

"Ah! I don't want to read it. When a stranger can come in and turn the town against a neighbor, usin' papers and writin', then it don't matter what it says on the paper. Now, help git my hogs across. The boy and I got a long way to go."

Exeter stiffened. "Tom, I said I don't want to lay a hand on you. So the boys and I will keep the hogs here on the bank, kind of in custody. I'll give back the hogs, after."

Woodbridge noticed for the first time that the men had spread out in a circle around the hogs. They had sheepish expressions. But earnest.

As he looked across the river, he could see people gathered on the opposite bank, watching.

He glanced at Stranger-boy. Then he looked at the men surrounding his hogs. He couldn't believe it, but it was a fact. He had no choice.

Woodbridge knew every beam inside the store. He knew every face. Yet today he felt estranged from his neighbors, and the store was a foreign and hostile place. The square-faced Dutchman who sat at the little table facing the crowd was no longer Jim Dolk. He was the justice of the peace. The six men lined along the counter were no longer Woodbridge's neighbors. They were the jury. And Woodbridge himself was no longer the village hog farmer who blasted out his opinions at will. Suddenly he was the defendant, and he stood accused before his fellows.

The stony face of Mesopotamia watched from the puncheon benches which had been moved in to the store from the church. It sat stolid and self-conscious, but determined. Woodbridge thought it must look comical to Blair. But perhaps Blair didn't know that these same faces, prior to this, its first trial, had sentenced Flannerty, by crowd verdict, to fifty lashes on the bare back for stealing salt. Then he realized that Blair was already talking.

"And further, Mr. Magistrate," he was saying to Jim Dolk, "the statute clearly specifies—you can read from my copy here—that the master shall teach the indentured boy to read, and—"

Woodbridge was on his feet. "Can *your* boy read, Dolk? Why should the Stranger-boy read if yours can't? If this is a sample of your seventy-five-cent justice, I'll take the old way!"

Blair cut in.

"I'll have to object, Mr. Dolk, to Mr. Woodbridge's talking ahead of turn. The plaintiff speaks first. Then the defendant can answer at length."

Dolk said: "All right, Blair. Anyway, Woodbridge, it looks like he's right. It's printed here."

"How am I supposed to teach the boy to read when there's no school here?"

"What about that, Blair?" asked Dolk. "Doesn't Woodbridge have a point?"

Veronica entered the store and sat down on one of the front benches.

Though he was the first to point out his own honesty, Blair made some friends in Mesopotamia by his answer.

"In honesty, I must admit that he does have a point. If there is no opportunity, the master is excused by law."

Veronica Woodbridge, who sat in the front row, smiled in relief, but the smile disappeared abruptly as the law man continued.

"But I am prepared to prove that Woodbridge did have opportunity. Woodbridge himself borrowed from the Taylor Printing Company in

Chillicothe no less than fourteen books on fourteen separate occasions last summer. And if he could take out fourteen books for his personal edification and instruction, he could have employed those same fourteen volumes for the instruction of his indentured servant, the one called the Stranger-boy."

Faith Hawkins, who made a great show of book reading, turned to look at Tom Woodbridge as if he had trespassed against her domain. Jim Dolk, from the bench, turned to Woodbridge in frank astonishment. Mike Stikes stared at the defendant as though he had just been told that Woodbridge was an agent for the English. Asa Buttrick smiled. Blair paused to let the information sink in.

Woodbridge himself felt relief. He had felt unable to cope with Blair the lawyer. But if he was going to be so foolhardy as to make up far-fetched stories, then he would be easier to handle. The hog farmer rose from his bench in the rear of the room, and answered with no excitement.

"You lie, Blair, I've not been to Chillicothe, and your own client should be the first to know it, since he transacted my only business in Chillicothe, the purchase of two crocks of hog-colic tonic."

Jim Dolk looked relieved. "You heard him, Blair. You know what you're saying?"

Sam Hosmer was studying the face of the handsome young lawyer, who did not seem as upset as he should for a man caught flat in a lie; he seemed even to be letting the court have its play, as though it suited his purpose. Dolk asked again for proof. Blair took his time. When he spoke again, it was not until well after the room had quieted, hungry to see how he would answer. His voice was controlled and low.

"The Taylor Press loans books for a fee. On their receipt ledger appears fourteen times the signature of Thomas Woodbridge, Jr., of Mesopotamia."

Woodbridge broke in: "You just hung yourself, Blair. I'm not named for my father. There is no Tom Woodbridge, Jr.!"

Sam Hosmer noticed that Blair waited as if inviting more from Woodbridge, but Tom had finished. All eyes were on the lawyer, and he held his best for the last.

"I was not so foolish, Mr. Magistrate," he said, "as not to bring the Taylor Company's receipt ledger with me. Will you examine it, sir?"

Mesopotamia, sitting at its first trial, stretched its neck as if to read the ledger on Dolk's table, twenty feet away. Dolk looked up at Woodbridge in surprise.

"He's right, Tom. It looks like your hand. Fourteen times. Thomas Woodbridge, Jr."

Mesopotamia leaned forward.

Even among his enemies, no man had ever called Woodbridge a liar. The color left his lips and cheeks. His big fists knotted until the knuckles went white. Speech failed him.

Old Sam Hosmer was sensitive to the moods and tempers of Mesopotamia. He wanted it to run itself, but he knew the instant his hand was needed.

"Now you sit down, Tom!" he commanded. "Your turn will come. Let this due process of law continue. Go ahead, Blair."

Blair was sensible that the due process of law continued in the room at that instant only by courtesy of Sam Hosmer. He also apparently knew that his big point had been made. He continued in a lower key.

"The statute also requires," he explained, "that the master furnish two suits. Does the Stranger-boy own two suits, Mr. Woodbridge?"

Hosmer interrupted: "Uh . . . Blair, it would be in the interests of your due process of law if you didn't address the defendant directly for a while yet. Ask the boy."

"Will the Stranger-boy answer?" asked Blair.

"I got the one I'm wearing," the boy said. "And when Miss Veronica finishes the sleeve . . ."

Veronica Woodbridge held up the knit coat that she was still working on.

"I must concede that fulfills the clothing requirements," said Blair. He seemed somewhat uncertain. "We yield the floor to the defendant."

Dolk said, "It's your turn, Woodbridge, to— Yes, Sam?"

"One moment," said Hosmer; and Mesopotamia hushed to listen to its patriarch. "Mr. Blair, here, has seemed to conduct himself pretty fair-minded and thorough. But one thing I thought he skipped too light. We all know it, of course, but he never did *prove* that the Stranger-boy can't read."

Dolk said: "That's right, Blair. You didn't."

Blair rose. "Mr. Hosmer is correct. We did not. Will the Stranger-boy step forward? Uh . . . we seem to have nothing here for him to read."

Hosmer said he had the Bible.

Asa Buttrick was on his feet. "No. Not the Bible. He might quote from memory."

"Not likely," said Blair, "if the magistrate opens the book at random."

"Then it's got to be at several places," said Buttrick. "Not just one. And Dolk will turn the pages."

Dolk flipped open the Bible, turned it around so that it faced the boy, who stood stiffly in front of him. "Read, boy," he ordered.

"How much must I read?" asked the boy.

"I'll stop you. You just read the lines I point to. I'll skip around. Read, boy."

No sound came from the boy, and Dolk was about to close the book when the boy's voice came out in a clear, hesitant monotone.

"And he spake unto them saying—Judge not according to appearance."

Dolk looked surprised. He flipped several pages with some deliberation and then pointed to another verse.

"For—a wise son—maketh—a glad father."

The hard-bitten face of Mesopotamia broke in that instant into a sheepish grin, and Veronica Woodbridge's eyes filled. The crowd started a babble of conversation that almost drowned out Jim Dolk, who was pounding on the table with the handle of his knife.

"Just a minute!" he yelled over the noise. "Woodbridge still has his say, if he still wants it. Do you say or don't you, Woodbridge?"

Woodbridge stood up and looked around the room. The noise died.

"Yeah, I've got something to say."

He walked to the first row, where the Stranger-boy sat at one end, alone.

"This Blair seems to know his mandamuses and his writs of this and writs of that. I'm askin' him now, for me, to go wherever he has to go . . . to get the Stranger-boy's name changed . . . on the records. I want it on a legal parchment. Can that be done, Blair?"

"There is a procedure for doing so," said Blair. "How do you want it changed?"

Even Blair ignored the fact that no one had bothered about the court's formal verdict.

Woodbridge's voice dropped a bit.

"If the boy be willing, as it seems he was once," he stumbled, "change it to . . . Thomas Woodbridge, Jr. . . . legal, and by due process of law."

# Chapter 16: THE TAXPAYER
## (1807)

EXETER'S title as tax lister shriveled, to his mortification, in the face of the hog farmer's mountainous indifference, and his resentment was further compounded by Woodbridge's interrupting to point out certain hogs.

Uneasily, Woodbridge gazed north to the farrowing pen. The week before farrowing was a time for holding the breath. In the hog farmer's gamble with nature it was the hung moment while the dice stopped rolling. He hardly listened as Exeter rambled on.

"The way they're gonna work the taxes, Tom, they're gonna take and rate all the land in three rates: first, second, and third. Ten dollars a hundred acres you pay on first rate. Seven on second. Four dollars a hundred on third rate."

Woodbridge didn't even acknowledge the explanation. Be a sad day when anybody had the gall to charge taxes to a man who owed only himself for what he got. The redhead's eyes concentrated instead on more imminent threats. He looked at the mass of cut timber on the north slope. The trees were cut, but now they had to be burned off before the new field would be ready to plant. He hoped he had cut off a big enough patch to support the new batch of piglets that was coming. He hoped Slasher could burn it off Monday.

He surveyed the eighteen sows he'd put in the special pen. In a week now, barring any trouble, the eighteen should turn to about two hundred, for the Bedford litters had been averaging eight and ten piglets each. Of course, they weren't like woods pigs. Plenty of damage could happen between now and the farrowing. But in this critical week Woodbridge watched them continually. He walked into the far-rowing pen four and five times a day. He called them by name. He scattered the feed so there'd be no fights. He kept them happy and content.

These problems closed Woodbridge's mind against Exeter's senseless tax chatter until, incredibly, Amos leaned against the top rail of the farrowing pen and began making marks on a piece of paper, an effrontery only comparable to Woodbridge's wrath.

"What the devil you doin', Exeter?"

"Countin' your hogs."

"What for?"

"The taxin', like I said."

"You're out of your mind, Exeter!"

But the redhead found out, that afternoon at the store, that Exeter was not out of his mind. Woodbridge heard Sam Hosmer with his own ears.

"We'll meet here Monday afternoon," said Hosmer. "Each man'll name off his property, and we'll decide which rate it is, first, second, or third."

Woodbridge exploded. "A-a-h! Are we to help the hangsman hang us!"

"This is different," said Stikes. "We're payin' these taxes to ourselves for things like Flannerty's share of the cost of the jailhouse."

"Hogwash!" said Woodbridge. "Y'want to pay taxes for only one reason. We elected Exeter tax lister, and now he wants to function and collect his 7 per cent!"

"That's nothing to do with it, Tom," said Hosmer. "County says we've got to pay taxes. Exeter, have that stock count ready by Monday afternoon."

"What's this about stock?" asked Woodbridge. "The state and county tax is a land tax. Not stock."

"True, Tom. But we need some improvements around town. While we're at it, we're collecting a town tax. It's within our rights. Tax meeting's Monday."

"You're lookin' at one that won't be there, Sam."

"You figure you're better'n everybody else?"

"No. But I take it personal you decided on a stock tax."

"Ye've been figurin', I suppose, that on a stock tax you're the one that's going to pay most."

"That's only half. I got it all figured, too, that if it was a land tax Shuldane and you would pay the most. And I got it figured, also, that any time it's between me and Shuldane, you'll always side with Shuldane."

"Don't you ever figure, Tom, that the more stock you own, the more you owe this village?"

"I figure the other way around. Besides, what about Shuldane?"

"Tom, what I'm tryin' to say to ye—" But the older man didn't finish. The contraction of his face was not anger but disappointment. "Tom, we don't seem to understand each other. I wanted ye on my side in this. But with ye or without ye, I'm going to put the tax through. And if ye're not at the tax meeting, I'll let the law take its course."

"I won't be there, Hosmer; nor many others, if I carry any weight!"

On almost any issue, lately, a certain number of men watched to see what Tom Woodbridge had to say. In fact, men were already being called "Hosmer men" or "Woodbridge men." But on taxes it looked as though Woodbridge stood alone.

Something in the grimness of Hosmer's face in the store that day caused Tom to talk to Jonathan Blair later.

"What I'm askin' ya, Blair: If a stock tax hits me almost all alone, haven't I got good law-court reason not to pay? Especially if I can show they ganged up on me?"

Blair's open face had lately taken on a strange earnestness which no longer patronized the issues of Mesopotamia.

"Yes, Tom. I could win your case against a stock tax for you. Wouldn't even be very difficult. And I've half a mind to do it. It would serve you right."

"Serve me right?"

Blair's relaxation as he examined Woodbridge was the lethargy of disappointment.

"Woodbridge, Shuldane was right. I was wrong. The West won't belong to your kind. It'll always belong to the Shuldanes. They'll stand up and foot the bill, and then they'll walk off with the cream. I had the idea that when Shuldane finally came out here some day, he'd be surprised to find himself up against you, a new kind of force. But when Shuldane comes, he'll find just what he figures to find—a runaway apprentice who won't pay his way."

Blair turned and left the redhead rooted in anger, staring after the lawyer's disdainful back.

On Monday morning, the day of the tax meeting, Woodbridge met Stanley-the-Slasher on the West Road to Hussong's cabin.

"We'll start the burning at noon, Slasher. Be there a little early if you can."

Slasher looked surprised.

"Tom, I'm not going to run your burning this afternoon. I'm going to the tax meeting."

"You bargained to run the burning of that field this afternoon."

"I'm breakin' that bargain, Tom. There's talk of a school for the babes from the tax money, and a road and a bridge."

"A-ah!"

"*After* the meetin' I'll run your burnin' off before dark."

"Don't bother, Slasher. Because I'll be doin' the burnin' *during* the meeting!"

The timbers on Woodbridge's north slope, above the shed, lay in windrows, just as Slasher had cut them. Slasher had the knack, though, of burning off a field so that the flames all worked to the center. The land was thus cleared in a single burning without leaving any big un-burned stumps and logs to ox-haul off the place. Besides that, the land had a good coat of potash on it from the firing. Slasher's trick for clearing a lot in one burning was worth twenty men working steadily for a week. Veronica pointed this out to her husband.

"I can't help that," answered Woodbridge. "Stranger-boy and I can tend to the burning ourselves! This afternoon!"

Mitchell and Adams arrived at the cabin. Woodbridge went out to meet them.

"We'll have to do it ourselves," said Woodbridge. "Slasher backed out. You bring shovels?"

Mitchell looked at Adams in surprise. Adams spoke. "Tom, we didn't come for the burning. We stopped by for you to go to the tax meetin'."

Woodbridge turned without answering and walked north with Stranger-boy to the slope that was covered by a morass of cut timbers.

Since the wind was from the east, Woodbridge piled his tinder under a stack of twigs at the east end of the field, and prepared to ignite it with the lock of his rifle.

Inside Sam Hosmer's store, the taxing continued, but with a certain hollowness. The center hitching post had been left conspicuously vacant. Hosmer glanced out the door occasionally as Exeter read the list.

"Hope Emerson. Fifty acres, at the second rate. One cabin. One horse. Six sheep. That correct?"

"It's correct," said Hope, "except that ledge behind the cabin with the cave in it should go for third rate. About ten acres."

Exeter looked at Hosmer, who nodded absent consent.

"Jim Hawkins. Fifty acres at the second rate. One single cabin. One horse. Two cows. That right, Jim?"

"Knock off one cow," said Hawkins. "She'll butcher before tax time."

"Lot Webster. Four hundred acres. No improvements. That's one of them absentee settlers. What rate is that land?"

"All absentees pay the high rate," said Hosmer. "Not likely they'll come a thousand miles to complain. Continue."

"Elnathan Shuldane, at the first tax rate—"

Jonathan Blair was on his feet.

"Gentlemen, as you know, I've power of attorney for the Shuldane lands. Naturally, Mr. Shuldane expects to pay the great share of the land tax. But he wished me to point out that to tax at the first rate the residue from 20,000-odd acres is an undue burden. And the four thousand acres to the east is hardly first rate."

"I see Nate's point, Jonathan." There was a challenging sparkle in Hosmer's blue eyes. "But on this I'm afraid we'll have to classify his land at his own estimate."

Jonathan Blair waited. But Hosmer merely held forth the clipping from the *Columbian Centinel*. "You see, he advertises here, Jonathan, 'All lands offered for sale in the Mesopotamia tract are exceedingly tillable and of the first rate.' Nate set his own rate."

Blair's grin acknowledged Hosmer's good-humored victory, and to the village's surprise Blair sat down without a fight.

There were some in the room who were not surprised, though. Jim Hawkins, for example, felt that Blair could not make so much of a fight even if he wanted to, since some people had cooled to Blair because of his mission to prosecute Slover Navarre. Navarre had to be caught again, first; but when he was, Blair was to prosecute.

Hosmer suddenly looked out the door and stood up straight with obvious pleasure. As Veronica Woodbridge entered, he ordered Exe-

ter: "Hold up a minute. Here comes Veronica to declare the Woodbridge property! Come in, Veronica, and sit."

But Veronica was distraught.

"Fire! Our place! Hurry! Shovels!"

The meeting disintegrated to an excited babble as Hosmer went
forward to get more details from the breathless Veronica. As Hosmer
and Veronica talked, the strong sentiment of Mesopotamia was pitched
across the store by Morgan Brady.

"Count me out! His place can burn to the ground if he's too good to
pay the tax with me!"

There was a rising murmur of agreement, but Hosmer yelled, "Grab
your shovels and get out to the Woodbridge place!"

Fitchburg's whine was well reasoned: "Sam, I don't see why we're
turnin' ourselves inside out for a man that wouldn't come six miles
to report for taxes!"

"You fools!" yelled Hosmer. "That fire don't know his fields from
yours! Now get movin'!"


Tom Woodbridge was stripped to the waist. His skin was fire-red,
and it glistened with sweat as he struggled to hitch the bull plow to
the ox. He was glad to see Hosmer, but he took no time for thanks.

"It's headin' for the cabin and the hog pens, Sam! Have 'em dig a
fire trench through the sod north of the pens over there. I'll plow a
trench through the corn on this end!"

The wind took the blaze slowly toward the Woodbridge development. Voices wouldn't carry over the hot wind, so Hosmer took each
man by the shoulders and pushed him into position, indicating with
gestures the projected fire-trench line. Those without shovels clawed
the turf with sticks and bare hands.

Veronica had moved the document box out of the cabin into the
wagon when she noticed that Zabeth was gone. She searched frantically
around the cabin.

When the plow was hitched, Woodbridge was already enveloped in
a thick white smoke from the wet cornstalks. He slapped the ox with
the lines, but the beast would not move. Woodbridge yelled for the
Stranger-boy, who appeared through the smoke.

"Get this animal movin', boy!"

But the boy turned away. Zabeth had followed him faithfully into
the smoke. Torn between Woodbridge's emergency and Zabeth,

Stranger-boy turned around and led Zabeth out of the smoke. When he reappeared, the ox was paying for the delay as Woodbridge lashed the animal.

"He's afraid of the smoke, Mr. Tom! It won't work!"

"It's got to work! Make him move!"

"I'll try. You lean on the plow!"

Stranger-boy moved to the huge animal's lowered head and talked softly into the great white ear.

"Don't stand there talkin'!" yelled Woodbridge. "Move him!" And the rein lashed against the animal's flank.

The boy continued to talk, putting a slight forward pressure on the head harness.

Hosmer materialized through the smoke.

"Hurry up, Woodbridge! We got a trench goin', but the fire's skirtin' the end of the trench between you and us!"

"Let the hogs out of the pens, Hosmer! Except not the farrowing pen! You understand? Not the farrowing pen! If they run loose in the woods, I'll lose every litter!"

Hosmer disappeared in the smoke.

Stranger-boy stripped off his shirt and threw it over the ox's head, maintaining his forward pressure on the harness. He rearranged the shirt to expose the great white ear, into which he talked.

"It's all right. I'm right here on the fire side. Nothin' can happen."

Incredibly, the animal leaned forward so that it had to put a foot forward. Burning twigs landed on the ox. The boy brushed them off. The ox strained into the yoke, leaving behind the heavy bull plow a broad-turned furrow of black wet dirt. But there would have to be many more furrows to stop the crackling flames from jumping across. Choking and talking, Stranger-boy led the ox back and forth through the smoke.

Stikes took shape in the smoke.

"Woodbridge! Hosmer says he's got to let the sows out of the farrow pen. They're jumpin' and rantin' around against the fence. Gonna kill theirselves, sure!"

"Don't touch that farrow pen, Stikes!"

But as Tom said it, he knew it was too late. An ear-splitting squeal preceded the sound of cracking wood, and through the smoke scrambled three delirious sows.

"They broke out," said Woodbridge, and his voice held such defeat as to unsteady Stranger-boy who guided Ox.

By the time the flames flickered through the hog pens, the fire had lost its momentum. The barren ground inside the pens offered no fuel. The air cleared. The smoldering north slope of the Woodbridge place was black and covered with exhausted men who started for home without comment. Hosmer had already left.

Woodbridge's left arm was around Veronica, who held Zabeth. His right hand rested on the shoulder of Stranger-boy, who was pouring water over Ox's head. Tom's voice was hollow as he looked at the blackened pen posts and the black, smoking field.

"Lost the hogs, Veronica."

"At least they didn't burn to death."

"Lost 'em, includin' the farrow sows."

"But the cabin's safe, and the babe."

"We can round up some of 'em in the woods. But we'll likely lose every blasted litter."

Veronica made them all eat supper, just as though nothing had happened. She even made Stranger-boy and Zabeth wash as usual. Woodbridge watched her in wonderment, as he had three years ago on the day of Rontondee's raid.

As they ate he said: "Veronica, you better go down tomorrow and list our property for the tax, what we got left. After all, the people put out the fire."

"I will. But Tom, I think it best you don't go on feeling they did it for us. They were pretty curled up at us."

"I know. The people kilt the fire to save their own places. Not ours. But it was to our benefit there was people handy."

"Always is, Tom."

"I guess a man should pay somethin' for that."

Watching his wife go about cleaning up the table as though it were any day in the week reminded Woodbridge that Ox and Prince and the mare had to be fed.

Veronica, watching her husband from the window, saw him walk listlessly into the charred hog pens, shake the loose corner post, and slap it with a lingering paw. He started to fix it, then stopped, shut the gate automatically, and started to lock it. Then he dropped the chain and started toward the cabin. Veronica was wishing that she could tell him what to do, when she saw him suddenly stop and cup his hand to his ear, listening. A strange parade was in progress. Veronica ran out and stood beside her husband.

Up from the hole in the woods where the West Road entered the clearing, there came a grunting column of white hogs. Every ten or fifteen head or so there'd be a man: Stanley-the-Slasher, Mike Stikes, Amos Exeter, Jim Hawkins.

Woodbridge stood transfixed.

Slasher arrived first. "Where you want 'em, Tom?"

Woodbridge could not answer, but Veronica indicated the first pen, and the column clattered by.

"Old man Hosmer detailed some of us to round these critters up durin' the fire, 'fore they got too far," said Slasher.

"Answer him, Tom," said Veronica. But Woodbridge only stared.

For twenty minutes the hogs came up the path. Stranger-boy checked them off: "Thirty-three, thirty-four, thirty-five. There's Cleopatra. Thirty-six, thirty-seven . . . "

"Don't count 'em, boy," said Woodbridge at last. " 'Tain't seemly at a time like this."

Sam Hosmer was aging. He was badly out of breath when he came up the slope at the tail of the column.

"I guess that's all of 'em, Woodbridge. You count 'em?"

"I—ah—I'm in a poor position to be countin' hogs that don't rightly belong to me."

"Sure they belong to ya—by grace of the people of Mesopotamia, to be sure—but you're payin' for that privilege."

"Don't get you, Sam."

"Well, I take it, it'll be all right if Exeter comes out tomorrow to count 'em for the tax listin', won't it, Tom?"

The lands and chattels of Mesopotamia were duly listed with the county treasurer, properly classified as first rate, second rate, third rate. The carrying charges of civilization had come to Mesopotamia Twp., as it was spelled on the tax roll down at county.

# Chapter 17: THE TRIAL (1809)

MESOPOTAMIA was laughing behind its horny hand.

Twice, Jonathan Blair had been down to the Chillicothe court of quarter-sessions. And twice the court had disbanded with no decision against William Hogland.

Mesopotamia, in part, was smiling at Blair. It had heard the reports.

Here was the handsome Mr. Blair, with his Harvard brand of law, backed by the power of the Shuldanes, the Daytons, the Youngstown Youngs, the Symmeses, and all the big ones; but he couldn't close a case against William Hogland, who was defended by an unknown woods lawyer from Zanesville. Nothing could better tickle the capricious whimsey of the upcountry.

A few, though, like Sam Hosmer and Hope Emerson, were puzzled by certain things about the trial. For example, Blair, who now held Navarre's seat in the legislature, had done some strange voting there, according to Buttrick's reports.

As the trial strung out, and the leaning of Judge Calvin Pease seemed to favor Navarre's acquittal, the Federalists began a movement in the state legislature to impeach the three judges.

Now, when the subject came up in a heated Statehouse debate, it was Blair who stood up and said, "Gentlemen, I remind you that the judicial term is seven years, and the judges do not sit at the pleasure of this body, but hold office above it and independent of it."

Worthington had answered this speech. "May I ask Mr. Blair how, if the court does not sit at the pleasure of the legislative, how is it that they were appointed by us? And do you tell us that the power to appoint does not contain also the power to remove?"

The argument reached a point where the Federalists, Blair's party, stood on the floor and demanded impeachment. But the impeachment motion was never carried. The obstruction was a lucid and impassioned speech by Jonathan Blair against his own party.

And back in Mesopotamia they discussed these things.

"I tell ye," Hosmer said, "there's more to this Blair than ye see when

255

ye look at him. He only had to support the impeachment and he had
the judge licked."

"No, you miss the point," Buttrick said. "Blair doesn't want those
judges removed because then he'll have to start all over again with his
trial."

Woodbridge's explanation was, strangely, the most logical. "You're
both wrong. I been mixed up against Blair more than any of ya," he
said. "And once you know him, it's easy to figure. If Blair opposes the
impeachment of the judges, how are those judges gonna look at his
case? Y'mean t'say he ain't gonna look like their hero?"

There was no answer to that.

"And y'mean t'say it ain't possible Blair rigged up this whole fuss
in the legislature so's he could turn out to be the judges' herdsman?
You'll see. Blair will win his case."

The redhead suddenly saw the guilty look on all their faces, and
turned behind him to find the cause.

Jonathan Blair walked into the store.

Woodbridge blustered. "All right, so ya heard what I said, Blair!
Is it true or not?"

Blair excused them with a tired smile.

"It's such a good plan, Tom, I wish I'd thought of it. But the fuss
over the impeachment of the judiciary is none of my making. Not
Judge Pease's either, nor the legislature. What you're seeing here is
only an echo of the big battle in Washington. John Marshall says the
court sits above the Legislative and the President. Tom Jefferson says
the court is just a hired hand to ratify the legislature. The same argument will break out in every level of every state."

"What's that got to do with Navarre?" asked Woodbridge.

"Navarre just happens to crystallize the issue. Actually, he doesn't
count."

"Maybe he don't count with you, Blair," challenged Morgan Brady.
"You wasn't around when he pulled Rontondee off our necks."

The room went silent, to the discomfort of Blair, who left the store.

Hope Emerson followed him out and overtook him.

"Blair, I'm still lookin' for a title patent to come through on my
place. They told me I had to go to the land office in Chillicothe. I'd be
obliged if you'd see me through that paper signin'."

"It's simple enough, Hope."

"I know, but if you was going to be there anyhow."

"Sure. I'm leaving tomorrow."

"I'll come down with Brady, day after."


The courtroom at Chillicothe was the same room that the legislature used. Judge Pease sat in the middle. Judge George Tod sat on his right hand, Judge Samuel Hutchison on his left.

Pease's gray hair pointed straight forward on top and came straight down on the back and sides, with no attempt to swirl it backward in a handsome flourish like Judge Tod's mane.

Pease sat relaxed, but very straight against the back of his chair, and watched the pleading attorney at all times with quiet eyes in an expressionless mask. His bearing did not imply that the furnishing of judgment was any greater calling than the furnishing of horseshoes, but it promised that if his business were smithing, he would deliver the best horseshoes available. There was no sophistication, yet neither was there any naïveté which would invite superficial handling of the issue.

There were two other judges. Judge Tod lounged in his chair, and during the long, unbroken arguments counted the links in his watch chain and thumbnailed at a spot on his waistcoat. Judge Hutchison, who was a busy farmer, went over his accounts during the dull speeches.

Slover Navarre, the defendant, observed all this as he sat before them, whittling a bone handle for a knife. Taken feature by feature, as he sat in the chair, Navarre was not at first a striking figure. In fact, those who came to the trial for the first time found it hard to believe that he was the cause of this great trial, which had become the principal diversion of Chillicothe and the test battle between the Jeffersonians and the Federalists and between the large landholders and the bounty-warrant settlers, between the absentees and the frontiersmen.

But after the second or third day of watching, Navarre strangely changed in one's eyes to the point where he was the dominant figure in the room. This was perhaps because of the great calm contempt which he wore on his face.

As one watched him seated quietly in the center of the furor, it did indeed seem quite possible that this man was the "Governor of the Squatters." As one watched his immense composure it even became possible to see in him a threat to the nation.

Navarre looked up from his whittling to grin faintly at the broad, solid back of the attorney they had given him: Captain Boley Travers. Travers was chunky and earnest and, in Navarre's opinion, stupid.

It was amusing, both to Navarre and to the crowd, to see the flagrant admiration on the face of Boley Travers as he watched his opponent at work.

Jonathan Blair paced back and forth before the bench, delineating his fluent, well-poised argument.

The argument was well poised, all right. So much so and so well rehearsed and so unimpassioned that it puzzled Judge Pease, who revealed his perplexity, however, only by his intensified concentration.

Blair was reading a letter from the former Secretary of War, Henry Knox, to the President of the United States Congress:

> ". . . therefore, sir, it is unnecessary to mention the manner in which the arrearages of pay due the late army was settled, or the present state of those arrearages. It is sufficient to observe that the soldiers were convinced that had Congress the ability, the payments would have been complete. But too many now have been compelled by economic necessity to sell their bounty warrants for next to nothing. Those veterans who still retain bounty warrants now consider the lands promised them as their only resource against poverty in old age. Uninformed of, or not comprehending the delay in surveying the lands due to them, they already feel that the government intends to default.
>
> "In any plan for the disposal of the Western Territory, if a tract be not quickly surveyed and assigned to these warrant holders, they will be prevented from the benefits intended them by Congress. Circumstanced as they are, they cannot enter into competition with rich speculators for the land, which will be the case if they are not quickly assigned lands which are surveyed and ready to occupy in small parcels. I have the honor to be sir—"

"Damnation, Blair!" Judge Pease hammered the table. "I can't follow you. Am I to construe this as evidence of misdemeanor on the part of Hogland and the squatters?"

"I'm building to demonstrate, sir, the motivation for large-scale invasion of the public domain by squatters."

"Huh! Seems to me you don't mind throwing a damned charitable light on your opponent."

"I'm willing the court should see the duress and the predicament of the squatters, trusting the bench to distinguish between sentiment and law."

"Huh. Proceed. But do not play around corners with me, sir."

Judges Tod and Hutchison were roused by Pease's explosion. They now leaned forward sheepishly to concentrate.

Blair next read an excerpt from Colonel Rufus Putnam's letter to the Secretary of the Treasury, written from Marietta, Ohio:

"It is supposed that these intrusive settlers or squatters amount to upwards of three hundred families on the shores of the Muskingum, six hundred on the Scioto, and daily increasing. The professed design at first was to purchase the lands upon which they set down if the land will be only offered to them for sale by the United States. I do not conceive any mischief coming from them except as they are cultivating soil and damaging timber which is the property of the people of the United States."

Pease scratched his chin, and studied Blair carefully.

"I'm establishing the numbers of squatters, sir," Blair explained.

Blair submitted that afternoon several other letters:

From Territorial Governor General Arthur St. Clair to the United States Senate:

"Furthermore, a very considerable number of people are settled upon the Scioto without benefit of title. It is believed their numbers are upwards of 2,000. When driven off by troops, they express an intention to purchase and pretend great injustice. But I warn the Senate at this time that should their numbers increase at this same rate, it will be impossible at the end of a year to assemble sufficient troops here to drive them off."

From Winthrop Sargent to the United States Secretary of State:

"Sir: Since my arrival upon the western waters, I have received certain information of intrusion upon the lands of the United States even to an extremely excessive degree. I have information locating the numbers of persons so intruding at 2,500. The altercations between these lawless ones and the United States troops have already resulted in beyond 200 casualties."

From Winthrop Sargent to the United States Secretary of State:

"I must, sir, repeat the very great increase of intruders upon the lands of the United States who are lessening the value thereof by a waste of timber and who are increasing under able leadership and will very soon become most formidable. Indeed, they are already arrogant in the strength of their numbers and talk of taking over the Territorial Headquarters here. Unless the Territorial Governor takes firm action soon, none may be possible. These observations, sir, are the result of my sense of duty and will, I trust, be received in good part. Winthrop Sargent."

Judge Pease reflected that a very inexperienced or naïve attorney, not sensitive to the emotions of westerners, might cite Winthrop Sargent in support of his cause. A naïve attorney might not know that the haughty Winthrop Sargent had left enemies thick and clustering among the rough, unlinened leaders of the West. That was why Judge Pease leaned forward, puzzled.

For he did not believe that Jonathan Blair was a naïve attorney.

"Let me ask you something, Mr. Blair," said the judge. "Are you aware that you may quote from state letters in private chamber without submitting them in open court for the scrutiny of your opponent?"

"Yes, sir. But I welcome the defense to examine them."

Pease leaned back and looked at his hands.

"H-mm. Naturally, I don't discourage your fairness, Mr. Blair." But he looked steadily at Blair for a long moment with cold eyes worthy of the bench.

Tod and Hutchison alerted to the byplay, but Pease said, "Adjourned until tomorrow."

At the land office Blair quickly scrawled out a form for Hope Emerson, an application to trace land title.

When that was done she said: "I watched in there today, Jonathan. Is that all it is? I thought it was more of a thing."

He was surprised that she had been there.

"Jonathan," she continued, "is your side winnin'?"

"It won't be known until the judges write a decision."

"I mean do ya *think* you're winnin'?"

Blair grinned. "I didn't know you were interested in law, Hope."

Her seriousness reprimanded his light answer.

"I'm not. I'm interested in Navarre, though."

"Oh."

"You want to convict Navarre?"

"Why, naturally. You know which side I'm on, don't you?"

"Not any more, I don't."

"Huh? Everybody in the state knows I'm trying to convict Navarre."

"Do they?"

"What kind of talk is this? Everybody knows I'm Shuldane's attorney!"

"I s'pose. Somehow, watchin', I got the idea you hadn't made up your mind which side you was on."

"What are you saying?"

"I got the notion, watchin' in there, it'd be a bad thing if Navarre went to jail, if he was sent there by a man that didn't really want to send him there."

He looked at her with a blank face.

"Wouldn't be so bad for Navarre." She looked straight ahead as they walked. "He knows his mind. And Navarre'd get free anyhow."

"Then nobody loses," Blair laughed.

"Somebody would."

"Who?"

"Ever see a she-lamb tryin' ta follow two opposite-minded bucks? It makes her half dauncy in the head."

For the first time since the long trial had begun, Jonathan Blair ran lightly up the tavern stairs, whistling. His grip was firm as he opened the door to his room. He lifted the coverlet of the bed and was hauling a large black book out from under it when he froze in the bent position.

"Hello, Jonathan."

Blair pushed the book back under the bed and turned to shake hands with Lot Webster.

"Uncle Nate thought you might like some assistance on the case, Jonathan."

Caution came over Blair.

"Thoughtful, Lot. But—ah—things are going well."

"Oh, understand, Jonathan. No criticism. You've worked like a dog on it. Nate just thought the court might be getting used to your face. Little new blood beside you might help. Show of strength, I guess, and so forth."

"Oh?"

"Don't get it wrong, Jonathan. Nate made it clear I'm strictly your assistant. You still do the talking."

"Well, Lot, I think you might as well go back. Don't think I'll need to take your time."

But Webster opened a dispatch case.

"Then, too, Jonathan, not being as close to the case as you all these months, we might have some fresh thoughts here. We outlined another approach here. Only for your approval, understand."

Blair sat down slowly and read the proposal. It was shrewd, hard-hitting, brutal, the more so because as he read Blair noticed many things which had occurred to himself long before Shuldane ever thought of them.

1. Develop comparison, Hogland same type operation as Blenner-hassett-Burr treason. Plans build new empire, seek Spanish aid in secession of N.W. Territory from U.S.
2. Demonstrate squatter election making Hogland governor is direct attempt overthrow Territorial Government.
3. Killing of U.S. troops. Cite comparable in *Sea Hawk* mutiny.

"What do you think of it, Jonathan?"

"Very good."

"I could present it tomorrow."

Blair took off his coat and unbuttoned his collar and cuffs.

"Tell you what, Lot," he said. "My best point is coming up tomorrow. I've been working up to it. Let me do that first. Then, depending on their reaction, you go into your story."

"Fair enough." But Webster's tone was guarded.

The court was more alert next morning. Obviously there had been some talk around town last night. And as the people noticed the new attorney sitting with Blair, heads swayed together and then nodded to each other.

Under Blair's arm, as he walked back and forth before the judges, was a large black book.

Blair began by building toward the concept, "How much usurped area becomes invasion, and how much appropriated land is merely a crime, a larceny?"

He delineated the long story of squatter usurpations. Coupling this to his estimate of the number of squatters, he arrived at a possible total of 200,000 acres of land which the squatters had stolen. But never did an attorney treat so fairly with the victims of his prosecution and the motives for their usurpation.

Finally he laid the black book before Judge Pease, who, when he saw the cover designation, was surprised: *Volume IV, U.S. Revolutionary Bounty Land Warrants.*

"The land office has made this Doomsday Book available to me, sir, for your examination."

"And your point?" asked Pease.

"I wish to demonstrate the proper way of settling in the public domain, sir. To show by these warrants how the eventual holders carefully substantiate every acre they claim by turning over to the government a bounty warrant in payment. I have not made an exhaustive tabulation. But I wish the court to compare the payments of the major holders in the west AGAINST—" Blair blasted his tone up to alert the other two judges and the defense attorney "—AGAINST the number of acres which they actually occupy."

Tod and Hutchison, both large holders, looked up. Throughout the room there was a surging forward, as though the book could be read from the back row. Blair looked around the court. He saw General Duncan MacArthur, who occupied two thousand acres but who had only turned in warrants for one thousand. MacArthur looked worried. He saw Judge Symmes's cousin, present on Symmes's behalf. Symmes had sold twice as much land as he'd ever paid for. Blair saw Haga and Salter and Stanberry glaring at him. He saw represented about a half-million acres of stolen ground. High echelon, refined, cultured stealing it was, done in the shuffling of papers. Still stealing, though, if swindling were a department of larceny.

But Blair said something else.

"I presume, sir, that I may have the clerk make the tabulation I suggest so that my statement may be in effect notarized for the court."

Pease looked puzzled, but he said, "That would be in order."

Blair saw Lot Webster looking at him with a puzzled expression. Then he saw Navarre lean close to Boley Travers. And Travers was suddenly on his feet, saying, "Would the court also present the defense with a copy of the tabulated comparison when it is complete?"

"It will," said Pease.

Judge Tod and Judge Hutchison leaned forward to whisper to the impassive Judge Pease between them. They pointed to various names in the book. But Pease said, "The requested computations will be made."

Lot Webster was assembling his papers, preparing to take the floor. The spectators were anxious to hear the new attorney.

Pease was therefore taken off balance when Jonathan Blair said, "Your Honors, my side rests its case with your wisdom."

The courtroom flushed into a buzz of whispers. But Blair knew that he faced worse than a whisper when he returned to his table. Lot Webster was standing. His face was livid and the veins in his temple were swollen.

"Blair, what in God's name are you doing? You haven't won this case yet!"

As the hubbub grew louder to cover his voice, Webster yelled louder at Blair, who only listened, buttoning his coat, as a man does who has finished a job and is leaving.

Webster was left standing in a rage of frustration as Blair walked toward the door. Glancing up under the brim of his hat, he saw the quiet, strong face of Hope Emerson, who sat among the low gallery of cloth-dressed watchers in her buckskins. Although she was not joining in the general courtroom hubbub, her face was as startled as the rest.

He passed close enough by her that she could say to him, "Looks like that lamb finally made up its mind, Jonathan. Gonna be a ever-lastin' surprise to the whole flock."

Even Captain Boley Travers knew what to do when a readymade brief like Volume IV was shoved into his hand.

As far as Mesopotamia could see, Jonathan Blair had suffered a serious defeat. He was not the great lawyer. Almost everyone was glad that Navarre had got off, but that didn't change the fact that Blair had been licked, and they dropped him several notches. Not obviously, at first, but definitely. It showed in a hundred ways, and young Joe Hussong no longer called him "Mr. Blair," just, "Jonathan, when you goin' back East? Everybody says you'll probably be leavin', since the trial. They're surprised you're still here, after."

It was even more surprising to most that Mitchell and Adams, the former squatters and disciples of Navarre, should be the very ones to insist on building a cabin for Blair on the common even though twenty inches of snow smothered the village. After all, Blair tried to jail Navarre. Yet despite the bitter cold the men turned out.

The trees cut down to build Blair's cabin widened still more the hole in the forest over Mesopotamia, or Hosmer Village, as it was called by those who remembered when the trails that crossed here were only the width of a Wyandot's heel.

# Chapter 18: THE CHRISTIAN (1811-1812)

BY 1811 the heel of the Wyandot had grown wide and mighty, especially in the person of Chief Rontondee.

The very Reverend Seth Gershom had seen it grow in boldness and in stamping power, and the minister was glad to be leaving the North. With a benign smile he supervised as Captain Michael loaded his ministerial effects into Morgan Brady's wagon outside the hut.

It was all right for Clay and Calhoun to demand war with England when they sat in Washington, but war with England up under the Greenville Line meant war with Rontondee in a red coat. The Wyandot Rontondee spoke English. Not American, but good Anglican Episcopalian English learned under the tutelage of General Sir Henry Proctor's British garrison just a little north, along the shore of the Erie Lake. Rontondee carried an English rifle that fired English powder. And as Tecumseh banded together the Indian nations from Erie Lake to New Orleans, Rontondee ventured farther and farther south, visiting the Indian mission and the western fringes of Mesopotamia.

The Reverend Gershom smoothed his robe over his knees, anticipating the new clothes he would buy in Steubenville. A robe was not strictly within his right. But his black bombazine suit had worn thin, and the robe had helped him immensely to command the imaginations of the mission Indians. Now, with a blessed recall to Steubenville, he would need new clothes.

Gershom felt good to be leaving, and he smiled. But Captain Michael scowled and prodded his son Silver Pigeon, who spoke earnestly.

"Brother Gershom, do not go. The Yankee militia marches soon against the redcoat. With you gone, they will drive us away—as they did our cousins at Greentown."

Gershom addressed the boy's father, not realizing that lately the messages from the handsome Indian boy were as much his own as his father's.

"Captain Michael, I have taught you a practical Christianity which allows you to use your brains. Do not worry. Put the bags in the wagon."

Neither Indian moved, nor did Thomas Running Fox, who spoke from a cynical slouch. "Strange the White Spirit calls Brother Gershom to Steubenville when his red brothers need him so much at the mission."

"I have nothing to do but obey when the bishop calls me, Running Fox."

"Does the bishop know we mission brothers will be run out by white militia which does not know a Christian Indian from a British Indian? Could he not leave you with us until after the fight?"

Gershom was impatient. "I have assurance from all authorities that you will be safely left alone. Put the bags in the wagon."

Morgan Brady, who was waiting to haul the reverend's baggage and anxious to be heading south of the Greenville Line, stuck his head in the hut. "You got a visitor coming, Reverend Gershom."

The column of troops was led by Armstrong—Major Armstrong. When the major halted, the troops fanned out in a semicircle which could observe most of the mission huts. Armstrong dismounted and walked toward Gershom, who stood majestically robed in the hut doorway.

"Good morning, Reverend Gershom. I came to wish you a good journey on behalf of Mesopotamia and to escort you down to where the road begins."

Gershom studied the major.

"Very kind of you, Major, but pray, how did you know I had not left yesterday as I announced?"

Armstrong struggled, then abandoned his courtesy. "Since you put it that way, Reverend, why did you not leave yesterday as you announced?"

"Seeing your column of troops, I'm glad I did not. Now what is your real errand?"

Armstrong was stripped bare.

"Frankly, Gershom, these Indians have got to go. They'll be taken up to the reservation on the Maumee along with the Greentown Indians and the others. We can't raise any militia out of these towns with Indians so close. The settlers won't leave their families unguarded."

"These mission Indians are the best neighbors you could have," said Gershom.

"They've been good Indians. But Rontondee's men have been seen visiting here. Mesopotamia doesn't trust the mission. Your Indians'll be safer elsewhere anyhow."

"If the whites who know them don't trust them," said Gershom, "what will happen to them if they move where they're not known?"

"Can't help that, Reverend. They've got to go. Especially since you're leaving. The colonel isn't sure just how long this Christianity of yours would last all by itself."

"Come in and explain yourself, Armstrong."

While the major was unstrapping his waist-flattering but overtight side-arms belt, Gershom paced the dirt floor, for the most part giving his back to the major, taking time to think. The major's two booted feet plunked onto the puncheon table, showing Gershom a large "U.S." burned into each sole. Gershom concluded that the major was one to respect signs of authority, and he planned a sermon. As he paced back toward the door, he winced as he saw Captain Michael happily unloading his personal gear from Brady's wagon. He whirled toward Armstrong and extended a long bony finger from which fell a graceful loop of robe.

"Major Armstrong, sir! You take upon yourself a great responsibility! The Indian mission here was not established by any mere Territorial or state authority. The mission here is not another ordinary settlement of friendly Indians to be moved about like the Greentown Indians. This was to be the beginning of a long-range experiment in Christianizing the entire race. A bloodless pushing back of the Indian boundary."

Gershom's hawk eyes riveted the major.

"Will your commanding officer stand back of you and assume the responsibility for disrupting this over-all plan, Major?"

As Gershom pronounced the word "Major," it sounded like a call for the tap boy in a tavern. Armstrong's feet came slowly off the table.

"Well, Reverend, I don't believe the colonel is aware of any unusual implications. I have blanket instructions for deporting all Indian settlements to a reserve well north of the Greenville Line."

"He'll be aware of the implications soon enough, Major. As soon, in fact, as it takes the report to get from the bishop to Washington."

"Still, my orders are clear."

Gershom softened.

"Son, you've stumbled into a big thing. I don't want to see you in trouble. I'd best stay on here another two weeks while you ask for clarification of your instructions."

"That would be very good of you, sir." Armstrong was grateful. "Ah —however, I shall have to disarm your Indians."

Captain Michael and Running Fox looked quickly to Gershom, who resumed his thoughtful pacing.

"I'd stand open to negligence if I left them armed, Reverend."

"Very well." Gershom's tone was wounded. "We'll deliver up our rifles, though it puts us at the mercy of both Rontondee and the settlers, the same kind of settlers who burned out the Greentown Indian settlement."

"I must at least have the rifles, Reverend."

"Bring in the twenty-eight rifles, Captain Michael!"

Captain Michael did not move. Running Fox said, "It is not wise, Father."

"Bring in the rifles!"

Brady was by now standing in the doorway, watching. He marveled at the control Gershom had achieved over the Indians, though he also wondered which side Gershom was on. Unwillingly, Captain Michael and Running Fox left the hut.

Gershom reached for a piece of parchment under his bunk. He uncovered the gourd of soot ink and the turkey-feather quill, and scribbled aggressively with his bony hand.

"What's that?" asked Armstrong.

"You may take the rifles." Gershom continued writing. "But I must ask you to deliver them to Governor Return Jonathan Meiggs on your way south, along with this message."

He wheeled the parchment in front of Armstrong, who read:

DEAR GOVERNOR:

I have instructed Major Armstrong to deliver to you these rifles which you inscribed and presented to the mission Indians in the ceremony some years ago. The Christian Indians were loath to part with them, but since it must be, they wished them returned to you that they might help you in any crisis now facing you.

In case this confiscation of the guns is some error, I wish you not to blame the young major, as I believe him to be carrying out the order of his superior.

REV. SETH GERSHOM

John Armstrong, Major, U.S. Army, was not overly scarred by combat, yet he was singularly experienced in the battle of the chain of command. He could visualize accurately the huffy endorsement Governor Meiggs would scribble on the bottom of the note as he forwarded it to the colonel at Cincinnati. Major Armstrong could see himself standing at attention before the colonel, and he could hear the colonel saying: "Major, half of our mission is to get along with the local militia, who are commanded, as I thought you knew, by the local governor. Perhaps this type of leadership is too subtle for you, Major."

Armstrong pushed the letter back to Gershom.

"Perhaps you'd better keep the rifles until I come back, Reverend."

The people of Mesopotamia were somewhat disappointed to see Major Armstrong ride back through the village so soon. However, he explained that he had extracted a firm promise from the Reverend Gershom to keep all foreign Indians away from the mission.

The clergyman's promise, however, was impossible to keep. Rontondee's hostiles continued boldly to enter the mission area to borrow and steal grain. Nor did Rontondee's Indians defer to Gershom's robe. To retain reverence among his own Indians, Gershom adopted more symbolism. He was never seen without his robe. He drank only from his silver-lace goblet, and he ate only in private, seeming to exist on divine air.

Gershom was on the point of sending for Brady again to carry him to Steubenville, when Silver Pigeon knocked on the door, after the new mission rule, and entered the hut.

"Father Gershom, Captain Michael says six Wyandots and three Delawares are here."

"Tell Captain Michael to get them out of here immediately."

"They will not leave. They are hungry."

"Then tell Running Fox to come with me. We must go to Meso-potamia to create some diversion before the whites see the foreign ones here."

Amos Exeter had built a small addition to the south end of his new cabin, which was on the common north of the blockhouse. On the south wall of the addition to the cabin was pegged a paper which was signed by one Emanuel Ault, county recorder. It was a license to keep a tavern.

In the corner stood a hogshead of whisky on top of which usually rested twelve gourds. Today, though, the gourds were all in the hands of the twelve men who lowered the level of the whisky and raised the tone of their voices.

"If Exeter's right," Buttrick said, "and if there are six of Rontondee's devils visiting the mission, we're fools to wait until tomorrow! We should go today! Clean out the mission by morning!"

Stikes ran a rod down the bore of his rifle and pulled it out, but as the door opened the cleaning patch dropped forgotten to the floor. Exeter was pouring a gourd full of whisky, which ran over onto the puncheons as he stared at the newcomers. The voices shut off as Exeter closed the spigot.

"What is the occasion, gentlemen?" The bass voice of Seth Gershom made the room small.

"I admire your courage coming here, Reverend," said Buttrick. "The village is just arming to come to the mission. The red bastards got to go!"

"How so?"

"We've a report that you've broken your promise. Exeter saw a red-coated Indian at the mission. We're not having any Greentown mas-sacre here!"

"There would have been no massacre of whites at Greentown," said Gershom, "if the whites had only evacuated the Indians; but when they burned the empty Indian huts they invited Indian retaliation."

Exeter was bold in his own house. He grabbed his rifle and pushed for the door. It started a general movement.

"Wait!"

Gershom's piercing command stopped them long enough for him to step in front of the door.

"Make it good, Reverend. We're not much minded for talk."

Gershom was suddenly humility. His voice faltered.

"You win," he quavered. "You are right. We will go."

"Brother Gershom!" said Running Fox. "We will be killed if we go."

"Quiet, Running Fox. We must go."

"That's good sense you talk now, Reverend," soothed Buttrick.

Running Fox studied Gershom narrowly, and edged toward the door.
"You do not speak for Running Fox, Father."

"The men are right, Running Fox. The Indians must go."

Gershom's voice now shed humility in favor of a practical trading
tone.

"Now, gentlemen, you're all fair-minded men. You will, of course,
have the grace to buy the Indian property. The huts, the fields, the
granary, and the livestock which they must abandon. Asa Buttrick,
which Indian farm will you buy? The big one?"

Running Fox's face was a mask of hatred as he glared at Gershom.
Buttrick was less sure of himself.

"Well, Reverend, I don't really have any use for a hut or for plowed
land. I admit that it's fair . . ."

Gershom's tone stiffened.

"Which will you buy, Hawkins?"

Hawkins didn't answer, and Gershom quickly circled the room, asking each man until he came to Brute Christofferson, who said, "Well,
Reverend, a piece of land and a hut way up there isn't much use to
me. I couldn't farm it."

"True," said Gershom, "but, of course, you must occupy it. Otherwise Rontondee's hostiles will. They'll be your new neighbors."

Gershom's velvet-covered threat sank the room into stillness, and the
silence was his victory.

Christofferson said, "Ah . . . Reverend, maybe you and those Indians
better stay still. Uh . . . they'll be safer near us. We can protect
them."

Gershom glared fiercely until the grin faded from Running Fox's
face.

But it required the peak of Gershom's wit to stay ahead of the dangerous, vacillating, frightened population of Mesopotamia. As belated
copies of the Scioto Gazette drifted upcountry to Mesopotamia, and
the people read of the mounting tension between England and the

United States, the prospect of Seth Gershom's departure for the rich parish at Steubenville faded.

On the maps in Washington, no doubt, the boundary of the United States of America was a nice wide crisp line, broken up by stout-looking symbols depicting outposts, blockhouses, and observation posts labeled "Greenville Treaty Boundary Line." But the Reverend Seth Gershom knew that this line showed only on maps.

And Rontondee had no map.

In Washington a war with England would mean ships and troops along the length of York State. But the Reverend Gershom knew better. War with England would first be a single-file column of arrogant Wyandots running down through the mission, stealing, burning, and shooting, and then moving south to Mesopotamia. War with England would first be a big red buck with a lascivious leer ripping the blouse off Veronica Woodbridge while the girl Zabeth screamed wildly until she was silenced by an ax. War with England would at the first be Captain Michael and Silver Pigeon and Running Fox refusing to go with Rontondee against Mesopotamia. Then it would be black, burned flesh of mission Indians lying swollen and shiny on the ground with mouths open, showing teeth. And Gershom didn't want to be there.

By June, Seth Gershom was riding south to see if the parish in Steubenville was still open to him. He had gone almost as far as Mesopotamia, accompanied by Running Fox, when he was met by a mounted party. There was no greeting. Buttrick simply said, "You heard the news, Gershom?"

"What news?"

"Hull has surrendered Detroit to the British."

"Oh."

"I should have known it would be no surprise to an Indian lover."

"I admit it's bad," said Gershom. "But I don't see what it does to us."

"What it does! It only gives Tecumseh and Rontondee a clean sweep from the Erie Lake all the way south, with nobody at their backs but British, feedin' 'em powder and whisky and rifles!"

Gershom did not answer.

"That means your little mission will make just a nice little stoppin'-off place for 'em when they come down this way, killing and raiding. So the mission's got to go."

"Gentlemen, there are no foreign Indians at the mission."

"That so?" asked Buttrick. "Then where would you be going now?"

"I was on my way to Steubenville to see if the parish is still open for me."

"That's good, Reverend, because you're out of work up here. The mission's finished."

Gershom looked down at the back of his horse's neck. No one spoke until the minister had finished his thinking.

"Gentlemen," he said, "I have a suggestion. If what you say is true, obviously the mission is in danger from two sides. From you on the one side and from the British Wyandots on the other. That is not your concern, of course. But it seems to me that if you fear hostile Wyandot attacks, you should leave the mission alone. Place spies among us. That way you'd have sufficient notice of any infiltration. You could alert Mesopotamia."

Brady laughed. "What more could we ask? He's made us a damn' sight better deal than we were gonna give him!"

The sense of it was apparent. They left Brady and Exeter to be the spies for the first week. The rest turned back to Mesopotamia.

Buttrick called to the minister, "Well, Reverend, if you're bound for Steubenville, might as well ride along with us."

Gershom stared longingly to the south, but his hands manipulated his horse slowly back to the north, following Running Fox, who was looking back to see what the preacher would do.

It was a week later that Woodbridge went into Exeter's tavern to find Brady doubled up in laughter. He could hardly speak.

"Did he ever work it beautiful on us!" laughed the wagoner. "That Gershom! You got to give it to him!"

Exeter did not find it so funny. But Brady continued.

"Treated us as pretty as you please, all the time. But we ain't in his mission two hours when it's plain as day what he's up to. Maybe we think we're spies. But for him we're protection. There's two of the red devils followin' me everywheres, and two followin' Exeter. That means that if any of you from the village comes up to do any dirty work, Gershom's got himself a couple a fine hostages—me and Exeter."

"How do you know that was his plan?" asked Buttrick, loath to give Gershom credit for cleverness.

"Simple. I spotted two of Rontondee's Indians in the camp, and I called Gershom on it. 'Oh,' says he, 'they're hostages. Notice how they're followed everywhere they go'?

"I'm just thinking what a cute-minded preacher he is when I looks around and sees these two red devils followin' *me*. And Gershom grinnin' like a horse eatin' briars."

What was funny to Brady was not funny to Mesopotamia. Buttrick and Exeter were already saddling up. Others followed.

Though the door threatened to shake off the hut, Gershom did not answer until he had risen from his bed and carefully put on his robe. Captain Michael and Running Fox heard the excitement in the night and came.

Buttrick was spokesman. "Gershom, we're here to search every hut!"

"What for?"

"We got word there's outside Indians at the mission!"

Gershom noticed that it was almost dawn.

"Gentlemen, if that is true," he said, "we shall be most humiliated."

"You'll be worse than that."

"Captain Michael and I will lead you through each cabin immediately."

"Let's get going."

"First, Asa, will you pray with us?"

"Quit the praying and—"

"Asa Buttrick!" intoned Gershom, "how is your daughter Margaret since we last asked blessing for her?"

"I'm sorry, Reverend. Go ahead and pray. But make it short."

Gershom's long arm shot out over their heads and the group bowed to prayer.

"Captain Michael, you listen closely," said Gershom, "for if you have permitted foreign Indians to come among us you will need concentrated devotion. Our Father, have mercy on the soul of Captain Michael. If he has broken his trust, let his spirit fly in chagrin through the night immediately. Let him search through the cabins of Jahanin till he findeth the cause of his downfall. Let him search among his brethren for the evil spirit. And let Captain Michael have no help, but let him combat his devil alone. Let this be a penance. Are you ready to do your penance, Captain Michael?"

"I ye et sa tigh. A yagh kee, Father Gershom."

"Amen."

"Ho ma yen de rang."

And Captain Michael was gone in the darkness.

They left Exeter and two men outside Gershom's hut to insure that no ambush threatened the inspecting party. The tour of the huts proceeded without excitement. The blinking, puzzled Indians in each hut presented themselves for inspection docilely, and the party proceeded back to Gershom's hut.

"Hey, Reverend, what about that hut over there? We didn't go in."

"I'm sorry," said Gershom.

The suspicious group hurried to the cabin. Inside, Captain Michael knelt on the floor in prayer, his hands clasped tight in front of him.

"That's that penance business, I suppose," observed Buttrick.

Gershom, last to leave the cabin, was the only man close enough to the Indians to perceive that the sheen on Captain Michael's cheekbones was not his natural complexion, but sweat. He noticed, too, that Michael's breathing was still heavy and that his knife was missing from his belt. In an unfamiliar gesture, Gershom gently touched the shoulder of the Indian as he left the hut.

When Gershom had safely shepherded the party back to his own hut, he noticed with satisfaction that the momentum of their rage had largely spent itself. In the waning night they looked tired.

"Where is the rest of your party?" asked Gershom. "The ones we left here to cover you?"

"I think we might better ask that of you!" said Buttrick, and suddenly the men were alert again and suspicious. The hogshead was forgotten. Brady and Woodbridge and Mitchell rushed outside, but they returned almost immediately.

Brady reported: "Horses are gone. Tracks back down the trail. They got tired of waiting, I guess."

"That's a funny thing for them to do," said Stikes, alarmed.

But now Gershom was alert. He moved slowly toward the door. "Let us step outside, gentlemen, to see if there could be a reason for the abrupt departure of your friends."

They walked to where the horses were tied. Brady tripped and stumbled. He regained his balance and exclaimed, "My God!"

Gershom was alert, like an angry hawk.

"What was that, Brady?"

"Nothing. Tripped over a stump. Scared me."

But Gershom's robe swept in the dark to Brady's side. Brady stepped back, and Gershom stooped to the ground and groped with his hands.

It was a long time before he stood, but when he did slowly rise his left hand held the loop of leather thong that carried the cross that Running Fox wore around his neck. The leather was cut, and the reverend's right hand was covered with blood.

Gershom stood with his hands outstretched. No man spoke. Gershom's face became terrible as his eyes slowly circled the group. His mouth hung open, a black hole. When his eyes met Buttrick's, the trader's jowls jiggled as if he'd been struck.

"Well," struggled Buttrick, "it could just as well have been the other way around."

Brady started to agree, but he stopped, for it seemed to him suddenly that the face of Seth Gershom was about to loose the lightning of the terrible swift sword. The minister sucked air into his cavernous lungs. His great mouth opened wider, and his voice split the dawn.

"Captain Michael!" he thundered. "Ne mat re zue enu mah!"

Gershom looked in the gray light like some gigantic bat as he flung off his robe, twisted it into a tight roll, and flayed it across Buttrick's face so that the large wooden button resounded against the trader's head. Buttrick clutched the robe in instinctive defense. Gershom jerked it forward with such force that it tore the nails off Buttrick's hand. As the trader stood looking at his bleeding hand, Gershom's bony fist smashed into his face.

"Stop him!" yelled Buttrick.

"Stop him, nothin'!" answered Brady. "They're comin'! Get out of here!"

The white men leaped to their saddles and clattered south on the trace.

It had been a long time since Captain Michael had seen the Reverend Gershom out of his robe. And as the great gaunt Christian sat in the hut drinking whisky, Michael noticed that he drank from a plain gourd. The silver-lace goblet sat on the table. Gershom saw Michael looking at it. The minister reached for the glass-lined goblet and shattered it against the wall of the hut.

Michael did not speak, for in the terrible face he saw for the first time a great, beauteous strength befitting a representative of the Great White Spirit. In his primitive wisdom the Indian saw on the face of Seth Gershom a raging awareness of the burden of human misery. And through the doorway he saw the sun come up on Gershom's wrath.

The mission Indians crowded around the body of Running Fox and around the doorway of Gershom's hut.

Captain Michael motioned them away and quietly pulled the door shut after him. He pointed to the closed door.

"Owa he. The Great Spirit tin de Father Gershom."

# Chapter 19: THE EXEMPTION (1812)

STRANGER-boy didn't want to stay and listen, but to leave might cause curiosity.

Mike Stikes never just "dropped in" without long cause, despite his casual air as he leaned against Woodbridge's farrowing pen. And lately there was only one thing on Stikes's mind. The tall man braced to speak, but Woodbridge bent to cuff a cantankerous sow who nipped at an orphan piglet trying to pirate a meal.

"Miss Veronica got that milk cookin' for these orphans, boy?"

"Yes, sir."

Stikes spoke.

"Just happened by, Tom, to see if you wanted to go down to militia drill with me."

Woodbridge gazed at 163 scampering piglets.

"Mike, you're lookin' at pure gold on the hoof. Hundred sixty-three of 'em. Knock off, say, twenty crits I'll cull out. Twenty more at the outside that won't get by the winter. Still leaves a hundred breeders. Each one worth ten, twenty times an ordinary hog. Look at 'em, will ya, Mike!"

But the frontier was still pale from the news of Hull's surrender at Detroit, and Stikes said, "What about the drill, Tom?"

"Tarnation! Will ya never let me be, Mike!"

Stikes was silent.

"I'm tellin' ya for all time, Mike, if the others got time for that left face and right face and squads by the left, let 'em play soldier! Myself, I got hogs!"

Stranger-boy picked up his bucket and left.

"With Hull givin' up Detroit," said Stikes, "there's nothin' between your hogs and the English, not to mention fifteen hundred red devils."

"Stikes, we're no worse off than before. Congress never did give us troop protection out here. You got no business goin', anyhow, Mike. Everybody told ya you're not fit. Ya fought one war already."

Mike had a way of remaining silent so that you could hear it.

"If it's shootin' you're after," defended Woodbridge, "it'll likely's not be right here in Mesopotamia. Why go runnin' off?"

"My brother was with them regulars they massacred at River Raisin."

"Oh. I didn't know, Mike."

"That makes it personal between me and the King."

There was no conscription. But as the little settlement prepared to furnish a platoon of militia to fill out the company that was going from county, the stern, frost-bitten face of Mesopotamia composed itself into an unenlightened but tyrannical impressment. Because of his age, nobody wanted Mike to go, but since he was going it left little excuse for others.

The unspoken draft had worked its way to the very hearth in the cabin of Thomas Woodbridge, where Veronica sat sewing a dark-blue stand-up collar to a wool coat of the same material. Cut onto the bottom of the coat in back was a short squared-off badger tail of cloth. At the base of this appendage were two brass buttons which Zabeth polished with the hem of her dress. Woodbridge did not overlook the almost loving care with which Veronica stood the roll collar in position.

"Little too broad in the shoulders, isn't it?" asked Woodbridge.

"Jonathan does not lack for shoulders," answered Veronica with two pins in her mouth and a needle in her voice. "Especially in this emergency."

"Seems to me I remember once he did."

Veronica bent her head to her work.

"Seems to me, too, if the governor can make him a lieutenant," furthered Woodbridge, "he could give him a uniform, if it's needed."

"The governor requested that all officers supply themselves with uniforms to face up to those fancy British officers. Other officers will have wives to make theirs."

"The milk warm yet for the pigs?" snapped Woodbridge.

The care with which Veronica set the uniform down irritated Woodbridge, though not so much as the eagerness with which she picked it up again when the Stranger-boy took over the milk chore. The lad swung the iron frame out from the fire and unhooked the iron kettle. He started silently toward the cabin door with the kettle, but Woodbridge snatched it roughly from his hand.

"The young ones I look after myself," he said, and went out.

The boy's suddenly empty hands returned slowly to his sides, and without taking his eyes from Woodbridge's back, he said, "Zabeth, if he should be asking, the mash is already mixed, and I'll be back in time to feed it."

He reached his squirrel rifle from beside the fireplace and went out. It took Zabeth a long time to hum her way carelessly around the room to the back window so Mam wouldn't see she knew there'd been sparks. When she looked out, it was in time to see the back of Stranger-boy and the mare heading for the village.

"Is Stranger-boy a man now, Mam?"

"No. Seventeen is not quite a man, Elizabeth."

"Well, is it enough of a man to go to the militia and to court with girls?"

"What gave you that idea?"

"Well, the men don't any more take the heavy end from him in a heft, nor ask does he want to spell a mite."

"*Rest a bit* sounds better, Elizabeth."

"Rest a bit."

Zabeth studied her mother curiously, how she sat so pretty. Even the way she broke the thread was different from the other women. Her mother cut it with a scissors instead of biting at it like Mrs. Flannerty.

"They call him Young Tom instead of Stranger-boy," continued Zabeth. "And his feet near drag the ground on the mare."

Veronica held the coat up as it would sit on Jonathan Blair's deep chest.

"And Camelia Flannerty was joshing him," said Zabeth. "Said his shirt was too small for his chest. But she said it like it was becomin' enough."

Veronica suddenly put down Blair's uniform coat with a blushing haste.

Woodbridge was no more lonesome at home than he was at the store the following morning when he found himself in a chilling minority. Exeter informed him that nothing required him to report for militia drill, but since all men were registered for militia he would have to pay a money fine for each drill he missed. Nor could Exeter resist adding, "Guess you won't object to furnishin' the platoon with a little penalty money for whisky even if ya don't want to go help us keep out the Englishman."

"English invasion!" scorned Woodbridge. "You sure you're so tarnation worried about the English? Or did Mr. Blair here dangle some fancy uniforms in front of you?" He wished he hadn't said it when he remembered about Stikes's brother.

Stikes said: "It's not uniforms, Woodbridge. The whole country is turnin' out to get even for Detroit."

"The whole country?" asked Woodbridge. "Not so fast, Blair. When President Madison ordered out the state militias, how many did Massachusetts send?"

"None."

"Connecticut?"

"None. I admit. But that's why we've got to do it."

"You mistake yourself there, Blair. We been standin' between the East and the Indians for so long they take it for granted. The regular army has been drawin' pay for sittin' around in forts and barracks. Now let them earn it."

"Ye got some right on your side, Tom," said Hosmer. "But the regulars aren't enough. That's why the Ohioans are all turnin' out."

"Are they, Sam? Is that why Governor Meiggs has got to offer $16 bounty money to every so-called volunteer? That don't look to me like no rush to the colors. Meiggs asked for five thousand men. How many's he got so far, Blair?"

"About twenty-five hundred."

"And hog-tyin' 'em to keep 'em. If you men want to hear bugles playin', go ahead to Detroit. But if it's in your mind to protect your kin, y'better take off the soldier suits and stay right here with me! Good day to ya!"

As Woodbridge mounted and rode east, the little militia platoon returned to its drills, which Blair studied from a book sent up from

Fort Washington. They were to march north to Fort Meiggs on December 16, in company with the platoon from Boxford's Cabin, to join in the coming invasion of Canada.

Woodbridge knocked at Hope Emerson's cabin and was admitted.

"Veronica said I was to pick up two yards of tow linen. I was to be particular to get the soft kind where you boiled the flax in lye water, as it's to go next the skin."

"It must be some very special skin," said Hope, "because I must charge you a dollar a yard for it."

"It's to be lining for a coat."

Hope went to her shed for the cloth. Woodbridge started to sit on the chair, but stopped with his legs bent as he noticed a dark-blue coat hung over the back of the chair. It was not of the fine-quality wool that Veronica was using, but it was cut much the same, though there were yet no sleeves on it.

When Hope returned, he pointed to the coat; his wrinkled forehead asked the question.

"For Lieutenant Blair," she explained. "I should be tendin' my critters, but Blair works so hard studying that drill book he's not time to clothe himself proper. We can dress our lieutenant as good as the next."

Woodbridge slowly folded the piece of linen she'd given him.

"Veronica must be makin' a coat for Zabeth, she wants the lining that soft," said Hope.

"I s'pose that's what it is," said Tom. "Thanks."

At home he started to tell Veronica about Hope Emerson's coat. But Veronica was at that moment working on her coat with such an infuriating look of contentment and joy that Woodbridge maliciously withheld. He had not seen such life in her face when she made his own hunting shirt.

As the leaves fell, Woodbridge raced to finish the sheds for the 163 young Bedfords. He hardly tended the woods hogs, which he let roam in the forest, mostly under the care of Young Tom. Woodbridge was not one ordinarily to take pleasure in craftsmanship with his hands. But because of the young pigs the very swinging of the ax to fell the shed foundation logs was a thrill, like counting money. The man and the boy swung alternately .

"It's about to pay us now, boy. The hard part's done with. We'll not be sellin' hogs for pork much longer. Only for breeders."

"But with the war on . . ."

"All the more need for heavy lard hogs. Countin' Cleopatra and Boss, it's 308 Bedford sows we've got, and nine good boars. I've heard of no other Bedfords in the West. They'll have to come to us for 'em, boy!"

"But they don't seem to value 'em like you do, sir."

"They don't know yet, boy. They think one hog critter is like to the next. Only England knows the Bedford. That's why the King's got rules against shippin' 'em out."

The beech fell to the north. They stripped it to a clean timber, and the ox began to haul it down the slope toward the hog pens. Woodbridge in his eagerness led the ox down the slope at a pace so brisk that it jaggled the loose skin that hung off the animal's sharp breastbone.

"If the King ever found out about Boss and Cleopatra gettin' off his islands and out here to Ohio—"

"Slow down a mite," called Young Tom from the rear, where he guided the tail of the timber. But almost as he spoke, the front end of the log gouged into the land and struck a rock. The jolt yanked the yoke cruelly back against the ox's shoulders. But the huge animal dug in and strained to pull the log over the immobile rock. He pulled the draw pole right out of the iron mooring that held it to the yoke.

Woodbridge quickly cut a new draw pole, threw it in the wagon with the iron mooring, and headed down the West Road. Stikes could drill the pole, cut the iron mooring, and forge it onto the new pole.

Stikes was not in his shop. Woodbridge went over to Hosmer's Store. He stepped on the porch and heard Blair's voice float out from within.

"Then on your command, Mike, the second rank fires in volley, and passes the rifles back to the third rank for reloading."

Woodbridge didn't want to go into the store. Lately, as the militia prepared to leave Mesopotamia on December 16, there were fewer words than usual between Thomas Woodbridge and his townsmen. But the draw pole had to be fixed. He opened the door to the store.

"And the third rank," explained Blair to sixteen men seated on the floor, "does not fire at all until called to relieve— Hello, Woodbridge. You come down to sign up?"

"No," snapped Woodbridge, "I didn't come down to sign up!" The hog farmer softened a little. "But—uh—don't want to interfere, either.

Just want to see Mike Stikes a minute. Could ya come over to your forge, Mike?"

"Can it wait till tomorrow, Tom? I'd like to get this point the lieutenant's makin'."

"But, Mike, my draw-pole hitch is fractured. I got timber needin' to be hauled for hog sheds. If I don't get the young ones under better cover, they'll catch their death of cold."

"We might catch our death of bullets if we don't learn this tactic right. I'll fix it tomorrow, Tom."

Seth Gershom paced back and forth the length of his hut. He wore no robe, but his hands were folded behind him in the churchly manner he had cultivated into habit. But he could find no such restful position of habit for his churning brain.

Gershom's flaming wrath had cooled to a coal of smoldering cunning. After the murder of Running Fox, the mission Indians had boiled for a vengeful raid to Mesopotamia. And that was one of the many things that bothered Seth Gershom at the moment: the fact that he had half wanted to let them go. He had stopped them; but he was privately afraid he had held them back for only one reason. News had come to Gershom the following day of the terrible massacre of Ohio militia at Frenchtown by Tecumseh's Indians; and because of that news Mesopotamia would be at this moment coiled up like a spring, hoping for the sight of a mission Indian. Perhaps they were not even waiting.

But even this was not Seth Gershom's chief worry as he paced the hut. More powerfully was he concerned with the fact that the Indians had obeyed him. There had been no dissent, only acceptance, given together with a back-breaking load of trust.

Six months ago he could have ridden to Steubenville without a backward glance. Today he was imprisoned by a ruinous web of human misery more imperious than an order from the bishop. More difficult, too, than any diocesan assignment; namely, to save the lives of twenty-six Indians surrounded by hot-blooded distrust. After the news of the Frenchtown massacre came the news of settler reprisals along the Greenville Line. Gershom was scared, Captain Michael was scared, and Silver Pigeon was scared.

"Father Gershom," said the boy. "News from Mesopotamia."

"I told you to stay away from the settlement," snapped Gershom.

"Militia marches north on sixteenth day of December."

"So?"

"On the way north they will move the mission Indians with them to Black Swamp."

"Why have they not told *me*?"

"Young Tom said they will tell you. But not until there is no time left for Father Gershom to think."

Gershom continued pacing the hut, but faster.

"Father Gershom, if we move from the mission, we will not get twenty miles alive."

"I told you we will not move!" snapped Gershom. And the two Indians watched him pace up and down the hut.

"Go now! Leave me alone!"

So that the militia platoon could continue last-minute preparations for leaving, Mesopotamia sent its young men to deliver the ultimatum to Gershom. The oldest Flannerty, the Hussong boy, the Fitchburg and Mason boys. They asked Stranger-boy to go. But he refused, and Tom senior said it was for the boy to decide. They went well armed.

The Hussong lad entered Gershom's hut and explained that the mission Indians were to pack up their belongings and be prepared to leave to the north on December 17th, when the militia platoon would reach the mission.

"And I'm to bring back an answer, sir," concluded the lad, "whether or not you'll do it peacefully."

Gershom sat silent.

"I take that to mean not, sir."

Gershom did not answer. His hawk eyes bored into the wall.

"Then I was to ask one more question, Reverend. Will you come to Mesopotamia Wednesday night to give a blessing to our militia?"

At this final presumption Gershom rose.

"Get out!"

The boy scrambled.

Gershom wove the floor with his pacing as his scheme fell apart in his hands. The plainest logic in the world the settlers couldn't understand. It had been a mistake to appeal to their logic. What was there left in them to talk to? If not to the logic of the general populace, what peculiarity of what individual?

For Seth Gershom to kneel and pray in private was to begin cutting an oak tree with a hand knife. For between Seth Gershom and the God for whom he was agent, there was a certain embarrassment in private. They supported each other in public, but that was a professional agreement.

But now a weakness seeped through Gershom. He remembered the light on the faces of the men at the seminary. He sank to his knees. He did not put it in words, for the pulpit-worn language of Gershom would be an insult at this time. It was all there in his mind to be read easily enough if the great Truth were true.

How could Gershom face the twenty-six Indians if the militia came on the 17th and took them away? How would Captain Michael look at him? What had Running Fox thought as he died? Even if the Mesopotamia platoon delivered the Indians safely to a new location, how would they defend themselves against whites who didn't know them?

Gershom waited there on his knees, hardly breathing, straining to induce the answer, the light. He removed the rolled-up robe from underneath him so that his bony knees would suffer from the splintery puncheon. He even began to listen for an audible voice.

None came.

Anger colored Gershom's face. He rose suddenly and fired the bunched-up robe at the wall of the hut. He grabbed one of the Communion gourds and slammed it to the floor, where it splintered.

"Good God!" he roared, and it was half curse, half literal. "Why can't the stupid fools understand it's for their own good! Why can't their miserable brains comprehend that if the mission leaves they'll suffer for it! Rontondee will make them pay through the scalp. Why can't they see that! Why can't *You* see that!"

Gershom froze suddenly with a second gourd raised over his head. Shaking with intense excitement, he set the gourd down gently, lest he disturb the idea.

Suddenly something was very clear to Seth Gershom. This platoon of madmen did not want to understand. Why did they want to go? Why were they so anxious to go to war? Who was the leading spirit? Not Hosmer. He wasn't going. Blair? No. He led them, but by appointment from Chillicothe.

Gershom remembered now. It had been Stikes who had started the platoon.

Gershom remembered seeing the tall white-haired blacksmith marching with the platoon, his white hair rising above the heads of the others, jaw set in concentration. He remembered now hearing the villagers beg Stikes not to go. Here, then, was the one man in the platoon who wanted to fight.

Gershom suddenly reached down to scoop the disheveled ministerial robe off the floor. He yelled, "Silver Pigeon!"

The minister was brushing off the robe when Silver Pigeon arrived.

"Go catch those boys from the settlement! Tell them I will come Wednesday night!"

Silver Pigeon's dark, handsome face was a reproof.

"To bless their militia, Father Gershom?"

"Just tell them I'll come Wednesday night."

Pigeon left slowly.

As they entered Mesopotamia on Wednesday, Gershom ignored the greetings as he privately rehearsed his part. Captain Michael ignored the hostile stares of the villagers. Silver Pigeon returned them.

From his accustomed elevated position at the east end of the blockhouse, the Reverend Gershom studied the crowd.

Hosmer saw the clergyman's eye taking attendance, and he explained: "Mike's not here, Reverend. The poor man's burdened something awful with work."

"Get him," commanded Gershom.

When Hosmer returned, Stikes entered, wiping his sweating face on his corded, hairy forearms, and then his arms on his much-scorched leather apron.

Gershom rose between his two Indians, and the rustling crowd hushed. In the stillness of the evening, the minister's resonant bass voice reached the settlers through their backbones.

"You can put on your hats," he said brusquely. "For this is no sermon. This is a warning."

The injured look on Stikes was replaced by sudden attentiveness. He felt that Gershom was addressing him in particular, which was true.

"I'm not here to bless your militia. For you will not now be fools enough to send your platoon. You've reason enough that the governor will excuse you. You will need every able-bodied man here to defend yourselves and your families in what you are about to face."

The sternness wilted in Gershom. He ran a bony hand over a bowed cranium and became utter dejection.

"You've probably already heard," he faltered. "It's true. I cannot control the Indians any longer. They leave tomorrow."

Mesopotamia's stare darted to the Indians. The Indians looked at Gershom.

"They leave tomorrow, though I've told them they will not live a fortnight away from their homes."

Captain Michael watched Gershom in amazement, and he stepped behind him to be beside Silver Pigeon, whose eyes grew startled.

"You have won," said Gershom. "They know they are not wanted and they will not stay."

Silver Pigeon's eyes widened in anger, and he stepped toward Gershom. But as he did so, the iron-brown fingers of Captain Michael pinched between the muscle and the bone of the boy's right arm.

Gershom straightened up, and his voice shifted suddenly back to a roar.

"But know this! Their departure and the disasters which befall them will be charged—just as surely as you sit here tonight—against the village!"

Silver Pigeon opened his mouth, but closed it quickly as the pain clamped his arm once more. Gershom's voice fell to a threatening monotone.

"For the eyes of a half-thousand Wyandots will be watching and will hold you responsible. Therefore look to your powder and your blockhouse and *keep your militia home to defend yourselves*—for Rontondee and Tecumseh are strict bookkeepers."

As they sat with open mouths, waiting for more, Gershom strode straight down through the center of the puncheon benches with such strides that Captain Michael was pressed to keep up. Mesopotamia sat stunned, as had been intended. Seth Gershom had used his talent.

It was impossible to deny Mike Stikes his say. Gershom's ultimatum had been so short that Mike's face was still sweaty; and in that aspect of heated righteousness, he commanded.

"The militia's got to march. The Indians got to stay."

He paused to stare down any dissent, but there was none, and Stikes took charge.

"Buttrick, you go down to Boxford's Cabin. Bring back those men we sent away, the ones that want the mission Indians to stay. And tell 'em to bring proof we mean the Indians to stay. Wagonloads of it."

Buttrick stood dazed.

"I mean *now!*" barked Stikes. Buttrick moved.

Stikes dispatched Exeter to the southeast on the same errand, and Adams to the little cluster of cabins that lately rose to the east. He told Brady to hitch up his large wagon and go from cabin to cabin collecting anything the settlers could spare: corn, roots, potatoes, maple sugar, salt, cloth.

The first part of the caravan, namely, Brady's wagon, reached the mission by midafternoon Thursday. The horses and the men were exhausted. The Indians stood silently watching. The white men entered Gershom's hut. Buttrick was spokesman.

"Reverend Gershom, you saw our wagon, no doubt. Squash, wheat, flour. And more coming. Can you make the Indians stay?"

Gershom was reserved. "I can only represent your gift favorably to them."

"We brought powder and some salt. Salt is $8 a bushel now," said the trader.

Gershom hauled up the cask of whisky. Beside Gershom sat a stranger, a cherubic red-faced young minister in black who leaned forward tensely as Gershom leaned back in a degree of relaxation. The young cleric's face reproved the cask until Gershom frowned at him.

"A sometimes very important form of communion in frontier mission work, my young friend," instructed Gershom. "Will you drink, gentlemen?"

When the Mesopotamians and Gershom had all drawn whisky, and when Gershom had shoved a gourdful into the reluctant hands of the chubby minister, Buttrick renewed his pressure.

"What do you think it would take to keep them here, Reverend Gershom?"

Gershom shook his head gravely.

"Well, what is something that *might* keep them here?"

"Hard to say. Though I happen to know they could use seed. Not the squaw corn. But some good Kentucky white."

"I'll get 'em all they can use! What's more, we'll plant it for them. Right, Stikes?" Buttrick looked around for corroboration.

"They could use an ox," said Gershom, "and a moldboard plow, some potash, a bullet mold, and some priming wires and brushes."

Buttrick gulped, but Stikes nudged him and Buttrick said: "You'll get them. All of it."

"And it would be a great convenience to them," said Gershom, "to have some iron nails, a saw, a couple of wagons, some sheets of glass, and some tobacco."

Buttrick reddened, for he knew a hard trader when he met one. But he wrote it all down in a pocket ledger, using Gershom's quill.

Gershom shoved his long legs out in front of him. He tilted back his puncheon bench against the wall, and finished off his whisky. Brady grinned.

As they left, Woodbridge watched the young round-faced minister lean forward. "What shall I tell the bishop, Brother Gershom? Does this now mean you can take over the parish in Steubenville?"

"Can. Always could," said Gershom, pouring another draught.

"Then when should they expect you in Steubenville, sir?"

"They shouldn't. Because I won't be there." Gershom drank. "I'll be right here," he said.

Woodbridge noticed that the minister wore no robe this day. Yet it seemed to Thomas Woodbridge that the gaunt clergyman wore some special mantle not made of cloth. The hog farmer took a new look at Seth Gershom.

Well he might. There was a new Seth Gershom to look at.

On the Friday morning before the militia was to leave, Woodbridge went up to Stikes's forge to get the draw pole which was long promised.

Stikes was usually a gentle man. But inside his own forge he moved around with such brisk assurance that a man's instinct was to get out of his way. Under the bristling white hair Stikes's gaunt face was stern as he tonged the dull red iron off his anvil, plunged it into the forge, and pumped the great bellows, ignoring the shower of sparks which lit on his hairy arms and went out.

With both hands occupied, Stikes nodded his white mane toward the corner. The redhead looked and saw that his pole was untouched. Stikes's nod made neither explanation nor apology.

On Friday afternoon when Tom returned to the forge, he saw that the draw pole was still untouched. Blood surged to Tom's head.

"All right, Mike! Ya put me off twelve days already! Must my hogs freeze to death before ya fix my draw pole?"

Stikes wiped the sweat from his face, which was fierce red from the hot iron.

"What would you do in my place, Tom?"

The gaunt smith ran his eyes around the cluttered room and resumed his hammering.

"I've got to straighten this gun barrel for Hawkins. He'll like to shoot hisself instead of the English. Then I got Amos Exeter's old gun there needs a new frizzen. Fitchburg's piece needs a whole new lock."

"You think guns are the only thing needs fixin'?" bristled Woodbridge.

"Lately. Seems so."

"While you're gone, who's gonna look after shoeing the horses?"

"Then the trigger binds on that little hand gun of Blair's," continued Stikes. "Sam Hosmer's old barrel I got to rebore if he's to protect the homefolks. Might get to your draw pole tomorrow."

There was a pause in the hammering. "What you lookin' at?" asked Stikes. "Oh, that? Yeah. I got to put a new stock on that little gun for the boy or he'll like to blow off a shoulder."

"What boy?" asked Woodbridge quickly.

"I guess you know whose gun that is better'n I do, Tom. And I guess he's growed up to it like you wanted."

Woodbridge stared at the small rifle, and colored.

Mesopotamia could on occasion become the loneliest place in the West, or so it seemed to Thomas Woodbridge as he left the forge and drove past the drill platoon, which ignored him in the seriousness of their maneuvers on the common. Woodbridge didn't know what they were doing, but one thing he noticed. Jonathan Blair was wearing a new dark-blue coat with a high roll collar. Looking beyond Blair to the porch of Hosmer's Store, he noticed something else: Hope Emerson sat watching the coat as it marched back and forth across the common.

Woodbridge nudged Prince forward slowly, and the wagon rattled south toward the river past Flannerty's cabin. He saw that Flannerty's cart had one wheel banded with iron, while the other wheel had only the bare wooden fell. Likely, Stikes hadn't the time to reband the other wheel.

As he drove past Buttrick's place, Woodbridge noticed the iron hinges and the iron salt kettles. Sure was a lot of iron in a man's life when you stopped to count up, which you did when you couldn't get your draw pole mended.

Woodbridge crossed the river to the south and turned right onto the West Road. The lonesomeness of the day caught up with him again.

There was nobody to wave to at Widow Hussong's cabin. The children had gone in to watch the platoon drill. He noticed the iron head on the ax that the Hussong boy had left stuck in a stump. With Stikes leaving, the boy had better keep that ax inside and covered with bacon grease.

Christian Kilgore's place was empty. Kilgore was going with the militia. Beyond Kilgore's cabin the trail was always lonesome because there were no more cabins until the Woodbridge place, not counting the Stranger's lean-to, which was empty.

That's why it was a cheering sight when Veronica came riding toward him on the mare. But when she came up close and stopped, the happy flush on her cheeks took all the joy of it away, leaving Tom that much more alone. For he saw that she carried a carefully rolled bundle of dark-blue wool from which protruded a couple of brass buttons. And he knew that that accounted for the flush at the base of Veronica's throat, though it could be she didn't know it herself.

"Shouldn't you have him come out to the cabin?" said Woodbridge. "To try it on? If it doesn't fit, you could fix it."

Veronica studied her husband, at first puzzled, then firm.

"It'll fit," she said.

But as she turned the mare toward Mesopotamia, Woodbridge caught her arm. "I already told him to come out to the cabin," he lied. "I figured you'd want to give it to him there, though I didn't spoil the surprise of it."

Veronica bristled under Woodbridge's roughness.

"It'll fit," she repeated, and tugged her arm away. But Tom's hand did not release her.

She looked up into his face, surprised. The diagonal line was in his cheeks, and his voice was soft. But it was his deliberately quiet voice. It was the heavily reined-in voice she'd first heard when he folded up his bounty warrant and refused Shuldane's offer. It was the measured voice she'd heard in the church meeting at the blockhouse, answering Seth Gershom. It was his right-or-wrong voice that would face down a man or a townful of men.

"Wife, I've reason you should not go to town."

She turned the mare and followed Woodbridge, leaving him in front with his loneliness. As he rode, he reflected that the coat would fit right enough, what with the way Veronica had studied the lawyer's person all these years. It would fit every curve of his handsome being.

Veronica went into the cabin. Zabeth looked in Tom's empty wagon while he unhitched.

"Where's the draw pole, Pap?"

"Stikes has got too much work," he answered. "Never will get the hog sheds built, it looks."

Zabeth's reply brought his head up quickly.

"Young Tom's already got the base logs laid and the walls partly up, Pap."

"What!"

Woodbridge walked out of the shed and looked up the slope to the north where Young Tom worked.

"How?"

"He cut a draw pole with a fork in it like a hook. He hooked it over the ox yoke."

In wonder, Woodbridge mused aloud: "By himself. By himself he did that."

"Yes. Young Tom's a man I think now."

"Well, Zabeth, I better go feed the shoats, then."

"He did that, too."

"The new litters, too?"

"He said you'd druther do it yourself, but he reckoned you'd be late. Said there wasn't so much trick to it as—"

Zabeth clapped her hand to her mouth.

Woodbridge watched the lad's ax swing rhythmically and powerfully up on the slope. He suddenly noticed five years' growth in the boy. He looked as if he could build the hog sheds alone. And as Tom's eye followed down the line of existing sheds, it struck him forcefully that the boy had in fact done most of the work on most of them.

"Zabeth, have you seen young Tom's squirrel rifle around lately?" Zabeth's eyes became busy with some mystery at her feet.

"I'd not know where he might have it," she stumbled.

Woodbridge reached for his saddle.

"You goin' again, Pap?"

"Tell your mother I'll be late home," said Woodbridge, "and no supper for me."

Woodbridge rode northwest to Mitchell's place, then northeast to Elisha Adams's farm. From there he forded the river to the east and tied up at Exeter's cabin. Exeter asked him to sit for supper.

"Can't, Amos. Got some more stops yet."

"What you up to?"

"Did you say you broke your stonecutting drill on Blair's well?"

"Yeah. Did. Why?"

"Stikes'll be leavin' with you and the militia tomorrow afternoon. Better take the drill down and have him put a new point on it tomorrow morning."

"You worried you might be needin' a well drilled while we're gone?"

"Well, me or somebody. But Stikes wants to clear up all the little odd chores around town before he leaves."

"Just like Mike."

"Yeah. And better bring your plow blade in to be sharpened for next spring. He might not be back."

"You're bein' a mite too farsighted for good grace, Woodbridge."

"Mike said get there early. Good night."

Woodbridge crossed over to the Cuyuga Trail and stopped at the Fitchburgs' and the Masons' and the Dolks'. He went to every cabin on the trail, ending at Hope Emerson's place.

"Hope, you got any ironware needin' attention by Stikes before he leaves tomorrow?"

Hope Emerson looked down from her commanding doorsill.

"My sickle does need re-edging, Tom, but I hate to work Mike t'death before he gets gone."

"We've got to get all the tools in shape before Mike goes, Hope."

"Not quite seemly, is it, Tom, for you to be so much worried about after the boys go?"

Woodbridge's face stung, but he said, "Stikes said get the stuff there early."

Woodbridge didn't go to Hosmer's cabin or store. But he stopped at Slasher's, the Flannertys', and late at night he reached the Widow Hussong's cabin.

"Mrs. Hussong, I could take any iron pots or gear you might have that needs fixin'. I'll be driving down to Stikes's in the morning."

But the Widow Hussong, perhaps remembering Jess at that moment, was cool.

"No, I'll not burden my pans upon a man who goes to fight."

Her tone was an indictment.

In his own shed at last, Woodbridge took his time forking down hay for Prince. For he knew that inside the cabin Veronica would be still smarting over the coat she had made for Blair. In the morning he would bring Blair out to try on the coat, asking him not to wear Hope Emerson's coat. A lieutenant could use two coats well enough.

It would be a bleak night in the Woodbridge cabin. It would also be a bleak morning on the common tomorrow.

Woodbridge rose early next day, but as he turned left off the West Road to come up out of the river ford into Mesopotamia he saw that he was late.

The animated crowd around Mike Stikes's forge obscured all but Stikes's white hair from Woodbridge's view. As Woodbridge approached, he was startled by the crowd, for it was beyond his expectation.

Scattered in front of the forge was such a collection of split-ox yokes, broken plow points, dull scythes, and unspoked wheels that it looked like the refuse of the whole state. There was Flannerty's wagon that needed a wheelband, Aaron Fitchburg's leaky salt kettles, Elisha Adams's wrecked clodbreaker, Mitchell's bull plow with a broken blade, and such a tangle of linkless swingletrees, leaky pots, bent hinges, worn-out wagon brakes, and blunt ax blades that Stikes stood knee-deep in rusty iron.

As Woodbridge climbed down from his wagon, good-natured and suddenly understanding grins broke out among the crowd. But on Mike Stikes's face, as he looked at the mass of work to be done, there was despair.

"I can't possibly do it," he pleaded. "Take me three months! You should have brought it before!"

A grin made Hope Emerson look quite fair. "Well, I don't know about this other stuff, Mike," she hollered, "but if my flax combs aren't fit with new wire teeth this town's going to be naked of linen while you're gone!"

Stikes ran a scraggy hand through his white mane, while he searched among the items for Hope's flax combs. Before he found them, Exeter yelled, "Mike, there's got to be a new point on that drill of mine or this town'll suffer for water!"

"That swingletree chain of mine's got to be fixed," claimed Hawkins, "or I'll leave Faith in an awful fix."

Stikes's face was a lined mass of injury as he faced the crowd. "I'm sorry, folks. But it's impossible! The militia's movin' out in a few hours. I won't even have time to finish—" He looked around at the tangle of iron, searching vainly for something he could finish by the time the militia would leave.

Hosmer didn't face his friend, but he said: "It's plain, Mike. You got to stay."

Stikes presented two upturned palms.

"Sam!"

"You got to stay, Mike."

With grinning faces and warm slaps on the back of Mike Stikes, Mesopotamia examined each other's goods. The Widow Hussong got the spirit of it, and went for her kettle to be mended.

Woodbridge was inside looking around at the guns in Stikes's forge. He found what he sought and was coming out of the shop with an object wrapped in buckskin when he saw through the crowd Veronica's mare tethered beside Blair's horse. Unless Young Tom had ridden the mare in, it meant that Veronica had not waited.

His eyes searched the crowd and he found her on the outer edge standing with Blair. She was looking at the new coat that Blair wore. Apparently Blair was describing it, for he fingered the buttons and showed her the linings of the pockets.

Woodbridge could see that under Veronica's arm there was a large roll of blue cloth with a little brass showing. Blair was talking to her, but Veronica was not answering. She lent Blair her ear, but her eyes were searching the crowd directly in front of Stikes's shop. When she saw Woodbridge, her face set in stern resolution. She left Blair abruptly and swept toward Woodbridge with such swiftness that her skirt molded itself softly against her and she unbalanced Hope Emerson as she brushed through the crowd.

Veronica did not meet Woodbridge's eyes. She grabbed him abruptly by the wrist and led him out behind the crowd, along the front of Stikes's cabin, around the corner, and out of sight. Not stopping there, she led on around behind the forge.

To be led by the wrist before the whole town like an overgrown school lout was all right with Tom if it would release Veronica's anger or pain at finding Blair already in possession of a coat made by Hope Emerson. But it had gone far enough. He jerked his wrist loose, spinning her around to face him, and his voice was a whip.

"Well, I told you to wait till I brought him to the cabin!"

But he found himself fighting the smell of pine soap close to him.

The bundled blue coat with the brass buttons was rolling on the ground. A cool hand pulled down on the back of his neck, and it was the yielding, infinite kind of kiss that left her only to explain, "You found out about Hope's coat when you picked up the linen, I suppose."

It was just after two o'clock when Exeter rolled on the drum in front of Hosmer's Store. The townspeople stood around the south edge of the common, watching. Veronica and Woodbridge stood together and watched, too. The platoon men all waited with their families until their names were called. Then one at a time they stepped out onto the common and fell in ranks opposite their gear, which was laid out in two rows.

Blair called the names.

"Brady!"

"Here!"

"Dolk!"

"Here!"

"Christofferson!"

"Comin'! If I can ever get this cobweb of pack straps straightened out."

The crowd chuckled as Brute Christofferson struggled to get his massive torso through a tangle of leather whang strips that tied his pack.

Blair called on down through the roll, and the men stepped away from their families and into the ranks. He called "Stikes!" and then corrected quickly in his new military vocabulary: "As you were. I mean, Stranger-boy Woodbridge!"

There was no answer. Blair looked around the crowd and called, "Young Tom!"

An uneasy stillness swept the group as heads turned left and right.

"Young Tom Woodbridge!"

A deep voice from the back of the crowd bellowed out, "Mike lost my boy's rifle somehow. No point in him goin' without it."

The bystanders looked at Woodbridge and then quickly over to Stikes's shop. Even at the distance across to the forge they could see Mike standing with his palms up in bewildered explanation, and the boy standing in front of him, talking fast and pointing emphatically to the place where the rifle had been.

They saw Blair run a pencil through one of the names on his list, and then they saw the disturbance in their own group as Tom Woodbridge threaded his way forward to the front of the crowd and out toward the platoon. Strapped to his back was a tight dark-blue roll from which one sleeve flopped as he strode between the first and second ranks of the platoon. The crowd's question was on the surface of its silence. Even Sam Hosmer looked surprised.

But Thomas Woodbridge, the hog farmer, had no time for questions and explanations. He stepped into the gap that was Stikes's place.

"All right, Blair! Let's get this war started. I got only three months till farrowin' time, y'know!"

In the month of December in the year of 18 and 12, sixteen men from Mesopotamia marched out the West Road and then turned north up through the gorge towards Fort Meiggs and General Harrison and the English Lake.

On the Woodbridge place Veronica lifted a squirrel rifle from the back of the wagon. She concealed it carefully under her cape, and called for Young Tom to come unhitch, feed, and stable Prince.

"And take good care of him, Young Tom, for it'll be a long war."

# BOOK III

# Chapter 20: THE HOMECOMING (1814)

Bᴜᴛ it was not a long war.

It was long enough, though, for Mesopotamia to build a hut on the common and to move Captain Michael and Silver Pigeon into it, carrying the hostage idea a step further.

It was long enough for Sam Hosmer to close in the porch on the store so that he could add to his stock such items as rope, glass, shingle rivers, colored cloth dyes, crockery, real coffee, needles, harness leather, factory candles, resin splinters, and even three and a half yards of silk.

It was long enough for Asa Buttrick to establish a bank account at New Orleans and one at Baltimore and one at Cincinnati so that he could drain the silver out of the great triangle. Without moving from the Cincinnati dock, he learned to route flour, pork, whisky ginseng, tallow, venison, and black walnut timber downriver to New Orleans. That built up his New Orleans bank account so that he could consign from that city to Baltimore a hull full of slaves and rope, the slaves loading the rope, thereby saving dock charges. The black men, once converted into a balance in Buttrick's Baltimore account, formed capital for a consignment of fancy eastern goods for Cincinnati which, not valuable at downtown Cincinnati, became important property when transshipped to Steubenville, Dayton, Zanesville, Chillicothe, Lancaster, and Mesopotamia.

Mike Stikes learned how to beat out a solid iron moldboard plow, and found out about Dan Heaton's iron furnace at Yellow Creek, near Youngstown.

It was a long enough war for a foresighted man like Elnathan Shuldane to see that the time had come at last. The time had come when twenty thousand acres of woods, held for twenty years, would begin to pay off. And it was time to stretch one's credit for more. It had been a long pull, but now was the time to dispense with agents and go out and stand on the ground, to be ready for the big immigration.

There would be need of assistants—good, loyal, smart assistants, men to be put into the legislature and the land offices and the county government to make sure that the flood of immigrants would be funneled into Mesopotamia.

It was a long enough war for Zabeth to learn that Young Tom was too busy to be a sociable brother and that Lot Webster and his younger brother Armitage, who had come out with Shuldane, were compensations. Arm, especially, was handsome, and he had seen everything there was in the world to see.

It was time for Veronica to be glad of that, for Elizabeth was fourteen, and tanned and lithe. She needed to be exposed more to the manners of the Webster boys, less to those of Camelia Flannerty and Joe Hussong . . . and Stranger-boy.

It had been a long enough war for Woodbridge to see and understand that Tecumseh fought, in a way, for the same as he. Tecumseh fought against the lines on the land, and the legal writing which kept him off it. Tom remembered the bounty warrant and the survey that had made him a squatter, and he understood Tecumseh.

But it had also been a long enough war to spatter a piece of lead into Morgan Brady's cheekbone and send him screaming off into a swamp on the Canadian shore of the Erie Lake to sink in the mud so horribly that when they pulled him out Woodbridge no longer understood or cared about Tecumseh, except that he should be dead.

Woodbridge had had time on the long marches to count up how many Bedfords he'd likely have on the place now. He had seen the need, too, for heavy, fast-growing hogs in the North and West, and he knew that the struggle had been worth it. Now was the time to reap the profit of fifteen years' breeding.

He was surprised at the difference a few more fallen trees made on the common at Mesopotamia. What with the larger Hosmer Store and a few more cabins, he might not have recognized it. The common had once stood in the shade; now it was completely in the light. The deep, damp forest mulch had been scuffed away, leaving a dry powdered dust over a hard baked base.

But no single development so changed the face of Mesopotamia as the massive shadow that fell across Hosmer's Store from the south end of the common. The mass that obstructed the setting sun was of smooth square timbers, and it was two stories high.

As though Woodbridge had not seen it immediately, Exeter said, "Cripes, somebody bought the Shuldane Reserve lot!"

"Maybe," answered Woodbridge.

"Well, somebody sure'n hell built on it."

"Yeah. Somebody."

"And look at them big double front doors. Milled wood, that is."

"Yeah."

For an instant the structure dominated the common, until the crowd of wives and sons and daughters clustered around the men of the platoon.

A tall fourteen-year-old girl clutched Woodbridge's arm with brown fingers and steered him to the rim of the crowd. Her hair was chestnut brown, and her skin was so dark that her teeth were extremely white in her wide smile.

"Mam thought she'd best wait for you t'home, Pap."

Woodbridge grinned.

"I thought she'd of broke you of sayin' 'Mam' and 'Pap' by now. At least that's the same."

If there's an instant between light and dark, this was it. It wasn't until Woodbridge took the lines of the wagon that he knew he was driving a different horse.

"Prince died, Pap."

They crossed the ford to the south and turned west over the road. Strange windows blinked at them through the trees.

"That's the Wheelers' and the Wrights'," explained Zabeth. "Came together."

They crossed Hussong Creek. The bridge had been widened.

"And that's the Culpeppers'. They're from Virginia." Zabeth's voice dropped. "That's the Denaros'. Onions, they grow."

Woodbridge grinned. "Denaro might feel the same about hogs," he said.

"And there's Adams'," Zabeth pointed.

"Adams? Elisha Adams?"

"Moved in town," she said without explanation.

When they came out from under the cover of trees into the Woodbridge clearing, Zabeth spotted the lantern.

"Mam couldn't wait, I guess. She's out meetin' you."

It was a proud thing for a redheaded hog farmer, up from apprentice, to step down from a wagon and take against his chest a soft woman like Veronica and to have the crisp crinoline of her best skirt blow around his mud-crusted boots.

It was a proud thing for Zabeth to have a pap with a forearm like the squared-off draw pole of a bull plow, instead of one corded and wrinkled like Mr. Stikes's; and hair that came down to a solid V at his forehead, instead of wispy like Margaret Buttrick's father's. She swelled with pride as she looked at her father's skin, which was tight over his cheekbones, and only wrinkled into powerful folds of leather below his ears when he bent his big head to kiss Mam. And how he squashed her, and kissed her on the neck so she shivered.

But he let her go suddenly, for a stranger loomed behind Veronica. The voice was deep and reserved.

"Hello, Tom."

The palm of the hand that came out from behind the lantern was hard and smooth, and barely allowed Woodbridge a fair grip before it squeezed.

The man raised the lantern to identify himself, and Woodbridge said, "Stranger-boy!"

Inside the cabin Woodbridge sat and watched Young Tom. He noticed that he didn't throw the new base log to the back of the fire pit, but reached in and lowered it gently with controlled strength. He saw his tanned but not dressed buckskins stretch tight over his legs as he sat down. He noticed that the boy no longer thumped around the cabin, but moved carefully, as though he'd learned that a cabin is not indestructible.

Seeing it, Woodbridge felt good and he said: "Now we'll go, boy! I've seen a piece of the country, and already there are people up along the lake over to the east. Settlement called Cleaveland. There'll be more, too, soon as they move the Indians out. And they'll all crave pork. Not woods hogs, but heavy lard hogs that'll yield two hundred pounds of ham and bacon and side meat and a winter's cooking fat left over. And we'll have it for 'em, boy!"

"Tom, I've got to tell you—"

But Woodbridge brushed the boy silent.

"There's almost a hundred people at Cleaveland, too. And four hundred in Dayton. Eight hundred and sixteen down at Columbus! The cry's gonna be for meat. Not just barrels of meat, but tons of meat. And the answer's gonna be hogs. And we've got 'em, haven't we, boy!"

"Tom, I got to tell you that—"

"Sure, we've got 'em! Let's go see how many!"

Woodbridge walked to the door, and Stranger-boy rose, as did Zabeth and Veronica. But Woodbridge paused, with his hand on the leather door pull, full of what he'd seen and heard.

"I met a man from Cincinnati, telling how there's a boat on the river. I suppose you've heard. Steam engine works it. Says it can take a barrel of pork out of Cincinnati on Monday and put it on the New Orleans wharf in twenty-one days."

Woodbridge sat down again, and he talked of soldiers who had told him how the southern part of the state was filling up. How some weren't even stopping in the Ohio Country any more, but going right on west to the Indiana Territory.

"How'd you like to be startin' all over again, Veronica?" he teased.

He expected her to throw up her hands in horror, but she lowered her head and took the question at face value. "Could be we'll have to, Tom."

He laughed and came over to her chair. "Nope. You'll never have to go through it again. Though they do say there's no land-title trouble out there. They learned their lesson from Ohio, and they laid off the Indiana Territory accurate."

Because the talk poured out of him, they never did go out to the hog pens that first evening, and Veronica decided to let his home-coming night pass in peace.

But the boy was ready in the morning. He got up early and waited outside. He didn't have to wait long.

Woodbridge came out into the daylight, looking around as though everything were new to him. The boy wanted to say "Good morning." But it wouldn't sound right, besides not being true. And every word that was said this morning would be remembered many times in the months ahead.

Nothing happened when Woodbridge looked at the lower pen and saw the weeds growing up in it.

"Abandoned the lower pen, eh, boy?"

"No, sir, I—"

"Good idea," said Woodbridge. "Prevents hoof itch to let it lay idle a season. Though you should have planted it to grass or clover."

He strode north toward the second pen. Young Tom heard the cabin door open and close, and he saw Veronica following after them. He motioned her back, but she wouldn't shirk the hard part; she came up the slope.

The second pen was grown over with weeds also, and the cutover stumps had sprouted shoots that were covered with leaves turning red. Woodbridge increased his pace now as he marched toward the third pen. The boy was hard pressed to keep up without running.

Woodbridge stopped. The pen was empty. His face was red now, but not from the exertion or the crisp fall air. He turned to the boy and asked with laborious restraint, "Where are they, boy?"

"Tom, it began when the man came up from Cincinnati."

"Never mind that!" Woodbridge grabbed Stranger-boy's arm. "Where are they?"

"He said the troops needed—"

But the sentence was chopped off in a grunt as Young Tom landed on his spine so that his head snapped against the ground.

"What did you do with 'em!"

Woodbridge was hoarse with apprehension. Both his hands grabbed the boy's shirt at the chest and yanked him to his feet with rage-born power.

"Where are the hogs?"

Stranger-boy brought his own fist down on Woodbridge's two fists, which tore the front off the boy's shirt. Veronica by now was clawing ineffectually at Woodbridge's back as he threw his heavy fists into the sides of the boy, who stepped back from most of the blows. Perhaps that was the worst thing the boy could have done, for it enraged the redhead, who flailed recklessly at the lad. Nor would he have stopped had it not been for the piercing scream of Zabeth, who ran up from the cabin.

Woodbridge looked around to see Veronica lying flat on the ground behind him.

"You knocked her down!" charged Zabeth with fourteen-year-old fury.

Woodbridge dropped to his knees beside his wife, and Zabeth scorched him.

"Serve you right if she died!"

She ripped the rest of Young Tom's torn shirt off him and stuffed it under Veronica's head. Tears dropped from Zabeth's cheeks.

"She's too good for you anyway! She held on to the hogs till no one'd speak to her in the town! The man tried to buy 'em four times before Mam gave in! The town said if the men weren't too pure-bred to be shot in the war, your hogs weren't too pure-bred to be eaten by the troops!"

Zabeth slapped her mother's wrist while Woodbridge bent over her helplessly. Zabeth sent Young Tom for vinegar "or anything sharp-smelling," all the while hardly interrupting her diatribe.

"Oh, you'd a been ashamed if you'd seen the way they snubbed her and closed doors to her! That's why she wasn't in town to meet you. All because of her tryin' to save your blessed pigs! And Stranger-boy, too. They'd hardly speak to him. And right they were, too. If you didn't come back, Mam said it shouldn't be because you were dyin' of the hunger. And she let the man buy the hogs. And us tellin' ourselves it was the right thing. And thinkin' as long as you come back, what else mattered? And maybe the pork'd be the savin' of your life. She even saved breeders, too, but the militia confiscated them. And then you comin' home and knockin' Mam down. Mam! Wake up! Pap, if she don't rise up, I'm wishin' you never came back!"

But Mam did rise up. Mam was one to look awful fragile and sweet, but she had a streak of iron in her spine. And Pap, he acted sometimes as mean and hateful as Wolf when he showed his corner teeth and stiffened his back hairs at the Indian smell. But that would fool you, too, because sometimes a certain word to Pap was like throwin' fire into a fence corner of dried leaves; but all it took to put him out, if you knew it, was a bucket of cold water, like stackin' Mam's worth up against a herd of hogs.

But then Pap was an uncommon sort of person, she decided, not noticing that a half-hour ago she had been willing that Pap hadn't come home from the war. And right now she wished she could coddle his head like a baby and take away his troubles, that beaten he looked.

If just the hogs were the worst, why, that part was over. But she knew she'd learn a lot about Pap yet, before this day was over.

Limp with defeat, Woodbridge hitched up the new horse, who was skitterish to the redhead's rough touch.

Zabeth climbed onto the wagon seat beside her father, for if he were going uptown he'd find out soon enough. Someone had best be standing by; and better Zabeth than Stranger-boy, she guessed.

As the wagon jostled into the village, Woodbridge got up strength to speak of it.

"This man that bought the hogs, you met him, Zabeth?"

"Yes. He seemed a good man, Pap. Came back five times in person."

"His name?"

"John H. Piatt."

"Big merchant in Cincinnati. He's bought from me before through Buttrick. Always good as his word, anyhow."

The wheel rims bumped over the cold hard ground.

"He said nothin' of breedin' them?"

"No," answered Zabeth. "Said he couldn't pay breeding prices as they were just for pork for the troops."

Zabeth saw a chance to sneak the news into Pap so's he'd hardly notice, while he was placid and limp like this. She began slowly.

"He seemed like he'd once been an awful rich man."

"Once been?"

"He had a fine suit, but it was fraying at the cuffs and he looked tired."

"Tired?"

"Said he'd lost a lot of money. The government asked him to ship rations and supplies up to Gen'ral Harrison, but when he sent in his vouchers the Congress balked and asked questions and like that. They've only paid him for a little part."

"Huh."

"But he'd sigh and say he'd keep shipping rations and powder to the soldiers as long as he could raise credit to pay with. Said the country had been good to him. It was time he paid back."

But Pap's thoughts weren't following, she could see. Usually he understood everything you were going to say before you were half through, and added some besides, that you didn't even know. But he wasn't understanding this, so she changed the talk to what she'd wanted to ask.

"Was there a lot of shootin', Pap?"

"Yes."

"Like when Rontondee came? Or more?"

"About the same. Only it was in the woods."

"Pap." She stole a guarded side glance to see if it would be all right. "Pap, did you kill any men?"

"We killed a lot."

"I mean you."

Woodbridge untwisted the lines and flicked the new horse lightly.

"Did you, Pap?"

"Zabeth, you'll hear all about it 'fore it's done."

The wagon rattled toward Mesopotamia.

"Well, did Mr. Blair, then?"

"I don't know."

"Why?"

"He got transferred right away. Up to the staff, they call it. Mord Mason commanded the Mesopotamia platoon."

"What's the staff?"

"Danged if you didn't ask one we'd all admire to know."

The wagon splashed across the river to the common, where there now rose a great massive square house made of smooth-faced logs. The center of the village had shifted.

In testament to the personal power of Elnathan Shuldane, witness the events on that morning in Hosmer's Store. The town's platoon, disbanded, was assembled there. It should have been their day, but Shuldane stole it from them with their wholehearted consent and support.

In Shuldane's position a less able man might have stepped lightly and covered his success with some modesty in view of the fact that Thompson and Morgan Brady were dead and Mordecai Mason's hand was gone, and all of them were ragged-looking.

But Shuldane's handsome waistcoat and his invigorating talk represented to Mesopotamia good things to come. A wave of hope was crossing the frontier. And Nate Shuldane's gold chain confirmed it. They wanted to see no more worn buckskins. They wanted Nate Shuldane. They wanted him to prosper, and they wanted to go along with him. For Shuldane's was a big, generous, outgoing prosperity that made Asa Buttrick's seem small and selfish. They listened hungrily.

"They'll be coming by wagonloads, gentlemen, now that we've licked the British and Indians. More than that. With the steamboats now, they'll come by the hundreds. I'll see to it we get our share up here. They'll come with money in their pockets, and they'll want land. Land that's in settlement. And that's just what we've got for sale. We're the ones that took the chance. Now comes our reward."

He was putting the colors on the picture that was already in every man's mind. But he painted it bigger and bolder than any of them dared. Shuldane told how land in the Miami Valley had gone from $2 an acre to $5. From $5 to $10. From $10 in some places to $20 an acre along the streams.

"And we'll see the day, and soon," he said, "when we'll refuse $40 an acre."

"How sure are you of that, Nate?" asked Exeter.

"This sure, Amos. I've bought the next township over. Took all the credit I could get. But I'll make out. And you will, too. I advise you all to look over that tract."

"That proof enough, Amos?" asked Caleb Wright.

Shuldane went no further. He didn't try to sell any of his new 20,000 acres. He merely stood there, full of confidence, looking like money itself, and Mesopotamia yearned to follow his lead and his wisdom.

To Mesopotamia it was further evidence of Shuldane's largeness that he extended his hand when Jonathan Blair entered. Blair, studying Shuldane, did not move to accept it. But Shuldane said, "Good you're back safe, Jonathan." He took Blair by the hand and the elbow.

"Wasn't sure you'd think so," said Blair. "After the trial."

Shuldane's candor was winning. "I'm only human, Jonathan. I wanted you to win. But you tried your best . . . I presume."

Blair studied every crevice of Shuldane's face. But he could find no sneer. Only the large benign voice, "I'm just smart enough, Jonathan, to appreciate ability like that."

"Ability," Shuldane had said. Not loyalty. Well, that was accurate. His trial had been able.

Despite himself Blair swelled, and the old admiration for the master came back to him. Perhaps Shuldane admired a trick, whoever won. Anyway, Blair shook hands.

It was not a fault in Shuldane's perception that he ignored Woodbridge's entrance. It was intentional. He deliberately continued to talk to a group of six men at the far counter in the store when he heard Woodbridge's voice near the door and noticed the head of red hair above the others.

Shuldane had read the few signs available. He knew it was a different Woodbridge he would meet. He knew it not only by the fact that Woodbridge held title to 140 acres, but also by the way men mentioned his name with a certain cold regard. He noticed, too, that Woodbridge did not snap his head around immediately to see who called, but proceeded about his intent, leaving the caller to hustle across his path if he wanted to. He knew it by the way his own daughter, Veronica, refused to move into his big house on the common during Woodbridge's absence. He knew something of Woodbridge by the way Elizabeth said, "Pap wouldn't set much store by that." Shuldane had also noticed the terrible stoic resistance with which Veronica and that castoff, the Stranger-boy, had held to the hogs despite the village. He laid that to Woodbridge.

It was part of Shuldane's strength that he would trouble himself to find out these things and be guided by them. But he held aloof an extra moment to abash Woodbridge. To invade the boy's own town and take it from him in his presence would work as well on the town's mind as on the redhead's. He continued to talk to the six men. What he did not know, though, was the degree of stature the young man held. He learned that when his audience turned away from him to see what brought Woodbridge to town.

Hosmer shook Tom's hand, as did Stikes and Adams and Mitchell. There were a few Woodbridge didn't know. Zabeth was proud of the way they greeted her Pap, like maybe he'd done something in the war he hadn't told at home.

Shuldane moved over toward Woodbridge to greet him as a father-in-law should, but the redhead was already in earnest conversation with Adams.

"But why did you sell, Adams? You knew I wanted a piece of that! It was our agreement you'd sell me the piece that abuts the gorge, and Mitchell was savin' me the piece that neighbors my west line!"

"Mitchell sold too, Tom."

Woodbridge stared through him.

"We couldn't afford to hold it, Tom, at the price offered."

"By who?"

Adams pointed to Shuldane. Hence there never came a chance for greeting as the two men faced each other.

Shuldane said: "Yes, Tom. I bought the whole township. I offered Veronica the same price for your place. She wouldn't sell. But the offer still stands."

"Sell? Nothin'! I'm buyin'! I need that land around me. Especially now with my Bedfords gone!"

"I need it too, Tom. What with the road goin' alongside the stream in the gorge, and the stream falling off as steep as it does, it's the natural place for mill sites and the like."

"Shuldane, will you sell me just the piece to the north?"

"Afraid we couldn't make you a suitable price, Tom."

"To the west, then?"

"Couldn't give you a decent price."

"To the south, then."

"Same condition."

"Well, hang the decent price, then!" flared Woodbridge. "Name a price! I've got my hog money!"

The redhead looked around in annoyance as Zabeth pulled at his leather shirt. He shook her off.

"Come on, Shuldane, you've cornered me. Name your price," he challenged.

But Zabeth caught her father's arm.

"The hog money didn't come yet, Pap," she said. "What I told you about the gover'ment and Mr. Piatt."

Woodbridge wilted. This time he heard her.

No one had to speak the words. It had already been spelled out. Woodbridge was surrounded, on land and on paper. And just as quickly as the realization sank into the still faces of Mesopotamia, that quickly did Thomas Woodbridge lose height before their eyes. For every man in the store was familiar with the dreams of Thomas Woodbridge. Every man in the store knew that though Woodbridge had made a paying thing of raising Bedfords in pens, no man could afford to pen up woods hogs and feed them hand-grown corn. There wasn't enough corn on 140 acres to make any differences in the weight of a woods hog. A woods hog you just let run and find what he could, and that took a lot of ground. It took a lot of cheap ground. Had to be almost free ground.

As the force of it sank into Woodbridge, his jaw went slack, his shoulders sagged, and he turned to leave the store.

"Tom, I knew this would hit you pretty hard," said Shuldane, "especially after losing your herd, no matter how good the cause they went for."

Woodbridge turned back to Shuldane, who continued.

"So I think I can help you. You taught me quite a bit about hogs. I've looked into it ever since that night when you brought me two Bedford shoats for dinner in Concord."

Shuldane grinned, and a few others joined him. For there was a sly and private legend in Mesopotamia as to how Tom Woodbridge had acquired his first two white hogs.

"I'd like to go into the hog business myself, Tom. You were right about those Bedfords. They will make a man rich. I tried to get another pair from England. But they wouldn't export."

Woodbridge studied Shuldane closely.

"However, somehow a boar and a gilt got loose from that shipment Veronica turned over to John Piatt. You'd know how a thing like that could happen." Shuldane grinned. "Well, I was able to get hold of them at a price. Thought I'd like to start a Bedford herd of my own. My interest chiefly is to enrich our township here. If you'd step outside with me, I think we could make an arrangement in private that would solve your problem and mine, too."

There were relieved smiles in the store, for Thomas Woodbridge had come to stand for something; and though affection was not a common attitude toward the redhead, no thinking man wanted to see him go down. For when Tom Woodbridge couldn't make out, few men could. It was good to have a big man like Shuldane around, too, and perhaps now the redhead would realize it.

Outside the store, Shuldane said, "Perhaps you'd best run along, Elizabeth."

"Zabeth can listen," said Woodbridge. "What is it?"

"You've had a lot of experience with Bedfords, Tom. How about you starting my herd? We'll work together, just like before. I've got the Bedfords. You've got the experience."

Woodbridge turned on his heel and climbed into his wagon.

Shuldane walked back into the store, and no man could avoid sympathy for him. "A man is never a hero to his own son," he sighed. "I can't do business, it seems, with my own daughter's husband."

And by the angry look on the face of Mesopotamia, it became apparent that Thomas Woodbridge was on his own.

As the wagon came up out of the ford and turned west, Woodbridge's face was a frozen mask. His jaw was set, and he snapped the lines sharply across the back of the startled new horse.

"From now on, Zabeth. From now on!"

He called for more speed from the animal.

"From now on, it'll be the Woodbridges for the Woodbridges, and the devil with 'em all."

Christian Kilgore looked up, surprised by the rumble of the racing wagon. He waved, but Woodbridge did not see him and Zabeth could not let go the seat.

"From now on, Zabeth!"

There was something mighty frightening about Pap, even when you knew him.

"There's land in the Indiana Territory where a man can hold enough to own his own town. And the survey lines are honest and there's no meddlin' with 'em. And when we get a stake, Zabeth . . ."

The wagon rattled up into the Woodbridge development. They knew by looking at his face that there was nothing to do but keep quiet. The redhead leaned silently on the rail of the first pen all afternoon, staring. Occasionally he'd kick his foot against the bottom rail, until it finally broke loose.

Occasionally Veronica would rub the back of her hand across her eyes, which were red and wet.

Young Tom tried to keep busy around the place. But with the hogs gone, it was hard to be busy.

The homecoming was a terrible thing.

# Chapter 21: BIG ONE

STRANGER-boy was about to speak, but he held back.

Perhaps the worst moment at the Woodbridge development came the next month, when Woodbridge got back from Cincinnati.

Zabeth had never seen Pap so low. Usually, no matter what happened, he could get mad enough to bust a way out of trouble. But today he slumped by the fire. He didn't even volunteer to tell what happened in Cincinnati. He talked wild about Indiana Territory and starting over again out there. Zabeth noticed that Mam finally had to ask him about Cincinnati, timidly, for she figured it was her fault about the hogs.

"No," he answered. "Piatt can't pay."

"Later perhaps?"

"No, I tell you. Never!"

"Did you ask him to sign a note?"

"He's already signed a note to you!"

"But I mean another, with longer terms."

"No. No."

"It would have been proper to ask."

"I tell you with him a note don't matter. If he can pay, he'll pay. If he can't, he can't. The poor devil's licked."

"But a note gives you grounds to file suit for some kind of settlement."

"Veronica, the varmints have got him choked to death with law already. He'll be in jail for life. For feedin' the blasted militia he'll be jailed."

Veronica knew the stopping place.

"It's more proof," shouted Woodbridge, "you got to look out for yourself. Ask no help. Give no help. The well-meanin' ones like Piatt get sunk. They can't help ya. The smart ones won't help ya. And as for lookin' to the government for anything, they're so fouled up—why, they even let the British walk right into Washington. We'll get us a stake and try the Indiana Country, where we can get enough land. Forget 'em all."

Young Tom decided it couldn't get much worse if he spoke.

"Tom, I'd like to show you something."

Woodbridge ignored him.

"On top of it all," he said, "Shuldane has brought his Bedfords in. Looks like they're out of Cleopatra. Exeter's going to raise 'em for him. Partnership."

Veronica made no answer. She could not understand her own father. It seemed he could have given the hogs to Tom. But she would not speak against him.

Zabeth understood better than Mam about Grandfather Shuldane. She knew that Veronica had never really caught the vision of the Bedfords. Mam knew they were very special and different from woods hogs, but she'd not the idea by half, not by a tenth, even, how very special. But Grandpa knew now, like Pap always knew, that the man who had the likes of Boss or Cleopatra had more than the worth of a thousand acres. More even than ten thousand or all of Ohio. That's why Grandpa Shuldane was even willing to go partnerships on a farm with Pap. Because Pap knew how to raise them. Knew how to raise them so fat they could hardly walk. Pap knew how to bring 'em back to life from half dead. He could guess to within an hour when a new litter would come, and he'd be there to see nothing went wrong. Pap was almost a doctor of pigs.

"If Young Tom had only saved out Cleopatra and Boss!" anguished Woodbridge. "If only that!"

"We did, Tom. But when the soldiers came, they wouldn't listen. They took them all. Not only our stock. Adams' and Mitchell's, too. The boy tried to stop them. They pushed him away. They said Major Armstrong told them where to come."

Woodbridge consigned the boy to hopelessness with a listless wave of his hand. "It's a good thing I leased the school lands, Section 16," he said. "At least I'll have forage ground for a few woods hogs."

"Tom, would you come look at what I got to show you?" asked Stranger-boy.

"I'm not gonna look at the ill-got product of any damned fool mixin' a good Bedford blood with any woods pigs. It's sick'nin', even the thought."

"Would ya just look, Tom?"

Zabeth's brows lowered, and her voice snapped Woodbridge's head around.

"Won't hurt you to look, Pap!"

Woodbridge followed the boy up the north slope into the woods.

It was a four-mile ride, for the woods hogs had had to forage farther and farther away from the development to find feed. As they came onto the old Adams place, Woodbridge saw the herd. Among the black-brown woods hogs there scampered here and there a black and white spotted one.

"What the devil are those?"

"That's what came from the crossing," said Stranger-boy.

Woodbridge rode faster and dismounted when he got near.

"Are they young ones?" he asked hopefully.

"No. They're full-growed."

"A-ah! Y'see, then! They're even smaller than the woods critters. Shaped better I will say, though. Square in the haunches and straight along the back. But they're runts!"

He got to within ten feet of one.

"Look at 'em. They're no-'count bastards. Hardly meat a family for a week, they're that puny! Pigmies, they are!"

"It's up farther I want you to look," said Stranger-boy.

"If it's more of these, I'll be turnin' back. It sickens me."

"It's only a ways yet."

As they came to a rise of rock, Woodbridge saw a line of vertical log posts carefully formed into a pen in the woods. He dismounted and walked over, Stranger-boy running ahead. The boy stood at the edge of the pen, nervously watching Woodbridge.

Thomas Woodbridge stood with both hands on the fence posts and said no word. The hog grunted and skittered away toward the rock, where she stood scowling back at Woodbridge.

The redhead never took his eyes off her while he threw one leg up onto the top of the posts and pulled himself over with a cautious motion. The huge sow lowered her head and feinted at him, but Woodbridge walked steadily toward her. The pig made mean guttural threats. Her snout quivered, and the moisture on it gleamed ominously. She stamped her hoofs in the mulch and charged. But Woodbridge raised a fist, and she halted in indecision. Slowly she retreated toward the rock.

The spots were not like those on the others. The black spots were larger and fewer. They were almost like squares with rounded corners. Her jowls were heavy and sagged to the ground. Her hams were heavy, and the poll over her head was huge, covering her eyes. Great ears the size of squash leaves flopped forward over the savage face, vibrating as the hog quivered. She was mean-tempered, but more solid than any Bedford that Boss had ever sired. She was not quite so large as Cleopatra, but she was as square as the counter in Hosmer's Store. Woodbridge did not speak. Almost he feared she would disappear.

A warmth spread through Stranger-boy as he watched the man. He said, "Just that one came like that."

"Out of how many?"

"Maybe fifty."

"You know its sire?"

"Not positive."

"You know its mother?"

"Not for sure. But it's one of four I can pick at sight."

"You know which litter?"

"If it's out of the one I think, it's a second litter."

"This one had any young?"

"No, I kept them away from her till you should say, sir."

"Get the wagon!"

Zabeth had never seen Pap so lively and enthusiastic. Nor, since the war began, had Stranger-boy looked as he did tonight, a young man instead of an old one. His earnest face was crudely handsome in the candlelight as he strained to stay alert to Woodbridge's quick questions. Not like Arm Webster, of course. But she could see how if he had a haircut and a cloth shirt, and wasn't so shy, he'd be as good.

The two men sat at the eating table in the cabin with the old Bedford notebook in front of them.

Veronica hummed quietly as she moved around the cabin. Zabeth had not heard Mam hum in a long time.

Woodbridge made lines on a piece of paper and referred to the Bedford notebook.

"Now you remember, boy, every fourth litter Cleopatra would spring just that one crit with the black foot?"

"Yes."

"We always culled it out because it was so puny."

"Yes."

"But once we didn't, remember? We raised it up, bred her, and her second litter had three black-footed ones?"

"I remember."

"Now! If you can narrow down the Big One's dam to four of those woods hogs, all we got to do is keep trying. Changing off boars, perhaps her second litter one time will give us three like her."

"But we'll need the use of a Bedford boar, sir."

Woodbridge pushed back from the table, and stared into the fireplace. He stood up and walked back and forth slamming his right fist into his left palm rhythmically.

Then he sat down again.

'There'll come a day, boy. There'll come a day Exeter will be in trouble with Shuldane's Bedfords. There'll come a day one'll get awful sick, and Exeter'll be beside himself to doctor it. He'll come apleadin', boy. Then I'll know what to do.''

Stranger-boy saw trouble, but he didn't answer. He didn't want to spoil anything. It was fine just the way it was.

# Chapter 22: SECTION 16

LIFE was no longer simple on the Wood-bridge development in Hosmer Village. A year made a big difference, what with Veronica wanting clapboards and an addition to the cabin so that Zabeth could have her own room, and Stranger-boy wishing to go with Asa Buttrick to Cincinnati to work as Buttrick's account keeper during the September trading.

But one thorny nuisance probed the side of the hog farmer with galling persistence. With an unchallengeable countenance of concern for village welfare, Shuldane was stirring Hosmer Village to call Thomas Woodbridge to account for his eight-year custodianship of a piece of property which belonged to the people.

Section 16 of every township surveyed from the Bounty Lands was reserved by law to the people of the town for the support of schools; that is, by leasing this section of land money would accrue which was to support a schoolmaster and a school building.

In 1809, when nobody cared any more about schools than Tom Woodbridge, Hosmer Village trustees had leased Section 16 to the hog farmer. The rent he paid was 6 per cent of the negligible assessed value. But in addition he had signed to make certain improvements on the school tract so that when the time came for schools Section 16 would be valuable enough to finance them. For eight years now, no man had cared a hang about the land. Then suddenly "Section 16" became a fighting phrase in Hosmer Village.

It was hard to point to the beginning of the trouble. But it could have been the day they all waved goodbye to Margaret Buttrick when she left for an eastern school, and Faith Hawkins turned immediately to look at her own daughter May.

It could have been the day Silver Pigeon came to see Young Tom.

Old Captain Michael was no longer a romantic figure even to the village children. When the stench from his hut on the common began to reach even to Exeter's tavern, they burned it and moved the chief down behind Buttrick's cabin on the riverbank. But Mr. Shuldane saw future store sites in the strip of shore.

Now Captain Michael had no pride of race left, nor pride in the title "Captain," for lately it had become a white man's joke. But in one possession Captain Michael could equal or surpass any white man. The chief had a son, Silver Pigeon, who was straight as a gun barrel, and bright and loyal.

"Stranger-boy, could Pigeon take the chief up in Mr. Woodbridge's timberland and build him a hut? It would not show."

"They kicked the chief out again, Pigeon?"

"Yes. Mr. Shuldane did."

"I don't think Tom would want the old chief on the place. You see, he's figurin' to clear more ground. Chief'd just have to move again soon."

"The chief is too old to take the trail."

"I've a notion," reflected Stranger-boy. "Tom leases a section of woods from the town, Section 16. The school lands. Take Captain Michael up in those woods and build a cabin. Way back from the road."

"What if Mr. Tom finds out?"

"Might not matter. But I'll see he don't."

"Thank you."

"Oh, one trouble, though," added Young Tom. "In September I go to Cincinnati with Mr. Buttrick to keep accounts for him at market."

"Cincinnati?"

"Yes. Tom says no. But I'm counting he'll change his mind. While I'm gone, though, you'll have to keep the chief back in the woods. Hidden."

"I will."

And to the old chief, when Pigeon explained the new arrangement, it was a kind of omen.

The word "school" had a special significance, and he clutched at it in his hard-won English.

"It is *school* lands you call it, Silver Pigeon?"

"That means nothing to us, Hayesta. Some day the white man—It is too much to explain. Come."

"Silver Pigeon! Now comes school for Silver Pigeon! White man will not laugh at Silver Pigeon."

"Chief, quiet. We have work to make the hut."

But the chief would not be quiet.

It was in Hosmer's Store in May that Amos Exeter, the appraiser, reminded Woodbridge that August 15 was the day set for reappraising the school-land section. That would raise the value on which Woodbridge paid 6 per cent.

"Now what brought that up?" Woodbridge demanded.

"Matter of fact, that crazy old chief was around here blabberin' about school lands," said Exeter. "That reminded us we got to reappraise that section. And Mr. Shuldane said he wants to take up the lease on that piece to develop it so it'll support a school."

"Exeter, your office has gone to your head. Nobody's gonna raise that appraisal on me or take my lease."

"The land's worth more just because the whole village is worth more."

"Not that land. I only use it for grazin' woods hogs. Slim rootin' at that!"

Sam Hosmer spoke with calm authority.

"Since you take that attitude, Tom, that land had better be worth more than when you took it over. In the lease you agreed to clear fifteen acres of it, five acres to be planted in timothy, three acres in fruit, seven acres in plowed land."

"A-ah! The town was glad enough to just get the interest."

"I'm not denyin' it," said Hosmer. "But the land's for supportin' a schoolhouse. And if Mr. Shuldane will improve the land better than you, he should have the lease."

"It don't prove out, Hosmer. I'm supposed to improve the lands and make 'em worth more so I can pay more rent and taxes, as a *penalty*, mind ya, for improvements I make *myself*. Hah!"

Hosmer turned to Exeter.

"Amos, if the improvements on the school lands aren't made by Woodbridge by the day of reappraisement, you can cancel the lease and make a new one with Mr. Shuldane, or whoever'll offer the best rent for it."

On his way home Woodbridge rode along the north side of the river for a look at Section 16 to see what he could do about it. It would be hard to make in a few months the improvements that were supposed to have been made over a period of nine years. But he needed the land for the woods hogs until the spotted herd grew to paying proportions.

Tom's theory of breeding Big One had worked; not exactly as he had planned it. But in the third litter out of Big One there had been four strangely spotted hogs which had grown large and square, like the Big One. One of these had been a boar. And by experimenting with the boar they had brought a whole litter of the large spotted hogs, and these had been even larger. The herd was growing, and they were more rugged than Bedfords. They had almost the toughness of woods hogs, and carried more flesh than a Bedford. They grew fast. One went to 270 pounds on Hosmer's scale. Things were going well—until the Section 16 business.

Woodbridge walked up into Section 16. That was when he came across a miserable hut in the woods. It was ill built, a covering of bark over the thinnest structure of small log poles. Inside, it smelled of smoke and ham. Untended embers smoldered dangerously in the simplest of fire pits. The shack was a filthy fire hazard.

Bracing his feet in the deep leaves Woodbridge shoved against the corner of the hut. He set it to rocking.

From behind him a voice split the quiet.

"Sa cati arin ga!"

Woodbridge turned quickly.

"Yours?" asked Woodbridge.

Captain Michael shuffled forward with a grim face. The righteous accusation on the Indian's face, coupled with Woodbridge's present problem of the school lands, ignited the redhead.

"Well, damn it! It's not enough ya sneak onto my property and squat! Ya had to go and stir up a whole townful of trouble for me!"

"School land! School for the Silver Pigeon. Soon."

"Why, you fool! Even if there is a school here—you think we'll tolerate red brats in it?"

Woodbridge shoved against the shack, and it leaned at a sharp angle.

"Get out!"

The chief was no longer much of an Indian. But in that hateful instant he straightened into a fearsome image of Tecumseh and Rontondee and Blue Jacket. His vibrating silence radiated a curse.

"Don't stare at me like that, ya red devil! Get out!"

The chief left. But as Woodbridge rode back home he felt that somehow he had made a mistake. He went back the following day to look for Michael. But the shack was empty, the fire was out, and the Indian's plunder was gone. Woodbridge straightened up the shack and cut three stout poles to brace it.

The third day he went to the hut again, but it was deserted. Nor had anyone seen Silver Pigeon or Captain Michael in the village or around it.

In the weeks following, the people of Mesopotamia took to riding out past Section 16 pointedly to see if Woodbridge had begun any of the required improvements on the land. Woodbridge just as pointedly remained away from the section.

Exeter was having trouble raising the delicate Bedfords for Shuldane. But Woodbridge and Stranger-boy had developed one of their special spotted boars and eighteen spotted sows which almost always produced the special type of hog which they took to calling the Mesopotamia Hog.

It was in June that Stranger-boy brought up the subject of the school lands again.

"We'd better start the improvements on Section 16," he said, "while I'm still here to help."

"And just where would you be going?"

"You said perhaps I could go keep accounts for Mr. Buttrick at Cincinnati in September."

"You'll not be running off to bookkeep for any man. And as for improvements on Section 16, there'll be none."

"I'm afraid there will, sir."

"What!"

"I heard talk about prosecutin' us, sir, for not improvin' the land under the lease. The lawyer and Mr. Shuldane were talking."

If the change that came to the Ohio frontier in 1815 had burst upon Woodbridge with a sudden clarity like a bad survey or statehood, he could have battled it and won or lost. But instead it seeped under his skin with a disturbing annoyance, like Veronica hungering for an addition to the cabin and clapboards on it; like Asa Buttrick sending his daughter Margaret back East to school, as if she were better than Zabeth; like Stranger-boy hankering to go with Buttrick to Fort Washington, which styled itself Cincinnati. It shortened Tom's temper and changed his heroes, and as they hoed the corn side by side he told Stranger-boy about it as though it were his fault.

"Rifles are rusting while flooring goes into the cabins," he charged.

Stranger-boy kept silent lest he remind Woodbridge, while he was on the subject of change, about wanting to go with Buttrick to Cincinnati.

"And Shuldane," continued Woodbridge, "while we was scratchin' holes in the turf deep enough to get a few seeds in, he was back East eatin' himself fat and buyin' more bounty warrants. Now that the work's done, he's out here paradin' around in a forktail coat and yawpin' about the big migration that's comin'. He's our Congressman in Washington. What does he know about us?"

Strange things were now valued in Hosmer Village: brass fire carriers, bed warmers, itinerant cobblers who made lefts and rights from separate lasts.

"And now we got barn mice, pigweed, house flies and bartenders—the signs of civilization. Huh! And you, wantin' to run off bookkeepin'!"

Veronica chose that day to ask Tom to have Buttrick stop at Dayton and inquire the price of clapboards from the mill there.

"Clapboards!" repeated Woodbridge. "Veronica, I'll build the new room we need for Zabeth. But clapboards come after the smokehouse is built. And that's a time off yet."

By the time the smokehouse was finished, Mrs. Hosmer had an iron stove, Faith Hawkins had a linen dress, and Mrs. Buttrick had cloth sheets. But Veronica asked for none of these. She wanted only a wing for the cabin. And since the smokehouse was done, it was time now.

That's why she bit back the tears in July when Tom came back from town. He brought heavy objects in to the cabin which he clunked onto the floor with a flourish.

"I had Buttrick to bring you back one of these iron beds with the brass knobs like Mrs. Buttrick's."

Veronica bit her lower lip and stared silently.

"Well, don't you like it?" he asked.

"Tom, is it to be instead of the wing on the cabin?"

The big hog farmer's red face was transparent with surprised guilt.

"We need new fences, Veronica," he said.

He searched Zabeth's face for encouragement, but the girl studied the bed as though it were a hog in the house.

Woodbridge looked at Veronica in the light of the glass window that high-lighted a glint of wet on the side of her cheek. Suddenly he dropped the end piece of the iron bed.

"Zabeth!" he ordered. "Ride into town and get Stanley-the-Slasher. Tell him to come out here right away. And to fetch along his tools!"

Zabeth stood puzzled. But Woodbridge called to Young Tom.

"Boy, put the stone to our axes! And hitch up the ox for timber draggin'!"

"But we promised that cured pork to Fort Tawa tomorrow, sir. Shouldn't we start loading?"

"We promised a wing for the cabin, too, boy! Get the axes!"

On the fourth day of the building Veronica noticed the men stretching a twine from the corner of the old cabin way out to the far end of the shed.

"But, Tom, we don't need it that big. I want only one more room."

"You've waited overlong. While we're buildin', we'll build big." And he yelled to Slasher, "Carry your end a little more north!"

Slasher's answer floated down to the corner of the cabin, "Golly crimus, Tom! We're long enough already for two rooms."

"We're buildin' three," answered Tom. "Can't do this over every year. Move it out!"

Tom's energy swept the improvement beyond Veronica's dreams. Nothing interfered with the progress, not even rain. At times like this he was superb. He cut only black walnut. He insisted the logs be hewn almost square, like the timbers in the Shuldane house.

When the addition was finished, it was larger than the two halves of the original cabin, and better built, for the square timbers gave solidness to it.

The new addition ran north-south, perpendicular to the length of the original double cabin and to the shed, and joining them both. Thus the entire improvement formed a U with the open end to the west. You could walk from the main cabin through the addition and into the shed without ever going outdoors. This Zabeth did many times, in wonderment.

Perhaps the greatest tribute to the house came from Stanley-the-Slasher. Slasher's graying stubble of a beard nodded from side to side as he admired the house from the south. He studied the smooth juncture between the old cabin and the new, which he had told Woodbridge was impossible. Woodbridge had insisted, though, and Slasher had joined them so tight a moth could hardly find the crack.

Slasher shook his head and walked over to the southeast corner of the house. With his knife he carved into the southern base log, "S. Slasher."

As Veronica measured the windows for curtains, Woodbridge said, "Wife, do you think it's time we had folks in for a—well, just for sociability?"

"It would be more fitting, Tom, to wait till there's a natural reason for it. At harvesting, perhaps. Might appear we're a bit showy."

"A-ah! You ashamed of the house I built?"

"Of course not, but—"

"Saturday night, then, we'll have them."

Veronica faced the week with mixed emotions. She was thrilled with the house. Particularly did she like the effect on Elizabeth, who walked more sedately through the rooms now that the cabin had become a house.

Saturday night, because of all the preparations which were being made, they sat to an unusually light supper. Stranger-boy was somewhat puzzled by the inattention to his important news.

"Tom, I think the young boar in this last litter will be the likes of Big Two, or better. He's squarin' up solid in the haunch, and he's heavy shouldered. He could be the second boar we're lookin' for."

But Woodbridge rose suddenly from the table and went into the new living room of the house. When he returned to the table he said: "I was afraid I'd mislaid that special sour-mash whisky I had from Buttrick for tonight. But it's there, all right."

"If he lives up to what I think," continued Young Tom, "he'll give us a replacement for Big Two, and—" But Young Tom never finished the sentence. He stared at the door to the new part of the house. Woodbridge stopped his mug halfway to his mouth and set it down slowly, by accident on his trencher. Veronica looked at Stranger-boy and then turned to follow his stare.

Zabeth came.

She did not bounce to the table, but rather swept across the floor. It seemed that way, at least, not so much because of the change in her demeanor, but because the long strides of her legs were invisible beneath the stiff cloth of the new dress. She seemed to glide on top of a stationary flare of crinoline. In an unfamiliar gesture she swept the skirt smooth underneath her as she sat. The motion of her arm stretched the crisp cloth so tight against her trunk that Young Tom turned abruptly to his trencher. But he was compelled to look again. And the margin of whiteness that bordered her brushed-back hair was a discovery to him, uncovering small white ears which had not been browned by the weather. She was a stranger.

When Woodbridge failed to pass her the common platter, but only sat and stared, Zabeth said defensively, "Well, Mam said I should wear the dress tonight account of the company."

Woodbridge smiled proudly, not taking his eyes from her as he passed the meat.

"You should have let Arm Webster buy you those slippers in Cincinnati, Elizabeth," said Veronica.

"My boots don't show, Mam. They're covered."

Stranger-boy said, "I could put a touch of harness soap to the boots."

"It's a good thing you've a brother," said Veronica. "Give him the boots." Veronica used the word "brother" a lot lately.

With some annoyance Zabeth swung her feet out from under the table. She raised the interfering crinoline for Stranger-boy to yank off the boots. He started to yank them as he had done perhaps a hundred times when she was a youngster. But The Dress changed all that. He stopped and held out his hand for the boots, and he was glad to be out of the cabin and in the shed.

As dusk lowered, the family sat in the large new living room. It was not the lack of furniture that left the room so extremely empty. Except for the Woodbridges, the room was devoid of people.

Veronica sat quietly sewing. Stranger-boy sat straight with his boots close together, toed in slightly, making an important occupation of examining the knuckles of his large hands.

Woodbridge rose to walk back and forth.

"It's too early yet for them to get here," said Veronica.

"I'd judge it a quarter beyond eight already."

Woodbridge sat down, and the room was silent except for an occasional muffled kicking from the stall in the shed. Young Tom was now studying his forearm. Zabeth studied the roof rafters.

Woodbridge split the silence.

"Well, we'll celebrate by ourselves then!"

He was on his feet drawing the bung from the keg when the tension was relieved by the arrival of Jim Hawkins. He admired the house satisfactorily, but Veronica looked back to her knitting when Hawkins made his explanation.

"Sorry I couldn't bring Faith, but—ah—she hasn't been feeling good all this week." Hawkins looked lamely around the empty room, adding: "And—uh—Judith Dolk told me the babe was down with something. And Exeter said to say he was lamed up some."

"Seems kind of funny," said Woodbridge. "I saw Exeter ridin' by here yesterday. Didn't appear lamed any."

Hope Emerson burst in without knocking. She walked to the keg and held out a noggin for Woodbridge to fill.

"'Lo, Tom," she said. "Nice house. No wonder nobody came. Near as big as Shuldane's." She drank with unashamed pleasure. She shamed the tenseness out of the room. But it was quickly replaced when Blair entered.

"The Masons and the Fitchburgs wanted me to say they wouldn't be able to make it, Tom. Sickness."

Woodbridge emptied a noggin and muttered, "Devil of a lot of sickness came over this town since yesterday."

Handsome young Arm Webster arrived with a package under his arm, wrapped in the Scioto *Gazette*. Webster was the kind of person whose presence was felt. And as he stood there, handsome and self-assured, accepting a cup from Woodbridge, everyone in the room noticed something about him.

Stranger-boy noticed first of all that Webster drank with his elbow high and that while he drank he looked out to the side at the little tip of boot that peeked from under Zabeth's dress. He noticed also that under the coat sleeve there was bulging muscle.

Veronica noticed that there was a good expanse of white cuff below the sleeve and that there was a poise and confidence about Webster that would carry him surely into the higher councils of the West, and could carry a girl like Elizabeth with him, to the better living.

Blair saw in Webster a reflection of himself minus fifteen years—but with an important difference. In addition to his own cleverness, he saw in Webster an unbending surefootedness. The wide-set eyes stared as evenly at his seniors as at his juniors. Blair envied Webster, though he could not thank him for the reflection of his own vacillating career.

Arm Webster turned to Blair with a candor which immediately put the older man on his guard.

"I'd very much appreciate some advice from you, Mr. Blair," said Webster.

Blair nodded. "Any time."

"How many signatures are needed on a petition to run for the legislature?"

Blair swallowed.

"From what district?"

"From this one."

Despite his best effort, Blair's surprise stood for an instant so naked on his face that young Webster saw it.

"Your district, Mr. Blair. Uncle Nate said you'd likely be going East on important business for him. Advised me to run for your seat next election."

Blair curled up inside. He'd seen Shuldane use this gambit before, but always young Blair had been the knowing bystander, dispassionately admiring the tactic. He'd never been on the receiving end.

"Uh—I hadn't heard about that," said Blair.

His voice was vacant, but his head was full. He noticed the few people in the room staring at him. That was part of the master's plan, too, to have the boy ask the question naïvely in front of a group, handing to Blair both a graceful retreat and an unmistakable ultimatum to get out of the way, coupled with a public announcement of his new candidate.

"You didn't answer my question, Mr. Blair," said Arm.

"Answer the boy, Jonathan," urged Hope Emerson, who leaned mannishly against the wall. Blair looked up at her suddenly to see what she meant, but Hope turned a careless glance to Webster.

"He just doesn't want to scare you, Arm," she said, "because the truth is you'd have to have about a hundred bushel of signatures on your little old petition to run against Jonathan Blair."

She turned her head casually to Blair, but her eyes raked him from head to foot and challenged him.

With a surge of vigor Blair took Arm's cup and his own and refilled them, shoving one toward Webster.

"She puts it a little strong, son," he said heartily. "But you'll need about fifty bushel, and you'll have to be fast on your feet. Good luck."

Young Webster was at a slight loss, but he drank and returned the toast. He recovered quickly enough, too. As the room watched him, he walked pointedly to the corner where he had placed his package.

"Uncle Nate sent along a little housewarming present to the Woodbridges," he said. He took the package neither to Veronica nor to Tom, but to Zabeth.

The girl unwrapped the newspaper from the large rectangular object and stared, immobilized. Candles, reflected from the shiny gift, lighted her face, but the flush came from within her. For Zabeth looked for the first time into a silver-backed mirror.

The girl's sudden experience was so personal that no one should have been watching. But Arm Webster stood grinning. What Zabeth saw in the mirror was the created product and total of fifteen years of Tom Woodbridge and Veronica and Prince and Jock and Wolf and Cleopatra and Boss and Ox and the big woods. But Arm Webster, by handing her a mirror, got credit in a way for the whole thing.

No one seemed to see Stranger-boy leave to get wood for the kitchen cooking fire.

When they had all gone, Woodbridge looked at all the clean cups which had not been needed. The food would keep. But something had spoiled that night.

Thomas Woodbridge had built his house too large.

Slumped in a chair at the far end of the room opposite Veronica, Woodbridge thought back over the past week. He could see now the echoes of envy that had rattled off the high walnut gables of the Woodbridge addition, permeating every transaction, squeezing a tinge of vinegar into every encounter. Nor had it been too intangible to be measured in the higher prices Fitchburg charged him for curing salt.

He remembered the tight cold face of Mesopotamia when he had announced in the store about the big doings tonight. Huh. All of a sudden they all were sick.

Woodbridge fired his cup against the new wall, startling Veronica.

"All right!" he roared. "All right! So it *is* a big house! They talk about it, huh? Well, I'll give 'em somethin' to talk about!"

"What do you mean, Tom?"

"Veronica, you're gonna have your clapboards!"

"Tom, I'd as leave postpone the clapboards a few years yet."

"You wanted 'em before! For five years you've been wantin' clapboards. You went without all the fancy what-nots they got in town. Now you're gonna have clapboards! I'll be leavin' for Dayton in the morning."

Veronica walked over to him, but a knock on the door surprised them both.

Woodbridge went into the old cabin and opened the door. His voice was edged with flint.

"Come in, Sam."

Sam Hosmer walked into the old part of the cabin. "I wasn't comin', but the wife began to feel better, so I came," he said.

He walked through the doorway by the fireplace into the new addition. He rubbed his hand over the wall timbers, admiring Slasher's work.

"Nice broadax trimming, Tom."

"The whole place is gonna be better yet by twice. They haven't really seen a house yet," said Woodbridge to Hosmer's back.

Hosmer bent to look at the grooved fit between the sill and the wall.

"I was just tellin' Veronica. I'm going tomorrow for clapboards."

"Oh?" Hosmer absently flicked shavings out the window corner with a blunt fingertip. He sat down in a chair, giving up his weight to it with an old man's full appreciation. He was still running his eye around the room.

Veronica said: "Sam, we didn't have you build it because—well— Tom just started it one day after we got up from table. Then it just grew. Guess it's a little too large."

Hosmer's leather wrinkles crinkled into a smile.

"You're a kind, womanly woman, Veronica; and you're smart, which ye need to be, bein' married to this wild boar here."

"Where do I get clapboards, Sam?" asked Woodbridge abruptly. "The best ones."

Hosmer didn't answer.

"Y'might as well tell me, because I'm gonna have 'em!" insisted Woodbridge.

Hosmer's voice was surprisingly passive.

"Why, of course, Tom. Ye should. Was there any question?"

"Well, I thought—that is, Veronica thinks the people will object."

"No. The people want you to have clapboards. In fact, they'll demand that ye have clapboards, Tom. They'll even put them up for you, same as they plastered the cracks in my house and store."

"What are you talkin' about, Sam? Doesn't work that way with me."

"Works that way all over, Tom. It's very simple."

"Hah! The devil you say!"

"Well, Tom, ye remember I decided I'd like to plaster up where the chinking was between the timbers of my place?"

"Yuh."

Veronica noticed tonight how much of the fierceness had gone out of Sam Hosmer's face, as it had from Captain Michael's and from Slasher's.

"Well," continued Hosmer quietly, "I decided same time that Fitchburg and Mason and Exeter and Stikes would prob'ly like plaster chinking too."

"You're a long time gettin' to clapboards, Sam," said Woodbridge.

"So I just made it so's everybody else that wanted could get plaster too. I ordered in eight barrels out of Pittsburgh."

"Plaster ain't clapboards," said Woodbridge.

"'Twas at the time, y'might say."

"Listen to what Sam is trying to tell you, Tom," urged Veronica.

"Tom, build your house as big as y'like," said old man Hosmer. "Just be sure when y'do it that y'take your neighbors up a notch alongside of ya. And if y'do that, Tom, somehow they always see to it you got the best one."

"A-ah! You're talkin' nonsense, Sam. How can one man clapboard the whole town?"

"Town needs a sawmill," said Hosmer. "Wouldn't be more'n a matter of $500 countin' mill, dam site, and saw blade."

"Huh, that might not be much to you, but—"

"Oh, but it is," said Hosmer. "It's a very lot of money. Maybe too much."

"Oh, I don't know," bristled Woodbridge. "I could probably raise it. That'd show them, by Gor! I get your point!"

"Not quite, Tom," said Hosmer. "If your money bought the whole saw and the gears and the shaft and the water wheel, why the clapboards that were made there would tend to be just a shade too thin, or too thick or too green."

"What difference whose money?"

"But now if the blade was bought with some of Stikes's money, and the gears with some of Slasher's and some of mine and some of yours and some of Buttrick's . . . why then I think that saw would mill the straightest, finest, most wonderful clapboards in the West, Tom."

A grin slowly lighted the redhead's face.

"Y-e-a-h," he breathed. "Yeah. Sam, I never knew you knew so much about—uh—clapboards."

During the following week Tom was in good spirits. For while he built a new pen for Big Three, and while he fed the hogs, and while he cleared more trees off the north slope, he thought about Sam Hosmer's idea, and it pleased him. The family knew he felt good, because out of a clear sky he said: "I reckon it might be good experience for Stranger-boy to go to Cincinnati for a couple a months to bookkeep for Mr. Buttrick. Might learn a few handy tricks for sellin' our Mesopotamia hogs."

Young Tom worked especially hard that week in thanks. And as they worked together, Woodbridge explained how he'd worked out Hosmer's idea.

"Y'see, boy, if Stikes, Buttrick, Hosmer, and I put up $50 each, and if Hawkins and Adams and Fitchburg and some others put up $25, we could get the mill set up, doin' the work ourselves. Then we could hire Slasher to run it. And each of us could bring in the timber off our own places and have clapboards for only the cost of the labor. And we'd get our original money back sellin' clapboards to the others in town and maybe make a little, too."

"Only trouble," said Young Tom, "won't Mr. Shuldane want to put up all the money and own the mill?"

"Yeah, he'll want to do that all right. But I aim to get the men together Monday while he's down to Chillicothe."

"Young Webster's likely to speak for him, though, in his absence, or Mr. Blair."

"Blair won't, I dare say. As for Webster, I'll chance that."

As Veronica watched Tom drive off the place, she commented to Zabeth, "I hope they all go in on the project, else Tom'll get mad and we'll be the only clapboarded house."

"You wanted clapboards before, Mam."

"But right now it wouldn't be the right thing to do."

Tom Woodbridge didn't believe in this forever banding together to get things done. More was accomplished when one man just up and did it. But on this clapboard thing, it made sense. But his speech was so set in his mind by the time he reached town that he wasn't prepared for the surprise when he walked into the store.

Against the counter leaned Captain Michael.

There was no malice on the old Indian face now. But there was a kind of insulting secret there. To Woodbridge's greeting the Indian kept silent, only nodding in benign acknowledgment. It ruffled the redhead.

"Well, where the hell have you been all summer, Michael?" he roared, trying to bridge the gap with brashness.

"Take Silver Pigeon to school. Colonel Johnson's Choctaw Academy. Father Gershom told me. Kentucky. All Indian boys."

For some reason the news unsettled Tom. But he proceeded to his business, addressing the men who stood there.

"Got an idea I want to put up to ya. Gonna cost ya some money. But it might make ya some, too. I got it figured out that for forty-fifty dollars apiece—less if there's more than nine-ten of us—we could—"

Woodbridge stopped because Elnathan Shuldane came into the store. Tom had believed Shuldane would not be in town.

Beside Shuldane came Amos Exeter, who carried a paper in his hand. Exeter walked into the center of the store.

"Glad you're here, Tom," he said. "You gonna be ready for the reappraisal of Section 16 on August 15?"

Woodbridge flared.

"Exeter, I told you I'm not improvin' any land to raise my own rent and taxes. It's against good sense."

"Suit yourself," said Exeter. "I'm only tryin' to give you good warning. Mr. Shuldane here wants to take over that lease of yours, which he can do if you haven't improved those lands. And I want everybody to know it so's there'll be no bellyachin' when it comes time we take it away from you."

"You'll not take away what's leased to me by the town on legal paper."

"If the improvements aren't made," said Exeter, "that'll break your lease."

Exeter looked to Hosmer for confirmation, as did Woodbridge. Hosmer nodded.

"The land belongs to the people for a purpose, Tom. The value must advance."

With the hurt, vengeful anger of a man who came to do a favor and stayed to be rebuked, Woodbridge challenged the room in general. "I'm so far from improvin' that land that you're drivin' me just the opposite. And when you get there for your blasted reappraisement, the land may not be worth the paper your lease is made on. Good day to ya!"

"Tom, don't go takin' off that timber," said Exeter, "or anythin' foolish like that. Tom! Come back here!"

But Woodbridge was already punishing his horse over the West Road. At that moment he would have swapped the best breeder on his place to even the score against the merciless march of improvements in Hosmer Village.

As the hog farmer passed his smokehouse on foot, voices from inside caused him to stop and listen. The Stranger-boy and Silver Pigeon were talking. Silver Pigeon's voice had dropped into his chest noticeably over the summer. He was saying: "So after Woodbridge and the chief had that argument in the woods, the chief was angry. He took me over the trail to Colonel Johnson's Choctaw Academy in the Kentucky. All Indian boys. He made me study. I learned mostly numbers and Bible reading."

"Maybe you could teach me some numbers, Silver Pigeon," said Young Tom. "'Twould help me to work for Mr. Buttrick."

"I thought Mr. Tom wasn't to let you go."

"He changed his mind. I can go for two months."

"Then I think we cannot be friends longer, Young Tom," said the young Indian.

"Huh? What do you mean, Pigeon?"

"It's what I came to tell you. The Mr. Buttrick hears of my learning the numbers. He tries me. And he says I had learned them better like a white boy. He chooses me to take instead of you to Cincinnati, Stranger-boy."

Tom Woodbridge turned away from the smokehouse, shaken. He threw the saddle on New Horse and rode slowly over to the school lands. The fight was suddenly gone out of him. He studied the timber on the land, and the creek and the black bottom soil beside the creek. But you can't raise the value of the wilderness in a week. It takes time to clear the land, to plant crops.

Woodbridge tied the horse and tramped farther up into Section 16 than he had ever gone before. If he could find and develop a salt spring on the place, it would improve the value overnight. Desperately he searched the area. But the strange truth was that Thomas Woodbridge was no longer interested in merely meeting the terms of the lease.

For the next three days he tramped around the school land tract searching for something that would miraculously change the unimproved land to a place of value.

On the morning of August 15th, Amos Exeter, the appraiser, and

Jim Dolk, the constable, approached the school land tract, Section 16. Along with them came Fitchburg, Buttrick, and Shuldane, in case there should be any trouble with Woodbridge. In the event there should be any general trouble, others came along: Hosmer, Stikes, Hawkins, and a few more.

As they approached the tract, it looked as if they might be needed. Exeter said, "Smoke comin' up back there."

"Wouldn't put it past the redhead to be mad enough to be burnin' up them black walnut timbers," said Fitchburg.

"Or worse," added Buttrick. "When he sees red, nothing counts."

"Doubt if he's doin' that," said Hosmer. "But we'd best hurry a bit."

They tramped up to where they heard the axes striking. Woodbridge and Young Tom were there. The hog farmer continued his chopping, leaving the group standing in awkward silence.

Exeter mustered his official tone. "Woodbridge!"

"Yeah." Tom continued his work.

"We're here for the reappraisement."

"Well, get to reappraisin' then."

"Well, first off . . . " Exeter hesitated, unsettled by Tom's serene composure. "First off, I'm servin' notice that I'm raisin' the valuation of this quarter-section right here to $7 the acre. You ain't made it worth that. But the comin' migration pushes it up there."

"All right," said Woodbridge, clearing away some small brush. Woodbridge's inattention annoyed Exeter, but he struggled on.

"Now what improvements you got to show that'll raise the value up to about $10, which is what it needs for you to hold the lease?"

Woodbridge raised his ax and brought it down so that it slashed into the stump of the maple and stuck there.

"Ten!" he said with his hands on his hips. "Why, Exeter, this land's worth $20 the acre if it's worth a dime!"

"Huh?" Exeter was taken unawares, and the others were suddenly attentive.

"Don't ya see that sawmill over there? That makes this place worth $20 an acre to any man!"

"What are you talkin' about, Woodbridge? There's nothin' there but the chief's old hut."

Hosmer followed Woodbridge's pointing arm, and he rubbed his chin.

"Don't ya see that wheel turnin' right opposite that stake?" continued Tom. "Don't ya see the mill shack standin' right there where that twine squares off the foundation?"

The wrinkles around Hosmer's mouth were shaping themselves into faint enjoyment as he studied the twine. Annoyance showed on Shuldane's face. Exeter looked from the string to Woodbridge and back several times. "I—I—don't get—"

"Don't ya see them wagons rollin' up to take out clapboards at twelve and a half cents a yard?"

"You mean," struggled Exeter, "you plan to— But you always said that stream was too slack-watered to seat a mill."

"Sure," said Woodbridge. "But don't ya see the dam staked out there, buildin' up the pressure ta turn that wheel? Don't ya see it?"

"I don't see anything but the creek," said Amos.

Shuldane stepped forward.

"We've had enough nonsense. Get on with this, Exeter. Any mills that are built will be over on the old Adams place in the next township. What's all this mill nonsense?"

"Y'all see it, don't ya?" asked Woodbridge of the crowd.

The grin spread through the crowd, except on the faces of Shuldane and Buttrick and Fitchburg and the puzzled Amos Exeter, who said: "Well, Tom, I guess I get your plan all right. But we can't credit ya with the improvements until it's already finished. You can't build it in less than a year."

"Well, we better, mister!" yelled Woodbridge. "This is the school lands, y'know! You want your kids growin' up more ignorant and want-witted than a wild Indian? You want Captain Michael t'have the smartest kid in the whole improvement? Well, I don't!"

"But I can't mark it up at county," said Exeter, "until I see it on the ground."

"Are you challengin' the word of your neighbors?" asked Woodbridge. "Callin' 'em all liars?"

"I'm calling this absurd!" said Shuldane with a reddening face. "And I'm—"

Woodbridge cut him off.

"You see a sawmill, don't ya, Jim?" asked Tom.

"Yes, Tom."

"You, Captain Michael?"

"Yah. Mill. Make boards. Make school."

Shuldane's face darkened. But the frosty face of Mesopotamia cracked slowly into broader grins, and leaned with the redhead, who asked, "You see it, Mike?"

"Sure do, Tom. Blade ain't in yet. But I got a piece of Revere steel that's just right for the saw blade."

"You see it, don't ya, Sam?"

"Plain as day, Tom," said Hosmer. "Plain as day."

"All right, then," said Woodbridge. "Mark it down there, Exeter. Section 16, southwest quarter. Reappraised: $20 the acre."

"It won't be the truth," minced Amos, looking helplessly at Shuldane.

"It will be," charged Woodbridge, "if you'll all drop those fool papers and grab holt of some axes and git on with this here improvement! Ya usually open a schoolhouse in September, don't ya?"

Sheepishly the Stranger-boy pulled back a piece of canvas under which there somehow happened to be twelve axes.

# Chapter 23: LAND!

IT was no fancied, imaginary ailment. Veronica noticed that it was a definite, real, and physical twitch that flickered over Woodbridge's cheeks when he heard the sound of an ax. The noon meal was only half over when he dropped his fork and got up from table.

Veronica had heard the ax, too.

"They've a right to be there," she said.

"I know. I know!" he said. And he walked out of the house.

The big redhead walked to the east boundary of the Woodbridge improvement. So often lately had the sounds of invading axes brought Woodbridge out to walk his boundaries, that there was a faint but straight path beaten along the survey line. He could no longer hear the ax, but he started walking north along the line.

Even back when you didn't hear an ax from December to December, Woodbridge had known this time would come. Ever since he first broke his plow point for listening to the Stranger's ax bite into the solitude, Woodbridge had known the axes would close in one day. The trees would fall. And now the time had come. Men who had thought so little of the possibilities as to sell their hundred-acre bounty warrants for twenty cents an acre now rushed to buy the same land for $2 an acre, $5, even $10. Men who had bought their hundred-acre bounty warrants with their own Revolutionary blood and then sold them to Shuldane for $20 now mortgaged their farms and their sons' farms to buy more of the same land at $5 an acre. For the rush of settlers was said to be coming, and the craziest land boom in history was on.

The warrant buyers who held plenty of certificates were riding high. Warrant buyers who had only a few were scouring the eastern seaboard, buying warrants from veterans' widows who were not yet aware of the rise in western land values. Warrants were being swindled, forged, and stolen.

Woodbridge caught himself talking out loud, stopped, then drifted into it again, as he walked his boundary.

Stikes mortgaged his forge to take a hundred acres of Shuldane's new township. And Stikes not knowing Hackelberry corn from Gourdseed! Exeter, as clutch-fisted as there was in Mesopotamia, had mortgaged to take a hundred. Aaron Fitchburg, the shut-pocketest man in town, had taken 125 acres. He'd paid down only two eagles, and not worried about the balance. Why should he? Credit was easy.

Interest was high, but what of it? No thought of payin' principal anyhow. Keep up the interest. Renew the note. Nobody cared.

Woodbridge heard the ax again, and he stopped dead still, listening. But he couldn't tell which direction the sound came from. He came to his northeast corner.

It seemed like yesterday that they'd marked that corner with Sargent's survey crew. He parted the brush and found the cuts in the stump. They had healed over with the years so that he could hardly read the marking: "N.W.¼, Section 15, Twp. 7, Range 5." The marking no longer comforted him.

He turned west along his north line.

So sure were they that every foot of land was to be worth a king's ransom that they were putting stone corner markers on the new lots. It was a part of the lightheadedness that had come over the town. Like Jim Hawkins paying $18 for that fandangled fanning mill that blew the chaff from the wheat when you cranked it, as if waving a blanket wasn't wind enough. Like the women dressing the children in cloth pants, even the Flannertys. Like Jonathan Blair blabbering about starting a county newspaper in Mesopotamia. Huh!

Seemed that anybody that had anything at all to sell was asking and getting fancy prices.

Woodbridge came to his northwest corner and turned south.

As he tramped along, Woodbridge saw a bright unnatural object ahead, and he walked faster. As he approached, it became a pole with the bark peeled off. It stuck up in the ground, and a path had been cleared through the brush from the pole to the north. Around the base of the pole the ground was trampled by human footprints, and the pole was planted about two rods below Woodbridge's north line and deep in his soul.

Unreasonably, perhaps as Tecumseh had felt, the pole angered Woodbridge. For there are few trespasses that jolt the blood to the temples like even a six-inch overstep against a land boundary, personal or national. It is the basal insult. He grabbed the pole, pumped it loose, and hurled it like a javelin to the north. It landed flat and bounced along the floor of the forest until it turned sideways and cracked to a sudden stop against the legs of a tripod. On top of the tripod was a transit, and raising up from behind the eyepiece of the transit was a startled, angry human head.

The man moved out from behind his tripod. He was short and stocky, and he stood wide-based and defiant.

"What in God's name are you doin'?" he yelled.

But his indignation returned upon him a hundredfold from Woodbridge, who yelled from his boundary line: "Keep your God-damned poles off my property! If I catch it there again, I'll ram it right through your gut!"

The solid figure preserved a menacing silence as he approached. Standing in front of Woodbridge, with his feet wide apart and his hands on his hips, the man faced Tom's rage with the confident amusement of one who knows his rights. Every part of him gave the impression of broad granite strength. The eyes were set shallow in his head. His close-cut hair did not stand up, but lay close to his scalp, slanting forward. The wide jaw blended into his short neck in a straight line of squat power. The only flabby flesh on the man was the long, mobile upper lip, which he continuously tucked under his lower teeth, pulling it out slowly as he studied the big hog farmer. The gesture pulled his mouth into a disdainful grin as he waited patiently for Woodbridge to stop ranting.

"Apparently you didn't recognize me, Woodbridge, without my beard."

"You! Ault!"

"Emanuel Ault is the name. You'll hear it a lot."

"I thought your kind that traded in blood-bought bounty warrants had no use for land. I'd hardly expect you to be takin' up acreage."

"I'm not. Land is no good except as it can be bought and sold and traded."

"Like bounty warrants," charged Woodbridge, "and a soldier's discharge pay."

"That's right," sneered Ault. "And the only man that makes by it is the man that keeps it moving through his hands. I wouldn't be stuck with a piece of it. I'm just developing this tract for sale."

"I thought it was Shuldane's. But whatever you're doing with it, stay off mine."

"I'm not on yours."

"You're sure'n hell standing on mine right now."

"Get out your patent, if you've got one. You'll see it reads 140 acres 'more or less.' "

"Patent hasn't been issued yet, but I know about that clause. That's just lawyer talk."

Ault smiled.

"Sure it's lawyer talk. But it's put there because when they surveyed this part here they made mistakes."

"There was no mistake here," bristled Woodbridge. "I saw to that!"

"Then you were ahead of your time, Mr. Woodbridge. Most surveyors didn't bother with the little matter of the curvature of the earth and the offset for magnetic declination. And according to my measurements you didn't either. If they let that discrepancy compound itself for the whole length of the range, there'd be a township up north that would be half the size of the others. So the surveyor general directs that we go back and take a little off the northwest corner of each township. That means you owe a little piece back to the government."

Ault walked back to where the pole had landed, while Woodbridge pondered his words.

That his 140 acres should be related to the entire earth was, strangely, not a remote concept to Thomas Woodbridge, for he habitually thought of the earth as the fringe left over surrounding his boundaries.

His loathing of Ault increased as he saw the irrevocable logic in the squat man's words. As Ault shoved the pole back in its hole, the redhead was flooded with apprehension.

"You might as well get accustomed to having neighbors, Woodbridge, because you're going to have a lot of them. I've cut the Adams tract up into four lots of fifty acres each. And I'm measurin' off eight more on your east line."

"Are they spoke for yet?"

"Yes."

The Mesopotamia Hog caused some attention in Mesopotamia when Woodbridge talked about it. But not much.

Mesopotamia never really thought much of the Mesopotamia Hog until a gray-haired stranger came to town. Zabeth was in the store and saw it happen.

The man was tall and heavy, and he wore a good cloth shirt and good wool breeches tight to his legs. Through the gray mud on his boots, Zabeth could see that they were good army boots like those Major Armstrong wore. He tied up a large dappled stallion which was spattered to the hocks and looked as if he'd come a piece.

Zabeth followed the man into the store, as did several others who lounged outside.

He had a likable openness as he addressed Hosmer, and a certain interesting firmness.

"David Marcusson, sir, is the name. I heard about a special hog in Mesopotamia. I've come to see it. Could you direct me, sir?"

Hosmer liked the man right away, Zabeth could see. So did the others. Though she noticed that Amos Exeter left the store abruptly.

Mike Stikes thought he recognized Marcusson, and said so. It turned out they didn't know each other. But that somehow led to army talk, and Marcusson said: "When General Harrison released me, I took my own warrant for a thousand acres and bought some others and took up a township in the Indiana Country. General Harrison arranged a judgeship for me there. But my principal interest is building up farms in my township."

That led to questions about the Indiana Country land, and did they get sick wheat out there and what would he raise?

"We're in an ideal corn area. Get fifteen bushels to the acre without cultivating. One man who has turned his land three seasons and cross-plowed got thirty bushels to the acre. So we want hogs. Our idea is to pack 150 bushel of corn into a hog, then pack the hog into a barrel, and pack the barrel onto a boat for New Orleans."

He smiled pleasantly. That was when Exeter returned, and right behind him was Elnathan Shuldane. Right away Zabeth could see that Grandpap and this Mr. Marcusson would have a lot in common. So could most everyone else, by the way they pulled back with their small talk to let the two men meet.

After the introductions Grandpap Shuldane said: "Colonel Marcusson, Mr. Exeter and I will take you up to see the hogs. But wouldn't you first come over to the house and take a meal?"

"Thank you, sir," said Marcusson, "but I'd prefer to go to your hogs directly."

As they started toward the door, Shuldane asked, "I'd be interested in knowing who told you about the hogs. I'm trying to spread the reputation, but it goes slowly."

"John Piatt at Cincinnati told me. Said he'd bought some for his trade and they cured up nicely. He said the strain started by a lucky accident."

Shuldane grinned proudly. "It was no accident, Colonel. These are out of Cleopatra by Boss, carefully smuggled in from England direct from the Bedford herd at Woburn, England."

Marcusson stopped as if he'd heard wrong.

"Bedfords?" he asked.

"Pure-bred," smiled Shuldane. "Cleopatra and Boss were the first in the West."

"But I didn't come to see Bedfords," said Marcusson. "Fine baconers. But I want a good heavy lard hog . . . and not a white hog that'll sunburn on our hot plain."

Shuldane looked at Exeter, and the loungers in the store unfolded their ears with interest.

"Piatt talked about a black and white spotted hog," said Marcusson. "Very heavy. A tough hog."

Zabeth spoke up. "He means Big One, Gran'pap!" she said.

Marcusson's face lighted.

"That's the name, miss!"

It was not a minute later that Zabeth and Mr. Marcusson were mounted and westbound for the Woodbridge development, though Zabeth wished she could have stayed in the store a little longer to see the men's faces and hear their talk.

Mr. Marcusson and Pap got along right from the start. Started right out on hogs. She noticed Pap glowed like he'd found a man who talked sense, though Pap did most of the talking.

Finally Mr. Marcusson got in a question edgewise.

"And can you get this hog every litter, Mr. Woodbridge?"

"No. But I get it more often now. I'm still trying various crosses."

"How?"

Woodbridge started to answer, but he stopped in the middle and grinned evasively.

"I'm sorry," said Marcusson. "Of course. None of my business. I was so interested I forgot myself."

"That's all right," said Woodbridge, and it was a further sign to Tom of the flamboyant, inflated times that the pleasant newcomer wanted to go right into the deal, without quibbling over the terms.

"I make no bones, Mr. Woodbridge. I want the Mesopotamia Hog. Naturally, you want to protect your breed. What arrangement would you accept? I'll respect your wishes if they're at all reasonable and your price is fair."

"Well, if I sold you breed stock, Mr. Marcusson, would you keep them only in Indiana Country? That is, not sell into Ohio?"

"H-mm. Quite a rigid stipulation. But, yes, if you'll sell only to me in the Indiana Country."

Then Mr. Marcusson frowned and bit his lip. "There's one trouble about that, though, Mr. Woodbridge. What will you accept in payment? We're having a little trouble about money. That is, there's plenty of credit, and plenty of local paper money. Our own brand. But damned scarce gold or silver or government notes."

"Same thing here," said Woodbridge. "But I might be most interested in land."

Their faces both brightened, and they talked eagerly as they went into the house to dinner. Veronica liked Colonel Marcusson, but she looked up sharply at the talk about Indiana land.

"I'm having a little trouble on my boundaries here," said Woodbridge. "Gettin' hemmed in. The survey is clouded. And they haven't mailed me my title patent from Washington yet. Worries me."

"Tom, I wish you could see the Indiana Country!" said Marcusson with excitement. "What a team we'd make! You have the breed. I have the land."

"I mean lots of it," said Woodbridge. "Like a whole quadrant or a township to myself."

"That's what I mean, too," said Marcusson, and the two smiled at each other in such enthusiastic complicity that Zabeth thought they acted more like boys than like men.

Veronica said, "You gentlemen are forgetting that it's bad enough trying to bring up a young lady this far west without going back into the woods more."

When Marcusson left, Woodbridge really missed him. But he had concluded a most liberal contract for himself. Marcusson was to get four branded sows to be shipped by the Ohio River from the Cincinnati wharf, but Marcusson was to ship back to Woodbridge half of the young boars from the first litters. He was also to kill off any crits which threatened the breed. Woodbridge believed Marcusson would do it.

Marcusson was to deposit the money with John H. Piatt in Cincinnati, who would release it to Woodbridge when the bill of lading was presented. Woodbridge also believed he would do that.

"It's beginning, Stranger-boy! It's beginning!"

Marcusson's coming charged Woodbridge with the same speculative fever that was sweeping Mesopotamia and the West.

Woodbridge went up to Hosmer's Store to ask about buying a piece of land in Shuldane's new township survey.

Zabeth was with her father, and it seemed to her that Sam Hosmer looked at Pap differently. It was probably a revelation to him that the first time a stranger found the town of Mesopotamia, it was not because of Mr. Shuldane, or Mr. Blair, the lawyer, or Arm Webster, the candidate for the legislature, or Mike Stikes, the fine gunsmith. It was because of a breed of hog named the Mesopotamia Hog, created on the farm of Thomas Woodbridge.

Woodbridge asked about the land.

"Tom, you'll have to see Emanuel Ault," said Hosmer.

"Aren't you still Shuldane's agent?"

"Mr. Shuldane's trying to get his business holdings organized better,

Tom. Exeter's handling his hogs. Arm Webster's handling his business down at county and down at state capitol. Ault's handling his land. I got my hands full with the store and my own land."

"Is Ault acting as agent or partner, or did he lease the land from Shuldane, or what?" asked Woodbridge.

"Don't know exactly how it works," said Hosmer. "I think it's more than agent. Think he kind of half-owns it or something. Anyway, see Ault."

Woodbridge went instead to Shuldane.

Shuldane was a bigger, smarter man than Ault, and he wore a pleasant face.

"I'm glad you came to me, Tom. It's time we got together."

"I'm needin' a piece of your land, Nate."

Shuldane looked up startled when the redhead called him "Nate."

"And I don't take to your man Ault," added Woodbridge.

"Tom, you've come a long way. You're up where we can do each other some good. You'll have your land, and you can pick your location."

Woodbridge was surprised.

"For how much money?"

"Money is only a symbol, Tom. Money is for storekeepers to fool with. Big men deal in a different coin."

"Suits me. I'm shy of money anyhow."

"Tom, I've got the Bedfords. You've got this new bastard breed— this—this Mesopotamia, you call it, that you're strugglin' with."

"Wait a minute," said Woodbridge. "You don't understand. The Mesopotamia is a better hog for the area. The Bedford is a better baconer. Nicer hams. But it's smaller boned. More delicate. The Mesopotamia is rugged. It grows bigger, and it's more of a lard hog. It's a better hog for where the weight of meat on the table counts more than linen on the table."

Shuldane brushed a hand toward Woodbridge in gentle deprecation.

"Tom, stop that bargaining talk. You taught me about Bedfords. They're the best. You know it. But you didn't teach me how to raise them. Exeter's lost fifteen by colic, and four litters this month were stillborn. You pick your piece of land and raise my Bedfords."

"No, thanks, Nate. I want a clean deal for the land."

Shuldane's eyes chilled. He looked steadily at Woodbridge.

"Then see Ault," he said coldly.

"Do you own that land or don't you?" bristled Woodbridge.

"See Ault. Good day to you!"

Even Veronica had the fever.

"Tom, they say that land with water on it will go to $15 an acre before the year is out."

"I'll have no dealings with a warrant-buyin' devil that sells land like it was lottery tickets."

"They say there are settlers coming into Cincinnati wharf so fast now there's no place for them to sleep. They're already paying $20 an acre as far north as Dayton."

"It don't add up to me, Veronica. How can a man pay $20 an acre for land? First year all he can do is get up a cabin. Second year his second payment's due, and he's got no income. Third year he's got his first decent crop, but it'll hardly cover his borrowings of seed and salt and feed. Fourth year, if nothin' happens, he gets a crop, but he's got to sell it against men that got their land for a dollar an acre. Looks to me like the fifth year the mortgage forecloses."

"You used to have confidence in the land, Tom. You used to say a man couldn't go wrong."

"But not this fast. How can you pay $20 an acre here when it's still cheap in the Indiana Territory?"

Stranger-boy came in late, and they sat to the night meal. The lad ate lightly, with an apparent excitement.

"Where've you been?" asked Tom.

Young Tom dropped his spoon and took from his pocket a paper which he unfolded in front of Woodbridge as if no more words were necessary.

Woodbridge picked up the paper and held it out a little from his eyes, as had become his habit lately.

Young Tom was disappointed when Tom put down the paper and resumed his eating in silence.

The meal was about over before Woodbridge said, "Where'd you get money for fifty acres?"

"Didn't need much," said Young Tom. "Mr. Ault said I should hang onto my gold, as it would get scarce. I paid only $20 and the rest on credit."

"Credit!"

"He took a mortgage against Big Four."

"You mortgaged Big Four!" Woodbridge stood up and pushed back his chair.

"You said he was mine," answered Young Tom.

"I didn't say he was yours to make a damned fool of me with!"

The boy stood up too, straddling his chair.

"Is it so foolish to take land that'll be worth four times what I paid at the end of the year?"

"It's worse!" yelled Woodbridge. "You could lose everything we got!"

"It's only my hog I put up for security."

"Only your hog!" sneered Woodbridge. "And if Ault forecloses and takes Big Four, and if he breeds him to Shuldane's Bedfords—then what happens to the value of my herd? Answer that!"

The possibility struck the boy silent. But he recovered.

"Tom, I didn't think," he said. "But I got a year to pay. I'll get it paid, all right."

"You didn't think is right!" said Woodbridge. "You fall in with this fritterin' nonsense that's goin' around, and think suddenly in one year you're gonna come by more cash than you saved in your whole lifetime."

"He said not to worry. I could renew the note, Tom."

"Yah. He *said*. See what he says when the note comes due!"

Suddenly Young Tom saw himself as the downfall of Veronica and Zabeth and Woodbridge. He saw Woodbridge bending over each precious litter in hot weather and cold, bringing them safely to life. He saw Woodbridge's sweating back twisting ceaselessly to swing the ax, building eighteen separate pens to keep the sows separate in an effort to tell which combination of boar and sow produced the Mesopotamia hog. He saw Woodbridge's wrinkled forehead bending over the herd book, trying to find the sure key to the complex, seldom-predictable puzzle of the blood lines. And then he saw himself throwing all that out the window in one careless transaction.

"Tom, I promise ya, nobody'll get Big Four."

But Woodbridge turned his back and left the cabin.

When the dishes were done, and Zabeth and Veronica were alone, Veronica said: "You'd best put on the dress, Elizabeth. Arm Webster is coming to take you to the four-handed reel at the blockhouse."

"All right."

"All right, but what?"

"All right, but isn't it showy for Mr. Buttrick to have this just because Margaret's come back from school in the East?"

"Some. But well meant, I think. He wants Margaret well thought of, and not left out of things now she's back. It's natural for a father."

"But there's probably only Margaret and Arm Webster and Mr. Blair and a few like that will know how to do this reeling."

"There have been other dances here, Elizabeth. You've not been aware of them because—" Veronica dried her hands and examined Zabeth proudly until the girl blushed. "Because it's only been just lately you've been noticed."

When the dress was on and Veronica had yanked it smooth in places and fluffed it up in others, Zabeth found Stranger-boy seated on the ground on the north slope by Big Four's pen. He was studying two pieces of paper, the land title and the note. His forehead was as wrinkled as the papers which he gripped roughly in his fists, as though he would wring any deception out of them.

Zabeth sat down beside him in a rustle of stiff cloth and a breath of pine soap that caused Young Tom to swallow and look at her.

"It isn't even writ in English," he said.

Without taking his eyes from her, he released the paper as she reached for it.

"Mr. Blair taught us about land contracts at the blockhouse school," she said. "Everybody wants to know lately. There's so much buyin' goin' on."

"What does that mean, 'heirs and assigns'?"

"That means the land belongs to you or your children or anyone you sign it over to."

"And on this other one. Ten per centum per annum?"

"Means you'll pay him a tenth more besides what you owe him every year for carryin' you."

"They sure try to catch you up."

"Don't see how anybody can hurt you with a piece of paper," said Zabeth.

"Your father sets a store by papers like this."

"Yes, but if they worried him, Pap would go see Ault and have him give back the money and tear up the papers."

"I'll go now," said Stranger-boy with relief.

She reached up her arms for him to pull her up, as she had done a hundred times since he had first used the stunt to laugh her out of childhood tantrums. She would stiffen her arms and legs, and the wind would rush by her face as he pulled her up.

But tonight he hesitated.

"Well?" she asked.

He took her hands and pulled her up easily. But this was no stiff little girl. For when she was on her feet, there was yielding in her arms, and the air that touched her was scented, making him realize suddenly that he was still holding her wrists after the reason was gone. As they walked down the slope to the house, Young Tom looked straight ahead. But he felt her walking beside him more clearly than if he looked at her. Something emanated to him which turned the familiar Zabeth into a land of mystery and excitement, changing everything. Four times now she'd worn that dress, and every time there had been the same fragrance and the same compelling strangeness that closed Young Tom's mouth.

"I'll go as far as the blockhouse with you," she said.

Veronica came out of the house in time to notice Young Tom saddling New Horse and the mare.

"You'd best wait here for Arm, Elizabeth," she urged, "with the dress and all."

"Young Tom has to go in to the village. I'll company him."

"But Arm Webster said he'd come for you."

"Be the neighborly thing," answered Zabeth, "if I save him a trip."

And they rode into the village.


Emanuel Ault tucked his upper lip under his lower teeth and pulled it out thoughtfully. Young Tom had finished his little speech, but receiving no answer from Ault, he felt called upon to continue.

"You see, Mr. Ault, I guess I had no business buying the land. I didn't think where I'd get money like that."

Ault's eyes studied the boy with amusement. His hands were on his hips, and his upper lip continued to work up and down, depriving the boy of the comfort of an answer.

"You see, Mr. Ault, I've really no property except the hog. If I've got money to buy anything, I'd best pay back Mr. Tom for my rearing."

"You made a good buy, boy. Now stick by it like a man."

" 'Twould be more manly under the circumstance to undo my deal, Mr. Ault."

"A contract's a contract, Tom."

Ault stood rocking from his toes to his heels. Young Tom stood staring at the ground until the silence proved it was final.

"I can see your mind's made up then," said Stranger-boy, "but in that case I want to cut my debt down as low as possible from the start. So here's $10 more. Mark it against my debt and change this paper."

"You might as well learn about a contract now, boy. When there's interest involved, you pay on the day it says on the paper. Not after. Not before. A contract's a final promise, just like the promise on a dollar bill."

Young Tom was surprised, and he looked down at the money in his hand.

"You mean to say you won't even take—" Young Tom interrupted himself and slowly pocketed his money.

"Mr. Ault," he said in an earnest manner that took a shade of the complacency out of Ault's gray eyes, "if this means you're gambling I won't pay on time and forfeit Big Four, you've missed a figure. I'll pay. But I'm glad we went through this."

He turned and led New Horse and the mare back to the common. From the common he traveled north of the river out to Section 16, where Captain Michael's cabin was.

The old Indian was scraping the hair from a lye-soaked deerskin when Young Tom rode up.

"Silver Pigeon here?" asked Stranger-boy.

The old chief shook his head.

"I wondered if he'd been able to sell those special smoked hams I sent down with him and Mr. Buttrick. He said Mr. Buttrick knew a fancy market for fancy food."

"Silver Pigeon stay Cincinnati. Work with Mr. Buttrick."

Captain Michael reached somewhere in his loose hanging leather jacket and brought out a handful of paper money which he held up.

"Silver Pigeon," he said.

"He must do well at the Cincinnati wharf. No wonder he didn't come back with Mr. Buttrick."

The chief's leather face folded in a mischievous grin. His two bent hands described the shape of an hour glass and the grin widened.

"Much squaw."

Young Tom went back to the common.

The light and the noise of stamping feet and the music of the organ and Denaro's fiddle in the blockhouse made the rest of the village seem dark and lonesome. Young Tom tied both of his horses in front of the blockhouse and then stood in the shadow by the door looking in.

The couples marched arm in arm to the music for a while. Then they stopped, broke into pairs of couples, and joined hands and made some motions that wouldn't make sense in daylight, but looked all right tonight with the music and all.

Young Tom was conscious of light footsteps. Camelia Flannerty came up behind him, half in the light and half out.

"Looks kind of funny to see Joe Hussong doin' that," she said.

"Yeah," answered Young Tom, but he noticed something different about Camelia. She was that close to him he couldn't look to see what it was very well. He continued to watch inside. He saw Margaret Buttrick there with Joe Hussong, and the dress she wore was even beyond the one Zabeth had.

"But it don't look so hard to do if you study it a spell," said Camelia.

"No, it don't," answered Young Tom. And he saw now that it was Camelia's hair that was different. She'd been to some trouble about it; and to avoid standing right in the doorway and yet still see in, she had to bend a bit, and she became a disturbing presence near him.

"And your sister's in there," she said.

"Yeah," said Tom. "Perhaps you and I—"

But he stopped, for the line was forming and marching toward the door. At the head of the line was Arm Webster, laughing and strutting to the music with his arm stuck out like one of those tailoring advertisements in the Scioto *Gazette*. And hanging onto the arm just as natural as if it were her pap's was Zabeth, laughing and flushed in the face. Webster put his arm around her waist, and Young Tom's scalp tingled. He could see where Webster's fingers came around the other side of her, high up where they crushed the cloth in, pulling it tight enough to outline the lovely young womanliness of her for everyone to see.

It burned Young Tom. For though he could see by Webster's laughing and pointing to the fiddler that he was making a careless light joke about Denaro's music, Young Tom figured Webster was not thinking about the music so much. He was thinking the same as Joe Hussong was thinking, and Hussong was looking back over the pale Margaret

Buttrick's shoulder apparently to hear the joke between Webster and Zabeth. Young Tom knew about Joe Hussong.

He wondered how Miss Veronica could let anyone outside the family touch Zabeth. But he decided that Miss Veronica would think it was all right with Arm Webster, because while he touched her he talked about the music. That was probably what was meant by "manners": to talk about the music, whatever else you did.

The promenade passed by the door and then came around again. Webster's arm was even tighter around Zabeth now, so that it pulled her skirt up a little from the floor, showing the fancy thing underneath that even Stranger-boy had never seen before, living in the same house with her all this time.

Zabeth's face was flushed and laughing.

Camelia Flannerty was stirring at Young Tom's elbow now, but he stood still.

As the line approached the door, it turned out of sight again. Joe Hussong was on the end of it this time, without a partner. As he came past the open door, he saw Camelia outside, and he yelled, "Camelia! Come in here!"

Hussong stepped outside and reached his hand to her. Camelia looked at Young Tom for a hesitant instant and then allowed herself to be pulled inside by Joe Hussong.

Stranger-boy went over to Exeter's tavern. He put down three cents for a mug of whisky.

"Gone up to six cents, Young Tom," said Exeter. "Land boom, y'know."

The lad paid six and listened to the town's latest deals.

But mostly he heard Denaro's fiddle across the common.

When he started home, riding New Horse and leading the mare, he passed the blockhouse and noticed that Arm Webster's fancy rig was gone. Unconsciously he nudged his own horses into a trot out the West Road.

A little west of Denaro's cabin he came up behind Webster's carriage lingering along. Voices drifted back to him, tinkling, and he felt like an intruder. Later the voices died out, and he felt more so. He dropped back about twenty rods and followed the rig onto the Woodbridge development.

But as he followed, he was glad that Ault had made him stick to his deal. A man like Stranger-boy would have to be twice as good to be even with a man like Arm Webster. But that could maybe be done. Emanuel Ault would get his money all right, Stranger-boy told himself . . . somehow.

The next morning, at breakfast, Veronica tried to be gentle. There were few things she wouldn't give to Young Tom. But there *were* some. And though she spoke gently, Stranger-boy could tell that her words had been thought over all night. Perhaps even over the years.

"It could be you'd hurt Arm Webster's feelings, following home like that last night," she said.

"It just happened that way, Miss Veronica. It wasn't planned."

Woodbridge looked up from his trencher. "What's the matter if he did follow apurpose?" he challenged. "Be glad if a brother looks out for his sister."

"If you put it that way," said Veronica with an inflection that pointed up "brother," "then it's different."

Zabeth asked Stranger-boy about his talk with Ault.

"I'll keep the land," said Stranger-boy. "Besides, Mr. Ault said a contract is a promise as final as the promise to pay writ on a dollar bill."

# *Chapter 24: THE TABULATOR*

BUT the promise on a dollar bill was far from final.

It was in 1817 that the eastern creditors and absentee owners yanked the bottom out from under the bloated western currency.

Tom Woodbridge never did understand money. That is, he never understood why a dollar was worth a dollar today and half that the next, when it was after all only the symbol for a hog anyhow; and the hog never changed at all.

And so he held a lofty scorn for all the worried talk at the store about how the United States Bank at Cincinnati had shipped an $800,-

ooo wagonload of gold back East and was going to use strictly paper money in the West; about how the government land office and the tax office would only accept certain types of paper money in payment for land and taxes; and how this would be dictated by the United States Bank, which was run from the East.

Any day of the week you could see men in the store comparing different sizes and colors of bank notes and asking worried questions of one another. For there were thirty kinds of paper money in use in the West, and only a man just up from Cincinnati or Chillicothe knew which were still good and which had gone bad overnight. In seven weeks seven Ohio banks closed, and their notes became worthless as soon as the word got out. The Zanesville Bank and half a dozen others whose notes were still good were spreading rumors that they were about to fail, and then buying back their own depreciated notes at bargain prices. It was a crude but desperate effort to equalize the ratio of their overissued notes to their pitiful reserves of specie.

The terrible slide estranged Mesopotamia from itself. Buttrick came back from Cincinnati and went to settle his store account with Hosmer.

"What kind of money ye gonna pay with, Asa?"

"Bank of Marietta dollars."

"What's wrong with them that you want to unload 'em in such a hurry?" asked Hosmer.

"Nothing. They were in good standing in the Cincinnati trade day before yesterday."

"*Good* standing?" Hosmer cocked his head.

"Well," Buttrick crayfished some, "they were only discounted 10 per cent."

"I'd just as leave carry your bill a spell longer, Asa. Keep your money."

"You may never get it the way things are goin' to hell, Sam, if you don't take it now."

Hosmer paused. For Buttrick spoke the truth.

"All right, Asa, I'll take your Marietta dollars. But I'll discount 'em 20 per cent."

"No, sir. You can knock down 10 per cent, Sam, but no more. Take them or leave them."

Hosmer chewed the inside of his cheek and looked around the store, studying the shelves.

"All right," he decided.

He took Buttrick's $77 worth of Marietta notes and he scratched the trader's $70 debt off the book.

Buttrick said, "Thanks, Sam," and turned quickly for the door. But before he got out, Sam said, "Just a minute, Asa."

"What?"

Buttrick watched uneasily as Sam bundled up the Marietta notes and plunked them in the middle of the counter.

"Just happens I notice I need twenty-two yards more of that gray wool blanketing," said Hosmer, "next time you're up through Steubenville. I'm payin' in advance."

Buttrick walked slowly back to the counter and picked up the Marietta notes reluctantly.

"Twenty-two yards? Huh, Sam?"

"Yeah," said Hosmer, relieved.

Western paper money was generally discounted 10 per cent right in Hosmer's Store. Easterly, at Pittsburgh it was discounted 20 per cent. At Baltimore and New York it was discounted 50 per cent and more, depending on the reputation of the issuing bank. In Boston it was unacceptable at any figure.

The money deflation was so brutal that Woodbridge even began to forgive Stikes and Hawkins and the rest for their overexpansion in land. As he watched them try to get paper money that would hold its value long enough to pay off their mortgages, he burned with them.

He saw Stanley-the-Slasher exchange a year's cut of walnut timber for a handful of good paper bank notes on Friday. Then he saw the anguished defeat on Slasher's face on Monday when his handful of paper wouldn't buy two new ax heads from Mike Stikes.

He saw the frightened frustration on Jim Hawkins's face as he pitched a whole wad of Owl Creek bank notes into Stikes's forge. It was pay for two cows. Only a week ago Owl Creek notes had been almost as good as silver. Today they wouldn't buy a cigar. Owl Creek assets had been discovered to consist of two sets of fine engraving plates and a keg of nails covered with a thin layer of silver coins.

And out on the Woodbridge place the hog farmer hurled his angry financial policy at the brute ears of Big One, dam for the now well-known herd of Mesopotamia hogs.

"So let 'em keep their blasted bank notes! Don't need 'em anyhow, eh, Big One? When you got the best breed sow in the West, you don't need money anyhow. Huh?"

Big One grunted assent as she nipped at an impertinent piglet.

"From now on," said the redhead, "any man trades with me talks corn or flour or salt or tanbark or iron. There ain't enough shinplasters this side of York State to buy Mesopotamia breed stock."

The hog grunted amen to this and then looked up at the newcomer. Blair said, "They got you talkin' to y'self, Tom?"

"Hello, Blair. Yeah. I'm that chawed up about the deal Slasher got from your fancy money-jobbin' friends in Chillicothe!"

"Slasher's deal is exactly why I came to get you to support the newspaper I want to start, Tom."

"Seems a mighty gap 'tween Slasher's deal and your newspaper, but I don't doubt you can talk your ways acrost somehow."

"The county needs a newspaper, Tom. And it could straighten out the money tangle."

"Can't see it, Blair. What good is it but to elect you to the legislature?"

"A newspaper can show men that we've got to reverse the balance of trade."

"If this balance needs mendin', it's not likely it'll be done in Mesopotamia."

"We've got to," said Blair. "England is dumping thousands of tons of manufactures on the East Coast."

"You're too roundabout, Blair. The trouble's right here somewheres."

"The East in turn is dumping thousands of tons of goods in the West," continued Blair, "for which they'll only accept our silver and gold. But there's nothing we can ship back East for which they'll pay us in metal money. We've got to make people understand that before they drain every grain of gold out of the West."

"A-ah! Blair, you're fiddlin'. The state's fallin' apart. Every man's overmortgaged. Banks foreclosin' left and right. And you want to fritter around with a blasted newspaper! No support from me, Blair. And that means from Mitchell and Adams and young Hussong and a dozen others!"

The money strangulation estranged Mesopotamia somewhat from Sam Hosmer, for it became uncomfortable to sit idly in the store in the presence of old Hosmer, who was creditor to almost every man in Mesopotamia. Men gathered more often now in Exeter's tavern; and

Blair's proposed newspaper somewhat relieved the gloom there next day.

"The day comes I can't get all the news I need from Faith Hawkins," said Exeter, "then I'll chip in to start your newspaper, Blair."

Encouraged by the laughter, Exeter expanded.

"Then after we get you elected, Blair, what do we do with the paper? Feed it to the stock? Or won't it be that tasty?"

But the laughter shut off like Exeter's whisky spigot when Emanuel Ault walked in.

Ault stood in the center of the silent tavern purposefully searching the crowd.

Then he marched directly over to Mike Stikes. Stikes straightened up under the gaze of Ault, who stood silent, resolutely stretching his upper lip out from under his big undershot jaw. Stikes fidgeted some, and then asked: "You bring my receipt, Ault? I left the payment at your cabin."

Ault reached into his pocket, but what he pulled out was not Stikes's receipt. It was a handful of Steubenville bank notes which he deliberately placed on the bar in front of Stikes.

"Sorry, Stikes. Steubenville bank notes won't do. Government just declared 'em unacceptable at the land office. That means they're no good to me either."

"I can't help what the land office says," exploded Stikes. "It's money! You got to take it!"

"You knew they were no good, Mike. That's why you left 'em at the house instead of payin' in person."

Stikes's intent study of the bottom of his copper mug was a confession. He slammed his mug down on the bench.

"What's a man to do!" he challenged.

Blair said, "Mike, that's why we need a newspaper."

"Newspaper, hell! We need money!"

"I'll accept metal money or any good bank notes, Mike," said Ault. "But I got to have 'em tomorrow, or I take back the deed."

"How can I . . ." Stikes gave up, helpless.

"Somebody gave them to you," said Ault. "Have him make good."

From under shaggy eyebrows Stikes looked over at Aaron Fitchburg. Fitchburg said, "Mike, when I gave them to you they were . . ."

"I know," said Stikes, and bent his head.

"Tomorrow, Mike," said Ault, and left amid a frustrated, sullen silence.

"The bastard is always in the right," fumed Christofferson. "And he never sleeps."

"A-ah!" Woodbridge hammered the wall. "And last week Steubenville notes were the best in the state! You'd best all do like I do. Don't use money. Pay in trade."

"Except that won't always work, Woodbridge," said Exeter.

"Huh?"

"You got to pay cash for your taxes. Which 'minds me yours are due. I'll accept metal money or U.S. bank notes. Chillicothe paper, Dayton Trust, or Miami Export Company currency."

It was a shock to Woodbridge when he told Veronica that he had to use part of their Dayton Bank money to pay the taxes.

"Tom, we haven't enough."

"What! Not even for that? It's only $62!"

"But we don't even have that much in the lock box. We could pay it in Miami Export Company notes."

"They discount those too heavy. Fifty per cent."

"What else is there?"

"I'm shipping two boars to Marcusson in Indiana. I'll have him pay in Bank of Indiana notes. They're good any place."


Hope Emerson was impatient with Blair. He stood by and talked while she held the ewe between her legs and sheared the wool.

"Here. You hold her while I shear."

But he pushed down on the frightened animal in such an awkward manner that she smiled.

"No. Not like that. Here. Catch her by the front legs, like this. No. Up under her chest."

Gingerly Blair sank down to his knees and held the sheep, stiff-armed.

"You see, Hope, they all blame the banks and the traders. And it's true in a way that the banks caused it. But that's only a manifestation."

"Y' mean the wildcat money is only like your headaches, when I keep telling you the real trouble is Exeter's whisky."

"That's right. The real trouble is there's nothing being shipped east that the East needs badly enough to pay in gold. But they're dumping cloth and iron beds and plow blades and clocks out here. And they won't accept our paper money at a decent exchange. Only gold and silver."

"You can't stop 'em from that if we're dauncy enough to pay."

"If the people knew. If there was a newspaper to explain things."

"Then why don't you get it started?"

"I am. The Jeffersonians are going to listen to me at their next committee meeting at Chillicothe. The paper won't have any source of revenue much besides subscriptions. But if they decide the election will be close, they're going to back my paper. Sam Hosmer's willing to help, and Stikes and a few others."

"Goin' at it the long way, Jonathan. Sounds like one of Mr. Shuldane's roundabout arrangements. Don't think you'll ever get it."

Hope put the sheep back in the pen and grabbed another. Briskly she placed Blair's hands on the animal in the right places.

"Besides," she said, "you're going to need the paper to get elected. Shuldane's weight'll all go behind his nephew, Arm Webster. What you get you'll get yourself."

Hope picked a thistle out of the wool.

"Why don't you start your paper the way Stikes or Hosmer or Woodbridge would go about it?"

He grinned. "How?"

"Just start."

"It's not as simple as starting a store or a forge or a farm," he said.

"Think that's simple, huh?"

"I didn't mean that the way it sounded, Hope. But for a paper you need a press and type and a paper source."

"Go get them, then," Hope said, concentrating on the shearing.

His grin faded a little.

"Go down to Cincinnati and find out who's got them and get one."

"But the money."

"Figure that out later. Get the press. Like I got that land off Ault. May lose it, like everybody else. But . . ." She shrugged her shoulders and straightened up to rest her back.

Blair was gripping the sheep extremely hard now, and there was no smile on his face.

"I could have Buttrick get me a secondhand one out of Pittsburgh," he was saying.

The sheep squirmed and pranced in pain from Blair's grip.

Hope bent over and unclasped his hands, and when she smiled her face was calm and strong, and it looked to Blair as though nothing could frighten her. The touch of her hand was not as hard as the hand looked, and Blair noticed it.

He went to Cincinnati the next day.


The way Woodbridge arranged for his payment for breed hogs, which he shipped quite regularly now to David Marcusson, was to send them down to Cincinnati by Buttrick. Buttrick put them on an Ohio River keelboat for Indiana, and presented the bill of lading at the John H. Piatt bank in Cincinnati. The Piatt bank then released funds from Marcusson's account to pay Woodbridge.

When the payment arrived on the Woodbridge place, it caused some excitement. Zabeth and Young Tom were surprised at the bulk of the paper-wrapped money. But when they were unwrapped, Veronica said, "Why, those are just animal skins."

"Yes and no," said Woodbridge, spreading them out proudly. "That's the currency of the Bank of Indiana. The only kind of notes that can't depreciate and can't be counterfeited. Next to gold and silver, it's the safest money in the West."

"How do you count it?" asked Young Tom.

Woodbridge spread the skins out on the table, exploring them.

"Don't know yet myself."

"I see," said Zabeth. "On the inside here. See, the raccoon skins are marked 'One Dollar.' "

They discovered then that the possum skins were marked at fifty cents, mink twenty-five cents, and rabbit twelve and one-half cents.

Young Tom and Zabeth went with him when he rode to town and walked into Exeter's tavern. He plunked the furs down on the bar.

"Here's my taxes, Amos. Give me a receipt."

"You lucky dog, Woodbridge! Where'd you get them Bank of Indiana skins?"

"I sell *my* hogs, Amos. You could, too, if you'd ever learn to raise 'em. Y' can't keep tavern and raise fancy hogs, too."

Some of the men smiled. Exeter scowled. The men studied the skins with interest and envy.

But Exeter was counting the skins carefully. Finally he looked up.

"This won't cover your tax, Tom."

"Why not? There's $62 worth there."

"Half of them are counterfeit."

"You fool! Y' can't counterfeit fur!"

"See for yourself," said Exeter, holding out one of the dollar ones. "See how neat some rascal sewed coon tails on them possum skins?"

The color rose up in Woodbridge's neck. He studied the skins. There was nothing for him to say.

As Tom left the tavern, Blair fell in alongside. There was an excitement in Blair's manner lately that Woodbridge had never noticed before.

"Tom, Buttrick got my press."

"More power to ya."

"Now we can tell the settlers about the dangers of banks issuing twenty and thirty times as much paper as their specie reserve. Agitate for laws against money jobbing and wildcat currency."

Woodbridge stopped suddenly and faced the lawyer.

"Blair, you're not wastin' all this talk on me because y' think I understand it. You got your press, y' said."

Blair's handsome, dark face struggled under the difficulty of his proposal and the unnaturalness of his position.

"Tom, Buttrick's holding the press until I make payment. I—uh—I wanted to offer you stock in the press."

Woodbridge's callous surprise was unintentionally cruel.

"*You?* Borrow money from *me?*"

"Not borrow, Tom. It would be . . ."

"Darnation, Blair."

Woodbridge was transparently reflecting on the reversal of their positions since the lofty young lawyer had lounged in Shuldane's study in Concord. But he snapped out of it.

"Look, Blair. What's your press to me? Besides, you just saw what happened to my money."

"A press is the one thing that can fight that, Tom."

"Too slow, Blair. Too slow. My taxes are due *now!* Can your press get me money that'll stand up *now?*"

It was hard for Blair to swallow the rebuff, but not as hard as he expected. For though he was not accustomed to the role of supplicant, neither had he ever had anything so much worth begging for.

Woodbridge stopped off at Christian Kilgore's to see if Kilgore could pay him anything.

"I can pay ya, Tom. But I'd be doin' ya dirt. Have ta pay ya in Steubenville notes. Will if you say."

"No thanks, Chris."

Veronica got out the lock box and counted out the Woodbridges' Miami Export Company dollars.

"Too bad to use them, Tom," she said, "if Exeter discounts them by half. Be better to hold them."

"Got to use 'em, Veronica. It's all we've got."

It was Thursday when Woodbridge took the Miami Export notes up to Exeter's tavern. Hope Emerson was ahead of him, talking to Exeter. Ault was there also. Lately you could come into the tavern almost any day of the week and find Emanuel Ault taking back land he had sold from men who couldn't meet even the third and fourth payments. Ault always stood alone.

Woodbridge listened to Hope's transaction. He had an admiration for Hope Emerson, as did everyone else. He particularly wanted to see her make a good sale on the land she had bought from Ault. And he hoped she could make the payments. But right now she was paying the taxes on her regular farm to Exeter. He heard Exeter say: "Sorry, Hope, but Job Hill sent word up from county. Those notes are no longer acceptable for taxes. They're all right in general trade down around Cincinnati, I understand; but the state won't take 'em."

Hope sighed, more from disgust than from worry. For Hope Emerson didn't worry, or seemed not to.

She turned from the bar to Ault.

"Ault, I'm offerin' them to you, then, against my second payment on the land."

Ault shook his head.

"Sorry, Mrs. Emerson," said Ault.

The man's stolid complacency burned Woodbridge, and he stepped toward Ault to intercede. But as he did so, he got his first look at the notes Hope Emerson held in her hand. It stunned him.

Hope's money was Miami Export Company bills.

In a daze he put his own money slowly back into his pocket, but not before Exeter glimpsed it.

"You want to see me, Tom?" asked Mesopotamia's tax collector.

"No." Woodbridge turned to leave.

"I got a notion, Tom, how you can raise good solid money for your taxes."

"How?"

"I'd be willin' to pay hard money for that boar you call Big Two."

Woodbridge stared at him in silent disbelief.

"God damn you, Exeter!"

Woodbridge got hold of Buttrick.

"When you goin' back to Cincinnati?"

"Friday."

"Want you to do me an errand."

Woodbridge told Buttrick to take his Miami Export Company notes to Piatt and ask him somehow to change them for John H. Piatt bank notes.

"Piatt doesn't have much say in the Piatt bank," said Buttrick. "He lost ownership control when he went to debtor's prison. He's just an employee in his own bank now."

"I know it. But he's that uneasy in his mind about what he did to me once that he'll probably work it somehow, if I judge him right."

As Woodbridge started for home, Mike Stikes hailed him. Mike reached in his pocket and pulled out a piece of paper on which Tom had scrawled, "I owe Mike Stikes two hogs, payable on demand, for iron nails for house."

Woodbridge looked at the paper.

"Sure, Mike, You can have the hogs now. Advise ya to wait till fall. But you can have 'em now if ya say."

Stikes shifted his weight uneasily.

"'Tain't that, Tom. I don't even want the hogs yet. But I was wonderin' if you'd take and tear up this note for two hogs. And write me out two separate ones for one hog each so I can pay Hosmer half."

On Monday an old scene was repeated in Mesopotamia. The Caleb Wrights gave up.

They were not the first. They would not be the last. Exeter postponed the auction of their land until after they left. Wright and his wife did not look back. Only the children waved out the back of the wagon.

Frontier finance became frenzied as men tried to get hold of cash that would hold its value as long as it took to run with it to the tax collector. Foreclosures became a weekly occurrence, and taxes, though small, became a frightening threat, especially to Woodbridge, since Exeter was tax collector.

Exeter had been unable to produce much of a herd from Shuldane's Bedfords. They got sick. They died. They miscarried. He had no system for breeding, and the hog deteriorated in his hands, becoming runty instead of larger.

Meanwhile, Woodbridge's Mesopotamia Hog was beginning to bring an occasional stranger into town, and gained attention on the Cincinnati wharf. Shuldane made Exeter smart under sarcastic comparisons. And Exeter thought about Woodbridge's taxes.

But Buttrick returned in two weeks with Woodbridge's John H. Piatt currency. Woodbridge fingered the bills on his way to the tavern. They crackled with crispness, because John H. Piatt currency didn't circulate much. When people got it, they held on to it.

Exeter was not in the tavern, so Woodbridge went to Hosmer's Store. It took an impossible number of bushels of corn to buy one yard of Hosmer's broadcloth. But if you paid in gold or silver, it seemed like nothing. Tom Woodbridge went over to Hosmer's Store to test his money.

All the cloth that had come onto the Woodbridge place in the last few years had gone to clothe Zabeth. It was time Veronica had some.

Woodbridge asked, "How much for seven yards of that dyed cloth, Sam?"

"Three hundred bushel, Tom."

"No. I mean in money."

"What kind?"

"John H. Piatt money."

Aaron Fitchburg and a few others in the store perked up, and Sam Hosmer himself now showed interest.

"In that case cost ye only $36, Tom."

"Then give me four yards."

Tom counted out $20' worth of John Piatt notes.

"Put the odd forty cents to my account, Sam."

"I'll drop the forty cents, Tom."

The men gathered around the Piatt notes.

The reception to the broadcloth in the Woodbridge house permitted Tom to expand. "That's what good money will do!" he said.

The news that there were John Piatt bills in town had preceded Tom to the tavern next day, and there were a few there to watch him pay his taxes, just to get a look at the money. There were a few there who just wanted to share the triumph of a man who had gotten hold of some good money, and they hoped he would slap it down in front of Exeter with a good verbal tongue-lashing.

Woodbridge walked to the bar and laid his money in front of Exeter.

"There y' are, Exeter! There's your blasted money! Give me a receipt!"

Exeter covered his disappointment with the business of counting the money.

Elnathan Shuldane did not much frequent Exeter's tavern. He did not, in fact, much frequent Mesopotamia, lately. But on certain occasions he came to the tavern. As he did everything else, Shuldane came in very good grace. He came to tell of affairs at Chillicothe and Washington, and he did it skillfully, de-emphasizing his own importance. He came usually in an open shirt and scarred-up boots. In explaining the current emergency to the men of Mesopotamia, he did not make the mistake of oversimplifying.

He explained the strangling policy of the Bank of the United States, which would honor only its own notes. As he talked, he seemed just another farmer caught in the unjust parity between western paper and eastern gold, but to thinking men in Mesopotamia that only heightened Shuldane's standing. Though it was no longer so easy for him, Nate Shuldane always took care to be good-humored in the tavern, as he was now.

Seeing Exeter counting the money on the bar, Shuldane laughed jovially, in a pleasant full voice.

"Ho-ho, what are we holding here? A burning? Well, add these to the pile!"

Mesopotamians had seldom seen Asa Buttrick move so fast and with so little thought for his bearing. But he was instantly at Shuldane's side.

"Not yet, Nate. Hold on just a minute longer!"

"I got stuck with a few myself!" laughed Shuldane, puzzled by Buttrick's anxiety, but ignoring it. Shuldane was opening a bulky leather wallet.

"Wait a minute!" pleaded Buttrick. "It's only taxes he's payin'. No harm in that!"

But Shuldane had already tossed a pile of bills in front of Exeter. They also were John H. Piatt bank notes.

Exeter looked up. Buttrick grabbed up Shuldane's money and handed it back to him.

"Go ahead. Take your receipt, Woodbridge!" said Buttrick.

But Exeter was alert now, and he withheld the receipt.

"What's this about?"

"Hand him his receipt," said Buttrick. "Nate's business can come next."

"Didn't sound to me like Mr. Shuldane was giving me money for any business," said Exeter. "What's wrong with them Piatt notes, Nate?"

Shuldane was quick, and Mesopotamia saw him try to join ranks with them. Except Blair, who saw only a magnificent actor.

"Nothing's wrong with them," said Shuldane. "I was handing you those to pay part of my taxes, too."

But whether on purpose or by ingenuousness, it was apparent that Shuldane was lying. It was also apparent that Exeter knew it. Shuldane could be excused now for telling the truth.

"I'm sorry, Tom," he said. "I thought everyone knew. Piatt is back in debtor's prison. John H. Piatt notes won't buy the ink to print 'em."

Woodbridge glared at Buttrick.

"It didn't happen until I'd already exchanged your Miami notes, Tom," explained Buttrick. "I thought if I kept quiet you could get your taxes paid. No harm in cheatin' the government. They got us into this."

Buttrick's explanation stuttered to a stop, leaving the room in hung silence. The redhead's mouth pulled back in a bitter curse, but no sound came out. The blood pounded up his thick neck, swelling the veins into great cords. Seeping under his red hair and across his forehead, it made the freckles show dark against the red skin. The blood pounded in his temples like an auctioneer's gavel.

Buttrick started to resume his explanation, and Shuldane formed an apology on his lips. But the electric hatred that radiated from the redhead stopped them with their mouths open.

"Shut up!" he gasped.

He doubled his fists and looked around the room.

"A-l-l right! All right! Blair?"

Blair was startled. "Yes, Tom?"

"You always wanted to start a fool newspaper! Now's the time! Can you get that paper out tomorrow?"

The quivering anger in Woodbridge's voice froze Blair's tongue, and he stood with his mouth open.

"Oh, I'll get it paid for!" said Woodbridge. "Can you get it out or can't you?" he yelled.

"Yes."

"All right. I want that paper to tabulate every miserable rag of currency in this miserable state every day, at its true value!"

Woodbridge's voice sank to a threatening vibration.

"I want that tabulation to come out every day so's a man can find out what God-damned kind of money he's holdin' before he loses his blasted shirt! And if the value of a dollar changes twice a day, I want that paper to come out twice a day! Y'understand?"

Woodbridge's fist hit the bar, and three tumblers fell off; but no man moved.

"If we got to be cheated, then by God at least every man will be cheated equal!"

Which was how the *Tabulator* came to be published.

# Chapter 25: BIG FOUR

THE strangling money slide also estranged Mesopotamia from Jonathan Blair.

Men did admit inside their cabins that the *Tabulator* had given almost every man a chance at least once or twice to slip out of town and change some bad bills for better ones before he got stuck with worthless rags. The standings of all the different kinds of currency were always listed in the upper right-hand corner of the front of the *Tabulator:*

    Owl Creek Bank notes . . . . Bank extinct
    Miami Export bank notes . . . . Discount 50% most places
    Bank of Kentucky notes . . . . No information. Dubious
    John H. Piatt Bank . . . . Acceptance varies. Good in Cincinnati

The list always included twenty-five to thirty kinds of currency. And for this every fair man thanked Jonathan Blair.

But there was something uncomfortable about Blair lately. He seemed to be trying to say something he wasn't quite saying, in his talk and in his paper. Those who got a glimmer of it didn't admit it even to Blair, though they would give him a fleeting wink of encouragement.

Many of the settlers also thought there was something wrong with a grown man who sat scribbling in his cabin in times like these. Some reflected that Blair had never lived up to the bright promise of the handsome, impressive young man that had come out to Mesopotamia as Shuldane's emissary in 1800.

Blair spent a lot of time now in the tavern, too, drinking. Didn't dress as well. The war was over four years, yet he still wore the old lieutenant's coat Hope had given him. He was no longer the bright up-and-comer. He was over a line where he should have made good by now. Aggression was no longer becoming to him. Arm Webster was the comer now. Though when a man had a question about a boundary or a legal paper, he was more likely to go to Jonathan Blair, even if the price of the information was to sit and listen to him rant about the "balance of trade."

Blair was dangerous to be around, though, because he had so little to lose. In a year when Emanuel Ault had become a name to worry about, Blair insulted the man to his face.

How it happened that men who had fought Indians and hunger and sickness could now fear such a newcomer as Emanuel Ault was hard to understand. But each man's timidity was in proportion to his holdings.

Because Ault seemed to hold most of the mortgages, Blair should have been more careful. But he ran small articles like this:

"In the matter of Emanuel Ault, consider how he came to be here. Why did he come here? Who brought him? If some-one brought him, why would they select an individual with precisely Mr. Ault's very real and valuable abilities? Perhaps it was because"

The article came to the bottom of the page abruptly, and it looked as though the editor had forgotten to finish it. At first no one paid much attention. But a few, like Zabeth and Aaron Fitchburg and Jim Hawkins, studied them. They were tossed aside by Stikes and Dolk and Woodbridge with the remark that Blair was drinking too much in

Exeter's tavern. But others, newcomers like Wheeler and Culpepper, winked and passed the paper along.

Such writing caused gossip about Blair.

Hope Emerson paid no attention to the paper. But she listened closely to the gossip. She then went directly to Blair's cabin, the *Tabulator* office, and shook Blair in his bed.

"Jonathan, get up and clean up this mess!"

She picked up the mussuk bag of whisky and emptied it out the front door. She picked his clothes off the floor and flung them on the bed.

"Get up and get dressed and shave your face and try to look like a man."

Blair grinned from the bed. His dark face was a little too heavy now, but still handsome with white teeth. Whisky weighted his breath and slowed his speech.

"Get up," she ordered. "Dress."

"Can't very well dress with you in the cabin," he grinned.

"I been considered a man long enough, it won't matter," she said. "And this mess'll keep my back to you."

She pushed the chair under Blair's desk, grabbed the broom, and the dust began to rise. Blair dressed.

"What's the cause of this one?" she asked. "You must have drained Exeter's still."

She stirred up the fire and washed out the frying pan and looked for something to fry in it.

Blair's voice was relaxed and somewhat maudlin under intoxication.

"Went to see the Central Committee in Chillicothe to support me for the legislature," he said. "They laughed. Said they'd heard from Shuldane my paper . . . no more influence than . . . county clerk."

She set him down at the table, and he ate as though he hadn't had a decent meal in a week, which he hadn't.

"Then went to see Gov'nor Allen. Said he heard I'd alienated most of the big landowners. Said I'd be . . . drawback to the party. Said young Webster . . . his choice. Shuldane's got me surrounded . . . Chillicothe 'n Columbus 'n Cincinnati. Even down County."

"Seems a funny way to get elected from this district," said Hope brusquely, "going to all those high places."

"Seen it work too many years, Hope. Know all about it. Y'work from the top. Higher the better. Work li'l above the top if poss'ble.

Sat at the feet of the master too ma'y years. I know. Seen li'l men strugglin' up from the groun'. Seen 'em come almos' to the Holy Grail. Seen big han' push 'em down . . . down."

"Huh. Maybe. But maybe that was in the East. Maybe you should work from the bottom. Seems t'me Sam Hosmer knows only people on the bottom."

"Hope, you're talkin' li'l things. I mean big."

"Seems to me I remember a fellow named Slover Navarre or William Hogland or whatever name you want. Seems to me he got strength from the bottom, and in turn the bottom lifted him right up like he was king for a minute."

Blair sat up and stared out the window. He put his fork down.

"The bottom?"

He laughed.

"The bottom, Hope! The big rough bottom! The big rifle-totin' bottom with no hand linen and no gold in the house. They almost made Navarre governor!"

But then Blair remembered what he had lost for Navarre's sake.

"And it seems to me," continued Hope, "that Woodbridge didn't know any high ones. Except a pair of high-blooded pigs. That's lower than the bottom. He don't pussyfoot aroun' with the high ones. Says what he thinks, like you ought." She pointed to the *Tabulator*.

"No. Not so fas', Hope. Not too fas'. Still got to pussyfoot a li'l. But same time, work for the bottom. The big bottom that has no gold in the house and no *fear*. No fear, tha's the part." Blair's face clouded. "But they got fear already," he said. "Gettin' worse all the time. Fear of mortgage. Fear of tax sale. But still . . ."

Blair pushed aside the trencher, reached for his quill pen, and began to scratch.

The next issue had two strange articles:

"The Northwest Territory could be the one place where democracy is not a code or a creed, but a natural circumstance, like the distance between our houses. This natural circumstance leads us to different laws than we had in the East . . . such as the requirement that one man shelter another in distress. Since our laws are different and born of our surroundings, let us also choose lawmakers who are of ourselves. Let us not import lawmakers with eastern ideas. Let us elect lawmakers who know that the absentee landowner's land has become valuable only because of the settler; and that the absentee should therefore be heavily taxed, and the settler lightly."

The second article was in the upper right-hand corner:

"TO BE READ AND PASSED ON TO STRANGERS,
TRAVELERS, AND NEIGHBORS

Will those who remember the circumstance of a certain William Hogland being tried for treason, be hereby apprised that the attorney, Jonathan Blair, is candidate for the state legislature."

On a Tuesday night he sat in the tavern arguing pleasantly, at first, with Stikes, Exeter, Brute Christofferson, and Culpepper.

Arm Webster was rolling dice with young Hussong, Wheeler, and some others.

Culpepper said: "Mr. Blair, some of us can't figure you out. Everybody in the town knows you're a tarnation smart man. Yet you run a piece in your paper as much as askin' the squatters and no-'counts to vote for ya. That don't look like a very good bed you're makin' for y'self, sir."

"I'm willing to sleep on it, Culpepper."

"That's your business, sir. But it don't seem very cunnin' of you, sir, because at the same time you're admitting that you are the man that prosecuted their leader, William Hogland."

Blair smiled wistfully. There was his dilemma. It seemed that Blair was destined never to stand on a clear-cut platform . . . for or against.

How do you explain to a man—Culpepper, for example—that at a certain moment in your prosecution of William Hogland you became his defender without seeming so? How do you say that and retain his respect? You don't.

Blair could predict Culpepper's reaction: "Then, sir, if that's how you felt, why didn't you come out flat on Hogland's side, sir?" How do you answer that, when you've not answered it yourself? You don't. Especially when you don't even know whether Slover Navarre ever understood what you did, nor what happened to him.

Christofferson said: "Mr. Blair, it looks to me you're imaginin' things when you say our lawmakers are large landholders. Tryin' to raise our dander now about Mr. Shuldane. He turned over most of his property to 'Manuel Ault. Young Webster's got no holdin's that I know of. You make us out kind of timber-headed. How could we let a thing like that happen without noticin' it?"

"We let a lot of things happen, Brute. It happens I took a trip down to the land office and copied off the real holders of these townships up here. I've got the type set right now. Going to run the paper off tomorrow. The list'll be in it. And you'll be surprised about who owns what. About who's really closing down the mortgages around here, and who's just acting as hangman."

"I can name the owners on all four sides of me," said Brute.

"Can you, Brute? Tell you what. You go ahead and name them. Then when you're through, I'll go over and press off a proof of tomorrow's *Tabulator* and bring it over here. Go ahead."

Suddenly Blair's arm was jostled, splashing some of his drink on the bar. Arm Webster brushed past him and went out the door.

"Now there's a man doesn't want to hear you," said Blair, louder than necessary. "Go ahead, Brute."

"Well, on my north there's a piece Ault holds. Trying to sell it. And on my west, that's Ault, too. On my east I butt against Woodbridge for a little piece. Then Ault has the rest."

Blair grinned. "That's enough, Brute. I'll be right back."

Blair walked out of the tavern. He groped across the dark common to his cabin. He was still grinning in the dark, from the whisky and from anticipation of the surprise he would create. He shoved open his door. But halfway open it stuck as something rolled underneath it. Blair squeezed in sideways. He lighted a splinter in the fireplace and with it lighted a candle. When the candle sputtered up, Jonathan Blair sobered.

Spread all over the floor was the type he had locked up in the frame. Resting half on the floor and leaning against the desk was the top of the press. Spreading slowly on the puncheon floor was a pool of black liquid—ink. As he watched, the floor sucked it in like a blotter.

Jonathan Blair grinned. He grabbed the shattered top of the press and walked back across the common and into the tavern.

A circle of eyes in the tavern converged on the shattered press screw in Blair's right hand; but Blair looked only at Arm Webster, who continued rolling the dice. The other players stopped the game and looked at Blair.

Blair addressed Stikes, but he kept his eyes on Webster.

"Mike, can you fix this tonight?"

Mike took the press screw from Blair. His long fingers caressed the splinters in the thick wooden screw. His voice was charged with accusation.

"Blair, you'd ought to know better'n treat a fine piece of wood turning like that! That took somebody a week of labor."

"I didn't break it, Mike. It was tampered with. Got to have it fixed by tomorrow." Blair's eyes fixed on Webster.

Mike looked up. He ran his hand through his white hair.

"Could be," he speculated, "that Mordecai Mason's cider press screw could be rigged somehow. How'd all this happen anyhow?"

Arm Webster interrupted petulantly: "Come on, Hussong, you trying to get out of this game? Roll the dice."

"It's your roll," said Hussong absently, still looking at the broken press screw in Stikes's hand.

"So it is," said Webster. He pulled the dice from his pocket and rolled them, with relief. But they rolled farther than he intended, to the center of the floor. When they stopped rolling, one die turned up a four. The other turned up an *S*. It was a block of type.

Blair bent over and picked it up. He tossed it in the air, caught it, and studied Webster, still grinning.

"Craps, Webster," he said.

Woodbridge sat with his head in his hands. It was beyond belief. The owner of over 380 of the most unusual hogs in the West could not raise $24 in cash that was good enough to pay the rest of his taxes. He could trade them for a whole township of land in Indiana. He could trade them for a whole barrelful of western currency of all colors and descriptions. But he could not trade them for gold or for United States bank notes, because there were none. People weren't parting with United States notes and gold.

Something was wrong when it took a barrel of western flour to buy one pound of eastern coffee. Ten barrels of flour now to buy one yard of plain cloth. Five hundred bushels of corn to buy one yard of silk. And no number of hogs would bring a dollar of gold. There was no gold. There was no hope.

"Look at me, will ya, Veronica! I'm better off than most any of 'em, but I can't raise $24 worth of decent paper! The thing is crazy! If I can't do it, nobody can. Why should I worry about it!"

"Tom, you've more reason to worry about it than the others."

"How so?"

Veronica gave him no answer.

Zabeth spoke up: "Mam doesn't want to say it about Gramp, Pap. But that's what's worrying her. She knows Mr. Exeter's cottonin' up to him. And since he didn't do so good with Gramp's hogs, it'd be a feather to his cap with Gramps if he was to put our hogs up for tax sale so's Gramps could bid for them."

"My place up for sale!" derided Woodbridge. "Exeter wouldn't dare!"

"Maybe not if it weren't for Mr. Ault," said Veronica.

"What's he to do with Exeter?"

"I think he's crowding Amos as far as managing things for Father. I think it worries Amos some."

"People won't stand for puttin' my place and stock up for tax sale!"

"Not ordinarily," said Veronica. "But don't forget there's hardly a man's not beholden to Mr. Ault or Father by some kind of mortgage."

"A-ah! And then there's that fool land deal the boy's mixed up in with Ault. That'd give Ault the edge over Exeter, too, if he could get Big Four for Shuldane."

"Sometimes I hope the Stranger-boy loses his land," sighed Veronica.

Woodbridge looked up sharply.

"The devil with his land!" said Woodbridge. "Don't you realize, if he loses his land he loses Big Four?"

The color rose in Veronica's white throat. She whirled to face him. "And don't you realize, Tom Woodbridge, if he doesn't lose that hog, you'll lose something else?"

Woodbridge was puzzled and annoyed by her excitement.

"Lose what!" he said. "What else matters? If we lost Big Four to Shuldane, he'll not make the same mistake again, as he did with the Bedfords."

"There are some things more important than a hog!"

"What's more important than a Mesopotamia hog? It's been the makin' of us!"

Veronica's eyes were wet.

"Don't you know yet?" she hurled at him.

"I do not."

Veronica turned to her daughter abruptly. "Elizabeth, go to the well and get water for supper."

Zabeth looked surprised. Young Tom always brought the water. But she left.

"Don't you know what a man gets next," said Veronica, "after he gets his land?"

Woodbridge looked up at her sharply. Then he broke into a grin. "Aw, you don't mean him and Zabeth."

"I mean exactly that. Stranger-boy is good. But he's no husband for Elizabeth . . . to take her to a one-room cabin and turn her into a woods woman like Lucy Adams or Mrs. Flannerty or—or Hope Emerson!"

Woodbridge was still grinning. "I know that. Not my Zabeth. Young Tom'll get some girl like Camelia Flannerty. Why, he's a brother to Zabeth. Lately, in fact, he pays her no attention, even when she's prettiest."

"You blind fool, Tom! That's just it."

"How can that hurt?"

"Don't you see? Don't you see he dares not boost her into the saddle any more? He dares not lift her down from the wagon like before? If she should pass him the meat and touch his hand by so much as a flick, he pulls back like it was lightning and bends down his head. Don't you see that?"

The smile was gone from Tom Woodbridge's face.

"Why, she's just a babe," he said.

But she was not a babe.

And as Young Tom walked briskly into Hosmer's Store he knew it.

"Hello, Mr. Hosmer," he said. "Did Mr. Buttrick and Silver Pigeon come up from Cincinnati yet?"

"No, Stranger-boy. Expectin' them, though. 'Least, Mrs. Buttrick is expectin' Asa."

Stranger-boy waited outside.

Folks that were here from the start and went through all the troubles were having trouble finding how to pay for just salt and coffee. It wouldn't ease their feelings any to see an Indian boy like Silver Pigeon handing over good United States Bank notes to an ordinary stranger-boy like Young Tom.

Buttrick and Silver Pigeon arrived shortly. Pigeon's shiny black hair had one of those store haircuts that left smooth edges around the ears and a nice smell. He counted the money out to Stranger-boy earnestly, explaining carefully about it.

"Only $8 this time, Stranger-boy. Six from the special smoked hams you sent down by Brute Christofferson for the Cincinnati Club. Two for the fancy barreled pork."

"I don't see where you took out any commission, Pigeon."

Pigeon waved his hand.

"I want you to get the land. Then maybe Captain Michael can have a cabin on a small corner of your place. How much more you need now to pay this Ault?"

"Only $29 more."

"Ah. We will make it. More ready for down trip?"

"Yeah."

Young Tom folded the money carefully and patted his pocket. The roll felt large to the hand. He walked to the store to look at the *Tabulator* which Hosmer always had pegged up inside. He planned to check the money chart to make sure Bank of United States currency was still at the top of the list. But the sparks in Sam Hosmer's voice made him dally just outside the door. Not since the Rontondee fight in the blockhouse had Stranger-boy heard old man Hosmer's voice rasp at it did now when he said: "You're crazier'n hell, Exeter! Take that notice down off my notice board!"

"I can't help it. The man owes taxes."

"Ye're gettin' ridiculous, Exeter! Don't try to tell me Tom can't pay his taxes. I can see about Flannerty and Wright and some of the others. But if the state goes sellin' out from under a producer like Wood-bridge, it's crazy!"

"He owes, don't he?"

"How much?"

"Only $24, but—"

"Twenty-four dollars and you're goin' to announce tax sale!"

"I give him two months already."

"Give him two months more! There's no better credit than Wood-bridge's. Why, every man in town holds his note for somethin', and none of 'em worried or pressin' to collect!"

"But those notes aren't payable in money. They're payable in pork. That's why nobody's worried. Woodbridge can always pay his debts in hogs. But he's got no cash for taxes."

"Who has? Now you get on back home and stop meddlin'."

"I'm sorry, Sam. If it was anybody else, maybe I could. But there's certain ones watchin' this one special. Tom's got to pay—one way or another."

The sudden sound of ripping paper reached Stranger-boy.

"Get out!"

Exeter walked out of the store. He brushed past Young Tom, looked back for a moment, and then rushed over to Blair's cabin.

Stranger-boy felt the roll of bills in his pocket. It felt very small now.

Veronica knew it was serious because polite Brute Christofferson didn't even wait to be asked in. He just walked over to where Woodbridge was eating supper, laid the *Tabulator* on the table, and pointed with a huge finger that obscured the very item he indicated.

"Blair said to get it to you right away, Tom," he mumbled. "Said to tell you he had to print it. Legal announcement."

Woodbridge exploded, "Why that—"

"Mr. Blair said to tell you to take it serious. It's not just a routine tax sale announcement. Something kind of funny behind it."

Woodbridge calmed down and stared at Veronica. Then he said, "Brute, you hold my note for ten hogs, owin' to you for haulin' that barreled pork to Fort Tawa for me."

"I'm in no hurry, Tom. Rather take 'em one at a time next winter, slaughtered and smoked."

"That ain't the point. I can pay any time," said Woodbridge. "But I'd raise that note to fifteen hogs if you'd loan me any good currency you got, Brute."

"If I had any, Tom, you could—"

"I believe you, Brute." Woodbridge absently waved him quiet. "Thanks, anyway. There's others hold my hog notes for curin' salt and tanbark and labor. I'll ask them. Somebody can loan me some good money."

But nobody could.

It had been Woodbridge's custom to pay for all the items he used on his farm, now a considerable amount, in personal IOU's. The promissory notes were payable in hogs, which he paid whenever the creditors desired. Hosmer usually took his hogs cured and barreled. Fitchburg preferred his smoked.

Woodbridge canvassed all his note holders and offered to increase his debt to them in return for the loan of some negotiable currency. He could get none.

Veronica would not have recognized her words as part of a plan. If she had, she might not have said them.

"Young Tom, I've heard no talk from you that worries about your next payment on your land, so it's likely you're saving, and will meet your payment to Mr. Ault all right."

"Yes, Miss Veronica. I've special reasons lately to see nothing goes wrong with my land deal."

"Your payment, though, is not pressing. That is, not like Tom's taxes, for instance."

Stranger-boy put down his spoon slowly.

"Miss Veronica, would there be more meaning than you're saying?"

The question made her face herself. "I guess I was hinting for you to help Tom with his taxes."

Young Tom continued eating uncomfortably and silently. He noticed Zabeth's lower lip protrude.

"You see," defended Stranger-boy, "it's important I hold on to that land."

"Why?" asked Veronica.

"Tom says don't try to get credit or a wife without you own your own land."

Veronica and Zabeth gave no answer.

"Besides," struggled Stranger-boy, "I promised Tom on my honor they'd not take Big Four. If I gave him money for his taxes, I'd not make my payment on time. We'd lose Big Four."

Stranger-boy was not accustomed to long stretches of talking. But their silence demanded he continue.

"And the way I've studied out Tom, he'd rather I stick to my own worries and he stick to his. He'd rather have that than excuses why I couldn't hold Big Four. As for the taxes, if Tom's drove to the wall he'll find a way out."

Zabeth suddenly flared. "But must you wait until he's drove to the wall! Can't you see he's worried! He's not here eatin', like you!"

She pushed back her chair and left the room. Stranger-boy did not look up. He was suddenly aware that his large body had demanded more than a third of the food on the table. As if to make up for it some, he carefully placed his fork and knife neatly on the edge of his trencher. He put his unused white butter back on the common plate. His young forehead was wrinkled with doubt, but his voice was resolute.

"I think I'm doin' right, Miss Veronica."

In the afternoon he was riding into town with Woodbridge for a wagonload of tanbark from Mordecai Mason.

They rode in silence a few miles.

"I'll have to go in and beg with Exeter," said Woodbridge. "About the last critter I want to beg from. But maybe it won't hurt me."

Woodbridge dropped off the wagon in front of the tavern. Stranger-boy followed him.

"No, you go on up to Mason's," said Woodbridge.

"Thought maybe I ought to come along," said the boy.

"Why?"

"Might have to do the same thing myself some day. Ought to learn how."

"You gonna miss your payment to Ault?" snapped Woodbridge.

"No, sir."

"Oh. All right."

Inside the tavern Woodbridge was relieved to find no crowd. Ault was sitting in a corner making some entries in a land book. But he left shortly after Woodbridge flatly told Exeter that he didn't have the tax money.

Strangely enough, Exeter acted quite reasonably about it. But very shortly Ault returned, and with him were Nate Shuldane and Arm Webster. When they entered, Stranger-boy was surprised at the sharp change in Exeter's tone of voice, almost as if he wanted no doubt about who it was had Woodbridge over the barrel.

"Nothin' I can do about it, Tom. If you can't raise the cash, your place goes on the block." He looked up for Shuldane's approval.

"You'll roast in hell first, Exeter."

"Won't help ya to talk mean, Tom. Men more deservin' of sympathy than you have been losin' their places."

"Can't you see how ridiculous it is!" yelled Woodbridge. "I own more actual goods than most any man in town, but just because I can't raise a few pieces of certain colored paper you want to close me down."

"Ridiculous part 'pears to me that such a high and mighty man as you can't raise your tax money when most of the rest of us poor devils get by. Us that live in smaller houses than yours."

"That's natural. Since you got that stock tax on, I got the biggest tax. You'd be in the same fix, but for your not bein' able to raise a hog past weaning without it dyin'!"

The wry grin that came to Shuldane's face scoured Exeter's soul. And there was no doubting Exeter's intention this time.

"Woodbridge, you can do as you like. The sheriff has his instructions."

Stranger-boy fell under the spell of the friendly resonant voice of Elnathan Shuldane, who now stepped in like an indulgent father among troubled, squalling children.

"Tom," he said, "let's keep our troubles in the family. I could manage some cash."

It was a marvelously soothing voice, and Nate Shuldane's shaved face seemed wise and powerful as he relaxed easily against Exeter's bar. However, Shuldane stiffened slightly when Arm Webster overzealously pulled out some kind of previously prepared paper and laid it on the bar in front of Woodbridge. Shuldane reached over slowly to retrieve the paper, but Woodbridge snatched it. He read it for a second only.

"Half and half!" he scorned. "Don't you ever quit, Nate? Half and half! So you had this all figured out!"

Young Tom expected to see the paper ripped to pieces. But instead Woodbridge studied the paper thoughtfully. That, more than anything, showed Stranger-boy how bad it was with Woodbridge.

Young Tom asked, "How much do we owe, Tom?"

But Woodbridge was reading the paper.

"How much do we owe, Tom?"

"Too much. Just a few miserable dollars. But it's too much."

"How much, though?"

Woodbridge was annoyed. "Twenty-four dollars! What's the difference? It might as well be—"

But before he finished, Stranger-boy stepped up to Amos Exeter. He reached deep into his breeches and pulled out a small roll of green bills.

Carefully, so as not to make a mistake either way, Young Tom Woodbridge counted out twenty-four bills.

"We'll be needin' a receipt, Mr. Exeter," he said.

The stunned silence that followed illuminated Amos Exeter's bare soul like flash lightning on a dark night. His decency was too paralyzed to hide his ugly disappointment. There were few things he could have said to unload some of his misery. But he managed to find one of them.

"Well, Woodbridge, you're saved by a boy."

But it was a quagmire. Any effort to lift one foot out of the financial quicksands of 1818 forced the other foot that much deeper in the muck. And Young Tom's assistance with Woodbridge's tax bill immediately brought his own land contract into jeopardy.

Silver Pigeon could sell no more of Young Tom's specially smoked hams at Cincinnati at any price in good money. The West was throttled. Merchants paid their debts in IOU's. Hardly any independent bank notes were acceptable. And the economy was so starved for good money that if you had United States Bank notes you could buy a fancy carriage for $5. And if you had three more good dollars you could buy a good horse to pull it.

Young Tom dumped a bucket of mash into the trough and watched Big Four bury his snout in it. The broad, bent-over ears jiggled as Big Four gorged himself, ignorant that he carried in his brute body the ability to sire thousands of progeny for which men would confiscate each other.

Young Tom looked at the assertive, solid mass of hog flesh and he marveled that this ugly monster could be the reason for the building of boats that ran in the Cincinnati-New Orleans trade. It was the reason for the cutting down of forests to make barrels for pork shipping. It was the reason for the making of laws in the legislature, ordering how many pounds would be in a barrel. It was the cause of men carefully guarding secrets on how to smoke or pickle to achieve a certain taste, for it looked like a man with a special method of smoking or pickling could build an empire.

Young Tom looked at Big Four and he realized that he was the end product of eighteen years of breeding back to two stolen white piglets, Boss and Cleopatra, who were in themselves the result of twenty years' breeding in England.

He looked at the trough of mash. It would be easy to poison the hog so Ault couldn't have it. But chances are there'd be some way they could make Woodbridge deliver another equal boar in its stead.

The hog looked up to see if that was all.

Young Tom decided he could probably substitute another hog. But he quickly realized that Ault would have made it his business to know the difference. Besides, the loss of another boar to Shuldane would be almost as disastrous.

For a half-hour, at least, Young Tom stood looking at Big Four. He realized that Emanuel Ault would stop at nothing to take Big Four for Shuldane.

Stranger-boy walked into Hosmer's Store.

"Have you got the money to pay him, boy?" asked Hosmer hopefully.

"Almost."

Hosmer shook his head sadly.

It amounted to a court trial. In fact it was a trial. Because when Ault came in, Sam Hosmer slipped out of the store and returned immediately with Jonathan Blair, casually, as if he'd met him on the common. Strangely, Arm Webster drifted over and Shuldane came behind him.

When Stikes looked out the front of his forge and saw Shuldane going to the store, he took off his leather apron and sauntered over. He called to Hawkins, who also came, as did others.

Young Tom was uncomfortable and puzzled by the crowd that developed so quickly.

Woodbridge and Zabeth arrived in time to see Ault counting Stranger-boy's money on Hosmer's store counter. He counted all the bills and pronounced, "One hundred eighty-four dollars." Then he began to count the large pile of silver coin. The room hushed, for every man in the store knew the Stranger-boy's debt was $230 plus 10 per cent, or $253. Ault's voice sounded like Seth Gershom enumerating the fires in Hell.

"Two hundred and nineteen, twenty, twenty-one."

He pushed one coin aside. "Don't like the sound of that one, boy. Two hundred twenty-two, twenty-three, twenty-four."

Ault slid the money back toward Young Tom.

"Twenty-nine dollars short, boy. You forfeit Big Four. Sorry."

There was no overt reaction from the crowd. They expected it. But Woodbridge didn't.

"You said you had the money, boy!"

Young Tom flinched for he had not seen Woodbridge come in; but before he could answer, Exeter said, "He darn near did have it, before he paid your taxes, Woodbridge."

"Why didn't you tell me you didn't have it?" charged Woodbridge.

"Because I thought I could get Mr. Ault to make a settlement. Take my money and cut down my fifty acres to forty."

"A settlement from Ault? Huh!" Woodbridge looked around the room. "Couldn't you tell they were layin' for ya? Did you think—"

Sam Hosmer cut him off.

"Tom, let the boy make his proposition to Ault. Maybe he'll accept it. Specially with all of us here to kind of help him decide about it."

"Well, I wanted to ask Mr. Ault to take my money and cut my title to forty acres," said Young Tom.

Ault looked at Shuldane, then stretched his lip out from under his bottom teeth and shook his head.

"Then take my money and cut my acres to thirty," said Young Tom.

Ault shook his head again.

Blair stood up. With his hands behind his back, he walked to the center of the store.

"I suggest, Ault, that you accept the boy's proposal. It leans over backwards in your favor, since you made him a very unfair mortgage. In a simple land contract the land itself is traditionally security for the payment. By binding him also to forfeit a valuable breed hog, you approach usury."

The sides shaped up firmly as Arm Webster jumped to his feet.

"That makes no difference, Jonathan. If a man voluntarily signs to those terms, he's bound."

"You're right enough, of course, Webster," said Blair. "But let Ault have the decency to consider that the pile of money the Stranger-boy offers him, in those particular notes, are now worth many times more than when the deal was consummated. While the piece of land is worth much less."

"You and I know that," grinned Webster, "but the state doesn't acknowledge deflation. Witness their law which makes it a felony to depreciate any bill from its face value."

"That law is unenforceable," said Blair, "and broken every day in the week right here in this store. Since this is no courtroom, let's leave out all theoretical law."

But it was a courtroom to all purposes. And Blair's face was troubled, for his jury was Mesopotamia. And Mesopotamia was frightened.

Also, he had no case. He cared little for the fate of a swine, and he understood less how one fat boar could become so valuable. But he did

understand that in the carcass of the miserable hog named Big Four
was centered all the contention between the men who had made the
West with their fists and the men who would confiscate it with their
brains, between the producers and the manipulators. The miserable
hog split Blair's brain from his heart and his past from his future, and
he cried out: "God damn you, Ault! Leave the boy his hog!"

Blair's ineffectual outburst added to Shuldane's stature as the latter
now stepped calmly forward like a tolerant father interested only in
the principle involved.

"Men," he said, unruffled, "let's not lose our heads over a hog. If
we're going to live together, we've got to pay our debts. Sam, if we all
bought from your store with no obligation to pay, that wouldn't work,
would it?"

It was a skillful question. Sam Hosmer was worried about the bills
owing to him.

"No," he muttered. "But Nate, this is different."

"Sure, it's different," said Shuldane reassuringly, "so out of consideration for the boy's brave effort, let's give him his land, Mr. Ault."

There were sighs of relief around the room.

"But," continued Shuldane, "to uphold the principle, let's make him
pay over the surety as an example. I believe in this case it's a hog, or
something."

"You know God damned well what it is!" exploded Woodbridge.
"And you know damned well the land isn't worth a hair off that hog's
ear! That hog can father a herd that'll set a man up for life!"

Shuldane looked hurt.

"Well, if you're going to be that way, Tom, the fact is your boy
doesn't have a legal leg to stand on, does he, Mr. Blair?"

Blair studied the floor. He squeezed his left hand so hard with his
right that the end of his fingers turned red and his ring cut into his
skin. He said nothing.

Ault addressed Young Tom. "Then you'll deliver Big Four tonight?"

Young Tom looked at Woodbridge, whose face was a mask of pain
and reproach.

"Deliver him tonight?" repeated Ault.

Stranger-boy seemed about to answer, but instead he stepped over
to Blair and wrote on a paper in front of Blair. Blair's face snapped
alert and serious.

"Let me see the mortgage paper, Ault," he said.

Ault's expression challenged his right to it. But Hosmer stepped from behind the counter and took it from him, handing it to Blair. Hosmer's snapping-turtle face concentrated on Blair. He didn't know what was going on, but he sensed hope.

Blair handed the paper to Shuldane.

"Read it," he said.

Shuldane read and handed it back.

"It's clear enough, Blair. The boy's got to give up the hog."

"I know that," said Blair, studying the paper. "But what I'm gettin' at is somethin' else."

"What?"

"Nothing in there says how the hog's got to be delivered."

"For God's sake, Blair, what do you mean?"

"I mean he can be gelded."

The tense face of Mesopotamia cracked into a smile. Every head turned to Ault, who snatched the paper back from Blair and studied it, as if to find new meaning.

Blair placed his hand on Young Tom's back. There was genuine pleasure on the lawyer's face.

Arm Webster was zealously on his feet.

"Now wait just a min-ute, Blair!"

But Elnathan Shuldane was quicker than his nephew.

"Sit down, Arm," he commanded.

Be it said in tribute to Shuldane's self-discipline that there was a grin on his face.

"Hard luck, Ault," he said. "But the boy's got you there. Blair's right, of course. I recommend since this turn of affairs that you be big about it. I wouldn't make the boy destroy the boar. It would be no good to you that way. The sporting thing would be to let him keep it."

Stranger-boy's hands trembled with relief as he took back his money. He handed the land title over to Ault, who snatched it.

The grins in the room all shared the Stranger-boy's relief. And some were obviously grins of admiration for Elnathan Shuldane, who was obviously a big man. They listened respectfully to his last word.

"Just one thing, though, men," said Shuldane. "Mr. Blair has hereby established a sort of precedent for our village. He is perhaps our ablest lawyer."

Shuldane threw a silencing stare at his nephew, Arm Webster, and continued. "So we look to him for guidance in these matters. And Blair has in effect ruled that in any contract among us . . . what is not explicitly prohibited is allowable. Let us be guided by that in our future arrangements."

As the men filed out of the store, they reflected that Shuldane was a big man. Except Jonathan Blair. He remained seated, studying the floor. For he knew Elnathan Shuldane well enough to know a warning when he heard one.

# Chapter 26: THE DEBTOR

NOTIFICATION of the arrival of a letter at the store in Mesopotamia these days was often a terrible announcement.

Immediately and publicly it brought up the question: Did the receiver have the money to pay for the letter? Sam Hosmer had been forced to withhold all mail until the addressee reimbursed him for the collect postage.

In the second place, a letter often meant trouble, usually a death in the family back East, like the letter Denaro got about his wife in Boston. Denaro would likely not stay on now, for he had been preparing a place for her.

The arrival of a letter often humbled the receiver, as in the case of Hope Emerson. "Sorry, Sam, I don't have the money with me. I'll fetch it tomorrow." But the letter remained in the pigeonhole for a week, and the village grew curious.

Woodbridge came in and plunked down a pie-shaped quarter chiseled from a silver dollar. Hosmer handed him a fat letter, well thumb-marked by the carriers and the curious.

The act called Hosmer's attention to Hope Emerson's letter, and she being present, he handed it to her.

"Sorry, Sam. Didn't bring any silver," she said. "Tomorrow."

Blair was there picking up the exchange newspapers from which he got his national news for the *Tabulator*. He said, "I've got some coin, Hope."

He flopped some coppers on the counter and handed Hope the letter, which she received coolly.

She pocketed the letter and proceeded briskly to the business of selecting a coil of rope, a process which did not require much concentration, for Sam stocked only two sizes of rope. Blair was somewhat put out.

"Open it, Hope, and see if your brother can send you the money to pay Ault."

Hope opened the letter slowly and examined it.

"Well, can he?"

"He's—ah—not very clear about it." She hesitated. "I'll take it back to the cabin and study out his meaning."

"On a question like that, how can he be vague?" asked Blair. "Here, let me see it."

While he read it, Hope Emerson's tanned face deepened in color. Blair frowned.

"Why, Hope, he leaves no question. He says flatly he can't send the money. How could you—"

But as Blair and the others looked at Hope, who stood there clutching the envelope, they understood simultaneously, and for the first time, that Hope Emerson could not read.

Hope Emerson left, and a depression settled over the store. Of all the foreclosures, people most hated to see Hope Emerson and Mike Stikes lose the land they had bought from Ault.

Since most of the purchases were made within the same frenzied period of land buying, the payments all fell due at about the same time, putting everyone in the same position. Ault would have his land all back to sell over again. He would also retain the first payments, which the defaulting buyers had forfeited.

Woodbridge's letter was from David Marcusson. He asked certain questions about the preparation of the pickle for curing pork and about the feed for firming hogs. But the part that worried Veronica was the main part of the letter that Tom had left on the ledge of the fireplace. The handwriting was large and bold:

Tom, it seems to me that during this money trouble, the only way you will get the worth out of a Mesopotamia hog is to sell for land. The vast difference between the Mesopotamia hog and these scrawny beasts now being raised means that breeder animals cannot fail to bring fabulous prices when men again have cash that's worth its face value. My neighbors here wish to buy of me faster than I can raise the animals. Meanwhile, I know that for half of your herd out here you could put yourself in possession of a half-township of good Indiana land, perhaps a whole township. Since there are not good dollars to be had anywhere in the West, I have been selling my breeders for land. You should do the same.

Your servant,
DAVID MARCUSSON
Marcusson Twp.

P.S. The hog Big Sixteen, which I had from you, has thrived well. Now weighs 360 pounds and bids to equal your foundation sow Big One. Her unborn offspring are sold for the next five litters.

Veronica replaced the letter on the mantelpiece and stood staring at it even after Zabeth came in.

"What's the matter, Mam?"

Veronica shook off her concentration.

"Nothing, Elizabeth. In fact, I've good news for you."

"Me?"

"We've changed our minds. You may go with Arm Webster to the political dinner-ball in Columbus. Your grandfather will be along. He's to make a speech to the delegates there."

"But Pap said I was to have nothing to do with Gramps."

"Come to your room. We'll see to your clothes. And there are some things to tell you about governors and the like."

"Mam," asked Zabeth warily, "will this mean a big ruction between you and Pap?"

It was on a Tuesday evening that Blair came out to the Woodbridge place. His arrival thankfully interrupted the argument about Zabeth's sudden departure for Columbus.

It always shocked Veronica to see Jonathan lately. But she was careful not to let him know it.

Blair had come to see Woodbridge.

"Tom, they're going to foreclose Hope's land this week."

"I know it. And Stikes' and Hawkins', too. Hate to see it happen to those three."

"No. Not Mike."

"Not Mike?" Woodbridge was surprised. "Why not?"

"I think he made his payment, somehow."

"Don't see how. He couldn't loan me any hard money for taxes."

"I don't know," said Blair. "But I hate to see Hope lose her land."

Veronica looked up from her sewing to study Jonathan.

"I despise to see it, too," said Tom. "But I can't see anything to do. Same with Adams and Mitchell, though they should have known better'n to sell what I got for 'em on their bounty warrants."

"It's the balance of trade," said Blair. "If only the West had something the East wanted badly enough so they'd pay us in gold or silver."

"Blair, you've preached me that a year now. But that don't help Hope any to pay Ault."

"I know," shrugged Blair.

The first wave of uneasiness went through Thomas Woodbridge on Wednesday, when he went to Hope Emerson's cabin.

"Hope, I can't help you make your payment. But the least I can do is pay you what I owe ya. Might help. You hold my note for five hogs for wool we got from you. You can have the pork now, any way ya want it, smoked, pickled and barreled, or just butchered."

Woodbridge found something strange about Hope Emerson this morning. Usually the clear, fearless eyes met you squarely. But today she bent her head over her flax combs, picking fibers out of the iron teeth.

"Tom, it's good of you to offer. But I'm in no hurry on those hogs."

"Yeah," said Tom. "A hog ain't nothin' when it's cash y'need." He turned to go. But she seemed to want to say something.

"Tom, I won't be needin' any cash."

"Huh?"

"I made my payment all right."

"You what?"

"Matter of fact, Tom, it was you helped me out."

"Me?"

"Tom, will ya set a minute? Somethin' I'd like t'say."

Tom sat down on a puncheon stool. Hope sat opposite, like a man, leaning her elbows forward on the knees of her buckskin skirt.

"Tom, you been close to losin' your land at times. I mind when you first came, and the trouble you had."

Woodbridge was puzzled. Hope resumed her nervous fiddling with the flax combs.

"Point is, Tom, you know what a thrashin' caterwaulin' sets up in your stomach when they go to take your ground away."

"Yeah. Sure."

"Well, Ault came 'round to see if I could pay. I showed him everything I had on the place and asked him what would he take."

"Yeah."

"Well, I had some silver in coin. He took that. It wasn't enough. So he said if I wouldn't tell anybody—so's the others wouldn't get the idea they could do the same—he'd take your hog notes in payment for my balance. Said it was a favor to me."

Woodbridge was surprised.

"I know'd you wouldn't like the notion of dealin' with Ault. But it was a way to save my place. And it don't really make much mind who gets the pork, me or Ault, does it?"

Woodbridge stood up slowly. "No. I guess not."

He walked to the door.

"No," he repeated. "Pork's pork. And if my pork'll hold your land, Hope, that's all right."

"Thanks, Tom."

"Just seems funny, Ault doin' anybody a favor and settlin' for so little. But then there ain't many wouldn't do you a turn, Hope."

As he left, he grinned. "Maybe Ault's took a kind of sneakin' notion after you, Hope."

She grinned back.

"If he had a notion, it'd be a sneakin' one, all right."

But her casual jest wiped the grin from Woodbridge's face.

"Yeah. 'Twould."

Woodbridge rode uneasily back west to the center of the village. He was about to pull up in front of Hosmer's Store, but there was some excitement there, centered around three strangers.

The strangers were not ordinary settlers or immigrants. They had not the nervous eagerness of eastern migrants who had worn out their cloth clothes and their confidence on the trek west. Instead, they stood stolid and easy, answering questions rather than asking them.

Their two wagons were not the lashed-up settlers' rigs sagging under

a poor selection of household goods and peopled with anemic offspring
and resigned women. These were the most unusual wagons Woodbridge
had ever seen. They were great rugged carts. The fore wheels were the
size of Tom's wagon wheels. The back wheels were to a man's shoulder,
with rims over half a foot wide. The spokes were great poles. The beds
of the wagons were huge yawning boxes, yet seeming not wide enough
for the capacity of the axles, as though some overcautious builder had
provided a ridiculous margin of spare strength.

The horses were immense, with mountainous withers and great muscled haunches that shimmered restlessly under the inactivity. They
were a light powdery brown with white manes and tails. Brute Christofferson stood admiring the huge draught horses.

The three visitors belonged to their teams, though they were even
more strange. They stood staunch, placid, and confident. And they
wore great broadbrimmed black hats with low crowns, black jackets,
and gray wool trousers that tucked into wrinkled leather boots. They
stood together as though arraigned against the crowd, yet in relaxed
attitudes.

Sam Hosmer raised a hand and called to Tom. But Woodbridge
was that centered on his own thoughts, raised by Hope Emerson,
that he wished no interruption until he had talked to Mike Stikes.
And since he did not see Stikes in the crowd, he drove his wagon
through the chilling shadow of the Shuldane manor over toward the
forge.

Stikes was just leaving. Hawkins was with him. Tom was sure they
heard his hail, for they both looked at him. But they looked away
strangely and proceeded toward the store. He called again, but they
seemed not to hear. It was the strangest behavior Woodbridge had ever
seen.

When Tom drove onto the Woodbridge place, Veronica had already
heard about the Quakers from Stranger-boy, and she asked Tom about
them.

"I didn't ask. They're there, that's all."

It was noontime of the following day that Brute Christofferson
stopped by and dropped off a copy of the *Tabulator*. He laid it in front
of Tom and pointed with a thick finger to the upper right-hand corner.

"Look, Tom."

Tom studied the place Brute indicated. It was an advertisement saying that a certain traveling dentist would be in the town on Monday next.

"What's that to me?" asked Tom.

"Nothing, but that's the place where Blair usually lists the fore-closures. See. There are none."

Tom took the paper and turned it over.

"No. There ain't," he observed. "What do you make of it?"

Veronica came over to look.

"Tom, it means things are mending," she said.

"I don't see Blair printing anything about the balance of trade being turned about. That's what he said was needed before good times could come."

"Mike Stikes and Jim Hawkins didn't lose their land," said Brute. "They paid Ault."

"Funny how they'd get the money so fast," said Tom, wrinkling his forehead. "Awful funny."

Veronica went back and sat down quietly. It could be that things were on the mend and that Tom would forget about Marcusson's inviting reports of the Indiana Country.

"What are those Quakers doin' here, Brute?" asked Tom.

"They don't talk about their business. Except to say it's with Shuldane. I thought Mrs. Woodbridge might know about it."

But Veronica didn't.

It was at the night meal that Young Tom suddenly got up and walked out the door to return immediately to the table. To Veronica's questioning glance he said, "She's coming."

There had been no mention of "she," but shortly they heard Zabeth's voice outside. And in a minute Arm Webster was at the door with her. He declined to stay to dinner, and left immediately.

The Zabeth who sat at table was a different girl from the one who had left for Columbus.

She had the grace not to babble about her experience, but when asked her talk came fast, though you could see that she was holding back so as not to belittle those who had stayed in Mesopotamia.

"But it looks we've perhaps put Cousin Webster in too small a pen," she said. "Down there he's whole hog and then some. Made a talk in front of all the men, and them clapping their hands and talking of big things for him and all."

Young Tom ate in silence with his head down. Zabeth could hold back no more, and her enthusiasm for the great things she had seen shrank the walls of the Woodbridge place and diminished Hosmer Village.

"And there were two big houses with paint on them, and four brick ones, and men with low shoes and hand linen at the table. And there's eight hundred people already, and they say it'll be bigger than Zanesville and Chillicothe."

"See anything goin' on as you came by the common?" asked Woodbridge.

"Oh, there is no common, unless you mean the statehouse yard."

"I mean here in Mesopotamia!" snapped Woodbridge. "Everything ain't in Columbus, you know."

Zabeth colored. "No, Pap. I didn't see anything."

"Nothin' goin' on about those Quakers yet?"

"Oh, those? We caught up with them on the road. Then we stayed the night at Boxford's Cabin so Arm could make another talk. The Quakers went on ahead. They were to wait here for Gramps."

"About what?"

Zabeth made her voice as gentle as possible.

"I think it's about hogs, Pap."

"Hogs! Why are they seeing *him* about hogs?"

"I don't know, Pap. They talked a long time on the road. I couldn't hear."

Woodbridge got up from the table abruptly.

"Come on, Stranger-boy."

When Big One was hoisted into the wagon, Tom and Young Tom drove in to Mesopotamia. They had the low sideboards on the wagon, and Big One's back loomed above them. It was dusk.

The Shuldane place was dark.

"They must be up at Shuldane's pens now," said Woodbridge, and they took the north road up between the Shuldane house and Hosmer's Store along the common.

Men on the porch of the store turned to go inside with that mysterious aloof shyness Woodbridge had noticed in Hawkins and Stikes in the tavern.

At the Shuldane farm the road came out of the woods, and it was light enough to see the three broad hats silhouetted. They were flanked by Exeter and Shuldane, who seemed to be talking rapidly and pointing to the Bedfords. The three stolid Quakers stood planted, two with their arms crossed over their chests, occasionally nodding their broad-brims slightly in acknowledgment of remarks and looking where Exeter pointed.

As he approached the group, Woodbridge pulled over very close and slowed enough so that Big One stuck her massive jowls over the side-board in curiosity. Seeing the horses and the five men, she gave a gurgling grunt and backed to the far corner of the wagon, but not before the large Quaker had seen her.

He immediately stepped to the road and called.

"Would thee stop, friend?"

Woodbridge pulled up on the reins, and the three broad hats approached his wagon. Shuldane and Exeter came reluctantly behind them.

"Thee must be the Thomas Woodbridge that David Marcusson sent us to," said the center one. "My name is Mathew Yoder."

Woodbridge nodded.

"And this surely is the Mesopotamia swine that we wanted."

The big Quaker's face was shiny clean and in its directness held a child's good will. Yet the skin itself was porous and pocked, and the jaw was not to be meddled with. Yoder did not introduce the other two, but said, "Thomas, we were sad to hear from Elnathan Shuldane that thee stopped selling the Mesopotamia hog."

Woodbridge was so intent on Yoder's face that he hardly heard Yoder's words. The big Quaker apparently gave no man a title, yet his simple "Thomas" somehow gave a man a place in the world somewhat above "Mr."

"What did you say?" asked Woodbridge.

"I said we were sorry thee stopped selling."

"Stopped selling?"

Shuldane broke in. "What I meant, Mr. Yoder, is that Woodbridge is hardly in a position to make a sale now, due to a circumstance which Colonel Marcusson could not know about."

"Perhaps Thomas Woodbridge would explain this himself," said Yoder, "since we traveled from Marcusson Township in Indiana to see his swine."

"I'm selling, all right," said Woodbridge. "Come out to my place and see them. Better come in the morning. Hogs look bigger than true size in the evening." Woodbridge grinned. "Isn't that right, Amos?"

In a confidential gesture Shuldane took Yoder's elbow, but the big Quaker unobtrusively dropped his arm and said gently: "Thee perhaps would now show us to the inn or sleeping place, Elnathan. Thee may not wish our company another night."

Within a few minutes of their arrival next morning, the three earnest-faced men had won over the Woodbridge household. They strode north with Woodbridge to the pens, and the questions were polite, but pointed.

"Thee say this is her fourth litter, Thomas?"

"That's right, Mr. Yoder. Nine piglets each time."

"And of the nine, thee raised how many past weaning?"

"Six from the first three litters and eight from the last."

"And thee warrant her at nine, then?"

"No. I warrant no hog for anything. But I feel pretty sure of it, sir."

"I like that statement. And thee need not 'sir' to me. I am above no man, and none is above me."

The three Quakers examined the whole farm. They challenged no statement, but Woodbridge had the distinct feeling they were quietly accepting certain of his claims, and rejecting others. They asked questions about feeding and colic and breeding. And they even furnished Woodbridge with some information.

"Yes, Thomas, we drove them as far as Vincennes to market, and we find thy hog is quite a fair walker. We bought some from Marcusson."

"But I thought it would be too heavy and small-boned."

"Naturally, they don't manage as well as the woods swine. And they lose about twelve pounds in seventy-five miles."

"You drove them seventy-five miles?"

"Aye. More. One must drive slowly. But we have driven them a hundred miles. Thee hast a better swine than thee know, Thomas. Which takes us to the price. We wish to be fair. Yet we must conserve."

There was no haggling. Woodbridge's price was high, but they knew the value of his breed. It was agreeable to the Quakers that Tom should ride up to the town and consult Blair about the value of their strange paper currency, which Tom did not recognize. If their paper was not listed, or was listed low, they would set aside Indiana land for him, if he would trust them.

"Except first one question to be answered, Thomas. This Elnathan

Shuldane said there was certain reason thee could not sell. We wish no entanglements. Be thee free to sell?"

"Of course I'm free to sell. Shuldane just wishes he had them. He can't seem to raise hogs."

"I noticed his animals were runty, some of them. We will go, then, Thomas, to see your friend Blair."

They made an impressive caravan driving into Mesopotamia.

Emanuel Ault was riding west, and it pleasured Woodbridge to lead the big Quaker wagons past Ault so that the latter could see the two loads of hogs he had sold. This was the biggest sale. This was proof. Woodbridge hoped all the doubters would see the transaction.

When they got in farther, Mitchell and Adams came out of their cabins to watch, as did Christian Kilgore. The Hussong widow was not home, for she kept house for Shuldane and Webster. But young Joe Hussong came out to stare and to wave.

The wagons creaked up to Blair's cabin. The editor was not in.

They tethered the teams in front of Blair's cabin and walked to the tavern. Halfway to the tavern Woodbridge's attention was attracted south to the river, and he was surprised to see Emanuel Ault riding toward the Shuldane house. He was surprised because he had only a few minutes before seen Ault riding west and because Ault was galloping his mount, a gait which did not become Ault's calculated manner.

Tom continued into the tavern. Blair was at the bar talking to Hawkins, who greeted Tom with the same timid expression that Woodbridge had noticed before.

Tom spread the Quakers' money in front of Blair.

"Jonathan, I sold some hogs. These gentlemen here are agreeable I should check with you to see if it's good money. Issued off a bank in Vincennes."

Blair looked at the black and white certificates.

"Never saw it before, Tom. But I'll go over to my cabin and get *Porter's Currency Manual*. See if it's listed. Wait here."

The Quakers stood silently waiting for Blair's return. Their inactivity made Woodbridge even more aware that the tavern was suddenly becoming busy. Kilgore, whom they'd passed recently at his cabin, was there, and so was young Joe Hussong. Ault was approaching, and Shuldane was with him. Woodbridge decided that it could be curiosity about the largest sale of hogs ever to leave the Woodbridge place. Yet it was strange.

Blair came back with his book. He stepped inside the cabin and looked around in surprise at the sudden assemblage. He looked especially at Shuldane. But finding no explanation, he opened the book in the center of the room for Woodbridge and the three Quakers, who crowded around the book respectfully.

Blair ran his finger down to the middle of the page. But while he talked to Woodbridge, his eyes studied Elnathan Shuldane, who returned a bemused and benign smile, unflinching.

"Here's your answer, Tom," said Blair. "As you can see, the Vincennes bank was as good as most. But now their assets are down to one-fifth of their issued notes."

"Make it plainer, Jonathan. Is Mr. Yoder's money good or not good?"

"Probably be all right if you lived near that bank where you could watch withdrawals closely. But out here—well, they're discounting it 50 per cent in Cincinnati, 75 per cent in Pittsburgh. Up here you ought to discount it about 60 per cent. No offense to you, Mr. Yoder. I'm judging by the book recommendation."

"I understand thee well," said Yoder. " 'Tis my aim to give the right amount for value received. But thee must decide."

Woodbridge's forehead wrinkled as he studied the book. It helped him none. But he stared at it with immense concentration, hoping to wring from it the answer: How much paper does it take to equal fifty-two hogs, fifty-two hogs that could start an empire? In land, he knew what he would ask. It would be a small county. His square finger scaled the column of mysterious figures. Then it stopped abruptly, not because of the book, but because the voice of Arm Webster bawled across the room.

"I counted fifty-two, 'Manuel."

"In both wagons?" asked Ault.

Though he didn't know what it was about, exactly, Woodbridge sensed a trespass. The color seeped up the back of his neck, and he leveled a question at Ault.

"Just what are you countin', mister?"

Ault moved out of the corner, to the center of the tavern.

"I meant to talk this over with you in the privacy of your place, Woodbridge. But since I noticed you were selling off a large number of hogs, I had to act quick."

"I don't see's any action from you, quick or otherwise, is called for if I decided to sell off my hogs."

Ault's lip gripped lightly by his lower teeth gave him the despicably knowing appearance of a man who enjoys a dangerous secret. It sent the blood pounding up around Woodbridge's ears and under his close-lying red hair to throb in his temples, giving further advantage to Ault, who was composed.

"Neither my customers' wagons nor my hogs concern you now or any other time!" blasted Woodbridge.

"No," said Ault calmly, "*your* hogs are no concern of mine. But I have to make sure it isn't *my* hogs you're selling."

Ault reminded Stranger-boy of Joe Hussong teasing Wolf by causing the animal to run after a stick which he only pretended to throw. And Tom was like Wolf, who finally flew into a snarling rage.

"God damn you, Ault!" yelled Woodbridge. "What hogwash is this?"

"Well, the fact is, most of the hogs on your place belong to me."

The ridiculous statement didn't register with Tom.

The Quakers folded their arms.

Sam Hosmer, who had come to investigate the crowd, said: "Ault, stop standin' there like a mule in shade. What's this nonsense?"

"No nonsense, Sam. Here it is."

Ault reached into his pocket and pulled out a fat calf's-ear wallet from which he drew a packet of small finger-marked papers bound together by a leather whang. He dropped them on Exeter's bar with a thump. They bounced and then lay still.

Woodbridge reached for them with a shocked expression. He flipped through them.

"My notes!" he marveled.

"One hundred and sixty hogs," said Ault. "And if my count is right, the Woodbridge herd is down to 180, after the last four big shipments."

Final realization was as slow to come to Tom as to the crowd in the tavern. No wonder there had been no foreclosures. He thumbed through the notes: all his debts to all the people of the village for salt, tanbark, barrel staves, iron hoops, haulage, cloth, potatoes, the building of his new house.

He flipped them over and mumbled the endorsements he found on the backs of them.

"Pay to the order of Emanuel Ault. Signed Hope Emerson."

"Tom!" protested Hope, "I never knew all of them were doing it."

"To Emanuel Ault," continued Tom. "Signed Mike Stikes."

Tom searched the crowd for Stikes, who looked stricken.

"Tom, it was a case of keeping my land. I had no idea—"

"To E. Ault," read Woodbridge. "Signed Hawkins."

Jim Hawkins broke under Woodbridge's inquiring glance.

"Tom, he told me I was the only one. Then I found out he did it for Stikes, too. But I thought it was just us two."

"To Emanuel Ault. Signed S. Slasher."

Woodbridge was drained of strength. He flipped through the rest of the notes and tossed them on the bar. His eyes circled the room.

"Now wait a minute, Ault," said Hosmer. "You can't do this! Tom would have had those notes all paid off to the lot of us, except we like to take the pork from him as we need it, instead of all at once. In exchange we all take our pay from him when it suits his breedin' season. Ye can't take a man's hogs when the sows are carryin' young!"

Ault picked up the bundle and read from the face of the notes.

"Payable on demand," he quoted, as a man who has said all there is to say.

Blair bent his head, as he heard the words. Why hadn't he figured this?

Hosmer flared, "That's a sneakin' thing, to go around buyin' up a man's debts like that!"

There was no response.

"Can he do it, Blair?"

They all watched Blair pick up the notes and flip through a few. He tossed them back on the bar.

"Nothin's against it," he said.

Mike Stikes said, "Ault, if I'd know you was up to this, I'd a jammed those notes down your gullet 'fore I'd signed 'em."

"That goes for me," said Slasher. "You told me it was a special favor to me only that you was acceptin' them. I was to keep quiet about it."

"Wait a minute," said Hosmer. "Looks to me like Woodbridge has got you over a barrel anyhow, Ault. The way the market is for pork right now, if you close in on those notes you aren't gonna get enough out of them to equal the amount you took 'em for."

"I'm not collecting pork," said Ault. "The notes say 'hogs.'"

"Well, sure!" said Woodbridge. "But the way I been deliverin' those hogs is in a barrel, butchered or smoked or pickled. Not live breed stock!"

"But the notes say 'on demand.' Well, I'm demanding *now*. And right now the hogs are *alive*. That's the way I'm takin' 'em."

Ault looked at Blair.

"Isn't that right, Mr. Blair?" he asked unctuously.

Blair stared down at the floor, and Ault twisted the lawyer's own precedent into his soul. "Seems to me in the case of Stranger-boy and Big Four we pretty well set it up that we're gonna use the 'strict interpretation' on these matters."

Blair looked at Elnathan Shuldane, who returned him an insultingly benevolent smile.

Yoder picked up his money regretfully but firmly. "Thomas, we cannot enter into thy contention. We shall return the swine to thy pens."

Yoder and his two Quakers walked out the door, leaving the tavern suspended in silence. Men lowered their eyes as Tom Woodbridge looked around the room in flooding desperation.

Shortly the lugubrious creaking of the great Quaker wagons rolling away played a kind of mournful Amen to Woodbridge's lifetime hopes. Ault stepped to the door to make certain the wagons were heading back west to unload the hogs.

Stranger-boy, from his position near the bar, could also see the wagons go, and he was sick with guilt. His brush with Ault over Big Four had given Ault the legal lever he needed to take almost the whole of Tom's herd.

Blair was thinking of his part in the same argument over Big Four, and how he had paved the way for this. He remembered now how quickly Shuldane had given up in the case of Big Four. He saw how thoroughly Shuldane had set the stage for taking the whole Woodbridge herd.

He saw what he had known all his adult life—that Elnathan Shuldane was formidable.

But while Blair thought about it, Stranger-boy acted. He reached casually over the bar and picked up the packet of notes. A dozen eyes turned immediately to watch the motion. But Stranger-boy stood still, idly flipping through the notes as Woodbridge and Ault and Blair had done a few minutes before. While the boy studied the notes, Ault said to Woodbridge, "I'll be out to pick my hogs tomorrow morning."

Stranger-boy, idly tossing the notes in the air and catching them, saw Shuldane glance quickly at Ault and begin to speak. Then he saw

Shuldane catch himself, and Ault said: "Oh, I'm not worried about waiting until morning. Woodbridge would rather cut off both his arms than slaughter any of the good hogs."

Shuldane relaxed.

Stranger-boy sauntered across toward the door, carelessly handling the notes in full view. But when he had crossed in front of Woodbridge, Arm Webster held out his hand with a grin.

"Wouldn't be goin' anywhere with those, would you, Young Tom?"

Stranger-boy abandoned the casual pose and broke for the door. But suddenly he was in mid-air over the extended boot of Emanuel Ault. The notes had been snatched out of his hand. Stranger-boy sprawled on the floor with both palms full of painful splinters. Ault bent over to pick up a piece torn from one of the notes. Suddenly his reddened face crashed into the floor as both of Woodbridge's huge fists pounded down on the back of his head.

Woodbridge dived for the notes that Ault dropped. But when he closed his hands over them, they were once removed from the notes by the thickness of a pair of hands belonging to Arm Webster.

Woodbridge's large hands completely enveloped Webster's and he crushed until he could feel Webster's hand bones mash against one another. But Webster held on.

With a great red strength surging up from a lifetime of threatened hopes, Woodbridge swung Webster by the hands like a wheat flail. The younger's man's body lashed through the air with a whipping sound to slap flat against the face of the bar. An instant later his heels cracked against the bar as his body was flattened there for a half a heart-beat before it thumped prone to the floor, limp.

The brutality brought Hosmer instantly in front of Woodbridge, who lunged for the notes.

Exeter stooped to pick up the notes that had rolled from Webster's flaccid hands. Woodbridge shoved Hosmer aside, but he was grabbed from the rear in the maddened bear grip of Ault's thick arms. Ault was strong, and his grip slipped only a little as Woodbridge surged from side to side. The grip held long enough for Fitchburg and Exeter and others to grab hold of Woodbridge.

Between breathless gasps Ault panted: "You'll be lucky—I leave a roof over your head—Woodbridge. Have 'em ready for me—'morrow morning!"

# Chapter 27: THE DROVER

IT was not the kind of thing that happened to people in Hosmer Village, not since the days of Isaac Shane. Stories like it had drifted up from county, from Boxford's Cabin, and from Columbus. But it did not happen to one's neighbors. And although the men talked about it in the tavern all through the following week, they spoke without conviction, as though they expected any minute to find that it was not true. They expected daily to hear some simple story which would explain away the whole mystery.

Veronica could not believe it was happening to her. Yet it was true enough.

Thomas Woodbridge and his hogs were gone.

Veronica found it equally difficult to believe the revelation which was being unfolded to her in her own house. But she was tempted to believe it for two reasons: the speaker was the most persuasive of men, and he was her father.

Elnathan Shuldane was a hard man to hate. The very incongruity of the mighty Shuldane in the role of humble supplicant lent sympathy to his plea, and he knew it.

His handsome face was tired, but he smiled, and Veronica had to credit him with courage. It was his due.

"My dear," he said, "I'm not asking you to tell me where he is."

"I tell you I don't know, Father."

He smiled and waved his hand.

"Perhaps. But I'm only asking that you tell the town he will bring the hogs back."

"But I have no idea that he will."

It must be said in Shuldane's behalf that he did not enjoy the guessing game with his daughter. For it was a mystic power of Veronica's that in her presence one wished to be honest. Something about her induced the feeling that any good act toward her would be recorded to one's favor in the ledgers of Kingdom Come. But at the moment

403

Shuldane could not afford to trade in futures. His life's work was at stake. He tried an assumption.

"How far," he ventured, "will a wagonload of corn take 186 hogs?"

"I don't know that he took a full wagonload of corn."

"If you know so little, you can tell the town you expect him back. Otherwise the hog notes Ault collected for me become worthless."

"I'm afraid that's not what you're interested in, Father. Because the town people will only honor those notes for their value in pork. That kind of trifling value won't do you any good."

"Veronica, I'm down to that now. I've been the biggest land gambler of them all. Everything I have is in these two townships of land. It was a good gamble. It still is. More settlers will come to buy. But meanwhile, just as the settlers owed me for the land, I owe the government. The Jeffersonians in the government have no love for my kind. They're pressing for payment. I have no funds."

Veronica studied him, searching for the truth. She was shaken.

"But if that's the case, pork money won't do you any good. Pork money doesn't come that big."

She talked herself out of her gullibility.

"No, Father, your interest in the notes isn't for the pork. You want Tom's herd alive."

"You've a hard opinion of me, Veronica."

"No, Father. I have a love for you, and a pity. You can't stop short of Tom's herd now. For these two townships you've invested a life. Not just for the townships, but for the control, the power. I think you'd like to stop now. I think you'd like to be just the gentle father of Mesopotamia. But you'll not stop at anything to hold the land now, because you've too much in it. I've seen you trample on smaller things than Tom's herd to get the land. You wouldn't hold back now."

"Veronica, even if I could find Tom, he'd never turn over those breeders to me. He's demonstrated that," said Shuldane, not without admiration.

"Then what sense to support the notes by lying to the town? They'll only honor them for the value of the pork."

"I'm down to where even that counts. Mesopotamia prime pork is not to be sneezed at. It might at least pay the interest I owe on the land."

"You're not that desperate, Father. And pork wouldn't pay a sixteenth of the interest."

Her words were true and hard, but she melted with sympathy for him as he sighed and stood up. His shoulders sagged into the good cloth of his coat. He reached for his hat and stood looking at the floor, resigned. He could have been waiting for her to relent. Or he could have been thinking.

"Well, at least, my dear," he ventured, "tell the people you're not moving to Indiana for a while."

"But I'm afraid we are. He'll send for us when—"

Her hand clapped to her mouth. She turned large brown accusing eyes on her father.

"Indiana," he repeated, and he left.

Shuldane covered his irritation. It was hard enough to bear the fact that Ault had become so bold as to enter the house freely and strut into the study, carrying himself like a partner; but when the crude agent presumed to speak of his daughter, it made Ault's price too high.

"No," snapped Shuldane. "She wouldn't promise to tell the town that Woodbridge would be back. But she probably won't say to the contrary, either. I don't think she's sure herself what's happening. Now where are the notes?"

Without handing over any notes, Ault said: "Then if we act quickly, we can unload these notes back on the village. But before I'll do that for you, you'll need to bring my pay up to date. And I'd rather have it in land than in your bank currency."

But it was not this easy to beat Shuldane down.

He flapped the pen down on his desk. His face was a stern reproach. "You surprise me, Ault!"

Ault stood rocking confidently on the balls of his feet.

"I picked you because I thought you were big enough. But I see you haven't lifted your ideas above where I found you, making a few paltry dollars on bounty warrants! I should have known! If you'd been big enough, you'd be the one who owned these two townships here. Instead of that, you settled for a small margin from me, and you're satisfied to be my agent. Do you want to be just that forever?"

Ault stopped rocking, his broad face torn between insult and greed. To see great visions is a great power. But Elnathan Shuldane had the still rarer power to pass the vision to others.

"How do you mean?" asked Ault.

"What exactly do you think you could get in the village for those notes?"

"Well, we could get walnut timber from Slasher, wool from the Emerson woman, ironwork from Stikes, salt from Fitchburg. We could get—"

"Ha!" Shuldane rose from his chair and gave Ault his back as he looked out the window. "A mess of pottage, Ault. Don't you know there are men in the country who will give a fortune for Woodbridge's hogs? Men who understand what he's done?"

"Where?"

"On the better farms in the West. On the rich farms. Woodbridge's own customers, for example. Marcusson in Indiana, and those Quakers. They understand what he's got."

Shuldane relented with a confidential smile.

"That's where Woodbridge is going, I'm sure. To Marcusson in Indiana."

An admiring grin began to break timorously over Ault's face.

"He's just saving me the problem of delivery," smiled Shuldane. "Because when he gets to Marcusson's place, I will be there ahead of him. I will have transferred the notes to Marcusson, explaining that Woodbridge is on his way with the stock. The sale will be completed when Woodbridge makes the delivery for us."

Ault was sheepish in admiration, and quick to obey Shuldane's imperious voice.

"Now let me prepare for the trip. I leave in the morning. See I have the notes with me."

It was not until Ault returned to his cabin that he regained his composure. Shuldane had not paid him. And if Shuldane were in Indiana, it would be hard for Ault to know exactly how much he got for the hog notes. It would be still harder to collect his share. In his cabin in the darkness he cursed his own weakness.

In the morning Shuldane was dressed for the road and mounted. Ault handed him the tanned calf's-ear pouch that contained the papers. Shuldane put it in his saddlebag and rode south.

Woodbridge did not ride. He walked, west.

It was lonely, but the loneliness did not bother him as he followed his hogs. It was extremely slow, paced to the waddle of Big Four, who led the column which walked ahead of Woodbridge. But the slowness did not bother him, nor did Captain Michael, who shuffled along silently at the head of the column. The nearly empty wagon rumbled along behind, and Woodbridge looked up at the sky. As the trail jogged and twisted, the clouds above Woodbridge jogged and twisted with his progress. Thomas Woodbridge had the world tuned to himself once more.

The country was flat, and as they moved west they more frequently came out from under the canopy of the big woods into small openings. The trail was a wagon axle wide, but obstructed by hearty second growth, for it had not been much used since it had served as General Harrison's supply trail against Tecumseh.

It was on the eastern edge of one of the clearings that Captain Michael raised his rifle over his head and stopped the column. Woodbridge came up to join Michael, who pointed with his rifle northwest to a long low log structure three times the length of an ordinary cabin, an old abandoned outpost.

"War house," explained Michael in typical detail.

"It's empty," said Woodbridge. "Let's keep moving."

"No! Look first." Michael began to move around the edge of the clearing, staying to the cover of the woods.

However, there was a sudden disturbance among the hogs. Big One skittered backward, buckling Woodbridge behind the knees so that his rifle fell among the animals. He recovered it quickly, but he did not rise, for a voice said, "Don't get up yet, mister."

Woodbridge looked into the black hole in the end of a Kentucky-type rifle. Looking to the north, he saw the apologetic expression of Captain Michael, who faced a similar threat. And to the east a third man rose up out of the undergrowth. The last took charge, addressing Woodbridge's captor.

"I got them, Amassa. Go on up and tell the old man we got pork enough for a regiment. Take these two with you."

The gun was in Woodbridge's back, and he walked beside Captain Michael into the gloomy interior of the low rambling hut. He found himself standing unarmed in the gloom before a bearded specter who ignored him while he washed his dirty feet in a clay bowl. An Indian woman took the bowl away and the washer pulled a pair of stiff buckskin leggings over his wet feet. While he laced them, he said, "Whattya got this time, Amassa?"

"Big column of hogs."

The leather-clad one continued lacing his leggings. As Tom's eyes grew accustomed to the darkness, he made out several other figures in the hut. One was inspecting stacks of trade goods. One was an elderly man with a wooden leg who sat at a crude desk writing painfully by the meager light of a narrow gun port.

"How many hogs?" asked the bearded one.

"A hell of a lot of 'em, and odd-lookin' critters," said Amassa. "Awful fat ones."

The leather-clad man snapped alert. He looked straight at Woodbridge, and then sprang up on elastic legs.

"Good God!" he said.

Woodbridge looked, and yelled, "Navarre!"

The man called Amassa was startled. But he quickly ran to the door and yelled out, "Better leave them hogs be!"

"What you doin' here, Slover?"

"Same as before. Only we're winning out here, Tom. We're gettin' land for the people, complete with titles. There's more comin' every day. Lot of 'em are men that was foreclosed in Ohio. Squattin' over here."

"What's the old man doin' over there with the quill?"

"Makin' out land titles and warrants."

"He's a land agent?"

"Might say so." Navarre grinned. "Least he worked in the government land office long enough to know how the Presidents all sign their names."

Woodbridge's jaw dropped slowly.

"He got a bad turn," continued Navarre. "He was custodian of the warrant books in Washington. One book got stole somehow. He got the blame."

Woodbridge was remembering what he'd heard about the trial of Navarre, and something about a Volume Four that was missing.

"Oh, don't worry about him," Navarre said slyly. "I figure to take good care of him. Kind of owe it to him, I figure."

"But the titles he makes out can't be—"

"Can't be challenged very easy," grinned Navarre, "him knowin' exactly what patent numbers were issued against the warrants that was pasted in Volume Four—which unfortunately is awful unhandy to check against, it being missin'."

Woodbridge grinned.

"And Loretta?" asked Woodbridge as he studied the young Indian woman.

"Back in Pittsburgh. Them that's headin' west and looks to be in need of warrants or titles, she tells 'em how to find me."

"How come you're located right here?"

"This is right on the boundary 'twixt Ohio and the new state of Indiana."

"That don't tell me anything," said Woodbridge.

"Boundary dispute. Awful hard to arrest a man if you don't know is he in Indiana or Ohio."

Woodbridge shook his head in appreciation.

"Will they ever get the land straightened out, Slover?"

Navarre sighed, and dismissed the impossible, heartbreaking riddle.

"Where you bound, Tom?"

"Marcusson Township, Indiana."

"Good man, Marcusson. What you goin' for?"

"For good."

The good humor left Navarre's bearded face.

"You're leavin' Sam and Asa and Hawkins and Blair and them?"

Woodbridge told the whole story. But Navarre seemed to listen without sympathy. By the middle of the story he was whittling a stick viciously. At the end he whurtled a bullet of tobacco juice out through a gun port and wiped his mouth with the back of his hand.

"Maybe, Tom. Maybe."

"Maybe what? I didn't ask ya nothin'!"

"But I dunno's it's workin' out so good for me," said Navarre irrelevantly.

"What, for God's sake?"

"Takin' the back way out."

The visit was soured.

Woodbridge accepted feed for his animals and some jerked venison for himself and Michael. Navarre seemed not to lack for corn, so Tom loaded up the wagon, which was nearly empty, and silently they resumed droving to the west.

Woodbridge looked up to see if the clouds still followed him, but the sky was overcast. Shortly it began to drizzle and later to pour, pelting down even through the thick overgrowth.

When Wolf returned to the Woodbridge development, Young Tom did not respond to the animal's ecstatic, excited greeting, for with peculiar concentration he was studying the Wolf's ragged coat, which was full of burrs. Stranger-boy stooped to pick the burrs out, and peevishly ordered the excited animal to stand still. But when he gripped the flanks, he softened his tone, for his hands sank deep into the fur before he could feel flesh. Wolf was all ribs.

There were patches where the fur was missing, and his right ear was ripped. Stranger-boy lifted the paws. They were worn pink on the bottom, and the claws were worn short. Wolf had come a long way.

The animal ate voraciously, and then clawed Young Tom's side and ran away, only to look back. Not being followed, he returned to stand up and paw Young Tom's chest. Then he ran away again, farther this time; but he returned, running in frenzied circles around Young Tom.

Keeping his eyes on the animal, Young Tom backed slowly to the shed for a length of rope. He tied Wolf to the shed while he went up into the school lands, returning in an hour with Silver Pigeon.

The preparations were simple. Young Tom put a copy of the *Tabulator* in his pocket, and took his rifle and two loaves of bread.

After borrowing Christian Kilgore's horse for Silver Pigeon, they untied Wolf, who led out the West Road, up north through the Gorge. Where the ruts bore to the left up toward Fort Tawa and the old Wyandot mission, Wolf went off the road even sharper left, westerly, up a creek bed that tunneled through a narrow cut.

"Short way to the old Harrison War Trail," said Pigeon. "Get off the horse."

They led the horses up the creek bed to a place where Wolf spiraled in ever-widening circles. He stopped repeatedly and stood stock-still. Then he resumed his circling with greater vigor. Finally he went up the left bank of the cut and headed still more westerly across a flat carpet of pine needles. Wolf raced quickly along under the lowest branches; but the men remained dismounted, fighting their way through dead, dry underbranches.

"Wolf! Wait!"

Their faces and hands were scratched, and the horses were irritable by the time they came upon a faint trace that seemed to head a little southwest.

"Don't see how he could get a wagon through there," said Young Tom.

"Could have divided the column. Sent the wagon around toward Tawa. Captain Michael would know a way. Hurry. The Wolf is already gone."

Since Colonel Shuldane knew that the food on the keelboat to Indiana would be foul, and the food on the road to Marcusson Township even worse, he lingered over his brandy and cigar at the Club of the Cincinnati. The former Revolutionary field-grade officers who comprised the club were many of them old men now. Most were dead. Many who had gone back into active service in 1812 had, instead of increasing their rank, lost it. Or, like Hull and others, they had come out embittered to find their glorious Revolutionary service records clouded by errors in a new type of warfare which demanded longer supply systems, longer marches; a war which put the old generals under upstarts from the Indian wars like Harrison, Croghan, Armstrong.

The only old-timers Shuldane found in the Cincinnati Club were ones like himself, who had been young enough for quick field commissions in the Revolution, smart enough to take advantage of the post-Revolution bounty warrants to build land empires, and old enough to guide the hand of Congress in protecting their empires. But such men had no time to swap leisure war stories at the Cincinnati Club. They had business to transact, for if the large holdings were to be kept intact against the Jeffersonian tendency to tax them away and to tighten government credit and sell in small parcels, then they must stay alert.

So the Cincinnati Club no longer offered chivalrous war stories murmured modestly in the language of sport. It offered only good food and a place to trade.

For Shuldane, tonight, it meant only food, or so he thought until he recognized at a table to his right the editor of the Cincinnati *Western Spy*. The editor faced Shuldane, but did not see him, for he talked earnestly across his table to a man whom Shuldane recognized from the back as Colonel David Marcusson. And while Shuldane seemed to be relaxing as he stared aloft into his cigar smoke, he was instead very much alert.

Marcusson was saying: "I thought you'd be interested. I come representing a group of forward-looking Indiana farmers. We've organized a state agricultural society and we're going to import the best stock. Legislature set off eight Indiana townships to pay for it."

The editor made some notes and asked, "But specifically what brings you to Ohio, Colonel Marcusson?"

"I'm going up the Miami River to Mesopotamia. Farmer name of Woodbridge."

As Marcusson leaned forward eagerly and lowered his voice, Shuldane could catch only a few fragments: "I'm empowered to offer him . . . goes to three hundred, four hundred pounds . . . finishes off firm on just corn . . . come from as far as Illinois Territory just to look at these animals."

The editor took voluminous notes, shook hands with Marcusson, and left.

If Shuldane had been a lesser man, he would have been sitting at Marcusson's table an hour later. Instead, Marcusson was sitting at Shuldane's, and the latter was saying, "Yes, Tom is this minute droving the hogs west."

"To my place?" asked Marcusson with unskillful pleasure which undercut any bargaining position he might have had.

"Well," Shuldane blew a cloud of smoke and studied it, "yes, in a way. We planned to stop at your farm. I was to meet him there, in fact, to see if you were interested in any of the hogs before we delivered them to the Quakers. We've had a fine offer—in fact, I must say, a spectacular offer."

Marcusson's face clouded.

"The Quakers are fine people," said Marcusson, "and excellent husbandmen. But they work clannishly. They might hold the Mesopotamia hog among themselves until the price rose beyond our average farmer."

Shuldane pushed out his lower lip thoughtfully. "I can see your problem," he sympathized.

"The object of our agricultural society is to make breeding boars available to the small-acre man and lift the whole level of stock in the state. Be sure you come to my place first. We can make you a good offer."

Shuldane nodded with reserve.

"But you say *we*," probed Marcusson. "Are you and Tom together now? Can you deliver ownership of Tom's hogs?"

Shuldane produced the calf's-ear purse and pulled out two of Woodbridge's hog notes. Marcusson studied the endorsements.

"It surprises me that Tom would share control of his herd, Colonel. With no disrespect to you, I'd like to wait and talk to him."

Shuldane was suddenly astonishingly agreeable to the suggestion, and he hastened to put away the leather case containing the rest of the notes.

"I'll return at once to Marcusson Township and wait for Tom and the herd," said Marcusson.

Shuldane seemed not to hear, and his dark face was turning red. "Very well," he said, controlling himself with amazing discipline in view of the shocking condition which he found in the calf's-ear purse. He had just discovered that the top two notes and the bottom two were the only ones in the purse. The rest of the contents of the packet was blank slips of paper. Totally blank.

"Perhaps you and Tom can settle matters together," said Shuldane. "As a matter of fact, I could well improve the time by returning to Mesopotamia, where I should talk to Mr. Ault, my agent—rather, my former agent."

Stranger-boy and Pigeon overtook the column of hogs a half-day's ride west of Navarre's cabin. Woodbridge was glad to see them.

"I lost four of them along the way," he explained, "and they're all down in weight, but not so bad I couldn't fatten 'em up in eight, ten days of good feed. We must of come a hundred ten, twenty miles already." He noticed the boy's lack of response. "You mean to tell me that ain't pretty good, boy?"

"It's good, Tom. But the whole thing's wrong. We got to turn around."

The calm statement was so staggering that Woodbridge knew he had misheard. As they walked along, he glanced sideways at the boy's earnest, troubled face, and continued.

"Now that we've found we can walk 'em over a hundred mile, there'll be no stoppin' us. Right, boy?"

"There'll be no stoppin' us, Tom. But we've got to turn around and go back."

"I thought I heard wrong before," bristled Tom. "When did you start sayin' what we got to do and got not to do?"

Stranger-boy's face fought with itself as his wrinkled forehead apologized for his resolute jutting chin.

"I asked since when do you decide about the hogs?" Woodbridge prodded.

"Since I promised they'd return, Tom," answered Stranger-boy. "I promised in front of them all at the store. Exeter was pokin' fun at the notes, and I said the notes would be worth everything writ on the face of them."

"How'd you come to fret yourself about my word?" snorted Woodbridge.

"Exeter was laughing at Ault," explained Young Tom. "He offered Ault a half-cent glass of whisky for one of your hog notes. They were all laughin', and makin' more jokes like that."

"Y'needn't of stewed on my account for a joke from Exeter."

"I didn't. But Miss Veronica was there and it peeved her, so's she spoke out and allowed the note was worth everything it said on the front of it. Exeter laughed and he said maybe Mrs. Woodbridge would like to redeem the note right there and then. Miss Veronica didn't have nothin' to make good with, and she got kind of wet-eyed."

"Huh!"

"So I reached in my pocket where I had the United States Bank notes that Ault wouldn't take on my mortgage. I threw a handful of 'em on the counter and said we'd redeem that note all right."

"You God-damned fool! U.S. Bank money you gave for that hog IOU?"

"It stopped the laughin'."

"I can't help your foolishness, boy," said Woodbridge, not unkindly.

But at that moment Stranger-boy looked ahead to see Captain Michael and Silver Pigeon starting the hogs across a small stream with some difficulty. He yelled: "Never mind that, Pigeon! We're turnin' around anyhow! Turn 'em back!"

The presumptuous order snapped Woodbridge's head toward the boy in disbelief and brought the red flooding up under his freckles.

"What are you saying?" Woodbridge turned to the Indians and yelled, "Send 'em across!"

But the Indians stood bewildered, because Young Tom yelled: "Turn 'em around, Pigeon! Like I said!"

His last words ended in a grunt, for Woodbridge's great red hand landed flat on his chest and grabbed a handful of his shirt. The hand twisted relentlessly so that the leather of the boy's shirt forced him to his knees.

From his humiliating position, looking up, he yelled in heedless defiance: "I'm sorry, Tom. But they're goin' back, no matter what!"

The complacent challenge curdled Woodbridge's blood, and he brought his flat hand across Stranger-boy's face in unhinged passion. Though it left a white handprint outlined in red, it was one of those futile, insulting blows which do not hurt the flesh so much as they sting the soul.

Stranger-boy's fist thudded impulsively against Woodbridge's chest. Hate and rage foamed to a splenetic thunderhead in Woodbridge, and he abandoned himself to his vindictive fists, which pounded against the boy's upraised forearms. One blow crushed through to the boy's chest, sprawling him on his back.

Stranger-boy regained his feet, still yielding backward.

Shock gave way in the boy's face to grim stubbornness, and he began to return the blows, awkwardly at first; but the lad was strong, and a boyhood of loneliness released itself in wild crashing blows that gradually backed Woodbridge off and bruised him into the defensive.

Woodbridge stumbled backward under the punches so fast that he fell. The boy was on him with his fist raised and quivering and his knee in the redhead's chest. Tom grabbed a short log and swung. It was rotten and broke behind the boy's neck; Woodbridge was on his feet, swinging hard but increasingly slower punches as Stranger-boy gasped, "They're goin' back, Tom! You hear? Back!"

Pigeon raced toward the fight, but Captain Michael's outstretched moccasin sent him sprawling.

"No!" warned Michael sternly. "Every tribe choose own chief!"

Woodbridge's breath came in rasping gasps now. His arms were heavy. He stumbled once more. Stranger-boy's fists were rocks. Woodbridge could only raise his heavy forearms to shield his head. He staggered backward against a tree. There was water in the boy's eyes and abandon in his right fist. Woodbridge ducked. Stranger-boy's fist jarred into the tree. A bow string twanged up the length of his arm, which went limp at his side.

Woodbridge instantly grabbed the dangling wrist and twisted it up behind the boy's back and shoved him toward the tree. It was hard work, and the redhead's ire was spent. He wanted rest. But he jammed Stranger-boy against the tree, braced his feet, and raised his fist.

But the fist never fell. Stranger-boy struck too deep.

"You hit 'em in the back, all right!" the boy panted. "Ault's givin' your damned notes back to the townsmen!"

Woodbridge jerked Stranger-boy around to face him.

"For God's sake! Are the fools acceptin' them?"

"Yeah. They're takin' 'em. Hosmer, Stikes, Fitchburg, Mason. They're takin' your notes in exchange for honest goods—timber, salt, whisky, ironwork."

Woodbridge let go the wrist, and the two men stood swaying face to face.

"Why? Why?"

"They figure you'll make good on 'em somehow. The poor fools. Hosmer made a speech. He said so."

As his chest heaved from his exertion, Woodbridge stood with his feet planted wide apart, swaying. Hosmer passed before his eyes, leading the townsmen out to his place to rebuild the cabin that Tom had burned as an Indian signal. Stikes, with his white hair singed from fighting the field fire at the Woodbridge place on the day of the taxing, led a column of captured Bedford hogs up to the No. 1 pen. Woodbridge could see Jim Hawkins, too, after the Rontondee raid, taking home two of the Bedford hogs that Woodbridge couldn't feed. He saw Asa Buttrick reading a petition to the county commissioners to make the Woodbridge Strip into a good road.

He thought he could see Hawkins and Adams and Mitchell and Stikes and Hosmer putting his hog notes in their jeans, with perhaps a shade of doubt, but with a shrug. He saw them handing the notes to their wives for safekeeping. He saw Faith Hawkins accepting the note reluctantly from Jim, demanding an explanation. He thought he could see Hawkins motion her quiet and go about his business.

Woodbridge called to Captain Michael, but he could not raise enough voice from his parched mouth over his deep breathing. He flung a hunk of rotten log to splatter near the hogs, attracting Michael's attention from the business of keeping them herded. He raised a heavy arm overhead and motioned to the east.

The mass of hogs swarmed in a swirling circle which picked up speed. Michael drove his staff into the ground in front of Big Two and yelled. The swirling circle of hogs uncoiled into a narrow column which rumbled back onto the trail—eastbound.

Slover Navarre set them to a meal such as Tom Woodbridge had never had. The Indian woman did some wonderful thing to the hunks of venison which Navarre's roughnecks took for granted. Though he noticed they did not take her for granted.

But Navarre had a greater treat than the venison for Woodbridge after the meal. The others, except for the woman, left the hut. Navarre took Tom to the table where the clerk's papers were.

"Tom, when your boy went through on his way back to Mesopotamia, I showed him this. He said to be sure and show you when you came through."

Navarre handed Woodbridge a copy of the Cincinnati *Western Spy*. "One of the men brought it up yesterday. Read that."

As Woodbridge labored through the article, a wondrous smile spread over his face. For the *Western Spy* editor had written a story about an amazing breed of hog which was bringing fabulous prices in Indiana, sired by a great boar named Big Two. He read the article twice.

Navarre took credit for Woodbridge's smile, and he said, "He's right, isn't he, Tom?"

But Woodbridge's smile faded. It was costing him to turn back east. It was not too late to turn west again, especially if they felt this way about his hogs in Indiana.

"Sure he's right, Slover," said the redhead thoughtfully. "It's the best hog in the country. Gains a pound a day if it's fed right."

Navarre's smile faded and then returned, together with a chuckle.

"Naw, you read the wrong article. I figured you knew all about your own hogs. This one here."

Woodbridge read the one Navarre indicated:

"MESOPOTAMIA EDITOR OPPOSES
WEBSTER FOR LEGISLATURE SEAT

"Jonathan Blair, Mesopotamia newspaper editor and attorney, will attempt to defeat Armitage Webster of the same place for the legislative seat. Blair is the man who has claimed that he can rectify the financial calamity by legislation which will foster a reversal of the balance of trade. He claims that western men can pull themselves out of this mire by finding products to ship east for gold. He proposes to tax Federal Banks here as a temporary source of revenue and with the hope of driving them out of the state, since he claims they contribute to the impoverishing drainage of hard money from the West by their refusal to honor western paper.

"Mr. Blair's scheme, though little understood, is not without merit, we think. But Blair will not see the inside of the new state-house at Columbus, for he is matched against the nephew of Colonel Elnathan Shuldane. Older subscribers will remember that Blair, as a young attorney, failed Shuldane and the large land-holding block of Symmes, Dayton, Steuben, and others in an important court assignment over the trial of William Hogland, Squatter Governor.

"Though he was once considered the agent of large eastern land-holders, Blair's voting and his recommendations on taxing of absentee owners and his opposition to the Federal Bank have put him in disfavor with his own sponsors. He has at the same time been rendered ineffective to the opposition party, who are not able to trust his reversal."

"Why didn't you tell me the boy was in trouble?" asked Navarre. "He's right as he can be. The West has got to ship stuff east and demand gold. Same time we got to stop buyin' eastern goods and payin' out gold. It's like he says. It don't balance out."

What never made sense from the lips of Jonathan Blair seemed like a flash of wisdom from Slover Navarre.

"See what he's sayin', Tom? Buy with paper and sell for gold. That's what the East is doin' to us. They got us chiseled down to nothin'. Then they send out a U.S. Bank that won't honor western paper but insists on gold when they sell us eastern stuff or government land."

"Yeah," said Woodbridge slowly, "but we got nothin' to sell to the East. What have we got they can't get cheaper at home?"

"Blair's got it figured. He's a smart man, Tom."

"Don't seem so smart as I used to think, Slover."

"How so?"

"He's not doin' so good. Shuldane's got him whipped. Even young Webster's got him whipped, like it says there."

"That bad, eh?"

"Even I whipped him once, if you remember."

"Don't take too much credit on yourself for that, Woodbridge. You didn't whip him with your brains. Blair's not a meat and potatoes critter like you and me. Blair's a kind of—he's a heady sort of critter."

"Huh!" Woodbridge snorted in annoyance. "For that matter, you saw him get whipped at your own trial! What call have you got to stand up for him?"

"More'n you think, Tom. Don't ever think Blair got whipped at my trial."

"He lost, didn't he? You got off free!"

"That's what I mean. That law fella they put on my side couldn't 'uv defended his own mother."

"But he beat Blair!!"

Navarre sat staring at Woodbridge with a grin that was close to contempt.

"You blind fool, Woodbridge! Is that what all you people think?"

"Think? We know. Blair got beat by your law fella."

"Blair never got beat by nobody except Blair. Blair got beat because he was feedin' the questions out so that even that numskull they gave me could see how to answer. And the ones he couldn't figure out, I could. Blair laid it out so clear that even Shuldane could see what he was doin'."

Woodbridge was silent. As he looked back over Blair's career, he could see it all now. It explained a lot. But suddenly his humility vanished, and he charged: "Well, blast him, it's his own fault! If he wanted to get you free, why'd he pick a sneakin' way like that to do it? Why didn't he stand up like a man and tell Shuldane he was quittin' the case?"

Navarre's cheek bulged with tobacco and criticism.

"Took more of a man the way he did it, because he's smart. If he resigned the case, they'd just put in another lawyer—one that could beat that timberhead that was defendin' me. Blair knew that."

There was a long silence while the truth soaked into Woodbridge.

"Blair's smart," continued Navarre. "Smart enough to figure out about the balance of trade, and smart enough to do somethin' about it for the people, if the people are smart enough to put him in the legislature."

"But they aren't," said Woodbridge dully. "The people think like I think."

Navarre called for Fawn, and when the Indian woman came he spoke a short sentence to her in Wyandot. To Woodbridge he said, "When you start back tomorrow, I'm goin' with you, Woodbridge."

"Why?"

"There's a lot of people can be made to think like I think."

But Woodbridge didn't start back the next day. Big One's skin was usually packed so full of hog that her bristles stood out like spines. But now her coat sagged, and she was listless and thin. Woodbridge laid over two days and fed the herd heavily on Navarre's corn.

Stranger-boy reached the Woodbridge place in Mesopotamia from the rear. In the three-sided enclosure between the shed and the old house and the new addition, he dismounted quickly and ran under the archway between the original east cabin and west cabin. But with his hand on the door he stopped, for in front of the house he saw Mr. Shuldane's large black stallion tied.

He softly opened the kitchen door a crack. There was no one inside, though Mr. Shuldane's and Miss Veronica's voices came through from the new part of the house. But what surprised him in the kitchen was the bareness of the corner shelves. And in the center of the kitchen stood several kegs and a large chest packed with household goods. As he stood with the door open, he strained to pick up the voices.

"I'll be ready when he sends for me, Father."

"You're a fool to go out there, Veronica. It's nothing but woods. You've been through it once."

"I know it. That's why I don't want Elizabeth to go through it. I want you to keep her in the big house in the village She likes Arm. They'll be good with each other. They'll have a good life."

"All right, Veronica. Mrs. Hussong will move in with us as full-time housekeeper. She can look out for Elizabeth."

So intently was Stranger-boy listening that he didn't hear Arm Webster and Zabeth drive up, and he was caught at the door. To divert the impression, he began closely examining the door, as if he'd found something wrong with it. Webster laughed at his effort.

Zabeth ran to him with excitement.

"Young Tom!"

It pleased Young Tom that she was so glad to see him. There was an awkwardness as she put her hands on his shoulder, then on his arm. There had never been established any system for greeting her brother after an absence, for there had so rarely been an occasion.

"Did you find Pap?" she asked.

"Yeah. He's coming back."

Zabeth ran into the house. "Mam, you can unpack! Pap's comin' back!"

Veronica's face lighted up as she saw Young Tom. She rose and came to him.

"He's headin' back, Miss Veronica."

She looked with concern at Stranger-boy's torn clothing. He put his scarred knuckles in his pocket when she looked at his hands, but not before Shuldane saw them.

"The hogs with him?" asked Shuldane.

Stranger-boy wasn't quite sure what might be going through Shuldane's mind.

"Can't say for sure, Mr. Shuldane," he answered.

"What do you mean? Have you seen him?"

"Yeah. I've seen him."

"Then are the hogs coming back with him or not?"

"Who knows what Tom might do between then and when he gets here?"

"Damn it, boy! Give me a straight answer!"

Stranger-boy presented a problem to Shuldane. What can you do with a man who's so low he has nothing to lose and nothing to gain? Stranger-boy gave a broad blank face to Shuldane, neither hostile nor obsequious.

It was that same afternoon that Stranger-boy faced the problem directly. When he entered Hosmer's Store, a large group was assembled there. They all looked at Stranger-boy as he entered, but they did not interrupt Shuldane to greet the boy. And Shuldane was like a father to the group.

"I want to make good for my son-in-law," he was saying. "The village is like a family to me, as you know."

Shuldane paused, and Polly Stikes's eyes blinked back the dampness of sympathy for the lonely man. Some remembered Veronica's leaving him, and reflected that Nate Shuldane had indeed had a lonely life.

"For that reason," he continued, "I must warn you of something which has happened, and explain how I intend to mend it. It's my fault, in a way."

Shuldane looked at Emanuel Ault with a cryptic grin, and for the first time Mesopotamia noticed a lack of composure on Ault's face, a combination of fear and humility and uneasiness, as if for the first time he was not sure of what would happen.

"Mr. Ault, here, during my absence has made purchases from most of you. You were good enough to accept my son-in-law's hog notes for the goods. Now, suddenly, it appears that Tom Woodbridge will not be back to honor those notes."

Blair studied the master with honest confusion on his face.

Ault studied Shuldane with self-reproach. He had allowed Shuldane to forgive him for stealing the notes, and under the charm of Shuldane's magnanimous forgiveness he had joined forces with him again. But now he wondered if he had been wise.

"I should like to take up these notes from you under any system you find agreeable. I can't let my family default to the town."

There was a stir of conversation in the room in response. Mesopotamia was touched.

Stranger-boy looked around the room. He was surprised that a few words could so cloud the issue. He didn't realize that it was not the few words that were so telling. It was years of reputation and kept promises that Shuldane was trading on. Young Tom stepped to the middle of the store.

"Don't give up the notes!"

It gave him their attention. He was not even self-conscious, for he spoke from urgency.

"Don't let go of those notes to Mr. Shuldane! Tom's coming back! That's why Mr. Shuldane wants the notes. Tom's coming back!"

"But are the hogs comin' with him?" asked Fitchburg.

Stranger-boy looked at Shuldane, who was waiting for the answer with interest.

"Yes."

"When?" asked Exeter.

"He should be here tomorrow or day after, I'd think," said Stranger-boy.

Others questioned him. Faith Hawkins asked about Veronica's packing up. Shuldane relaxed and let the argument continue. When the boy had them pretty well convinced that Woodbridge would return, Shuldane said with persuasive composure: "I cast no aspersions on the boy's sincerity. I think he believes what he says, and I admire his devotion to Woodbridge. That's as it should be. But I'm afraid the boy has not seen this."

Shuldane pulled a copy of the *Western Spy* from his pocket and shoved it across the counter.

Sam Hosmer read about the great value of the Mesopotamia hog in Indiana. It seemed to explain clearly enough where Tom Woodbridge would be.

"What about this, boy?" he asked.

"I know about that!" said Stranger-boy. "Tom knows about it. But I tell you he'll be back! I can promise he'll be back! I know!"

For the next three days Stranger-boy watched anxiously to the west. Mesopotamia watched Stranger-boy.

Captain Michael led the column of hogs as they approached Mesopotamia. Wolf ran on both sides of the column, nipping at adventurous pigs that strayed, heckling sluggish ones that hung back. Woodbridge and Slover Navarre walked at the rear of the hogs. Their horses and Tom's wagon followed them. They were approaching the turn where the Harrison Trail intersected the Gorge Road, where they could turn south into Mesopotamia.

Woodbridge had been quiet and thoughtful most of the way. Now he asked questions like a man trying to sell himself something.

"You figure Blair's right, then? You figure they got gold in the East, Slover, and they'll give it out?"

"They won't give it out unless we got somethin' they got to have, and until we're standin' where we can say, 'Gold or nothin'.' "

"These hogs look pretty good, considerin' they walked over two hundred miles," said Woodbridge irrelevantly.

"How do I know, Woodbridge? A hog's a hog in my sight."

Captain Michael up ahead had reached the fork. He started to turn south, Big Four lumbering along behind him.

Woodbridge cupped his hands to his mouth and threw his voice against the wind. "Take the left fork, Michael!"

Captain Michael stopped and looked back, puzzled. The hogs closed up toward the head of the column.

"No," answered Michael. "Right fork."

"Left fork, I said!"

Pigeon rode his horse back to Woodbridge.

"Mr. Tom, the right fork goes into Mesopotamia. The left goes up toward Fort Tawa."

"But it hooks into the trace from the East, doesn't it? Goes northeast along the Greenville Line and towards Pittsburgh, doesn't it?"

"That's right, sir, but—"

Woodbridge put one hand to his mouth again. With his left hand he pointed northeast.

"Take the left fork!" he yelled.

Michael unslung his rifle from his shoulder and carried it across the front of him, alert.

The column turned northeast.

# *Chapter 28: THE LIAR*

As he walked toward the store, Young Tom saw Exeter step out of the tavern and angle toward the store also. He felt a sudden hush from the direction of Stikes's forge, and he realized that Stikes had suddenly stopped pounding. He saw Stikes casually unstrap his leather apron and idle toward the store. He sensed a flicker of curtain in the Buttrick house, and presently Buttrick was converging with the others toward the store.

Young Tom was puzzled, not because they thought he was lying, but because under their silent inquisition he began to *feel* like a liar. But he guessed it was the same as when Mr. Shuldane told a lie and felt in his heart that he was telling the truth.

He made Veronica's purchases in the store and turned to leave. But Fitchburg said, "You still say he's comin' back, boy?"

"Yeah."

"Joe Hussong rode in over the West Road this morning. Said he crossed no signs of Tom."

"Can't help what Joe says. Tom'll be here. Today likely."

"You been sayin' that five days now."

" 'Twould be only natural if Tom stopped to rest the hogs a day or two."

The boy dropped off Veronica's goods at the house. Then he walked slowly to the top of the Gorge, giving his hopes more time to come true. But as he stared through the Gorge and up the road to the north, he saw no column on the deserted road. He moved north a few steps and then a few steps more to uncover a little more of the horizon. But he stopped the fruitless procedure.

His back itched under his coarse woven shirt, and he started to pull it off over his head. But when he did so, a breath-taking pain stopped him. Awkwardly, with his hand, he felt his back up under his shirt. The infected abrasion from the fight with Tom had become attached to his shirt again. He knelt by the source of the Gorge stream and wet his hand. He placed his wet hand in the middle of his shirt back, but he couldn't quite reach the place. And as he worked thus clumsily, Zabeth's voice caught him in the graceless position.

"Got a bite?"

He colored.

"Somethin'."

"You come up to look for Pap?"

"Yeah."

"You sure he's comin'?"

"Yeah."

"Then why do you fret about it?"

"Shouldn't, I guess, seein' I'm sure."

Stranger-boy moved away to let her dip a drink from the spring, but she wasn't approaching for water.

"Stand still," she said. "Let's see what's on your back."

He moved away as she reached for his shirt. But seeing the surprised look on her face, he realized the presumption of the motion. After all—a sister. He pointed awkwardly to the place on his back; and if he rolled his shoulders forward to give more breadth to his back, well, she didn't notice. She quickly rolled the shirt up under his raised arms until he straightened in pain.

Then she rolled it more slowly, pursing her lips.

"O-oh. Kneel down," she said.

The fabric was meshed into the abrasion from the fight along with grains of soil and the points of pine needles. An angry white-rimmed inflammation circled the place.

She worked slowly, extricating a thread at a time, unaware that her hands lightly touching his back from time to time sent ripples racing over him. From her concentration she asked, "How'd it happen?"

"Fell."

He felt her hands stop suddenly on his back.

"No," she stated. "Not likely."

Her hands resumed their work, and he felt the shirt let go.

"Now pull it off," she ordered. The shirt came off over his head.

Her cool left palm hovered lightly over his back as her right hand sopped water on the abrasion.

"Hurt?"

"No." He said no more lest it be obvious that to him the treatment was worth a little pain. From his bowed-forward position, with his hands braced on his knees, he could see her skirt swishing this way and that behind him, reflecting the energy with which she now washed the whole area of his back to prevent further infection.

"Stand up straight," she ordered, and though it was an impersonal command, as to Wolf, it was more concern for his person than Stranger-boy had ever experienced before. She bustled around him now, arranging a bandage which she had torn from the bottom of his shirt.

"You need a new shirt anyhow. Raise your arms now."

The strip just barely reached around Stranger-boy's chest, and she stood in front of him tying the knot with the little bit of overlap. He looked down at the straight part in the top of her hair.

Her face was matter-of-fact, just as he had seen it when she concentrated on currying the horse; still, her efforts were expended on him, and her concern suddenly made her something he wanted for life. He wanted the business-like face, the round brown arms, and whatever mystery it was that filled the dress so vibrantly full of life so close to him. He wanted the cool busy fingertips that occasionally touched him below his ribs with exasperating lightness. He wanted the matter-of-fact spirit of her that set about repairing any part of him as though he were a possession of hers to be tended. He gazed down at her in deep absorption.

"You still didn't tell me the truth about your back," she said, without looking up from her work. "Nor about the scabs on your knuckles."

Stranger-boy's breathing snapped apart her bandage knot for the third time.

"Hold your breath in for a minute," she said, struggling with the knot. "Could it be that you and Pap had words—or worse?"

She looked up in annoyance to see what caused the pulsatory drumming of his chest and to ask what held his tongue. He saw the instant of surprise on her face; but the question was pressed out of her softly against Stranger-boy's chest, and the breath of her own words reflected warm against her own cheeks from the face of Stranger-boy, whose lips closed over her mouth.

She stiffened in surprise and pushed against him. Her struggle was ineffectual, but he let her go.

If she had sputtered or scolded it would have helped. Instead she snatched the parted ends of the bandage together, jabbed the pin of a dress ornament through them, and left with resolute finality.

Stranger-boy flooded with regret as he watched her go, for he'd owned more of her before than he ever would again. Henceforth he would be to her not even a brother.

When Zabeth had changed back into her doeskin skirt and shirt, Veronica looked up from her sewing with displeasure.

"You'd best think about putting those things aside for good now, Elizabeth."

"I prefer 'em."

Zabeth saw the shadow cross Veronica's face.

"Aw, Mam, it's not that the dresses you made aren't awful fine; it's just these suit me better."

There was a lot Mam didn't know about. A lot that went right by her all her life, Zabeth thought. Mam was that kind of person. People just naturally looked out for her pretty much. Even when they froze her down because she wouldn't let Tom's hogs go during the war, they were partways admiring her for fighting for Tom's property. And even now, with Pap gone so long and no word from him, nobody pried much under what little she gave out.

The wide-eyed part of Mam sometimes nerved up Zabeth, like now, when Mam sat so patiently sewing up Pap's old blue shirt.

"What makes you think it's worth sewing, Mam?"

"It has a year or two in it yet."

"I mean, will he ever be back for it?"

Veronica dropped the work into her lap and looked reproachful.

"I only mean it's tarnation funny, Pap not being here. And everybody saying . . . "

"Saying?"

"Well, wondering."

Veronica's face took on some severity, and Zabeth suddenly realized Mam was going on forty. It was the only time you thought about it much.

"Zabeth, your father will not leave us in trouble."

"I'm sorry, Mam."

But Zabeth could see Pap boiling off in a good mad and not coming back. Mam couldn't see that. Zabeth wondered if Pap could be two different people, one kind of man to her mother, another kind to herself. In fact, could it be that every person is what you think he is, which is different from what everyone else thinks? No. Because look at Young Tom.

It was no good to talk of things like that with Mam. Mam didn't know much, lately.

Veronica watched her daughter walk back and forth in the cabin, and said, "You came running down from the Gorge a minute ago."

"Um-hm." Zabeth stopped walking.

"Stranger-boy back yet?"

"Why—why I don't know, Mam."

"Elizabeth, Arm Webster was by. Said he and your grandfather would like it if you'd come in to supper tonight."

Zabeth received the news with genuine enthusiasm.

"But you'll have to dress up."

"I will. I will."

Veronica watched her daughter hurry to prepare, and she smiled hopefully. Young Webster, she hoped, could make an evening interesting.

Young Tom had no errand of importance in the store, but he had come in principally because the men seemed to expect that he would not come in. He was conscious of Sam Hosmer's scrutiny as he fended questions.

"If you don't believe me, you can ride out the trail and meet him," said Young Tom.

"We've already been out that way, some of us," said Fitchburg, "and didn't see him. Could be, though, we took the wrong trail." Fitchburg lowered his voice and spoke like a man sneaking up to pull the string on a wild turkey trap. "Could be," he said, "that Tom's in trouble, and maybe you'd ought to lead us out to where he is. Tomorrow."

The silence begged for an answer.

"All right," he conceded.

But then his eyes lighted up.

"But perhaps you won't want to go. Because here comes Silver Pigeon. He was with them."

Pigeon entered the store. He carried himself now among white men with a bold assurance not altogether pleasing to Hosmer Village, but conducive to respect. It was almost as though he remembered the days of the mission and some unreturned favors.

Stranger-boy walked forward to grasp him eagerly by the arm and shoulder.

"Pigeon, tell the men where Tom is and when he'll be here!"

Pigeon looked around the room and then at Stranger-boy as though he didn't understand.

"Just tell them that Tom's on his way back," said Young Tom.

"What does Pigeon know about Tom?" asked the Indian.

Stranger-boy stared at his friend in disbelief. Then he pleaded: "Pigeon, don't you understand? Just tell the men where Tom is!"

"Why should Pigeon know?"

A buzz of conversation broke out in the room.

Pigeon's face was an exasperating blank of bronze.

Aaron Fitchburg rolled his insinuation slowly into the middle of the expectant hush that fell over the store.

"Looks like we'll be wantin' you to lead us out there, Stranger-boy," he drawled, "like we were just sayin'. We'll come by the house to-morrow."

Young Tom had ridden halfway home when Silver Pigeon caught up to him. It took the space of a mile before the Indian could get Young Tom to listen to him.

"Don't you see what I'm doing, Stranger-boy?"

"Yeah. Makin' me a liar in front of Mr. Blair and Mr. Hosmer."

"I bring a message, Stranger-boy. Tom says to load the small cart with corn and come with him. He's north of here. Eastbound over the Cuyahoga Trace."

Stranger-boy stopped.

"Eastbound?"

"He says nobody's to know. You're to come."

"What about Miss Veronica and—"

"And your sister?"

"Yes."

"Tom said you'd know what to do."

"Where's he going?"

"To the East. All the way east."

"Pigs can't walk so far."

"No. That is true," agreed the Indian.

"There is no way to feed them, either."

"No. No way to feed them."

"No one has ever driven pigs so far. It can't be done."

"No. It cannot," said Pigeon without expression.

"Then why?" asked Stranger-boy. "Why?"

Pigeon shrugged. "Like the hog itself," he said. "It is impossible for any man to raise a hog that grows so fat."

Stranger-boy grinned.

"Come on," he said.

When Fitchburg and Mason and Exeter stopped by next morning, asking for Young Tom, Zabeth found that he was neither in the shed nor in his room. His bed had not been slept in.

The men looked at each other in a conspiracy of silence that ratified their suspicions. They rode back to Mesopotamia.

It was a strange procession that moved east across Ohio: two Indians, three white men, two horses and wagons, a wolf that acted like a dog, and a long column of extraordinarily huge brown and white hogs.

The column moved very slowly. Woodbridge estimated their rate of travel at ten miles a day. Infrequently they would come to a small cluster of five or six cabins. At such times the settlers would come out to marvel at the size of the unusual hogs and to ask where they were from and where they were going.

Invariably they would exclaim when Woodbridge gave his destination, saying that it would be impossible to drive hogs so far. Some would cite instances of men who had driven cattle half the distance with severe loss of weight and numbers. But halfway through these explanations they would become aware that the square-faced, ageless redhead was not listening. From under the bleached eyebrows the unresting blue eyes would be playing ceaselessly back and forth over the backs of the strange hogs, as if counting.

While the wayside advisers talked to him, the redheaded one with the big hands would chomp on whatever food they had given him and his crew. And while the others sat down to eat, the redhead would remain standing. He would occasionally raise a long arm and point, perhaps with a knife blade full of steaming potato, to some wriggling in the bushes. The old Indian would then shamble off into the brush where the redhead had pointed. There would be grunting agitation in the foliage, half Indian and half animal, and a snorting, chastened hog would lumber reluctantly back to the herd. And all the while the redhead ceaselessly watched; forever counting, checking, examining.

Occasionally the preoccupied redhead would split the air with some odd name like "Samson" or "Big Ten" or "Rosebud." And then, incredibly, from all that sea of hog rumps, one curious head would rise from the greedy feeding. The redheaded one would fold back the hog's flopping ears and look into the animal's eyes. He would force open the great jaws and examine the tusks. He would feel the flanks, and occasionally he would give an order for one to be hoisted into the wagon and the wagon to be bedded with straw.

The settler women along the route watched whenever this happened, and smiled at the tenderness of the rough redhead for his animals. The men, however, watched with something like awe. In the man's caressing care of his hogs they saw, not tenderness, but an unbelievable hardness akin to greed. The redhead hardly noticed the straining of his men to hoist a 450-pound sow into the wagon, but his face and shoulders twitched with concern for the hog. And suddenly, while the settlers and the drovers were just settling to the exchange of tobacco and lighting up, the redhead would yell: "All right! Get 'em on the road!"

And the drovers would look up surprised, and scramble to it, and the strange procession would be gone—except for one man.

The skinny, leather-clad one with the beard would remain behind a while to talk urgently to the older men. The newer settlers stayed to listen, too. But they noted that the bewhiskered one was well respected by the older settlers. He talked with a rough urgency about a strange idea, involving what he called the balance of trade. He leaned heavily upon some abstruse fraternity involving squatters, and he talked of a man named Jonathan Blair, which brought reminiscent grins to some. And when he left, he took with him a promise.

Thus, as the column of hogs moved east, the word spread through the big woods from cabin to cabin and from settlement to settlement . . . "Jonathan Blair."

Every stray woodsie who saw the column coming, every degenerate Indian, every lonely farmer-settler, every ferryman saw something impressive in the strange oncoming procession. Most of them saw the largest hogs they had ever seen. But when the column had passed them and gone out of sight, the keener ones saw something above and beyond that. Vaguely, they felt good.

Part of this impression was inspired by the size of the amazing hogs, part by the talk of the whiskered one about Jonathan Blair and the balance of trade, but mostly by the leaning-forward demeanor of the redheaded drover who acted as though his hogs were the salvation of a nation.

But up ahead with the column, Woodbridge himself saw more clearly the undoing of twenty years' labor at every turn in the trail.

It rained two days in a row, and Big Two went off his feed along with a dozen others.

Certain of the sows reached farrowing time, and Woodbridge stayed behind with them, placing the piglets and the sow in the wagon. But the wagon was filling up with piglets, and in the third week it was becoming a problem. The entire herd was seriously losing weight, and Stranger-boy began to fear that Tom Woodbridge had made a mistake. But that was not the worst.

For Thomas Woodbridge senior feared the same.

Jonathan Blair leaned against the board in Exeter's tavern. Through the door he looked out on the stagnant common of Mesopotamia, Ohio, and as he looked a slight smile played over his lips. It was not a smile of amusement, but the slight widening of the lips of a man who puts together the pieces of a puzzle with not much hope for the result. Behind him, motionless, stood Amos Exeter, a man of some ambition, a man whose ambition outstripped his capacity, but none the less a man to be considered in the puzzle.

Across the stultified common, Mike Stikes stood in the doorway to his forge with his apron on, ready to work, but not working. When Stikes's shop was neat, times were bad. Mike Stikes looked over at Blair, then stepped back into his forge to rearrange his tools on the wall.

Blair now looked opposite the forge to where Sam Hosmer sat on the porch of his store, motionless. For Sam Hosmer to be idle detracted from him and from humanity. But there were no customers, nor did he wish any, for they would have no money with which to pay.

To the south, on the riverbank, Asa Buttrick's house was silent.

To the west was the Woodbridge cabin, containing Veronica who never came in town lately. Too many questions to be answered.

In the center of it all stood the great Shuldane house. The widow Hussong walked listlessly in and out as she prepared the meal for Shuldane and Webster. But there were no interesting comings and goings there of settlers and important strangers. There were only two horses tethered motionless in the rear. Blair knew they belonged to government men who had come to see Shuldane about his overdue land payments.

The town was strangled.

Down in Columbus, Governor Ethan Allen Brown sat equally motionless, for there was no money to carry out his canal program.

Yet Blair's imagination played farther and farther away from Mesopotamia. For despite all this stagnation, there was a stirring out in the big woods. Almost a month now Stranger-boy had been gone from the town. Somewhere out in the woods he was doing something.

Woodbridge had been gone even longer, and wherever he was he would not be standing still.

Two other strange events had broken the impoverished monotony. Two weeks ago a ragged stranger had come to Blair's cabin and printing office. Through a grin he had said: "We're with you, Mr. Blair. We're going to put you in."

The stranger would explain no more. But he had grinned as though Blair was supposed to know the rest, and the man had carried a tattered copy of the *Tabulator,* one with a balance-of-trade editorial. And only a week ago a letter had come. Enclosed was a clipping from the *Tabu-*

*lator.* A balance-of-trade editorial. The handwriting was crude and cryptic:

DEAR LT. BLAIR, ESQ.:
We are going to elect you. But when you get down there to Columbus . . . don't forgit.

As Blair looked at the hot, lifeless common of Mesopotamia, he thought about these things and the fact that Silver Pigeon had asked for a bundle of *Tabulators* before he left, containing the balance-of-trade argument. He had said Navarre wanted them. And the ragged stranger had mentioned a column of hogs. So it must be that Navarre was with Woodbridge, and Pigeon was with Woodbridge, and perhaps Stranger-boy and Michael. And they must be some place northeast of here, and they must be taking the hogs some place.

Could it be that . . .

Blair leaned forward like a spectator wishing a horse over a jump.

As the column worked east, the men noticed a chilling change in Woodbridge. He joined no more in the comments about the country they passed through. His speech was short, bone-tired. His eyes were always ahead. When the men came together to eat, Woodbridge sat off by himself, or moved ceaselessly through the herd. Silver Pigeon passed the water to Navarre, and commented on the change in the redhead.

"Yeah," said Navarre. "Seen him that way once before, years ago, when he was surveyin' the fifth range with Major Sargent. Gets awful narrow-minded." Navarre sliced off a thin layer of pork with his keen blade. "Narrow, like the edge of a knife," he added with a grin.

Woodbridge himself, though he paid little attention to the trail, except as the road was too hard or too soft or too dusty for the herd, paid especial attention to certain trivial signs which the others ignored or took for granted. He took great hope, for example, from the great interest in the hogs displayed by the settlers in the place called Sandyville.

And in the small town called Winesburgh one farmer approached Woodbridge with an offer for Big One. The offer was ridiculously low for what Woodbridge had in mind. Yet the man had singled out Big

One without previous knowledge that she was grand dam for the herd. And though the offer was low, it was still high for a hog.

Woodbridge noted that of all the farmers who gathered to look, the one who had made the offer was the most successful-looking. The man obviously did not believe it when Woodbridge told how far he had driven the hogs. But on the other hand—and Woodbridge watched closely—he was not shocked when Woodbridge said he planned to sell only for gold.

At Winesburgh Tom had no trouble getting corn to load into the small cart, for the prosperous farmer was delighted to sell him all he could load in exchange for two of the piglets in the cart. He also agreed to house and feed four sick sows until Woodbridge could come back to claim them.

As they moved east, approaching the Ohio River and Pittsburgh, Woodbridge observed slightly better clothes on the people, and very few buckskins. They passed a tavern made of brick; and at places the trail widened out so that one wagon could pass another without pulling off the road, if you could stand the dust.

But the rider who now approached him paid no heed to the dust. From his position at the rear of the herd, Woodbridge saw him stop at the head of the column to speak briefly to Stranger-boy and then continue on back. The rider swung around and fell in beside Woodbridge, who rode on the seat of the wagon in an attempt to get above the worst of the dust.

"My name's Bullit," he said.

"Woodbridge is mine."

Tom glanced over at the man, who looked straght ahead, allowing himself to be studied while he talked. Woodbridge found it difficult to make an estimate of Bullit, who spoke like a man accustomed to meeting the world on a combatant level, but dressed like one privileged to avoid it. His clothes were good, but dusty. His hair and his beard appeared to be familiar with barbering, but they were decidedly undone, apparently by a long ride at a fair speed, with perhaps an overnight pillow on the flanks of his mount. He was talking important words, but as though they were of no importance.

"Heard about this column coming in," he said. "Heard the stock was some better than average. Market's slow. Needs something pretty good to do any business. Thought I'd ride out and have a look."

"And now you've looked?"

"They were right. Your animals are some different. Look like they'd be good baconers, and they look about 250 pounds. Can you speak for the owner?"

"If there's anything worth speakin' about."

"Like to make him an offer."

"For who? And what market you talkin' about?"

"Pittsburgh, naturally."

"And how'd you hear about these hogs?"

"Don't know, exactly. Talk was around the market."

They rode along in silence. Bullit looked frequently across at Woodbridge, and finally said: "Well, what about talking to the owner? I can offer $3 a hundredweight."

There was dust on the part of Woodbridge's hair not covered by his broadbrimmed hat; there was dust, too, on his face and shoulders, and a powder of dust thickened his eyelashes, but gravel rattled in his voice.

"There's nothin' to talk about, Mr. Bullit."

"Huh?"

"You heard me."

Bullit had no way to be warned that under the coat of dust Woodbridge's face was red with rage, nor that his paltry offer had trampled on twenty years of a man's life. But he got an inkling.

"You talk like a God-damned fool!" said Woodbridge. "You talk about baconers when you're lookin' at lard hogs! You act like you were talkin' about ordinary pork, when you known damned well you never seen hogs like these in your life! You name slaughter prices when you're lookin' at a herd of breed hogs that any farmer'd give his right arm for one boar! And the money you name wouldn't buy a hair off that little one's rump!"

Bullit accepted Woodbridge's tirade as though he were accustomed to it. He rode in silence, waiting out Woodbridge's temper.

"I see you're the owner, then." He smiled. "I should have known. But you see, this is one of the largest herds I've ever seen come in. So I expected perhaps a more . . . " Bullit looked at Woodbridge's dust-covered leather shirt. "You're right, Mr. Woodbridge. I knew they were mighty fancy hogs, and you got a right to be proud of 'em. What do you call 'em?"

"Mesopotamias."

"And you developed 'em?"

"That's right. Me and my boy."

"And you been protectin' the breed?"

"That's right. I only sold to men as understood the value and didn't go mixin' in any other strains."

"And you worried with it, and sweated with it for probably quite a few years, and now you've got something extra fine."

Woodbridge nodded.

"And you brought 'em all the way from . . . "

Woodbridge didn't fill in how far he'd come.

"And now you're going to try to make it pay," said Bullit with a disturbing concern.

"It's gonna pay, all right. I got to get $100 a head for some of them boars. What you laughin' at?"

"What I'm gettin' at, Mr. Woodbridge. 'Twould seem like you'd be in an enviable position right now. And deserve a good reward."

"Yeah?"

"But see where you've gone and put yourself? You're gettin' farther and farther from your farm. Harder to turn back. Your animals are losin' weight at about twelve pounds every fifty miles. And you're goin' into a strange market where the only buyers are slaughterhouse men and packers."

Bullit had a way of talking that undermined a man.

"They're not interested in how you bred the hogs. They're interested in buying the cheapest per hundredweight. Because when those barrels of pork get down to New Orleans, it don't much matter what kind of pork is in 'em. Just so's every barrel weighs 198 pounds net. How you gonna tell a packer like that about your fancy breeding?"

Woodbridge made no answer. There was none.

"I hate to see you go into a market like that, Woodbridge." Bullit read the effect of his slim daggers of panic, and sliced for the heart. "Could you maybe turn back, Woodbridge? Save yourself a lot of grief."

"Are you crazy! Them hogs have run theirselves all the way from— They come too far already."

Bullit remained silent to let Woodbridge listen to his own answer.

It was a mile later that Woodbridge spoke.

"Now look here, Bullit, you didn't come ridin' all the way out here to meet me without thinkin' I had somethin' special. If you thought I'd have trouble selling, you'd have stayed right there in Pittsburgh and waited for me."

Bullit's grin could mean that he'd been uncovered, but to a worried man it could also mean, "Wait and see."

There was a little more talk, but always Bullit said just enough to be within the truth, just little enough to worry Woodbridge.

"Five dollars a hundredweight, Woodbridge. And I take 'em off your hands right here."

Woodbridge waved him away, but as he watched Bullit ride ahead and out of sight he had a sinking feeling.

In two days they arrived at the Wellsburgh Ferry on the Ohio River. Tom didn't recognize it for the same river he had come down when he came into the Ohio Country. But he didn't take much time to look at it, either. Because when he brought the tail of the column up to the shore he saw all the hogs massed there.

"Well, get 'em on the boat, boy! What you waitin' on?"

"Tom, the man says five cents a head to take 'em across."

Tom looked stupefied, but he turned to the smug ferryman.

"What you sayin', mister! We been payin' two cents a dozen for ferry rates!"

"This is the Uhia, mister. Five cents a head."

The argument that followed was futile, for the ferryman had the upper hand.

"Besides," he added, "what I hear about them hogs, you oughta be willin' to pay ten cents a head."

"What have you heard about these hogs?" asked Woodbridge hopefully.

"Well, I heard they was . . ." But the ferryman jerked a thumb over toward the toll shanty. "There's the gentleman told me," he said.

Woodbridge looked at a figure who lounged in the doorway. The man blew a cloud of cigar smoke.

"Seven dollars a hundredweight, Woodbridge. Take it or leave it."

Bullit snapped his cigar into the river and slid his hands into his pockets without moving from the doorway.

Slover Navarre fired a bullet of tobacco juice near Bullit's feet. "River's still full of water rats, Tom," he said.

When they counted all their money, they had more than enough to pay the ferry.

"But we can't pay out our cash for that," said Woodbridge. "We'll need it for feed. Unhitch New Horse, Boy, and ride north. See if there's another ferry. You do the same to the south, Pigeon."

When Young Tom and Pigeon had left, Captain Michael and Navarre proposed a plan for crossing the river that would eliminate the
argument in a hurry. But Woodbridge shook his head.

"That's what they deserve, but I can't chance it. Might give grounds
to impound the hogs."

Bullit came over to join them, but under the sullen scrutiny of Michael and Navarre he did not repeat his offer.

Stranger-boy and Pigeon returned toward late afternoon. Neither had
found a ferry. Woodbridge was honed thin on worry, and he dozed.
But he woke in time to see the fog rising off the river, and he yelled:
"Stranger-boy! We got to get 'em out of the damp!"

"Back up the bank?"

"No. We're goin' across!"

He called them all together for a minute. And soon the hogs were
loading onto the ferry under the watchful count of the ferryman. Three
loads went across, and Navarre and Captain Michael and Pigeon kept
them assembled on the opposite shore. The last load was fairly small,
and it contained as well the small cart and Woodbridge and Young
Tom.

The ferryman had two helpers who drove their poles to the bottom
on the down-current side to keep the ferry from drifting while the
ferryman pushed it across.

In midstream Woodbridge handed the money to the ferryman.

"Hold it till we get over," he said. "I got to keep pushin'."

"No. I want you to count it now so we can get the argument over
with," said Woodbridge.

"What argument?" The ferryman locked his pole and counted the
money.

"Hey!"

"That's right," said Woodbridge. "We're payin' ya two cents for
every five hogs. No more."

"Is that so?" asked the ferryman. Promptly he shipped his pole.
"Happens we've dealt with your kind before, mister. We'll sit right
here. Just hold her against the current, men, until our swineherd pays
us our money."

"I figured that would be your move," said Woodbridge. "Stranger-
boy, heave a little of that corn along the edge of the deck, close near
the rail, all on the same side."

The ferryman's confidence diluted as he watched Young Tom spread corn along the down-current side, just inside the gunnel. But when he saw the hogs run for the one side and felt the deck tilt under his feet, he yelled: "Ya damn' fool! Get them hogs back in the center!"

"A little more corn, boy," said Woodbridge.

The ferry tilted so sharply that it gave the current a strong purchase on her bottom. The pole men held only by the greatest effort.

"A little more corn, boy!" said Woodbridge.

But the ferryman had had enough.

"All right! All right! But get them hogs back in the middle!"

On the east shore they climbed above the steep bank, away from the cool fog, and spent the night.

Bullit overtook them about noon the following day, and he seemed displeased to see that another of his trade had fallen in beside Woodbridge. The new man's name was De Camp, and he spoke quickly and with authority.

"You see, Woodbridge, it's one of the unfortunate aspects of the market that the closer you get to it with your stock, the further you weaken your bargaining position. First place, your stock loses weight, spirit, condition. This herd of yours has been driven way too far already."

"If I told you how far they've come, you'd think they were in damned fine shape—except you wouldn't believe it."

"They look like they've come a hundred miles or more."

"They've come closer to five hundred."

De Camp remained silent. There was no point in calling a man a liar this early in a trade.

"Then you'd better get them off your hands now, Woodbridge. I'll give you $4 a hundredweight right here. Cash."

"I got to get twenty times that."

De Camp threw up his hands.

"Woodbridge, can't you see every step you take is cutting your chances? Can't you see the price has dropped $3 on you just in the last ten miles?"

Woodbridge was silent, not under De Camp's reasoning, but because he began to see what kind of dealing he would have to overcome. But he didn't realize quite how bad it was until Stranger-boy asked a simple question.

"Mr. De Camp, how did you know what we were offered before?"

De Camp looked stricken.

Woodbridge looked at De Camp with sudden surprise, and then he grinned and put his hand on Stranger-boy's shoulder as a tired man leans on a good son.

"They got gold here in the East, Young Tom," he said. "But it'll take a hateful lot of gall to git it out of 'em."

# Chapter 29: THE MARKET PLACE

BUT it turned out that Pittsburgh was not the East. At least not far enough east. Depression was there, too.

Woodbridge found no physical building that he recognized. Though Pittsburgh was now a sprawling city of thirteen hundred houses, Tom recognized the same stifling inactivity that smothered Mesopotamia. But here the idlers had thirty taverns in which to idle in comfort. And as the redhead and Young Tom passed up Front Street and down Liberty, men nudged each other and pointed and grinned. Buckskins were rare in Pittsburgh now.

Tom and Young Tom gazed at the strange signs on the idle, silent buildings: "Pittsburgh Foundry . . . Cannon, Shot & Pig Iron"; "Thomas Cooper Brass Foundry"; "Blackwell & Page . . . Window Glass, Bottles, Lanterns"; "Foster & Murray . . . Shovels, Spades, Scythes"; "Monongahela Distillerie."

There were wagonmakers, boat builders, tallow chandlers, and silversmiths; and the Woodbridges stopped long in front of a bootmaker's shop. They walked along the river front, where a hundred boats of all descriptions were tied up: broadhorned flatboats beginning to disintegrate and used mostly now for houseboats; swift keelboats, more luxurious now but still simple, powered by human brutes with immense shoulders thickened from shouldering the poles and calf muscles overdeveloped from straining up and down the catwalks. But Tom Woodbridge and Stranger-boy stood longest before three smoke-snorting giants that nuzzled the wharf. They had heard about steamboats. But today the word took meaning. Stranger-boy wanted to stay and watch, but Woodbridge yanked his sleeve.

"We got hogs to sell, boy."

Long after Woodbridge had left, Young Tom remained gawking at the giant paddlewheels. He stared at the men in shiny pants who walked aboard the wonderful vessels without looking up from their newspapers, just as though they walked from Hosmer's Store to Exeter's Tavern. But he noticed that these people were also staring at him. Stranger-boy looked down at himself, touched the buckskin of his left sleeve, then looked back up at them in understanding, and turned away. As he left, he stole another glance. They were not looking unpleasantly, just curiously, as he had looked at them. In fact, one man with white stockings smiled and threw his newspaper down to Stranger-boy.

Young Tom picked up the paper, the Pittsburgh *Gazette*. He read it as he walked along to join Woodbridge.

The hogs were penned between two long cargo houses where there was little shore activity. As he approached the herd, he saw Pigeon and Michael standing watchfully on opposite sides of it, while Navarre stationed himself on the water side. Woodbridge was on the inland side of the herd, but he was surrounded by a crowd of men who were laughing.

As Young Tom approached, he heard Woodbridge rasping defensively: "Laugh, blast ya! But did you ever see hogs this size?"

By the dwindling of the laughter, Woodbridge had made his point. But a well-dressed man said: "I know, mister, but $100 for a pig! My God!"

"Not for a pig!" defended Woodbridge. "But for a boar that can sire a whole herd like this!"

"I know. I know. But nobody around here can pay like that."

Half of the crowd was interested in the discussion with this presumptuous, fierce-eyed farmer in buckskins who talked about $100 pigs. Half stared at the silent, stoic old Indian and at the handsome young Indian opposite him. Older men pointed to the Indians and expanded a little as they explained to younger men about the difference between Wyandots and Mingoes and Delawares.

But around the outer rim of the crowd were a few silent ones who paid no attention to the Indians nor to Woodbridge nor to the strange dog. They stared silently at the hogs, some with their hands on their chins. And Stranger-boy noticed that they turned occasionally to look silently to either side of the herd. Following their glances, Stranger-boy saw on either side of the herd, standing relaxed, at a good distance off from the hogs, with faint smiles on their lips, Mr. Bullit and Mr. De Camp . . . waiting.

The crowd was a changing group. New ones came as others left. But always De Camp and Bullit remained quietly standing.

Finally the curious crowd thinned to four men as dusk set in. Mr. De Camp and Mr. Bullit converged on Woodbridge.

"You see what you're up against," said Bullit.

"The damned fools don't understand!" said Woodbridge. "They're blind!"

"Mr. De Camp and I," said Bullit, "have gotten together. We can offer you $7 a hundredweight for—"

"Why talk 'hundredweight' when you're talkin' about breeders!" exploded Woodbridge. "Don't you know you're not payin' for pork!"

"All right," said Bullit. "Make it $20 a head for the boars and $10 a head for sows."

"A-ah!"

"Then suppose you name us a price."

"I did! I'm takin' home $100 a head for them boars!"

Bullit smiled.

"Not only that, it's gonna be in gold!"

Bullit laughed out loud, and was joined by De Camp. Smiles spread among the other men.

"Come on, De Camp," said Bullit, turning to leave. "The man's mad."

"Not according to the *Gazette*, Mr. Bullit," the Stranger-boy said.

Young Tom handed his paper to Tom, with the article folded outermost. Bullit went around behind Woodbridge and looked over his shoulder, where the editor had printed:

The exchanges from the Cincinnati *Western Spy* describe an interesting, if true, agricultural development in the West. The editor speaks of a brown and white spotted hog which grows to tremendous proportions there, for which western farmers pay great premiums. The owner, it is said, holds such a great value on these animals that he will not sell for western currency, but insists on material exchanges, such as land. The article claims that certain Indiana agriculturists are formed together to offer whole townships for these beasts.

The incredible story is somewhat corroborated by an exchange paper, from a place called Vincennes, which came into this office and which reprints the Cincinnati editorial. . . .

Bullit and De Camp left without comment. But as they walked away, Young Tom noticed that Bullit was talking intently.

Woodbridge said, "Boy, we've got to get these hogs on higher ground for the night, out of the damp."

The place they found was up above the wagon yards on Liberty Avenue. It was a good distance from the houses and offered a fair cover of trees. It was a good thing, because a cold September rain chilled the canyon called Pittsburgh.

Slover Navarre went to find Loretta Shane, his wife.

Captain Michael was one of those woodsmen who needed but a half-hour to domesticate any given piece of landscape, and by midnight it looked as if he'd lived there forever as he sat sheltered under a lean-to made from the tail gates of the wagon and the cart and some light branches. His rifle was already carefully wrapped in an oily rag for the night, and a good smell came from the cook fire he had built.

Silver Pigeon fed the horses and arranged the canvas over the wagon beds. Stranger-boy fed the hogs thriftily from the dwindling supply of corn. Woodbridge walked silently among the hogs, followed by Wolf, who could not feel the desperation in the redhead's voice.

"What in the hell is a man to do?"

During the first three days quite a few curiosity-seekers stopped by the piece of woods and looked at the hogs. Some were farmers, deeply impressed by the size of the hogs and by the fact that they'd been driven about five hundred miles. These men meant no insult when they made their offers to buy boars for $15 and $20 each. It was more than they had ever offered for a pig. Woodbridge ceased to be angry with their offers, for he saw they were sincere. And he spent long hours showing his notebook to the men and pointing to certain boars and explaining their ancestry. Occasionally he captured one for them and had them feel the firmness of the flanks. He explained patiently that you couldn't feed on just anything and then try to firm up in the last four weeks on corn. It had to be corn all the way.

The farmers appreciated the information and asked many questions. Some came back repeatedly and brought newcomers. Some brought copies of the Pittsburgh *Gazette* and asked if Tom's hogs were the hogs referred to.

One man named McMasters offered $25 for Big Four. When Woodbridge shook his head, McMasters asked reasonably enough, "Then if $25 won't buy him, will $5 rent him for stud service for two days?"

Tom looked at the wagon which now held only a scattered layer of corn one ear deep.

"What kind of hog would you match him to?" he asked.

"Just the regular critters that grow around here. We haven't got a good hog in the county. Nobody's done any breeding, and importing's out of the question."

"No. I couldn't let you do that," said Woodbridge sadly. "Like to, but I've seen what happens when you let a good strain breed wild."

McMasters seemed to understand, and he gave way a step or two to make room for the two men who approached Woodbridge. The tall one called Bullit spoke.

"Woodbridge, you should have a more practical idea of the market by now. Mr. De Camp and I are bringing you a last offer. Twenty dollars a head for all the pigs . . . boars, shoats, even the young ones."

Woodbridge's face colored, but he did not answer.

Stranger-boy came up the road on foot and handed Tom a packet of currency.

Woodbridge did not accept the money. Instead, he looked up in annoyance.

"Where's the corn?" he demanded.

"It's arranged for, Tom."

"Arranged for! I want it *now*!"

Stranger-boy stole a glance at Bullit. "I'll explain about it later, Tom."

"Can you explain to the hogs, too?" asked Woodbridge, showing the strain.

Bullit's voice was quiet.

"Wisely, the lad is trying not to say it in front of me, Woodbridge.

But obviously he has found out that your paper money won't buy corn or anything else. Not worth the paper it's printed on. Is that right, son?"

Stranger-boy denied it. But his lie was shallow, and Bullit's quiet voice resumed its logical destruction of Woodbridge's life work.

"And every day you wait here, Woodbridge, you'll be in worse shape. How you going to put that fat back on 'em without corn? How long can you wait before you face the facts? What you going to do when snow falls?"

Woodbridge's angry hands jammed the money in his pocket.

"How long can I wait, Bullit?" he challenged slowly. "I can wait till hell freezes over!"

Without removing his glare from Bullit, Woodbridge spoke to Young Tom. "Boy! Tell Navarre to find some likely timber for building hog sheds good enough to keep off snow."

Navarre had ways of finding things. And as the second week wore on, he furnished rations for the drovers, old deck planking for hog sheds, oats for the horses, whisky and tobacco for the men. But he was unable to maintain the tremendous quantities of corn needed to build up the herd to weight.

McMasters came back many times to look at the hogs. Sometimes he brought friends, and Woodbridge noticed that men were coming from farther and farther east to look at the hogs. One man from Harrisburg offered $40 for Big Four, payable in Spanish silver dollars. Woodbridge declined, but he offered instead a much lesser boar with slimmer flanks, and a ten-month-old gilt. The easterner accepted.

Woodbridge turned around and bought corn from McMasters. At sundown he counted out the silver to McMasters with especial slowness because he was aware of the approach of Mr. Bullit for his daily visit from the Pittsburgh docks.

Bullit concealed his surprise well when he spied the two wagonloads of corn, but he couldn't cover his dismay as he watched Woodbridge count out the silver.

With more enthusiasm than was wise in a good trader, Woodbridge said, "Now you are sure I'm payin' ya enough, McMasters? I don't want to trim ya, because I may be needin' more corn." Woodbridge looked directly at Bullit. "Lots more."

McMasters, who knew what Woodbridge was up to, grinned and said, "You can have all you can use at that price."

When McMasters had left, Bullit said, "Woodbridge, I'm leaving in the morning to go out to meet a herd of Bedfords that's coming in."

"Bedfords?"

"I'm only telling you because if you change your mind tonight about taking my offer, come in to the dock. You'll find me or De Camp there. Might even better our offer a little."

"Bedfords?"

"If we don't see you tonight, we'll not be troubling you any more. We probably won't want your hogs if we get the Bedfords."

"What do you know about Bedfords?" asked Woodbridge.

"Why do you ask that?"

"Because I never heard of any Bedford herd within drovin' distance of here. It's an English breed, and there's an embargo on 'em."

"Sure. But there's a few got out of England."

"Funny you'd know about 'em and I wouldn't."

"How so?"

"Why, just because a man that talks about buyin' breed hogs by the pound ain't likely to appreciate Bedfords."

"Well, I hope you come in to see me tonight. Because if I get these Bedfords you and I won't be doin' any business together."

"If the man's smart enough to own Bedfords, he won't take any offer you'll make him, Bullit."

But as Bullit rode away from him, Woodbridge experienced a twinge of panic and jealousy. It was a big country, and there could be Bedfords in it somewhere besides the ones he'd brought to the West. Without taking his eyes from Bullit's back, Tom called for Stranger-boy. When the lad came over, he said: "Stranger-boy, you got a good head on you. Come along and see I don't make a fool of myself. Keep your eyes open."

Together they saddled up and overtook Bullit, that is, they caught up to where they could just silhouette him against the faint western light. As he dipped down into the canyon, they had to close up on him to avoid losing him in the darkness.

Bullit walked his horse thoughtfully to the Eagle Hotel and tied to the rail.

"We'd best tie ours somewheres else," said Stranger-boy.

Woodbridge dismounted and handed his lines to Young Tom, who disappeared, returning shortly without the horses.

Bullit walked into the Eagle Hotel and talked to a few men there. Mr. Bullit was apparently a considerable man in the town. Woodbridge and Young Tom watched from the outside until Bullit walked up the stairway. Bullit stopped on the landing, looked down over the loungers, and then disappeared up the steps.

Woodbridge entered the hotel and crossed toward the stairs. The idlers looked up with interest at the unshaven redhead in the buckskins and at the younger one who followed him.

A clerk with flowing white shirt sleeves coming out from the armholes of his vest walked over to intercept their path, but Woodbridge's foot was on the first step before the clerk asked, "Looking for something?"

Woodbridge didn't answer, but mounted the stairs two at a time.

As his head rose above the top of the stairs, he saw Bullit's back moving swiftly down a long hall. Bullit turned off the hall and Woodbridge followed. But, gaining the top of the stairs, Woodbridge found that doors opened off the whole length of it, and that he had no way of telling which one Bullit used.

They walked the length of the hall, listening at each door.

At the second door from the end, they heard faint voices inside. One was Bullit's, and he was saying: "I tell you the redhead is serious when he says he's going to get $100 for those boars. And in metal money. He believes it. Besides that, the word is getting around despite everything I can do. Farmers are interested."

For answer there was a grunt, and Bullit continued.

"And he's settling down to wait it out. He's got himself a supply of corn—that he paid for in silver. And he's buildin' sheds to protect 'em from snow."

There was a deeper grunt.

"You're going to have to raise your offer," said Bullit.

"Can't. Not in gold, anyhow."

Bullit laughed.

"When the day comes you can't borrow more money, nobody can—against holdings like yours."

"Then nobody can," came the answer. "Because I can't. Don't have enough equity in my land."

The voice, though very faint and distorted through the door, had a familiar sound to Woodbridge. He was extremely curious to see what great man it must be who could talk thus peremptorily to an agent of Bullit's stature.

Woodbridge missed an interchange of words in the exhaustion of his own breath, which he had been restricting. But he heard Bullit say:

"Yes, he got quite excited when I mentioned Bedfords. I gave him until tonight. Said I'd meet him on the docks."

"Then get down there."

"Why should he get so excited over this Bedford talk? Are they better than what he has?"

"It's a long story. Get down to the wharf."

There was some moving around in the room, and then the more refined voice said: "Bullit, you've had two weeks now to make the transaction. Perhaps I should have commissioned De Camp for the main effort and you to assist him."

"I'll get them, if they can be got.'

"See to it, then, if you value forwarding privileges to Cincinnati." The inflection and the command reinforced by conditions were unmistakably this time from the throat and mind of Elnathan Shuldane.

Woodbridge and Stranger-boy left the Eagle Hotel quickly.

Woodbridge found Higgins's Hardware Store closed. But several men sat on the step. Woodbridge selected the old man in the center.

"Will you open up, sir?"

The old man ended a long story reluctantly and opened his store.

Woodbridge had a strange feeling inside the store. He looked around at the rope and canvas and lanterns and axes. He wished he had time to explain to the old man how he knew about his store; but it would take a long time, and the old man was exasperatingly slow as it was, insisting on getting behind the counter and removing his coat before he was ready for commerce.

"Nails," said Woodbridge.

"That's the wisest thing a man can take to invade the western woods, mister. Nails. You'd ought to have a lantern, too."

"No, just the nails, and a canvas bag to put 'em in."

"You'd ought to have a lantern to light up the West, mister."

"I'm not invadin' the West. I'm invadin' the East, in a way of speakin'."

But he wished he hadn't spoken, for it stopped the old man, who now, for the first time, took notice of Woodbridge's buckskins.

"Oh, yes. I see. You been already."

"One more handful of nails, and that'll be enough," said Woodbridge.

The pleasure was gone out of the sale for the old man, and he bent to the nail barrel.

When he was out of sight of the loungers around the store, Woodbridge took a few silver coins from his pocket and sprinkled them over the top of the nails in the canvas bag. With Stranger-boy he proceeded to the wharf.

On the dock Bullit offered Woodbridge a black Conestoga cigar which the hog farmer declined.

Then, as if he were not pleasantly surprised that Woodbridge had appeared, Bullit leisurely offered a cigar to Stranger-boy, who pocketed it for Navarre. As the agent lighted his cigar from a sulphur splint which he pulled out of a little bottle, Stranger-boy noticed in the flare that Bullit's eyes were studying Woodbridge with great interest. The agent screwed a cap on the bottle, which he flourished into his waistcoat pocket.

"Well, Woodbridge," he said at last, "I think you did the right thing by coming down. I can take them off your hands tomorrow at $20 a head and you'll be free of your troubles. I'll buy the corn you have on hand at whatever you think is right and—"

"I didn't come to sell," said Woodbridge.

Bullit straightened up from the warehouse wall and removed the cigar from his mouth, which remained open.

"You're pretty good at beating a man down in his price, I've noticed," said Tom. "I'd rather have you buyin' *for* me than *from* me."

Bullit's face vacillated ludicrously between mock modesty and suspicion of insult.

"You still going out to meet this herd of Bedfords in the morning?" asked Woodbridge.

"What herd? Oh, yes. *Yes.*" Bullit recovered, and then added, "Well, that is, if you and I can't work out a satisfactory trade for your Mesopotamia herd."

"Well, we can't work out a trade for my herd the way you're talkin'. But I might buy these Bedfords from you. How many are there?"

Bullit had lost control of the interview.

"Why, I'm not just sure," he faltered.

Woodbridge opened the front of his buckskin shirt. From inside he pulled out a rather large and obviously heavy canvas bag which he clanked down on the loading dock. He let Bullit stare at it for a long moment, leaving his own hand on it.

"I'd like you to buy me fifty of those Bedford hogs, Bullit. You can keep everything you can make on $75 for boars and $30 for sows."

Bullit was speechless until he managed feebly, "That's the money there?"

"That's right." Woodbridge carelessly brushed the lip of the bag open, exposing a flash of silver. "Is it a contract?"

Bullit puffed on his cigar and studied the bag.

"Or could it be, Mr. Bullit, that there aren't any Bedfords? Could it be, maybe, that little story is just one of the bargaining tools of your miserable trade?"

Bullit threw down his cigar, but he didn't move, nor look up. Woodbridge held him there by force of scorn just as motionless as if he trained a gun on his head. Bullit was demolished. The principal attitude of his profession was shattered. He stood like a teen-age boy.

"There he is, Stranger-boy. What do ya think of him? There stands an agent with his bare soul showin'. How do you like him? That's the man that was gonna rob us as sure as if he stole the hogs right out of our pens. There's one of the miserable critters that's bleedin' the West dry—payin' us in paper and sellin' to us for gold."

Bullit made no effort to repair his prestige.

"It's all right, Bullit. You're good at it. I got to say that for ya. I expect you're one of the best. And I need the best, right now. Only, you'll have to be a little smarter if you want to work for me. And I expect you do, seein' as I've got the stayin' power to outlast ya."

Woodbridge patted the canvas bag.

Bullet's face was pathetic as he looked up, groping for Woodbridge's meaning in which he pitifully glimpsed some vague profit for himself.

"I guess it won't strain your conscience too much to switch sides, will it, Bullit? Long as we understand each other, we can work together. I want you to sell my hogs at my price. I can tell you how to do it. And your share will be this."

Woodbridge patted the canvas bag.

Bullit agreed with considerable enthusiasm. He would start tomorrow.

"No. Tonight," said Woodbridge.

It must be admitted that when Bullit once took the assignment, he knew what to do.

"I'll go over to the *Gazette* office. I saw to it there was nothin' in the *Gazette* about these bein' the same Mesopotamia hogs that was wanted in Indiana. I can undo that. Then we'll move a couple of the big ones down onto Wood Street where the crowds are."

Woodbridge agreed, but he was more interested in having Bullit head east to Harrisburg and to Lancaster County where the Quakers were.

"I suppose you know your way around the state government and Harrisburg, don't you, Bullit?"

"Yes."

"All right. Now you got to know about hogs. Come on out to the herd. You're gonna sit down and do some studyin'."

"Studying?"

"Yeah. This is gonna be a kind of new experience for you. When you're through, you're gonna know why it is you don't have to do any lyin' to sell Mesopotamia hogs. All you really got to do is tell the right people where the hogs are."

It was past midnight, but Bullit showed no fatigue as Woodbridge explained from his crude book the ancestry of his hogs. How they gained a pound a day and were marketable six months from birth. How a packer could pay himself back for the cost of slaughtering by just saving the lard. Bullit got the idea quickly, and beyond that he got some ideas of his own.

"Why wouldn't it pay for packers here to band together and buy good breed stock to start the farmers raising Mesopotamia hogs? Why, they could even afford to give away the breed animals at first."

"Sure they could," answered Woodbridge. "But first I want to get the word all the way east to Harrisburg. Remember, I'm sellin' only for metal money."

In the morning Bullit rode east.

Almost in Bullit's eastbound wake, an intermittent but increasing stream of westbound farmers drifted west into Pittsburgh, seeking out a man named Woodbridge.

They were generally prosperous-looking men, though some were not, and they had in common empty wagons and a directness of question. Stranger-boy was somewhat ashamed, for as he watched Tom answer the men, and as he watched the eager faces which hung on his words, he realized that no one at home had set such a value on what Thomas Woodbridge carried around in his head. He saw that men hungered for even small fractions of what Tom Woodbridge knew about hogs. Obviously, these strangers had no Tom Woodbridge. He wished Hosmer and Stikes and Exeter and Hawkins could see this.

"How do they dress down, Woodbridge?"

"Depends on who's doin' it," answered Woodbridge calmly. "Myself and my boy, we can get 65 to 80 per cent of weight in dressed meat. Little waste. Bones are light."

"How's your hog at rootin' for itself?"

"No good, mister. You got to treat him like a baby, in a way. But in return it'll put on a pound of pork for every five pounds of feed, providing you don't expect him to live on stocks and greens. You got to feed him corn. He'll not return ya somethin' for nothin'. Nothin' will."

They seemed to like his answers, and there were more questions, especially from the men in the broadbrimmed Quaker hats who began coming from as far east as Harrisburg.

"Does thee hold the notion that the swine takes its shape from the sire and its disposition from the dam?"

"I've not been able to tell. But it does seem to me that all the young of Big One have been more sweet-tempered. And I can always tell a son of Big Four at a hundred feet."

"Then if a man was to buy a boar of thee, would he be allowed a look at the dam and the sire? Would thee know it?"

"We've got 'em pretty well marked on the ear. If you pick your stock, I can locate the boar and likely the dam."

"Then would thee give me a price on that swine there?"

Woodbridge looked where the Quaker pointed.

"You've picked well, sir, but I'm not sure Big Four's for sale. But I'll sell you one that's his image."

"Thee must have a price in mind that would satisfy thee for the one thee name Big Four."

"I suppose I have. All I know, sir, is I've turned down $350 for him."

The Quaker turned to his companion, and Woodbridge turned to more questions.

Men walked among his hogs and marveled. Woodbridge's face was anxious, but illuminated as Stranger-boy had never seen it.

The bidding went up on Big Four, and Woodbridge grinned. Always the bidder settled for a lesser boar. But it vindicated a lifetime of labor. There were men who were glad to pay $100 in gold or silver for a boar.

Buyers were not to be hurried. Some came back three and four days before they even made a bid on a hog. They must see the dam and the sire, and the more cautious wished to see the granddam and the grandsire. They must see them in the morning light as opposed to the afternoon light. They must feel them and slap them, and often they must send back for more money.

Stranger-boy had never seen Tom in such a mood. The man was at home with himself and the world these days. He treated the men who came like long unseen brothers, and it seemed quite natural. No man ever introduced himself. He merely asked a question about this boar or that gilt. And suddenly Woodbridge had known the stranger a lifetime.

Michael and Pigeon seemed to enjoy it. They worked with Woodbridge with quick interest and curiosity.

And Navarre. He grinned at Woodbridge. Or rather he grinned at the world, which had apparently slipped up and made a mistake, allowing a western bounty-warrant settler to come into this. Navarre, who was custodian of the money, fingered the gold eagles, half-eagles, and quarter-eagles. He grinned at the Spanish pistoles and doubloons, the Queen Anne crowns and silver Virginia pounds. Through Tom Woodbridge a kind of victory came also to Slover Navarre.

But the grin disappeared, and he quickly locked up the lock box in the bottom of Woodbridge's wagon and grabbed hold of his long rifle as he watched an incongruous figure advancing through the hogs toward the wagon.

The out-of-place gentleman, who had apparently unerringly picked out the wagon as headquarters, walked gingerly through the hogs, stopping to examine none. He stepped, where possible, on stones or timbers, avoiding the muddy ground, and on his face Navarre recognized the insufferable brand mark of minor officialdom.

The official's official arrived in front of Navarre, tapping his chest with the roll of paper and looking all around. Finding no one better, he said, "Who's in charge here?"

Navarre spiked a bolt of tobacco at the official's feet and split his beard in a grin.

"I said, who's in charge here?"

"Far as you're concerned, I am. What d'ya want, sonny?"

"Name's Mr. Clinton. Judge Branckton's court."

"Your name's '*Mr.* Clinton'? Or is it just Clinton and you gave yourself a title?"

Clinton bristled, but he unfolded the paper and handed it to Navarre, who increased Clinton's temperature by not taking it, but only reading it, leaving Clinton in the attitude of a lackey holding a sulphur stick to a hotel guest's cigar. Clinton's outstretched arms began to shake with the effort, for Navarre read it very slowly.

"'Ordnance declaring the presence of the large herd of hogs unhealthful and constituting an illegal trespass on the grounds of' . . . Hey! Mr. McMasters! Who owns this ground here?"

Clinton rolled the paper up, but Navarre said, "Not so fast, sonny. I ain't finished."

In the presence of McMasters and, later, Woodbridge, Navarre finished reading the paper ordering them out.

McMasters said: "Don't worry about it, Tom. You can bring 'em over to my place as long as you want to stay."

"Doesn't matter what you do with them," said Clinton. "Just get them out of here by sundown."

"What about my sheds?" asked Woodbridge.

But Navarre's hand was on Tom's arm.

"No point in movin' 'em, Tom."

"But it's an order. They might try to confiscate."

"No. They won't, I don't think." Navarre turned his talk to Clinton. "Sonny, this Judge Branckton, he happen to be a member in good standin' of that iron-heeled, overstuffed outfit that calls itself the Cincinnati Club?"

"The judge is a retired colonel and a member of the respected Cincinnati."

"Uh-huh. He happen to be talkin' lately to another honored member named Shuldane?"

"I believe I've seen Colonel Shuldane in the judge's chamber."

"Uh-huh. Then you just go tell the judge—or Shuldane, either one—that all Tom's got to do is move up the road a ways to McMasters' place. So the whole scheme won't work anyhow. After you tell him that, he won't ask you to cause us any trouble, and he'll forget all about that 'unhealthful' talk."

Clinton was puzzled. "If you want to take that chance," he said.

Navarre waited until Clinton had left, and then turned to Tom.

"But it looks to me like you'd better send one of us back to Mesopotamia, Tom. That looked like Shuldane's last desperate try here. Wa'n't up ta his standards by a damn' sight. He'll be headin' back home t'make trouble, I'll bet. Somebody ought to go back just to keep watch."

"Yeah," said Woodbridge. The redhead looked at his small crew, and his gaze settled on Young Tom.

"Can you find your way back, Stranger-boy?"

"Yes."

"Give him some money to fend with, Slover."

# *Chapter 30: THOMAS WOODBRIDGE*

STRANGER-BOY found a new kind of loneliness in Mesopotamia which he had not experienced before. It was in a way the loneliness of wealth, and this conspicuous kind of loneliness was more uncomfortable to the boy than any.

It was the boots.

Stranger-boy's boots had worn out on the long droving east, and Woodbridge had bought him a new pair. Though he pulled his trouser-legs down over his uppers and kept the toes of the boots dusty, still, amid the complete desolation which now shrouded Mesopotamia, the boots were flagrantly, obtrusively new.

He was not prepared for what he found in Mesopotamia, or rather, what he did not find. He did not find Tony Denaro. Grass grew up in the ruts that led to Denaro's barn, for Denaro was dead.

Denaro's death was not in itself so stark as the cause of it. And the cause was poverty in Mesopotamia.

As they looked at the new boots in the store, they explained that when the bilious fever came to Denaro, Hosmer could buy no quinine. Paper money would not buy one drop of quinine nor calomel nor elixir of vitriol.

When the fever spread up the road from Denaro to Lucretia Kilgore, Sam Hosmer sent Brute Christofferson all the way to Columbus in search of a medical doctor. Christofferson could get no real medical doctor to come, for he had nothing to offer. But he did persuade a young man who was under preceptorship and who had "attended the lectures" at Transylvania Medical College in Kentucky. The young man looked good to Christofferson, for he had a genuine pulsometer with pink water in it and he owned a kit containing sage, opium, geranium, magnesia, jalap, Grauber's salts and Jesuit bark. But on the return to Mesopotamia the young doctor was commandeered at a crossroads where there was a large house like Shuldane's. The people offered the young man metal money to stay. Denaro died.

The hard heels of Stranger-boy's new boots scraped harshly on the store floor, and though he tried to carry himself with humility, the firm square leather under him gave him an arrogant straightness amid the moneyless people.

He learned more. In Cincinnati woods hogs brought only $1.00 apiece, wheat $0.20 a bushel, corn $0.08, flour $3.00 a barrel, whisky $0.12 a gallon. It didn't pay to carry anything to any market. Sheriff sales had almost stopped, for no one had money to buy farms even at fifty cents an acre.

Immense amounts of bank paper had perished, not in the hands of bankers and traders in Cincinnati, who foresaw trouble, but in the hands of farmers in Mesopotamia who had given full value for the paper.

Credit was ended. Distress stretched from Hosmer's Store to the big Shuldane house and all the way down to Boxford's Cabin and Columbus . . . and beyond to the Ohio River.

Paper money had turned Mike Stikes to a gaunt idler who sat in the doorway of his forge, shaking his white head. The leather apron was still molded to his skinny legs, but the fire in the forge was out. The fire in Stikes was almost out, too, Stranger-boy saw.

Exeter was surrounded in the tavern by loungers. Hosmer was surrounded on the porch of the store by loungers. The founding fathers of the Bounty Lands were scarecrows of wrinkling flesh and withered spirits. The founding mothers were now silent stoic women trying to cure bilious fever by applying fresh-killed pullets to the wrists and ankles of the sufferers.

The sons of the founding fathers were growing up poor.

In the hush any movement was plainly evident. Hence it was no wonder that every dull eye on the common sparked when the monotony was relieved by the sight of Emanuel Ault moving from the Shuldane house across the common to Jonathan Blair's cabin and newspaper office. For Ault to go into the cabin of Jonathan Blair was as unlikely as for Arm Webster to go to Blair's cabin. Yet Ault was doing just that. The only influence which could make him do that would be an order from Elnathan Shuldane.

Ault stayed only a minute. Then he left and walked to the tavern.

Before the speculative gossip was well started, Mesopotamia saw Jonathan Blair step out of the doorway of his cabin. They saw him stand with his hands on his hips, facing the Shuldane house. Then they saw him turn around and go back into his cabin.

"Whatever Shuldane wants, he won't get it out of Blair," said Hawkins to the porch in general.

"Dunno about that," said Joe Hussong. "He's coming out again."

And as surely as they watched, Jonathan Blair was walking toward the Shuldane house. He pivoted, though, and turned back to his cabin. He put his arms behind his back as though he were addressing a jury, which in fact he was. And the jury before which he argued was Jonathan Blair. He lost, apparently. For he turned once more and walked slowly toward the Shuldane house and disappeared inside.

In Shuldane's study Blair remained standing.

"Have a chair, Jonathan."

"Never mind that, Nate. I came for one reason only. Ault mentioned the legislature."

When he saw the quick pleased smile flicker over Shuldane's face, he knew he'd said the wrong thing. He had shown Shuldane how much he wanted to be in the legislature, which the older man had obviously wanted to know. Shuldane, on the other hand, had revealed nothing.

It was hard for Blair to tell anything about Shuldane any more. For example, the scuffed-up boots on Shuldane's feet could mean that he didn't have money for new ones, or they could mean that he didn't want anyone to think he had money for new ones, or they could mean that he wouldn't wear new ones in front of Mesopotamia, who could not buy new ones.

Shuldane swung the boots down off the carved walnut table, but he remained relaxed with fingers locked over a good solid torso. His face was pleasant.

"Jonathan, you still want to be in the legislature very much."

Blair did not answer.

"Besides that, you've gone beyond me a long way, Jonathan, because now you don't want the legislature for a personal prize. You want to be there to *do* something. You want to be there now as you never did before. And I'm afraid you'd be pretty effective if you made it."

No matter where it came from, it was good to be understood. Blair raised one foot to an empty chair and leaned on his knee.

"Yes, Nate, I want in. But what's that to do with you? If I get there I'm going to run that U.S. Bank right out of the state. I'm going to tax it to death. I'm going to make it impossible for the bank to commit its debtors. Judicial officers will not be authorized to acknowledge its conveyances nor protest notes payable to the bank."

"You're probably right," said Shuldane. "The bank has been no good, though I was instrumental in setting it up. But you'll never get elected on that premise in this state."

"Did you call me over here to tell me that?"

"No."

Shuldane leaned forward across the table.

"Jonathan, I want to make a trade." Blair drew off, but Shuldane continued. "I'll put you in the legislature."

"You'll what?"

"Even knowing what you plan to do—and mind you, I now think you're capable of doing it—I'll put you in the legislature."

A wave of excitement passed up over Blair's chest and face. But caution came back.

"You think you're still in a position to do that?"

Shuldane smiled.

"Jonathan, you've a low opinion of me. But give me my due, at least."

"Yes. You probably can."

"I'd get pledges from McLean and Worthington and Allen and Corwin."

The names were all the right ones. And Blair knew Shuldane could do it.

"Pledges in my hands in writing?" asked Blair.

"If you insist on that, I'll have it done that way."

"Why should you?"

"I want something big in return."

"What?"

Shuldane smiled.

"Jonathan, our destiny seems to be bound up in this land and the bounty warrants. That's what brought us here. That's what split you and me apart when we should be together. That's what lost me my daughter. That's what's buried us in a depression. I'm land poor, Jonathan. Bounty-Land poor."

"I know I'm not expected to weep. What do you want?"

"It was the bounty warrants you used to whip me in court, too, remember? A clever job, Jonathan, if it's been worth the price."

"What do you want?"

"I believe it is Volume Four that's missing from the Land Office in Washington, Jonathan."

"What do you want?"

"I believe it's a black book pasted full of Bounty Land warrants."

"What do you want?"

"I want those warrants."

Blair brushed a hand at Shuldane and pivoted toward the door.

"Jonathan!"

Blair turned back to face Shuldane.

"Don't forget what you could do in the legislature, Jonathan. You might get the debtor law off the books. You could make a try at the bank." Shuldane leaned forward and smiled and leveled his voice at Blair's soul.

"You could even justify a lifetime, Jonathan. A new beginning for you. Think it over."

"That book disappeared when Navarre disappeared. They say he took it."

"Credit me with knowing what 'they say,' Jonathan, and with knowing where Navarre's loyalty should be."

"Suppose I had the warrants," Blair proposed. "Or suppose I could get them. What would you do with them?"

"I could turn them in against my overdue land payments."

"But they're canceled. They've been used."

"You and I know there are ways of fixing that, Jonathan."

"But there are more than enough there to pay your land debts."

"Then you *have* got the book."

"I mean *if* I had it, there would be more than enough."

"I know that, Jonathan. But I don't want any more land to pay taxes on. If it means anything to you, you can be sure I won't be turning them in for more land."

"What then?"

"I don't have to go into all that," grinned Shuldane. "I've made my offer. Will you do it?"

"No," said Blair, and he left Shuldane's house.

But from that instant he was a fretting, worried, thinking man.

Blair was certain that once in the legislature, he could either kill the bank or force it to honor some of the western currency in metallic legal tender. He also felt that he could legislate a more favorable balance of trade, or at least influence it. It might even be possible to put, or threaten to put, a duty on eastern importations, bartering for respect for western cash and forcing western manufactures.

And since Shuldane was responsible for most of Blair's misfortunes, it seemed as though some Almighty Chief Justice was now offering to make Shuldane the instrument of Blair's recovery. Yet, to the knowledge of Jonathan Blair, no man ever used Shuldane without paying too dear a price.

But as he tried to explore every possible motive Shuldane might have, as he tried to think one step beyond Shuldane, Blair found no trouble in the offer.

The printing press was heavy, and Blair labored to shove it to one side. With his fingers he felt along the cracks in his cabin in the puncheon floor until he found a hand hold. When he lifted, a section of the floor came up. Blair reached into the hole and pulled out a large black book. With a rag he rubbed off the mold. The pages were crinkled with dampness, and he placed the book in front of the fire. He opened it and began to study the pages.

The door pushed open. Blair grabbed his coat and threw it over the book. He looked up in irritation at Stranger-boy Woodbridge.

"Odd comp'ny you're keepin', Mr. Blair, it strikes me."

The conversation was brittle with pique on Blair's side. The boy was patient until Blair lashed, "Seems to me you might have stayed around to help the town in its trouble, and to take care of Veronica and Zabeth! Why isn't Tom back here!"

"Seems to me, Mr. Blair, you're losin' faith in your idea. Seems to me while you sit here and rant about the balance of trade, Tom's out doin' somethin' about it."

"What?"

"While you're talkin', Tom's out changin' the balance of trade that you said got unbalanced."

Blair broke into a loud laugh.

"Look, boy, the balance of trade is a broad concept. One man doesn't do anything about that alone."

"Then you never really believed in the idea, Mr. Blair?"

"Of course I do. But not Tom Woodbridge nor anyone else is going to change it all by himself."

"You think *you* can do something, don't you, Mr. Blair? Isn't that why you want to be in the legislature?"

"Yes. But that's different. That's a joint effort. Trouble with Tom, he won't join with anybody."

"Tom works best alone, Mr. Blair. Maybe there's too much joinin' together. Maybe all this joinin' together is why some people just sit around and talk while some others—like Tom—go out and get the thing done all by theirselves."

Blair looked thoughtful, and the boy continued.

"Anyway, I'm askin' you to help, Mr. Blair. I'm askin' you to help me see to it the men hold on to those hog notes of Tom's. I'm askin' you to see to it Ault or Shuldane don't get 'em."

Blair laughed, but kindly now.

"Son, you've nothing to worry about there. No one puts any value on those notes. If Tom is selling those hogs as you say, no one can collect anyhow. The notes call for hogs. The men see no worth in the notes."

"No, but Mr. Shuldane does. He was up there. He knows the hogs are worth money. Metal money. Money that bought these boots."

"Stranger-boy, money that buys boots isn't enough to save the West."

Stranger-boy left, but he withdrew only to Hosmer's Store. As he looked across the common, his lower lip pushed out because he saw Jonathan Blair walk to the Shuldane house with a package under his arm, wrapped in copies of the *Tabulator*. The lad frowned.

With his back to Blair, Shuldane turned the pages of Volume Four.

"This will do very nicely, Jonathan. The ink's already faded. A good penman can handle this easily. Some of them won't even have to be changed. Never in the history of the world, I daresay, was land ever handled so carelessly by any government."

"That's right."

"I take it it's a contract then between you and me."

"I hate to have it called a contract," said Blair. "But I suppose it is."

"Fine. Then I'll get you letters from at least six of the main leaders. It'll not only get you in. It'll give you some weight when you get there."

Blair walked over and picked up the book.

"You get the book when I get the letters," he said.

Shuldane smiled.

"A fair enough precaution, Jonathan."

Blair left with his book. Inside his cabin he looked back out the window toward the Shuldane house; and he was somewhat disconcerted to see there Elnathan Shuldane and Emanuel Ault standing side by side, looking back at the *Tabulator* office.

Veronica had trouble adjusting to Stranger-boy. It was good to have him back. It was good to have him carrying the water, feeding the few pigs which had been left behind because they were so young. It was good to have him clean up the shed and take the rust off the equipment. It was especially good to have him say that Tom was doing so well with the hogs in Pittsburgh and that Tom would be back. But it was hard to understand why the boy spent so much time up on the common, standing in front of the store.

As he knelt in the evening to shove a new backlog into the small living-room fireplace he said: "It's a nice lot of firewood Brute Christofferson cut for you, Miss Veronica. I know'd he'd take good care of you."

"Brute's been good," she answered. "But he's been busy most of the time. He didn't cut the firewood nor fetch the water."

Stranger-boy looked up.

"Who then?"

"Arm Webster's been the helpful one."

She didn't see the disappointment on his face; but he saw the eagerness on hers, and he knew she wanted to tell him more. But she withheld, for Zabeth's running footsteps came in from the outdoors. From the kitchen her voice floated in to Veronica and Stranger-boy.

"Mam! Has anyone done anything about it?"

"About what?" asked Veronica.

She stepped down into the living room, and as she did so the room changed for Stranger-boy, who still knelt at the fireplace.

Zabeth's new radiance was an unearthly substance to Stranger-boy, a thing that couldn't be made from the common clay of Mesopotamia. And the way in which she took herself for granted, as though there were nothing special about herself, only added to the yearning in young Tom.

"About what?" repeated Veronica.

But Zabeth saw the lad, and her eyes asked Veronica to drop the matter.

"But he knows by now, surely, Elizabeth," said Veronica. "If he doesn't, I don't know who should be told before your own brother."

Stranger-boy rose slowly. Already he had read some unwelcome announcement in Veronica's extra tenderness toward him. The two women, both beautiful in their separate ages, presented a barrier of loveliness that somehow excluded him.

Veronica started to speak, but Zabeth cut her off.

"No. I should be the one to tell him, Mam."

The effort with which she now composed her face so as to deliver the message mercifully yet without apology was apparent, but he helped her none.

"I was about to ask Mam about the minister, Young Tom," she said. "It's to be Arm Webster and me."

Stranger-boy stood up from the fireplace dumbly. Zabeth's words brought the color to his face. He stood demolished, unable to conceal the emptiness in him.

Spontaneously, in a flush of pity, Zabeth moved to him. Her arms were around his neck.

"Young Tom!"

His right arm clamped the small of her trunk. His left hand enclosed the back of her neck under her hair as he bent her backwards, bruising away her sisterly kiss . . . demanding a different kind.

Veronica rose. "Young Tom!"

Zabeth stiffened under the embrace. Stranger-boy took her wrists from his neck and shoved her back into her chair.

He left the house.

Shuldane had worked fast, for in little over a week he was back with his pledges for Blair. He delivered them to Blair's cabin. Blair inspected them carefully. They seemed to be all right.

"Now if I may have the book, Jonathan," said Shuldane.

Blair put the letters in his pocket carefully. Then he smiled.

"Nate, the letters seem to be in order. But it's some time yet before election. Just to make sure of the sincerity of these letters, just to make sure nothing goes wrong between now and election, I'll hold on to the warrant book until after election."

Because Blair had expected Shuldane to fly into a rage, he was not prepared for the gentle smile that came to Shuldane's face.

"Jonathan, did you think I had not prepared for this contingency?"

"Well . . ."

"Didn't you think I'd have to protect myself against such a move? I've got to have the warrants *now*. The government won't wait on me any longer."

"That's not my problem, Nate."

"I'm afraid it is, Jonathan. You see, I took the precaution of taking a little security when you brought the book to my house that day. I lifted out one of the warrants."

Blair's face was a question mark.

"If you'll trouble to look into the warrant book, Blair, you'll find one of the warrants missing. Tom Woodbridge's. I've filed claim to his place. He'll have nothing to show to prove he owns it as long as the warrant's in my hands. No patent was ever issued before this book was stolen from Washington. So of course Washington Land Office can't substantiate the claim."

Shuldane watched the realization come over Blair's face like a shadow.

"I just happen to figure you wouldn't be the type to let that happen to Woodbridge," grinned Shuldane. "At least, not to Veronica's husband, to put it another way."

Blair was silent, stricken.

"I know you wouldn't keep the book here in your cabin," said the older man. "But whenever you're ready, I'll swap you the Woodbridge warrant for the book."

He left Blair knotted in frustration.

As the herd of Mesopotamia hogs above the wagon yards on Liberty Avenue in Pittsburgh diminished, the crowd of men increased and the prices rose beyond all reason. The situation had so reversed itself that the buyers no longer asked, "How much for that one?"

Instead, Woodbridge asked, "What will you give me?" And often as not when the buyer answered, the stranger next to him added $10 to the figure, and while Woodbridge contemplated it, a third voice would add $10 more. Thus a sort of auction evolved over each of the few remaining hogs. The buyers were from farther east than Harrisburg. There were even some from Atlantic Coast cities, and they carried gold.

It was a thrilling experience for Woodbridge. Yet it gave him a pang of regret, too. For he remembered how he had sold the first boars for $60 and $70. Now, when there were only a handful left, he was getting $300, $400, and men were bidding over $500 for Big Four.

But that was when Woodbridge stopped.

"Nope. He's not for sale, gentlemen."

There was a buzz of discontent. One angry voice called out: "I'm all the way from York State, Woodbridge! My town all pooled its funds to buy a breeder pair. You gonna send me back empty-handed?"

"Sorry, stranger. Seems mean, I guess. But nobody was cryin' over me the last twenty years while I was tryin' to raise these critters."

There was another buzz of objection.

Woodbridge hollered: "Come back here this time next year. Maybe I'll be here again."

Leaving the crowd dissatisfied, Woodbridge turned to Captain Michael.

"Michael, put Big Four and Big One in the small cart! We're goin' home!"

While Michael and Pigeon were closing up the camp, Navarre was putting the last of the silver and gold into the document box which was bolted to the floor of the wagon. Navarre now continually carried his rifle loaded.

Woodbridge had saved a young boar and a young gilt for McMasters. He could get $200 for the pair if he wanted. But he gave them to McMasters.

"That's just because you was willin' to let my herd on your place if I'd had to. I don't guess you were thinkin' money when ya offered."

"Tom, I don't know what to say to you."

"Don't say nothin'. Just get me a piece of paper so's I can write out the pedigree for ya. They're out of Big One by Big Four. That'll make their young'uns worth a plenty one day."

It was one of the very few times in Tom Woodbridge's life when he could afford to be downright extravagantly generous.

As he arrived at the boat landing, he had another pleasurable feeling, for standing on the deck were Pigeon and Michael in brand-new boots and cloth shirts. Woodbridge had done it for them, and it thrilled him. Navarre had two huge canvas bags full of hardware he was taking back to his squatters. They contained shot molds, medicines, ax heads, rifle locks, lanterns, rope, canvas. Navarre still wore his old buckskins, but on his feet were new boots. And at his side was Loretta Shane who held a boat ticket back downriver. It made Woodbridge warm to know that everything was bought by Mesopotamia hog flesh.

In a way they were all bought by Cleopatra and Boss. The money in Woodbridge's wagon today began to be generated twenty years ago.

On Woodbridge's own feet were new boots. In his wagon were new shoes for Veronica and Zabeth, and there were other things.

Blair had been right. The balance of trade had become unbalanced. There were few things the West could sell the East; but there were some things for which you could make them pay through their cold blue noses. Woodbridge patted the pocket of his shirt, feeling for the large notebook, containing the family tree of the most famous family of hogs in the West—or rather in the East, now.

As he walked up the gangplank of the weird steam vessel, he noticed a sharp animation among his group of men around the wagons. And as he approached, he saw that Navarre was sitting on the locked document box in the bed of the wagon. His rifle was pointing at a well-dressed man who was arguing violently. The people on the deck were watching with interest. As he approached, Woodbridge saw that the well-dressed one was Bullit, and he argued with feeling.

"Navarre, this boat won't leave here until I get my bag of money."

"I don't know nothin' about any bag of money for you, mister. Sure you helped out. But not till after you tried to cheat us out of the whole herd."

"You ask Woodbridge. He knows about it!"

The crowd was enjoying the argument. But Navarre was grim, and he said: "Ask him yourself. He's right behind you."

Bullit turned and was relieved to see Woodbridge.

"Yeah," said Tom. "He earned his commission, Slover. Pay him $1,000."

Navarre did not budge. His jaw dropped in amazement.

"I know what you mean, Slover. But the fact is, he got 'em started comin' to us. He made two trips to Harrisburg. Besides, it's worth $1,000 not to have his kind workin' against ya."

With sullen disappointment, Navarre slowly unlocked the box. He covered the box guardedly with his back as he counted metal into a canvas bag. With a piece of leather thong he tied the top of the bag in a knot so tight that it squeezed the oil out of the leather.

He tossed the bag at Bullit, who caught it with a smile and tugged at the leather thong. The knot would not budge. The whistle blew, and the crew ran for the gangplank.

"Won't come undone real easy," smiled Navarre. "You better make for the shore and open it later."

Navarre's smile broadened as he watched Bullit run for the gangplank and the shore. It broadened still more as the steamer backed slowly into the channel. He watched Bullit kneel on the shore to struggle with the knot, which was apparently beginning to yield.

Navarre nudged Captain Michael, who was also watching Bullit.

"Captain Michael," he said, "we'd better move on aft. If he gets that knot open, we just might get a fist full of flyin' nails in our face."

The Indian's mass of wrinkles twisted into a boyish grin, and the steamer surged into the current.

Mesopotamia was supposedly thinking over Mr. Shuldane's proposal. He had called a town meeting a week ago and made them an amazing offer. That is, the offer was not so amazing as the fact that he should trouble to make it at all.

"In the first place," said Christofferson, "why should he offer us land warrants in exchange for Woodbridge's hog notes if all he wants is to do us the favor of collectin' on them for us. You don't put up security when you're gonna do a man a favor."

"Well, it's just Shuldane feels Tom let us down. He feels responsible for Tom and wants to make it up to us that hold the hog notes."

"Funny he takes all that responsibility on himself," said Brute. "I been lookin' in on Veronica about once a day to see she's all right. She don't seem to feel like apologizin' to anybody for Tom. And there ain't anybody hates to hurt anybody worse'n she does."

"Yeah. But she's loyal, too," said Exeter, by indictment. "If Tom wasn't comin' back, she'd not give him away, if it was meant to be a secret."

"If that's what you think, Exeter, why didn't you give Shuldane your hog notes and accept the land warrant he offered?"

"Well, Stranger-boy raised such a fuss, and said we'd all be fools to give up the hog notes. He said Tom was comin' back to make good on them."

"He said that once before," Fitchburg reminded them. "Remember?"

"True," said Exeter. "But he said Tom was gonna make good on them in a way that would surprise us all."

There were some deprecatory snorts. Several men turned to Sam Hosmer for an opinion. But Sam Hosmer had no opinion. That is, he had an opinion, but he didn't even want to face it himself. Sam Hosmer was a disappointed man. He loved Mesopotamia. He loved every man in it.

He had no notion that Mesopotamia was filled with heroes, but he had believed it was full of men who were capable of heroism. However, he saw nothing of heroism in the conduct of most men in Mesopotamia lately. He was a very old man, and he had continually looked first to one and then another of the men to take over the leadership of the town. He had looked to Woodbridge at one time; but Woodbridge was interested only in hogs, it seemed. He had looked to Blair at one time; but Blair was a man of fine ideas and talk and clouds and whisky. He had looked to Shuldane; but Shuldane's affairs were too large to give much room for the worries of the town. Also, in the last few years, Hosmer could no longer understand Elnathan Shuldane. Sam Hosmer had looked to the very young men; but in Joe Hussong and Arm Webster and Stranger-boy he found no image of himself. Hosmer had been hopeful of the new men, Culpepper, Wright, Wheeler; but they had not weathered so well as the original settlers.

Now, as the men talked in the store of Woodbridge's hog notes and Shuldane's offer of Bounty Land warrants, Sam Hosmer found no hope in the discussion. His wrinkled face was immobile, his jaw was clamped, and he looked out on the common.

Stranger-boy came in near the end of the discussion in time to have Ault fling a question at him. "If Woodbridge wants to make good on the notes, what difference does it make to him who holds them?"

Stranger-boy started to answer but he was frustrated by Ault, who said he had to leave at once for Columbus.

The argument was dropped when Hosmer bristled: "Let each man make up his own mind what to do. Shuldane is going to hold a meeting next week. Then you'll have a chance to take your pick."

That perhaps would have ended the argument for the day except that toward suppertime all those who were near the common heard a clattering of horse hoofs which brought startled faces to the windows. Those who had seen Ault leave for Columbus just a few hours before were amazed to see him now gallop up to the Shuldane house. He dismounted and ran into the house without even tying his horse, which walked over to the trough in the yard and drank thirstily.

It was but two or three minutes after that that Arm Webster came out of the house and walked briskly to the tavern. He came out of the tavern and walked to the store.

Stranger-boy was feeding the hogs on the Woodbridge place when Webster rode up. Webster had not come to see him, but something in Webster's haste made Stranger-boy grab an armload of wood and head for the house.

While he stacked the wood by the fireplace, he heard Webster talk to Veronica.

"Nate has decided to hold his meeting right now, Mrs. Woodbridge; and since it concerns Tom's notes I thought it was only fair you'd be there."

Veronica said: "Thank you, Arm. I'll come in right after supper."

"No, Mrs. Woodbridge. The meeting is right now."

"Why now? Everybody'll be getting ready for supper."

"Who knows why Nate does anything when he does?" shrugged Arm.

Stranger-boy did not wait upon Veronica's decision. He was out of the house, saddled and mounted, before Webster finished talking.

The men in the store were silent, not so much out of interest in the subject, but because of the puzzling haste in which the meeting had been called. The silence and the lantern light in the store gave Elnathan Shuldane an excellent theater for his logical and skillful presentation.

His handsome face showed sincere concern. His forehead was wrinkled in appealing internal struggle, and his words were exactly right.

"I wouldn't have called you away from your suppers this way if the burden of this thing wasn't so urgent within me. I think I have a good chance to find Tom, if I hurry. I think he's sold some of his animals, and I think that if I present him with some of the hog notes he will see the justice of our claim. I think he will either give us the animals called for on the notes, or he will give us the equivalent in cash. Heaven knows our little town is starving for the lack of it. If we'd had ready metal money, we might have saved Denaro and Mrs. Kilgore."

Shuldane's voice was low. He seemed to keep it from quivering only by great restraint, and no man could challenge his earnestness. After all, Shuldane wouldn't have to worry about anyone.

The room frowned at Stranger-boy as he disturbed the silence by moving over to Zabeth. He took her by the hand and led her outside the store.

"Zabeth, ride quick down the south road. I think you'll run into Tom. Tell him to hurry."

Zabeth kept a puzzled silence. Stranger-boy took both her wrists and squeezed. "Hurry, Zabeth. Don't you see why he's in such a hurry to get the notes?"

"No, I don't. Gramps is trying to help."

Stranger-boy's hands moved up to her shoulders and gripped. She struggled to break away.

Webster, who had followed them out, now cracked a fist down on Young Tom's forearm, causing him to let go.

"What do you mean sending your sister out on the road alone at dusk!"

The word "sister," coming from Webster, stopped Stranger-boy suddenly, but he recovered and appealed to Zabeth.

"Please hurry!"

"All right, Tom," she yielded under his intensity.

"You'll not go alone, Elizabeth," said Webster. "I'll go with you."

"No, you won't, Webster," said Stranger-boy. "You'd take her any place but where she needs to go."

Zabeth untied Stranger-boy's horse, backed him around, and mounted. Webster moved for his own horse, but Stranger-boy grabbed his wrist and pulled him out of sight of the store window. Webster whirled in anger, but pain silenced him, for Stranger-boy twisted his arm and jammed it up behind his back until he was helpless. Zabeth

paused to wait for Webster. She was puzzled at the two men standing
motionless, one partly behind the other in the dark. But Stranger-boy
yelled, "Hurry!" Webster said nothing, and she urged New Horse into
a gallop.

Stranger-boy released Webster, who started for his horse again.
Stranger-boy sprang onto Arm's back and shoved him to the ground.
Webster was up quickly and swinging a club-shaped broken swingletree which he had picked up. Stranger-boy yielded backward before
the flailing swingletree until Webster flung it. Stranger-boy twisted so
that it missed his chest but caromed off his left arm, bruising it senseless. Webster charged in, yelling: "You'll learn to mind your business, hired boy! And don't ever let me see your hands on that girl
again. Just forget this 'brother' business. You're not that or anything else!"

"You overspoke yourself, Webster!"

Stranger-boy could not lift his left arm to fend him off, but with the
killing determination of a man who has one blow left, Stranger-boy
drove his tight balled right fist into Webster's face. The blow was followed with the full force of the lad's body and the full weight of his
hate.

Webster sagged like a half-filled bag of corn.

Stranger-boy unhooked the reins from the nearest horse and bound
Webster's hands behind his back, and his hands in turn to his feet
with the knees bent. He dragged him behind the store and left him face
down.

In the store all heads turned to the panting Stranger-boy, who
listened for Shuldane's words above his own breathing.

"So it's essential that I take the notes tonight," he was saying. "In
exchange I'll issue these land warrants. In case anything goes wrong,
at least you'll have the land, which is more than you have now with
only the notes."

Fitchburg stepped forward and slapped his notes on the counter.

"That's good enough for me, Nate. And it's you we'll be thankin'
if we get anything out of 'em."

Shuldane reached for the hog notes, but Stranger-boy's hand slapped
down to cover them. In the heat of his exhilaration the lad's shyness
was gone. "Don't be fools!" he yelled.

Critical eyes turned on him, but the boy's excited face demanded a
hearing.

"Don't you know why all the hurry? Can't you see the notes are worth something big enough for Shuldane to go after?"

Sam Hosmer spoke. "Boy, if you're wrong, you're doin' an injury to the town and to Mr. Shuldane that won't be forgot."

There was an angry outburst of corroboration from the men. But Hosmer raised his hand for quiet. "And if he's right, Nate, you're a livin' lie, and may God have mercy on your soul."

Shuldane was surprised at this from Hosmer. But his reply was overpowering.

"What proof do you offer, Stranger-boy?" he asked.

"None, but if I guessed right why you're in such an all-fired hurry to get hold of the notes, there'll be proof enough here soon."

"Then let's wait a spell longer," said Hosmer, "to give the boy's proof a chance to show up."

Shuldane was a picture of injury. His voice was quiet.

"I see, Sam. Well, it seems a little too much to ask that I be put to defending myself for trying to help. And I'm convinced that I must act now to do any good. But I'll not try to force my aid on any man. I'll leave now. Any that want to follow my plan are free to see me."

To many, the sight of Elnathan Shuldane walking toward the door was salvation walking out of this life. Polly Stikes walked forward with Mike's hog notes.

"Mr. Shuldane, there's no reason you should help us now, but if you're still willing, here's our hog notes."

As Shuldane reached for the notes, others dug into their pockets. The general movement was only halted by a clattering of horse hoofs outside the store.

As the crowd watched, Zabeth swung down off New Horse and rushed into the store.

"Pap's comin'!"

The crowd surged out onto the porch and onto the road.

Up from the south through the dark came the creak of a straining wagon. It loomed suddenly in front of the store, and a cloud of dust settled. The crowd did not rush forward to the wagon, for Thomas Woodbridge was not a man to be clapped on the back even in the heat of affection, much less in an estranged moment of doubt and wariness like that of this homecoming. More cooling still was the severity of the expression on the face of Slover Navarre, who stood in the bed of the wagon with his rifle meaningfully slung across his front.

Woodbridge's face had changed in the last few months. It was thinner, even more self-possessed, and covered with dust. He looked silently at the crowd until Veronica stepped forward.

The redhead climbed slowly down from the wagon seat and took her hand.

"Sorry it had to be done this way," he said. "But it's over now, Veronica."

As she stood by his side, his eye scanned the crowd until he found Stranger-boy. There was not an ear in the crowd that did not notice a new depth to the redhead's voice as he said, "Good work, son."

Stranger-boy did not come forward. It was enough, what he had heard.

As Woodbridge moved toward the store, a path cleared through the crowd. Over his shoulder he called, "Bring it in, Slover."

Inside the store the lantern barely held the shadows to the corners, and the circle of faces that stared at Woodbridge looked white. A natural hush fell over the room as Navarre came in with three canvas bags which he set on the counter in front of Woodbridge. The second wagon had caught up by now, and Silver Pigeon carried a similar canvas bag which he also placed on the counter. He was followed by Captain Michael, who did the same.

Woodbridge did not touch the canvas bags which so intrigued the crowd. Instead his pale-blue eyes moved slowly around the room. When they had completed the circle, he said slowly: "Zabeth tells me there's a big question on your minds. I guess you've a right to it. And I guess I've got an answer that'll make it up to ya for waitin'."

The moment was almost more than Stranger-boy could bear. He sought out the face of Jonathan Blair, who now stared at Woodbridge in fascination.

"It may surprise some of ya," continued Woodbridge, "but we've got a man here among us that we owe a lot to. That's Jonathan Blair. He's been tellin' us that it's the balance of trade that's needed mendin'. And we been laughin' at his words. But it turns out he was right. And it's been fixed now, least as far as Mesopotamia's concerned."

The crowd turned to look at Blair, who stood as surprised as any of them. Blair's face was a battleground of emotions. He was touched to the heart by the faith of the redhead in his theory, but he was appalled at the presumption, or ignorance, by which Woodbridge actually thought one man could do anything about it.

"There's a lot of ya holdin' my notes for hogs," said Woodbridge. "Well, I haven't got the hogs any more. But I got somethin' a sight better. I got gold."

Hosmer looked again at the bags, and every man turned to his neighbor.

To Amos Exeter it was beyond belief, and he bawled out, "Aw, Woodbridge, what are you—"

But he never finished, because Slover Navarre ripped the leather tie off one bag and tipped it so that the lantern light touched a gleam from the gold and silver coins. Over the buzz of conversation that broke out, Woodbridge said: "I want every man that holds my notes to step up to the counter. And I want Jonathan Blair to be the first."

There was another buzz of amazement in the store which quieted when Blair approached the counter.

Woodbridge spoke to Navarre. "Count out every man $100 gold for every hog I owe him, Slover."

Navarre did not comply. He looked up at Woodbridge reproachfully.

"Count it out, Slover!" ordered the redhead. "That's a good guess at the average we got for 'em. The God-damned days of skimpin' and starvin' are done now the blasted balance of trade's been balanced!"

# Chapter 31: HIS HEIRS & ASSIGNS

By mid-November there was a spaciousness in Mesopotamia as the wind ripped the leafy cover off it, and there was an energizing frostiness in the wind that swept across the river and up between Hosmer's Store and Stikes's forge.

But it wasn't the air that so livened the town, Stranger-boy thought. It was gold.

As he rode beside Woodbridge, he heard Stikes hammering. The forge was once again an embrangled jumble of junk. A good sign.

The tavern was active. The customers no longer nursed half-cent mugs to kill a deadly day, but rushed in instead for a full three-cent jolt, and then rushed out again like men who valued their time.

And Stranger-boy knew that as the wagon passed, heads turned from the bar to take a new and respectful appraisal of Tom Woodbridge. He detected the slight pause in the buzz of voices, and then the resurgent renewal of talk as they passed. New hard-heeled boots rang on the tavern floor where previously the shabby leather on purposeless feet had made no sound.

There was a group outside the *Tabulator* office talking to Blair as he prepared to go somewhere. From the center of the group Blair hailed Woodbridge, who reined New Horse to a stop and climbed down.

Blair disappeared in his cabin and returned, handing Tom Woodbridge a paper. It was yellowed, much handled, and torn at the folds. Tom unfolded it, and then his eyes darted at Blair from under a corrugated forehead of amazement.

"My warrant, Blair! How come you—"

"Don't ask too many questions, Tom. Shuldane had it. I traded him something for it."

"But my place! There'll be no record in Washington!"

"That's the point. I'm going down to Steubenville. I could put it back into the land office for you if you wish, and see a patent's issued properly."

Woodbridge flipped the warrant over and studied the wrinkles on the back, where it outlined his boundaries, and said:

Which land with all appurtenances thereto shall belong to Thomas Woodbridge and/or his heirs & assigns, forever.

Signed: WINTHROP SARGENT, *Col.*
*Principal Surveyor*

"No, Blair. I'll give you some money to pay for my land with. This, I think I'll keep."

"What for?"

"Well, if you must know, I'm gonna give it to Young Tom. The God-damned thing belongs in the family."

Blair grinned.

"Can you stop at the land office, Blair, and pay for my acreage in metal, and get me a good ironbound receipt? I'll give you the exact boundaries. I'd be obliged."

"The other way around, Tom. I'm the one that's obliged."

"You're obliged to no man, Blair. You figured out about shiftin' the balance of trade."

"It's one thing to figure. It's another to get up and do. And when you proved the theory and brought back metal money, the people heard about it all the way up to Cleveland. That's why they voted for me."

Woodbridge snuffed, as though with a nose cold. "I dunno. Navarre had some'at to do with that, too, y'know." Then he changed the awkward subject. "What takes you to Steubenville, Blair?"

"There's a Society of Manufacturers there, headed up by Bazaleal Wells and Seth Adams. They want me to come down to explain about the balance of trade, and show how they can work it, too."

"If they're that fired up about it, they'd ought t'come to you, 'stead of you goin' there."

"Well, it's a large group. Besides, I'm going to use the occasion to enlist some downstate support for the tax legislation I want to start against the U.S. Bank. No state ever taxed the Federal before. It'll take a lot of talking. I want to do my talking while I'm still considered an expert."

Hawkins winked at Kilgore in approval of Blair's tactics. The group also looked at Blair with a new possessive affection.

Hope Emerson walked up to the gathering carrying a bulky package wrapped in *Tabulators*. She said hello to everyone. But then she turned and left.

"What's the hurry, Hope?" Blair called. "You didn't come for just 'hello.' "

"Nothin' important, Jonathan. I'll come back later."

"Come on back now. What is it in the package?"

"Just some wool I brought over to show ya."

The men insisted that she bring it back, but instead of handing it to Blair she opened the cabin door, tossed it inside, and turned to leave.

"I'll just stow it in there for now," she said.

But Blair reached in the door, hauled out the bundle, and opened it with his new briskness.

Mouths opened as the dark-blue contents were unwrapped.

"Pretty fancy wool, I'll say," whistled Hawkins.

Blair held up the so-called wool. Hope's tanned face colored, and she stammered, "Well, I figured any honest-to-gosh representative out of Mesopotamia oughta be dandied up as good as them Federalist no-'counts from Cincinnati at least."

The silence was a perfect tribute to the beauty of the dark-blue frock coat, but it left Hope standing embarrassed, not knowing whether to go or stay.

"A fancy coat don't help a man any in lawmakin'," she said, "but there'll be some down there that'll think it does."

Blair took off his old coat and put on the new one. His exaggerated motion of pulling out his shirt cuffs was a burlesque, but you couldn't help notice that even out here in the woods it looked natural on him. And there were some who remembered when Blair used to make little motions like that without smiling.

He pulled the handsome coat closed in front of him. Hope had even calculated precisely the eight-year change in his girth since the lieutenant's coat she'd made him. But he could find no way to button it.

"Slasher cut some walnut-wood buttons," said Hope. "But he said they didn't suit for the statehouse. Said they'd brand you as an upstate woodsie."

"I didn't say the buttons wa'n't good enough for Blair," said Slasher. "I said they wa'n't good enough for the coat."

"In Columbus there'll be good bone buttons," said Hope. "At the store."

Blair assumed a frown.

"I'm supposed to get the buttons myself!" he accused.

"It's not such a darnation chore as all that," flared Hope.

"For a busy legislator it is," said Blair. "And I asked you once to come along and handle those affairs for me."

Brute Christofferson grinned and colored like a girl. The others grinned and were self-conscious, except for Hope Emerson, who knew a matter of fact when she saw one. She pulled down the front of her doeskin jacket and brushed it off absently.

"Jonathan," she stated, "at Columbus it's a velvet-clad kind you'll be needing, as I told you. A person that's set a china table and can fit her feet in slippers and read a thing or two."

Blair pursed his lips and nodded in acknowledgment of her good sense.

"If you're to be felt down there, you must shake off the woodsie and talk up to them if you're to make anything of this chance. At your age you'll not get another such," she said.

Blair stroked his shaved chin and nodded. Hope turned to leave, but Blair asked, "Hope, did you sign that land-patent application that I'm going to drop off at the courthouse for you?"

She pulled a paper from her side pocket and unfolded it. "Can't make much sense to it, but if you wrote it out I reckon it's legal. Here."

Blair took the paper, examined it, grinned, and hung the paper on a nail on the door.

"Don't think I'd go hangin' it on a nail if it's so all-fired valuable as you said, Jonathan."

"The others might want to see what kind of contract you were making."

Christofferson was already reading it, and his grin brought the others over. As they read, smiles grew on their faces until, as they finished reading almost simultaneously, they began to pound Blair on the back. Brute Christofferson took Hope by the shoulders. "You gonna let that slippery rascal get away with this, Hope?"

Hawkins ripped the paper off the door. "If you want to get out of this, Hope, I'll rip it up. It says here: 'I, Hope Emerson, do hereby enter contract to furnish to J. Blair a lifetime's worth of common sense, self-respect, and courage; and I hereby authorize the minister to publish the banns of marriage between self and the said J. Blair. Signed, Hope Emerson.'"

The laughter that began never got well started, for the sight of Hope Emerson at that moment was one of the great events in the history of Mesopotamia. Her head was tilted slightly to one side and forward. The corners of her mouth turned up in an uncertain smile which flickered quickly into suspicion of a jest and back again to trust.

It was too much for Christofferson, who said: "God damn it, Blair. Tell her it's for sure!"

A few Adam's-apples went up and down, and every man's body strained to hurry Blair, who slowly put his arm around Hope's soft doeskin jacket.

"It's for sure, Hope," he said quietly, "if you'd sign again with full knowledge and free will."

Most towns in the big woods turned any day of the week into Sunday whenever Seth Gershom arrived. But at Mesopotamia he always tried to arrive on the real Sunday.

Mesopotamia owned Seth Gershom. They had seen the small specks of gray sprinkle his sideburns. Then they had seen the sides of his head turn gray. Even the narrow rooster's comb of black hair that stood upright on top of his head was yielding to the gray. But they had also watched the face grow younger. The hawklike profile was still as sharp as ever, but occasionally they saw the circuit-rider grin, and in his homeliness they found a great strong beauty. Now that he no longer used a robe in the pulpit, nor cared for one, the women made him a rich befolded one, which he never remembered to bring.

Seth Gershom also owned Mesopotamia, for as he looked down now on the congregation in the blockhouse he no longer rehearsed himself on the names before he rose. He no longer even prepared a formal text. He looked down on the parish and talked.

He had relaxed even to the point where, as on this morning, he published the banns of marriage in a routine singsong voice.

"I publish the banns of marriage between Hope Emerson, of Mesopotamia, and Jonathan Blair, of Mesopotamia. If any of you know cause or just impediment why these two persons should not be joined together in holy matrimony, ye are to declare it or forever hold your peace. This is the first time of asking."

The minister's smile was reflected all over the blockhouse. He paused, allowing them time to look around at Hope Emerson and smile.

Then he proceeded to his next routine chore.

"I publish the banns of marriage between Elizabeth Woodbridge and Armitage Webster. If any of you know cause or just impediment why these two persons—"

The Reverend Seth Gershom looked up from his text, for what was happening now had never happened before. Rising slowly, as if in a stupefied trance in the middle of the blockhouse, was Stranger-boy Woodbridge.

Gershom did not know what was coming. But keeping his eye on Stranger-boy, he continued from memory: "—why these two persons should not be joined together in holy matrimony, ye are to declare it. This is the first time of asking."

The boy's words were as slow as an oxen's trudging . . . and as inexorable.

"I so declare," he said.

It was as if Chief Rontondee had appeared at the service.

The stunned people sat looking at the lad and then at Elizabeth and then forward to Seth Gershom. When Gershom took no action, a slight murmur of whispered exclamations spread into a gabble of conversation that burst quickly into babbling surprise.

Gershom had never faced this situation before, but he raised an arm, and the blockhouse hushed in anticipation.

"On what grounds do you make this protest?" asked Gershom.

Stranger-boy stood with his feet wide apart, his hands hanging open at his sides. His head was bent slightly forward, but he looked up doggedly at Gershom, risking no glance to the right or left. He thought hard for an answer.

"What grounds—the protest?" asked Gershom.

Stranger-boy stood silent.

"It's quite within your right to declare against the marriage; but the impediment must be just and it must be stated."

The boy had been compelled to his feet by impulse. Now that he stood, he could make no case for what he knew.

"Does the objector wish to state his just reasons in private?" asked Blair.

But there was no just impediment. Stranger-boy bit his teeth hard together to see better through the glaze of water welling in his eyes, and he sat down.

Now that it had begun, the great party at the Woodbridge place became a delusion. All the signs of festivity were there, but there was no festivity.

The men and women talked quietly in groups, and Thomas Woodbridge wondered why it was always this way in his house. At Hosmer's Store there was always loud talk and laughter. At Blair's office there was always earnest discussion and interest. At Exeter's tavern there was always relaxed good feeling. Woodbridge remembered now that on the few occasions when men had come to his house, it had always been as it was tonight.

There were glass drinking vessels which Hosmer had bought from Columbus carefully packed in wood shavings, and resold to Veronica.

There were gleaming brass candleholders for the seven candles, and there were sparkling glass chimneys on the six oil lamps. There was special Monongahela whisky bought through Buttrick from Pittsburgh for conviviality. But there was no conviviality. There was merely awkwardness.

A man's life is governed by slighter influences than he admits even to himself. And though Woodbridge would proudly admit to being the originator of an amazing breed of hogs in a country where that was a twenty-year accomplishment of difficulty and significance, he would not admit that this party was the object of it all. Nor perhaps should he, for it was not wholly true. The object of raising a four-hundred-pound lard hog that will reproduce itself is to give to mankind a source of good and plenteous meat.

Yet on this night Woodbridge was vaguely conscious of nights twenty years ago when he had walked by the great Shuldane house in Concord envying the light which shone out from the tall narrow windows on both floors to light up the shiny black paint of fifteen and twenty carriages standing outside. He had pictured a man inside the house, among his fellows, and he had seen warmth and heard noise and music. And young Tom Woodbridge had felt envy.

But in his house tonight there was similar noise and light and Christofferson's fiddle, yet Tom Woodbridge felt awkward among his townsmen. He even looked awkward as he stood beside the fireplace with a glass in his hand. In the first place his face was so clean-shaven that the guests and he were aware of his extra preparation. And few people ever saw Woodbridge without his hat. The red wavy hair came to a firm V on the forehead, which was crossed by a diagonal line separating the tender whiteness above his hat line from the weathered skin below. The face belonged outdoors with a hat on.

Unfortunately, as the guests from time to time looked at the severe face of Tom Woodbridge, which smiled uncomfortably from time to time, they did not know that he wished them to carry on with their talking and laughing and merely allow him to walk around in it. Somehow talking and laughing did not come naturally here.

Veronica also was somewhat apart. For on this great night she could not bring herself to chat with Faith Hawkins about the new schoolteacher who was to replace Blair at teaching Mesopotamia's children, nor could she talk to Mrs. Hosmer about the letter from Concord telling about all the deaths and births. For, though the party was for Elizabeth, tonight was in a way to be Veronica's triumph, too. After the wedding Elizabeth would go back East with Arm Webster. She was even glad Arm had lost the election to Blair, since it was the cause of his return to the seaboard.

Veronica moved over with Tom, who stood by the fire watching the party. The Bounty Land warrant hung framed over the mantelpiece.

"She doesn't seem to be enjoying it like I thought, Tom."

"Well, she's broke up over the way it hit Stranger-boy. You must have known the boy would take it pretty hard, Veronica. So this young Webster better be all you think."

"I didn't go to hurt Stranger-boy, Tom."

Woodbridge put his arm around her.

"I know."

"I guess there are others think Stranger-boy should be the one."

"I suppose," said Tom. "I guess that's why Stikes and Hawkins and Hosmer didn't come tonight."

"It's not their daughter, Tom. It's ours."

"That's right. To hell with them. It's Zabeth's the one to be suited anyhow."

"There's a knock," said Veronica. "Perhaps they've come."

They went together to the kitchen door. Woodbridge opened it and then stood silent, as did Veronica. The guest himself made no effort to step over the threshold, but remained quiet for a moment. He was alone in more ways than one.

When the silence became worse than awkward, Elnathan Shuldane raised his palm.

"I didn't come without a reason," he said.

Veronica reached out to him.

"Come in, Father."

Shuldane waited until Woodbridge said, "Come in, Nate."

As he stepped over the sill, Shuldane said, "I'd not have ventured it except I come with a sizable marriage present for my granddaughter. Could have conveyed it by Arm. But—ah—a man's own grand-daughter . . ."

"I'll send her to you," said Veronica. But she did not find Elizabeth in the main room. She looked through the house, for all rooms were open to accommodate the crowd.

Shuldane joined the group where Stranger-boy, Silver Pigeon, Joe

Hussong, Christofferson, and Buttrick talked. He was cooly received. But it must be said in his favor that Shuldane neither bent nor flinched under the affront. It was never safe to attribute such conduct wholly to courage, for there was always the greater likelihood that Shuldane's confidence in any given situation was due to sound knowledge that he retained in his manicured fist or in his well-tailored sleeve the last and final trick.

Blair, who was talking state affairs for the information of Kilgore and Slasher, and to the humiliation of Arm Webster, looked over to see Shuldane. It surprised him; but he had business with Shuldane, and he left his group to join the other.

"Nate, I heard from Ault that you and he were buying more warrants and going west to buy a new township."

"Yes, Jonathan. Warrants are cheap now. I shall try again." Shuldane's hair remained mostly black. His face flesh was not so mobile, and his erectness was by effort, but there was quickness in his eyes. His weak smile encompassed twenty years. "I'm a little old for it. But this wouldn't be the place for me any more after what . . ." Shuldane looked over at Woodbridge. "After what I've learned."

You can't follow a man like that as long as Blair had without a spark of resurgent admiration. You couldn't put your foot on his neck at a time like this, but neither could you be careless.

"Reason I asked about the warrants, Nate," said Blair quietly. "Ah—that warrant book."

Shuldane laughed.

"No. I'm not going to use those to take up land, Jonathan. If the stakes were something else, maybe yes. But just for land, when you can still buy warrants cheap—I thought you'd give me more than that, Blair."

"Then you'll give me back the book?"

"Wouldn't you let me be the one to turn it back in to the government Land Office through General Harrison?"

"Why?"

"With you in the Ohio legislature and your Jeffersonian friends in Washington, my kind don't have many friends left in the government, Jonathan. I'll be needing to ask a few favors. It would give me a little credit, of a kind."

Blair finished his whisky and set his glass down reflectively.

"That's probably all you want of it, Nate. But I can't be sure. I've seen you—"

"I know. Do this, then. Go with me. Let me carry it and hand it over. But you can be with me every step of the way. Harrison will be in Columbus soon."

"All right."

Veronica could find Elizabeth nowhere. She put on a shawl and went outdoors in the frosty November night. Up by the shed she saw the thin light-colored dress in the darkness, and she went to her daughter.

"Why out here, Elizabeth?"

"Be hard to leave this place, Mam."

Veronica didn't answer.

"Be hard not to be with Wolf and New Horse and—and you especially, Mam."

A thrusting swell throbbed into Veronica's throat, and a salt-flavored pang stung the roof of her mouth, but she steeled her lips shut.

"Be hard to be with men that don't cuss like Pap, and work and roar and sweat."

"That such a recommendation?" Veronica could say no more safely.

"Now take Arm. I don't even know what he looks like with his shirt off . . . nor how he'd be with a sick horse. You suppose, Mam, he's got a back like Young Tom's with a groove down the backbone and muscles risin' on both sides that could get under a foundered horse and lift up? Or would it be a back more like—well, Young Tom's is the only one I've seen."

"Arm Webster's got a fine enough back, though that has little to do with it."

"I suppose it doesn't, Mam. Yet suddenly it seems to."

"You should know by now, Elizabeth."

"I should. Yet tryin' to think tonight how it would be, it seemed always Arm was in his coat with the felt in the tailoring so's I couldn't picture exactly how he is. Or else in a fine shirt that the pleats gave him his shape."

There was no answer.

"And it seemed suddenly Arm has always been under pleats to me. It seemed maybe it was the pleats that started me herdin' him 'round. Or did I start? How did it all start, Mam?"

They had wandered out onto the West Road, the part which was still called the Woodbridge Strip. They turned around and headed back to the house.

"Now take Young Tom. If it was a man like that, I'd know how to do for him, what to feed him, and the like. Fact, with him not around I'll hardly—oh, Mam, how did this all get started?"

Wolf followed them between the east and west halves of the old cabin, out back.

"I guess, without squarin' off to the fact, I been wishin' all along that it was Arm that was my brother and Young Tom that was . . . Well, it'll be hard to imagine Young Tom workin' around the place without me followin' him around. Be hard to leave here, Mam."

"It's hard to leave anywhere, but the memory's that short it's only a while."

"You know about picking up and leaving, don't you, Mam?"

"Yes."

"And if you still want me to go back East, it looks like maybe your memory wasn't so short."

Veronica put her arm around the girl's waist, and they walked in the court-like space between the shed and the cabin and the new addition.

"Do you think if I have a daughter in the East I'll be wanting her to come back here when she'd grown, Mam?"

Veronica had never thought of it so, and she gave no answer.

" 'Course, I know you love me. . . . To see me go away from you means you think it's going to be a lot better there for me . . . else you couldn't do it."

Veronica thought about it, and she found herself trying to see Elizabeth's face in the darkness. For Zabeth's remark was strange indeed, and twisted things considerably.

"Then I keep thinkin', too," said Elizabeth, "of him standin' up there at the Reverend Gershom's meeting."

"Who?"

"Young Tom, of course. And everybody staring at him. And him not caring what they thought, and having no good answer for the reverend."

They walked in silence for a long while, until Veronica spoke from a long review of her life. "Elizabeth."

"Yes, Mam."

"When a man will stand up in front of a whole church full of his friends . . . and enemies . . . and expose himself to ridicule and think nothing of it . . ."

"When a man'll do that?"

"When a man'll do that . . . then there's not much else he wouldn't do for you either, Elizabeth."

Elizabeth Woodbridge squeezed her mother's waist.

"You'd know something about that too, wouldn't you, Mam?"

Elizabeth went back into the house before her mother, who stayed a while to look at the outside of her house, the windows with the yellow lights, the people inside by the windows. She looked at the archway between what had once been the east cabin and the west cabin. The west cabin was dark now, a storage place only.

As she stood in the small courtyard taking pleasure in the clean frost of her breath in the moonlight, she heard the impatient snort and stamp of a long-standing horse. It was none of the guests' horses in front, for it came from behind the shed. Wolf heard it too, and he disappeared around behind the shed. Wolf returned directly and stood before her, mincing impatiently from one front paw to the other, as he did when in need of a language, and backing toward the end of the shed.

When Veronica began to follow, he immediately turned and ran around the end of the shed. It was easy to see what was wrong. In the excitement of the preparation for the big affair, Tom or Stranger-boy must have left New Horse hitched to the wagon. As she unhitched the handy new spring fasteners from the wagon tongue, she reflected that New Horse was no longer new. He was, in fact, old.

The wagon, however, was practically new. That is, it was the same wagon Tom had brought from Concord twenty years ago; but it had the third set of wheels that Mike Stikes had made for it, and a brand-new tongue. The sideboards on the wagon bed had been replaced twice.

She led New Horse around to the front of the shed, wondering how he happened to be left out tonight. As she reached for the wooden bar which served as a handle to slide the door back she felt how smooth the bar had become. It was so deeply indented that her hand slipped into the hand hold even in the dark. The notch had not been cut there. The wood had been worn away by the palm of Tom's hand.

She realized that Tom Woodbridge had left a wake of wear behind his life—wearing out wagons and horses and barns and tools. But Tom himself had increased. Suddenly it came to her that Tom was not as worn as any other man his age inside the house. His face was ageless. At twenty he had looked older, at forty he looked younger.

Veronica forked down some hay in front of New Horse and returned to the house. Thinking about him, she naturally looked around the room for Tom; but when she found him she was somewhat concerned, for his face had that extra shade of color which only a few had learned to notice as the beginning of trouble. Approaching the group she heard Tom's voice.

"Seems to me you might have told me about this, boy!"

"I was going to, Tom, as soon as things settled down," said Stranger-boy. "Didn't want to cause any stir, with Zabeth's wedding and all."

"Where the devil are ya plannin' t'go?"

"West a little, Tom."

Stranger-boy's explanation fell into a shocked vacuum, and he felt compelled to soften the sharp edges.

"It's not as if I won't be back to see you and Miss Veronica, Tom."

"But, lad, I'd figured it would be you and me. We got everything ahead of us, soon's we can get some good foundation stock."

"I been ridin' on your back long enough, Tom."

"Ridin' my back! Everybody in this room knows you been carryin' a man's load since you was twelve."

"The fault is ours, Tom," said Veronica. "Everybody knows it, but I don't know's we ever troubled to tell him."

Woodbridge swallowed.

"You're right, Veronica," said Tom. "Look, boy, it's half and half. Anything you want. We'll split the place right down the middle. That means land, stock, wagons, and cash."

The silence was more painful to Stranger-boy than to anyone, though it was bad enough all around.

"What d'ya say to that, boy! Half and half!"

Stranger-boy's task was tripled by the genuine anxiety on Tom's face, and by the offer which he knew Tom thought was superior. The boy looked at the floor, but he said what he had to say . . . just as slowly and yet as surely as he had once led the ox and the bull plow through the wall of fire.

"It's more'n I got ever a right to ask, Tom—but the fact is, I covet more'n even that."

Tom's face fell, and the others looked surprised. But it became suddenly clear as the boy raised his eyes from his boots to look directly at Zabeth, who stood talking to Arm Webster.

"Don't you reckon it'd be better all around if I was to go?"

Oddly enough, the uncomfortableness was ended more favorably for all by a remark from Elnathan Shuldane.

"I never had a son, Tom," he said. "Yet I had an apprentice once that I was slow to value. Seems to me, listening to what Stranger-boy says—ah—the same was said to me once."

There was a knock at the door, but before Veronica could open it Sam Hosmer was standing in the kitchen. He was dressed for the affair except for one incongruity. Over his shoulder was slung a rifle. It had been a long time since men carried rifles on social visits in Mesopotamia.

Behind Hosmer came Stikes, also carrying a rifle. And the two held the door open for Jim Hawkins, who staggered into the kitchen room carrying a large wooden box. Since he had hold of it, he didn't stop short of where he intended it to stay, and he struggled on into the main room, where he dropped it in front of the fireplace with a thud that rattled the framed warrant which hung over the fireplace.

Hosmer and Stikes did not leave their rifles in the kitchen but brought them into the main room. Veronica and Tom were surprised, not so much at the entrance of the men with the rifles as at the fact that no one else was surprised. The room livened up with smiles and talk now, almost as if this was what they had all been waiting for.

Christofferson now began filling whisky glasses, and the talk rose to an unselfconscious abandon. Woodbridge looked around. This was the way he had always wished it could be in his house. The people were no longer stiff, like people accepting a too-calculated hospitality.

Standing beside Tom, Veronica said, "It must be a present for Elizabeth and Arm."

Christofferson, wishing to make it clear that he was in on it, said: "No such thing, Miz Woodbridge. This ain't no present for anybody, 'less it would be for the whole town."

The crowd was already forming around Hosmer, who was catching his breath. They quieted down even before Hosmer was ready, for he still breathed hard.

"Wait'll ya catch your breath, Sam," said Kilgore. "You shoulda let somebody else go on that detail."

"Tom," Hosmer began, but he had to wait a spell yet. He unbuttoned his jacket in the sudden heat of the room. Veronica noticed forcibly that Sam Hosmer was more worn than the handle on the shed door. His crinkled face had a transparency, and the pupils of his eyes were not sharply demarked from the whites, which were shot through with blood lines and brownish yellow. The wool jacket seemed a burden to the shrunken frame. Mrs. Hosmer also seemed to notice it, especially in the crowd.

"Tom," he resumed, "this isn't exactly a party matter. Yet we wanted a time when everybody was together. Isn't even a present for Zabeth, like you might guess." He paused again.

"Take your time, Sam," said Stikes.

"Fact is, it's an extra job we're puttin' on your shoulders. That's the way it always happens to a man that's worth a damn."

Tom Woodbridge observed that the town had put a lot of jobs onto Sam Hosmer over the years.

"Fact is, Tom, we want to know have you still got those hog notes you took from us?"

Woodbridge looked at Veronica.

Veronica went to the document box and came back with the notes.

Hosmer reached for the notes. Tom impulsively reached to intercept them, but Hosmer snatched the packet from Veronica.

"You got the list, Blair, of which man turned in how many notes?"

"Yes, Sam."

"Well, Tom, we want to take these hog notes back from you."

"But I already paid—"

"And we figured out that this town would still be in bad trouble if it hadn't been for what you did with those hogs. We figured out with Navarre how much you kept back for yourself, after you paid off the notes, and it ain't much. We figured out also that you ain't got no herd left except Big One and Big Four and a few young'uns. And we figured out that when you got a herd, the town's got good livin'. When you got no herd, the whole town's less 'count."

Hosmer paused under the effort.

"We figured out, too, that when you got hogs, these pieces of paper are better'n gold, Tom."

Stikes stooped to unlock the big wooden box. Hosmer lifted the lid with his toe.

"We collected this here gold, what ain't been spent, to get us back in shape. Ain't a man here wasn't willin' to put back in. We want you to give us the notes back and take this here metal money, or any part of it, and start the new herd—bigger and better than the last one."

Veronica looked up at Woodbridge. The hog farmer swallowed. His face colored under the tribute, and his forehead wrinkled under the responsibility.

"But, Sam, then I got it to pay back all over again."

"Yes and no. Tell him how it works, Blair. You got it all set up down at statehouse."

Blair stepped forward and held out an incorporation paper.

"Tom, it amounts to a bank. Here. 'Mesopotamia Hog & Trust Company.' The gold goes in the bank as assets. The bank loans to you ... or anybody, in fact, that the stockholders are willin' to loan to."

"Who are the stockholders?"

"All of us that turned our gold back."

"But what do all of us use for money if the gold is in the bank?"

Hosmer pulled the dirty hog notes from his pocket.

"These."

Veronica's hand went to her mouth. "But those are nothing but scraps of paper with Tom's name signed to them, Sam."

Hosmer riffled through the packet of notes, some of them torn, all of them dirty. He slapped them against the palm of his hand.

"That's all it ever took to make a piece of paper into legal tender, Veronica. A good man's signature mark."

Tom Woodbridge was dazed. He heard Blair explaining the technicalities of the bank arrangement to some of the men. Sam's explanation had been oversimplified. But Blair apparently would handle the legal part.

Veronica stood beside him. The people looked at the Woodbridges with pleasure from various parts of the room, but they left Tom and Veronica pretty much alone, for the box of gold and silver on the floor said everything that could be said. It took some time for the excited conversation to die down. But when it did, Shuldane came to them, where they stood by the fire.

It was apparent that Elnathan Shuldane had been impressed, but he made no attempt to cover the past.

"Veronica, I'll be getting on. The present I'd like to give to Zabeth and Arm is the house on the common on the Shuldane Reserve. I'd rather like to tell her myself."

Veronica melted.

"I'll get her, Father, right now."

But Zabeth was not to be found, nor was Stranger-boy.

In the confusion of the search which now began, Thomas Woodbridge's eye happened to notice the blank space over the fireplace where only a few hours before there had been a framed document, the Bounty Land warrant.

Blair saw Woodbridge looking, and the two men stared at each other.

"I guess the lad can cash it in," said Tom. "It's endorsed over to Thomas Woodbridge. That's his name, too."

# GEORGE WASHINGTON, PRESIDENT, THE UNITED STATES* AMERICA

To all whom these presents shall come,

Greeting:

Know ye that in consideration of military services performed by:

Jonathan Woodbridge, Private

as a member of the Continental Establishment in the Great Rebellion, there is granted to said veteran in lieu of monies:

100 acres

in the United States public domain known as The Northwest Territory, to be surveyed from the tract known as The Military Bounty Lands. Said tract and all appurtenances thereto shall be to said

Jonathan Woodbridge

and/or his Heirs & Assigns, to have and to hold, *forever*.

G. WASHINGTON

Indorsement: To Thomas Woodbridge, son & heir, J. Woodbridge. (Tom, do not yield up this share in the Bounty Lands until ye hold in hand the deed.)

Indorsement: To Thomas Stranger-boy Woodbridge, by T. Woodbridge, 1840

Indorsement: To Alycia Stranger-boy Blair, by T. S. Woodbridge, 1870

Indorsement: To (*Obliterated*)

Curator's Handwritten Note Attached:

This defaced document forwarded to Mesopotamia Historical Society from Pacific Coast, 1952. As I did not have opportunity to confer with previous curator of the society, I do not know much about it. But an accompanying note said it belonged here.

Probably some early type of land conveyance to veterans used in pensioning off old-timers after revolution. Mrs. J. Stranger-boy Blair used it to qualify for membership in D.A.R.

Any information on this might make a nice little filler for the *Quarterly*.

CURATOR